HARD-BOILED DETECTIVES

ABOUT THE EDITORS

Robert Weinberg, one of the foremost authorities on pulp magazines, is the author of *The Weird Tales Story,* for which he won the World Fantasy Award.

Stefan R. Dziemianowicz is a contributing editor of *Crypt of Cthulhu* and the author of *The Annotated Guide to* Unknown *and* Unknown Worlds.

Martin H. Greenberg has more than three hundred anthologies to his credit. He is professor of regional analysis and political science at the University of Wisconsin–Green Bay.

HARD-BOILED DETECTIVES

23 Great Stories from
Dime Detective magazine

Edited by Robert Weinberg,
Stefan R. Dziemianowicz
and Martin H. Greenberg

GRAMERCY BOOKS
NEW YORK • AVENEL, NEW JERSEY

Copyright © 1992 by Robert Weinberg, Stefan R. Dziemianowicz, and Martin H. Greenberg
All rights reserved.

First published in 1992 by Gramercy Books,
distributed by Outlet Book Company, Inc., a Random House Company, 40 Engelhard Avenue, Avenel, New Jersey 07001.

Dime Detective is a trademark co-owned by Argosy Communications, Inc. All rights reserved. Artwork copyright © 1938 by Popular Publications, Inc. Reprinted by permission of Argosy Communications, Inc.

Printed and bound in the United States of America

Library of Congress Cataloging-in-Publication Data

Hard-boiled detectives : 23 great stories from Dime Detective magazine
  / edited by Robert Weinberg, Stefan R. Dziemianowicz & Martin H.
  Greenberg.
     p.   cm.
   ISBN 0-517-06009-4
     1. Detective and mystery stories, American.   I. Weinberg, Robert
E.   II. Dziemianowicz, Stefan R.   III. Greenberg, Martin Harry.
PS648.D4H38   1992
813'.087208—dc20   91-23828
                                                                        CIP

8 7 6 5 4 3 2 1

ACKNOWLEDGMENTS

The following stories, which were originally published in the date indicated issues of *Dime Detective Magazine,* are reprinted by arrangement with Argosy Communications, Inc.:

"Hell's Pay Check" by Frederick Nebel, December 1931. Copyright © 1931 by Popular Publications, Inc.

"The Crime Machine" by Carroll John Daly, January 1932. Copyright © 1931 by Popular Publications, Inc.

"A Burial Is Arranged" by John Lawrence, 1 March 1935. Copyright © 1935 by Popular Publications, Inc.

"A Man's Last Hours" by William E. Barrett, September 1936. Copyright © 1936 by Popular Publications, Inc.

"Something for the Sweeper" by Norbert Davis, May 1937. Copyright © 1937 by Popular Publications, Inc.

"Footprints on a Brain" by D.L. Champion, July 1938. Copyright © 1938 by Popular Publications, Inc.

"Strangler's Kill" by Merle Constiner, August 1940. Copyright © 1940 by Popular Publications, Inc.

"You Slay Me, Baby" by Frederick C. Davis, July 1942. Copyright © 1942 by Popular Publications, Inc.

"Sleep No More My Lovely" by G.T. Fleming-Roberts, September 1943. Copyright © 1943 by Popular Publications, Inc.

"I'll Slay You in My Dreams" by Bruno Fischer, September 1944. Copyright © 1944 by Popular Publications, Inc.

"No Minimum for Murder" by Julius Long, January 1945. Copyright © 1944 by Popular Publications, Inc.

"A Dish of Homicide" by Hank Searls, November 1949. Copyright © 1949 by Popular Publications, Inc.

Copyrights renewed and assigned to Argosy Communications, Inc. All Rights Reserved.

"The Hand of Horror" by Erle Stanley Gardner—Copyright 1933 by Erle Stanley Gardner. Reprinted by permission of Curtis Brown, Ltd.

"Nine Parts Devil" by Max Brand—Copyright 1934 by Popular Publications, Inc. Copyright renewed © 1962 by Jane F. Easton, Judith Faust, and John Frederick Faust. Used by permission.

"The Lady in the Lake" by Raymond Chandler. This is one of the stories that Chandler later expanded into a novel. From a collection entitled KILLER IN THE RAIN. Copyright © 1964 by College Trustees Ltd. Reprinted by permission of Ed Victor Ltd.

CONTENTS

INTRODUCTION

When discussing national art forms, Americans point with some pride to jazz, the Broadway musical, and even rock and roll music. Few, if any, think to mention the hard-boiled detective story, which comes as no surprise: Like the character it glorifies, this particular genre has always occupied a place on the fringe of public acceptance.

The hard-boiled detective story originated and flourished in the pulp fiction magazines of the 1920s, 1930s, and 1940s. Like any art form, it emerged both as a reaction against its predecessors and a response to its time. Detective fiction had always tended to concentrate on the fine art of detection. Edgar Allan Poe's C. Auguste Dupin and Arthur Conan Doyle's Sherlock Holmes, the models for most fictional detectives of the nineteenth and early twentieth centuries, took on seemingly insoluble problems and, through superior powers of deduction, solved crimes by noticing clues overlooked by less discerning colleagues. The word *superior* must be stressed, for the traditional detective was always an uncommon character. Educated and often independently wealthy, he had the leisure to train his intellect and took a dilettante's delight in the mental stimulation a mystery afforded— the more difficult the better. The enormous burden of apprehending master criminals and restoring the social order was to the traditional sleuth a matter of *noblesse oblige*: He did what was expected of a man of his unusual capabilities.

The pulp magazines changed all that. Created in 1896 to provide the public with cheap reading material, pulps rapidly became the main source of popular fiction in the United States, proliferating and diversifying to satisfy every taste.

Without a doubt, the most fertile pulp fiction genre was the mystery-detective field. Between 1915 and 1955 nearly two hundred mystery-detective magazines flooded the newsstands. Some lasted only one issue. Others, like field leader *Black Mask,* lasted a quarter century or more. All contributed to the genesis and evolution of the hard-boiled detective, a tough remake of the classic detective who preferred street smarts to intellect and physical action to contemplation, and whose most sophisticated tool of detection was a smoking .45.

It isn't difficult to understand the hard-boiled dick's appeal or how he supplanted the traditional detective when one considers the age that gave rise to him. With the passage of the Eighteenth Amendment to the Constitution on January 16, 1920, America officially entered the Prohibition era and not coincidentally one of the most violent periods of lawlessness in the nation's history. Over the next thirteen years, mobsters like Al Capone, Legs Diamond, Lucky Luciano, Bugsy Siegel, and Dutch Schultz enjoyed a notoriety normally reserved for world leaders as they supplied Americans with endless quantities of bootleg liquor, ran prostitution and gambling rackets, and fought bloody turf wars in cities across the nation. Rampant corruption in high levels of government and law enforcement became a recognized part of the social norm as racketeers sought to buy influence and protection for their illegal activities. Even average citizens threw in with the criminals by patronizing speakeasies and stashing bathtub gin.

In a climate of such moral ambivalence the exploits of the traditional detective seemed at best impractical and at worst naively unrealistic. The hard-boiled detective, on the other hand, thrived in society's gray areas. Though on the side of law and order, he knew from personal experience that it was sometimes necessary to break the rules to bring justice. His unorthodox methods might include lying, bluffing, stealing, or even killing, but they were never worse than those of the criminals he fought and were always justified by the ends they achieved. In contrast to the sophisticated classic sleuth, the hard-boiled detective was an obvious product of his rough environment: He spoke its language, fraternized with its citizens, indulged in its vices, and blended inconspicuously with its tawdry scenery.

Nevertheless, he was a man of principle, afflicted, as Frederick C. Davis put it, "with an ingrown sense of obligation." For all his wisecracking arrogance, he never thought of himself as anything more than a working man paid to deliver the goods.

He also delivered action, which was no doubt one reason why he so dominated the landscape of the pulp era. Produced in an era marked by two world wars and the Great Depression, the pulps had their entertainment duties cut out for them, and the hard-boiled detective proved one of their ablest performers. Through him, readers enjoyed the vicarious pleasure of taking swift and decisive action against recognizable foes, and thus indirectly fought back against the anonymous social and domestic pressures that overwhelmed their daily lives.

Unlike the majority of popular fiction types, the hard-boiled detective has a known birthday and place of origin: the June 1, 1923, issue of *Black Mask,* in which Carroll John Daly introduced Race Williams, the progenitor of all hard-boiled detectives. The story in which Williams made his debut, "The Knights of the Open Palm," pales in comparison to the countless imitations it spawned, but it laid the groundwork for what we recognize today as the hard-boiled genre. Williams is a rugged individualist, the only person in an entire town with the gumption to take on the Ku Klux Klan. He has a smart lip, but he backs up his tough talk with action, and though he takes some lumps he dishes out more. When he finally walks away, he leaves behind a body count of Shakespearean dimensions. More important is the way Williams describes his profession: "I'm what you might call a middle-man—a halfway house between the dicks and the crooks." Right from the start, it was established that the hard-boiled detective was a character beholden to no one but himself, a maverick whose tactics were not only outside the law but perhaps just a hair shy of the criminal.

Over the next eight years, the hard-boiled detective kept almost exclusive residence in *Black Mask,* where the crimes he fought quickly took a backseat to the elaboration of his character and the demands made on it by his milieu. These were the years that exposed readers to the early tales of Erle Stanley Gardner, Raoul Whitfield, Paul Cain, and Frederick Nebel, and treated them to the adventures of Raymond Chandler's Mallory and Ted Carmody (both prototypes for Philip Marlowe) and Dashiell Hammett's incomparable Sam Spade. It was Spade, the cynical antihero of *The Maltese Falcon,* who forged forever the image of the hard-boiled detective as a lone figure of conscience serving a society rife with criminal tendencies.

Then, in 1931, Henry Steeger and Harold Goldsmith created *Dime Detective,* the one legitimate rival of *Black Mask. Dime Detective* was one of several genre titles in Popular Publications' "dime" line that flaunted its low price—in this case a nickel less than *Black Mask*—to appeal to Depression-strapped consumers. As added inducement, it was able to lure *Black Mask* regulars like Gardner, Nebel, Chandler, Norbert Davis, and Frederick C. Davis into its pages by paying them the princely sum of four cents per word—one cent more than *Black Mask* and quadruple the going pulp fiction rate.

Dime Detective made only two stipulations to its authors: there were to be no novel serializations and the characters they created could not appear in competing magazines. Beyond that, they were given relatively free rein to write what they chose. The result was a looser and more varied magazine than *Black Mask.* Though undeniably influential, *Black Mask's* pursuit of the straightforward hard-boiled tale produced a literate but limited legacy. *Dime Detective* on the other hand allowed both humor and horror into its fiction and wound up accommodating some of the unlikeliest crime stoppers to make the printed page. In its later years, it also published a good many non-detective crime stories written in the grim *noir* style that would become the trademark of Jim Thompson, David Goodis, and other writers of the paperback originals that helped put the pulps out of business.

The twenty-three stories selected for *Hard-Boiled Detectives,* one for each year that *Dime Detective* published between 1931 and 1953, offer a representative sampling of the magazine's fare. *Dime Detective* began publication slightly before Popular Publications conceived its line of "shudder" pulps, magazines filled with lurid stories that suggested supernatural explanations for their weird mysteries. Such tales would achieve their bizarre perfection in *Dime Mystery Book, Horror Stories,* and *Terror Tales,* but they can be found in nascent form in early issues of *Dime Detective.* For example, Gardner's "The Hand of Horror," in which a palmist detective must read a victim's severed hand, and John Lawrence's "A Burial Is Arranged," with its background theme of premature burial, suggest more than a touch of the Grand Guignol.

Counterbalancing stories set on the weird fringe were the classic hard-boiled detective tales. "Hell's Pay Check" is the second of forty-four stories Frederick Nebel wrote about his footloose private eye Jack Cardigan of the

Cosmos Agency. Cardigan debuted in the first issue of *Dime Detective* and was portrayed as the epitome of the rumpled hard-boiled dick in this passage from one of his 1934 adventures: "Cardigan was standing in the vestibule of the head sleeper, cuddling a cigarette in his palm. His battered fedora was cramped down low on his forehead, his old ulster was wrinkled, its shapeless collar bundled about his neck." The same description could have fit Raymond Chandler's John Dalmas, another of Philip Marlowe's immediate ancestors. "The Lady in the Lake," which Chandler expanded into a novel of the same name in 1943, is one of only seven stories he contributed to *Dime Detective,* yet it established him as the magazine's version of Dashiell Hammett, the paragon of quality that other writers aspired to.

At the same time, Dalmas is the sort of private eye that detective writers tried to wreak variations on. By the end of *Dime Detective*'s first full year of publication, the hard-boiled detective was ten years old and getting pretty set in his ways. To keep him from growing stale, writers sought new angles on his character that would make his exploits seem even more interesting. Thus, in "The Crime Machine," Carroll John Daly introduced Vee Brown, a detective who fights crime to earn the peace of mind necessary to write popular songs. Norbert Davis's Just Plain Jones, the cop with aching feet who limps through "Something for the Sweeper," is a forerunner of his wacky Bail Bond Dodd and Max Latin series, rare examples of hard-boiled humor. Hugh Cave's Peter Kane, who was bounced from the police force for his alcoholic binges, plays Cyrano de Bergerac to a former sweetheart who marries his best friend in nine stories written between 1934 and 1942, among them "Ding Dong Belle." At least two detectives moonlight as newspapermen, a profession they usually hold in as much contempt as the police force: Dean "The Blue Barrel" Culver of William Barrett's "A Man's Last Hours" doubles as an anonymous crime reporter cum gossip columnist, while the alias of Frederick C. Davis's Bill Brent, hero of "You Slay Me, Baby," is Lora Lorne, adviser to the lovelorn. A unique mixture of the hard-boiled and armchair detective can be found in D.L. Champion's "Footprints on the Brain," the first of twenty-nine stories about Inspector Allhoff: His legs shot off in a bungled police ambush, the crusty Allhoff forces the young cop responsible to work as his partner, continually confronting him with his guilt in the only sadomasochistic detective team in pulp history.

As far as the publishers of *Dime Detective* were concerned, the drawing card for series detectives was that each attracted a core group of readers who bought the magazine when he was featured. Over the course of *Dime Detective*'s 273 issues, nearly one hundred different detectives made appearances, and as late as 1949 important ones like Hank Searls's Mike Blair, the hero of "A Dish of Homicide," were still being introduced. By the mid-1940s, though, the format of the hard-boiled tale had begun to change. The adventures of the detectives in any given issue were matched, and sometimes outnumbered, by a growing volume of offbeat stories in which average people find themselves succumbing to criminal impulses or implicated in crimes they are forced to solve to save their skins.

The model for this type of tale was the short fiction of Cornell Woolrich, whose 1942 *Dime Detective* story, "It Had to Be Murder," was filmed by

Alfred Hitchcock in 1954 as *Rear Window*. Following Woolrich's lead, many new writers for the magazine downplayed the detective element of their crime stories to reflect on the pervasiveness of crime in society. Julius Long's "No Minimum for Murder" features series detective Clarence Darrow Mort, but is more interesting for advancing the idea that petty motives are often behind the most heinous crimes. John D. MacDonald, a *Dime Detective* find, wrote "The Man From Limbo," about a shell-shocked war veteran who stumbles upon an entire town in ignorant collusion with its corrupt politicians. G.T. Fleming Roberts and Bruno Fischer both contributed stories in which suspicions of murder threaten the sanctity of the home. Perhaps the most telling story from this period is William McGivern's "Death Comes Gift-Wrapped," wherein a hard-boiled detective oversteps the boundaries of his profession far enough to be convicted as a murderer.

Such changes in content were minor when compared to other changes that began to affect *Dime Detective*. In 1944, wartime paper shortages and rising printing costs forced an increase in the magazine's cover price to fifteen cents. This wasn't nearly as devastating a blow as the abdication of Raymond Chandler, Carroll John Daly, Frederick Nebel, Norbert Davis, and other name writers to more lucrative work writing books or for Hollywood. Although their absence opened the magazine up to the work of such new writers as William Campbell Gault and Robert Turner, and occasional contributions from William Tenn, Cyril M. Kornbluth, and Murray Leinster, who were better known for their work in science fiction, it signaled the end of the hard-boiled detective's heyday. The last issue of *Dime Detective* was dated August 1953, two years and a month after the final issue of *Black Mask*.

Some writers for *Dime Detective* enjoyed their greatest success after their pulp careers ended. Erle Stanley Gardner, for example, went on to create his immensely popular Perry Mason, and John D. MacDonald his critically acclaimed Travis Magee. In most cases, though, their reputations—and the characters that had earned them—died with the magazine. Not one of the hundreds of hard-boiled detectives who did their own small part keeping our country safe between 1920 and 1950 enjoys the immortality of Sherlock Holmes or even Dick Tracy, and the adventures of only a few have achieved lasting fame through perennial book reprints. It is left to anthologies like *Hard-Boiled Detectives* to remind readers of America's hard-boiled heritage, and to champion the reputation of a character who probably would have shrugged off all the attention.

——STEFAN DZIEMIANOWICZ
New York, 1991

Hell's Pay Check

FREDERICK NEBEL

Chapter 1

DEATH ON ARRIVAL

THE CHANGE IN the tune of the train wheels roused Cardigan. He used a broad palm to wipe steam from the rain-wet coach window. The train was crossing the Wabash River. Beyond were the lights of the city.

Cardigan bent over, dropped a magazine into an open grip, started to close it. On second thought, he drew out a .38 revolver and slipped it into his hip pocket; closed, locked the grip.

He rose, a big, shaggy-headed man with a burry outdoor look, shrugged into a wrinkled topcoat, put on a faded fedora that had seen better days. He lugged his bag to the nearest vestibule. The locomotive's bell gonged more resonantly as the train pulled into the station.

Cardigan swung down to the platform, shook his head at a barging porter, tramped heavy-footed through the waiting room. He dwarfed an average-sized man. His shoulders rocked. He slapped open a door with the flat of his hand, felt a gust of rain and raw fall wind. He moved along slowly, looking at the license plates of parked cars. Then he stopped before a large black sedan and was regarding the windshield curiously when the front door opened and a man in a chauffeur's cap stepped out.

"Mr. Cardigan?"

"Yeah."

The chauffeur saluted, pivoted, and opened the rear door. He took Cardigan's bag, and Cardigan climbed in. The bag landed after him. The chauffeur climbed in front, started the motor, clicked into gear.

Cardigan leaned back, rolled a fresh cigar between his lips, nibbled off the tip, spat it through an open window. He lit up and watched wet buildings flash past. The car turned into the main drag, where trolley bells clanged, auto horns honked, and red neon lights scrawled advertisements in the rainy dark.

"Wet night," said the chauffeur.

"Lousy."

"Train was on time, though."

"Yeah. How far out is this place?"

"It ain't far. Say, you're that private dick made such a haul out in St. Louis in the summer, ain't you?"

"Better keep your eyes on the road," Cardigan said.

They shot through a railroad underpass, rolled through a tatterdemalion part of the city. The chauffeur's ears stuck out from his head. He kept wiping sweat from the inside of the windshield. Cardigan was uninterested in the scenery. He was rather fascinated by the way the chauffeur's ears stuck out.

"Much further?" he asked.

"It ain't far," the chauffeur said.

Cardigan squinted at the back of his head, took two long, ruminative puffs. "Stop at the next cigar store. I want to get some pipe tobacco."

"Mr. Edwards'll have plenty."

"That's all right. I said I want to get some pipe tobacco."

"All right, then, all right."

A minute later the chauffeur pulled up to the curb and Cardigan opened the door, stepped out and strode into a cigar store. The windows were opaque with steam. Cardigan slipped into a telephone booth, looked at a yellow slip of paper, made a call. Half a minute later he stepped out, picked up a tin of tobacco, and went outside.

"I'll ride in front," he said. "Lucky he had my brand."

"I don't smoke a pipe," the chauffeur said, and rolled the car from the curb.

They rode in silence for a few minutes. Then Cardigan drew his gun and pressed it against the chauffeur's ribs.

"Now where the hell are you really going?" he said.

"Hey, what the—"

"Cut it out, you fat-head! Keep your hands on that wheel and don't try handing me a line."

The chauffeur was gripping the wheel hard with both hands. He didn't look at Cardigan. He stared intently through the windshield, his body tense, his shoulders hunched.

"Take the first right-hand turn," Cardigan said. "Go around the block and back to the city."

"Cripes, chief—"

"Lay off, lame-brain—lay off. The next time you try to act like a chauffeur—act like one. You've been a heel so long that you're heel-conscious." He jabbed his gun hard against the man's ribs, snapped, "Turn right!"

The man heaved on the wheel. The car skidded on the wet pavements, grazed a tree, slewed badly but held its balance. Behind, on the main street they had left, brakes ground and tires screeched. Cardigan looked back and saw a curtained touring car skidding to a stop.

"Step on it!" Cardigan muttered.

"Geeze—"

"Step on it!"

The sedan gathered speed. Looking back, Cardigan saw the touring car in reverse. Then he saw it swing into the side street. The sedan swung right again, skidding, and the man at the wheel groaned and cursed.

"Right at the next," Cardigan said, "and back to the main drag."

"What a sweet spot you put me in!"

"I'm glad of that."

"They'll think I'm two-timin'!"

"Swell!"

The chauffeur snarled, "You ain't sittin' so pretty yourself!"

The rear end slewed wildly as they took the next right. The rear left wheel struck the opposite curb. The car heaved, slammed back to all fours. The chauffeur threw out the clutch, raced the motor to keep it from stalling, meshed gears again savagely and skidded on the get-away.

The beams of the touring's headlights sparkled on the rain-beaded rear window of the sedan. The chauffeur sank deep in the seat, gritting his teeth, gripping the wheel low. Cardigan twisted around and hunched down on the floor.

A gun banged in the wet dark. The rear window fell out with a crash. A hole appeared in the center of the nonshatterable windshield, with spider-web lines radiating.

"Look!" cried the chauffeur. "Look at that!"

"To hell with that! Step on it!"

"Me—I'm gonna stop!"

Cardigan trained his gun on the man. "You stop and I'll cave in your chest!"

"Oh, Gord! They think 'm two-timin'!"

He swung left into the main drag—wildly. The wheels rasped on the wet pavement, screeched over trolley tracks. The big sedan shuddered. Miraculously it retained its balance, careened away, with the chauffeur's foot so hard on the throttle that the wheels lost traction momentarily and the rear end swung from left to right. Then the wheels gripped and the sedan shot ahead.

Another hole appeared magically in the windshield. The chauffeur choked and stared at it with horrified eyes. Then he saw a pole directly in front of him. He heaved at the wheel violently. The car slewed, skidded, turned sidewise. It swung all the way around and across the tracks—and around again. The chauffeur gripped the wheel hard, his mouth open, his eyes frozen with horror.

The right front mudguard slammed against a pole. A window fell out of the car with a crash. Guns barked and lead ripped through the sedan's body. The chauffeur screamed and heaved up and another bullet knocked him down again. The touring car roared past.

Cardigan pushed open the door, pawed glass splinters from his face. He looked once at the chauffeur's head. Another look was unnecessary. He hauled his bag out of the back of the car, ran with it across the sidewalk, back of a ramshackle house with boarded windows.

He ducked through a gap in a rotten board fence, screwing his feet into wet earth with each step to kill his footprints. He went along back of the fence, then paused in some tall grass, started to reach for his handkerchief; changed his mind. He tore off wet grass, made a pad of it, scrubbed his face and tossed the grass away. The grass and the rain were cold.

Cardigan shivered and threaded his way on back of other board fences, reached a side street and walked away from the main drag. A police siren moaned through the night. By dead reckoning Cardigan walked into the city limits, his coat collar up. The mirror of a chewing-gum slot-machine showed him that his face was not as bad as he had supposed. He sighed, whistled to himself and walked across the sidewalk into a taxi.

"Sixth and Diana," he said.

At Sixth he got off, walked north on Sixth, turned right at the first intersection and entered the Hotel Flatlands.

The man sitting behind the enormous flat-topped desk of aged mahogany drew slowly on a large pipe shaped like an inverted question mark. He was massive himself, in keeping with the room's furnishings. Middle-aged, bald, except for offshoots of grayish hair above the ears, he had a large nose, a fighter's jaw, a broad, impressive forehead. Through black-ribboned pince-nez he gazed at the stocky youth who sat quivering on a straight-backed chair.

"Be calm, Otto," said the big man.

"Yes, sir. Y-yes, sir." The stocky youth's teeth chattered.

The big man frowned concernedly, rose and went to an eight-legged Boulle cabinet. From it he took decanter and glasses. He carried them to the desk.

"Not Napoleon, Otto, but brandy nonetheless."

He gave the youth a stiff jolt. Otto threw it over, choked, spluttered, grimaced. The big man chuckled, but the look in his eyes was not one of humor. Worry was there and a haunted light shimmering deep in the pupils.

Rain thrashed against the French windows.

Otto began stuttering. "I—I couldn't do anything, sir! They walked up to me—and I could see how their hands were in their pockets. They made me walk away from the car and they kept me in a touring car after one of them took my cap. They held guns against me there. Then after maybe an hour they told me to get out and walk away and say nothing. Our—your car was gone. Then they went too. I—I—"

"You could have done nothing else, Otto. Pull yourself together. That man Cardigan telephoned a second time and I thank God nothing serious has happened to him. He's on his way out."

The old Negro in black livery came in. "Mr. Cardigan, suh."

A moment later Cardigan filled the doorway. He had left hat and coat with the butler and stood chafing his hands and staring keenly into the dimly lighted library. His shaggy hair stood out around his head.

The big man rose from behind the mahogany desk, held out his hand. Cardigan crossed the room, shook it, peered levelly at the pince-nez.

"This is Otto Shreiner, my chauffeur," the big man said.

Otto rose and bowed. Cardigan took him in with a piercing look, said nothing.

The man with the pince-nez said, "Leave us, Otto."

Otto went out. The grandfather's clock ticked solemnly.

"Brandy, Mr. Cardigan?"

Cardigan said: "Thanks," poured himself a tot, sniffed the aroma, then drank it. He squinted one eye at the empty glass. "Well, Mr. Edwards, what's on your mind?"

"Sit down, won't you?"

Both sat down, facing each other across the flat-topped desk. The old man took off his pince-nez, leaned back. "First," he said, "my name's not Edwards."

Cardigan, starting a fresh cigar, did not look up until he had it going smoothly. Then he spoke impersonally. "And then what?"

"I am the mayor of the city."

Cardigan maintained his impersonal stare. "Once I worked for a governor."

"I said 'Edwards,' you know, on long distance because—" He shrugged and held his palms up, then fell into a moody silence.

Cardigan studied the red end of his fresh cigar and started speaking in a low, blunt voice. "All right, then, Mr. Holmes. I expected trouble, anyhow. I always expect trouble when a client telephones long distance, offers to pay all expenses, and adds—'details on arrival.' That's all O.K. by me. It's my business. But I'll be twice damned if I like to have trouble pile on my shoulder the minute I step off a train. I'll stand for almost anything, but I hate to get mixed up in a murder before I know what all the shooting's for."

That ripped Holmes out of his moody silence. He half rose, remained that way, exclaimed: "Murder!"

"And why I'm sitting here right now, Mr. Mayor, is one of the reasons why I believe in luck, a rabbit's foot and words like abracadabra."

Holmes fell back into the chair, gripping the sides. "But—you said—murder!"

"Don't take it so hard. It happens every day. Besides, the guy that got it was a hood anyhow. He was the nice little boy that played chauffeur and started to take me places. But I had a hunch the minute we started that something was wrong. So I phoned you from that cigar store and asked what your chauffeur looked like."

Holmes squared his jaw. "Did you have to kill him, by God?"

"Me? Hell, no. His pals did it. Trailing us in another car. When I made the hood turn around his pals got sore and opened the fireworks. I ducked out and kept my mouth shut. Did you report the theft of your car to the police?"

But Holmes was still thinking of murder. "Murder—murder," he repeated in a faraway voice.

"Did you?"

"Oh— Well, Otto did. At the railway station."

"What did he tell them?"

"Just that three men had forced him away, held him prisoner for an hour, then let him go."

"Did he say he was waiting for me?"

"No."

"I've got to be sure. I've got to be sure because I want to know how I stand with the cops."

"Otto is in my confidence."

Cardigan got up and took a turn up and down the room. He stopped and looked at the mayor. "Where did you telephone me from, your office?"

"No—here. Right here."

"Any other phones in the house on this line?"

"No."

"All right. Then your wire was tapped. You'll hear about the murder soon enough, and your recovered car. Tell that chauffeur of yours to keep his mouth shut. You keep yours. Your enemies, whoever they are, know I'm working for you. That may be tough for you, but it's tougher for me. And now"— Cardigan sat down—"why am I here?"

Holmes leaned forward. "To recover a check for twenty thousand dollars that I made payable to one Roberta Callahan, a notorious woman."

"In other words, if this check gets to certain hands the notoriety won't do you any good."

"It will ruin me."

"You don't look like the kind of man would run around with a dangerous piece of fluff. Still, there was a governor—"

"I assure you I'm not," Holmes said with quiet dignity.

"Philanthropy?"

"Don't be droll. My son Edgar's a rather gay blade, and I did it for his sake. He became badly tangled with this woman and there was only one way out. I bought her off. I gave her my personal check for twenty thousand dollars two weeks ago. She immediately blossomed out in a new roadster, moved into a fine apartment—"

"You mean you want the cancelled check?"

"No—no. The check has not been through my bank. Don't you see? She cashed the check with someone—someone who is holding it against me. And I want that check."

"What makes you think some guy's holding it?"

Holmes tilted his jaw. "You know me—or of me, rather. The reform mayor. By Judas Priest, I am that! Edgar had to get himself involved with that—woman—and I, naturally being his father, had to get him out of it. Hence my check. And would a photograph of that check, printed in the daily tabloid here, help my reform platform? No—you needn't reply. The answer is obvious."

"Who would be holding that check?"

"Any number of persons. Our daily tabloid, the worst scandal sheet in the country. Or the Fusion crowd. Or Pat McHugh, the boss of the old party. Or somebody unknown to me who hopes to reap a fortune by passing it on to someone else. But there you are. There's the situation. I blundered into this because I'm not as smart-alecky as a lot of people. I'm entirely innocent. You might say that my son would come to the fore and admit the check was written to clear him. But the rest could hoot that down—and they could buy off the woman. You see?"

Cardigan had slid way down into the chair. He regarded Holmes through narrow-lidded eyes. Suddenly he knew he liked Holmes, saw his position. Cardigan, no reformer himself but a hard party down to the core, had a habit of admiring qualities which he himself did not possess.

He sat up, taking out a notebook. "All right now, Mr. Holmes. Give me all the names of persons you suspect, and addresses if possible. I don't suppose you asked the woman who cashed the check for her."

"I dare not go near her. I will pay the person who holds that check now the amount written on it—but I must have it."

"You'll get it," Cardigan said.

Chapter 2

DOUGH FOR A DICK

A T MIDNIGHT CARDIGAN lay awake in the dark of his hotel room thinking. The rain had stopped. The sound of a crosstown trolley came up sharply out of the street.

Elections were a month hence, and old Mayor Holmes had things to think about. A reform platform is a ticklish thing to stand on. Wiseacres are always ready to accuse you of trying to kid the public, of playing the wolf in sheep's clothing. A confessed mountebank is always colorful, a good man rarely popular.

Thus thought Cardigan—until a sound at the door dismissed philosophy and snapped him to the immediate present. He reached over to the little bedtable, got his hand on his revolver and sat up with the same motion. He heard the not quite silent movement of a key in the lock, a final click. Then a pause of utter silence. Then a vertical line of light appeared where the door opened on a crack. The door swung wide slowly, silently, and three men stood there. Two of them had guns drawn while the third moved into the background. One of the armed men reached in a hand seeking the light switch.

"That's far enough," Cardigan said. "One slight move out of any of you birds and the management'll be disturbed."

The two armed men remained motionless. Then one said: "Police, Cardigan."

"Show me."

The two men turned back their lapels.

Cardigan lowered his gun. "It's damned funny that I can't get a night's sleep without you guys prowling around here like correspondence-school detectives."

The horse-faced man snapped on the lights and said, "I'm Lieutenant Strout. This is Sergeant Blake. That's Massey, the house officer. You can go, Massey."

Strout closed the door in Massey's face. He put away his gun and Blake did likewise. Blake was a chubby-cheeked fat man with a sly, smiling face. Strout was tall, muddy-eyed.

"Let's see that rod," he said.

Cardigan reversed it and Strout took it by the butt. It was a jointless solid-frame gun. Strout smelled the barrel, examined the chamber, hefted it thoughtfully, tossed it back on the bed.

"That the only one you carry?"

"Yeah."

"Look around, Blake. There's his bag."

Blake ransacked Cardigan's handbag while Cardigan stuffed a pipe and watched him with mild amusement. Strout went through Cardigan's clothes, opened the dresser drawers. Blake left Cardigan's clothes on the floor beside the bag.

Strout sat down on a chair, struck a match on the veneered frame of the wooden bed, left a long scratch there.

"What were you doing in the mayor's car tonight, Cardigan?"

"Was I in the mayor's car?"

Strout spurted smoke through his nostrils. "Don't give me the runa-round."

"Well, was I?"

"You got in it at the railroad station and the chauffeur was killed twenty minutes later on Prairie Avenue."

"Says who?"

"Says me."

"Get your proof, lieutenant, and we'll continue."

"Listen, you," Blake said with his sly smile. "We've heard a lot about you."

Strout went on. "It was a stolen car. You got in and the chauffeur wasn't the mayor's chauffeur. He was all shot up when we found him and the car was busted. He was cold meat. You rode with him."

Cardigan put his bare feet on the floor, buttoned up the coat of his blue cotton pajamas, pointed his pipe stem at Strout.

"Now I'll tell you what I did. I came out of the station looking for a taxi. A guy with a chauffeur's cap on said, 'Taxi!' like that. So I thought it was an independent, and as it was raining and the car was handy I climbed in. I told him to drive to the Hotel Flatlands. After a while I began to wonder where he was going. I asked him and he said where I told him. He began to look queer to me, but I wasn't looking for trouble. So I got out at a cigar store and went in and bought some tobacco. I thought it out. I left the store and walked away. I walked back to the city and came here."

Blake laughed in a shrill, mocking tone. "That's a fast one!"

"Well, what are you going to do about it?" Cardigan said.

"What are we going to do about it?" Blake cried. "Damn you, you can't—"

"Shut up, Jake," Strout said dully and kept looking at Cardigan with his muddy, humorless eyes. "This is damned funny, Cardigan," he went on. "You were in a stolen car and the guy that drove it was murdered."

"With my gun, I suppose."

"Not with that gun there, but that don't say you didn't have another."
Cardigan laughed harshly. "And they pin medals on you guys!"

Strout blew cigarette ash to the carpet. "What did you come here for?"

"To sleep." He swung back into bed, pulled the covers up to his neck.

"I mean the city," Strout said.

"To get the hell pestered out of me by a couple of dumb clucks wearing badges."

Strout looked sullen. "None of your lousy cheap wit, Cardigan! You may have a name where you come from for being a pretty swell dick, but names are all the same to me on a police blotter."

The bed covers erupted and Cardigan was sitting up again. "Any time a client engages me it's just the same as if he engaged a lawyer. He gets my confidence and the benefit of silence."

"But there's murder in this."

"Because a heel in a stolen car starts taking me for a ride, for some reason I don't know, and I'm wide awake enough to slip out of it; and because a little later the heel is murdered with a gun that isn't mine— Listen, Strout, why the hell should I get all hot and bothered and tell you the story of my life? Do you mean to sit there in those pants and tell me I ought to get gray worrying about it? Hot dog, what school did you go to?"

Blake snapped, "This mutt is looking for a bust in the puss!"

"Yeah, and I suppose you're going to do it. Any minute now I'm going to break into convulsions!"

Strout pushed Blake back and said to Cardigan: "You come down to headquarters tomorrow."

"Like hell I will. If you want me to come to headquarters go get a warrant for my arrest. You got a lame tip somewhere, Strout, and you're trying to make me believe that it's red-hot. At your age you should know better than try that one. It was whiskered before I was born."

Strout got up, put his bony fists on his hips, regarded Cardigan with sullen eyes. "You're bright as hell, ain't you?"

Cardigan lay back in bed, pulled up the covers. "On the way out, Strout, douse the lights and lock the door."

Cardigan was singing deep-throated under the shower next morning when the doorbell rang.

"Wait a minute," he yelled.

He stopped the shower, climbed out and rubbed himself down with a towel and then alcohol. He heaved into a bathrobe, kicked his feet into mules and tramped through the bedroom.

A little plump man with pomaded sandy hair and narrow shoulders stood holding a derby chest-high with both hands. Thirty-odd, he had a clerical air. He wore expensive dark clothes.

"May I come in?"

"You're a new one on me," Cardigan said, "but come on."

The man crossed the threshold and Cardigan's hands darted to his person, slapped pockets rapidly. Out of the man's left pocket he took a small, dark automatic, palmed it.

"You see," he said, "I never know," and kicked the door shut.

The little man smiled. "You're a man of parts, Mr. Cardigan. I'm sorry to have intruded so early. Be careful—the safety may not be closed."

"I find that out the minute I touch a gun. It is."

"Truly a man of parts."

Cardigan said: "Now get this. I just got up. I haven't eaten yet. I'm a lousy guy to do business with most of the time, but especially before breakfast. Cut out the drawing-room tricks and speak your piece."

"A most definite man also. My compliments." Smiling, the little man showed exquisite white teeth and crinkly red lips. "Very well. I shan't be long. Primo: what are you doing in the city?"

"Answer: none of your business."

"Of course, you are here working for the mayor."

"The words are in your mouth, not mine."

"Doubtless you came here to regain possession—for the mayor—of a piece of paper. Green, let us say. And watermarked. You know—those little wavy lines? Correct?"

"You make me sick," Cardigan growled. He extracted six .25-caliber shells from the miniature Webley, shoved the Webley in the man's pocket, turned him about and shoved him to the door. "In a word—scram!"

The man turned, smiling with his shell-like teeth. "Would five thousand dollars interest you?"

"A thousand would, but what's that to you?"

"I have a friend who would pay you five thousand dollars for that little oblong strip of green, watermarked paper."

"I work for a living," Cardigan said, "and the agency I work for has a reputation. I don't think it would go nuts about doing business with you."

"But how about you?"

Cardigan took three long strides and gripped the little man by his shirt front. "Who the hell are you?"

"Please don't get pugilistic," the little man said in a tranquil voice.

Cardigan turned about with him, hurled him across the bed. "I've been here only twelve hours," he growled, "and I'm getting fed up on a lot of people."

He straddled the man, held him down by the throat with one strong hand, used the other to go through his pockets. He pulled out a wallet, keys, some envelopes. Getting back on his feet, he said: "Now stay there," and began sifting the articles.

Presently he shrugged, tossed the lot back on the bed. "You can go," he said. "And tell that lousy tabloid you work for that they couldn't buy me for a hundred thousand! And mark me, little morning glory! If you go monkeying around here again things may happen to you. Cut—and goom-by!"

The little man rose, patted down his clothes, picked his derby from the floor and bowed at the door. His shell-like teeth gleamed. He backed out saying nothing, closed the door quietly.

When Cardigan went downstairs fifteen minutes later, Massey, the house dick, headed him off.

"What did that reporter from the tab want, Cardigan?"

"A short autobiographical sketch, Mr. Massey. Something like 'From Plowboy to Mastermind.' I said mine wasn't interesting. Referred him to you."

"And for that you gave him a split lip, huh?"

"He stubbed his toe and fell against a radiator."

"Yah!"

"Goom-by!"

Cardigan ate breakfast in the coffee shop, went out carrying his topcoat under his arm. Under the facade, he looked up and down the street. Across the way, diagonally, a man stood in front of a Western Union window. Cardigan walked west, turned south into Sixth, used a store window as a mirror and saw the man follow him.

He turned around abruptly and retraced his steps, putting a cigar in his mouth. The man who had followed had no time to duck. He slowed down, however. Cardigan came up to him, stopped, said: "Got a match, brother?"

The man was young. "Sure," he said, and passed a packet.

Cardigan lit up, returned the packet, said: "Spider on you!" and struck the man's lapel lightly. Beneath the cloth he felt the hardness of a police shield.

The man looked bewildered.

"Give Lieutenant Strout my love," Cardigan said, and rolled on, puffing enthusiastically.

The plainclothesman did not follow.

Chapter 3

THE GIRL IN 616

TEN MINUTES LATER Cardigan got out of a taxi in front of a six-story apartment house. He pounded a broad flag walk and tramped in through a broad, imposing entrance. The livery of the Negro elevator boy hurt his eyes.

"How is every little thing?" Cardigan grinned.

"What floor?"

"All right, be dignified—Six, colonel."

The elevator rose in silence. Cardigan got out at the sixth floor and walked on carpets resilient as sponge rubber. He stopped, raised a bronze knocker on the black door of 616, let it fall back.

A girl with a shock of blond hair opened it and looked at Cardigan with wide, baby-blue eyes. She had on blue pajamas and a blue peignoir trimmed with sand-colored old lace.

"Yes?" she chirped in a babyish voice.

"I have grave news for you," Cardigan said with a judicial air.

"Oh—what?"

Acting fatherly, he took hold of her hand, patted it with rough tenderness, the while he worked himself through the doorway and kicked the door shut. He scaled his hat into a velours divan, grinned broadly at the girl. She shrank back, drawing her peignoir about her small, rounded body.

"What—what do you want?" she asked, fear tailing her words.

Cardigan grinned. With his ungodly shock of hair and his heavy, powerful shoulders he filled the room. He indicated a loveseat.

"Sit down, Miss Callahan."

"W-what d-do you—"

He sudden crossed the luxurious living room, looked in the bedroom, the bathroom; turned and regarded the girl across the length of the room.

"Now let's put the cards on the table, sister. I know who you are and what you are, so don't try to pull an act on me or throw a faint or in any way try to kid me into believing that you don't know what it's all about. I may look like a gorilla, but I'm not going to slam you down. All you have to do is answer a question."

The baby-faced girl swallowed. "W-what is it?"

"Who cashed that twenty-thousand dollar check for you?"

Miss Callahan sat down on the loveseat, sinking into one of its twin cushions. She gripped her knees with white hands the nails of which were lacquered in red. Her baby-blue eyes dilated. She looked innocent and hurt.

"Come on, come on," Cardigan growled, thumping across the carpet. He was big, towering, inimical in a leather-faced way.

The girl made a sound that sounded like "Eek!" and drew her knees up to her breast, gripping her ankles.

"I—I don't know what you're talking about," she cried in a tiny, breathless voice. "I—I d-don't know you. What right have you got to come in here? You b-brute!"

"For God's sake, sister, don't pull a hack line like that. I tell you I know you. I know you got a check for twenty thousand. I know you cashed it—and not in a bank."

She jumped to her feet and began pacing up and down dramatically. "This is an outrage!" she cried. "I don't know you and I don't know what you're talking about. You forced your way in my apartment and if you don't leave right away I'll call the management and we'll see. Now"— she indicated the door—"get out!"

"Tone down, girlie!"

She stamped her foot. "Get out!"

He grabbed her. Her eyes popped and the flat of his hand stifled a scream. His hair stood up on his nape. He shook her.

"You fool! Pipe down!"

"Release the lady, Mr. Cardigan."

Cardigan stiffened, twisted his neck. The reporter from the tabloid stood with his back to the door holding the small Webley and smiling with his shell-like teeth.

"Naughty, naughty!" he mocked.

Cardigan released the girl. She reeled away from him, bounced into the loveseat and lay panting and choking out hysterical little sounds.

"So," grunted Cardigan, his big hands hanging at his sides, his face lowering.

"Just so, Mr. Cardigan. Observe the steadiness of this gun and act accordingly."

"Cool, ain't you?" Cardigan growled.

"As the proverbial cucumber."

"N-now who are y-you?" cried the girl.

"Your benefactor," said the little man. "I eavesdropped." He smiled politely at Cardigan. "You'll be going directly, won't you, Mr. Cardigan?"

Cardigan felt the red color of chagrin flooding his face and neck. He felt suddenly oafish in the presence of this cool little man with the gun and the steady hand. He crossed to the velours divan, picked up his hat. He kept looking at the girl and backed up toward the door. In a mirror back of the divan he could see his own and the little man's image. The little man was behind him, holding the gun, smiling.

Cardigan's right elbow shot backward and upward. It caught the little man neatly under the chin and snapped his head back violently to the tune of clicking teeth. Cardigan jumped to one side and pivoted at the same time. His fist traveled a foot and smashed against the little man's chest. The little man slammed against the wall so hard that he rebounded and ran into Cardigan's short left. That straightened him momentarily. The gun dropped from his fingers. Glassy-eyed, he went down like a balloon suddenly deflated.

Cardigan picked up the gun with one hand and with the other drew manacles from his pocket and lunged at the girl. The leveled gun cut her scream in the bud. He drew her from the divan, made her sit on the floor and manacled her to the unconscious little man.

"Now be quiet," he said huskily.

He began searching the room. He turned out all the drawers in a high, narrow secretary. He found a bank book showing a deposit of twenty thousand dollars two weeks ago. He scanned letters. He ransacked the living room and the bedroom with a vengeance. In the bedroom he knocked over a vase of flowers into a pink waste basket. Cursing his clumsiness, he picked them up, and spotted a small card and a small envelope lying in the wastebasket. The card had written on it: "Just a remembrance for a favor from you know who." A plain white card such as florists supply. And on the accompanying envelope, printed in green, on the flap: "The Shelman Florist."

Cardigan pocketed card and envelope and went back into the living room. The girl was shivering.

Cardigan said: "This guy here works for the daily tabloid, so look out for him. Why the hell don't you tell me who cashed that check and get the benefit of silence? Do you want to have your name sprawled all over the papers?"

"I w-wish you'd leave."

"You little scatter-brained fool, they'll use you eventually! This guy is looking for the same information I am, but he wants to spread it in the tab."

"I—have nothing to say."

Cardigan shrugged. He bent down, unlocked the manacles and put them in his pocket. He threw the Webley on the velours divan, started for the door.

"B-but this man!" cried the girl. "What am I going to do with him."

"Try ice bags or smelling salts. I wouldn't care."

He opened the door, went out, down the corridor. He punched the elevator button and went down with the stony-faced Negro.

The Shelman Florist Shop was in the small arcade of the Shelman Hotel. It was a small, chic cubicle with a floor of lozenge-shaped tiles. The attendant was a girl in a black jersey ensemble. She smiled brightly and Cardigan took off his hat, leaned on the black marble counter.

"If I asked you in a nice way, miss, would you tell me who sent flowers to Miss Roberta Callahan, 4111 Danneford, in the last day or two?"

"Strange request, isn't it?"

"Strange as strange. How about it?"

"I don't know." She tapped her foot and kept throwing little glances at him. "It's unusual. I never had it happen before. I don't know what to say. Who are you?"

"By one look at my ugly map couldn't you tell I was a detective?"

"No."

"You're being kind. I am."

She blushed. "Wait a minute."

She went to the rear of the shop, looked through a file of carbons. In a minute she returned. "I'd like to keep my name out of this," she said.

"Sure thing."

"They were ordered by a Mr. P. K. McHugh."

Cardigan went out finding the air a sweeter thing to breathe. P. K.—Pat—McHugh, the boss of the old party. Pat McHugh sending flowers to Roberta Callahan by way of remembering a favor she had done him! Pat McHugh, arch-enemy of the reform ticket and Mayor Evan Holmes—

On his way back to the Flatlands Cardigan picked up three different newspapers, went to his room and read them. Last night's murder was front-page stuff. The dead man had finally been identified as Carl Dorshook, alias Charles Dorn, alias James Matson. His record went back to Toledo, Chillicothe, Dayton, Pittsburgh, and Baltimore. According to the police, however, he could not be linked up with any local mob, though apparently he had been. Theft of the mayor's car enlarged the headlines and evoked a picture of the mayor in each paper.

Cardigan tossed the papers aside and thought things out. He knew the police were not through with him yet. He knew they couldn't hang anything on him but he also knew that they could make things uncomfortable for him. He wanted to protect himself, to steer away from any hint that he was working for the mayor.

He went out and took a high-speed train out to a suburb five miles distant. From the telegraph office at the railroad station he sent a code message to the main office in New York. Translated, the message said:

In a jam. Send a long wire. Make it a follow-up on a fake case to kid the cops. Use your own judgment.

He gave the address of the Hotel Flatlands. He suspected that Massey, the house dick, would get a copy of it, and he wanted it so. Because Massey would turn it over to Lieutenant Strout. He took the tram back to the city and at one o'clock he received a message.

The girl may also be using the name of Sterrit. Her hair is dark red instead of brown and she was last in Cleveland, not Springfield, Ohio. She has stenographic ability and can also play on the harp. If there is any place of amusement there featuring a harpist look into it. She affects an English accent and has a complex for using big words such as amanuensis and gymnosophist. Her parents are desolated, so show results and spare no expense in obtaining same. If you feel you need the assistance of another operative let me know.

George Hammerhorn,
President,
The Cosmos Detective Agency

Cardigan appreciated the message, excepting the nonsense about the harp. Certain that the mayor's wire was being tapped, he walked six blocks to a Postal Telegraph office, wrote out a message and saw a messenger depart with it.

He was in his room at two o'clock when Otto Shreiner, the mayor's chauffeur knocked. Cardigan put him on a chair.

"You can help your boss and me in a big way," Cardigan said. "At midnight I want you to come here to my room and stay here for an hour while I'm out. The night telephone operator comes on duty at that time and she's never heard my voice. At a quarter past twelve I want you to call her and ask her the time. At twelve-thirty I want you to call the Union Station and ask the best train to St. Louis tomorrow forenoon. At a quarter to one I want you to call the operator again and ask her to call you at eight in the morning. Got that straight?"

"Yes, sir."

"Try to speak like me. You know, rough, as if you owned the place or something. Get me?"

"Yes, sir."

"You took a room here all right?"

"Yes, sir."

"What room and what name?"

"I signed Henry Josephs of Indianapolis. Room 411."

"O.K. Stay in your room and use the stairs on the way down."

"I used them on the way up."

Cardigan slapped his back. "You'll do, Otto!" Then he let the chauffeur out.

The tabloid, Cardigan knew, had no political stand, no moral stand. It had a personal grievance against Mayor Holmes dating back to a day six months ago when the mayor, in a radio speech, had called it "a filthy, depraved rag"; this because two of the tabloid's reporters had broken into the home of a woman whose daughter had been slain in a love tangle. In an effort to steal photographs and letters, they had bound the mother and precipitated a nervous breakdown. On the other hand, the *Press-Clarion* was politically definite in its stand against Holmes, carried considerable heft in the south and east ends, and obviously would jump at the opportunity to undermine the mayor's character.

Cardigan knew for certain that the tabloid was after that check. He had a strong hunch that Pat McHugh possessed the check. And he wondered if the *Press-Clarion* had a finger in the pie too. The murder of Dorshook was an accident—a bad one. It was reasonable to suppose that some mob in the extortion racket had got wind of the check, had wanted Cardigan for purposes of extracting definite information. Thus Cardigan had three distinct groups of enemies. And he was hampered by the police.

Chapter 4

STRONG-ARM STUFF

A T THREE O'CLOCK he went down to the lobby for the afternoon editions. He was on his way across to the newsstand when he saw Strout and Blake come barging through the swing doors. He sensed trouble. A savage doggedness was in Strout's gait and manner and Blake wore a wily, bitter smile.

"Now don't give me any back talk," Strout chopped off. "Over to headquarters with you."

"What's this—another one of your bright moments?"

Blake gripped Cardigan's arm. "Ixnay on that back chat."

Cardigan looked disgusted. "Wait'll get my hat and coat."

Blake shook him. "You come right along!"

"You go chase yourself. I get cold in the head easily."

Strout muttered: "We'll go up with you."

In his room Cardigan took his time. "What have I done now?"

"Snap on it!" Blake clipped.

Cardigan picked up Hammerhorn's wire. "Have you seen this?"

Strout read it, looked up at Cardigan with his muddy eyes, looked down at the wire again. Then he tossed it on the bed and said: "Come on."

Cardigan said: "D'you know of any place around here featuring a harpist?"

Blake took a crack at Cardigan's ribs, from behind. Cardigan, whirled, cursed, his eyes blazing, but Strout grabbed him from behind. Blake snickered and went to the door, opening it, and Strout marched Cardigan out. They went to headquarters in a taxi.

In a dusty office on the second floor a uniformed cop sat in one chair and the Negro elevator boy from the Danneford Avenue apartment house sat in another. His eyes got round when Cardigan looked at him and then Blake knocked Cardigan into a chair and chuckled loosely.

"Is this the guy?" Strout said to the Negro.

"Yassuh."

"O.K." Strout sat on the desk, dangled one leg and turned his horse face to Cardigan. His eyes got muddier, his face dark and dour. "Now spout, big boy."

Cardigan knew it was no time for horseplay. He saw in Strout a good cop, a hard one, short on speech and not a man to be kidded when he was in deadly earnest. Blake was a wind bag, but he could be nasty too in a mean, sly way. The presence of the Negro was hint enough that something had gone wrong at the apartment house. More properly, in Roberta Callahan's apartment.

"Spout about what?" Cardigan asked.

Strout indicated the Negro with a nod. "This guy described you to a T. The minute he described you I knew it was you. You called on a girl named Roberta Callahan this morning. Right?"

"Tell me some more."

"All right. When you came down in the elevator the boy here says you looked red and mad and mean. What the hell were you doing in Roberta Callahan's apartment?"

"What proof have you I was in her apartment?"

"There are eight other apartments on that floor. We asked the occupants of those apartments if they'd had any callers. They hadn't."

"I thought the Callahan girl might have told you."

"She couldn't. She's in the hospital."

Cardigan felt a chill knife his spine. His brows bent. "Was I the only guy in her apartment?" he snapped.

"The boy says you were the only man got off at that floor before ten-thirty. She went out at ten-thirty. At two o'clock she was picked up on a road near the Wabash, unconscious. She was beaten up. She has a black eye and a fractured jaw and we don't know if she'll live."

Blake shook his fist. "By cripes, Cardigan, you can't pull off a thing like that!"

Cardigan glowered. "You horse's neck, do you think I'd beat up a woman? Outside of my personal habits in a job like that, d'you think the agency'd stand for it?"

"Listen," said Strout dully. "I don't know you except from what I've seen of you. You've been handing us the run-around since you hit the city. Now what the hell were you doing in her apartment?"

Cardigan folded his arms. "You read that wire, didn't you?"

"What of it?"

"I was on a tip that the girl I'm tailing was seen in the company of Roberta Callahan. I went there and saw the Callahan girl. She got touchy because I busted up her sleep and we had an argument. I was mad because I thought she knew something about this girl and wouldn't tell me. She finally threatened to call in the management if I didn't take the air.

"As I was about to leave, a man called on her and I didn't want to make a scene, so I left."

"Who was the man?" Strout asked.

"How should I know?"

"What did he look like?"

"Kind of small, I remember. It was dim in the room and I didn't bother to look at him close enough."

Strout looked at the Negro. "I thought you said he was the only man got off that floor before ten-thirty?"

"Yassuh."

Strout looked back at Cardigan. "Well?"

"Well? Well, they have a staircase in that place, haven't they?"

"Why the hell should anybody climb six flights when there's an elevator?"

"How should I know? Either the dinge is lying or the guy climbed the stairs."

"I ain't lyin'," growled the Negro.

Blake chattered, "It's this guy's lying! This big bum right here! I know his kind! He can keep a straight face all he wants but he's lying! He's a lousy two-faced liar! There's only one way we can make this baby talk!"

Strout looked at Blake absently, looked back at Cardigan. Blake jumped on Cardigan where he sat, planted a knee in Cardigan's stomach and gripped his throat with both hands. Cardigan wore a cold, crooked smile.

"Spring it!" Blake rasped.

Cardigan chuckled. "Nuts."

Blake struck him across the face with an open palm. The chair creaked. Cardigan jammed his hands under Blake's armpits, rose mightily and sent Blake sprawling across the desk. The Negro yelped. Blake fell to the floor, carrying a chair down with him. He came up spitting oaths and drawing his blackjack.

Cardigan was set for him. Strout turned and blocked Blake, took the blackjack away from him and shook his head. Blake cursed. Strout shook his head and shoved Blake into a chair. Strout dropped the blackjack to the desk and looked dourly at Cardigan.

A windy glitter was in Cardigan's eyes. "You pipe this, Strout! I've got a lot of power behind me and a lot of money—enough of both to make you and this whole police department take water! And as for that fat-head partner of yours, he'll get his jaw broken if he tries any rough stuff on me. I'm no heel! I'm no cheap back-alley gangster! I work for a salary and it's damned small considering what I have to put up with. And unlike you guys I get no graft."

"Shut up," said Strout.

"I'll shut up when I damned well feel like it! If you—listen, Strout—if you want to pinch me, go ahead and pinch me. You haven't got a thing on me. You know damned well I wouldn't beat up a woman. You pinch me and I'll be out inside of three hours. And what can you pinch me for? Because some heel tried to take me for a ride? Because I called on a girl who later was taken for a ride? Damn it, I've got a reputation! A big one! And not in any hick town, either! And I should throw a fit over a couple of hicks like you and Blake? You'll pinch me—yes, you will!"

Strout colored. "Can't a man ask you a question?"

"Oh, that's what you call it! That's what you call busting into my hotel room last night! That's what you call falling on me in a hotel lobby! That's what you call dragging me down here like a red-hot! Oh, what big eyes you have, grandma!"

He bent down, picked his hat off the floor, pinched it back into shape and slapped it violently on his head.

"I'm going out of here," he said, "and I'd like to see you stop me. And

I'd like to see you come around and bother me again. I'd just like to see you!"

He yanked open the door, shot Blake a look of scorn and banged out.

At eleven that night Cardigan walked into the Flatlands lobby, bought some tobacco at the newsstand. He asked for mail at the desk. There was no mail, but another fake wire from Hammerhorn supplementing information on the "runaway girl."

"I have to work in my room tonight," he told the clerk. "And I don't want to be disturbed by anybody."

On the way across the lobby he ran into Massey.

"I hear they had you down to headquarters," Massey said.

"Did you ever hear the story about a hotel detective who solved a great murder mystery?"

"No."

"You never will."

Cardigan went up in the elevator, checked his wristwatch with the elevator boy's, said good night, and strode to his room. At a few minutes to twelve Otto Shreiner came in and Cardigan impressed on him the necessity of making the three telephone calls. Then he put on his coat, turned up the collar, and pulled his hat down low on his forehead.

He went downstairs by the stairway. The stairway was enclosed, with a door on each floor, and was really a fire-escape. It terminated near the side entrance of the hotel, and Cardigan left unobserved and put his head into a brisk fall wind. The city had very little night life, and what it did have was not obvious. Cardigan used darkened store windows for mirrors and walked three or four blocks to make certain he wasn't being followed.

Roberta Callahan was still unconscious. Cardigan knew who had given her that beating—or pretty nearly knew—the little man from the tabloid. What Cardigan did not know was whether the beating had served its purpose and extracted information. Lester Sisson was the little man's name. Had he given her the beating alone or had he hired strong-arm men?

Cardigan hopped in a taxi and gave a West End street corner as his destination. Ten minutes later he got out and watched the taxi speed away. The wind clapped the skirt of his overcoat smartly. The sky had a wintry look, with tattered scud driving across the moon. The wind threshed in a big sycamore tree and telephone wires hummed. Cardigan got his bearings and moved up a wide, deserted street where substantial houses stood far back from the sidewalks.

He crossed an intersection and kept on. He saw the tail-light of a parked car halfway up the block. He crossed to the other side of the street. He walked with long, purposeful strides. He looked across the street at the car because he heard its big powerful engine purring softly. There was something familiar about the car. It was a big touring, with the curtains up. He looked straight ahead. Fifty feet further on he turned his head to the left and looked at the fieldstone house of Pat McHugh. It was dark.

Cardigan kept on, turned left into the next cross street and did some quiet and deliberate cursing. He was sure it was the car that had opened fire on him, killing Dorshook. Its presence in the street meant one of two things:

either the men were friends of McHugh or had come on a mission similar to Cardigan's. If the latter, were they certain McHugh had the check or, like Cardigan, were they taking a chance?

Cardigan stopped, looked up and down the street then scaled a low stone wall. He went through shrubbery in the rear of the corner house, fell over a croquet wicket in the back yard of the next and then came to a waist-high hedge that blocked the way to McHugh's grounds. He followed the hedge to the rear of the yard, squeezed between the end of the hedge and the stone wall it met there. He went back of McHugh's double garage and peered around the corner of it at the rear windows of the house. The hatchway to the cellar was open. The garage was empty, doors open.

He had not been able to see how many men were in the car. He did not know how many were in the house. He ducked from the garage to the hedge and crept along in the shadow of it, nearer the house. He stopped, kneeling, his hand closed on the gun in his overcoat pocket. He looked at the illuminated dial of his wristwatch. It was twelve twenty-five.

A couple minutes later he saw a shape materialize out of the hatchway. A tall man, topcoatless, dressed in dark clothes. He stood for a moment listening, a gun in his hand. Then he took hold of the open door, let it down slowly, softly.

Cardigan made the dozen feet in three long steps, jammed his gun against the small of the man's back as the latter was rising.

"Quiet!" Cardigan muttered.

The man frozen in a half crouch.

Cardigan whispered, "Stick your gun straight up in the air—arm high. Quick!"

The man's arm went up. Cardigan took away his gun, put it in his own pocket.

He said: "You should have dumped that car right after you bumped off Dorshook."

He could see the man's muscles flex, heard a breath being sucked in sharply. The man started to turn around.

"No, you don't!" Cardigan muttered.

"Who the hell are you?"

"A reporter from the *Press-Clarion*. Now hand it over."

"Geeze, looka here now—"

"Hand it over!"

The man whispered an oath, put a hand in his inside pocket, passed an envelope over his shoulder. Cardigan took it, put it between his teeth, drew out a smooth oblong of paper with his left hand, then shoved it and the envelope into his pocket.

"Now walk toward that garage," he said. "Along the hedge here, then across."

He kept behind the man, prodded him with the gun. He knew that if Roberta Callahan died he would have a tough time of it with the police. They had no proof against him but they could raise an unholy row, hold him if they had to and create a lot of undesirable publicity for the agency. In which event Cardigan knew he would stand a good chance of losing his job. He had to protect himself. He walked the man to the garage entrance and told him to keep walking till he reached the back wall. While the man did this Cardigan swung the doors shut, slipped on the lock, snapped it.

He heard the man jolt the doors a second later, heard him mutter fiercely: "Damn you, what you doin'?"

Chapter 5

CARDIGAN CRASHES THROUGH

CARDIGAN LOOKED AT his watch. It was twelve thirty-five. He backed away toward the shadow of the hedge. He had almost reached it when he heard a twig snap. He pivoted, saw a man standing by the side of the house.

He heard "Burt!" called in a hoarse whisper. He remained silent, motionless. Again—"Burt!" A little louder, almost stronger than a whisper. And eager—anxious.

After a moment the man moved cautiously into the rear yard. He looked at the closed hatch doors, at the rear of the house. He moved again, peering hard. He was nearer the garage now.

Again he called, "Burt!" in a whisper.

The man in the garage answered in a whisper. "I'm in here! Get me out! A guy got it!"

The other tensed, went swiftly to the garage. "Got it?"

"Yeah!"

"Who?"

"A guy from the *Press-Clarion*. Cripes, get me out!"

"Sh!" the man on the outside cautioned, and stood in a tense listening attitude. Then he examined the lock. "I'm damned if I can open it."

"You gotta! You get me outa here! Here! There's no windows—only the door here—"

"Quiet—quiet, loud mouth! . . . Lemme think . . . Hell, I can't force it—"

"Take a chance! Put a couple o' slugs through it! That egg— Listen, Louie—that egg knows I was in on the Dorshook kill. You gotta get me out. I ain't gonna fall for no rap on my lonesome. You get me out or you and Joe and—"

"O.K. Get back outa the way. I'll blow her off, then lam. Better not hang together. We'll join up at Cicero's—and don't you make any more cracks who takes a rap and who don't. O.K.—get back."

"Hey you!" Cardigan said in a low, blunt voice. "Scram!"

The man called Louis almost fell over with surprise.

"And watch that rod in your hand," Cardigan said. "You heard me—beat it!"

The pitch of his voice and the darkness made it hard for Louie to locate him. Louie began backing away.

"Louie!" cried the man in the garage. "Louie, you ain't gonna leave me here! So help me, if you lam out on me I'll shoot the whole works!"

Louie stopped. He looked over his shoulder. Another man was coming along the side of the house. He stopped and looked at the cellar hatch, then at the shape of Louie.

"Say," he whispered, "Sisson's gettin' nervous. He says we better breeze. There's a patrolman due through here any minute."

Louie backed up toward him, and the latter whispered, "Where the hell's Burt?"

"Louie!" Burt cried in a hoarse whisper.

The third man began: "What the hell—" Then Louie made a motion of his head, kept backing up.

"Come on, Joe," Louie whispered grimly.

"But Burt's in that garage! How— Say, what's the matter?"

"Come on, you fool."

"I'm gonna get Burt!" Joe lunged toward the garage.

"Scram!" Cardigan barked. "You heard what your pal said."

"Louie!" Burt pleaded.

Joe stopped in his tracks, made a half turn with his gun held low. Its muzzle whipped flame and thunder through the dark. Cardigan heard the bullet snap through the hedge. He fired the gun he had taken from Burt and the echoes barked among the houses.

Louie's gun exploded. Cardigan heard the snick of the bullet passing, the slap of it against the stone wall beyond. He threw a shot at the dim shape of Louie and ruined a drain pipe on the house.

Joe began yelling. "My God—my God!" and ran toward Louie. Burt hammered inside the garage.

"I'm hit!" Joe gasped. "I'm hit, Louie!"

Cardigan snapped: "You guys beat it!"

Joe, yelling, "Oh, I'm hit bad!" ran right past Louie, fell over a flower bed and squealed like a woman. Louie backed up swiftly, cursing. There was the sound of a motor roaring, of gears being meshed savagely. Joe got up out of the flower garden and looked toward the street.

He cried: "Sisson's ditchin' us, the louse!" He hefted his gun, yelled: "Hey, wait!" and staggered wildly toward the street. The touring car roared past in second, slammed into high violently.

"Hey!" screamed Joe; then— "You dirty—" Rage choked him. He raised his gun. Flame burst three times from the black muzzle.

"Good cripes!" Louie moaned. "Come on, Joe—come on!"

Rubber tires rasped on the rough pavement. The touring car slewed from left to right, blindly, like a harried animal. Then suddenly it headed for the curb. The chassis wrenched at the springs as the car hurtled over the curb. A sycamore ripped off the left rear mudguard. A low iron fence met the front tires, ripped them open. The radiator crumpled. The iron fence crumpled and the big car crashed head-on into a stone house. Glass snarled. The rear tires heaved five feet off the ground, slammed down again. The rending sound of tortured metal raked the streets for blocks.

Joe and Louie reached the sidewalk.

"Help me, Louie!" Joe gasped.

"Come on—run!"

Louie set an example but Joe found it hard to follow. He reeled along, coughing. Louie ran faster.

"Louie—lemme a hand—"

But Louie ran faster.

Joe fell down, braced himself on one arm. "Louie!" he cried savagely. "You hear me!" He raised his gun. He fired. Louie swerved, hit a tree with such force that he bounced back and crashed down in the middle of the street.

Cardigan wiped off the gun he had taken from Burt and tossed it in front of the garage. He passed back of the garage, crossed the two yards, paused an instant by the stone wall and then vaulted it and landed on the sidewalk. He strode swiftly away. Stopped once to hide behind a tree and watch two cops rush past, then went on. Five minutes later he boarded a city-bound trolley. He looked at his watch. It was twelve minutes to one.

It was three minutes to one when he got off, four blocks from the Flatlands, and entered an all-night drug store. He crowded into a telephone booth, called police headquarters. He pitched his voice high.

"You guys down there—take this or leave it. There's a red-hot in the garage back of 906 Magnolia Avenue. He was one of the guys bumped off Dorshook. . . . Who am I? Santa Claus to you, brother."

He hung up, left the drug store and walked to the Flatlands. At one he slipped in through the side entrance, ducked to the stairway and started climbing. At two minutes past one he entered his room.

"O.K., Otto. Beat it."

"Did you get it?"

"I did," Cardigan said. "Quick. Back to your room."

He rushed Otto out. Then he whipped off his clothes, got into pajamas, rumpled his hair, grabbed a magazine and climbed in bed. He took one look at the mayor's check, chuckled, slipped it in the back of the magazine, tore the envelope to bits and dropped them in a waste basket.

He put the magazine under his pillow. He reached for his briar pipe.

The clock's hands crept around to two. The hotel was quiet. Vagrant street sounds rose sharply. No one disturbed Cardigan. He knew that headquarters must be throbbing with activity. Surely Sisson had been killed in that crash. Press wires were humming. Still the hotel remained quiet. Cardigan yawned, turned off the lights.

Strout came in with Massey bright and early next morning while Cardigan, suspenders draping his hips, was lathering his face by the bathroom mirror.

Cardigan bowed elaborately.

"Swell morning, Strout!"

"Not so swell. Say, a guy named Sisson: Massey said Sisson paid a call on you once here."

"Oh—you mean that little morning glory from the tab. Yeah, he did. He'd heard about me and wanted my picture for the tab. See that rug in there? Well, he tripped over that and busted his lip against the radiator."

Strout looked mournful. "Sisson got bumped off last night."

Cardigan stropped his razor. "Too bad."

"It was funny. Two other guys got bumped off—they bumped off each other apparently. There was a third guy locked in Party Boss McHugh's garage. It was very funny. There was a fourth guy that slopped up the others' parade. The guy in the garage said he was from the *Press-Clarion.*"

"Reporters turning gangsters, huh?"

"That guy was no reporter."

Cardigan said: "How did the girl make out?"

"She died."

"You're here to make a collar?"

Strout shook his head. "No. Just before she died she identified the guy we found in that garage as one of the men. On the way out of the hospital the guy pulled a fast one and broke loose. We had to shoot him."

"What was all the fireworks around McHugh's house?"

Strout pawed his jaw. "Well there was one guy knows all about it. The fourth guy. And the fourth guy was the guy made a phone call to headquarters at a few minutes to one this A.M. And a gun we found was the one that did for Dorshook. Our ballistics man checked up."

"And what's that to me?"

Strout wore a bleak smile. "It's funny—how that mysterious phone tip cleared you up completely. The guy said he was Santa Claus."

"And I suppose now you're going to call me Santa Claus!"

"There are a lot of things I'd like to call you, Cardigan. But just now I'm too tired. You're in the clear now. O.K. But whatever job you are on—if I catch you in this town after tonight—"

"You knew I was leaving this morning, didn't you?"

Massey looked uneasy.

Strout turned and walked to the door. Massey opened it and went out first. Strout turned and stared sourly across the room. Cardigan, patting his face with a hot towel, grinned.

"Go ahead—grin!" growled Strout.

"Ain't I?"

"Sure. Grin!"

"Ain't I?"

"Damn it, laugh your head off!"

"Ho-ho! How's that?"

Strout disappeared, banging the door.

Cardigan hurled the wet towel at the door, heaved into the bathroom chafing his hands in high good humor and bursting into a lusty ballad of the levees.

The Crime Machine

CARROLL JOHN DALY

O F COURSE I paced my apartment nervously. In five minutes I was to meet and associate myself with the most dangerous, the most feared—and if Jack Ferris, editor of the *Morning Globe,* was correct—the most relentless hunter, and even killer of criminals. And it was this aptitude for killing; for meeting gunfire with gunfire, which had interested the *Globe* in the activities of this detective who carried the mildest of names—Vee Brown.

Vee Brown, after some pressure—in which Jack Ferris threatened to expose him as a ruthless killer—had agreed to permit a reporter to accompany him on his man-hunts and let the public see, through the *Globe,* that the new era in crime demanded that the hunter meet the hunted with his own weapons.

But there was more behind the *Globe*'s interest in Vee Brown than the recording of his cases. Jack Ferris had told me that Vee Brown enjoyed an outside income that permitted him an apartment on Park Avenue, together with a high-priced car and chauffeur. The source of this income was not known to Ferris. It was part of my job to discover it. What with the police investigation, the enormous bank balances of discredited officers, Ferris was anxious to be assured that in killing the enemies of the state this detective did not also kill the enemies of himself. Those criminals, perhaps, by whose crimes he had profited. But that, of course, was mere speculation.

Vee Brown had made one stipulation. That he could choose his own assistant from the *Globe.* And he had chosen me.

Why had he picked me? Certainly the name Vee Brown was unfamiliar to me. But why confuse further an already overstimulated imagination, when this Vee Brown himself would call on me any minute and take me out into the night—in a hunt for a killer?

And Vee Brown came. There were short quick steps, and a small, slim, dark-haired man stepped through the doorway.

I was half across the room when I stopped and stared. Then grasped the hand that was extended toward me.

"Vivian—Vivian Brown!" I gasped. "Such an idea never entered my head. And you! Surely—"

"Quite correct—Vee Brown." He grinned. "The 'Vivian' was dropped years ago. Honestly, now—Dean, didn't you even suspect me?"

I shook my head. How could I? Oh, I recalled Vivian Brown now—when I was face to face with him. But to connect the acquaintance of my college days with the gun-toting, gun-using detective was hard to do even now. Vivian Brown, who had failed at things physical! Yet I recollected his gameness. It had been admired—and joked about too. Vivian Brown's insistent and useless attempts to force his frail body into college sports.

It was half an hour before we were through reminiscing and Vee Brown came down to business.

"I didn't like it at first," he told me frankly. "This being dragged through the press. And then your name bobbed up in that 'big game' feature. We weren't very close at college, Dean, but I admired your athletic accomplishments—and perhaps now, there was the boyish itch to reverse the tables. Johnson had his Boswell, Sherlock Holmes his Watson, and—" he looked at me shrewdly with those penetrating black eyes, "Napoleon had his Waterloo," he finished.

Did he suspect, after all, the very thing that Ferris sought? The unfounded wealth back of Vee Brown's salary as a first-grade detective. But he was talking again. "You wonder how I got into the thing—eh, Dean?"

And I did wonder.

"Purely through my failure to make the mental desire conquer the physical weakness of my body. It is drilled into us that all men are created equal. I didn't believe it. Then it finally came home. We were created spiritually equal. That was the Divine power." He leaned forward. "But it took man, who made the pistol, to put the physical powers of each of us on an equal basis. Get the point?" He wagged the index finger of his right hand before me. "It's all there. I worked on it day and night for years. The difference between life and death lies only in the pressure of that single finger and the brain that controls it."

I jerked back in my chair. His hand had flashed down and up again with such rapidity that it seemed simply to waver slightly in the air. But now the hand held a heavy revolver, and the finger that had wagged in the air no longer caressed an imaginary trigger—but a real one.

I looked again at Vee Brown; his clear black eyes; his fine intelligent features; and the quizzical, somewhat humorous twist to his thin lips. He would not be my idea of a criminal, but neither would he be my idea of a fearless hunter of men—although there was something animal-like and graceful about his movements.

"Do you work entirely alone?" I asked.

"Entirely alone, and independent of instructions since I have been assigned to the district attorney's office." He came to his feet and walked across the room to the piano in the alcove. "I might talk to you for hours, but you see it all yourself. You play?" he asked suddenly.

"No. I lease this apartment furnished. The piano came with it."

Without a word Vee Brown sat down and strummed a few notes. "That's something I never mastered." He laughed harshly, rose from the piano, and lighting a cigarette stood before me.

"You are going to see and feel sudden and violent deaths tonight," he said.

"Do you always go out with the purpose of killing a man?" I asked.

"I never go with that purpose." He shook his head. "Nor have I ever regretted a death. Tonight it's 'Killer' Regan. He shot the watchman and the cashier at the Hudson Terminal Theater. She identified his picture before she died. He shot her three times in the stomach, though she never made a cry or move."

"You know where he is?" I asked.

"No, I don't. But I'll know tonight." His speech became more rapid and his tone more vehement as he talked. "Regan killed without reason. And he knows I know, and knows that I'll seek him out. And he knows that I'll shoot, and I know that he'll shoot. If there are any odds they're all in his favor. I'm getting information that may be true and may be false, or may be simply a means of cornering me—to be shot down as that defenseless girl was shot down." He paused a moment, jerked out his watch, snapped it open. "Come! It's close to midnight, and there's much to do."

"We're temperamental—all of us," Vee Brown said as we left the subway and walked toward Sixth Avenue. "I'm thinking, and my thoughts are all of the girl who died with a stomachful of lead." He paused a moment, then jerked out the words. "It's never pleasant to think, before the deed, that you might take a human life—unless you've built up a wall of hate."

"Don't you ever feel that there's another way?"

"I have no plans," he cut in quickly. "No specific instructions. Just an order. This time, to bring in Killer Regan—wanted for murder. And my order calls for me to produce a man or a body."

"Is—Regan in here?" I think that my voice shook slightly as we turned into a hallway beside a pawnbroker's shop.

"No." Vee Brown shook his head. "This is my bureau of information—and misinformation. The clever police clues and reasonings and deductions that decorate the newspapers are, with few exceptions, the squeals of stool pigeons. An unsavory system, that? Granted—but a necessary evil."

We passed down a narrow, ill-lit hallway, paused before a door on which Vee Brown tapped. A moment of silence; the shuffling of heavy feet and a tiny hole in the door as a panel fell back.

"This will be Irving Small," Vee Brown whispered, as the door opened and we slid through the narrow passage.

For a moment we stood in blackness. The door closed, a lock clicked, and a dim electric lamp flashed from under a worn shade upon an old table. I saw the bent figure peering at us in the darkness. He opened his mouth as if to speak, closed it again; and I caught the flash of watery blue eyes.

"My assistant." Vee Brown spoke sharply as the little man still watched me.

"I understood there was to be only one." Irving Small raised the lamp and held it out toward me as far as the silk cord would permit.

"You understand 'two' now," Vee Brown said simply.

"He goes too?" The yellow lips of the pawnbroker smacked.

"Yes—he goes too."

"It ain't safe. Leastwise, it's doubly dangerous—for you."

"I know that. But he goes nevertheless."

The clawlike fingers opened and closed long after Irving Small placed the lamp back on the table. He stretched out his right hand and took something from the hand of Vee Brown. For a few minutes his back was to me. He was counting softly to himself. Then he spoke over his shoulder. "It ain't any more than last time. Regan's worth more than that. It ain't very much."

"It's better than a cold, damp cell."

"Ehe—but not worth the price of a long box."

Another moment of silence, and Irving Small spoke again. "He's a desperate man. I hope you've left nothing behind to—that tells ill of me."

"Nothing. You've had my word on that."

"Ehe—I've had that." The lips smacked again—and then, "He's at Magna's. Second floor—last room—over the pianie. This is the night for it. He'll leave tomorrow. Magna's is watched. If you hold a police parade there'll be no show."

"There'll be no parade," said Vee Brown.

And that was all.

I breathed easier again when we reached the street. I was learning much about police work. Vee Brown had wanted information, and he knew where to get it. And he had bought it as he might buy any commodity.

"Stuffy place." Vee Brown stretched. "That's part of the system, except that I have my own private information bureau. It wasn't through luck that I first found Irving Small. It took time, and much work. But now—I hold twenty years over his head any time I wish to speak. I know you won't mention this until the usefulness of Irving Small is over and he has betrayed me."

"And that he might betray you I should think would be a real fear."

"It is." Vee Brown nodded vigorously. "I haven't the least doubt that he doubled on me tonight. I know that he was Killer Regan's fence."

"Then we won't go to—to Magna's." I guess I felt relieved.

"On the contrary, we will go straight to Magna's."

I pushed the question of his suspicion of Irving Small and why he walked into a trap, if he suspected treachery.

"Why—" he looked suddenly up at me as we passed a street lamp, "traps are a most interesting study. The game is—to get the bait out of the trap before the trap is sprung. Tonight the bait is Killer Regan."

"You'd walk into this trap—and drag me with you!"

Vee Brown stopped and swung on me suddenly. "You don't have to come." His eyes flashed and his lips set tightly. "Your editor has hinted that I shoot men down in cold blood, without giving them a chance. If you want to learn the truth you've got to face what I face—or you've got to believe what I tell you. It's not too late to turn back."

I guess several things shot through my mind as we faced each other there on the deserted street. But what decided my quick reply was the curl of his lips and the sneer in his voice.

"I'll go with you," I said. "But I hope you're playing a man's part tonight."

He hesitated—and when he spoke again the curl had left his lips and the sneer gone out of his voice.

"I am not acting as a man tonight," he said, "but as a machine—maintained by the state. A crime machine." Then suddenly, "Are you armed?"

I nodded my reply, for a high-caliber automatic was one of the first things I obtained when I left the office of Jack Ferris, city editor of the *Morning Globe.*

"That's Magna's," Vee Brown told me as we passed a dilapidated, neglected three-story building. "There's a fence and a gate in the rear, which is used for a hurried exit when the police make a raid. That'll be our entrance."

Well back down the side street was a dirty driveway which gave entrance to a storage warehouse. The wide wooden gates opened enough for our bodies to squeeze through. For some time Vee Brown remained at the crack in the big gate, peering out on the side street.

"Not a watcher—not a light—not a sound," he muttered as he shook his head. "Very clever or very stupid." He took my arm as we passed along the six-foot wooden fence. Somewhere, close to the middle of the block, he paused. "Since two of us are going in, you'll have to play your part," he said. "The little gate is about ten yards down. If you find it open, walk in. If you don't—climb over."

"And you?" For a moment the thought came that I was to be the bait that would spring the trap. But I didn't say more. It was the contemptuous tone of his voice as he dismissed my question that made me act. I simply turned and hurried down the alley toward the gate.

The gate was not locked. It gave easily beneath my pressure, but there was a dull squeak to it that sounded doubly loud in the clear stillness of the night. I thought that I heard the soft tread of feet beyond the fence. It was then that I first sought my gun and jerked it into my hand. The gate opened inward; I thrust it open and stepped back, raising my gun. But no figure darted out at me; no voice called for me to stand back; no—. And I heard it. The scraping of feet—and once a dull thud against the fence, further down the alley. I looked back in the direction I had come. The night was clear—it was only ten yards to where Vee Brown had been standing. He was gone.

For perhaps two minutes I hesitated between entering the gate and retracing my footsteps to the street in a search for Vee Brown. Again I heard the footsteps, a steady tread this time, that came toward me and the gate. Should I stay and face the one who came, or— It was too late to decide. The owner of those feet had already reached the gate and stood in the opening. I half dropped my gun.

"Come!" The figure spoke. It was Vee Brown. He was straightening his tie and rearranging his coat. A tiny trickle of red showed on his forehead.

"I missed him by a foot when I swung over the fence," Brown explained. "Timed it wrong, I guess. His feet against your squeak at the gate. I thought he'd search you out, and by dropping over the fence we'd have him between us. But he didn't. He sought the house." Brown's thin shoulders shrugged as he wiped the blood from his forehead. "After all, it was a close call—and I got the breaks."

The explanation in Vee Brown's cryptic words came to me as I followed him. The alley inside the fence was narrow. Fifteen or twenty yards down it we stepped over the body of a man. I shuddered slightly and looked down at the silent figure.

"He's not dead—just knocked cold." Brown answered my unspoken question as he jerked me by the arm. "We must hurry now. Our presence is expected. When this outside man doesn't report, suspicion may be felt within."

He was a different man now. His words came in quick, sharp, spasmodic jerks, and he seemed to raise his head and listen between each sentence.

As we hurried down the alley I could hear a hum that grew louder and louder. Then I knew that it was voices—many voices. Almost at once it died away and the tin-pan notes of a piano drifted to us, above the steady beat of a trap drum. I didn't have to be told that we were approaching one of those many dives that dot the city under the name of night club.

The music and the sound of dancing feet became almost deafening as I followed Vee Brown down a short flight of stairs and into a cellar.

"Stick close—and behind me." Vee Brown stretched out a hand to guide me as we crossed the damp, ill-smelling basement. "It's here that we strike the first blow, I think." I hardly caught his whisper. "And we must make it before the music stops. Now!"

I heard a door open before us, saw the dim light and the white face; the thick lips of the man who blinked at us, trying to pierce the darkness.

"Is he—" The man started, and stopped. His lips parted; his narrow eyes tightened to two slits, and a hand jerked to his side. But he never called out—he didn't have a chance. Vee Brown sprang forward; his hand flashed up. Metal shone for a moment in the light, then steel collided with bone— and steel won. Without a groan the man toppled forward into Vee Brown's arms. I saw Brown's feet slide back as he braced himself and eased the inert body to the floor.

The cellar door swung closed behind us with a dull slam—and the music stopped. Again the hum of voices and laughter, and the clink of glasses. But this time it was very close; almost as if we were in the room with it.

"You'll make note of that," Vee Brown whispered, close to my ear. "Remember that I struck with the barrel—not the butt. I don't want to appear a fool, in the paper. It's only detectives of fiction who are free from the danger of a bullet running up their sleeves." And there was a high-pitched note to his voice—and a slight ring of pride too, I thought.

"What was that?" He sung suddenly, raising his gun. But I had heard nothing. At least, nothing but the buzz of voices. For a full minute Brown tried to listen as we crouched back in the darkness.

"I could almost swear a figure moved—back there." He shook his head, and I thought that much of the elation had gone out of his voice. "Let's go on," he said finally. "I can't stand this waiting—this inactivity. It hounds and depresses me. I wouldn't mind so much being knocked over by Regan— but to be trapped here by this sort of flesh!" And he actually pushed the unconscious body slightly with his foot before he stepped over it.

"Inactivity" and "waiting." I could have laughed at the absurdity of the complaint, but I didn't. I said nothing, scarcely breathed as we slipped along the dimly lit hall, turned a corner sharply, and stopped before a flight of stairs.

"I've been this way before," Brown told me as we waited, our backs against the wall. "Every step is charged with its own natural burglar alarm. We'll have to wait until the music starts again. Every step groans loud enough to wake the dead. The dead!" he repeated, as he nudged me in the side.

"How do you like it?" he whispered—and I thought there was a challenge in his voice. "One flight up—last room—right. And Regan; Killer Regan, who put the lead into a young girl's stomach. Always think of that, Dean. Put your mind constantly on something like that, in the man-hunt. It steadies the nerves. And even now, when we flatter ourselves on doing well so far, we cannot tell. For often the obstacles that we overcome are planned just so—for us to overcome. No. The question for us to figure out is—are we coming to 'get' Regan, or is Regan waiting above to 'get' us? And in your honest answer to that question lies the *Morning Globe*'s opinion of the paid man-hunter of the law—Vee Brown."

For seconds that seemed like hours we remained in silence at the foot of the stairs. In the room beyond, the voices churned incessantly; in the hall behind us a man lay unconscious; and above—

My heart gave an involuntary leap. Did the man who put the lead in the dead girl's stomach lurk at the top of that black stairway?

I jerked erect. Vee Brown gripped me by the arm. The music had started—and so had we. Quickly we were mounting the stairs.

The old boards gave up their dead. Would others hear them? Would they announce our arrival to listening ears at the top of those stairs? Vee Brown didn't hesitate. In fact, we increased our speed. I reached for a step that wasn't there, half stumbled, felt the hand upon my arm jerk me erect—and we were at the top. At the top and still going: moving along the dark hall to the rear room, right—and Killer Regan.

Would the gunman be in bed? Would he be waiting for us at the door? Had he been listening at the top of the stairs and was now crouched back in the darkness? Would—

I sucked in a deep breath. I heard the knob of a door turn—and the slight squeak of hinges. Then saw, almost at once, a thin strip of light. Certainly Vee Brown did not waste time.

I could see into the room now; dimly illuminated by the soft glow of a heavily shaded lamp. The room was divided as the suites in cheaper hotels. There was a large arch effect, with a curtain pole across the top—but no curtains. Through this I could see the end of a bed and, I thought, the shape of a foot beneath the covers.

As I slipped through the doorway behind Vee Brown I heard him close the door gently. Then the click, as the key turned in the lock. If Killer Regan was in that room his escape was cut off—and I also thought, with a gulp, so was ours.

Vee Brown slipped the key into his pocket, and stepping across the room thrust a hand against the curtains before the window. He turned suddenly at my exclamation.

"There's a man in the bed." My voice seemed to come from a long way off as I clutched Vee Brown by the arm.

"Really. How observant!" Vee Brown glanced casually at the bed, knelt and looked beneath it, and stepping to a closet door swung it open.

I walked cautiously to the bed, my gun raised.

Vee Brown joined me. His gun hung by his side. He didn't move cautiously. He strode rapidly by me, reached the bed and threw back the covers. A couple of pillows and a pair of shoes were beneath them.

There was a thud behind us, as if feet had jumped upon the floor.

"Quick—right—behind the arch!" Brown jerked out the words. And I? I jumped to the left, collided with Brown, and saw the sad sort of smile on his lips as he muttered: "It didn't really matter, Dean. I'd advise you to drop your gun at once." And I heard the revolver that he carried in his hand drop to the rug. It was then that I saw the shadow that crossed the light and heard, too, the voice—gruff, vicious, with a ring of triumph in it.

"That's good advice, bozo. Drop the gun and stick up your hands. I was sitting pretty, on the fire-escape. If you'd opened them curtains the show'd be over now."

Mechanically my fingers opened and the gun fell to the floor. Funny, I didn't have the same sensation of fear now that the thing had happened. My first thought was—what a story for the paper! And my second thought, and hardly as pleasant—who would write the story, and would I read it?

"I didn't expect such a pleasure," the voice went on behind me as I stood with my hands in the air—Brown beside me. "Who may you be?" A gun in my back punctuated the final sentence.

"A cub reporter from a paper. Leave him alone, Regan. He—" Brown began.

I heard the curse, saw the shadow, and caught the thud as the man's arm swung through the air. Vee Brown swayed slightly, his arms half lowered— but they went up again at a sharper command.

"We'll have no advice. One more peep and I'll slap you away for good. It's a great moment, Mr. Vee Brown—and a personal one." He raised his voice above the din of the orchestra that shrieked out its music from below. "Swing around—both of you, and I'll boast a little myself—that Killer Regan's bullets weren't found in your backs."

We turned and faced him. Certainly if I didn't know fear before, I knew it now. Rat-like eyes; dominant chin and coarse, evil lips. There wasn't one redeeming feature in that hard, mean face. For the moment I thought of the girl with the stomachful of lead. Regan had finished searching me and was now searching Vee Brown for weapons. And I acted. My body slipped forward and my hands lowered. Threatening perhaps, but it was involuntary. Maybe I was going to spring on Regan—maybe I wasn't. I don't know.

Regan's left hand shot up and his gun cracked beneath my chin, straightening me. In a dazed way I knew that I still stood on my feet. And I knew too that Regan had backed us into the other room. But I also knew, with a little feeling of satisfaction, that Regan watched me carefully—and that, though he finished patting Vee Brown for weapons, his search was but a perfunctory one—his eyes ever switching to me.

"You let him go, Regan," Vee Brown nodded his head toward me. "He's from a newspaper. Nothing to do with you or with me."

"You're from a paper?" Killer Regan raised his voice again, for we must have been directly above the orchestra now, as the music was almost deafening. "Well—you'll have something to write for them. Something about Killer Regan. You can face a bit sideways and watch the show." Regan stepped around in front of us again, a gun in either hand now. "I'm going to shoot this boy detective to ribbons. There's one thing about frying a lad that has its good points. You can't burn him more than once."

Killer Regan raised his right hand. His chin shot forward; his thick lips curled. Vee Brown stood straight and tense, his eyes full on Regan's—and his hands stretched high.

"You guessed at me and brought the picture of my mug to the girl I croaked." I could see the gathering of hate in Regan's eyes as he talked. "She'd never have lived long enough to mark me if it wasn't for you. You've been a terror to them what lacked guts, but now—" His gun shot forward, his finger tightened upon the trigger, and deadly silence fell upon the room. The music, below, had stopped. Regan dropped the muzzle of his gun slightly.

"What—" Vee Brown smiled as he faced death. "Must have music with your murders, eh? But you won't be the first man who talked himself out of killing me. Now—if you had an ear for music you'd have shot sooner and talked less." Involuntarily, it seemed, he stepped to the right.

"You stand your ground!" Regan's sharp little eyes ran from Vee Brown to me, and both his guns raised and waved menacingly. "If you want it now, why—"

"But you don't care to disturb the peace, and—"

Vee Brown stopped. Regan grinned. The orchestra, below, had crashed into life again. I knew the piece. It was "The Gangster's March," that had lately taken the city by storm. And I read death in Regan's face. I had never seen it in a man's face before. In animals, perhaps. But I recognized it just the same. Not just a deadly purpose; not the will that forces a man to do something particularly loathing to him. No. It was a lust—a desire to kill. I saw his tongue slip out and lick at thick, dry lips. There wasn't a bit of doubt that only a second stood between Vee Brown and sudden and violent death.

I half closed my eyes, then opened them again. Vee Brown spoke.

"Don't be foolish, Dean," he said. "There is no danger to you. Keep your hands up."

Killer Regan's rat-like eyes flashed toward me for a split second; mine shot toward Vee Brown. And it happened. Just as the music reached the weird, high, cracking notes—like the staccato of machine-gun fire—Vee Brown plunged his right hand suddenly downward. Down and out. And that hand, which had started down empty, now contained flashing steel.

They fired together, I think. The roar of the bullets was lost in the clash of the instruments below, but plainly I saw the two spurts of orange blue flame.

I didn't jump forward. I didn't even lower my hands. I just stood there, frozen to the spot. For a moment I saw nothing but the dull white smoke, the blurred faces of two men, and the little pool of blood on Vee Brown's forehead, that broke suddenly and forming a tiny red stream rolled down his face. But Vee Brown still stood upon his feet.

Mechanically my eyes turned and rested full upon the face of Killer Regan. There was a gray, powdered, spattered hole right in the center of his forehead. And those eyes, that were malignant and glaring bright, now were dull, glassy, distant, filmy things.

I knew that I was looking at a dead man, yet he stood upon his feet. He didn't sway back and forth. His hands opened and his guns dropped to the floor. Then his knees bent—slowly, almost carefully—till they reached the floor. For a moment he knelt so, as if in prayer—then pitched forward on his face.

Vee Brown shrugged his shoulders and knelt beside the dead gunman. With an effort he turned him over on his back.

"Lucky I planted that gun in my sleeve," he said. "But I felt, dear Mr. Regan, that you were on the fire-escape. And that's the disadvantage of having a newspaper pass judgment on your ethics. How much easier to have shot through the curtains before the window!" He wiped the blood from his forehead. "Well—you missed and I didn't. But I don't like this playing to the gallery. Yet, the public must have its thrill."

He smiled at me as he stood up.

"There's your story—and hard to get a better one, even if we had rehearsed it." And then, the smile broadening into a grin, "You can put your hands down, Dean," he said quietly. "You were always my idea of a hero—and you look rather silly now. I should—" He stopped as he stepped over the dead murderer, one foot on either side of what had been Killer Regan. The music below had suddenly changed. The notes were soft and alluring now.

Vee Brown stood so, his right hand raised in the air, his index finger keeping time with the music, his shoulders swaying slightly. The sad smile had changed to a pleased, wistful sort of a smile, and his eyes were bright and—yes—laughing.

"Hear that, Dean," he said softly. "Even that gang of melody murderers can't take the beauty away from it. Can't you feel it rip you, like a southern night?"

"I—It's pretty." My voice came from between cracked, dry lips.

"Pretty!" He swayed back and forth above the dead man. "Why—all New York will sing it by tomorrow night. It's a masterpiece." He began to hum softly.

And I? It was loathsome—revolting. Here he had killed a man, and now stood above the body and discussed a new melody. I shuddered, half turned my head, took a step forward—and stopped, swaying dizzily. Things began to dance about the room; the hot blood rushed to my forehead; the floor began to rise—and I stretched out a hand.

Vee Brown was across to me—a hand beneath my elbow.

"I forgot, Dean. I didn't do it for bravado. There! Brace up, old man." As he led me from the room and down the stairs and out into the alley, he said, "Think of the dead girl and the stomachful of lead."

But I was thinking of something else. Of the dead man on the floor; of Ferris and his suspicion of Vee Brown's supposed wealth; of the song that was still on Vee Brown's lips. As if he read my thoughts he cut in on them.

"It's the music that gets me, Dean. There are two men in me, I think. An outer and an inner man, and the one is the relief for the other." He looked at me with that wistful, twisted smile as we reached the street and he hailed a taxi. "You didn't think of me when Ferris spoke the name Vee Brown. You knew me as Vivian. Now—what you wish most to know, and Ferris wishes most to know, stares you in the eyes every day; assails your ears on the radio and from every night club. Even the restaurants that have music. Don't you see—don't you understand yet?" He looked at my blank face. "Vivian. I'm Vivian. Why—the name is blazoned out on the most popular of our sentimental song sheets."

"You—you!" I gasped. "Vivian, the song writer. Who people wonder about, and whom the publishers won't—So that's where you get your money."

"Yes. That's the other side of me, Dean. The outlet for this passion of hunting criminals. Or perhaps the sentiment in my songs is—But I don't know. I don't know which man I really am—or if I am a mixture of both. It's a rather lonely life. You'll keep my secret and—and my shame." He was grinning now. When he left me to enter an all-night drug store to telephone police headquarters the grin was still there—and he was humming.

Vivian Brown. Vee Brown the anonymous writer of sentimental song hits! Hard to believe that? But why? After all, it was easier to believe that this slim, almost delicate little man was Vivian the song writer, than it was to believe that he was Vee Brown, hunter and killer of men. "Master of Melody" they called Vivian.

Killer of Men—Master of Melody. What a— But above all, I was thinking that I was through, *Morning Globe* or no *Morning Globe*—public or no public. Yet, thoughts are flitting things. I looked up as Vee Brown came from that drug store, still grinning and still humming, and despite my thoughts I knew that I was not through—but just beginning.

The Hand of Horror

ERLE STANLEY GARDNER

Chapter 1

MURDER MAIL

REED SAMPSEL STARED at the oblong package, which his secretary handed him, with evident distaste. The package was some nine inches in length, by five inches wide and five inches deep. It was wrapped in brown paper, tied with heavy cotton string, and was addressed simply to—"Sampsel the Seer."

"How did this come?" asked Sampsel.

"First-class mail," the secretary said. "There's a special-delivery stamp on it."

Sampsel looked at the package, noted the special-delivery stamp and the words: "First Class Mail." He tapped the paper with the tips of his fingernails, and said: "It sounds like a wooden box."

His secretary nodded.

Sampsel sighed and set the package down on his desk.

"Lord," he said, "how I would like to get away from those tags."

"What tags?" asked his secretary.

"Sampsel the Seer and Sampsel the Great," he said. "I presume it's part of the hocus-pocus that goes with this business. As a matter of fact, I'm carrying on a legitimate profession. A lot of the big corporations have people retained who size up character from the shape of a man's chin, or the slant of his eye. Why the devil shouldn't I be able to carry on a profession in which I tell something about a man's character from the lines in his hand, without having to wrap my advice up in all sorts of hocus-pocus?"

Edna Grace, his secretary, smiled.

She was a red-headed young woman who carried herself with something of an air—her manner seemed to indicate that she was very sure of herself, indeed. "You've got to hand them just so much hooey," she said, "otherwise they won't take you seriously."

Sampsel picked up a letter which lay on his desk, a letter which he had just extracted from an envelope that had been neatly slit down the side with a single stroke of the heavy steel dagger that he used as a paper knife. Clipped to the letter was a five-dollar bill and a rather smudgy, inked impression of a woman's hand.

"Write to this woman," he said to Edna Grace, tossing the letter over to her, "and tell her that she'll have to send a better print of her hand than this, if we're going to answer her questions. But you can tell her that she's inclined to be too restless; too much inclined to want things to happen all at once. Tell her that she should study the book of nature; that a farmer plants seed and then cultivates the ground at intervals, and waits for the crop to mature. If he pulled up the seeds every few days to see if they were sprouting, he'd never have a crop."

Edna Grace looked at him with calm, quizzical eyes, then nodded as she took the letter and made a few rapid notations in shorthand on the margin.

"How about the box?" she said. "You'd better open it."

He reached impatiently for the box, took the dagger, and slit the cords.

"Sampsel the Seer!" he snorted. "And the worst of it is I have to cultivate just that kind of background in order to get my stuff across."

Impatiently he pulled away the wrapping paper from the outside of the package. There was disclosed a neat wooden box, nailed tightly shut with small brads which were pounded in at frequent intervals.

Sampsel weighed the box appraisingly in his hand.

"A crystal?" asked his secretary.

Sampsel shook his head. "No," he said, "it doesn't feel like a crystal."

"You mean to say you can tell what's in the box by some psychic ability?" she asked curiously.

He shrugged his shoulders. "Who knows?" he said. "All I know is that I have certain feelings. Perhaps those feelings are the result of a disordered stomach; perhaps they are caused by the fact that my body is a living, vibrating organism that emanates vibrations which are similar to the x-rays and can penetrate to the inside of that box, and cause me to have an involuntary shudder—just as a current of cold air on the back of my neck will cause an involuntary muscular contraction of the skin, giving rise to goose pimples."

"Then," she said, "the box gives you a feeling of revulsion?"

He nodded and inserted the edge of the dagger between the top and the sides of the box. He pried the lid off and disclosed a layer of cotton. He pulled off the layer of cotton, and Edna Grace's scream rang in his ears.

Slowly, he put the box back on the desk, without taking his eyes from it.

Edna Grace screamed again.

"Stop it!" he told her.

She was clutching at the edge of the desk, her face ashen-gray, her eyes wide and staring. Her lips seemed bloodless.

"A woman's hand!" she said, in a voice that was tremulous with horror.

"A woman's hand," agreed Sampsel slowly. "And there's a slip of paper underneath the hand."

Delicately, almost tenderly, his fingers touched the cold skin of the clammy dead hand. It was the hand of a woman, with long, tapering fingers. There were no rings or ornaments upon it, and yet it gave the impression of culture and refinement. The nails were tinted a vivid red, and the crimson on the nails shone out as a flash of live color against the dead skin of the lifeless hand. It had been severed at the wrist, and carefully packed in the cotton-lined casket.

Edna Grace abruptly sank into a chair and sat staring at her employer with eyes that seemed to push from their sockets.

"What," she asked, in a faint, weak voice, "is on the paper?"

Sampsel took out the paper from beneath the hand. It was a single sheet of note paper, upon which a message had been printed, in pencil, and the lettering was sufficiently crude to make it appear that the person who had written the message had been inclined to make an attempt to disguise his hand writing.

FOR GOD'S SAKE SAY NOTHING TO THE POLICE.
OTHERWISE I WILL LOSE MY LIFE!

Sampsel stared at the scrawled message on the piece of paper, then read it aloud to his secretary.

"You mean that was written by the woman whose hand is in that box?" she asked.

Sampsel shook his head slowly. "No," he said, "I think it was written by the party who cut off the hand and put it in the box. It looks like a young woman's handwriting, despite the fact that an obvious attempt has been made at disguising the salient characteristics."

"What," she asked, "are you going to do?"

Sampsel the Seer stared at the dead hand with appraising eyes, in which there was a quickening interest.

"You remember several months ago," he said, "a woman brought me the imprint of a man's hand for a character reading? The man was a criminologist. You will remember that I deduced that fact from his hand before I knew anything about him from any other source."

His secretary frowned thoughtfully. "Yes," she said. "I remember the occasion. I was trying to think of the name."

"It commenced with an A," Sampsel told her.

"I have it," she said. "Arsen, Sam Arsen, the scientific detective and criminologist."

"Get him on the telephone at once," said Sampsel, "and tell him I would like to see him here if possible, upon a matter of the greatest urgency."

Edna Grace nodded and withdrew. At the door she turned for one last stare at the cold, dead hand with the crimsoned nails.

Reed Sampsel stared across the desk at Sam Arsen. "I should like very much," he said, "to heed the request which came in the package."

Sam Arsen looked with the apparent contempt which the scientist feels for one whose methods are less accurate or more subtle, as the case may be.

"You mean this request to refrain from notifying the police?" he asked.

"Yes."

Arsen shook his head. "You can't do that. You can't afford to take that chance. This is a matter which may doubtless prove serious."

"But it apparently means life or death to the person who wrote that message."

"Nonsense. That's simply some sort of a game to keep you from making the matter public."

"In that event," said Sampsel, "why did they send the hand to me in the first place?"

Arsen shrugged his shoulders.

"Well," said Sampsel, "what do you suggest?"

"You have," said Arsen, slowly, "probably destroyed any fingerprints which were on that wrapping paper. You have carelessly handled the paper which was in the box, and have probably destroyed or obliterated any prints which were on it. However, as a matter of precaution, I will check both bits of paper for fingerprints. I will make a microscopic examination of the hand, taking scrapings from beneath the fingernails, examining them under a microscope, making a chemical analysis when I have finished with the microscopic examinations. I will probably be able to tell much about the hand. I will also take prints from the fingers, and see if those prints are registered anywhere."

Sampsel showed interest. "You make inquiries concerning fingerprints by a system of numerical classification, do you not?" he asked.

The criminologist nodded.

"I wanted to consult you," said Sampsel, slowly, "because I have great faith in your ability. Your hand shows that you have extraordinary analytical abilities; that you are remorselessly methodical, and that you are destined to make your living from the apprehension of criminals."

"Bosh!" snapped Arsen.

"I beg your pardon?" said Sampsel.

"I said 'bosh,'" remarked Arsen. "I know you make your living out of that stuff, but I don't believe in it and I don't think you do either."

"And may I ask why?" said Sampsel, in a tone of frigid politeness.

"You most certainly may," he said. "I have no hesitancy in expressing myself upon the subject. I think that your so-called 'science' of palm-reading is all a bunch of cheap clap-trap designed to mislead the public.

"Of course you'll understand that I am not criticizing your sincerity. I am merely giving you the opinion of a scientist upon a pseudo-science which has no standing whatever."

The look of frowning annoyance left Sampsel's face. In its place there was a calm, tolerant smile which made his manner seem almost patronizing.

"Very well," he said. "Suppose I tell you something? Your science is purely objective. You think you can take that hand and perhaps tell something about it from a scientific viewpoint."

"I do," said Arsen.

"The reason that I happened to call you into consultation," said Sampsel, "is because a young woman brought in a print of your hand some months ago, and—"

"I know all that," said Arsen. "You told her a good many things about me. They were the truth. However, for a person in your position to get all the information concerning a person in my position is not particularly difficult. You said nothing which you could not have learned from my close associates, perhaps from having me shadowed for a short period of time, and from making shrewd deductions."

Sampsel smiled. "In common with most people," he said, "you take yourself far too seriously. Do you think that even had I known the name of the owner of the hand that was brought to me for examination through the medium of an inked print, that I could profitably have gone to all that trouble to find out about you?"

Arsen snorted. "Sure you could," he said. "It would have been worth it from the advertising standpoint."

Sampsel looked at the dead hand which lay on the table. "Does that hand," he asked, "indicate anything to you—not from future examinations or analysis which you are to make, but just as it now appears?"

"It indicates," said Arsen, "that the hand was severed at the wrist by a physician. I am quite certain that some skillful surgeon amputated that hand."

"And that is all it shows to you?" said Sampsel.

"That is all it shows now—yes."

"Very well," said Sampsel, "let me tell you something about this hand."

"All right," said Arsen, "what can you tell me?"

"Simply this," said Sampsel, "that the hand is that of a woman who has suffered much. She had a childhood which was unhappy. When she was a young woman, she was a victim of a treacherous betrayal of friendship. I can tell you that this young woman experienced fatal results which followed a surrender of reason to emotion."

"How," asked Arsen, "do you tell that?"

"You can see," Sampsel said, "that the line of the head curves toward the fingers and merges with the line of the heart, under the mount of Saturn. I have never seen that condition in a hand without its meaning a surrender of reason to emotion, with disastrous results."

The laugh of the criminologist was scornful.

Sampsel remained patient and persistent. "Have you ever noticed," he asked, "that a person's physiognomy varies with his character? For instance, a high forehead denotes intellectuality?"

Arsen almost mechanically touched his own high forehead with the tips of his fingers. "Naturally," he said. "The brain is the thinking organ. The more space it takes up, the larger it is, and the larger it is, the more intelligent."

Sampsel smiled. "And have you noticed," he asked, "that thick lips generally go with a passionate temperament; that a protruding jaw generally goes with an aggressive temperament?"

"Certainly."

"Yet," said Sampsel, "the organs of sense are not in the lips, nor is combativeness in the jaw."

Arsen shook his head impatiently. "We are getting beside the subject," he said.

"We are," Sampsel agreed. "I merely mention these matters in order to show you that unreasoning emotion might as well be shown in the line of the head and heart on the palm of a person's hand, as in the thickness of the lips upon a person's face. However, what mainly concerns me with that hand is the fact that it indicates an impossibility from the standpoint of palmistry."

"What do you mean?" the criminologist inquired.

"I mean that judging from the condition of the hand, and the texture of the skin on the back of the hand, which is an infallible criterion of age, the body from which that hand was severed was that of a woman of approximately thirty-four years of age. Judging, on the other hand, from certain peculiar configurations of the line of life, the line of head, and the line of heart, I would say that the woman met her death from very tragic circumstances at approximately the age of thirty years. She has, therefore, been living for years beyond the time which was assigned as her natural span of life."

Arsen pushed back his chair with an exclamation of impatience. "I am willing," he said, "to listen to reason. I am willing to make all reasonable allowances for your profession, but I cannot subscribe to such damned nonsense as that."

"In that," said Sampsel, "you are entirely right. I agree with you. It is something that I, myself, cannot understand. If I had met with such a condition in a living hand, I would have doubted the very fundamentals of my profession."

"Bosh and nonsense!" said Arsen.

He reached over, picked up the hand carefully, and dropped it into the cotton-lined interior of the box. Then he opened a bag and carefully placed the box, the pieces of wrapping paper, and the message which had been received, in it.

"You will hear from me," he said "within the next hour or two. In the meantime, I believe that it is imperative the police should be notified."

Sampsel shrugged his shoulders and spread his hands in a gesture of surrender. "I am leaving the matter," he said, "entirely in your hands. Will you please notify the police if you feel that it is necessary?"

The criminologist nodded. "I shall," he said.

Sam Arsen glanced about him at the tapestried interior of the study, sniffed the incense-laden air, looked at the crystal ball on the desk.

"If," he said, "you use palmistry, what's the need of all this stage setting?"

Sampsel the Seer smiled, a slow, patient smile. "If," he said, "you don't believe in things psychic, could I get you to accept an explanation that I am something of a psychologist, and that I utilize psychological factors in a profession which is, after all, merely an applied branch of psychoanalysis?"

Arsen nodded eagerly. "Yes," he said, "such an explanation sounds logical to me."

"I thought it would," cryptically announced Sampsel. "And you'll telephone me within an hour or two, at the most?"

"Within two, at the most," said the criminologist.

Sampsel the Seer poised a pencil between his thumb and forefinger as Arsen hesitated for a moment, with his hands on the knob.

"I know that you don't believe any of this sort of thing," Sampsel said slowly, "but, as a favor to me, will you be very careful during the next few days?"

Sheer surprise caused Arsen to stop in his tracks. "What do you mean?" he asked.

"Only what I saw in your hand, and the impression that I now get. I would suggest that you be very, very careful. It seems to me that a danger threatens."

The face of the criminologist flushed. He took a swift step through the doorway, glowered at Sampsel, and said: "Baloney!" then slammed the door.

Chapter 2

"AND THE HAND WAS GONE"

THE MORNINGS OF Sampsel the Seer were taken up by appointments; appointments made, for the most part, with wealthy people who came to Sampsel with problems that ranged from serious questions to the frivolous matters with which many idle people concern themselves.

It was nearing eleven o'clock when Sampsel got a break, due to the failure of one of his clients to keep an appointment.

He rang for his secretary.

"Edna," he said, "I'm going to take a chance. I want you to look up for me the records of women who were convicted of murder within the last five years."

She stared at him with wide eyes. "You mean the woman's hand?" she asked.

"Yes," he said. "I've been thinking it over. If such a woman came to me for advice, or had come to me five years ago, I would have warned her that the lines of her hand indicated she must be most careful to guard against some outburst of emotions which would culminate in a homicidal mania."

"Are those things shown on the hand?" asked Edna Grace, in a tone of sudden curiosity.

Sampsel the Seer looked at her frankly. "I don't know," he said.

"Then how can you tell— What do you—"

He shrugged his shoulders.

"There are certain lines of temperament shown in the hand; certain dangerous tendencies on the part of an individual. Sometimes by a proper warning, coupled with an exercise of the will, those tendencies can be avoided. If an intelligent attempt is not made to exercise the will, the tendencies are not avoided, and there is future disaster indicated. In the hand which I examined, there were such tendencies.

"Now, of course, when one knows the tendencies of a person, it is only a question of meditation to realize what those tendencies will lead to. For instance, a person who has the predisposition to extreme greed, and also a lack of generosity, will, frequently, turn out to be a miser. If there should be a banking stringency, such a person would undoubtedly rush to the bank and start to horde his money. Therefore, if I should tell such a person that he would probably have a large sum of gold in a safety deposit box on a certain date, you might question whether there was foundation for such a statement in his hand."

Edna Grace nodded her head slowly. Then she said: "A lot of what you do is based on deductive reasoning."

"Perhaps," he told her. "Perhaps it's a hunch. Perhaps it's some manifestation of the subconscious that we call psychic ability; I don't know. All I know is that I've been thinking over that hand, and I've come to the conclusion that there were dangerous homicidal tendencies—"

A pair of heavy shoulders appeared in the doorway, behind the form of Edna Grace. A man pushed his way into the room. "All right, buddy," he said, "suppose you tell us what you know about it," and he flipped back his coat lapel to disclose a gold shield.

"About what?" asked Sampsel.

"About this dead hand that came to you in the mail."

Sampsel spoke slowly and deliberately. "That," he said, "is a matter which Sam Arsen took care of. He was to notify the police, and, I believe, did so. He has all of the data; all of the information."

"You're still not answering my question," the detective said. "I want to know what you know about it."

"Simply that a package came in the mail," Sampsel told him. "It came first-class, and contained a woman's hand. I gave the hand to Arsen, and told him to do whatever he saw fit about it. With the hand, was a note, stating that if the police were notified, it would mean death to the person who had sent the package."

"Is that what it said?" asked the detective.

"Words to that effect," Sampsel remarked.

"All right," the detective said, "now tell us something about the hand—what did it look like?"

"Like a dead hand," Sampsel remarked, with some show of irritation. "What's the use of asking me to describe it from my recollection when you can see the hand itself by going to Arsen's office? He undoubtedly telephoned the police more than an hour ago, and they have had their experts make careful examination."

Sampsel was conscious that the eyes of the detective were staring at him with a peculiar, cold concentration.

"All right," the detective said. "Arsen telephoned the police all right, but that's as far as your statement checks."

"What do you mean?" asked Sampsel.

"The hand isn't at Arsen's office.

"Why, he took it with him," said Sampsel.

The detective shrugged his shoulders.

"What does Arsen say about it? Where does he say it is? What does he say happened to it?" Sampsel asked.

"He says nothing."

"What do you mean by that?"

"I mean by that," the detective told him, "that Sam Arsen was murdered in his office about fifteen minutes after he telephoned the police about that hand."

Sampsel stared at the detective, conscious of the eyes which gimleted him, and conscious, also, of the white face of Edna Grace which stared from one to the other.

"And the hand was missing?" asked Sampsel.

"The hand was gone. We went to the office in response to his telephone call. His secretary said he was in his private office and was expecting us. We followed her to the door. She opened it, and Arsen was slumped over his desk, with a peculiar wound on his neck. There was no sign of the hand, the note, or the box, but there was the paper that the box had been wrapped in, addressed to you, and sent first-class mail, with a special-delivery on it."

"That's right," Sampsel said slowly. "That's the way it came."

He paused, and there was a second or two of silence, which was broken by the noise made by Sampsel's chair as he pushed it back, stood up behind his desk, and took off the turban and robe which were a part of the background with which he surrounded himself.

"Cancel all appointments, Edna," he told his secretary. "I will see no one until I have cleared this matter up."

Edna Grace watched him with round, startled eyes. "Then," she said, "there was really some justification for that warning which you gave Mr. Arsen just before he left the office?"

The detective whirled to face her. "What warning?" he demanded.

"Mr. Sampsel," she said, innocently enough, "warned Mr. Arsen that he had better be very careful, because of an impending danger which menaced him."

The detective turned to Sampsel.

Sampsel said, in that same steady, level voice: "I warned him because his hand showed that he was entering upon a period of his life in which he was threatened by menacing influences."

The detective's lip curled scornfully, and his eyes made no attempt to disguise the suspicion with which he regarded Sampsel.

"Oh," he said, in a sarcastic tone of voice, and then, after a moment, added: "Yeah?"

Sampsel the seer, his face white and drawn, stood in the doorway of Arsen's private office and looked at that which lay within.

The detectives stood to one side, and watched him curiously, as Sampsel moved toward the desk. The body had been left as it had been found. It was slumped forward, the weight being partially supported by one shoulder. On the back of the neck was a livid spot; a spot from which there had oozed a drop or two of blood.

"All right," said one of the detectives, "tell us all you know about it."

"You have heard all I know about it," Sampsel said.

"What about this warning you gave him?"

"Just a warning such as I have given to hundreds of my clients. I warned one about an automobile accident no later than yesterday."

"Did the accident happen?"

"I don't know. I hope not. I told her to keep out of automobiles."

The detective snorted.

Sampsel stood, with his finely sensitive face displaying unmistakable evidence of the shock, staring at the dead man. One of the detectives pushed forward a piece of wrapping paper, on which was an address, some canceled postage stamps.

"This the wrapper that was around the box that came to you?"

Sampsel looked at it and nodded. "There's no trace of the hand or the box?" he asked.

"None," said the detective.

Sampsel looked down at the desk. There was a microscope placed in position, ready for instant use. There was no slide in the microscope. Sampsel bent forward to look at the hands of the body.

"Be careful not to touch anything," warned the detective in a low voice. "We're waiting for the autopsy surgeon before we move him."

"Do you notice," said Sampsel, "the very faint traces of ink that are on this thumbnail?" He indicated the thumbnail on the dead man's right hand.

The detective grunted an inarticulate something.

Sampsel made a careful examination of the desk. "There are no papers here?" he asked. "Nothing that would indicate what Arsen had been doing?"

"Nothing whatever," said the detective. "Just the microscope, that's all. Everything else seems to have been cleared away."

"And no one came into the private office?"

"No one."

"That wound in the neck was the cause of death?"

"We think so. We're waiting for the autopsy surgeon."

Sampsel inspected the wound. "It hardly seems to have lacerated the skin," he said. "It looks like a lot of little puncture marks arranged in a circle."

"You seem to know a lot about it," the detective said, "particularly, in view of that mysterious warning which you gave your friend."

"He wasn't a friend," Sampsel said. "Merely a business acquaintance. I called him in because I had confidence in his ability."

There was a bustle of activity, and a short, stocky man, with a vandyke beard, and a black bag, walked briskly into the room.

"All right," said the detective. "That's all from you, Sampsel. Get back. Here comes the autopsy surgeon."

Sampsel stepped back, his eyes still busy, taking inventory of the surroundings.

Abruptly he noticed a torn fragment of paper in the waste basket, which was beneath the table, on the side of the desk. The fragment of paper contained what appeared to be a smear of ink.

The detectives crowded forward, staring curiously at the autopsy surgeon who was examining the wound on the neck of the corpse. Sampsel leaned forward and his hand darted swiftly to the waste basket. With the technique of a stage magician, he swiftly palmed the piece of inked paper, and straightened.

One of the detectives said: "You can wait out in the other room, Sampsel."

Sampsel moved with quiet dignity to the outer office. As he left the inner office, one of the detectives slammed the door shut. A plainsclothesman, who stood in the outer office with a notebook in his hand, looked up at the sound of the slamming door, nodded to Sampsel.

"You'll be wanted for questioning later on," he said. "But you can go now."

Sampsel nodded, looked toward the white-faced young woman who was standing by a bookcase, her arm resting on the bookcase as though trying to relieve quivering knees of part of the weight of her body.

"May I speak to Mr. Arsen's secretary for a moment?" Sampsel asked.

"You may not," the detective said in a voice of cold hostility. "Get out."

Sampsel nodded and moved from the door. In the elevator, he took the bit of paper from his palm and looked at it.

It was the smudged impression of two fingerprints. One of the prints was very plain. The other was badly smudged, as though the paper had been moved suddenly, or the finger that had made the print had been jerked away.

Sampsel put the paper in his pocket and went at once to his office.

Edna Grace had a list of names prepared. "I got these over the telephone," she said. "They're the women who have been convicted of murder during the period you inquired about."

"All right," said Sampsel, "give me the information."

"Stella Lincoln, convicted of murder in nineteen twenty-eight, poisoned her husband for insurance."

"No," said Sampsel, "that's not the one. This would be a crime of emotional anger, something probably to do with jealousy."

His secretary nodded, moved a finger down the list which she held in her hand. "There was Martha Lenton, who killed Sally Blake in an argument over a man."

"Her husband?" asked Sampsel.

"No, just a man friend. Martha Lenton was buyer in the woman's department of a big department store. Sally Blake was a clerk. The man was a floorwalker that they were both sweet on. Martha Lenton killed Sally Blake, and the man didn't even stand by her at the time of the trial—simply walked out and left her to take the jolt."

"What happened?" asked Sampsel.

"She was electrocuted on March the fifth, nineteen twenty-nine."

Sampsel frowned thoughtfully for a moment, then suddenly started for the door. "I am going," he said, "to check all the facts on that case. I think it's the one I want."

"But," said Edna Grace, "that woman has been dead for four years."

As Sampsel went out of the door, he nodded thoughtfully. "Yes," he said, "four years would be about right."

Chapter 3

THE WOMAN WHO DIDN'T DIE

S AMPSEL THE SEER gazed across the desk, into the black, enigmatical eyes of Carl Moffat, the prison physician. "I wanted to find out," he said, "something about the execution of Martha Lenton."

The eyes of the prison physician were dark and inscrutable. Lights glittered from their lacquer-like surfaces with an almost hypnotic effect.

"Why," he asked, in a deeply resonant tone of voice, "did you wish to know?"

Slowly, Sampsel took a bit of folded paper from his pocket. "I," he said, "am a professional palmist."

He looked for some hint of incredulity or scorn in the eyes of the doctor, and saw none. The doctor gravely inclined his head.

"Many people," said Sampsel slowly, "do not believe in palmistry."

"Many people," Doctor Moffat assured him, smiling slightly, "do not believe in mental telepathy, or other well authenticated physical phenomena which come in the realm of that which we are pleased to term 'psychic.'"

Sampsel sighed.

"What you have said," he remarked, "simplifies my task greatly. I received this morning, through the mail, a package which contained the dead hand of a woman. The hand had been severed at the wrist. I have no idea why it was sent to me, or from whom. There was a note which accompanied the hand, requesting that I refrain from divulging the information to the police. I called in Sam Arsen, a criminologist and detective. He started to work on the case, and met his death under most peculiar circumstances. The police are inclined to believe it was murder, but they do not know the means by which the man met his death."

Doctor Moffat's eyes widened. His manner became excited. "Yes," he said, "go on. Please go on."

"That is all," said Sampsel.

"No, no," Doctor Moffat assured him. "There was some lead that brought you here—something that led you to ask the question about Martha Lenton."

"That," said Sampsel slowly, "was due to the fact that, from the marks in the hand which had been sent me, I believed the woman might have been betrayed into murder or homicidal tendencies by her emotions. The configuration of the hand, and the various lines in the hand indicated that such a woman had actually committed a murder and had been executed for it. The startling thing which was apparent, from an examination of the hand, was that this execution must have taken place some four years prior to the time the hand was cut from the wrist."

"In other words," said Doctor Moffat, squirming excitedly in his chair, "the woman had actually been dead for four years, and yet had continued to exist."

"To the extent that the physiological changes brought about by the process which we call age had continued to make themselves manifest," said Sampsel.

Doctor Moffat took a deep breath, seemed about to speak forcefully and at some length, then apparently changed his mind and let the breath out in a deep sigh.

"Well?" asked Sampsel.

Doctor Moffat fingered his chin, then slowly: "And there was something else?"

"Yes," said Sampsel. "I thought that Arsen would take fingerprints of the hand as soon as he reached his office, probably before he notified the police. I found an ink smear on his thumbnail, which led me to believe he had actually taken the fingerprints. I happened to glance in the waste basket, and saw a piece of paper, on which fingerprints had been taken. One of the prints had been blurred, so Arsen had evidently thrown the paper into the wastebasket, tearing it across, and had started to make fresh prints when he was interrupted by the murderer."

"And you recovered those prints?" asked Moffat.

Sampsel nodded. "Yes," he said, "I started investigating the crimes of violence committed by women during the period that I thought might be most productive of results, and found this case of Martha Lenton. I consulted the jail records, and was able to find her fingerprints. The print that I had was undoubtedly taken from the index finger of her right hand."

Doctor Moffat was now breathing heavily, as though he had been running. Apparently he was laboring under strong emotional stimuli.

"Tell me," he said, "was there anything peculiar about the death of Arsen? That is, was there any peculiar mark upon the body?"

"Yes," said Sampsel, "there was a peculiar bruise or contusion on the neck. It looked as though there had been a puncture wound made by quite a number of small needles."

Doctor Moffat stared steadily at Sampsel, eyes glittering with suppressed excitement, nostrils expanded. "Lord," he said, "but I am glad that you came!"

"What do you mean?" Sampsel inquired.

"You can belittle your powers all you want to, make it appear that you simply employ logical deductions, or apply basic principles of psychology; the fact is, however, that you have something of a knowledge of the things that are beyond the scope of the ordinary man's experience or reasoning."

"All right," said Sampsel, "what are you leading up to?"

"I am going to show you," said Doctor Moffat slowly, "a file of private records, a case history of something that is so weird and bizarre, I have never previously mentioned it to anyone. I am going to show you the case notes of a dead woman who did not die."

Sampsel stared steadily at Doctor Moffat, but Moffat made a gesture for silence, got up, crossed his office, unlocked a filing case, and took out a file.

"Before she died," Doctor Moffat said, "Martha Lenton started going into trances. Those trances were not the ordinary type of trance. They were a peculiar condition of suspended animation which went far beyond anything in my experience."

"Can you explain that a little more in detail?" Sampsel asked.

"Yes," said Doctor Moffat. "During the periods of trance, it was impossible for me to get any pulse; impossible to get any reflexes; impossible to get any signs of animation."

"In other words," Sampsel inquired, "the condition resembled death?"

"Resembled death so closely that I was unable to differentiate between death and life."

"Did these trances come on regularly?"

Doctor Moffat said: "I am satisfied that, toward the last, she acquired the power of putting herself in one of these trances consciously."

"How do you mean?" Sampsel asked.

"I mean that I came into her cell one morning about three weeks prior to her execution, and found her lying on her cot, apparently dead. I made rather a complete examination, and was satisfied that life was extinct. I knew that there had been some condition of suspended animation prior to that time, and I wished particularly to guard against giving any false reports, so I was careful to check my conclusions thoroughly before I started to report the case. I had gone to the door of the cell to make my report, when I heard a laugh behind me, and turned. There was the woman whom I had pronounced dead, sitting on her cot, and laughing at me."

"Was the laugh normal?" asked Sampsel.

"It was not what I would call normal," said Doctor Moffat slowly. "There was a strained note in it, a metallic something which sounded, if you understand what I mean, hardly human."

"I," Sampsel remarked slowly, "understand exactly what you mean."

"That," said Doctor Moffat, in a more professional tone, as though he had gained control of his emotions, now that he had made his first confession, "was the initial occasion when I was forced to recognize the ability which Martha Lenton had, or, rather, an ability which I felt some other entity had to bring about a condition resembling death. I felt that something had happened to her consciousness, that her body had been mastered or possessed by some other force.

"Now I am, of course, familiar with the general phenomenon of multiple personality; also of the secondary personalities which are developed in a hypnotic trance. I would say that Martha Lenton showed no signs of multiple personality or a secondary personality. It seemed as though there was a case of what we might call obsession."

Sampsel nodded, but said nothing.

After a moment, Moffat started speaking again. "There was a dog," he said, "a dog that I was very fond of. He had been with me several years. This Lenton women started to make strange statements concerning powers which she possessed. Among other things, she told me that she was going to kill the dog."

"Why?" asked Sampsel.

"I think she was enraged at me because I wouldn't cooperate with her in something she wished to do."

"Can you tell me what that was?" asked Sampsel.

After a moment, Doctor Moffat shook his head. "I would prefer not to, right at present," he said.

"All right," said Sampsel, "how about the dog?"

"She threatened to kill the dog," said Doctor Moffat. "It seemed an idle threat. She was, of course, confined to her cell. She could not leave; nor could she send anything out of the cell. My offices were in another wing of the prison, and there was no possible way in which she could have had access to the dog; yet she killed him."

"How?" Sampsel inquired.

"I don't know. All I know is that when I found the dog, he was dead, and just above his right ear was a small abrasion; something about the size of a dime—circular. It looked as though needles had been clustered together and pushed into the skin. To satisfy myself, I made an autopsy, and was able to find some evidence of poison, but, even so, I do not understand how it would have been possible for her to have brought death to the dog."

"Go on," said Sampsel. "Then what happened?"

"After that," said Doctor Moffat, slowly, "Martha Lenton seemed to possess the ability to die at will. She seemed possessed of strange powers when she was in this condition of coma. She could apparently ascertain what was going on about her; even seemed to have the ability to bring about physical phenomena far outside of the walls of her cell."

"I presume," said Sampsel, "that what you are leading up to is a matter in connection with her execution."

Doctor Moffat's face showed relief. "I am glad that you have grasped the possibilities of the situation so readily," he said. "It was a difficult matter to bring up, and I know it will be difficult to explain, but inasmuch as you already understand—"

"Yes?" encouraged Sampsel. "Go on."

"Executions," said Doctor Moffat, "are, at best, a gruesome business. Personally I do not favor them. However, I have my duty to perform as prison physician. You understand that the various individual types react differently to currents of electricity. The idea of an electrocution is to give a big enough shock to result in death, yet not heavy enough to bring about disfiguring burns. It is a matter of rather a nice balance."

"Go ahead," said Sampsel.

"For that reason," said Doctor Moffat, "the duty of the prison physician becomes quite important. It is necessary that he pronounce a person dead; otherwise there is a possibility that there might be a recovery from an unconsciousness superinduced by the electric current."

"And you pronounced Martha Lenton dead?" asked Sampsel.

"Yes."

"Was she dead?"

A look of agonized doubt came over Doctor Moffat's face. "I wish to heaven that I knew!" he exclaimed fervently.

"And in the event she was not?" asked Sampsel.

"Her body was claimed," said Doctor Moffat slowly, "by a person who appeared to be her brother. A subsequent investigation has convinced me that the documents which he had, as proof of his identity, were clever forgeries. The man took the body, had it placed in a coffin, and then completely disappeared. In all of the burial records, there is no record of the burial of Martha Lenton."

"All right," said Sampsel, "I can see that there are other things in connection with this case that you haven't told me about. What are they?"

Doctor Moffat placed the tips of his fingers together, and stared down at his hands. "There have been," he said, "several significant circumstances."

"Such as?" Sampsel prompted.

"Such as my inability to keep a dog. I have tried to keep dogs on five successive occasions. I am very much interested in dogs and very fond of them. In every case, the death of the dog has resulted within a period of less than two weeks from the time I brought him here to the prison."

"And the death has been in the same manner?" asked Sampsel.

"The same manner; the same peculiar wound."

Abruptly, Doctor Moffat lost his manner of professional calm. He got to his feet and twisted his hands together, as though in physical agony.

"You've got to help me," he said. "You've simply got to. You're the one man who can understand these things. I don't know how it's done. I don't know whether it's a case of obsession, or if it's simply hocus-pocus, but I know that I am going to be next."

"Next for what?" asked Sampsel.

"Next to be killed, of course," said Doctor Moffat, and, as he spoke, his hand involuntarily went to the back of his neck, the place where he anticipated the red death would leave its fatal trade mark.

Chapter 4

THE RED RING OF DOOM

S AMPSEL SAT IN Doctor Moffat's private office, going over the file of papers which had been handed him by the physician, papers which reported the intimate details of the strange case of Martha Lenton.

Doctor Moffat had busied himself with the routine duties attendant upon his office. The long afternoon shadows had given place to a twilight. A nurse, in stiffly starched white uniform, turned on lights for Sampsel.

"When do you expect the doctor to return?" asked Sampsel, looking up.

"In about an hour now, I think," the nurse told him, coolly consulting her wristwatch. "He's over in the hospital."

"Did you know anything about this Lenton case?" asked Sampsel.

She surveyed him with cool brown eyes, and said in a voice that was steady and unwavering: "Very little. I understood that she was given to fainting fits prior to her execution."

"Is that unusual?" asked Sampsel.

"I think not. It is, of course, a frightful ordeal, and a woman is so constituted that she is more affected by it than a man."

Abruptly Sampsel laid down the documents and stared at the young woman. She met his stare with those steady, frank eyes, and a manner which was purely professional in its cool efficiency.

"Does Doctor Moffat take you into his confidence on his cases?" he asked.

She shook her head slowly, deliberately. "Certainly not. I am merely an assistant, a trained employee."

Sampsel let his eyes drop to her hands. They were at her side, tightly clasped. She noticed the direction of his glance, and said coolly: "Were you interested in my hands?"

"I am a palmist," he told her. "I am always interested in hands."

"You'll pardon me," she said, "but I don't believe in palmistry," and moved toward the door. In the doorway she paused.

"There's another gentleman waiting to see Doctor Moffat," she said, "and he is a detective, or perhaps a reporter."

"Waiting?" asked Sampsel.

"Yes, he's waiting in the outer office."

"Did you get his name?"

"Bigelow—Mr. Frank W. Bigelow, I believe he said the name was."

She opened the door and stood for a moment on the threshold. "I think it's about this same case," she said.

There was a swirl of motion behind her. Sampsel saw a hand come to rest on her shoulder, saw her being pulled out of the doorway, and then encountered the wary, watchful eyes of a tall, thin man, who loomed in the doorway and said: "You're Doctor Moffat, eh?"

Sampsel waited until the visitor had pushed the nurse out of the way and closed the door before he answered.

"What was it that you wanted?" he asked, and he did not deny that he was Doctor Moffat.

"My name's Bigelow. I'm on the *Clarion*."

"What was it you wanted?" asked Sampsel, repeating his question in a monotonous monotone.

"I want to know something about Martha Lenton."

"What do you want to know about her, and why do you want to know it?"

"I understand she was executed."

"She was."

The reporter eyed Sampsel in shrewd appraisal. "Was there anything unusual about her execution?"

"Nothing," said Sampsel. "Why did you wish to know?"

The reporter's eyes continued to search those of Sampsel. "All right," he said, "I'll tell you why I want to know.

"A palmist received a woman's hand in a wooden package through the mail. He called in a criminologist by the name of Sam Arsen. You probably know of him. Arsen took fingerprints from the hand and then was killed. The hand and the fingerprints were missing, but Arsen apparently had made a classification of the fingerprints before his death. The figures representing those classifications were on his desk, and apparently their significance was overlooked by the murderer."

"Go on," said Sampsel. "You interest me very much, Mr. Bigelow."

"I thought I would," the reporter told him grimly. "All right, here's what happened: I chased down those classifications, figuring that the numbers referred to fingerprints. I found that if those figures related to a fingerprint classification, the hand that Sam Arsen had been examining was the hand of Martha Lenton, who was executed for murder some four years ago."

"Had the hand been embalmed?" asked Sampsel.

"We don't know; apparently not."

"Then," said Sampsel, "it wouldn't have kept for four years."

"All right," Bigelow told him, "have it your own way. Now I'm coming to something else."

"All right," said Sampsel, "what is it?"

"No one went into Arsen's private office. That is, no one that the secretary knew anything about, and she would have known had anybody gone in through the outer office. Arsen almost never opened the door of his private office in order to let visitors in from the corridor, yet he must have done so in this case."

"Most annoying," said Sampsel, "having a case of death, where it is impossible to get a clue as to the murder."

Bigelow lit a cigarette, glanced once more at Sampsel. "You're not the type of man I expected to see," he said.

"Indeed?" said Sampsel.

"Anyway," Bigelow told him, "I'm going to tell you something, and ask you a question."

"All right, go ahead."

"You have a teletype machine out here in your office, which is connected with police headquarters. Just as soon as Arsen notified the police that he was the custodian of a severed hand which had been sent to the palmist, the police teletype machines sent out the information in a broadcast, to ascertain if any officer had come in contact with any body from which a hand had been severed."

"Indeed," said Sampsel noncommittally.

"Now," said the reporter, as though Sampsel had made no comment, "I notice that the paper from the teletype machine is thrown into a special waste basket after it has been read either by you or by your secretary. While I was waiting in your outer office, I improved my opportunity to observe the premises, by prowling through that waste basket. I found that the item dealing with the dead hand has been cut from the rest of the paper and is missing."

"Yes?" said Sampsel.

"Yes," the reporter told him. "I want to know what is the reason for your interest in this dead hand, if there was nothing unusual about the execution of Martha Lenton. I also want to know why you rushed from your office, in your automobile, at such break-neck speed, almost immediately after the report came out, and where you went."

Sampsel raised his eyebrows. "I didn't go anywhere," he said.

"Oh yes you did," the reporter told him, "I've got all the dope on that. The knowledge that this hand had been severed, caused you to—"

"I'm just a bit hard of hearing," Sampsel told him, "perhaps you have me confused with Doctor Moffat. I am only waiting for Doctor Moffat, myself. Sampsel is my name, and I'm the palmist who received the hand through the mail."

The reporter stared at him with a face that showed surprise, mortification, then anger. "You certainly knew that I was taking you for Doctor Moffat," he said.

"I thought there must have been some misunderstanding," Sampsel admitted.

"Didn't you tell me you were Doctor Moffat?"

Sampsel shook his head. "I asked you what you wanted," he said. "When I saw you pushing your way into the room, I thought you must have told the nurse you wanted to see me."

"Well," said the reporter, "I do want to see you, now that you're here, and I want to ask you some questions."

"Go right ahead," said Sampsel, smiling.

"I want to know," said Bigelow, "how it happens that I find you here."

"I came to consult Doctor Moffat, and am waiting for him."

"Did you want to consult him about Martha Lenton?"

"I think," said Sampsel, smiling, "that I will have to ask you to confine your inquiries to matters connected with the hand which I received through the mail this morning."

There was a knock on the outer door. The door opened, and the nurse stared at them with calm, steady eyes. "Doctor Moffat," she said, "wants you to wait in the outer office."

"Did he say so?" asked Sampsel.

Her face remained expressionless.

"Those were his orders when he left on his tour of inspection," she said, "and I feel quite certain that he would not like it if he returned and found Mr. Bigelow in this private office."

Bigelow stared at her and said belligerently: "I don't know as I'm responsible to Doctor Moffat for my actions. It happens that I'm working for my newspaper. I'm getting some information from Mr. Sampsel that I desire, and—"

"And you also want information from Doctor Moffat," said the nurse very sweetly. "I am simply advising you that if you wish Doctor Moffat to answer any of your questions, it might be much better if he found you waiting in the other office. You could talk with Mr. Sampsel afterwards."

Bigelow let his eyes drift from the nurse to Sampsel, then back to the nurse, then nodded. Without a word, he walked into the outer office, and the nurse closed the door behind him, looked at Sampsel with that same sweet smile.

"It would seem," she said, "that you were very curious."

"Suppose I am?" Sampsel asked.

"I think," she said, "that your curiosity is somewhat ill-timed."

Sampsel started to say something, but stopped as he saw a shadow form on the ground-glass panel of the door which led from the private office into the corridor. It was a shadow, squat and misshapen—the shadow of a hunchback, with a long beak-like nose, and a pointed, protruding chin.

The nurse moved swiftly to the door, shot back the bolt, and opened it.

The hunchback leered at her with eyes that glittered with some strange excitement. He shuffled rapidly across the office.

"That's all right, Edward," said the nurse. "You don't need to attend to that now."

Sampsel became conscious of an odor of perfume; a strong cloying perfume which assailed his nostrils. Then the hunchback turned and fastened those glittering, gray eyes upon him.

"I'm the spider," said the hunchback.

The nurse caught Sampsel's eye, tapped her forehead significantly.

"Of course you're the spider," agreed Sampsel.

"I spin webs and human flies drop in those webs," said the hunchback, speaking in a harsh, metallic voice.

"Of course you do," Sampsel agreed.

"That's all," said the dwarf, "that I wanted you to know. I just wanted you to recognize who I am." He turned and walked across the office, through the door which led to the outer office.

The nurse smiled at Sampsel. "I'm glad you understand," she told him. "The hunchback is something of a privileged character. He has a peculiar mental condition, and Doctor Moffat thinks he can cure it, but, in order to do so, it is necessary to encourage the man in his hallucinations. One should never argue with an insane person."

Sampsel nodded and was about to say something, when there came to his ears a demoniacal outburst of shrill, metallic laughter.

He paused, and caught the sudden look of terror in the eyes of the nurse.

"What is it?" asked Sampsel.

She stood with her hands clenched, her face dead white, eyes bulging with terror. Apparently she tried to speak, but words did not come from her lips.

"It's in the outer office," Sampsel said, starting for the door.

She held out one clenched hand, as though to push him back, then nodded and turned toward the door. Sampsel heard the sound of a door slamming in the outer office, then pushed open the door and stood staring at the form of a man, crumpled down in a heap on the floor.

The room was filled with that heavy odor of cloying perfume.

Sampsel was conscious of the nurse rushing past him with a flutter of her stiffly starched garments, saw her bend over the form on the floor and tug at the man's shoulders. As the man's head rolled back, Sampsel caught a glimpse of a round, red mark, about the size of a dime, in the man's neck, right at the base of the head, just behind the right ear. Then the face rolled into view, and Sampsel saw that it was the face of Frank Bigelow, the reporter.

At that moment, the door of the office opened, and Doctor Moffat stood staring at them. "What happened?" he asked.

The nurse looked at him, and spoke the first words which Sampsel had heard come from her lips since the sound of that laughter had filled the office.

"Martha Lenton," she said.

Chapter 5

THE SPIDER AND THE FLY

DOCTOR MOFFAT FELT for the man's pulse, then turned the head to examine the small spot behind the ear. He raised his head and sniffed.

"Has Edward been here?" he asked.

The nurse nodded.

Sampsel spoke, watching the nurse's face as he talked. "If you mean the dwarf with the loud perfume," he said, "the man went into the office just before we heard the laughter. He must have been here at the time. I heard a door slam just before I came in the office. I think that somebody must have run from this room."

"It wasn't Edward who did this," said Doctor Moffat, "but he may have seen her."

"Her?" asked Sampsel.

"Martha Lenton," said Doctor Moffat.

"Surely you don't believe she did this," said Sampsel.

Doctor Moffat shrugged his shoulders, and reached for the telephone.

"We've got to report this," he said.

In a coldly professional tone of voice he communicated to the exchange operator his desire to speak with police headquarters. Then, after a moment's pause, his voice, sounding coldly efficient, went on in a swift report. "Doctor Moffat speaking. I am at my office in the east wing of the penitentiary. A newspaper reporter who came to interview me has been killed. Apparently it is a murder. The man has a small puncture abrasion through the skin on the back of his neck. He is quite dead. At the time, a Mr. Sampsel was present, and also Miss Edith Caldwell, my office nurse. They were in an adjoining room. That is all I know about the matter."

He hung up the telephone.

"You didn't mention anything about the hunchback," Sampsel said.

Doctor Moffat smiled. "The hunchback," he said, "had nothing to do with it. He wasn't here at the time."

"He went into this office," Sampsel insisted.

"And then went out again," Doctor Moffat remarked. "He was not in immediate proximity to the crime."

"I notice," said Sampsel, with some feeling, "that you were very careful to have me in immediate proximity to the crime."

"I reported the facts," Doctor Moffat said in a cold, impersonal voice. "Miss Caldwell, will you please step into this room with me for a moment? I desire to give you some instructions about some of the more urgent cases before the police arrive and take up all my time with fruitless inquiries."

Sampsel spoke hotly. "You desire," he said, "to tell her that she is not to tell the police anything about Martha Lenton, or the peculiar trances to which she was given prior to her execution."

Sampsel felt the dark eyes of Doctor Moffat boring into his with something that seemed to have almost the shock of a physical impact.

"We will discuss that matter later," said Doctor Moffat, and he held the door and the private office open for the nurse, who stepped into the room.

Doctor Moffat entered the room, banged the door shut, and Sampsel, casting only one swift glance to make sure that the door was shut, moved over to the waste basket near the teletype machine and looked at the paper in the waste basket. Then he walked back to the body of the reporter, knelt down, pulled back the coat, and found a folded wad of yellow paper in the inner pocket. Swiftly he took it out, and spread it on the floor.

The paper was one of the long yellow sheets which had been fed through the teletype machine, and which contained typewritten police reports. Sampsel noticed that there was no mention made of the report of Arsen, the criminologist. Apparently that had been cut from the sheet of paper, which was in two separate pieces, the edges of the severed parts showing evidences of hasty scissor strokes. There was, however, a report of the death of Arsen, the criminologist, with a mention of the peculiar wound which had been found on the back of the neck.

Sampsel was just replacing the yellow paper in the pocket, when the door of the private office opened, and Doctor Moffat stalked into the room.

"What are you doing?" he asked.

"I gathered that this man had taken some paper from your waste basket," said Sampsel, "and I wanted to see what was on it."

"That was paper that came from my waste basket?" asked Doctor Moffat, staring at the yellow paper.

"Yes, from the waste basket beneath the teletype machine."

Doctor Moffat strode over to the corpse, reached down and snatched up the yellow paper. He spread out the sheets, looked at the printed matter, wadded the paper into a ball, and flung it across the room, in the general direction of the waste basket.

"Snooping!" he said. "Reporters are always snooping. They can't be gentlemen."

Sampsel shrugged his shoulders.

Doctor Moffat stared down at him, with those black glittering eyes showing cold hostility.

"When the police arrive," he said, "you will be careful to say nothing concerning our conversations about Martha Lenton."

"May I ask why?" Sampsel inquired.

"Because," said Doctor Moffat, "you would not be believed. You would bring about an attitude of the police and the press which would result in a public ridicule which would sweep me from my office. You will kindly leave this matter entirely in my hands."

"And in the event I do not?" Sampsel asked.

Doctor Moffat stood with his feet spread slightly apart, his shoulders squared as though braced against an attack.

"In the event you do not cooperate with me in this matter," he said, "the police will understand that you deliberately led Mr. Bigelow to believe that you were the man he had called to see. In short, that you deliberately assumed my identity for the purpose of getting information from Mr. Bigelow. The police will further be advised that you had opportunity to inflict the peculiar wound on Bigelow while he was here in this room; that it was not until after Bigelow returned to the other room, that the poison took effect, and he burst into that hysterical laughter which preceded his death."

"That won't work," Sampsel said hotly. "The evidence will show the poison was instantaneous in its effect. It must have been. Arsen must have died instantly. This man must have died instantly."

Doctor Moffat sneered. "You seem to know a great deal about the poison," he said.

"I know what happened," Sampsel said. "And you're either going to have that hunchback brought into this case, or I'm going to tell the police that you're suppressing facts."

"Miss Caldwell," Doctor Moffat told him, "is very positive that she heard Edward leave the office prior to the time she heard the laughter."

"I am equally positive that he did not," Sampsel said.

"Let us not misunderstand each other," remarked Doctor Moffat in his cool, professional voice. "I am trying to restore reason to this hunchback. The shock of rough police questioning or the nervous reaction to any police accusations would probably be fatal to the progress I have already made. There is no need to drag him into this."

"I think," Sampsel told him, "I am going to talk with Miss Caldwell before the police do."

Sampsel strode across the room and through the door to the inner office. At the sight of the empty inner office he turned to ask Doctor Moffat where the nurse had gone, but the question was never asked, for the simple reason that the door of the outer office sounded to a peremptory knock. Doctor Moffat strode toward it, and Sampsel pushed the door of the inner office gently shut, and looked around him.

The room was quite empty. There was no sign of the nurse; nothing to tell him where she had gone. But the room was redolent of that odor of cloying perfume.

Sampsel stepped swiftly to the door which led to the outer corridor, shot back the bolt and walked down the echoing linoleum. Two plainclothesmen hurried past him. Behind him he could hear a hub-bub of voices coming through the doorway of Doctor Moffat's office. A door opened and two men appeared, robed in white, carrying a stretcher. One of the plainclothesmen stopped Sampsel.

"Who are you?" he asked.

Sampsel was on the point of making a reply, when the man caught sight of the stretcher bearers.

"You can't move the body," said the plainclothesman, "not until the coroner and the homicide squad finish their examinations."

"I don't know anything about that, sir," said one of the men. "We were just told to bring a stretcher to the office right away. Maybe the man's alive."

"Let's go see," said the plainclothesman, and he and his companion resumed their rapid walk, leaving Sampsel free to go unquestioned.

Sampsel paused for a moment, looking up and down the corridor, seeking some person of whom he could ask the question which was on his mind. But there was no necessity for asking the question. The form of the squat, misshapen hunchback crossed the corridor, and vanished into a doorway. Sampsel moved forward rapidly, turned the knob of the door, and found himself in a room. The hunchback looked at him with glaring, malevolent eyes.

"I'm a spider," he said.

"Of course you're a spider," said Sampsel.

"Human flies come to my web and I drain their life blood," said the hunchback.

Sampsel nodded his head. "Of course you do," he said.

There was a moment of silence.

"Can you laugh?" asked Sampsel.

The hunchback looked at him. "Spiders don't laugh," he said.

"Did you see the dead man in Doctor Moffat's office?" Sampsel asked.

The hunchback shook his head. "I'm not interested in dead men," he said. "Just flies—human flies."

Sampsel suddenly extended his arms and started running around the office, making high-pitched buzzing noises by holding his tongue against the roof of his mouth.

"I'm a fly," he said. "A human fly."

He heard motion behind him, and looked back over his shoulder.

The little hunchback, his eyes glittering as though they had been polished diamonds, his arms extended, lips curled back from fanglike teeth, was coming slowly and purposefully toward him.

Sampsel continued making the buzzing noises with his tongue. He turned, arms still extended, and caught the flash of motion as the hunchback sprang for him.

Sampsel felt the fangs of the hunchback at the back of his neck. He sank to the floor, the hunchback on top of him. He could feel the heat of the foul breath on his neck, could sense the feverish glitter of the staring eyes. Then Sampsel struggled for a moment, and lay still.

Chapter 6

PLACE OF THE LIVING DEAD

THE HUNCHBACK STRAIGHTENED, crooning to himself: "I'm a spider, I'm a spider. Human flies come to my net and I suck out their life blood."

Then he circled long arms about Sampsel's body. He lifted his motionless burden, and carried it as easily as though his victim had been but a child.

The hunchback moved with swiftness and stealth, apparently. He paused before what appeared to be a wall of the room, reached out with his foot and pressed a concealed spring. A doorway swung silently back, and the hunchback moved into the narrow dark passageway which was disclosed.

The heavy door of masonry swung slowly shut behind them, and a spring lock gave a dull click.

The steps of the hunchback sounded on cold stone, and came back in muffled echoes from the sides of the dark passage. Far ahead, a light showed vague and indistinct—a diffused light which seemed to come from an open doorway.

The hunchback crooned to himself as he walked: "I'm a spider, I'm a spider, I'm a spider. I spin my webs and catch the flies, I spin my webs and catch the flies, I spin my webs and catch the flies."

He came to the lighted room, at the far end of the passage. It was a room fitted up with operating tables, beds, a long bench, on which were glass retorts, and bottles of various colored liquids.

Over in one corner was a bed, and on the bed lay the form of a dead woman. The torso was entirely nude, and one of the arms showed a stump, where the hand had been amputated.

Next to that bed was an operating table, on which lay the unconscious form of Edith Caldwell, Doctor Moffat's nurse. Beside it was another operating table, over which were bright lights, beating down in incandescent brilliance.

The dwarf man walked across the long room to this operating table, placed Sampsel upon it, and stepped back a pace or two, staring at Sampsel, and droning: "Another fly, another fly, another fly," monotonously repeating the phrase over and over.

In a far corner of the room was a marble slab, and on this slab reposed a body, partially dissected. Yet, the color of that body was not the color of death, but the color of life—a life, to be sure, which was at a low ebb, but nevertheless still existent.

A door opened and closed. There were quick steps, then the voice of Doctor Moffat.

"What's this Edward?"

"A human fly, a human fly, a human fly, a human fly, come to the web of the spider. He wants his life blood drained," came the monotonous chant of the dwarf.

Doctor Moffat moved quickly across toward the operating table, and as he moved, muttered an exclamation of annoyance under his breath.

Sampsel flung himself from the operating table to the floor, just in time to avoid the reaching hand of the prison physician.

"Grab him, Edward!" shouted Doctor Moffat.

Sampsel backed toward the corner, behind the operating table. He saw the dark, glittering eyes of the prison physician, reflecting the glare of the incandescents, as the man rushed toward him. Coming around the table from the other side was the hunchback, his eyes diamond-hard, his long arms reaching out, the fingers like the tentacles of some devil fish, squirming with impatience to reach their victim.

Sampsel was unarmed. The swift, hasty glance which he was able to cast about him disclosed no weapon to his hand. He could see the murderous intent of the men who were closing in on him, and he raised his voice in a long reverberating shout for help.

He saw the look of sardonic mirth in the glittering black eyes of Doctor Moffat, and knew then that the chamber had been constructed to be proof against the screams of victims.

The dwarf's fingers closed on Sampsel's left wrist as Sampsel drew back his hand to launch a blow at Doctor Moffat. The power of those fingers came as a distinctly unpleasant surprise. They seemed to grip the bone with a numbing, crushing force.

"A human fly, a human fly, a human fly," droned the dwarf man.

Doctor Moffat rushed forward.

Sampsel managed to snap his right fist across in a blow which struck the physician on the side of the head, staggering him somewhat, lurching him against the operating table, and then on past Sampsel's shoulder. The physician stumbled, and his weight, lurching against the arm of the hunchback, broke the hold of those abnormally long and strong fingers.

Sampsel swung his left viciously, felt the thud of his fist impacting the temple of Doctor Moffat. The three men lurched into a tangled huddle in the corner, their bodies swaying. Sampsel flung his weight against the side of the operating table, and it tottered on its broad base for a moment, then fell over with a crash.

Drawers fell from the operating table to the floor, cascaded a glittering shower of surgical instruments which clattered on the masonry.

Doctor Moffat, cursing, whirled and caught Sampsel's vest with his right hand, holding him long enough for the dwarf to reach out and grab the back of Sampsel's coat with his gripping fingers.

Sampsel knew there could be no escape now, with these two men holding him. He could not exert sufficient force to break loose. There was only one thing to do, and that was to bore in, trusting to his ability to disable his adversaries at close quarters.

The great hand of the dwarf man came up, seeking his throat. Sampsel flung his head down and forward, lashed out with his right, kicked viciously as he whirled against the grip of the dwarf, jerked back, and heard buttons rip from his vest as the physician's hold was broken. He was conscious of the right arm of the dwarf grasping the back of his neck, felt the nerves ache with the sudden pain, then Doctor Moffat leapt upon him, throwing his entire weight upon Sampsel's neck and shoulders, bearing him to the floor.

Sampsel twisted, whirled and struggled. He felt his foot strike some round object on the floor, and his leg shot out from under him, precipitating them all in a struggling mass to the stone floor. He heard the dwarfed hunchback give a little inarticulate scream, felt the body shudder. He was conscious of a round object flashing in the rays of the incandescent, realized suddenly that Doctor Moffat was trying to press a signet ring against his flesh.

Sampsel flung himself back against the grip of the dwarf, to find, to his surprise, that that grip had now grown limp. The signet ring missed his neck by less than half an inch, and then Sampsel grasped the physician's wrist, twisted, pulled, caught the arm over his shoulder and heaved with all of his might.

He heard a bone snap, heard a scream of agony come from Doctor Moffat, then he fought to his feet and was free.

Doctor Moffat lay sprawled on the floor some five or six feet away. The hunchback lay in a limp huddle against the overturned operating table.

Sampsel flashed one swift look, and saw that one of the surgical knives, held upright by the edge of the overturned operating table, had penetrated the back of the hunchback's neck, and saw that those glittering, hard, feverish eyes of the man who labored under the delusion that he was a human spider, were already glazing.

Sampsel jumped forward, caught Doctor Moffat off balance, as the man rolled and struggled to gain his feet.

The physician screamed a curse, fell backward under the impetus of Sampsel's attack.

Sampsel found straps on the overturned operating table. He took these straps and strapped Moffat's arms and legs. Moffat's right arm was broken just below the shoulder, and he screamed with agony as Sampsel strapped the injured arm to the body. When he had tightened the buckle, Sampsel got slowly to his feet and looked around him. He heard voices, the sound of steps, and, suddenly, white, startled faces appeared in the passageway through which he had been borne by the dwarf man. The lights over the operating table glinted upon the steel of weapons, and a harsh voice said: "Put 'em up."

Sampsel the Seer spoke rapidly.

"Get a physician," he said. "Try to do something for the young woman who's on the operating table. The other one I'm afraid is dead. Get that woman to consciousness and get her story. How did you find this place?"

One of the detectives undid the straps which bound the nurse, then spoke slowly, his eyes shifting about the room. "We saw you go into a room. You didn't come out. We wanted to talk with you. We thought you might have had something to do with the murder. We looked around and found a secret spring that opened a door into this passageway. We heard the sounds of struggle and came in."

Sampsel nodded.

"Doctor Moffat," he said, "has been carrying out experiments with human victims. He got the victims from the execution chamber of the penitentiary, having tools who claimed the bodies as their relatives. I'm satisfied that he has a signet ring so designed that whenever he presses it against flesh, numerous needles, saturated in poison, push through from the interior of the ring, and bring instant death to the victim.

"He knew that his activities were about to be discovered, and he knew it in some way, from the hand that had been severed from the body of Martha Lenton. He killed Arsen in order to gain possession of that hand, and he killed Bigelow because Bigelow had uncovered evidence which indicated Moffat was the man who murdered Arsen.

"The doctor used the dwarf as an assistant. The dwarf thought that he was a human spider, and that the victims designated by Doctor Moffat were merely human flies that had come to his web.

"I sensed something of this when the nurse disappeared, and pretended to become unconscious while struggling with the dwarf. He acted mechanically and carried me to this place."

One of the detectives moved toward him. "All right," he said, "it's a good story, but stick 'em up anyway."

Slowly Sampsel elevated his hands.

"How'd you get all this?" asked the detective.

"Part of it by my knowledge of palmistry; part by my knowledge of psychology. I knew that the nurse was laboring under some great strain, and that she was trying to conceal something. During all of the time she talked with me, she kept her hands tightly clenched, a sign either of rage or an almost hysterical desire for concealment."

"Baloney!" said the detective.

There was the sound of motion. One of the detectives said: "Look out, she's sitting up."

Sampsel, his hands elevated, the detective's gun pointed at his stomach, turned his eyes and saw that Edith Caldwell was in a sitting position.

She stared at them with eyes that were wide, and seemed to be out of focus, as though she had been drugged or was talking in her sleep. But her voice was strong and firm.

"It's the truth. Doctor Moffat was carrying on his hideous experiments. He pronounced Martha Lenton dead when she was still alive, and revived her, after he had caused her body to be claimed by an accomplice. I knew that he had this room, and knew something of his experiments, but I dared not say a word because I knew that he would kill me. He has all of his offices wired so that he can hear anything which goes on in any part of the offices. I was selected as a trusty and nurse from the female inmates of the penitentiary because I had been a nurse before I was convicted of driving a car while I was intoxicated. I had an accident and a man was killed. I was convicted of manslaughter.

"Martha Lenton's life was a veritable hell. She died. I knew that if I could get some message to the outside world which would result in an investigation, Doctor Moffat's hideous torture chamber would be uncovered. I knew that I needed some proof other than just a mere statement coming from a convicted felon

"So I managed to amputate one of the hands from the body, just as Doctor Moffat was preparing to smuggle the body out and bury it. I got the hand mailed to Mr. Sampsel. I knew that he would be sufficiently interested to make an investigation, and I knew that the fingerprints of Martha Lenton were on file in every criminal identification bureau in the country. But the police were notified, and Doctor Moffat knew at once what had happened. He didn't know that I had taken the hand, but he knew that he had been betrayed. He killed Arsen and recovered possession of the hand. You can understand how easy it was for him to do that. He simply had to telephone to Arsen that he had important information about the hand, and ask Arsen to let him in through the exit door of his private office.

"I knew that Doctor Moffat left me alone with Mr. Sampsel simply as a trap. Had I said anything that would have put Mr. Sampsel on his guard, Doctor Moffat, who was listening over the concealed wires which led from the room, would have killed us both."

She paused and swayed slowly on the operating table. A detective rushed to her, placed his arm about her shoulders, giving her support.

Sampsel glanced at the detective who was holding him at the point of the revolver.

"As soon as I saw the teletype machine in Doctor Moffat's office," he said, "I knew that Doctor Moffat must have been familiar with the circumstances surrounding the death of Arsen. When he pretended ignorance, but became greatly excited when I told him the circumstances, I knew that he was simply acting a part. All of his story about Martha Lenton was simply to lay the foundation for the subsequent discovery of her body. He knew that he would have to get rid of it, and that he had to account for the hand which had made its appearance four years after the woman had officially met her death."

The voice of the nurse was vibrant with horror as she added her comment. "Four years," she said, "that were the same as death! Four years during which she was held much of the time in a state of suspended animation!"

Sampsel saw the detectives exchange glances; saw the detective who held him covered lower the gun and put it in his pocket.

Silently, purposefully, the two detectives moved toward the form of Doctor Moffat, stood staring down at him.

"All right, buddy," said one of the men, "we'll hear your story now."

There was no response. One of the detectives bent to make a closer examination and then jumped back and pointed.

"Look!" he said.

In some manner, Doctor Moffat had been able to turn the signet ring on his right hand, so that he had pressed the gold circle against the palm of his hand. As the detectives straightened the fingers, there appeared a small circular puncture mark against the flesh of the hand.

Nine Parts Devil

MAX BRAND

Chapter 1

TEN-GRAND RETAINER

E ACH OF THE DUMBBELLS weighed fifty pounds. Imagine a filled six-gallon pail. That was the burden which Clovelly shifted in each hand. He had finished the shadow-boxing and the skipping of the rope, together with exercises to develop speed and elasticity. Uncle Henry always had advocated slow, heavy movements which build muscle into a great bulk.

Dressed for the street, Clovelly might have been lost in any crowd of dapper young men. Stripped to shorts for the gymnasium which filled the uppermost floor of his house on Channing Place, he struck the eye as quite another picture.

The massive weights swayed lightly in his hands. Those side thrusts, which looked so easy, caused arches of trembling muscle to spring into view from wrists to elbow to shoulder to neck—flowing bridges of power. When he pushed the dumbbells above his head, a thousand snakes squirmed along his back. He began a queer dance in which the heavy weights seemed possessed of invisible wings which lifted Clovelly from his feet. And Jim Tolan, agape, from the shadowy corner to which the butler had just brought him, watched the mighty shoulders and shuddering outspring of thigh muscles.

"Geez!" whispered the detective to Williams.

"Beg pardon, sir?" said old Williams, keeping his eye from Tolan.

Clovelly checked his strange dance. His body, sunbrowned to a coppery darkness from head to foot, was bright with currents of sweat. As he dropped the dumbbells to the mat and stood in repose, all that Herculean strength disappeared and left him merely rounded and sleek.

"You said I was to bring Mr. Tolan to you whenever he came, night or day, no matter what you were doing, sir," remarked Williams. "So I ventured to bring him here."

"Quite right," said Clovelly. He waved his hand. "How do you do, Mr. Tolan. I'll be with you in one moment."

In spite of that strenuous workout, he was not breathing audibly. There was merely a slow, great lifting of his chest.

"Take your time, Mr. Clovelly," said Tolan. "Geez, but you're fit."

Clovelly stepped to the side of a pool which filled an end of the gymnasium. He took a running stride, bounded into the air, hit the padded end of a springboard, and floated upward from it like a bodiless mist. Shooting down, he knifed into the water and only left some softly spreading ripples. Tolan, staring with very wide eyes, saw a powerful stroke taking the body through the green water. In another moment Clovelly had whipped out of the tank.

"Be dressed in a moment, Mr. Tolan," he called, and disappeared.

Tolan leaned and grasped at the nearest dumbbell lying on the mat. His fingers slipped away from the weight. "Well, I'll be—" said Mr. Tolan. He leaned, took a more secure grip, and hefted the dumbbell. He was himself a strong man, so he pushed the massive iron as high as his shoulder. He pushed it still higher to the full extent of a trembling arm.

"Geez!" he murmured reverently, letting the weight drop to the padded mat. "I thought they was painted wood or something. But they're real. He'd never starve even if he wasn't one of the ten richest guys in America. He could go into the ring. I never seen anything like him."

This enthusiasm caused the freezing marble features of Williams to relax a trifle. He did not waste a glance on Mr. Tolan, but he permitted himself to say: "All the Clovellys are unusual. My late employer, Mr. Henry Clovelly, could climb that rope hand over hand at the age of sixty-five—that rope which hangs from the ceiling."

"Not using no legs?" asked Tolan, gradually lifting his head to look upward along the course of the rope.

"With his hands only," said Williams.

"Geez!" sighed Tolan. His vocabulary was not large but it was eloquent. Like the Chinese, he could give at least three meanings to every sound he uttered.

He had not finished gaping at the rope before Clovelly returned in gray flannels. He was not flushed to any great degree. He was not panting. His voice was as quiet and easy as though he had just risen from a lounging chair. He shook hands with Tolan and said he was very glad to see him; he was sorry to keep Mr. Tolan waiting. He led the way out of the gymnasium and down into the big library where dark woodwork was somberly enriched by the colors of the bound volumes.

They sat down in deep leather chairs. Mr. Tolan would have a drink. He took three fingers of Scotch and two squirts of soda.

"You ain't with me, Mr. Clovelly?" he said, looking at the empty hands of his host.

"If you'll excuse me, Mr. Tolan," said the deep, gentle voice of Clovelly.

"My Uncle Henry always used to say that every drink before dinner created a mental hazard."

Tolan blinked. "Yeah?" he said. "By the smell of this stuff, I'd back it to the limit if it was a hundred-to-one shot."

"Ah?" said Clovelly, blinking in bewilderment in his turn. "But now—perhaps you've brought me news?"

"I have, all right," nodded Tolan.

Clovelly almost sprang from his chair. "About Mrs. Shaney?" he breathed.

"Yeah, about her," agreed Tolan.

Clovelly sat very straight. He wanted to cry out something but he shut his teeth over the exclamation. Tolan took a long swallow and grinned. "This is the real quill," he said. "There's the real old whiskers in this stuff; it tickles all the way down. Yeah, I got news about Mrs. Shaney. But she ain't Mrs. Shaney."

"What do you mean?" cried Clovelly.

"She's just Al Champion, like she always was. She never married nobody, as far as I can find out. Shaney don't know where she is any more than you do; and he's just as crazy to know."

"Shaney doesn't know? She never was married?" echoed Clovelly, stunned. "But then what did it mean? What did it all—"

"Listen, Clovelly," said Tolan, "there's a lot that I don't figure because you never let me in on the lowdown."

"Lowdown?" echoed Clovelly, helplessly.

"My God, don't you even know what that means?" asked Tolan. "Have I gotta look in the Bible to find all my words? I mean, you always treat Al Champion like she was holy water instead of a cabaret entertainer."

"If you mean—" began Clovelly, coldly.

"No, no, I don't mean that!" Tolan broke in, rather wearily lifting his hand. "I know that Al Champion is nothin' but a little woolly white lamb with a pink ribbon tied to her neck. Even if some of the boys have wanted to tie that ribbon onto the working end of a rope. But leave that be. For as I make out, you're in a jam, Al Champion gets you out of it, you take her home to this place. She acts a little queer. You go to find her a drink—it's the fag end of the night and you don't want to wake up the servants—and when you come back, you ask her to marry you. Geez!" breathed Tolan, pulling out a blue-edged handkerchief to wipe his brow. "You wanta pour a couple hundred million into her lap. And after she bats her bright blue eyes a couple times, in walks Jay Shaney's mob all kind of bruised up—by you—and looking for trouble with guns. They've come to get her and you don't want to let her go."

"I think I understand you almost perfectly," said Clovelly, who had listened to this jargon with a look of utter concentration. "That's correct. Undoubtedly they had come to get her."

"Look here. Ever dawn on you that they'd come to get you, too?"

"But where would they have taken me?" asked Clovelly, surprised.

"For a ride—to hell!" said Tolan. "They would have flopped you. To make it straight Bible—they would have murdered you, Mr. Clovelly."

"I've suspected that before," declared Clovelly.

"Yeah, you suspected it, did you?" said Tolan. "Did you suspect that the reason that Shaney and his mob showed up was because the gal had given them a buzz while you were hunting for drinks?"

"She is as incapable of treachery—" began Clovelly in a ringing voice, his head raised.

"Yeah. Sure, sure!" agreed Tolan hastily. "I know she's as perfect as a sour fizz on a morning after. But lookit—suppose that she had tipped off the mob, while she still thought that you were trying to make the usual play for her, and then you walk in and talk marrying, and it knocks her for a row of loops. Mrs. Quarter Billion Clovelly; all that sort of thing. Then the boys show. She's gotta stop them from murdering you. She's gotta stop you from trying to fight guns with your bare hands. And she pulls one from the hip— a fast one. She simply announced to you that she's Mrs. Shaney and of course she goes home with her old man. That stops you. It stops Shaney, too. He's wanted that blonde for a long time. He takes her on his arm and shows the mob the way out. With one smart sock she wins against the two of you, keeps you as safe as a bullet-proof vest, and kids Shaney into thinking that she's already walking up the center aisle of a church with him. But then she ducks out on Shaney on the way back home. All he's got is the air. All you've got is that dizzy feeling. And all she's got is—I dunno what!"

"It was her adroitness that saved my life?" said Clovelly. "Is that what you mean? I believe it!"

"I'm glad you translate me right," said Tolan. "It's like talking to a foreigner, you were raised so far from Broadway. Now here's the funny gag. Once Al Champion has shaken Shaney, why don't she come back here and give you a call? Does she figure that when you wake up the next morning you'll think you've been through a slumming nightmare and that all you've got for her is a big laugh if she shows? Or is she lying low because she's afraid of Shaney and his gorillas?"

"She found me tiresome," explained Clovelly. "If you'll excuse me, sometimes it was as difficult for me to understand her as it is for me to understand you, Mr. Tolan. Not that I wish to imply that—"

"Listen!" exclaimed Tolan. "Nobody ever gets tired of a couple hundred million; not till the gal is right on Alimony Street. You couldn't make her tired. Not if she had to talk to you in sign language like a dummy."

"The mercenary nature which you attribute—" began Clovelly.

"Quit it, chief," pleaded Tolan. "She's the Queen of Sheba if you say the word. She ain't mercenary. But most of them blondes like to be pastured on the long green, is all I mean. The main thing is, do you wanta find her as bad as ever?"

"Yes!" exclaimed Clovelly. "If you can bring her to me, Mr. Tolan, the ten thousand I sent to your office is only a retaining fee. I intend a much larger reward."

"You intend what?" cried Tolan. "You mean you'll pay more than the ten grand for Al Champion?"

"When the thing is done, name your own price, Mr. Tolan. It shall be paid twice over!"

Jim Tolan snatched out the blue-edged handkerchief again and mopped his face with slow strokes. "Yeah. All right," he said. "I got some news about Al Champion that may be real. It's downstairs in the reception room."

"News? News of Alice Champion? Waiting downstairs?" cried Clovelly, brought from his chair by these tidings.

Tolan rose also, but more slowly. "Don't swaller the drink till it's poured," he cautioned. "What I got downstairs is a skirt that I picked up who says she knows where Al Champion is. I offer her up to a thousand bucks to lead me to the prize. She can't hear the gelt song but the nearest she ever came to real money before was in a book. Her line is that she knows where Al Champion is; that she's sworn to keep it a secret; that the only one Al wants to see is Mr. Clovelly; that the reason she hasn't come to David Clovelly before this is that she's scared of the Shaney mob. That's her line. How does it sound to you?"

"I must see her at once!" said Clovelly.

"Put on the brakes," urged Tolan. "This kid is a floozie with a Hollywood look and a marble front. She may be working a double-cross, for all I know. What I don't like is that she won't take the two of us to Al Champion. She'll show you the way, but she won't show anybody else. Sound her out, Mr. Clovelly. She's hard enough to bust a diamond drill; but I'll be there to help you along."

Chapter 2

A MAN'S OWN FOLLY

CLOVELLY COULD HARDLY WAIT to usher Tolan before him into the reception room where Parker, the second man, stood almost invisible against the stiff downward sweep of the great curtains. He stood on guard, as it were, over a slender girl in a flowery spring dress and a very dainty blue hat. She stood up with a smile so pleasant and with eyes so big, so brown, so gentle, that Clovelly knew at once that he could believe whatever she said. The doubt which Tolan had expressed about her was a brutal comment on Tolan himself, not upon this charming girl.

"You may go, Parker," said Clovelly.

And as Parker disappeared, with a faint struggle on his face that might have been toward a smile, Clovelly heard Tolan saying: "This is Rose, Mr. Clovelly."

Rose held out her gloved hand and Clovelly took it gently. "I didn't understand the lady's last name, Mr. Tolan," he said.

"Lady? Last name?" echoed the brutal Tolan. "Why, I dunno. What's the lady's last name, Rose—Jones?"

A very odd look appeared for a moment in the eyes of the girl. It disappeared at once. "My name is Rose Winston, Mr. Clovelly," she said.

"I'm delighted to meet you, Miss Winston," said Clovelly. "Will you sit down? Is it true that you can take me to Alice Champion?"

"It's on the level that you're David Clovelly?" asked the girl.

"I am he," said Clovelly.

"He don't wear his bank account, if that's what you're looking for," said Tolan.

She stood quite close to Clovelly, and looked up at him with such an obvious gleam of admiration in her eyes that he was moved and a little embarrassed.

"Al has told me a lot about you, Mr. Clovelly," she said. "But I didn't know you were so big! Of course I'm going to take you to her. She's been crying to see you. But she's been afraid."

"We must go at once!" exclaimed Clovelly.

"There's a car outside that'll hold the three of us," answered Tolan.

"Not the three," said Rose Winston. "Al was dead certain about that—that I mustn't bring anyone except Mr. Clovelly.

"That's a pile of bunk," said Tolan.

"Mr. Tolan!" exclaimed Clovelly.

"You know how it is, Mr. Clovelly," said the girl. "Who can a girl trust except the man that—"

"Now listen to me, Rose," said Tolan. "I'll be damned if I'll let—"

"I think we'd better start," said Clovelly. His face was towards the girl but his stern eye dwelt on the detective.

"Suppose that she's a decoy that Shaney and his mob have thrown out?" argued Tolan. "You might be going to Al, and maybe you're going to Shaney's guns."

"Mr. Tolan," said stern young David Clovelly, "my uncle, Henry Clovelly, often used to say that it is folly and a waste of time for a man to make up his mind twice about one subject. On this, I have made up my mind. I shall accompany Miss Winston, and I shall accompany her alone."

As he said this, he cast on Miss Winston a look filled with the greatest amount of brotherly affection and pure emotion that had been seen in New York for some decades.

Mr. Tolan said, with an equally profound emotion: "Ah, what the hell!"

He said this rather under his breath, while Clovelly marched past him, most tenderly ushering Miss Winston into the hallway, where he received, in answer to a very abrupt command, a hat and coat from Parker. As they got to the front door, Miss Winston did three things. She winked at the detective, she turned up her nose at Parker, and she gave Clovelly one of those slow-dawning smiles which always rouse in a man, or should rouse in him, the most upward and onward parts of his soul. Clovelly saw that he was trusted and it made him yearn to leap into flames for her should the occasion arise.

At the curb stood a limousine, sleek and long of hood. A uniformed chauffeur, when he saw Clovelly coming down the steps, instantly had the door of the car open and stood at respectful attention.

"Oh, but we mustn't go in your beautiful car, Mr. Clovelly," murmured Rose Winston. "The Shaney people—if they were to see it—how easily they could follow; and then who knows what would happen! You see, you're in my care. I hope you don't mind?"

"We'll do exactly as you wish," he said.

Tolan came running down the steps. He overtook the pair as they sauntered past the limousine.

"You're not going to make the trip in your own car, Mr. Clovelly?" he asked.

"Suppose that Shaney's ruffians were to spot that car; they could follow it too easily, Mr. Tolan."

"Yeah, but the limousine would be a claim check. If you disappear, we could call for you," said Tolan.

"Disappear?" echoed Clovelly.

"I really think that poor Mr. Tolan doesn't trust me," said Rose Winston.

"Yeah? I really wish that I'd never laid eyes on your mug," declared Tolan. "Look, Mr. Clovelly—"

"In addressing a lady," said Clovelly, more cold than ever, "there is a certain decent respect—"

"Yeah, yeah," agreed Tolan, with a wave of the hand. "But let me follow along and see where you go with Rose What-not, will you? If you should fade out of the picture, I'd like to know the door you went through."

"Well, there's no objection to his following us, is there?" asked Clovelly.

"Oh, none—of course not," said the girl, "except that I gave my word and honor to poor Alice Champion—"

"Of course you did!" exclaimed Clovelly, "and that settles it."

"It settles you, maybe!" muttered Tolan. "I'm telling you this. The more I listen to the chatter of Beautiful, here, the more I think she's crooked in this deal. But I'm not gonna argue. You've got a stone wall picked out and you're sure to ram your head into it. So long. The next time I see you may be in the morgue, but that's your business."

Clovelly was glad to get the girl away from Tolan. He explained, gently: "Mr. Tolan means very well. But he seems just a trifle harsh in his nature, at times."

"Yeah? Oh, he's all right," said Rose Winston. And she gave Clovelly one of those glances which one can see in the movies by the yard and reel— except that Clovelly never went to the moving pictures because Uncle Henry had not approved of them. "Gibbering shadows," Uncle Henry had characterized all movies.

Around the corner from Channing Place there were several taxicabs, but Miss Winston had a rather odd preference for a battered red cab that was driven by a fellow with a whiskey flush and a two-day beard.

The driver pulled open the door and the girl murmured the address to him. When they were settled inside, Rose Winston said: "There's only one thing—tell me, Mr. Clovelly—you do care a little for poor, dear Alice?"

"Ah, yes. I do!" said Clovelly.

She settled back in the seat, at that, and sighed with relief. "Then it's all right," she declared. "Oh, how happy Alice is going to be when she sees you!"

It seemed to Clovelly that the name re-created the great blue eyes of Alice Champion and the golden sheen of her hair, and he was lost in the dream of her for some time, only wakening to discover that the taxi was running rapidly through streets where children with soiled faces played from curb to curb. Vendors sat on stools at the entrances of their little shops, and an odd odor, half sweet and half unclean, drifted painfully to the nostrils of Clovelly.

He lifted his head and shook it.

"Not in a district like this—" he began, when the taxi plunged into the narrows of a side-lane and halted before a dark doorway.

"Here we are!" said the girl, cheerfully.

"It doesn't seem possible that I can find Alice here," said Clovelly. He looked up at the long face of the building, which seemed to lean back into the evening sky. Half the windows were shaded. More than half. The huge place seemed unoccupied.

"She had to come to a place like this to be safe from Jay Shaney!" whispered Rose Winston.

Of course that was it. Clovelly felt shame for his instant of doubt. And they walked past the doorway where lounged a youth with a long, yellow face, an eye as steady as an agate, a flower in his button-hole.

"Hello, Rosie," he said.

"Hello, Mickie," said Rose Winston.

It seemed to Clovelly just a shade unpleasant that she should know this fellow so intimately. He looked to Clovelly like a lizard—one with teeth and poison behind them.

However, they were now winding up a stairway, and Rose Winston clung closely to his arm. "I'm always frightened, going into one of these awful places!" she said.

At the landings, he saw nothing but blank steel doors. He had never before been in an apartment-house of this sort—but then, there were a great many things about New York that he did not know.

Several flights up, Rose Winston stopped, panting, and gave him one of her sweetest smiles.

"Al will simply scream with delight!" she said.

She fitted a key into a door. The lock clicked and the wide door pushed inwards. Clovelly stepped into one of the strangest rooms he had ever seen. It had three small windows, high in the wall; it must have been fully forty feet long, and the table and small group of chairs in a far corner of the chamber seemed lost in the bigness of the surroundings. They were not furnishings; they simply happened to be there.

Rose Winston was closing and locking the door through which they had come. A vague chill poured from the mind of Clovelly through his blood.

"We're almost there!" whispered the girl.

She crossed the room, unlocked another door, and pushed it open, exclaiming: "Al! Oh, Al Champion!"

There was no vocal answer to this appeal, for a moment. But then it seemed to Clovelly that feet were stirring softly in the next room and, suddenly, through the doorway filed three men of grim aspect. Behind them appeared Jay Shaney himself with his weary, swollen eyes and his prematurely bald head.

The door was locked behind Clovelly. The other doorway was filled with armed men. The windows were too small and too high. He had less hope of escape than a mouse that has fallen into a bathtub.

Shaney walked up to him, pausing at a safe distance because he knew what the swift hands of Clovelly could accomplish. Shaney pulled an automatic from his pocket in a leisurely manner.

"A penny for your thoughts, David," said he.

"Well," answered Clovelly, calmly, "I was remembering a saying of my Uncle Henry. 'A man's own folly is his worst enemy.'"

"Yeah, but how did you let her walk you up into a loft building?" asked Shaney. "What made you think that Al Champion would be living in a loft, eh?"

"The poor cluck didn't make any fight at all. Once he was hooked, I reeled him right in," said Rose Winston.

"What's the matter with his brains, Rose?" asked Shaney.

"He's noble. That's all," said Rose. "God, but he's noble! All I had to do was smile a couple of times and keep from yawning. And here he is. If he began to think, I threw Al Champion's name into him and wrecked all his ideas. You mean to say that Al is strong for this hypnotized dummy?"

Clovelly, looking steadily at her, flushed a little. Her own glance rested boldly upon him. She began to laugh.

"Even with the dick on hand to tip me off to him, he couldn't see anything in me but some man's daughter, some man's sister. What a lot of hooey *he's* full of."

"But to walk him up right up into a loft building! I thought you might get him as far as the street door, and that's why I had the gorillas ready down there. Rose, you're wonderful. She's wonderful, ain't she, Clovelly?"

Clovelly looked fixedly into the face of Shaney. The night-club proprietor might be more prosperous than ever but his looks were gone. The most delicate re-shaping of the smashed bridge of his nose had left it broad and bent inwards, more like the nose of a monkey. Where the lip had been split through to the teeth, a ridge of scar-tissue puffed one side of the mouth, and the badly broken cheekbone left a sag in the outline. He looked like a hasty caricature of his old self, a distortion of Jay Shaney—lady's man. The iron fists of Clovelly had, one unforgotten night, worked this damage, and by its apparent effectiveness he could guess the intensity of Shaney's hatred. He could expect from this man the consideration a tiger shows its prey.

He answered the last question by saying to the girl: "Miss Winston, it's true that I've never met anyone like you before."

"Winston?" laughed one of the men. "Where did you pick up that monicker, Rose?"

"Out of the air," said Rose. "One name wasn't good enough for David. All the ladies he ever drank with had two."

"Ladies?" murmured Shaney.

"Well, what's so funny about that, you dip?" snarled Rose.

"Take some air," ordered Shaney.

The girl withdrew. At the door she called back: "Sorry, Clovelly. But a girl has to make a living. You know how it is!"

She was gone.

"Sit down," said Shaney.

Clovelly walked to the table and took a chair beside it. The table was made for supporting heavy weights. It consisted of three thick planks bound at the ends and again in the middle with ponderous iron clamps. Behind his chair came two men. A third faced him from the farther side of the table. Shaney took a chair opposite his prisoner.

"Meet the boys," he said. "This is Stuffy beside me; that's Jig Whalen on your left and Slip on your right. Where's your other name, Slip?"

"In the soup," said Slip.

He was lean as a sword-blade and looked fully as dangerous. Jig Whalen was a dapper little lad not more than eighteen or nineteen, pink-cheeked and always smiling. Stuffy had his name undoubtedly from the flesh that loaded his face and the muscles that puffed his clothes about the shoulders.

"I tried out a set of strong-arm boys on you the first time," explained Shaney. "These guys handle rods. If you make one fast move, you're dead, Clovelly."

Clovelly nodded. He folded his hands on the edge of the table, and they were very cold. Something like the fear of the dark possessed him—the dark made visible. He turned his head and scanned the faces of the men behind him. Like Stuffy, they watched him with a thoughtful calm.

Shaney was lighting a cigarette.

"Rubbing you out is a pleasure that I've been rolling under my tongue for a long time, Clovelly," he said through a cloud of smoke. "You know why?"

Clovelly was silent, watching the strange twisting of the ruined face of Shaney.

"You've made an old man out of me—you've given me a monkey face!" snarled Shaney. He sat rigidly erect for a moment. Then, taking a breath, he went on: "But I wouldn't keep a dying man from one last drink; and I'll give you a last sight of Al Champion. Is that what you want?"

Clovelly hesitated, in thought. At last he said quietly: "I want that more than anything I can think of."

For a moment Shaney glared at him with inexhaustible malice.

Then he said: "I'm going to put you in an open cab. Open, mind you. You'll be between Stuffy and the kid, here. We're going to drive you straight through the thick of a lot of traffic. If you yap, you get a dose of lead where it'll cure the cramps. Understand? But we're not going to tie you. I'll take your word of honor that you won't try to get away."

"I'll give you my word of honor," said Clovelly.

He did not understand. That such a mercy should be suggested by Jay Shaney seemed totally impossible. But the words had been spoken. And, for that matter, how could he say that he understood any man or woman in this world! Raised as he had been, at the eccentric whim of Henry Clovelly, by bloodless tutors and usually in the wilderness, the world and the people in it were as new to him as to a child of five.

"He gives us his word of honor not to make a move to escape or to attract attention," said Shaney to the other three.

Stuffy said: "Yeah, and what does a word of honor mean from a bird on his perch?"

"Maybe it means a lot," answered Shaney. "But if he makes a move, let him have it, all of you."

"Sure, sure," said Stuffy, as though the order had been taken for granted. "You mean that we don't tie this mug?"

"If people get a look at him and see he's tied, wouldn't it raise hell?"

demanded Jay Shaney angrily. "If you've got a brain up there behind the fat, try to use it."

That was why they took Clovelly with his hands free down the same stairs which he had just climbed. It was dusk, now, and Stuffy walked ahead, lighting the way with the flash of an electric torch. One man walked at the side of Clovelly, Shaney and the fourth were at the rear.

"Start something, Big Boy," young Jig Whalen kept on whispering. It was he who walked beside the prisoner. "I've heard a lot about that shifty pair of hands. Try something, Big Boy."

But Clovelly moved with a sober quietness down to the street. Two men who were at the door turned suddenly inward and flashed on a powerful light, which shone up the stairs. The light was turned out at once. "Get the open cab, Slim!" commanded Shaney.

They waited inside until the car was backed up to the curb—an ordinary taxi to all appearances. Clovelly was placed in the rear seat between Shaney and Stuffy. On the drop seats facing them from under the half-top of the car were Jig Whalen and Slip. As they started, Clovelly cast a glance up to the lofty, receding face of the prison which he had just left and to which he would undoubtedly be returned. High on the top, like a pinnacle above a mountain, appeared a large penthouse whose windows were beginning to gleam.

"Summer place of a friend of mine," said Jay Shaney, following the glance. "They warm up a lot of nights in that dump!" And he chuckled a little at the reflection.

The car slipped rapidly across town and up. A half dozen times it paused with the stream of arrested traffic close to the brightness of street lamps with scores of people in sight. But Stuffy, under the flap of his coat, kept an automatic pressed against Clovelly's side. More than that, his own promise stopped the lips of the prisoner.

They entered a side street.

"There!" called Shaney. "Look up there—at the first balcony that runs across the face of that hotel. There—d'you see her?"

Clovelly stared up and saw her at once. There was no other figure on the lighted balcony except the one in the blue velvet wrap. He would have known her, he thought, by the gold of her hair and by the high, proud carriage that set her apart from other women. She saw the men in the cab at the same moment—she seemed to have been searching the traffic patiently—and leaning over the balustrade of the balcony she waved her sudden recognition.

The towering mass of a truck here slid in between and shut off the view. And when Clovelly looked again, she was gone.

Chapter 3

AL CHAMPION

THEY RETURNED AT ONCE, Clovelly half stunned, asking only one question during the journey. "Mr. Shaney, why in the world did you permit me to see her again?"

"I told you," said Shaney. "I'd give a drink to a man who's bleeding to death. That's all there is to it!"

But it seemed hardly likely that this was what set the eye of Shaney on fire and kept his distorted mouth twisting with unspoken words. They reached the huge loft building again and climbed the stairs to the room which was Clovelly's prison. When they reached it, they could hear a telephone ring and a voice speaking in the next room.

Rose "Winston" appeared through the inner door

"She's on the hook. The boys say that they're bringing her over," reported Rose. "When she got her eye all full of Handsome, she couldn't stay away."

"She's coming?" echoed Shaney. "By God, is she coming?"

"What's the matter?" demanded Rose. "Ain't that what you want? Ain't that what the whole gag's for? What's riding you now?"

"He's still cracked about her," commented sleek young Jig Whalen. "It sickens the old boy a little to know that Al is running herself into the fire for the sake of Clovelly."

"Shut your rotten mouth!" commanded Shaney.

"You mean," said Clovelly, slowly, "that Alice Champion is coming here?"

"Sure she is," said Rose. She walked up to Clovelly and eyed him. "But what does a headliner like Al see in a dumb bunny like you?"

"Back up, Rose," directed Shaney. "She'll be here—in five minutes. In less, maybe."

He looked desperately around the big room, dimly lighted by its one electric globe.

"And where's the easy chair and where are the flowers?" mocked Rose. "How'll you make her at home, Jay? She's gonna miss the style she's used to, and will that make her sour on Jay!"

Shaney smacked her face with the flat of his hand. Her head jogged with the force of the blow and her bobbed hair danced. But she gave no ground.

"You dirty little second-hand piker!" said Rose. "I wish Clovelly had bashed your face clean in when he was about it instead of giving you the permanent mumps."

"Throw her out!" commanded Shaney.

"Get out, Rose!" directed Slip. "Move!" ordered Stuffy.

"Try to get me out!" exclaimed Rose. "You pair of marked cards, you'll wish that you'd handled fire if you touch me."

Young Jig Whalen said: "Get!"

He sauntered slowly towards her.

"Don't touch me—you fat rat!" screamed Rose in a sudden panic, and fled from the room. The steel door slammed behind her with a noise like the explosion of a gun.

Jig Whalen lighted a cigarette. "I gotta take her in hand one of these days," he remarked casually.

"Listen at that outside door," commanded Shaney. "She'll be here any minute. When she comes in, keep your eyes on Clovelly. He's nutty about her and he's likely to make a break. Don't let him get his hands on one of you."

Stuffy, from close to the door, reported suddenly: "Somebody's coming up. Three or four on the stairs."

Clovelly held himself straight and stiff. Jay Shaney, putting a hand against the wall, braced himself like a man prepared to receive a great shock. There was a knock at the door. It swung open and Alice Champion appeared on the threshold with two men behind her.

"Thanks, boys," said Shaney. "That's all."

Stuffy closed the door in the faces of the two.

Alice Champion, throwing back the folds of her wrap, appeared in shimmering black satin with the gleam of a diamond pin on one shoulder.

"Hello, Jay," she called with a cheerful wave of her hand. "I heard you had him and I came right over to the morgue. I'm glad you haven't laid him out, yet. Hello, Jig; how's things. Stuffy. Slip, you look ready for Arizona. And here's my beautiful, big David! Davie, is it adenoids that gives you that misty look?"

She walked past Clovelly to Shaney and dropped a hand on his arm. "What's all the noise about, Jay?" she asked.

Clovelly raised his hand. He was instantly covered by the flash of three guns, but without heeding them he wiped his forehead. His wits were spinning.

"What's the line, Al?" asked Shaney. "You explain, will you, and then we'll all be ready to give you an encore. What's the act about?"

"It's called pulling the chestnut out of the fire. Davie is the nut and you're the fire and I'm the tongs, Jay," she answered.

"Yeah—you'll pull him out, will you? By God, Al, you're crazy about him—if you weren't crazy you never would have come here!"

"Crazy? He'd drive anybody crazy," said Al Champion. "Look at the booby now with his mouth hanging open, will you? I tell you he's only five years old and you treat him like a man! Jay, where's your sense of humor?"

"I've still got it," said Shaney, "but it's hard for me to laugh since this little boy of yours smashed my face for me. Al, you think you can bluff me into believing that you're not crazy about Clovelly?"

"You always were a little cock-eyed, Jay. I could like even a stuffed shirt if the stuffing was all dollars. But why wish such a cold dish as that on a poor girl, Jay? Be yourself!"

Shaney stared at her.

"Back up a little, Al," he said. "I almost believe you, when you talk like that. Far as I can see, he ain't your style."

"You have a little sense," said the girl. "I knew that or do you think I would have walked right into the fire for the sake of a lug like Davie?"

"You've got him out of the fire twice before, Al," said Shaney, his worshipful eyes on Alice Champion. "You can't kid me now. No matter how you throw the words, you're all burning up about him."

"Am I?" said Alice Champion. "Now let me tell you something. You see Handsome over there? Ask him if he wanted to marry me?"

"Clovelly!" exclaimed Shaney. "Did you ever ask Al to marry you?"

"I did," said Clovelly, slowly.

"By God!" exclaimed Shaney. "Two hundred and what-not millions!"

"I wouldn't have him," said Al Champion. "I'd rather be married to a dummy and talk sign language. I'd rather live on cold turnips and mutton hash. Have I been near him since the day he proposed?"

"No," admitted Shaney, "because you knew that I was watching."

"Have I even tried to come near him?" she repeated.

Shaney frowned suddenly, in doubt.

"And doesn't he mean millions in the pocket and diamonds in the teeth?" went on the girl. "Listen, Jay. You're being hysterical. When I heard that you were holding Big Boy—when I actually saw him with you—of course I came on the run. Go and rob the cradle and get a baby to bump off. That's all this big cuckoo is—a baby. Squeeze some hard cash out of him and then kick him into the street. He's learned enough to make him keep out of your way, after this."

Clovelly again raised his hand to his face and took a great breath.

"She don't like you, Big Boy," grinned Stuffy. "I always wondered how could Al carry on with your kind of a dummy."

"Al, I half believe you," said Shaney.

"Of course you believe me, Jay," said the girl. "Why didn't you give me a ring long ago, and I would have tipped you off to how I felt about things."

"I want more than money out of him, and I'm going to get it!" said Shaney.

"Oh, get what you please, then," said the girl. "I'm tired of talking about him. Who's got a drink in this crowd? Do what you please, but why not put him through the wringer and make him pay big? Don't turn your back on the easy money, Jay."

"Let's cut out the jabbering," said pink-cheeked Jig Whalen. "I'll rub out this account!"

As he spoke, deliberately, he raised his gun and covered Clovelly.

"No, no!" screamed Alice Champion. She got to Clovelly in a scurry and flash of white and stood before him with her arms thrown out, as though they might be able to ward off bullets.

"There you are, Shaney," said Jig. "She doesn't give a damn about Clovelly. Sure she doesn't! Look at her now! All she'll do is eat lead for him."

The girl, as though the strength had gone out of her in that one great effort, drooped back against Clovelly. And he, still bewildered, fumbling through the strangeness of what he heard, put an arm about her and leaned his head beside hers.

She moaned: "I've spoiled it all! Oh God, David, I've killed you!"

Shaney, white-faced, trembling, made a few paces up and down.

Stuffy was saying: "Well, now, damn it, doesn't that beat anything? She had me kidded. She *is* nuts about the big cluck!"

"Faithful unto death, for better and worse, and all that baloney," remarked Jig Whalen. "The trouble with you eggs is that you don't understand the skirts."

"What tipped you off?" asked Slip, curiously, hungry for information.

"When she came in through the door, over there," said Jig Whalen, "she opened her eyes and swallowed Clovelly before she said a word. Then she was able to talk."

Shaney faced Clovelly at last.

"Thanks, Jig," he said, and waved his hand. "Now, the rest of you get out."

"Wait a minute, Jay," said Stuffy. "You don't want to stay in here alone with them, do you?"

"I'm heeled plenty," answered Shaney. "And I want to talk to them a minute. I've got some things to tell them. Little secrets, boys!"

His face twisted with his smile.

Jig Whalen said: "Keep your back against the door. If you want us, kick the door and we'll be in."

The three of them left the room. Shaney, his back resting against the door, weighed an automatic in one hand.

"Break away from her, Clovelly," he said. "That's better. I've got to tell you what's coming your way; after that, I'll give you a couple of minutes to say good-bye."

Chapter 4

FACE OPERATION

JAY SHANEY, now that he was alone with the two, gathered his faculties together. He said at last: "Clovelly, you've smashed my face and you've put me in hell. But you come second, here. The girl comes first. Al, speak up and give me an idea. What am I going to do to you?"

She looked at Clovelly, instead of at Shaney, and with a desperate eagerness as though she knew that life was closing for her and she wished only to draw more and more of her loved one into her eyes.

"Clovelly showed me the trick," said Shaney, after another moment. "A face operation, Al. He operated on me. But he was quick and I'm going to be slow. I've got some vitriol in the next room. You understand? I'm going to put it on bit by bit. I've heard you sing, Al. Now I'm going to hear you screech and the big boy can stand by and watch what happens to that pretty face. Think it over. It'll take me a few minutes to get things ready for the operation. That'll give you some time for making love. Talk a lot; say a lot. Or spend your time thinking how you'll get away. It's all steel and concrete. You couldn't squeeze a dime through those windows. And the door to the hall is steel and double-locked."

He surveyed them with a long, almost affectionate glance, and then opened the door into the next room. A murmur of voices came out to greet him and died away again as the door was shut.

Alice Champion had slipped into a chair.

"What does he mean, Alice?" asked Clovelly.

"You heard him," said the girl, heavily.

"I heard him talk about vitriol and you—your face. Vitriol—but that's sulphuric acid. It would eat the flesh away."

"He means that. Drop by drop. While he sits by and looks on!"

Her head rolled loosely back as she looked at him. He took her face between his hands and leaned close over her. It seemed to him that death was already dimming her eyes. Her beauty was like that of a garden under rain.

"He's only pretending, in order to frighten you," said Clovelly. "There are no men in the world who would do such a thing. You know that it can't happen!"

"I know Jay Shaney," she said. "He'll rot the flesh from my bones. He'll turn my face into a skull and laugh. I'll scream. And then I'll have no lips to scream words with—I'll only make noises, like a beast. And he'll eat the sight and the sound like food."

The strength went out of Clovelly's knees and dropped him heavily to the floor. Still his head was as high as hers.

"You can't mean it," he said.

"I know what's in him," she answered.

"It's because of me. I've been the reason for it!" said Clovelly.

"I'm glad!" she cried out suddenly. "When I first saw you, David, I was bound straight for hell. It was only a question of picking out the way. I was making up my mind. I was picking my first man. I was going the way they nearly all go. I wanted enough clothes to set me off and so long as I made a flash in the eyes of the people that looked at me, I didn't care. But I've found you and I've tied to the thought of you even when I knew that you were too good for me to keep hoping. But, God, David, I've had happy hours just thinking about you, and how clean you are. I don't care what Shaney does. I don't want anything except to—"

Clovelly rose to his feet. He had hardly heard the last words, and the girl watched him almost in fear as he swung to this side and that, glaring at the walls and the impossibly small windows. What Shaney had said was perfectly true. The weakest point was steel—the door.

He bent over suddenly and ran swiftly forward. Drove his entire weight against the door, using the rubbery shoulder muscle as a pad to keep his bones from being shattered. The impact stopped him, crumbled him on the floor.

The girl ran to him. He was already rising to his feet.

"It's no good," she said. "You can see that we're helpless. Let's not stamp and rage like animals. There's still time for you to listen; and I want to tell you how I love you, David!"

Only with an aching misery he regarded her. It seemed to Clovelly that the God who made her must be watching her now, holding His hand until the last moment before intervening between her and a horrible destruction. He thought of Jay Shaney's contorted face and realized that the very Devil could not be possessed of greater malice.

Desperation grew in him. The foolish, soft hands of a human being— what are they until they are filled with a tool?

The chairs—they were heavy enough to have used against a wooden door—but against the strong steel they would splinter to pulp.

The chairs would not do, and there was nothing in the room that was moveable except the chairs and the table.

He got to the table with a leap and lifted. The top came clear of the heavy trestles which supported it. That top was a ponderous weight—two or three hundred pounds, perhaps. Yes, or more, much more.

But now, with bowed head, with the burden on his shoulders and his hands gripping the edges to make a balance, he moved with short steps until he was in a line with the steel door.

He saw Alice Champion with her hands gripped into fists and a silent prayer in her face. Then he leaned and ran forward. He took short steps. He lengthened them. He charged with bent knees, like a bull, and crashed the end of the table against the door.

The noise was that of an explosion. The recoil knocked him to his hands and knees, the clumsy weight slithering off his shoulders.

And when he stared at the door he saw that all he had accomplished was the knocking of a dent in the center of it.

But Alice Champion cried out: "It's springing, David! The whole thing is springing! Can you try again?"

Could he? He had the massive table like a feather on his shoulders again. He backed up to his distance, aimed that clumsy shaft, and once more charged. He had thought that he had given all his strength before, but it was nothing to the blind desperation which drove him now. The door crashed under the shock—the table-top and big Clovelly lurched with it half into the hallway.

Alice Champion was through the gap as he dropped the door.

He had turned toward the lower flight of steps but her voice murmured: "Up, David! You'll only run into guns down there! We've got to go up!"

Go up to what? To simply higher levels of the same prison? To lurk in corners till they were snared?

But as he turned after the girl, he heard the inner door of the room open and the voice of Stuffy exclaiming: "Hey, why all the racket? Why all the— hell, they're gone! They're gone! Shaney, they're gone!"

Clovelly, with long strides, stole up the steps beside the girl. Even the whisper of her satin dress seemed treacherously loud. And below them, spilling out into the hall, he heard many footfalls.

Above the voices rang the commands of Shaney.

"Go down slowly. Use those lights. Have the guns ready. Turn the switch that lights the steps, Rose. That's better! We've got them between the devil and the deep sea. The boys at the street will blast hell out of them. But go slow. Remember that Clovelly can break a man's neck like a stick of kindling wood."

The voices and the footsteps were hurrying down the steps, and at the same time lights suddenly flushed all the stairs with brilliance.

Clovelly and the girl, side by side, turned and stared at one another. They were not safe, but they had a ghost of a chance for winning, now.

Below them, at the next landing, the voice of Rose sounded.

"If I'd only known what kind of a man—if I'd only known what a man— I would have picked him for myself, the big, soft-headed sap!"

Clovelly failed to understand slang and therefore the greater part of this speech completely missed him; but it set Alice Champion to laughing, softly.

They climbed higher. At each landing they paused, and at each landing, when they leaned over the narrow, steep well of the stairway, they could hear the thin noise of voices below them.

By this time the searchers must have reached the street. They would guess that the fugitives had taken the upward way rather than the shorter cut towards safety.

"Is there an elevator? There must be an elevator!" exclaimed Clovelly.

The girl went on, unhurrying. They had twenty flights of steps still to climb and they were walking fast enough to make the legs numb.

"There's an elevator, but the juice will be turned off at this time of night. They'll never use the big freight elevator."

"Is there another lift for passengers?"

"Not for the lofts."

"But there's a penthouse on top of the building."

"Yes, there must be an elevator for those people."

"They'll get around to use that, then. They'll go around on the street level and go up in that elevator!"

"Maybe we'll be there before them—but that penthouse belongs to a friend of Shaney's."

"I heard him say so," agreed Clovelly.

"We're running into a new trap—but it's all we can do—"

She panted a little as they hurried on. But she was almost tireless. He remembered that she had been a dancer. That was why she did not crumple up from this effort. He himself, made of steel as he was, began to breathe hard. But he took her heavy velvet cloak with its fur collar over his shoulder and put a hand beneath her elbow.

And still the stairs went upwards, turning at the monotonous angles, giving them two or three half-running steps on the level of each hall landing, and then lifting once more. Endlessly. Not twenty, but a hundred times twenty.

And then the stairs ended.

It seemed a kindly miracle when they reached the very top with a trap-door over their heads.

No doubt there was a better way of getting out onto the roof, in some place, but they could not afford to search. Shaney and his men, or a part of them, might already be in the penthouse.

Clovelly lifted, found resistance, thrust up with all his might and snapped the frail latch which had caught. He stood head and shoulders above the roof level, with Alice Champion beside him, and found himself in the very middle of the riot of a gay drinking party.

Over her shoulder, the girl said to Clovelly: "It's Olaf Erickson. He's nine parts devil and one part man. We may be in the fire, now, if he's a friend of Jay Shaney. But keep the old head up and smile, David!"

A chorus of outcries greeted them from all sides; the voices of the women shrilled high and small. Two or three fellows with bulldog faces advanced aggressively. They looked like policemen in plain clothes; but no doubt they were privately hired by Olaf Erickson to keep his peace.

"What about this, Mr. Erickson?" demanded one of these men.

"If they haven't invitations, throw 'em down those stairs!" called Erickson.

Clovelly saw him, now, guided by the voice which had the deep and booming vibrations of a bass drum. It carried far even when the pitch was low.

The roof garden of Olaf Erickson was scattered with small tables but there was one longer than the rest with the host at one end of it in a capacious armchair. He was a monster with a pale, square face and a huge block of a body. His eyes had no perceptible color. They were like eyes carved from stone. And when he lifted his hand in giving his order it looked too big to be human.

"You show us your invitation," said a burly chunk of a man, advancing at Clovelly. "Let's see it or out you go."

"We have no invitations," said Clovelly.

"Whatcha mean bustin' in on a private party like this?" asked the bouncer. "Get out—the pair of you!"

And he thrust himself straight at Clovelly, as though he intended to execute his orders to the letter and hurl the intruders down the stairs.

"Put him under your arm, David!" whispered the girl. "I'll do the rest."

Clovelly caught the man by the wrists and stepped out onto the roof as the fellow pulled frantically back.

"Clout him one!" gasped the bouncer, to his companions. "He's Sandow, and he's smashin' my bones."

"Back up, boys," said Alice Champion. "I've got the invitations but I'm only showing them to Olaf."

And as she spoke, her voice soared away suddenly in the chorus of that rousing favorite, *Tony*. The first high, sweet note of that soprano struck the silence through the party like a stroke on a signal bell.

But the bouncers were not altogether deterred. One of them, slipping towards the rear of Clovelly, muttered: "I'll take him, Jimmy!" and raised a hand that had a short length of rubber hose in it. Clovelly swung Jimmy straight into the path of that descending blow, swung him with such force that the two men slipped together to the gravel. The third bouncer stepped over those sprawling bodies, changed his mind, and reached for a gun.

"Hold off, Terry!" boomed the gong-like voice of Olaf Erickson.

And the gun was not drawn.

Alice Champion, as she sang, was stepping through the measures of a slow dance, making the gray velvet of her cloak flow with the rhythm while she made her way towards Olaf Erickson. Hers was that song about Tony who had gone too far, too far with knives, too far with guns, too far with bootleg booze, so now he was too far away in that sunny Italy.

The fallen bouncers, coming to their feet, would have rushed Clovelly, but a tipsy guest intervened with his arms stretched wide to prevent trouble.

"Don't be so dumb!" he exclaimed. "Don't you see that this is one of Olaf's gags?"

Out of the house came a hurrying trio at this moment—Shaney, with Stuffy and Jig Whalen at his back. The sight of the girl and Clovelly stopped them for only a moment. Then Shaney stepped on and leaned at the shoulder of huge Olaf Erickson, talking rapidly.

Alice Champion's song had been taken up by the orchestra which was half-screened from view behind a green wall of potted plants. She was in the second verse, which described other ways in which Tony had gone too far before he went where he was now.

The face of Olaf Erickson remained the same pale, square blank. No one could tell whether those colorless eyes were understanding the rapid, mut-tered words of Jay Shaney or whether they were filled by the picture of Alice Champion as she danced.

But presently he lifted one of his vast hands and deliberately thrust Sha-ney to a distance.

The chorus of the song had hardly ended when Erickson thrust Shaney away. Then he beckoned with one thick forefinger, and the girl went smiling to him.

All the other guests were smiling, too, or laughing, or shouting for more—all except the two girls who sat on either side of the host. They, with pinched eyes and frozen faces, watched the coming of the singer.

Shaney, a little to the rear, had gathered his two hired men close to him. They were watching not Clovelly—and he found this strange—but the girl, constantly shifting their eyes from her to the vast Buddha-like counte-nance of Olaf Erickson.

Erickson said, loudly—it was impossible for him to speak otherwise—"Shaney wants that man. Shaney'll have him."

Alice Champion answered: "Are you afraid of Jay Shaney?"

"Ha?" boomed Erickson. "Afraid?"

The guests began to gather closer to hear this dialogue. Erickson shouted: "Get away, you mugs. Go drink yourselves drunk. Go on! Waiters—bring out more champagne. Bring more of that Pommery. Everyone who won't drink full glasses, send them home. You two go away, too. You are only a little pretty. You see this girl—aren't you ashamed to show your faces when she's around? Go away!"

The pair who had been sharing his attention rose, one to rush off in a fury and one to slink away with the exaggerated air and foolish step of a show girl on parade.

"Afraid?" said Erickson. "I am not afraid."

"Not of many things. But afraid of Shaney," insisted the girl. "I was a fool to bring my friend here. I thought he would be safe from Jay Shaney here. That was the reason I brought him. Because I thought you were the one man not afraid of Jay. I was wrong, I guess. I'll go away with him."

"Sit down!" said Erickson, pointing to a chair on his right.

Alice Champion slipped into it, cheerfully. Clovelly's collar began to strangle him. His throat was puffing with intense anger. He wanted to put hands on Erickson.

Some of the guests were in full evening dress; some were in flannel jack-ets. But the expanse of Erickson's white shirt was limitless. His white tie above it was almost buried under the deep flesh of his throat. The face, purple and pale, was almost as white as the shirt. All the front of his head was bald. To the rear it was covered with thick white hair. Yet he was not old. He had the weight of a stone and his features suggested a patience like stone, as well. Something told Clovelly that he could be as swift in move-ment as a youth. The more he looked at Erickson, the more he felt that a weight was leaning over him from above.

"Now that you are seated, we can talk," said Erickson. "Come here!"

He beckoned to Clovelly, and Clovelly came like a boy.

"Why are you here with this girl?" asked Erickson. "Who are you? What does she mean to you? What are you to her?"

"You know," murmured Clovelly, "that there are things one cannot say very easily. My uncle used to say that whenever we speak from the heart we should speak with reverence—as if we were in a church."

"This man talks like a book. What does he mean?" asked Erickson. "Come here, Shaney."

Chapter 5

MAN-SIZE

SHANEY STEPPED CLOSER, and his two men moved at his shoulders. The eyes of young Jig Whalen roved ceaselessly toward the women, but every glance returned to the face of Clovelly.

"This man talks like a book," said Erickson. "I don't know what he means. But you mean to have his blood, eh?"

"I do," said Shaney calmly. "I claim the two of them."

"You can't have the girl," answered Erickson.

Shaney's face grew pale, and not with fear. He seemed more of a man than ever before as he encountered the bald stare of the giant.

"Then I get the other—I get the man," he insisted.

"That ought to make a bargain," said Erickson.

It seemed to Clovelly that he was acting a horrible fairy tale that had come to life. Beyond them, blooming with yellow lights against the sky, rose the tall heads of the New York superstructure. The dull glow of the city invaded the sky still higher and dusted the faces of the stars. The voices of the city exhaled in a melancholy roar from the streets. This group of drinking, shouting, singing, laughing joymakers was held up in the flat of a great palm against the heavens for the consideration of unseen eyes, he felt.

"It *does* make a bargain—but you get all the best of it," said Shaney.

"Does this woman belong to you?" said Erickson.

"She promised herself to me." It was strange to hear him talk so frankly.

"A woman makes promises faster than a salesman," said Erickson. "She is here. You can't have her. Unless she wants to go. Now—you"—he turned to Alice—"what is this tall man to you? Do you want to belong to him?"

"Yes," said Alice Champion, looking at Erickson and not at Clovelly.

"Then I have to buy you," answered Erickson. "Here—and here—"

He took from a vest pocket a number of unset jewels—rubies, sapphires, emeralds, and one glaring diamond.

"Here are the things I keep to look at when I'm alone," said Erickson. "You take them. They're worth something. Take them. Put them in your pockets. Then go with Shaney. I'm tired of looking at your face."

He poured the jewels into Clovelly's hand. He held them for a moment, a flashing of small fires, hot and cold. Then David tossed them down on the table. They bounced off and rattled away on the tiled flooring. That sparkling shower caught the eyes of some of the dancers. They came swooping, with shouts. They picked up the gems like birds pecking up seeds.

Erickson laughed like a bellowing bull. "Let them go," he said. "They are a price, even if they're thrown into the sea. But what are you?" he demanded, staring suddenly at Clovelly. "A man? All the rest of these little things dressed up in clothes. Little apes trying to be men. They would curse their fathers and their fatherlands for the sake of a little ready cash. You— what are you?"

"I'll tell you about him, Erickson," said Shaney.

"Be still!" commanded Erickson. "It is a long time since I've shaken hands with a man. Give me your hand, and let me try you!"

He leaned over and gripped Clovelly's right hand.

It was like the presence of a vast electric clamp, a power that bruised flesh and bone and made every nerve numb. Clovelly, taken by surprise, had to rally all his strength to meet the grasp. He had the further disadvantage of a long, lean hand which was swallowed in the fleshy bulk of Erickson's grip.

But those daily exercises had made Clovelly's fingers like steel talons. Gradually they began to work into the powerful muscles of Erickson. The edge of Erickson's palm was a trembling bar, hard as wood, as the giant put on full pressure, but the curving fingertips of Clovelly began to compress the hard rubber of muscle. His whole arm shook with the immense strain. Erickson's face swelled. A color came into it. And out of the infinite depths a light came up into his eyes such as few men ever could have seen in them.

Clovelly's thumb gripped down over the bones at the back of Erickson's hand. They were strong as steel, but even that steel commenced to bend. Clovelly, leaning forward, his face closer and closer to Erickson's eyes, exerted now the last fullness of his power. The tremor of the opposing flesh became more rapid. The arm of the giant shuddered more visibly. His neck swelled with a mighty effort. But very surely the grasp of his hand was being mastered.

"Ha!" said Erickson, suddenly nodding and relaxing.

Clovelly let his own hand fall away. His fingers were white along their length, and purple at the tips with congested blood. The giant's hand was white, also—and crimson. It was banded like a flag. And from beneath the nail of one finger dripped blood. He held up his hand and laughed, watching the blood drop into a clean plate and splatter it with red to the edges.

"Ah ha!" roared Erickson. "Have I met a man, at last? We shall find out!"

And Clovelly heard a faint, moaning breath of relief from the girl. He knew that he had regained one glimmering hope of life.

The gleam still remained in Erickson's eyes. "You saw that, Shaney!" he exclaimed.

"A trick," said Shaney. "He's full of tricks. And there's poison under his hat. Erickson—listen—he belongs to me!"

"Does he?" said Erickson. "Perhaps. Now everybody sit down and get drunk. I have been trying to get drunk for years. Perhaps tonight will be better luck. Wait a little while, Shaney. Perhaps you shall have him, after all. You, Clovelly—look—find a woman and go and talk to her. Go away from me. I shall see you later."

Clovelly looked in dread towards Alice Champion and saw that she was nodding her head slightly, in token that he should be gone. He turned and faced the full sweep of the scene around him. There were still terrible obstacles. There were Shaney and his men; there was Erickson; there was the questionable position of Alice Champion. But gradually his vision cleared and he saw what was before him. The music, which had escaped his notice, began to seep back into his consciousness.

These people, whom Erickson had called apes in the dress of humans, were dancing, chattering at tables, and drinking. The champagne corks kept popping at irregular intervals, sometimes single shots, sometimes in small volleys.

He saw the glowering dark beauty who had rushed in such a fury from Erickson, sitting, chin in hand. With her steady eyes she devoured the picture of the giant and the blond beauty of Alice Champion beside him. If it was necessary for him to talk to one woman, this was she. He bowed at her table.

"Sit down if you want to," she said, without looking at him. "Who's this gigolo?" she added, indicating Jig Whalen who had stepped softly to the side of Clovelly.

"Pretty soon—five in the face—five forty-fives in the middle of the face. You haven't won. You've only put it off for a while. I'm watching you, Clovelly. You're as good as dead right now."

Whalen passed on to another table.

"That was pretty," said the girl. "I wouldn't think that Pink Face carried a rod. Is he one of Shaney's men?"

"I think he's the best of them," answered Clovelly, slowly. "I beg your pardon for sitting down here with you. But I was told to talk to someone."

"You do what you're told, do you?" asked the girl. "You crash the gate of the Erickson dive when your girl wants to try her luck with the rich Swede, eh?"

"Crash the gate?" echoed Clovelly.

"You mean you don't understand what that means?"

"I'm sorry," said he.

For the first time her dark eyes flashed towards him.

"What sort of a line is that?" she asked.

"Line?" said Clovelly.

"Come on!" she exclaimed. "Where were you raised?"

He sighed.

"It would take too long to explain," he answered.

She stared at him, before she answered: "Is it straight—the buzz that's going around—that Shaney is after you?"

"Yes. It is."

"For what?"

"For my life."

She made a small grunting sound as though she had been struck.

"You take it easy," she said.

"Can I reach the police from this place?" he asked.

"Can you reach out of hell and grab some of the blue out of heaven?" she answered.

"There's no hope?"

"Nobody leaves this place except by the elevator; and the key to that is in Erickson's pocket."

"But if people must leave—for business—for an engagement—"

"Nobody with business comes to Erickson," she answered. "Nobody that comes to him has any other engagement. Know who these boys and girls are?"

"I don't think I've ever seen them before," he answered.

She laughed. "That tall blond bird is a jewel smuggler. The girl he's dancing with used to do secret service until she found out too many secrets. The little mug that looks like a Chinaman is a Russian prince. His girl is a high-class pick-pocket. The young man with the clean bald head, at that table next to us, has a nickel mine in Canada and a murder trial's waiting for *him*. His girl is just one of those gals."

"One of what gals?" asked Clovelly.

"Come, come!" said the girl. "Be your age!"

"I'm sorry," said Clovelly again. "And what is Erickson?"

"Olaf? He's anything. He's everything. He's been a monk in Tibet. He's been a blackbirder in the South Seas. What he is now, nobody knows. No one ever knows what he is until he stops being it."

She stopped short.

"And what are you? If Shaney's after you—what are you doing here?"

"I'm trying to think of a way to get that girl away from Erickson. Can you tell me how to do that?"

"Sure," said she. "Put on a bullet-proof vest, knock all the men on the head, throw your friend Shaney off the roof, and after you've choked Olaf, take his key, open the door of the elevator, and just run the car down to the street. Isn't that easy?"

He looked fixedly at her, said: "I'd do anything!"

"Do you mean it?" asked the girl, frowning.

"Yes, I mean it," he answered.

"Would that singing blonde go with you?"

"Yes."

"Anywhere?"

"Yes."

"Well, I'll be damned," said the girl, softly. And she began to think.

"Olaf is getting himself drunk, perhaps," she murmured, aside from the main trend of her thoughts.

Erickson, rising from his place at the table, commenced to sing a tuneless song in his vast drum-beat of a voice. The sound flooded the air. The musicians vainly attempted to create an accompaniment. The dancing stopped. In his hand, Erickson held a huge beer glass filled with champagne. As he ended the song, he poured the contents of the glass down his throat. The champagne disappeared as though down a great funnel, in one endless flow.

"Murder—" said the girl beside Clovelly. "Death for you—and still you're thinking of taking the blonde out with you? Well, there might be a way—if you were three men instead of two."

"Tell me!" he pleaded.

"If you got the blonde away from Erickson, d'you think you could keep her away?"

"Yes."

"Do you know the inside of the house, there?"

He stared at the little imitation of a French chateau.

"I don't know it," he admitted.

"Straight through the hall off the entrance, and then down the corridor to the left, takes you right to the elevator door. And the key to that door is in the Swede's left vest pocket. Now you know what to do. I'll help. I'll get into the house. I have a way of getting at the lights. First they come on blinding bright. Then they flash out, and they'll stay out for a few minutes. It's a wild chance. Take it or leave it!"

"I'll do it—if it can be done," Clovelly answered without a moment's hesitation.

The girl drifted easily across the roof garden. He saw her pass inside the open front door of the house. Then Clovelly rose and sauntered to the edge of the roof, behind the table where sat big Olaf Erickson. He could hear Erickson booming out another of his tuneless songs.

"Your time's up, Clovelly!" David recognized Shaney's voice on his left.

He turned, suddenly, and saw Shaney and Stuffy before him. A footfall sounded behind him and Clovelly knew that that was Jig Whalen—more to be feared than ten of the others.

"Erickson's through with you," said Shaney. "There's going to be a little accident, damn you. And the way Erickson picks his guests, there won't be a single voice raised afterwards. Now, Jig—"

Then the lights, which shone softly on the roof garden suddenly increased a thousandfold, it seemed to Clovelly. He closed his eyes against the glare.

"What's wrong with the lights?" exclaimed Jig Whalen behind him.

"Damn the lights! Do your stuff!" commanded Shaney.

And as he spoke, a thick darkness dropped on them.

Even Clovelly, prepared as he was to shield his eyes from the glare of the lights, could hardly see his way before him for an instant. Then he leaped for the place where huge Erickson was rising from his chair, shouting, laughing.

In the Swede there was some spirit of fair play, no matter how vague it might be; and Clovelly called as he leaped near: "Erickson! Erickson!"

"Hai!" said Erickson. "The man with the hands!" and he whirled about, sending his big armchair crashing.

Clovelly did not strike for the point of the jaw because he knew that he might as well hammer at the jawbone of a whale. Instead he hammered his fist home under the ear.

Even that mighty shock was not enough to fell Erickson. He merely swayed back, his arms swinging loosely at his sides, a curse bubbling thickly out of his throat. In an instant, Clovelly's fingers were in Olaf's left-hand vest-pocket as he said: "Make for the front door of the house, Alice!"

She was out of her chair and running, in a dim white flash, as the tips of Clovelly's fingers found the cold metal of the key and snatched it out.

Clovelly dashed in pursuit.

Somewhere a familiar voice was shouting. That was Shaney, calling out to make for the house. Then the sweep of an electric torch found the white figure of the girl, steadied on it.

A gun spoke at the same time and Alice Champion swerved from view behind a screening palm. Was she hit by the bullet?

Clovelly, sprinting hard, overtook her at the front steps of the house. The whole terrace was confusion, but all other sounds were reduced to nothing as compared with the tremendous gong-like cry of Erickson as he roused himself into action.

It seemed to Clovelly that he could distinguish the grinding stride of Erickson from all the other noises.

A spot of light from an electric torch caught him in focus. An automatic started showering lead. Somewhere inside the hallway it found a glass target and shattered it with a great downpouring.

"Back—the corridor to the left!" he called to guide Alice Champion.

He tugged at the right-hand panel of the door. It was latched, but a second effort tore the latching-iron loose from its moorings and allowed him to slam that half of the door.

He could see the roof garden rather clearly, now—the dim figures of the women in the distance—the men flooding into the foreground towards the entrance to the house.

He gripped the edge of the other panel of the door and hurled it shut.

Bullets ploughed through the wood. A long splinter stung his face and brought a warm trickle of blood.

He found the heavy bolt and thrust it home. He fumbled for a key, but the keyslot was empty. The bolt would have to serve him as best it might to secure his retreat.

Now he was fleeing to the rear of the hall. He struck a chair, pitched headlong over it, staggered to his feet once more—and then saw a thin star of light in the rear corridor with the frightened face of Alice Champion behind it.

Clovelly ran at her, past her, to the glimmering metal door at the end of the hall. The key fitted it. He turned the lock at the same time that he heard a tremendous pounding begin at the front door. And through that door he could hear, distinctly, the thundering voice of Erickson. His blood turned to water. He could even now feel the hands of the giant ripping him as a child rips thin cloth.

The elevator door was open, but the trembling glow which came from the cigarette lighter of Alice Champion failed to show the elevator itself behind the glass doors. He had to press the recall button; a soft rumbling at the bottom of the shaft told Clovelly that the car was rising in answer.

But how slowly!

Some efficient tool was in the hands of the giant outside the front door, now. The blows that he dealt ended with splintering crashes which told of wood that was being smashed to pulp. They would be inside, within a moment.

They were inside now. The babel which rattled outside the house boomed suddenly, hollowly through the length of the entrance hall; and along the rear wall of it, played a sudden wild dance of many pocket torches.

Beside him David saw the trembling hands of Alice Champion, still cupped around the frame of her lighter. It showed her face turned up to his and let him see the wide blue of her eyes.

Then a shadow rose behind the glass doors. There was a light clicking sound and the hum of the elevator machinery ceased.

He had the doors torn open in a flash. They stepped onto the slightly swaying car. He jerked the doors shut as the torrent of people poured into the corridor and their lights flashed across the glass of the doors.

He had found the button for the street level. He pressed it. But only slowly, slowly came the response. Softly, as though there was a pride in slowness, the elevator began to drop. Looking up, he could see the first of the running feet reach the place. Then the view of them was erased by the level of the next floor.

Alice Champion's body slipped against him. She spilled an inert weight into his arms.

But they were dropping every moment. On the stairs above them footfalls commenced to beat rapidly; but these, also, diminished by degrees. He could be grateful for every inch of the height of the building, now. It would leave the pursuit that much behind him before the elevator touched the street level.

And now the car stopped as though on an air-cushion, without a jar. He pushed the door back, and, cradling the girl in his arms he made the side-walk.

From the building behind him issued not a sound of all the riot he had left behind him. The long dark street opened to either side.

"Lady a little sick, sir?" asked a man in a uniform cap. "Car sir? Right this way!"

It was a big limousine, furnished with an almost guilty softness of luxury inside. Into it he carried the girl. She was already stirring, making a mournful, small sound as the motor started and the big car trundled quietly away up the street, past the entrance to the loft building.

"Which way, sir?" called the driver.

"The park," said Clovelly.

He lay back against the cushion. The street lights traveled past him with a dignified slowness on either hand. They left the narrow alley for the width of one of the great avenues. They were turning north over empty pavements.

And then he was aware of the soft, smooth rushing of the Fifth Avenue traffic, like the flowing of a great and easy body of water.

Only after that he saw that the girl was sitting up straight, staring ahead with never a word.

They entered the park. The trees blew cloud-like past them. Tires whispered everywhere over the pavements. And now she sank her head against his shoulder, still utterly silent.

He knew that, for her, the dread of the future had not ended; they merely had passed another milestone on a journey, the final destination of which was unknown.

A Burial Is Arranged

JOHN LAWRENCE

Chapter 1

"WORSE THAN MURDER!"

I T WAS A nightmare job, and it was jammed down my throat. I sensed something queer—for all the good it did me—in my lawyer's hurried voice over the phone giving no more than a name and a meeting-place. From there, I felt as though I'd stepped into quicksand.

My watch said midnight when I paid off my driver in Little Italy, shivered on the curb till the cab had rounded the corner above. It was an ugly, black street. Icy wind whistled down the long, warped blocks of two- and three-story frame houses—unlit, squalid—the slums of the quarter, whipped my coat around me. I seemed to be alone in the thick, unbroken darkness, as I crossed over. In the light from my cupped flash, I re-examined my slip of paper.

There was no difficulty in locating my objective; the crumbling, square, two-story wooden structure that housed the barber shop. Dirty, sordid, odoriferous, it was distinguished by narrow, black crevices between it and its neighbors. Its upper story was as black as the lower, on front and side. Not till I groped into the backyard, did I see a bar of light through fire-escape rungs overhead. A blind flapped in a slitted-open window above me.

A dwarfed Italian answered the back door, said not a word as he ushered me up broad stairs to the rear of a hall above that contained a pay phone. He opened a thick wooden door opposite the phone, gestured me in, closed it behind me.

I got my first look at my ghost-like client.

He was Italian, plump, dark-eyed, with a thatch of stiff, gray-black hair, gray-black sideburns. He was dressed in perfectly fitting morning clothes, his black Ascot tie was held down by a black pearl. Derby and Chesterfield lay on the deal table. He whirled back from the flapping blind as I came in, and his olive face was ashen, haggard.

I looked into haunted, wild eyes, glanced down hastily at my slip. "Mr. Maresca?" I asked.

He almost snatched at it, choked, blurted huskily: "Please—please destroy that!"

I gave him no argument, burnt it without comment in an ashtray. The flame was brighter than the sickly bulb that lit the hot room. He sat tense at the table, kneading his plump hands, jerked fevered eyes to mine. "You—you haven't anything else—with you—that would connect us? No matter what—whatever happens—no living soul must know it's me you're—Mr. Blue—it could mean my life if anyone even suspected I'd retained you. You—you'll protect me?"

"Sure."

"I'm not crazy, Mr. Blue. I'm facing ruin—more than ruin—if anything goes wrong. I'll pay you a thousand dollars to see me through. It should be only an hour—two hours. It's inconceivable that anything should go wrong. Yet, if it does, to the last gasp, my name must be kept out of it."

"What do you want me to do?"

"I—simply meet a friend of mine downtown and take a package from him. Bring it to me."

My uneasy feeling began. "That's a lot of pay."

"It's worth it—to me!" He half rose. His voice shook huskily. "Mr. Blue, that package is my life's blood. It's got to reach me. If anyone else got it or anything unforeseen happened—and my name is linked to it—it could mean my complete ruin."

I groped. "Don't be afraid to tell me everything. This sounds like a blackmail proposition."

He swallowed. "Yes. It is."

"Then I'll have to know exactly what I'm expected to receive from your friend."

"A—a camera case; there'll be an oiled-silk envelope in it with papers."

"What papers?"

Sweat stood on his face. "Just—papers. For the love of heaven—don't cross-question me! Judge Frost led me to believe—"

"Judge Frost is my friend. He's been my lawyer for eight years—since my agency started. His sending me to you means I'll go all out for you. But the judge isn't a private cop; neither are you. I am, and I'm telling you the only sane system is to trust me with the works. Blind jobs inevitably go sour—"

"No, no, please—if I tried to tell you—you'd drop the whole—"

"I won't drop it. I *can't* drop it. Blackmail is delicate. I want to be able to block a double-cross, if any—"

"No one will double-cross me! I'm certain of it!"

"Mr. Maresca, the blackmailer doesn't live who wouldn't—"

"No not this one. You don't know the circumstances—"

"I'm begging for them. If you told the judge, you can tell me."

"I didn't tell him!" he cried hastily. "Nobody knows but my daughter and the one who has it. My God, I couldn't tell the judge! I couldn't tell anyone. Don't you understand?"

"I understand you've stepped out of line—else why blackmail? I'm ready for that. Because the judge sent you, there's no limit. You can take it as gospel that I'll go to bat for you—even up to murder. I mean that."

"Murder—yes!" His face was dingy, strained. "There—there can be worse than that."

"Not legally speaking."

He squeezed interlaced fingers. His eyes on my belt burned with the struggle inside him. "It's—an affidavit."

"Saying what?"

His eyes were like a trapped animal's. "My God—don't you see—I *can't* tell you! You wouldn't help me if you—"

"Forget that! I'll help you, in any way that's humanly possible, if you give me the whole story—everything. Because of the connection, I've got to help you."

His voice was almost a whisper. "You—you swear you'll help me—no matter what I've done?"

"If you do what I say."

"All right." He swallowed, repeated in a husky, desperate voice, "All right, I'll tell you."

He told me. A second later, I wished to God I'd asked him not to. Horrors are no novelty to me, but in nine words he sent goose-flesh starting out on my whole body.

He said: "I think—I may have—buried a man alive."

I tried to be incredulous. The effort petered out before the stark agony in his eyes. Then a dark spot cleared in my skull.

"You—then you must be John Maresca—the big parlors on Broadway— I didn't know—"

"No. That was my father." His voice was dry, breathless, his eyes pleading fearfully. "I've carried it on, since he died, ten years ago; though God knows I don't want—never wanted to be—an undertaker. Blue—I swear by the Cross—if I have done this terrible thing, it was innocently done. You'll believe that? Believe that it must have been some frightful mistake."

"God, yes. But how? Some doctor must have pronounced him dead. Why are you responsible? Even if—"

"He was embalmed. Rather, he was supposed to be embalmed. He died of catalepsy. His wife paid for the funeral—an expensive one. He was to be embalmed. The embalming would have killed him, whether he had passed on or not. On my books, it shows that I did it myself. But I can't remember. It's seven years ago."

He ran a shaking hand through his hair. "Four months after we buried him in Redlawn, his brother wanted to remove him to their home town— Montclair. They had found a will, or something. They got an order in the regular fashion. An undertaker from Montclair removed him, and reburied him in the Montclair cemetery. An undertaker named John Machen."

He put a hand inside his coat, licked his lips. His eyes were white-rimmed on mine. "I'm putting myself at your mercy. The judge said—"

"I won't let you down. That's right."

He took out a folded document. "Machen—this is a copy of what I'm buying tonight."

I took it from him, read the affidavit—

I, John Machen, being of sound mind, (etc.,) do hereby solemnly depose and swear that on an order issued by the court of (etc.), I did proceed to Redlawn Cemetery, and exhume the body of Arthur Peters, interred in grave (etc.) and did then transport same in my hearse to Montclair, N.J., for the purpose of re-interment in Montclair Cemetery. I further swear that, being moved by curiosity and studious intent, I did take the casket containing the aforesaid remains into my establishment at Montclair, en route, and there did remove the cover of the casket. I solemnly declare that my motive in so doing was to view, study, and seek instruction from the body contained, it being my impression that the embalming of same had been effected by a man well-known to be expert in our mutual trade, viz., Mr. Mario Maresca, of New York City.

I hereby swear that I found within, the body of a young man, in an advanced stage of decomposition, who had evidently been interred while wearing a gold watchchain, weighted at one end with a small gold penknife. The body was lying in a face downward position. The gold penknife lay near the hand of the deceased, on which the nails were broken. The blade of the knife was also broken, its missing part being imbedded in the rosewood wall of the coffin. Deep gashes in the wood, surrounded the head of the deceased.

I returned the casket to its original condition, and re-interred it, as ordered. I then proceeded to the offices of my attorney, and on his advice, am inditing this affidavit.

There was sweat on my forehead as I handed it back. "Where—where is he now—the body, I mean?"

"Still in Montclair cemetery."

He burst out: "He's dead now, Blue! Dead—and mostly dust. Nothing can help him now. I'm not inhuman. I've sweated cold sweat, night after night, these three years, thinking of the mad hell he must have experienced. It's over—done with. I can't make amends now. I can't conceive how I could do such a thing. Yet, I've always hated this work, and I may have. Am I wanting too much—to want to keep the poor devil in his grave? I've a family, Blue—a daughter. She—she wants to marry—she's engaged. If this terrible thing comes out—I have other interests now—real estate. They've ceased to think of me as an undertaker. I'm not ashamed of it. But—her fiancé's family—if they knew this! I swear—it's because of her, I want—I'm paying half of everything I own for this thing tonight. Blue—it will—it will save us!" He gulped. "You said—no matter what—you'd—"

"I know. I meant it. I'll handle it."

I fought to get the thing clear. "How long ago did it happen?"

"Seven years ago, I buried him. Three years ago, Brothers first showed me this cop—"

"Brothers?"

He swallowed. "Richard Brothers. He says he was Machen's lawyer."

"Where is Machen?"

"Dead. He died just a week before I got Brothers' first letter."

"Brothers demanded money in a lett—"

"No, no! It was typewritten anyway—just hints. When he came to see me, I wouldn't see him. Didn't even understand what he was driving at till he scribbled a note and sent it in by my secretary. Not one of his letters even had a written signature!"

"Letters! How many?"

"I must have half a dozen in my safe downtown—but they're useless— even the note in pencil—unless you see the affidavit. He showed me that and I paid. Then, three weeks ago, I heard something." He hesitated, held my eyes fearfully. "Then—somebody wrote the district attorney and told him the whole story."

I felt my stomach cool. "The D.A.'s investigating?"

"No—I don't think so. I was just warned that the letter had come in. Naturally, I became frantic. I begged Brothers, once and for all, to sell me the affidavit. I offered him one hundred and fifty thousand dollars. It happened that he wanted to get out of the country. He agreed. My trusted friend is taking the money—meeting his messenger in the Little Church Off Times Square at one-thirty tonight. Judge Frost recommended you—said I could count on you. At the last minute, I decided I couldn't risk—that I'd get you to take the silk envelope from my friend at the church door and—"

"You don't trust your friend?"

"My God, yes! But he's delicate—crippled. If someone should attempt to rob him, he—"

"You mean Brothers? After he's got your money, you think—"

"No, no—I think I know him. He won't—"

"Then who, for God's sake? The D.A.? Tell me what I'm up against. You think the D.A. might—"

"I'm not insane! The D.A. wouldn't know about the affidavit! I think he's dropped the whole thing. I heard he tried to find Peters' family and couldn't. It isn't that I'm afraid of *him!* Once I have my hands on this silk envelope and destroy it, nothing, nobody can ever open that grave legally. Certainly no judge would allow an exhumation on an anonymous letter—"

"I've got that. But who is this someone that might attempt to rob me?"

"Sainted Mother—that anonymous letter! The writer of that letter! Only my daughter knows—and Brothers—unless he's told someone. None of us would write to the authorities. Someone else must have found out. Might even know about my buying the affidavit—know that he could get a fortune from me for it! Or want to have it, for some other reason—" He added hastily, too hastily: "I don't know what."

I bored into his eyes. "Don't hold out. The anonymous letter means nothing. It was almost certainly sent by Brothers, himself, to do just what it did—force a lump sum out of you. Unless something else focused the D.A.'s attention on you, nothing could come of it—except a scare, and he knew it. The whole ugly mess adds up to this little silk envelope. I understand that. No one you've mentioned so far shows any likelihood of hijacking me. What's in your mind? Who haven't you mentioned?"

He wrung his hands, stared down at the table. "Nobody—nobody really. I—my daughter—she thinks—she suspects—" He broke off, met my eyes desperately. "I can't explain it. I've always thought that when a person loved another person, they—"

Then it happened!

Without the slightest warning, snarling flame and thunder belched from the half-opened window. I *heard* the lead smack into Maresca's back; his broken cry as he arched, his knees buckling. For a split second my breath was caught in my throat. The gun bit again and I dived headlong, digging frantically for my armpit.

Chapter 2

KILLER'S SANCTUARY

M Y SHOULDER HIT Maresca at the waist, flung him in a heap across the room. Blood sprang alive on his cheekbone as I did. The gun at the window racked twice more furiously, the second time in concert with the roar of my own gun. Glass exploded. I fired again, dived behind the table and shot again. No answering shot came. I half rose, ducked again— to draw fire. None came. Maresca was a huddled, sobbing heap in the corner. I flung myself out, dived for a wall, ricocheted to the window, tore out the blind.

The fire escape platform outside was empty. Jagged glass was in the windowframe. I flung the sash up. Furious, biting-cold wind roared in my ears. I ran halfway down, crouched, strained my ears. I could hear nothing. The gale drowned every sound. I hung there a split second, tortured in indecision, then drove myself back into the room above. I shot to Maresca's side, dropped on one knee.

He was on his face, crumpled. I saw the blood-soaked hole under his left shoulder blade. But he was still breathing, moaning.

The slug that had furrowed his cheek had knocked him unconscious. I ran out into the hall.

The dwarfed Italian and his twin brother were two white death masks as I burst out. They turned to run. I roared viciously at them and they froze, their hands shooting high. I dug desperately for a nickel, shot words at the doctor I phoned, then drove the Italians into the room with me.

They were frightened men. I could feel blood heavy in my face as I told them grimly: "If anyone knows about this it'll ruin Mr. Maresca! A gunman tried to kill him—and me—from that fire escape. I don't think the shots could have been heard above that wind. If the cops come—and you so much as open your mouths—I'll frame you for accomplices. If there's anyone else in the house, stop their mouths, too. Furthermore, I'll kill the lot of you! Understand?"

Pasty-faced, they nodded wildly like automatons. I held them there, silent, while I waited—every nerve strained for sounds that would say someone had called the police. Nothing happened. I glanced at my watch and set my teeth.

It was twenty minutes to one. Before the doctor arrived, it was ten minutes to one. I tried to make Maresca as comfortable as I could, I snarled at the Italians. They didn't know where Maresca lived. A card in his wallet told me.

When the doc finally arrived, he took one look and said: "Hospital, Cass. It's serious."

"He can't. He's got to be taken home. I'll explain later. Hire nurses—anything—but no ambulances! No one must know a thing about this till later, Mac. Play with me. You'll open hell up if you don't. On the level, give me a couple of hours—"

"Where does he live?"

I told him. He looked worried, finally said: "All right." And did a swift job of bandaging. Between us, we carried him to the cab. We shot northward.

A block from his house, I said: "I can't be seen near the place. I'll help you carry him up the steps, but I'll have to go before you open the door."

I did that. It was ten minutes after one when I was back in the cab, racing downtown.

I was a long way from the Little Church Off Times Square. My brain was numb. Every nerve gathered on the desperate hope that I could get my hands on the affidavit.

My eyes were glued on my watch, while the seconds flashed away. At half past one, the unknown messenger would expect me. When we hit Columbus Circle, it was thirty-two minutes after. When I shot out of the cab at the corner of Broadway, it was exactly twenty to two.

The church was three-quarters of a block west—almost to Eighth. Whistling wind lashed my face as I ran.

I didn't overlook the occasional, wide-spaced parked cars along the curb as I raced by. It was so black I couldn't be sure they were empty. I marked them down. I saw no light from the church. The whole street was black.

Then I was in front of the church, between two parked cars. Wind obscured every sound. I wavered there, tense, hoping against hope that I was in time, desperately scouring my brain for procedure.

Nothing happened. I ached there for five minutes, then I stepped grimly onto the curb. I jerked a gun from my shoulder holster, shot swift glances up and down the street as I put it half in my coat pocket. Two paces put me on the broad stone steps of the rakish, modern church. I swept my hat under my arm before I groped open the high-arched door and stepped silently into the dim-lit vestry.

Swinging, studded-leather doors at my left held small oval windows. I peered through into the church proper. It seemed deserted. I stepped through—and my heart sank.

I saw no one. The quiet peace of churches was on the place. Everything had the orderly, waiting look—utterly quiet. Rows of empty pews marched away from me, up to the altar in front. I came through all the way, let the door swing shut behind me, stepped aside into the aisle to avoid the rebound.

Then I saw it.

From the foot of a pew, halfway up, a tiny stream of blood was running. Already a sizable pool had collected, was shining, following the edge of the maroon carpet-strip that lined the aisle.

I ran to the pew. A thin, blond man lay on his side, on the floor between the pews. His near foot wore a built-up shoe—he was club-footed. He lay in a pool of blood, eyes staring, glazed, his throat slashed horribly—a grinning extra mouth. I reached for his flesh desperately. It was already cooling.

I jerked eyes to his pockets. Here was Maresca's messenger! My stomach cooled as I saw his pocket-linings turned out. I swung futile eyes around in a search for the camera case—or the oilskin envelope.

Somewhere, deep beyond the choir benches, a door slammed.

My gun was out in my hand, as I jerked erect. One split second, I registered again the stripped pockets—then I was plunging up the aisle, my eyes probing—

I saw the curtained door behind the choir benches, swung myself in, dived through it. I was racing down a long gray-painted passage. Something black loomed on the floor, halfway along its length, between the open doors of dressing rooms.

I stumbled as I tried to check myself, snatched it up. A camera case! Sweat came out on me as I read *Mario Maresca,* in neat gold letters, inside the cover.

There was a twisted rosette of ribbon on the floor under it. I snatched it up, with the camera, jammed it in my pocket, ran on, stuffing the camera case under my coat. I realized the passage ran through to the street above, sprinted grimly—

I flung my weight at the gray door that loomed ahead of me, burst out stumbling onto the windy street, the door banging behind me.

To my left, thirty yards away, was Eighth Avenue. I had one flashing glance of the man spurting north, around the lunchroom on the corner— and my gun flamed.

The lead whined, ricocheted. I tried to clap my hat back on my head as I flung around parked cars to get into the street after him, struggling with the camera.

A door in the side of the red building that housed the corner lunchroom burst open. A uniformed copper ran out, one hand tugging his gun from his hip, the other cramming food into his mouth. He dived directly in my path.

Panic shot through me. If I were caught and searched—questioned now—

I ducked my head instinctively, to shade my face, clutched gun and camera to my stomach, doubled over, coughing, reeling round in circles, groaning.

The cop reached me on the run, trying to shout questions through the food in his mouth. He grabbed my shoulder, waved with his gun, his big Irish eyes popping. I recognized him as McMartin, a three-striper, but there was no help for what I did. I swung my gun up under his jaw, hard.

Doughnut crumbs showered me. He made a choking sound as he went down. I grabbed for his head to keep it from cracking the cement. He eased down—out cold. In the side door of the restaurant, I saw the white-aproned proprietor throw up his hands and wheel, run out of sight, as I dashed on for the corner.

I swung round the corner—and the street was empty. I drove pavement under me, skidded to a stop at the corner above, swung hot eyes down the side street.

He was gone. I swung back, raked all directions. Suddenly my gun jerked up—but I checked myself.

From the corner just south of the lunchroom, a cheap brown coupe was lifting in a long, towering arc, out from the curb. In one steady swing, it whirled across the street, plunged west on the side street and was gone.

For a second, I stood there, disorganized. There was no possibility that the brown car could have contained my man. Yet who—

The distant wail of a police siren jerked me out of it, sent me flying down the side street, as chill realization of the danger I was in cooled my spine. If McMartin had chanced to recognize me, as he went down—

If they caught me now, with the butchered, robbed man back in the church—Maresca, even if he *could* come to the front for me, dared not— with the terrible evidence against him once more gone into—where?

I reached a cigar store, swung into a phone booth. For a full minute I sat there, breathing heavily, thoughts racing in my head. One was paramount. I must not land in jail!

Sweat ran down my back. The very streets were danger zones. My only hope was to find the affidavit and the man who had it. After that, Maresca could speak for me—if there were need for speaking. I told myself, grimly, that if I laid hands on the rat who had done this, the mystery would be cleaned up—by his own words. Because my hands were tied with my vow of silence, even the flimsiest evidence would be enough to hold me.

Then I got a brain wave. My hands were unsteady as I swung back, jammed a nickel in the phone, called Judge Frost's number. He must have caught something in my voice as I asked: "Richard Brothers—a lawyer. Do you know anything about him?"

He said: "What's the trouble? Yes, I do—in a way. The bar association started to investigate him for practicing without any authority. He vanished in the middle of it. We understood he was from San Francisco. Why? What—"

I told him. Just in time, I remembered that I was restricted as to what I could tell him. There was enough to put tensity into his voice. "Ye Gods! If you only had some sort of an alibi—any kind—I'd say you were here. Only that would be of no use."

I woke up. I said: "I'll look after that," and depressed the hook. I called another number. After what seemed a lifetime, a voice answered. I said: "I need an alibi, Al."

Chapter 3

LIQUID ALIBI

THE TAXI DROPPED ME before the garage on Fifty-second. I threw a look at the gray door just east of it, propped open. The heavily carpeted steps leading up to the second-floor speakeasy showed in the light from the landing. I strode straight into the garage.

Al Lascoine stepped from behind a car as I reached the rear, worry in his big brown eyes as they looked up at me. "I hope—"

I showed him the camera case. "I've got to get rid of this."

He tucked in his chin, tightened his lips and led me to a rubbish bin by the dumbwaiter shaft. I threw it in, poked it down among the greasy rubbish with a crowbar. When I finished, he said: "Let's have your hat and coat."

I gave them to him. He opened the dumbwaiter shaft. I climbed in, crouched on the top.

"Wait in the kitchen," he told me, "till I get there." He closed the door, and I pulled myself up.

I got off in the kitchen. The placid Chinese cook took one uninterested look at me, returned to his sizzling pans.

When Al came in, he lipped: "I'll douse the lights for a second. Ease through the swing doors to the end of the bar. There'll be an Old-Fashioned waiting for you."

I peeked through the door after he went out. The lights were blotted out.

When they came up again, I was leaning quietly against the bar, draining my Old-Fashioned. The place was full, the bar crowded. Ben, the bartender, was scribbling on a paid below the bar. He caught my eye as he straightened up, laid the tab on the register.

"That's all Ben," I said. "How much do I owe you?"

He brought over the tab, added it. "Four dollars, sixty-five, Mr. Blue—"

"What!" I howled and looked up at the clock. So did others.

"Listen," I said belligerently. "I've been here just one hour. I'm supposed to have drunk all that?"

Al came hurrying over, his soothing, "What's the trouble, pal?" getting plenty of attention from people around.

I beefed loudly. He scowled at the tab, then at Ben, shook his head, handed back the tab.

"You must've got somebody else's round mixed up, Ben. I seen Mr. Blue come in—sharp at one. He couldn't've drunk all that."

I paid two dollars and a half. Al accompanied me to the checkroom, hoping aloud that I understood how it was—a busy night—easy to get confused.

When we stood on the landing outside, I said: "How much, Al?"

He was shocked. "Cass! You know I wouldn't take a cent. Friendship means more to me than all the money in the world." His thin dark face clouded. "Only thing—that damn Chink—and Ben—and, damn it—the checkroom girl. I should have thought of that. They're damn bloodsuckers. I'm going to fire them tomorrow. But tell you what, I'll split a grand between them and they can take it and like it."

"You'll get it tomorrow," I told him. "You won't let it spring any leaks?"

His dark eyes glowed. "I've fixed you up before, ain't I?"

I piled into a cab in front—and faced the desperate question of where to go. It was three minutes before I told the driver Maresca's address and said: "A block or two from there."

I covered the last two blocks on foot, till I stood, wracked once more with indecision, in the deep shadows across from the homey, unpretentious house where Maresca lived with his daughter. It had a high porch, a long flight of steps. Light glowed through the door panel.

There was a black roadster parked before the door, empty, its lights on. I could see no one on the deserted sidewalks. I sweated, unable to make myself march up to the door. Yet I knew I had to. There was no one to see me. Then I thought of the back door.

I was stepping silently onto the curb in front of the house, before I really focused on the license plates of the black roadster. Something seemed to curl up inside me.

They were the serial numbers issued only to members of the district attorney's staff!

For a second I held my breath—as the harrowing implications of this sent water through my veins. Possible reasons threshed in my head—every one of them disastrous. I felt rooted to the pavement.

Sharp clicks sounded, coming down the sidestreet hurriedly—the heels of a woman, walking.

I slipped into the shadows, beside the steps, mechanically. I was making a feverish effort to remember those plates. I wasn't certain, but the grim idea persisted that the license number was that actually assigned to the D.A., himself—Angelo Picarro. If anything could make the mess worse, this topped the heap. A savage, uninspired man, he had been carried into office by the reform wave, and was taking it literally. At this time, his office had become sort of an extra police department, making wholesale arrests in a kind of frenzy. He appeared to see himself as a second Jerome or Seabury! He *had* jugged some politicians, but his blunders were fast out-running his triumphs, and he was becoming the most hated man in New York. A chill ran down my back as I imagined what *he* could do with a spot like this.

The heel-clicks rounded the corner, and I shrank back deeper in the shadows. To even attempt to enter the house was now out of the question, yet where was there to go? If—

The heel-clicks came abreast of the steps. I jumped, as they turned in, started up. I swung around the newel post, whispered sharply: "Miss Maresca!"

She gasped, whirled on me—a hatless, dim figure in a fur coat, a wrapped bottle in her hand. "Who—who is it?"

"Cass Blue."

I heard her sharp intake of breath as she ran back down quickly.

I hushed: "How is your father? Is he conscious?"

"No—no—he's still in a coma. You—you got it? You met—"

I told her as painlessly as I could, what had happened. I couldn't make that kind of news very painless. She cried out: "Oh, my God—"

"You've got to help me, Miss Maresca!" I urged her. "My only chance of getting it back and clearing us all is to do something fast. You're the only one that can help me. Why is the D.A. here?"

"What?"

"The D.A. That's his car. Did he arrive while you were—"

"Oh, no! No! That's Chick's. It's all right! Chick—my fiancé."

"Chick who?"

"Chick Picarro. Please come inside. It's all right."

"All right? My God—the D.A.'s son!"

She lashed distractedly: "I tell you it's all right. It's—it's Chick who brought us the warnings that might have saved us, Mr. Blue. I don't mean directly—he can't go against his father like that—but hints. We want so to get married. He'll do anything he can to help!"

A sudden thought popped out of my memory. I grabbed her arm. "Wait.

Just before your father was shot, he started to mention some obscure suspicion you had about someone in love with—"

"Oh, not—not Chick." She had hold of herself; only the desperation in her gasping voice showed her panic. "It was Mr. Giannini—the manager of dad's real-estate office. But dad sent him out of town—to Albany—yesterday, just so he wouldn't be here. He was in love with me before I met Chick, Mr. Blue. Please come inside. I've got to give this to the nurse. I promise you it's all right. I've got something to tell you."

She gave me no opportunity to argue, ran up the steps. I followed, protesting in a futile whisper. As we entered the musty hall, a nurse appeared in the stair landing, came down to take the bottle, and simultaneously a door opened at the left. A well-set-up, clean-limbed Italian youth in a well-tailored Chesterfield stood in the doorway, a soft hat in his gloved hand. His long-lashed, liquid black eyes were anxious, shifted from me to her. "Nina, I've got to get back to the office—really."

"Where can I call you if I need—I may want—"

"Either the office or dad's—or my place."

They kissed shamelessly. The girl made no effort to introduce me. As soon as the door closed, she turned on me, and the desperation came back in her face. "It's Mr. Brothers—he did it—I knew he was going to do it!" she burst out. "Dad wouldn't listen to me. He thought—"

"I know what he thought, Miss Maresca. Why do you—"

"Oh, he's evil, Mr. Blue. Nothing's too low for that—that—"

"You know where he lives?"

"No. He was at the Shilelah Hall. He hangs around there a lot."

"The political club?"

She nodded. "He's some sort of honorary official there. He made Dad take us all there last night. He always does when they have a ball or anything."

It was at that minute that my fingers in my pocket touched the rosette of colored ribbon I had picked up in the church. I took it out hastily. It was intertwined ribbons of orange, black and green, in the form of a miniature cap made to fit over some small object. "Does this mean anything to you?"

"Of course. They sold them at the Hall. They're the club colors."

"Who wore them?"

"There were five hundred people there. They all wore them. Where did you get—"

I groaned inwardly.

"It doesn't matter. Listen. If young Picarro goes to his father and tells him he saw me here, you know what will happen, don't you?"

"He won't! He won't! Can't you understand, Mr. Blue? He loves me. When we first wanted to get married—a year ago—he knew there must be something wrong when Dad said no. I couldn't tell him what it was—anymore than *he* can betray *his* father, now. I—maybe I hinted, but it was the anonymous letter that really told him the truth. He doesn't care. He thinks Dad must be innocent, and he'll do anything—anything to get the horrible shadow off us, so we can be—" She suddenly checked herself, her eyes desperate on mine. "If we told Chick everything now, he'd make his father help us, Mr. Blue. I didn't want to, without asking you, but I threatened Mr. Brothers that I would—"

"What? When?"

"Tonight—when they brought Dad in. I—wasn't going to tell you. I was frantic. I called him at the Hall; he was there. I told him Dad had every letter he'd written him, and that note, in his office safe, and if anything went wrong, I was going to give them to Chick and tell him everything."

"Wait! This is important. Exactly what did he say?"

"Nothing! He swore at me—terribly—and banged down the receiver."

"You told him your dad was still alive?"

"Yes."

"Where is your father's real-estate office?"

Her eyes darkened with fright. She stammered it out, put a hand to red lips. "What—what? Why do you look like that? If—"

I touched her arm. "I'm sorry. I've got to go, now. Don't worry."

"Where—"

"Excuse me," I threw over my shoulder, as I half ran out. "I can't tell you. A possibility just hit me. I'll call you later."

I was on the street in time to see young Picarro's roadster vanish a couple of blocks away. I ran down the steps, my eyes searching for a cab.

In that moment, from the black rim of shadow that the street lamp on the corner cast in front of the houses across the street, a man suddenly fell sprawling on hands and knees, as though he had overbalanced from something. He was up in a flash, threw a quick look at me, walked as fast as he could to the corner, and vanished round it.

If I'd had anything real in my mind, I might have ignored it, but I was down to the bone—grasping at straws so dubious that I didn't dare examine them too closely. The best I had was a vague guess that, for some reason, Brothers might strike for the notes in Maresca's safe.

I was not only alive to, but praying for, another lead—anything. It took me just a split second to slip after the man I had just seen. I darted down the block, till I came opposite the corner around which he had vanished, swung questioning eyes down the side street. I gasped.

I was just in time to see a car spurt away from the curb. It was the same cheap brown coupé that I had seen leave the vicinity of the church!

I roared, "Hey!" and launched into a futile run after it. I had a gun out, racing after the car, actually taking a bead on the rear window, before the disastrous consequence of a volley of shots, at this point, struck ice into my spine. I slid to a heart-burning stop. A corner swallowed the car.

Yet, even in the sudden storm of emotion, my brain had automatically noted the license number. Also, I could see a brilliantly lighted avenue ahead of me. One badgered second he hesitated, then hurried on. I jotted the license number on an envelope. When I came out onto the street of stores, I dived into a druggist's, phoned my office girl at her home, ignored her fretful protest at the hour, set her to work to trace the license.

For a second after I hung up, I stood irresolute. I swore it down savagely, pounded out and caught a cab, rapped directions for reaching Maresca's Cedar Street office, and told the driver: "I've got to get there in nothing flat or it's no use going. Don't drive up to the place—or in sight of it."

He shot away from the curb eagerly. I sat on the edge of my seat, trying to convince myself that I was not on a fool's errand.

It was a fifteen-minute drive before we were in the financial section. As we shot past Maiden Lane, I told him to slow down.

Chapter 4

CORPSE CUSHION

THE DISTRICT WAS COLD, gloomy, deserted. The tall buildings near Broadway vaguely visible in the raging dark, the occasional light seeming to hang far up in midair, isolated.

I told the driver: "It's about three blocks down and two over. Angle a block below, around the corner."

He started turning across corners. It was when we swung around the second turn that I saw the brown coupé for the third time, parked, empty, almost within reach of my hand as we sailed by.

I choked, "Stop!" at the driver, and he braked hastily. Half incredulous, I hopped out, ran back, one hand tight on a gun butt.

I found nothing but the cheap, brown coupé, empty of anything that a hasty search would reveal as significant. I swung quick eyes around. It struck me that the spot he had chosen to park was, in one direction, almost the same distance from Maresca's Cedar Street address as my own projected spot was in the other. It sent the blood through my veins. I took one more hasty glance around, ran back to my cab and said, "Go where I told you. I'll ride here," and clung to the running board, till he covered the block, turned round the corner south, and stopped.

I handed him money as I jumped down.

"Back up so you can just watch that coupé," I told him. "If anyone gets in it and drives away, follow him, and as soon as you get a chance, phone this number." I scribbled my office girl's number on one of my cards. "You'll have to explain what you're talking about, but then she'll understand. It'll be worth your while—plenty."

He had an interested gleam in his eyes. "O.K. What if no one don't come?"

"Stay here. I'll be back." I made a hasty calculation once more, as I started off at a silent run. I figured my spot would be around the next corner, midway the block, and it was.

I eased around the corner, hugging the building fronts, spent a full minute raking the shadows of the block, before I slipped down the narrow avenue. I was on the wrong side of the street, but I had no difficulty in gauging which was the address I sought.

It was a stunted, old-fashioned building. This part of the section had been missed by the march of skyscrapers. It sat, plain, unadorned brick, closed. There was not even a light behind its old-fashioned lobby doors.

The wind swept down the street, but from nowhere else could I catch the faintest breath of motion. The girl had told me the office was on the second floor. I stared steadily at it, seeking for a tell-tale flash of light or other indication that someone might be within. I got none.

I ran narrowed eyes down the block, tracked swiftly on past the building opposite, bent over, my eyes seeking for a building with an open lobby.

I found one five buildings away from the one that housed Maresca's office—a ten- or twelve-story semi-skyscraper.

I could see, in the skyscraper's lobby as I crossed over, a uniformed watchman tilted back in his chair by the elevators, reading a newspaper, half dozing. I cudgeled my brain, but I could not think of any merciful way to handle him. I had to move quickly. I fished out an old envelope from my pocket—a long one, approached the door, rattled it.

I saw him start, get to his feet, plod toward the door, frowning, a heavy key ring in his hand. There were two sets of doors between us. He opened the inside one, peered sharply through the glass before attacking the second.

I waved my letter in a carefree manner, and he inserted his key, opened the door just enough to get his body in the opening. I held the letter out so he had to turn his head to the right. I slid a blackjack off my hip as I said, "Can you get this to this guy first thing in the morning—" and tapped him.

I caught him in my arms as he would have slumped forward, held him a second while I shot another quick glance up and down the street, saw bare, empty cement. I carried him in and put him back in his chair, tilted back as though he were asleep, the paper across his legs.

This part of town was familiar. I knew that, unless the building extended through to the next street, there would be a court behind, adjoining other courts. All I asked was that none of the buildings between here and Maresca's would block the line of courts.

I got my wish.

Four minutes later I stood in the rear court of Maresca's building.

Just under the fire escape, I paused, listening tensely, but still the wind drowned any other sound. It sounded above the slight scraping noise as I jumped to grab the lowest stationary part of the fire escape, chinned myself, wriggled up till I was on my stomach, got to my feet.

By the time I reached the second floor, I could see perfectly by the brilliant street lights out front. I made my first circuit of the story on hands and knees, barely peeping into each window. After one round, I realized with mixed feelings that I could see into every room in the suite from one or another of the windows. The street lights, slapping against buildings adjoining and higher, were reflected down on this one with surprising strength. I spent a good minute at each of the windows, straining my eyes within. The conviction grew that no one was in the office.

I peered into what was evidently the waiting-room. A few feet from the window at which I stood, a wooden railing ran the length of the room. I figured the door must be in the same wall as my window. A small switchboard, on a stenographer's desk, sat just beyond the gate of the railing. Ranged against the far wall, opposite me, were three overstuffed leather chairs, a table. Directly inside the railing, its square back to me, was a large couch of the same material. Maresca believed in comfortable waiting rooms.

Anxious as I was, I spent another full minute staring into the room. Then I went to work on the window. I had a piece of glass tapped out, my arm through and the catch undone in a matter of seconds. I shot it up and was inside, my gun fanning the room.

Nothing happened.

I went through the railing gate, every nerve tense; began a silent, swift prowl through the various offices. Naturally, I used no light. The reflected glow from outside was not light enough to reveal detail, but it certainly would not conceal the figure of a man.

I found nobody in the office. The safe stood silent, in the outer office. I did not touch it, but I almost put my face against it looking for any sign of violence. It was undisturbed. Then the hope jabbed me that I had beaten the man in the brown coupé to it. Or had I? I had one chilling minute when it occurred to me that he might not have been headed here at all—that I might have muffed him entirely. I refused to believe that—yet.

My brain spun with wild guesses. The only one that stood up was that he was having more difficulty in gaining an entrance than I had had. He might even be below this minute. Certainly, if he were trying to pick the ancient lock of the front door in the full glare of the street lights, it would be an arduous job—if not impossible. And if he had had a key he would have been here before this.

I gave up trying to speculate on how he might enter the building. That was no concern of mine. If he entered the office—

I hefted my gun, my jaw hard. I sent quick glances around for a place to stow myself. The couch looked best. It was sunk in a patch of deepest shadow, its high ends would effectually screen me from the opening door.

Also, it commanded a full view of the safe—or, at least, of the black outline of the safe. I slipped quickly over to the huge deep-seated leather piece, groped for the high end of it, turned and eased myself down into the corner further from the door.

I sat on a man's face.

I'd sat down so hard that, for one wild, grisly minute, I couldn't get up. I clawed madly, threshed. Even with my rear I knew it was not a live man. I half fell, half threw myself onto the floor, one hand diving frantically for my pencil flash.

As it sprang on, I whirled it onto the lumpy automobile robe covering the seat of the couch. I jerked the robe away in a sort of frenzy, cold sweat drenching me.

He was a chunky, well-dressed Italian with a bald spot. There was terror in his shiny eyes, his contorted dough-like face. His tan overcoat was soaked with blood from his heart down. I could even see the rent in the fabric where the knife had entered. He was still faintly warm, but *rigor mortis* was setting in. I clamped my teeth, sent flying fingers over those pockets I could reach without soaking myself in his blood.

His pockets were full of trash. I flung one trifling item after another on the floor, without the slightest clue to his identity. I held the flash in my teeth, redoubled my speed. In my mind's eye was the picture of that brown coupé—the killer making his getaway. I found handkerchiefs, cigarettes, matches, money, keyring, a ring puzzle, a cheap watch, toothpicks, obscure memorandums in shorthand. Not till I slid a hand under him, felt for his hips did I get anything important—a brass key, attached to a multipointed brass star, and a small, crumpled pink slip.

On the brass star was stamped—*Hotel Royale—204.*

On the slip was an address—and the cryptic note, *B-Rear.* Hastily, I copied it on my cuff.

I gave up trying to find out who he was and jumped through the gate, dived for the hall door before my brain functioned. Outer doors of buildings like these needed keys, even from the inside. I reversed myself, spun back to the window.

As I went down the fire escape, I breathed a second prayer that the watchman I had sapped would not have come out of it yet. I made a swift guess, tried to estimate how long a time had elapsed, realized with a shock that it could not have been more than ten minutes. I scrambled over fences, caution thrown to the winds, till I was again in the cement court of the watchman's building. I dived down the areaway steps.

When I darted silently up inside the building, peered around, relief blew out my breath. The watchman still slumbered peacefully. I ran down the hill, snatched his keyring from his belt, fitted one after another into the lock of the inner door, then the outer. I made shift to hold both open, while I tossed his keys back along the tiled floor of the lobby, almost to his feet. I stepped back while the doors swung closed. I turned to run for the corner around which my cab waited—and almost tripped as I checked myself.

From the corner of my eye I saw an indentation in the building fronts, just behind me, five yards from the door I had just left. One spring carried me into it—just as a police radio-car's red headlamps whirled round the corner three blocks west.

I pressed myself flat against the back of the crevice, sweat running down my back, as the headlamps flashed across the mouth of my hole, almost afraid to breathe. I clung there, hoping desperately that they would go by without seeing me. The car screeched to a stop—*directly before me!*

For one second, I thought I was lost. I saw the earnest, worried faces of the two coppers as they piled out of the car, trotted straight toward me. It seemed incredible that they could not see me. Sweat broke out on me anew. I groped crazily for some story to give them—and then they were at the doors of the building I'd just left, pounding on the glass.

Nothing happened. I heard one of them say: "Look—the fathead's gone to sleep."

The pounding redoubled.

The same cop said: "Well! He's come to!" A second or two later I heard the door burst open and the old watchman's piping voice. "I was slugged! I was slugged! Some feller got me to open—"

"Save the fairy tale!" the cop snarled. "Go on and ring in. God's sake—job's are tough enough to get these days without going to—"

"No—no—I swear—he may be still in the building! This is no kid—honest to God! Please—look at my head!"

There was a second of silence, then: "What'd he look like?"

"I—I didn't get a decent look at him. Medium-sized guy—snap-brim hat."

"All right. We'll take a look." There was skepticism in the cop's weary voice. "And if you—" the closing door cut him off. I breathed again. I slid one eye around to make sure they'd both gone in, slipped out. Through the lobby doors I saw two blue backs sandwiching the watchman going down the hall and in that second I was past the door—just as the radio in the police car gave three peeps. I was slipping along the building fronts toward the corner, but they had left the loudspeaker on loud. Clear and concise it reached my ears—the last straw.

"Add to Message Four-six-five-eight, re Cass Blue, wanted for murder. He was reported seen in—"

I didn't hear the rest. I was racing across the corner, toward my still-waiting cab. I was almost to it before it struck me that its very presence meant the brown coupé must still be parked!

I lit on the running board wrenching at the door.

"What happened? Did anybody go to the coupé?"

"Not a soul."

"You didn't see anybody, but that police car—since I left?"

"Some guy beat it across there—the opposite direction you went. Maybe three, four minutes after you went in. I just seen him as he crossed the st—"

"What kind of guy?"

"Gosh, boss, I didn't—see, I was watchin' the coupé. I didn't hardly notice the guy, till he was half across the street there. Matter of fact, I thought it was you—till I heard his car start up."

"Car? He drove off?"

"Yeah. I'm pretty sure it was him. The wind went down for a minute, just about the right time for him to be—" he eyed me anxiously.

I swung wild eyes at the brown coupé. Debate raged in my head. I dared not stay in this vicinity. Yet if I missed the man in the brown coupé—

And then suddenly the explanation hit me. The murdered man in Maresca's office must be the man of the brown coupé.

I was getting fuzzy in the head from the frantic nightmare. My hand closed on the star-shaped key tag in my pocket. I snapped at the driver: "You know a Hotel Royale?"

He grabbed his red book, thumbed it hastily. "There's one here—down in the Italian quarter. It ain't very hot—"

"Get there—fast!" I said grimly. "Turn around here! Don't go down to that street ahead!"

He hastily started the car. I sat taut on the seat while we threaded back uptown.

We turned into the dingy Latin quarter once more. My watch showed ten minutes past three. We had to slow to a maddening pace as the driver fumbled his way.

By the time we drew up finally in front of the villainous-looking little hotel, within two blocks of the waterfront, I was crouched with my hand on the door. "Go back around that corner—and wait."

Through the revolving glass door of the six-story narrow building, I could see a tiny lobby, one elevator, and the shirt-sleeved attendant talking at the switchboard. I pushed in—and had my question answered before I asked it.

As the thuggish-looking desk clerk—if that's what he was—slid shiny eyes at me, he said into the mouthpiece: "No. Mr. Giannini ain't been here for two days. He's outa town—expected back tomorrow. No . . . yes."

I came to a bewildered halt, as something inside me jerked. I jumped over toward the clerk. "Here—hold them on the line—" but even as I did, his fingers had already jerked the plug. His face hardened.

"Say—who the hell do you think you—"

I reached over and grabbed his tie, pulled a gun with my other hand. I jerked him up against the counter. "Who was that asking for Giannini? Talk fast—and never mind the lip!"

He swallowed. "Some dame. I dunno who."

"She didn't leave a name?"

"No. No. She—"

I patted his armpits, hips, clipped through thin lips: "All right. Get over there and call this number." I gave him my office girl's phone. He backed over, swallowing, eyes on my gun, made the call. I picked up a phone on the desk, held my eyes steady on him, while I spoke.

My office girl told me: "The license plates were issued to an Italian—name of Giannini, seems to be manager of a real-estate concern, the Maresca—"

I clipped, "Thanks," grimly and hung up. To the clerk I said: "You got a long wait coming before you see Giannini again. I'll take a look in his room."

A rasping voice behind me grated, "No, you won't! Freeze!" and I went rigid, halfway around.

Chapter 5

FIRE WITHOUT FLAME

TWO MEN STOOD in the open door of one of the rooms opening off the lobby, covering me with guns. One was a thin, razor-faced Italian in cap and dark shirt; the other a huge albino. There was tense wildness in their thuggish faces. The gaunt wop's breath whistled through his nose. I saw astounded light leap into his eyes. "Lovely! Drop that rod!"

I dropped it. He seemed to be trying to catch his breath.

The albino started forward to pick up my gun, and the other shrilled: "Get back! It's the killer! Go out—tell Brothers—we don't get Giannini, but we got Cass Blue!"

The stupid-looking albino gasped, "Oh! Oh," turned and scuttled out the door.

"Get your hands high!"

I raised my hands. From the corner of my eye, I could see the starch-faced desk clerk with his hands flat on the desk.

The albino dashed back in, whispered hastily to the dark thug. The other's close-set eyes twitched. "All right." To the desk clerk he said: "Come out around that desk. One funny move'll finish you!"

The clerk came out, swallowing. "Listen guys—you don't need to worry about me. I seen guys get it under my nose! I never squawked—ask anybody—I never saw you guys—never saw this guy—"

The dark man bit: "Get out there." The albino swung behind the clerk, heaved him whimpering toward the door. To me, the dark man snapped: "Turn around."

He snaked my gun from the floor, grunted. "Sweating, huh? You'll be sweating plenty more, you chiseling rat. There's a black car, half a block down. Walk straight down into it, or I'll put one where it hurts."

His hands darted over me, patting. He got my extra gun and my black-jack, swore steadily under his breath as he prodded me out the door.

Ahead of us, I saw the clerk and the albino reach a huge black limousine; saw the cringing clerk heaved aboard.

The man at the wheel had his face turned toward me as we came up. In the dark I got no more than a general impression of a large head. His voice was dry, harsh, as he snapped: "Put him in the bottom—and watch him."

I was prodded in, the gun in my neck forcing me to lie in the bottom of the car. I tried: "I don't know what this is all about, big shot, but you're making a monkey—"

There was venom in his voice. "Shut up! You'll get a chance to talk—plenty—in a little while."

He sent the car shooting away from the curb. I opened my mouth again, and the albino's foot kicked my jaw. "Shut up!"

We rode. I got enough glance of passing things to identify Avenue A. I could feel the powerful car eating away miles.

Fifteen minutes without a break and we began to slow down. I felt the car veer, the brakes take hold as we swung to take a corner. The nervous, dark thug cried sharply: "Not this way—for God's sake, boss—the precinct station's on this street!"

The other grunted: "So what? You think the dick's going to squawk—with a murder and a cop-slugging alarm out for him?"

We went down the side street. Vaguely, I saw the green illumination flash across the car windows as we passed the precinct station lights. We went a block and a half further, turned north again, went a block and stopped. There was a second of silence. The albino breathed: "What the hell?"

"That building—the one set out by itself," the driver said grimly. "Take them in there—the top floor. It's a place where they work on those moving pitchers—homemade ones. And it's soundproof."

They tumbled me out. We were almost at the waterfront. Directly in front of us were half a dozen shadowy warehouse buildings; then, out in the middle of a space, as the big-headed man had said, a modern, four-story brick building.

The driver strode on ahead quickly. The clerk started whimpering in the darkness. I heard the savage *smack* of a blow, and the albino's thick, "Shut your damn face!" then the driver's rapid undertone.

They were invisible in the gloom ahead. The dark man's gun was steady in my back—too steady. I could hear his tense breathing.

We came up to the building door as the key was scratching in the lock. The driver told the albino: "Take that guy and lock him—" I didn't hear where.

To the thug behind me, the instructions were, "To the top." We went up three flights of stairs, onto a tiny landing at the top. The whole floor was evidently part of the office space. The leader unlocked the office door, went in. My captor's free hand closed on my collar as we waited.

A shaded, powerful lamp went on. It was clamped on a long gray table inside. The room resembled a laboratory. I saw a dozen similar gray tables, waist-high, ranged down the room, lamps clamped to each. The thick-headed man was looking round the room at the numerous windows. They were all heavily blanketed. He reached a switch in the wall, pressed it and brilliant overhead lights blinked on. I got my first real look at Richard Brothers—and it wasn't pleasant.

He was short, fat; his face the color of boiled lobster. Either a goiter or incredible fatness had produced a roll of red whiskery flesh that began under one ear and ended under the other, passing under his chin like an exaggerated double one. His eyes were black rectangles sunk in his face, his nose a blob. When he put his hard hat on the table, his scanty, sandy hair looked indecent, boyish.

As the door closed behind us, the dark man shoved me over sideways a few feet. I stood with my back to the front wall of the square room. On three sides, the walls were lined with counters containing sinks. Out of the corner of my eye, I could see in the wall behind me, the half-open door of a tiny, tiled lavatory. The ceiling was dotted every few inches with a tiny spigot—a sprinkler system, evidently a specially concentrated one. Considering this was a movie company, I presumed film was locked in the wooden cabinets overhanging the wall counters.

Brothers snapped at the dark man: "Frisk him—clean."

The dark man emptied my pockets. He piled everything on the nearest gray-painted table, and Brothers turned on the clamped lamp over the pile. I saw my two guns, my jack, my twisters, what few papers I had on me, all join the heap. Brothers stood beside it. I saw him take each of my guns, smell the muzzle closely, slip out the clip and examine that.

When I stood, clean, the dark man backed to the table beside Brothers, stood with a gun on me, his eyes sliding sideways over Brothers's shoulder at the few old letters I had had, which Brothers was reading carefully. There was nothing in them I worried about, but as I saw the dark man's attention drawn irresistibly, I started easing forward, an inch at a time.

I had covered nearly two feet of the five between us. A sudden flare of hope leaped in my stomach. I dared not shuffle anymore. Brothers had no gun in his hand. One leap at the dark man and—I swayed forward—

The door behind me came open and the albino came in. I was caught off balance, going forward, unable to check, as the three pairs of eyes jerked to me. The dark man gave a yelp, jumped aside, his gun flashing up. The red-faced man stumped back around the corner of the table, his hand going to a hip. The albino dived on me from behind, one huge fist swinging, to crash against my cheek, sent me whirling, stumbling. He dived after me, grabbed my coat-front, drove another pile-driver into my cheek-bone, and let me go. I saw a million stars as I went flying backwards, turning to crash into the wall, my hands up just in time to protect my face. I swayed there, half-stunned, shaking my head.

Brothers snarled: "You got lots coming, you mug! Ask for it and you'll get a little extra."

I stood as I was, while my head cleared.

I got my eyes to focus again—straight on an involved little metal and glass appliance on the wall two inches from my face. It took me a second to recognize it—but then I did! It was a thermostat!

It was like a shower of ice-cold water. I pushed myself erect slowly, turned and faced them. The dark man blurted shrilly: "Stay back! I'll give it to you right, next time!"

I picked my hat slowly from the floor. From numbness, my brain had sprung into activity so violent that it was bringing sweat out on my forehead. I put my hat on my head, regarded them all without expression. "All right," I said bitterly. "I suppose I can have a smoke—or are you too yellow to hand me my pills?"

The dark man snatched my package of butts from the pile, threw them at my feet with a wooden match. I picked them up, straightened slowly, grunted contemptuously, at the three of them. "What am I? A vaudeville performer? What the hell do you want—now you've got me here?" I lit a cigarette, puffed it to a long coal.

The two thugs looked at Brothers as he finished reading my last letter, put it down with the air of getting down to brass tacks. "That all he had on him?"

"Yeah."

He looked at me ominously. "Listen, gumshoe. If I turned you in to the cops, you know what'd happen to you, don't you?"

"I can see you turning me in," I said.

"Maybe you're right." His eyes narrowed. "Then think of it this way. Suppose I pull out that blow-torch on the counter there, and put it to work on you? Think your memory's pretty good?"

"Cut the chin-rattle," I said, "and give me the story. I know I'm in a spot, if that's what you're trying to say. What do you want?"

"I want the affidavit you copped off Mario Maresca's friend, when you shivved him, and I want the letters you got out of Maresca's office—including the note in pencil."

I folded my arms. I folded them in such a way that my right hand held the glowing cigarette behind my left shoulder blade. With my right little finger, I explored till I located the bulb of the thermometer attached to the thermostat. The glowing end of my butt went against the bulb. "What is this, a gag?" I asked him.

His eyes veiled. "I'm trying to give you a break, Blue. If you think I won't put you through the business—you're crazy. You don't know what you've stepped into. Where you got your tip-off I can't imagine, but you're out of your class and you better give, see?"

"Why the hell wouldn't I give—if I knew what you're talking about?"

"You trying to tell me you didn't stick a shiv into a guy in the Little Church Off Times Square? And bust into Maresca's real-estate office and take the notes out of his safe?"

"I'll admit I was at both places but I was too late—twice in a row. I got a tip-off from a finger. Where he got it, God only knows. If I could snatch the camera case that bird in the church had, and the stuff in Maresca's safe, I could sell them—to you or Maresca. I needed dough so I went for it. Only I flubbed it."

"You were tailed from Maresca's office building downtown to that hotel where Giannini lived. What's your answer on that?"

"I couldn't get the safe open in the office. The finger had the wrong combination. I knew the manager lived at that flea-bag, and I thought of squeezing it out of him." Then I added: "Use your head, Brothers. If I'd clipped anything from that office, and you've been on my tail ever since, I'd have it on me, wouldn't I?"

His eyes scoured my face. "You talk too smooth. What's the finger's name supposed to give you all this dope?"

I looked him in the eye. "I don't remember fingers' names."

"You do now!"

"Not even now."

His jaw hardened. He jabbed a long finger at an acetylene blow-torch on one of the counters. "Get that baby, Curt—and plug it in."

The albino blinked, swung to obey. I pulled my cigarette from behind me, gave it another long drag, returned it to the bulb of the thermostat. Three things were pulsing in my head. First—that the precinct station was less than two blocks distant. Second—that a thermostat in an office building could mean only one thing. It must be connected to the sprinkler system. Third—that if it were, there would undoubtedly be an alarm of fire put in when the sprinkler started to work.

Brothers snapped: "You know this means your finish?"

I shrugged. "I don't think even *you* guys are dumb enough to finish a guy for something he didn't do."

"You damn liar! I—"

The blow-torch burst into spluttering flame as the big albino put a match to it. I started to sweat. If I had guessed wrong—if the thermostat were not connected to the sprinkler—

"Now, wait a sec," I said. "You've got me where you want me. I'm not dumb enough to try and lie. What the hell's it all about? I'm not the kind of guy that crosses pals up—you birds are right—you know what I mean. Maybe, if I weren't playing it blind, I'd be able to give you the answer you want. Maybe I know—and don't know I know."

"You don't have to know—nothing!" Brothers exploded. "I want them notes out of Maresca's safe. We were waiting across the street when you went into the building down the way. We seen you sap the watchman— we'd picked the same spot. Then we seen you come out, and kept on your tail. Or are you going to try and tell us you never went down the line, and into—"

"I told you once, I did," I said. "But I couldn't get the jug open. Damn it to hell, maybe the stuff's still there—for all I know. Why don't you send one of your red-hots to give it another whirl!"

"Yeah. After you've made the place lousy with coppers. No, by God! A wise mug like you wouldn't go in there without the right dope. Listen—I'll make a deal with you. Give me the note in pencil, and I'll turn you loose. I don't care what you do with the rest of—"

"I tell you, as I hope to live, I never laid hands on any of them! Hell, are you crazy?"

His face was quivering. "By God—it's got to be you!" he bit off. "If it isn't—it's your tough luck. I'm going to burn strips off you, Blue, till you conk. You get that? I'll fry you alive, so help me—"

The first drop spurted from the ceiling.

It was heaven's gift that the first squirt lit squarely on top of my hat. Otherwise, I would have expected pure water; after one whiff of the stuff as it splashed, I realized differently. It was fire-extinguisher fluid! The sharp tang of sulphuric acid was corroding my nostrils!

And then the deluge. Like a terrific, furious thunderstorm, the fluid suddenly spat down from a thousand nozzles; clouds of white vapor billowed from the floor as it struck. The three thugs jerked their faces skyward, gasping—and I dived. I didn't think a few drops would hurt me. I whipped my hat off as I plunged, clapped it over my guns on the table, whipped them off together. The dark man shouted, fired blindly at me, but one hand was clutching his stinging eyes as he did. The bullet plowed into the open door of the lavatory behind me, smashed a mirror.

Like a giant wave of blackness, the lights went out.

I ducked as two guns flamed again. The three of them were shouting in panic as I flung myself into the shelter of the lavatory, slammed the door behind me, flattened myself against the wall inside, shot the bolt home. I set my hat down. Hastily, I groped, turned on the cold-water tap in the basin, splashed water over my face and head. I felt a slight stinging, but that was all. Outside, I heard them squealing, the crash of the furniture as they fought blindly for the door—

Then a fire engine's bell clanged wildly—and another. A police siren split the night. I heard one of Brothers' thugs roar: "Listen—the cops!"

It was like a stampede as they fought to get out the door. I heard their feet rattle down the steps, then a sudden yell as one of them fell, crashing, bumping.

I opened the bathroom door. The sharp sting of acrid gas sent me reeling back.

With a sudden desperate feeling, I realized I had come out of the frying pan into the fire. The cops!

Hastily I lit matches, looked into my hat. I got my handkerchief, peered anxiously at my two guns. Only the odd drop had spattered them. I had to make a wild guess. I chose one of them, wrapped it carefully in my handkerchief, stowed it in my hip pocket. The other I jammed in my shoulder holster, restored my other belongings to my pockets. I leaped up on the closet seat, examined the catch on the clouded-glass window. It was new, springy. I tried holding it halfway open, then slamming it down. Three times the catch snipped locked when closed. I opened the window, looked out.

A fire engine was already steaming, red-lighted, in front of the building. I could see firemen running in from the street. And a police cruiser was, even as I looked, screeching to a stop behind the engine.

Under the window of the lavatory was a narrow stone ledge, no more than six inches wide, completely unprotected. Above the window was a scanty ornamental scroll-work. My heart did flip-flops as I faced the desperate chance. Yet I had to take it.

I slid up the window, fixed the catch for the fourth time halfway open. I climbed out, sweat running down me in streams, got my feet on the six-inch ledge, knelt till I could get one groping hand up to the scroll-work above, heaved myself erect, trembling.

It was an almost incredible job to slam the window down, but as I did, I heard the click of the lock shooting into place.

There I hung, literally, by toes and fingers, with the wind whistling about me, and the dread certainty that if I were discovered, I faced my ultimate, indubitable finish.

I heard shouting voices, heavy, pounding boots inside the building.

They didn't find me—didn't open the locked window.

Chapter 6

A BURIAL IS ARRANGED

I WON'T GO INTO the fifteen minutes that I hung there, desperate, my fingers numbing. A searchlight started to play. Only the fact that it was directly in front of the building, its wide arcs missing me in the shadow, saved me from the most ignominious exposure. I heard feet, even in the bathroom. I didn't hear anybody say anything about the catch; but I knew that my gag must have worked.

I heard them tramping about in the film offices outside. Then finally, like a log to a drowning sailor, a voice crisp with authority: "There's no fire here. It's a false alarm. Those birds we saw beating it, must have been playing with this blow-torch and thrown the thermostat system. We'll send some repair men over and notify the owner. Come on."

I heard them clump downstairs. I heard—after what seemed eternity—the fire engine, then the police car, drive away. I made myself wait for five minutes.

I kicked in the window, got it open, fell back into the lavatory. The door was open, the fumes had gone from the outer office. One gun in my hand—still faintly fearful they might have left a guard on duty—I crept out to the hall, down the stairs, out into the night, still cautious.

Then I ran.

Two blocks of hard running brought me in sight of a cruising cab. I jumped in, breathing hard, my handkerchief-wrapped gun in my hand, barked the address at the driver—Dr. Hans Pfaff, on Central Park West.

The little German opened his apartment door—his lab was part of his quarters—in his pajamas. His round blue eyes lighted up as he saw me. I shoved the wrapped gun into his hand, hurried him to the lab in the rear. "Is there a fingerprint—just one—that isn't my own on this? It was handled by a guy—a few minutes ago. He took out the clip."

Pfaff's hands appeared in rubber gloves as though by magic. He ignored the outside of the gun, took out the oily clip, exclaimed, "Yah! Yah! A perfect thumb!" and I dived for his phone, begged over my shoulder: "Classify it for me—please—like lightning!" He hurried over to his microscope.

I got my raving office girl on the phone, silenced her wails. "Give me the phone number of our San Francisco correspondent."

She gave it to me, and I hung up on her outraged list of questions, let the hook up again and called the Schaeffer Agency on the coast. By the time I had the connection, Pfaff had put the print into a classification.

I said over the phone, "Cass Blue, New York. Get this thumb print," and gave the classification symbols to him. "I want to know—by wire here—as fast as you can get a man down to your local records office—if that bird has a record in your town. Bill me as usual."

I got a crisp "O. K." from the other end and hung up. Once more I called a number—Maresca's house.

Pfaff's shrewd china eyes were regarding me over his moon-shaped spectacles. He said: "I was listening to the radio tonight. You—didn't do it, did you Cass?"

"I did if the cops catch me before I crack the job. They'll tie it round my neck so tight it'll sink me. Give me another clear half hour without getting pinched and I've a fifty-fifty chance of nailing the world's foulest killer. I'll—Hello. . . ."

Hastily I made my voice smooth. "Miss Nina Maresca, please. She's expecting my call."

The voice said: "Miss Maresca stepped out about fifteen minutes ag—"

"Where? Where did she go?" Blood was suddenly thick in my head. "Did she take anything with her—a bag—or a car?"

The voice gasped: "She didn't say where she was going. She went on foot. No, she had no bag. She just went out without telling any—"

I slammed down the receiver. For one second, I sat there, numbed. Then my eyes fell on my cuff. Dirty, torn, it still carried the address I had jotted down from the dead Giannini's card.

I fairly overturned the phone table as I jumped to my feet. I shot at Dr. Pfaff as I ran for the door: "Catch that telephone, Hans! I told them to send it here. I'll call—though God knows if it'll be any good now. I think I'm too late."

I dived into my cab on the street below, rapped out the address from my cuff, said grimly: "Run right over any copper or anybody else that gets in the way. Jam down that throttle—and move!" We roared away.

Not till we were almost at the address did I realize with a wild, incredible feeling that we were back—within a pistol shot of Maresca's own house. The driver suddenly slowed, pitching me forward onto the floor.

As I jerked up, I had a gun in my hand. I was tense, one hand holding the door half open as we swung in, idled down a long line of old brownstone houses. The driver shot over his shoulder: "I think it's that one, boss—the second from the corner."

I threw him a bill and was out, making for the corner. The cryptic *B-Rear* was suddenly clear as day—the rear apartment of the basement. I ran on past, to the house on the corner, dived down the two steps to the areaway of *that* house, jammed home the bell by the grilled-iron door—and held it there. Light went on. I took my finger away.

A furious German householder emerged from the door, a poker in his hand, a wool gown around him. "What the hell do you think—"

I flashed my badge. He gulped, swallowed his words.

I half husked: "Got to get through to the rear. Let me in."

His hands fumbled with the door, his eyes wide, awed. I stepped in, eyed him ominously. "Go back into your apartment and stay there."

His eyes were on the gun in my hand. I saw him back in his own quarters, before I turned and darted for the rear door.

I came out into the backyard. As in all brownstone places of this section, it was the joint backyard of the two adjoining houses. My heart jerked, as I saw light behind the drawn blind of the rear-basement apartment of the second house from the corner—the address of Giannini's card.

My feet were silent as I shot across to the window. It was barred! Long bars covered the entire window from the outside, close enough together to exclude cats. The window was open at the bottom—only an inch—but enough to let in the breeze, and the breeze was swaying the blind—ever so little.

I flattened myself against the corner of the window, my eye glued to the edge of the blind, praying for—I groaned at my own stupidity.

A minute's search found me a stick in the yard. I slid it carefully between the bars at the bottom of the window till it just touched the blind, lay across the sill. Then I straightened. My toe touched the end of the stick projecting. I eased it forward gently, lifted the blind away from the window-frame—

I saw into the room—and caught my breath.

Sitting on a kitchen chair, his arms drawn over the back of the chair and bound round with ropes, a pad of adhesive plaster over his mouth, was Chick Picarro, the D.A.'s son. The room was in turmoil—rugs in bunches, other chairs overturned. There was no one else in the room that I saw, yet from the white-rimmed, turned eyes of the youth, I guessed that the person I was seeking was in the room beyond. I could not hear a sound above the now greatly diminished wind. One second I stood there, taut in doubt, then I turned hastily, groped for the rear door of the house. It came open and I was in the hall, staring at the door of the rear-basement apartment.

I dropped to one knee, my ear against the panel. It got me nothing. I straightened to a crouch, my hand closing on the doorknob. I twisted it cautiously—and I almost gasped as it opened under my hand.

I dived in, my gun fanning the room. Picarro's eyes were like saucers over his gag. A wild, smothered mumble came from him. His eyes jerked desperately toward the bedroom beyond. I didn't have to look. From the corner of my eye, I could see Nina Maresca, bound and gagged, lying across a bed in the inner room.

My eyes flew back to Picarro's. He still indicated the bedroom with his eyes again and again, desperate pleading in his expression.

I said: "Heard me coming, eh? Planned the stall. It gets you nowhere. You're pinched, you stinking life-taking skunk—"

He shot me in the gun arm.

Imbecile that I was, I hadn't realized that, with his arms hooked as they were over the back of the chair, his coat masking the position of his hands, he had a perfect set-up to hold a gun on me, close to his side. The attempt to get me into the other room was in order to have my back for a target.

His gun was a big one—a police special. The roaring slug tore up my arm from wrist to elbow, bored into the fleshy part of my upper arm with a shock that sent me staggering backwards. I got one flash of him springing up, the ropes and gag falling. As my feet hit a wastebasket, I went over hurtling—

I lit like a ton of bricks, half on a chair, my feet a flying tangle in the air, my gun flying from nerveless fingers. He fired again, and the slug parted my hair. He fired once more, and splinters from the chair splattered.

He flung out the door, slamming it behind him. I was half groggy from the fall. I fought wildly, struggled up, grabbed up my gun with one hand, dug out a pocket-knife with the other. I was staggering for the bedroom door, plucking at my knife to get a blade open trying to focus my fogged eyes—forcing myself to consciousness.

I saw the girl—truly bound and gagged, her terrified eyes bursting up at me. I slashed her ropes with one swift cut, tore the adhesive from her mouth in one cruel-kind yank. She couldn't keep back the tortured cry and her back arched from the pain, but even as she sobbed she was crying through it: "That rosette—when Chick was at our house earlier tonight—he had on a different suit. After you left, I thought I remembered seeing a bare stud in his buttonhole, like that rosette came from. I came over here to see if I was right. I found the affidavit—and the letters from Dad's safe! He came in and caught me. Then he heard the bell ring next—"

I cut her off. "Get to this address!" I flung Hans Pfaff's number at her. "Understand? Get out of here and go there as fast as ever you can! Be sure no police follow you there. Say I sent you. Understand?"

She nodded—and I was gone—racing out into the backyard. I didn't bother about the house next door. I ran straight for the fence that banked the street—a seven-foot wooden wall. I dived, jackknifed over, flung up my feet and dropped, raced for the corner.

I slid to a halt. My gun was in my right hand. A block west, racing, bent over, I saw a man running. I fired, saw him stumble. He spun, fired across his arm—two orange winks. I felt them snick past me before I heard the thunder of their report. I fired again just as my man swung round a corner, and, behind me, no more than a block, the sudden rising whine of a police siren put ice in my veins.

I ran. I saw the red headlights sweep into the street. I knew I must be visible to them—but I could not stop. I drove the pavement under me, whirled round in Picarro's wake. Half a block down, he was jerking open the door of his black roadster. I fired—and he staggered away from it. I saw him trying to raise his gun. I fired again as I ran on—and he dropped. I saw light reflected from his gun as it flew from his hand across the cement into the gutter.

I covered the last twenty-five yards like a madman. He was lying on his stomach, his knees drawn up, like a frog, sobbing, groaning.

I dived for him, scooped him up in one motion, and threw him into the car. I was around, into the driver's seat, had my foot jammed down on the starter, when the red searchlight of the screaming police car whirled round to settle behind me.

I sent the roadster literally off the road as we swooped forward. We were around the next corner before the coppers behind me could recover from the shock of seeing the D.A.'s license plate on the car they were pursuing.

I made the roadster do tricks. I went around corner after corner like a mad-man, my heart in my mouth half the time. Finally I heard the siren far off. I straightened out, shot over to Central Park and thundered south.

When I found the Seventy-second Street exit, we were in the clear. I sent the car squealing to a stop before Hans Pfaff's apartment house.

I took one look at my groaning companion. Blood was running from his shoulder, a shattered wrist, a hit leg. A doorman came running out. I rapped at him: "Get Doctor Pfaff down here—fast—a patient!" As he hesitated: "Go on—it's life or death!"

Pfaff came down, and between us, we carried Picarro in—not to Pfaff's office, but to the doctor who had offices on the ground floor. The other medico stripped clothes from Picarro.

"Three slugs," was the verdict. "None of them even dangerous."

"Patch him up—for now." I begged the doc, and at Pfaff's insistence he nodded. Picarro had gone unconscious from pain. I pulled Pfaff into a cor-ner. "Get hold of Sergeant McMartin—uniformed man. Get him to your apartment. Say nothing about me. Did the telegram come?"

"Yah, Yah," he said eagerly, "And a girl—she just came before you—" He handed me a telegram. When I read it, I could have shouted aloud.

"Get that copper—if you have to promise him a thousand dollars! I'll wait till he arrives. You can phone down to me from your apartment when he does."

He ran off. Men in his position can usually get a favor from any cop. It was exactly twenty-five minutes before the call came. The doc had patched my arm. Picarro had come to, had tried to bribe me, tried to plead, finally dissolved into a flood of tears and silence.

When I half led, half carried him into Pfaff's apartment, I thought McMartin would faint. He was sitting at one side of the sitting room, his seamed old face puzzled. When he saw me, he went white, shot to his feet, his gun half out. The girl, on a chair opposite, screamed.

His eyes were pinpoints of suspicion. "What's the gag?"

"Read this." I handed him the telegram. It read—

Print as per classification by phone, that of Red Beatty, wanted here on five-year-old homicide charge. One thousand dollars reward. He is apparently orig-inator of new racket. He seeks out well-to-do undertakers, finds instances where bodies they have buried have been exhumed and reinterred, and forces or bribes phony affidavits from the undertaker who did the moving. The affi-davit purports to prove that body was buried without being properly em-balmed, and that person was buried alive. This serves as basis for blackmail. He is wanted here for murdering undertaker who attempted to revoke such affidavit, having had him beaten so severely that he subsequently died, naming Beatty in ante-mortem. Also available are specimens of handwriting, photostats of which we are forwarding by first mail. If any available for comparison there, identification should be clinched. He is dangerous criminal.

Schaeffer Agency, San Francisco

per Jack Schaeffer

McMartin looked up, bewildered, flushed. "Well—is this guy supposed to be Beatty?"

"No. But Beatty can be had—he hasn't had time to leave town. He's such a queer-looking duck that he couldn't hide out. Get the radio room on the phone and I'll give them a description—also of two red-hots he's got. The dragnet's sure to catch him, if you make it strong. What do you say?"

McMartin's face was a study for a half-second. Then he clipped: "All right—but this don't mean—"

"Just get them! I'll explain the rest after the alarm's out!"

I pulled from my pocket the papers I had taken from Picarro downstairs, laid them before McMartin. "This is an affidavit—the kind he works his racket with."

McMartin's eyes were narrow. "So what?"

"These are notes he wrote Mario Maresca, the big-shot undertaker."

The sergeant's eyes widened. "Maresca! You mean—"

"I mean Maresca was being blackmailed on account of this affidavit. He made a deal to buy the affidavit back from Beatty, alias Brothers. I was at the church in your beat tonight to help with the deal. What had happened was that this"—I jerked a thumb at Picarro—"had been sent out by his father—the D.A.—to investigate an anonymous letter received a year or more ago at the D.A.'s office. The anonymous letter—I'm just guessing on this point—must have been sent by Brothers to set the stage for his blackmail. Anyhow, Chick Picarro was sent out to investigate the thing, a year ago.

"He tried to ingratiate himself with the family—to get a chance to judge if there was any truth in the charge. Maresca's daughter fell in love with him."

I looked at Nina. She dropped her eyes. "It's true, officer. I'm Nina Maresca."

I kept on giving it. "Chick pretended to be in love with her—got engaged to her. He worked her for information—for months. He realized he was onto something big, decided to cash in. From the girl, he knew enough of Maresca's plans to be able to guess at the rendezvous tonight. He went to the church, snatched the affidavit from Maresca's messenger and killed him in the process—at the church.

"I was chasing him, when I ran into you. Now, wait a second and think. I had a camera case under my coat with Maresca's name all over it. I'd sworn to keep his name dark. Remember, he was terrified this would come out—or that the D.A. would remember the anonymous note and start investigating again.

"I forgot to mention that this prince"—I jerked my head at Picarro—"had finally slipped a warning to Maresca that a note had been received. He claimed it was recently. I think he was just trying to get some action—make Maresca do something so that he, Picarro, could locate the affidavit and have a chance to get his hands on it. He got action, all right—more than he expected. He also found out that there was a specimen of Brothers' handwriting in Maresca's safe—which Brothers wanted.

"Picarro had, long back, gotten hold of ways to get into Maresca's office and safe. After he had killed the man in the church and gotten the affidavit, he beat it back to Maresca's to make sure there had been no slip-up—that no one had seen him. As soon as he was sure, he hightailed it for the office, planning to make the doubleplay.

"Unfortunately, there was a bird named Giannini working for Maresca, who was also in love with the girl here. Naturally, when he was cut out, he hated Picarro, and somehow, seems to have gotten suspicious of him. He was tailing him tonight. He was down at the church. He was outside Maresca's, and his car is now standing down near the office I speak of—on Cedar Street.

"Picarro got into the office, opened the safe and had the letters he was after in his pocket, when Giannini came in. He murdered Giannini. If that body hasn't been found, you can turn it up too. We'll drag a confession out of this rat before he leaves this room if I have to pull his finger nails out. At any rate, these two, Giannini and Picarro were both in that office! Whichever one got there first doesn't matter. Giannini was killed! The letters were taken by someone who didn't have to blow the safe!

"I found both the affidavit and the letters on Picarro here. And he'll confess. What about—"

The phone rang. Pfaff answered. He held it out to McMartin. "You, Sarge."

When McMartin hung up, his eyes were gleaming. "They already had those three birds up in Number Nine. They ran over a cop trying to burn up the highway."

I walked over and stood looking grim-jawed down at Picarro. "We've got you dead to rights, rat. Are you going to belch—or am I going to murder you by inches?"

He took one look at my eyes, looked away. "I'll confess."

I was at the indictment next day. I never hope to see anything so harrowing in my life as the moment when the D.A. laid down his son's confession and asked him: "Is this true, Chick?"

"Of course it's true!" The boy's voice was wild, his face still starch. "It's your fault—damn you—" he was almost sobbing. "You—and your heavy-footed playing around! Everybody in this town hates the name of Picarro! When all the public clamor that put you in office dies down, where do you think you'll be? Out in the street!

"We're pariahs—that's what! You left me without a chance to ever make a dime. When I saw a chance for some money, I took it. I didn't expect to have to kill anybody—but I did. Now, damn you, you know what your snivelling hypocrisy's done. Sure it's true! I'm guilty as hell and I'll fry! I hope you'll remember me, for the rest of your God-forsaken life, sizzling in the chair."

There was sweat on *my* forehead as the half-mad youth dropped into his chair and went into hysterics.

A Man's Last Hours

WILLIAM E. BARRETT

T HE CROWD WAS three deep around the roulette table despite the fact that it was early evening when the Twin Moons dining room could usually be depended upon to outdraw the betting-salon. Some plunger from out of town was running a big streak, and crowds usually follow sensations.

Behind the spinning wheel, Dean Culver sat with his eye-shade pulled low. He was the croupier, the man whom nobody noticed. Night after night, he sat in the most conspicuous spot in one of the town's most popular places and attracted no more attention than the furniture. He called the play, tossed the ball to the spinning mechanism, and plied his rake as the numbers came up and the chips went out or came in.

"Seventeen in the black."

He was paying off the plunger again. A light hand touched his shoulder. "Hanlon's office, Culver. I'll take over."

Larry Dane, the change-off man on the wheel, was standing just behind him. Culver nodded his head. "O.K.," he said.

It was done like that, a simple exchange between plays. The crowd never noticed the difference. One man or another, the wheel went around and around. Culver walked quietly across the room. He wore the regulation dinner jacket, and there was nothing to mark him apart from other men or to make him remembered. He preferred it like that. If once he attracted too much attention, he was through.

There were men playing at his wheel who would kill him within twenty-four hours if they knew his real identity.

He passed out into the big reception hall. It was quiet, dignified, furnished in taste, more like a parlor in a big hotel than like the rendezvous room of a gambling house. To the right of the door to the street there was a large dining room that was more than a mere front for the other activities of the Twin Moons. People dined at the Twin Moons who never gambled there. Culver swung left to the heavily carpeted stairs that led to the upper floor and the private office of Dollar Hanlon.

Hanlon was seated behind his mahogany desk, a big man with iron-gray hair, clear eyes and a firm chin. To Hanlon's left sat a red-faced man in a gray suit, Sergeant Driscoll of the homicide squad. Culver nodded his greetings and raised one eyebrow in the direction of Driscoll.

"Somebody been getting slaughtered around here?" he asked.

Hanlon grunted explosively. "Naw. But do you know what that fool, Doherty, did?"

"Let someone in with a soup spot on his vest?" Culver made himself at ease. Hanlon was the boss, but Hanlon could be kidded. Doherty was the downstairs man and greeter, and Hanlon kept him on the job while he forever grumbled about him. Hanlon didn't rise to humor this evening.

"Monk Menger got out of the pen today," he said. "Tonight, Doherty lets Sid Weyler into my place. Does that mean anything to you?"

"I'm away ahead of you." Culver's face was suddenly grim, the lines bracketed deep around his mouth.

They had taken Monk Menger out of a courtroom nine years ago with the word "frame" on his lips and a publicly registered oath that he'd kill Sid Weyler the day he came out. It was one of those things, but Monk Menger was out and the underworld would be sitting back and waiting. Monk Menger and Sid Weyler had been partners in the dope racket, and Menger had been a pretty big shot. He'd be a small-time punk if he didn't do anything about Sid Weyler now—and he'd had nine years to think about it.

Dollar Hanlon was worrying a cigar. "Weyler, the big heel, is stowing a feed downstairs now," he growled. "He'll take his time and then he'll play the wheel. Sure. He'll be right out in a public place where nobody can criticize him, and it's Menger's play."

"Doherty doesn't have to let Menger in, too."

"Naw. He'd be sap enough to do it though. It's when Weyler has to leave that we get burned. We always give big customers protection home with their dough when they ask for it. He's figuring on that."

Culver hadn't changed expression, but there had been no joke about his statement that he was away ahead of Dollar Hanlon on the first sum-up. He was the one who was usually picked to escort the heavy winners home. It would be very nice for Sid Weyler, if Sid could euchre Dean Culver into shooting Monk Menger for him. That way, Monk would die in a stick-up and there'd be no flare-back on Weyler, no cop theories on feuds that would stand before a jury. Culver shrugged and looked toward Sergeant Driscoll.

"There're still a few cops working for the city, aren't there?" he said.

"That's what I thought." Dollar Hanlon was glaring at the plainclothesman.

A faint smile crossed Driscoll's grim lips. "We don't pinch anybody for crimes that haven't happened yet," he said. "It just ain't legal."

He tapped the ash from his cigar against his heel. That was the cop position and they were sitting pat on it. Sid Weyler had been a pain to the cops for years, a slick labor racketeer who beat every rap that they tried to hang on him. Monk Menger, of course, was just somebody who was better off in the can. To have Weyler removed by Menger, under circumstances that made Menger's conviction a cinch, would be just too perfect from a cop angle.

Dollar Hanlon looked with irate helplessness at Culver. "We're it," he said. "For the first time since we've been open, we send a customer out to be killed. If we don't, we have to take on a job of killing to do, with a lot of lousy publicity on the side."

Driscoll was pulling on his cigar. "Culver could forget to load his gun," he said.

Hanlon pushed a box of cigars across the desk. "You're a big help," he agreed. "Here, make yourself sick. I'm talking to Culver. . . ."

He led Culver out into the hall. There was a moment of silence after they reached the little private conference room that Hanlon reserved for moments like this. Hanlon was shaking his head.

"Culver," he said, "Monk Menger's going to do it. I called a newspaper guy I know. They're keeping tabs on him. He's over at Zorro's and he's boasting that he's going to chill Weyler. He's got to come through even if he's got no more privacy than if he rodded somebody during a police line-up."

Culver smoked quietly. "So what?"

"So, the only play is for you to go over to Zorro's and cover Monk Menger. I'll send somebody else home with Sid Weyler if I have to."

Culver's lips twisted wryly. "You mustn't have anything in mind for the future that I figure in very much."

Hanlon matched him with a hard grin. "I wouldn't send you anyplace unless I figured that you'd come back, somehow."

Culver turned to the door. "That 'somehow' is the catch to it. But I'll try Zorro's," he said.

It took less than ten minutes for Culver to change into a suit of dark blue that had been worn often enough to be inconspicuous anywhere. It took him five more minutes to reach Big John Zorro's.

In all the city, there was no place like Big John's. You could order an Italian dinner there, and get a good one, or you could order hot money at discount prices, an honest gunman out of work or a neat piece of forgery. You'd be equally well served in all cases, and Big John would be as innocent as a baby of the whole transaction. Through the whole deal, he'd be just a big good-natured Italian who liked to "introduce my frands togedder." When he got his cut, he'd be as grateful as a child for his "gift."

Culver stopped outside for a moment below the glittering neon sign of red and blue, then shrugged and plugged down the three steps to the basement entrance. Big John was standing inside the door, as usual. He beamed when he saw Culver.

"Ah, good evening, Jones, my frand."

"Evening, John."

Culver allowed his hand to be pumped and hid his grin. It was one of Big

John's little pretenses that he knew everyone who came into his place and he called everyone "Jones, my frand." It was a good gag. If a man corrected him, he apologized—and had the right name thereafter. Occasionally, he would actually hit a Jones and that was perfect. Culver let the Jones stand.

About him the lights were dim, and his table was in a corner. There was a small dance floor surrounded by the favored tables of good spenders. Monk Menger had one of these.

He did not look like a man just out of stir. He was wearing dinner clothes and had a couple of girls of the chorus-girl type with him, one on either side. The others of his party were small-time chiselers who dated back to the days when Menger was a big shot. The tough boys, who counted, weren't present. They were waiting to see how Monk Menger made out before they joined any of his parties.

And Menger was boasting. He was pretty well lit, bragging about what he was going to do to Sid Weyler. Culver could read his lips. The man had ample lips to read. He was short, squat and ape-like with a big mouth and sloping jaw. He was throwing a party and before midnight, he was going to blaze down Sid Weyler.

"It will be a good act if it happens." Culver placed his order, then made his way to a phone booth. Every eye in the place seemed fixed upon Monk Menger's table. Culver passed, unnoticed. That, too, was a laugh.

If the people who patronized Zorro's knew Culver, for who and for what he was, he'd attract more attention than a dozen Monk Mengers—and he wouldn't figure to live as long. He slipped into a phone booth and called the *Morning Star.*

"Randall? This is the *Blue Barrel.* Catch an item fast, for tonight's bull-dog. Here it is. The inside on why a well-known labor racketeer will not be killed tonight by a well-known ex-convict is that preservation is the first law of nature, and that a man can be awfully sore and still not be sore enough to pull a trigger in a goldfish bowl."

"Hey—you're putting yourself on a limb." Randall's voice was startled. "Menger's got to—"

"I know. Take bets on it."

Culver hung up and slid back to his table. That item would go into type fast and it would appear in a first-page box with a cut of an automatic pistol at its head. People would read it and discuss it and believe it. The *Blue Barrel* was a local institution. What Winchell had done with a gossip column, the *Blue Barrel* had done with a crime-column—got out in front ahead of the headlines. There was one difference. Men had gone to jail, and men had died, because the *Blue Barrel* leveled at them. Like the weapon from which it got its name, the column fired slugs—slugs of type.

And Dean Culver, who spent most of his life as the unnoticed man in the green eye-shade, was the anonymous *Blue Barrel.*

He ate slowly, watched Monk Menger—and then he saw the frail youth at the table beyond his own. The man appeared to be in the last stages of tuberculosis, and his big, dark eyes fixed on Menger's table with a sort of desperate fascination. His lower lip was trembling, and Culver had the impression of chattering teeth behind the man's lips. The man's thin hand fumbled under the napkin on the table-top.

That was the tip-off. Culver was out of his chair as the gun cleared the napkin. The frail youth came to his feet, and the gun swung through a shining arc to level full on Monk Menger. Monk fixed startled eyes on Death's glittering symbol—and Culver suddenly dived.

The youth with the gun had a moment of indecision, warring impulses, desperate resolve. In that moment, Culver hit him. Culver's lips were pressed tight, his eyes were fixed on the gun. His left hand flashed clear, and he had the youth's wrist in his grip. It was like bending a toothpick back. The gun fell to the floor, and the weapon-wielder went as limp as a straw man. Culver swept him off his feet and slammed him back again into the chair that he had vacated.

The surrounding tables were in turmoil. Waiters were closing in, and Monk Menger's party was standing. Monk had the hand buried in his armpit, a belated gesture that did him no good—and that would have done him no good even if he had made it sooner. Culver shook the man he had grabbed.

"Keep your mouth shut, mugg," he said.

He waved the waiters back, a hard crew of huskies who could—and did—do many things besides wait on the customers of Big John. Big John himself was coming down the aisle like a human locomotive. Culver beckoned to him.

"Get us out, John, and quiet," he said. Zorro's eyes bit into him. As a casual customer, a man might be "Jones, my frand," but when that customer asked for anything, John had to know which Jones was doing the asking.

"This fellow should be pinch," he said.

"Sure. But I'm paid to follow him around and keep him out of trouble. I did."

Culver nodded toward the trembling youth and tapped his own forehead significantly. He had already started to propel him toward an exit. They were up against a wall with a phalanx of waiters between them and the diners at the tables. Big John was mad. Every available man of his that wasn't on this particular party, was busy around the dining room, attempting to restore order. Things had moved so fast that very few people had seen what happened, and rumors were flying. Somebody said that Sid Weyler had come in, and people were straining to see.

"I do not know this feller. I do not know you."

"O.K. You don't want a pinch in your place tonight, John."

"Me, I never want the pinch in my place. What the hell?"

"O.K. I'm taking the kid out, see? He didn't do a thing. Monk Menger isn't going into court to swear that the kid pointed a gun at him, I hope? You see how it is?"

Big John saw. It was a dirty situation from his point of view and, under ordinary circumstances, he'd have had a half-dozen huskies take Culver and the youth out in the alley. They'd be worked over plenty, and Big John would swear that he'd never seen either of them. Tonight, he didn't want anything to detract from the drama of Monk Menger's return. It was bringing Big John business, and there would be curious hundreds coming into the place for weeks if Monk Menger shot Sid Weyler tonight and the word got out that he had primed himself at Zorro's for the killing. There would even be saps who would pay an extra cover charge to sit at the table that Monk Menger had occupied.

"All right," he said. "You take him out quick. Never again come into this place."

Culver didn't hear the rest. He was hustling the kid along, and the kid was a limp parcel. They reached the sidewalk by a side exit, with a few assorted Italian oaths curling around their ears. Culver steered a course down the block.

"Mugg," he said, "you've got a lot to tell me."

They stopped at a white-lightning joint where there were booths, and where the customers who weren't too drunk to listen in on conversation were too indifferent to listen in. Culver studied his prisoner across the table-top, with grim eyes.

The fellow was no more than twenty-five but the white plague was strongly in the saddle. He was coughing hard when he came into the place, and had another fit of it when he took the drink that he needed. He had probably been a good-looking young man once. He was a walking skeleton now.

"What's your name?" Culver shot the question at him fast.

"Benny Pond." The youth was in that numb grip of despair where men don't take the trouble to lie.

"What's your racket?"

"Musician, once."

There wasn't any need to throw a question beyond that. It was too apparent what the man was today. He was a deathly sick, whipped dog. Culver had hit upon a theory in the split seconds between the moment when he noticed the gun under the napkin and the moment when he dove for it. He hadn't changed that theory since. Now he cracked it, his hard, direct stare fixed on Benny Pond's pale face.

"Somebody hired you to shoot Menger," he said. "Probably fixed it for your family to get the money. Sold you the idea that you wouldn't live to take the rap. Right?"

Benny Pond stared sullenly at the table-top. He didn't attempt to answer. Culver guessed again. "You've got a wife and kids, haven't you?"

The youth was startled. "Yes. Two girls. I—"

"Sure. They'd pick somebody like you. You fumbled your job. Now, your family won't get the money."

That shot went home. Benny Pond's luminous dark eyes bugged. "They— they got it. Before I tried to shoot—they didn't know, of course. But—"

He was frightened, breaking. Culver kept him on the run. "How much?"

"One thousand dollars."

Culver blinked. For one thousand dollars, this man had sold his last hours on earth, had whipped himself up to murdering a man whom he had never seen before—a thousand dollars that he would never touch himself. And some low heel of a human had trafficked pitilessly in the man's great need.

"They won't take it away from them—from my wife and kids?"

There was stark terror in the youth's face, terror beyond that which he had shown when he held the gun on Monk Menger.

Culver evaded the question. "Come clean, and I'll see what I can do about it. What was the proposition?"

It came tumbling out then. Benny Pond had been down and out and dying on his feet, faced with the certainty of leaving his family in poverty when he went. And one of the slimy rats who prey upon labor unions, and know too much about labor business, had made a date for him "with a man who could help him out." Benny Pond hadn't known the man's name, but the fellow had given him a gun and a thousand dollars in an envelope for his family, and told him that he'd be better off in a prison hospital than walking around.

"He—he told me it would be tough on my family if I double-crossed him. I—I tried—"

"Sure, kid." Culver stood up. It was the way he had figured the play, and it was a dirty business. "I'll see you through, you play my way and follow instructions. You're going to see the guy that hired you and you're going to tell him that you did the job, see?"

"But, I don't know—"

"That's all right. You're going to the Twin Moons. I'll tell you who to ask for. When he comes out, if he's the right one, you walk up to him and tell him that you did the job. That's all."

"But—"

"Sure—you didn't do the job. I know that. What's a white lie between friends? You're going to play ball."

Benny Pond swallowed hard. "Yes—yes, sir," he said.

At the Twin Moons, Culver let the youth go in alone. He slipped in quietly himself and stood near the telephone switchboard. He watched Benny Pond hand in the name by a haughty waiter—and he saw Sid Weyler come out.

Sid Weyler was short and had run to weight in the wrong places. He was flabby and his skin was dough-white, under any circumstances. It turned several shades whiter now when he saw Benny Pond. His normally pendulous lower lip dropped farther. He took a backward step, then reconsidered and came forward to face the music. In his swiftly shifting eyes there was written a war of resolves.

He wanted to disclaim all knowledge of Benny Pond, and yet he did not want to risk raised voices nor to call attention to himself by the type of argument that a frail, excitable invalid like Benny might be expected to stage.

Culver lounged by the switchboard. He was absorbed in the drama before him, and he didn't see the second invalid until too late. A tall, thin wreck of a man in an ill-fitting dinner jacket rose jerkily from one of the easy chairs in the reception hall—and he had a gun in his hand when he rose. On his face was the same desperate, hopeless resolve that had been on the face of Benny Pond.

Culver went for him lunging—but the gun cracked three times while he was crossing the reception hall.

An Italian waiter just inside the dining room door gave a loud shriek and dropped a dish-loaded tray. Sid Weyler clutched the gleaming-white shirt-front that was turning red with his blood, and his breath gurgled in his throat. He was folding forward when Culver brought his killer down.

The man was fighting like a wildcat. He was flailing with the gun and threshing around under Culver's grip. Culver missed two grabs for the gun, and then Sergeant Driscoll was in the picture with Dollar Hanlon at his heels. Driscoll twisted the gun away and the man went limp, his eyes desperate, defiant. Culver was breathing heavily.

"You can sweat the truth out of this guy, Sarge," he said. "Monk Menger hired him. It was Menger's out. Menger wouldn't have to kill a man who was dead already. This guy would keep buttoned up—but he probably got a grand for it. Tell him you'll take the dough away from his family if he doesn't come clean."

The expression on the thin man's face was enough to confirm Culver's guess, but he didn't want to look at the man's face. It was tough business. He turned away.

"Strange how the minds of two heels will work exactly the same way when they've been partners," he murmured. "Figure the odds against two men hitting on the same scheme at the same time!"

There was excitement at the door of the dining room. Culver took the few seconds that he had in the clear to cross to the cowering Benny Pond. "Beat it, kid," he said. "Nobody knows you got that money now. Go to Arizona with it. It's better than a hospital in the gow."

He didn't wait to see him start. Dollar Hanlon was in the group around a sputtering, half-hysterical Italian waiter whose tray was on the floor with a bullet-hole in it and who was loudly exhibiting a hand that had been bullet-grazed. Sid Weyler's face had already been covered by a handkerchief by a doctor-guest. Dollar Hanlon saw Culver and his brows pulled down to a scowl.

"A swell job, you did. A shooting in my place."

"Sure." Culver shrugged. "But at the door of the dining room, old settler. No damage in that. It advertises you." He waved to the waiter who was still carrying on noisily about his hand. "If that guy doesn't recover, you can have him stuffed, and attract tourists with him."

He turned on his heel. The flash-lead of the *Blue Barrel* for the morning edition was already shaping in his brain—

Look for the strangest defense in local criminal history in the trial of the man who sold his last hours on earth for one grand. And chalk up a believe-it-or-not. There would have been two murders, and two men with the same freak defense, if it weren't for a fellow named "Jones-My-Frand."

Elsewhere in the column, he'd have to work in a prediction that almost any jury would vote the hot-seat to Monk Menger who did his murder by proxy. The bet was a cinch.

Something for the Sweeper

NORBERT DAVIS

JONES LIMPED SLOWLY ALONG, his rubbers making an irregular squeak-squish sound on the wet cement of the sidewalk. He was not a large man and, walking as he was now, humped forward in an unconscious effort to favor his feet, he looked small and insignificant. He wore an old trench-coat with grease stains running jaggedly down the front. The sun was bright on the slick-black wetness of the asphalt paving, and he had his hat-brim pulled low over his tired eyes.

The houses on this street were gaunt, ugly and brown, and as alike as the teeth in a saw. They all had a wide flight of worn stairs leading up to the front door with another flight beside it leading down into the basement. They had all been built by one man, those houses, and he evidently was a person who believed in getting a good, plain plan and then sticking to it.

Jones was watching house numbers out of the corners of his eyes. He was coming pretty close now, and he began to walk even slower. His mouth twisted up at one side every time he came down on his right foot.

Ahead of him he could see a man's head and shoulders. The man was halfway down one of the basement flights of stairs. His head and shoulders moved back and forth in a sort of a jigging rhythm. Approaching, Jones saw that he was sweeping up the stairs of the basement. He swept in careful, calculating little dabs, as precisely as if he were painting a picture with his broom.

"Hi," said Jones, stopping and standing on his left foot.

The man made another dab with his broom, inspected the result, and then looked up at Jones. He was an old man, small and shrunken and wiry, with white, smooth hair that was combed straight back from his softly plastic face. He nodded silently at Jones, solemn and wordless.

"Hendrick Boone live here?" Jones asked.

The old man sniffed and rubbed his nose. "Who?"

"Hendrick Boone."

The old man considered for a moment. "Live where?"

"Here," said Jones.

"Yes," said the old man.

Jones stared at him sourly. "Thanks a lot," he said at last.

"Oh, that's all right," the old man said, and smiled.

Jones went up the stairs, grunting painfully, and, when he got to the top, leaned over and pinched the toe of his right rubber and muttered to himself under his breath. He straightened up and looked at the closed double doors ahead of him. There was a narrow frosted-glass panel in each one, and the pair of stiff-legged storks, with toothpick beaks depicted on them, leered disdainfully at him with opposite eyes. Jones looked around for a doorbell, finally located a little iron lever that protruded out of a slit in one of the doors. He pulled it down and then up again, and a bell made a dismal *blink-blink-blink* sound inside.

Jones waited, standing on his left foot, and the door opened slowly, squeaking a little. Jones touched his hat and said: "Hello. Is Mr. Hendrick Boone here, and if so, can I talk to him for a minute?"

"He's not here. He's really not here."

"Oh," said Jones.

She was a very small woman with gray hair that was puffed up in a wide knot on the top of her head. She wore thick, rimless glasses and behind them her eyes were a distorted blue, wide and a little frightened and anxious to please. She wore a long skirt that rustled and a white waist with lace stiff on the front. She had a timid, wavering smile.

"Where is he?" Jones asked.

"He's in the hospital."

"Hospital?" Jones repeated.

"Yes. He fell downstairs. Are you the man from the installment company?"

"No," said Jones. "I'm a detective, believe it or not. I know I don't look like one. I can't help that. I didn't pick this face, and, to tell the truth, I don't think so much of it myself."

"Oh, but he didn't do it! Really he didn't, officer! He couldn't have, you see. He's been in the hospital, and his condition is very serious, really it is, and he couldn't have done it."

"Done what?" said Jones.

She moved her hands a little, helplessly. "Well—well, whatever you think he did. Was it—windows again?"

"Windows?" Jones asked.

"I mean, did you think he broke some windows, like he usually does?"

"He makes a habit of breaking windows?"

She nodded. "Oh, yes. But only plate glass ones."

"Particular, huh? What does he break windows for?"

Her sallow face flushed slightly. "He sees his image. You know, his reflection. And he thinks he is following himself again. He thinks he is spying on himself. And so he breaks the windows."

"Well, maybe it's a good idea," said Jones. "Is he ever troubled with pink elephants?"

"Yes, he is. He often sees them walking on the ceiling when he wakes up in the morning."

"What does he do for them?"

"Oh, he always saves a half pint, and as soon as he drinks that they go away."

"I should think they would," said Jones. "I'm still talking about Hendrick Boone, by the way? Are you?"

"Yes. My husband."

"Oh," said Jones. "You're Mrs. Boone. Could I come in and sit down and speak to you for a moment? I've got some news for you, and besides my feet hurt."

"Oh, yes. Surely. Excuse me, please. I was a little flustered when you said 'detective'—"

The hall was dark and small and narrow with a carpeted staircase running up steeply just to the right of the front door. The wallpaper was a stained brownish-black. There was a hole worn in the carpet at the foot of the stairs.

"Right in here," Mrs. Boone said anxiously.

It was the parlor that stretched across the narrow front of the house. The furniture was stiff and awkward, mellowed with age, and there was a clumsy cut-glass chandelier that had been originally designed to burn gas.

Jones sat down on a sofa that creaked mournfully under him and looked down at his feet, wincing involuntarily.

"Now," said Mrs. Boone. She was sitting primly upright, looking very small against the high carved back of the chair, with her hands folded on her lap and smiling a little, timidly. "Now—you wished to speak to me?"

Jones nodded, still thinking about his feet. "Yes. Your husband was born in Awkright, Idaho, wasn't he?"

She nodded brightly. "Yes."

"Had one brother—by the name of Semus Boone?"

"Yes."

"Not any more," said Jones. "Semus Boone died a couple of months ago."

"Oh," said Mrs. Boone. She was silent for a moment. "We hadn't seen him for over twenty years. He didn't like Hendrick. He invited us to a Christmas party, and Hendrick took a drop too much and broke the plate glass window in Semus' living room. Semus was very angry."

"He must have gotten over it," said Jones. "He left your husband all his money."

"Oh!" said Mrs. Boone. She smiled vaguely. "Was it enough to pay his funeral expenses?"

Jones nodded. "Yes. And a little bit to spare. About a million and a half."

Mrs. Boone's hands gripped tight. Her eyes glazed behind the thick glasses, and her lips moved soundlessly. After a while she drew a deep breath. "You're not—joking?"

"No," said Jones.

"You're—you're sure there's no mistake?"

"No," said Jones. "I don't make mistakes—not when there's a million and a half in the pot. I've been hunting your husband for two months."

"A million and a half!" said Mrs. Boone dreamily.

"Yes," said Jones. "Your husband can't touch the principal, though. It's in trust. That's where I come in. I'm an investigator for the Suburban Mortgage and Trust Company. The company's the trustee—handles the principal. Your husband gets the income—he and his heirs and assigns and what not—for twenty years. Then the principal sum goes to certain charities. The income amounts to over a thousand a week."

"Oh!" said Mrs. Boone. "Oh!" Her eyes began to gleam behind the glasses, and she swallowed. "Sarah!" she called, and there was a gasping catch in her voice. "Sarah! Sarah!"

There was the flip-flop of slippers in the hall, and a girl came and stopped in the doorway. She had a wide red mouth and cigarette drooping in the corner of it that slid a smooth blue stream of smoke up past her cheek and the faded blondness of her hair. She was big and heavy-boned, but had a lazy, cat-like gracefulness. Her eyes were a deep-sea blue, set far apart. They were narrowed sullenly now, and she looked Jones up and down.

"Well," she said. "And now what?"

She wore a blue kimono with the sleeves rolled back and was wiping her hands on a towel. Her forearms were white and smoothly muscled. There were birthmarks on both of them.

"Sarah," said Mrs. Boone. "This gentleman here just came to tell us that your Uncle Semus died."

"Too bad," said Sarah. "What'd he do—bite himself on the tongue and die of hydrophobia?"

"No," said Jones. "As a matter of fact he had a heart attack."

"Somebody must have cheated him out of a nickel," said Sarah. "That would do it, all right."

"Don't speak ill of the dead," Mrs. Boone said in a gently reproving voice. "He left your father a lot of money."

"How much?"

"The income from a million and a half," Jones told her.

Sarah's wide set eyes blinked once and then narrowed slowly. "Oh yeah? What's the gag, mister?"

"No gag," Jones said. "I don't have anything to do with it. The trust company that handles the principal hired me to find you, and here you are. I'm through."

"A million and a half," said Sarah slowly. "About how much would that be a month?"

"Around five thousand."

Sarah's breath made a little hissing sound between her white teeth. "Five thousand a month! The old man will drink himself to death in a week."

"Won't make any difference to you if he does," Jones said. "The income will go to your mother in that case."

"Oh," said Sarah thoughtfully. "It would, hey? That's something that needs a little thinking about."

Jones got up. "I'll run down and see Mr. Boone before I leave town."

Mrs. Boone blinked at him, worried. "He's in the City Hospital. But, I don't know. He's really pretty seriously ill. I don't know whether they'll let you in his room."

"I just want to look at him," Jones said. "I'll have to put it in my report. You say he fell?"

"Yes," said Mrs. Boone. "He came home late, and he was—"

"Fried," said Sarah. "Drunk as a skunk. He crawled up the front steps and started walking around in circles looking for the front door and fell down again. He cracked his noggin on the sidewalk. He'll get over it, though, I'm afraid."

"Sarah," said Mrs. Boone. "Sarah, now. He's your father."

"That's your fault," said Sarah. "Not mine."

"Well, I'll be going," Jones said.

"Mr. Morganwaite," Mrs. Boone said brightly, getting up with a sudden swish of her long skirt. "I must tell him! He'll be so pleased! I won't have to worry—" She hurried out of the room.

"Morganwaite?" Jones said inquiringly, looking at Sarah.

"He's an old stooge we keep around to clean up the joint now and then," Sarah told him. "He takes care of the old man when he gets potted. You probably saw him when you came in. He was sweepin' the basement stairs."

"Oh, yes," Jones said. "Well, so long."

"So long," Sarah said. "Lots of thanks, mister, for coming around and doing a Santa Claus for us."

Jones smiled. "I got paid for it." He went down the dark hall and out the doors past the two storks that were still leering at him and the world in general.

The city hospital was a great square pile of brick, masonry and steel that covered a complete city block. Three hours after he had visited the Boones, Jones rode up and down on seven elevators and limped through a mile and a half of silent cork-floored corridors and finally located the section he wanted. He went in through a glass door in a glass partition that blocked off the short end of a hall. There was a middle-aged woman sitting behind a flat desk in a little cubby-hole off the corridor.

"Yes?" she said. Her voice had a low, practiced hush, and her face looked as stiff and white and starched as her uniform and cap.

"Hendrick Boone?" Jones inquired wearily.

She nodded. "Mr. Boone is in Room Eighteen Hundred."

"Hah!" said Jones triumphantly, and shifted his weight from one foot to the other. "Can I see him?"

"No. Mr. Boone is allowed to receive no visitors except the members of his immediate family. His condition is very serious."

"I'm not a visitor," said Jones. "I just want to look at him. Don't worry—it's not curiosity. It's my job. I was hired to find him."

"He's here."

"Look," said Jones. "How do you think that would sound in my report? I can't say I think he's here, or he's supposed to be here, or somebody by his name is here, or you told me he's here. I got to *know* he's here. I've got to see him. They're not paying me for guessing."

The nurse regarded him silently.

"Just a peek," said Jones. "Just open his door and give me a squint. I've got his picture and description. I won't say a word to him."

The nurse picked up a precisely sharpened pencil, opened a leather-bound notebook. "Your name, please?"

"Jones," said Jones.

"Your first name?"

"Just Jones."

The nurse looked up at him, and her lips tightened a little.

"All right," said Jones quickly. "Don't get mad. You asked for it, and that's really my name—just plain Jones. J. P. Jones. See, my mother had a lot of kids, and she always thought she ought to give them something fancy in the way of first names on account of there being lots of Joneses around. She named 'em Horatius and Alvimina and Evangeline and things like that. But she began to run out of names pretty soon, and she had an awful time with Number Twelve. She said: 'If there's any more, I'm not going to all this trouble. The next one is going to be just plain Jones.' So here I am."

The nurse wrote in her book. "Address?"

"Suburban Mortgage and Trust—New York City."

She closed the notebook, laid the pencil carefully beside it. "This way, please." She went along the hall to the last door on the right and, standing in front of it, turned to look at Jones. "You are not to speak to him. You understand?"

"Right," said Jones.

The door swished a little, opening slowly. The room was a small one, and the high iron bed was in the corner beside the big window. The man in the bed made a bulging mound of the covers. He was lying on his back, and there was a white bandage like an adhesive and gauze skullcap on his head. There was something the matter with his face.

The nurse made a gasping sound, and her starched stiffness seemed to crack. She ran across to the bed, and Jones trailed right behind her. She fumbled under the covers, found the man's limply slack wrist. It was a thick wrist, big-boned, and the hand was big and square and powerful.

The nurse's voice was breathlessly small. "No—pulse. He strangled himself—"

"He didn't have to do it, himself," Jones said. "He had some help." He pointed to the red blotches, slowly turning dark now, on the thick throat.

"Pulmotor," the nurse said, and started for the door.

Jones caught her arm, spun her around. "No. A pulmotor won't do him any good. Look at the color of those marks on his throat. Who came to see him this afternoon?"

The nurse jerked against his grip. "His daughter. She left a half hour ago. Said—he was asleep."

"He was, all right," said Jones. "You sure it was his daughter? Sarah? You've seen her before?"

"Yes—yes. Let go!"

"You sure it was Sarah?" Jones repeated. "You positively saw her?"

"Yes! She was veiled, but her arms—the birthmarks—"

"Oh, yeah," said Jones. "Anybody else come?"

"No!" She twisted free, ran out the door.

Jones looked closely at the face of the man on the bed. It was Hendrick Boone. Jones went out of the room. There was no one in sight in the corridor, and he went out through the glass partition and walked along the hall until he found a stairway and went down it.

In five minutes, he came out in the main entrance hall of the hospital and entered one of the public telephone booths beside the reception desk. He consulted the directory, finally deposited a nickel and dialed a number. He could hear the telephone at the other end ring and ring. It rang for a long time while Jones squinted at the black hard-rubber mouthpiece in front of him and muttered to himself inaudibly. Finally, the line clicked.

"Hello," a voice said casually.

"Is Sarah Boone there?" Jones asked.

"Who?"

"Sarah Boone."

"Where?"

Jones drew a deep breath. "Oh, it's you again, is it? Listen, Morganwaite, this is Jones, the detective that was there this morning. I want to know if Sarah Boone is there and by there I mean where you are. Now, quit playing around and answer me."

"No," said Morganwaite.

Jones choked and then recovered himself. "Are you saying no, you won't answer me, or no, she isn't there?"

"No, she isn't here."

"Is Mrs. Boone there?"

"No. She left as soon as she got Sarah's message."

"Message?" Jones said. "Sarah sent her a message?"

"Yes."

"How do you know?"

"Mrs. Boone told me."

"When?"

"When she got it."

"That's what I want to know!" Jones said explosively. "When did she get it?"

Morganwaite was silent while he evidently considered the matter at some length. "About a half hour ago."

"What did the message say?" Jones asked.

"I don't know. Mrs. Boone didn't say. She just left."

"What kind of a message was it? Telephone—telegraph?"

"No."

"Well, what kind?"

"A written message—in an envelope."

"Who brought it? Come on now, shake yourself and think hard."

"It was a boy," said Morganwaite pensively. "A boy in a gray uniform on a red bicycle. A small boy with freckles."

"Thanks," said Jones. He hung up, took out his handkerchief and wiped his forehead. Then he got up and walked quickly out of the hospital.

There was a taxi-stand across the street. Only one taxi was there now, and its driver was sitting disconsolately on the running-board cleaning his fingernails with a jackknife. He stood up when Jones approached and said, "Taxi?" in a not very hopeful voice.

"Is there a messenger service around town that specializes in red bikes and gray uniforms?" Jones asked him.

"Sure. Bullet Service."

"Have they got a branch office near here?"

"Sure, on Court Street. Three blocks down and one to your right."

"Show me," said Jones. He opened the door of the taxi, climbed in, and plumped himself down on the seat with a sigh of relief.

It was a small, neat office with a big plate glass window that ran clear across the front and had an enormous bullet painted on it with red lines trailing behind to show it was traveling at tremendous speed. There were several people waiting when Jones limped up to the high counter and leaned on it with his elbow, looking as mysterious and hard-boiled as possible in view of the fact that his feet were hurting him more and more all the time.

A clerk with a polished haircut and a vacantly cordial smile stepped up to the other side of the counter. "Yes."

"I'm a detective," Jones sneered at him. "Don't act funny. Just be natural. Treat me like anybody else."

The clerk gulped. "Police! What—"

"Shut up," said Jones. "I said act natural. I want some information about a party who sent a message by one of your boys to Mrs. Hendrick Boone at forty-five–fifteen Raleigh Street. Was it sent from this branch?"

The clerk nodded once, then again, and finally said, "Yes," in a frightened stage whisper.

"When?"

"About—about an hour ago."

"Did a woman send it?"

"Yes," the clerk said. He swallowed and then said: "Her name was Sarah Boone."

"So?" said Jones sharply. "And how do you know that?"

"Well, we have a rule about messages. A few months ago someone started sending poison-pen letters—anonymous—through our messenger service. Brought us a lot of bad publicity. Now, we require anyone sending a sealed message to sign it in our presence. This lady did."

"What'd she look like?" Jones asked.

The clerk stared. "Well, she was a woman—I mean, sort of young, I think. She was veiled. I didn't notice. She had a lot of birthmarks on her arms."

"Yeah," said Jones absently. He squinted thoughtfully at the clerk for a moment, then suddenly pulled one of the blank pads of paper on the counter toward him, picked up a pencil, and wrote rapidly *You're a liar.*

"I'm not!" the clerk denied, instantly indignant. "You—"

Jones slapped the pad down. "I thought so! You're a shark at reading handwriting upside down, aren't you? That's the why of your signature rule, to give you boys a chance to spot a poison-pen letter before it goes out. Now, what did Sarah Boone's message say? Don't stall me."

The clerk shifted uneasily. "Well, I can't repeat it, word for word. I didn't pay enough attention. I saw right away it wasn't anything like what we've been looking for. It was headed 'Dear Mother,' and it said something about a lot of serious trouble and for the mother to meet her right away at Ten-eleven Twelfth Avenue."

"Where?" Jones asked.

"Ten-eleven Twelfth Avenue. I remembered that on account of the sequence of figures—ten, eleven, twelve. I was thinking that ought to be a lucky address—"

"Maybe not so lucky," said Jones. "Keep this under your hat—if you have a hat. Thanks."

Half the pickets were gone out of the fence, and it swayed backward wearily toward the wet brown square of earth that had once been a lawn. The house was gaunt and weather-beaten and ugly, and it had boards nailed haphazardly across the windows on the lower floor. It looked long deserted. A sign beside the gate said *For Sale or Lease* and gave the name of a realty company.

Jones looked from the sign to the house and back again, squinting thoughtfully. He turned his head slowly. There were no other houses within a half block.

Jones said, "Huh," to himself. He dropped his right hand into the pocket of the trench-coat. He was carrying a pair of flat brass knuckles in the pocket, and he slid his fingers through the metal loops and closed his fist. He unfastened the middle button of the coat with his left hand and touched the butt of the .38 Police Positive he carried in his waistband. Then he nudged the sagging gate open with his knee and strolled aimlessly up the narrow walk.

There were some children playing in the street a block away, and their excited cries carried high and shrill in the stillness. Jones' feet made hollow thumps on the steps, on the damp-warped boards of the porch. The front door was open about an inch. Jones took his right hand out of his coat pocket and rapped with the brass knuckles. The echoes came back from empty rooms, hollow and thin and ghostly. Jones put his right hand behind him and waited. Nothing happened.

Jones closed the fingers of his left hand more firmly around the grip of the Police Positive and then suddenly kicked the door open and stepped to one side. The door swung in a dark, silent arc and banged against the wall. After about thirty seconds, Jones looked cautiously around the edge of the doorway and saw Mrs. Boone and Sarah.

Mrs. Boone was lying in front of the door. She wore a long, old-fashioned coat with a thin fur collar and an old-fashioned hat that sat high on her gray hair. The hat was tipped sidewise now at a grotesquely jaunty angle. She was lying on her back, and she had one arm thrown across her face.

Sarah was crumpled in a heap under one of the boarded windows, and the failing sunlight made a barred pattern across her broad face. A little trickle of blood on her cheek glistened brightly. One smooth white arm was flung limply wide. Jones could see the birthmark on it. The lax fingers just touched a stubby automatic lying there beside her.

Jones came inside the room, taking one cautious step, then another. He knelt beside Mrs. Boone. She was breathing faintly. There was a swollen, blue-black welt on her cheek. Jones leaned over Sarah and touched the smooth white arm. Then he suddenly spun around and ran out of the room. He ran down the walk, through the gate, on down the street. He ran two blocks to a corner drugstore, dodged into a telephone booth, dropped a nickel in the instrument, and dialed the operator.

"Ambulance," he said breathlessly.

Dusk was a soft-gray smoothness closing down slowly over the row of houses that were just alike when Jones stopped on the sidewalk in front of the Boones' and looked up the steep front stairs at Morganwaite. Morganwaite was sitting on the top step, leaning forward weakly, as if he had collapsed there. His broom was lying beside him, and he had the evening paper spread across his knees.

"Hello," Jones said, and climbed the steps slowly and sat down beside him.

Morganwaite's hand was trembling a little, and he touched the paper on his knees with his forefinger gingerly. "This paper—I picked it up. The newsboy—delivered it just like any other night. It says that Sarah killed her father and tried to kill her mother and then—had an attack of remorse and killed herself."

"It's mostly right," said Jones. "Only Sarah didn't kill herself. She isn't dead."

"Not dead," Morganwaite repeated dully.

"No. They thought she was, at first. I did, too. I never saw anybody that looked deader. But the bullet was a small-caliber one. It didn't penetrate her brain. Gave her a multiple skull-fracture. It's a toss-up whether she'll pull through or not. The doc thinks she's got a good chance. Funny thing— she's in the same room her father was in at the hospital. That's the wing where they put the head injuries, and it was the only room vacant. She doesn't know it, of course. She's unconscious."

"Mrs. Boone," Morganwaite said. "There—there was no mistake about her? She's—all right?"

Jones nodded. "Just a concussion and shock. She's not even in the hospital. She's staying at a private nursing-home."

"Sarah," said Morganwaite. "I can't believe it. I can't think she'd do that."

"People do," said Jones. He stretched his feet out on the stairs, grunting painfully. "Chilblains—I get 'em every spring. They're killing me. Ever have 'em?"

"No," said Morganwaite.

Jones sighed. "You're lucky. Can you look after things around the place here for a couple days? Mrs. Boone will be O.K. by then."

"Yes," said Morganwaite.

Jones got up. "Well—I've got to go. So long."

Morganwaite didn't answer. He sat staring straight ahead with eyes that were wide and unseeing.

There were two big stone pillars on either side of the broad walk that led up to the entrance of the City Hospital. Jones was leaning against one of them, a thin indistinguishable shadow in the darkness, with his hat pulled low over his eyes. He was peering around the edge of the pillar, up toward the entrance of the hospital. After a moment, he stepped from behind the pillar, walked quickly up to the steps, pushed the plate glass door open.

A thick-set man with square, heavy shoulders was standing just inside the door. He wore a blue overcoat and a black felt hat, and he had a thin white scar on his face that ran from the corner of his left eye straight down across his cheek to the line of his jaw.

"Jones?" he asked softly.

"Yes," said Jones in a surprised voice.

The scarred man stepped forward and picked up Jones by the front of the trenchcoat. He swung Jones around and slammed him against the wall.

"Careful," said Jones. "Don't step on my feet, or I'll kill you."

He said it in such a murderously calm voice that the scarred man let go of him. Jones straightened the front of his coat with a jerk and a shrug of his shoulders. "You don't have to tell me," he said. "I know you're a cop."

"Yeah," said the scarred man. "Maybe you didn't think there were any cops in this town. Maybe you think you've been playing a little game of hide-and-seek with yourself. What's the big idea of trying to make us look like monkeys?"

"I can't help what you look like. You wanted to see me, you said."

"All right. You've been in this case from the first. In fact, you started the ball rolling. You found Hendrick Boone. Did you stick around? No, you ducked out before we got here. You found the other two. Now, just what do you think you're doing?"

"Trying to find a murderer."

The scarred man stared at him. "Are you so dumb you haven't figured it out yet? Sarah Boone did for her father and tried to do for her mother so she'd get the money her uncle left."

"Did she?" said Jones.

"Why, sure. What—" The scarred man's hard eyes narrowed. "Oh, so you've got something else up your sleeve, have you? All right, then. Who is the murderer?"

"The person I was following. You can come along and take the credit for the arrest, if you don't bother me with a lot of dumb questions."

The feet of Jones and the scarred man were soft and noiseless on the cork flooring. They walked side by side, tensely, and ahead of them was the bright, clean glitter of the glass partition that blocked off the short corridor where Hendrick Boone's room had been.

Through it they could see the nurse sitting behind her desk and looking up into Mrs. Hendrick Boone's thick glasses and shaking her head in a blank, surprised way. Jones nodded at the scarred man and then reached down and turned the knob on the glass door very softly.

"No," said Jones. "Sarah isn't here. That was just a gag to see if I couldn't get you out from under cover. You really killed Sarah. She's in the morgue. Your feet are too big, Mrs. Boone."

Mrs. Boone's skirt rustled silkily. Mrs. Boone's white-kid gloves made a blurred streak rising above the collar of her old coat, flipping down again. The knife was a flat, hissing glitter coming at Jones.

The scarred man ducked with an inarticulate cry. Jones dove under the knife and it smashed through the glass partition and rattled on the corridor floor beyond. Jones' shoulder hit against bony knees. There was a strangled cry, and Mrs. Boone's coat ballooned clumsily, falling.

Jones got up, drawing in a long breath. "You were a big help," he said to the scarred man. "Thanks." He looked at the white-faced nurse. "Sorry, Miss. I didn't figure on any knife-throwing."

The scarred man pointed. "She—Mrs. Boone—she killed her husband and daughter?"

"No," said Jones. "Of course not. Morganwaite killed them. What do you think I just tackled him for?"

"Him?" the scarred man said blankly.

Jones leaned down and picked up Mrs. Boone's glasses and loosened the collar of Mrs. Boone's coat and pulled it down. Morganwaite's face looked white and peaceful and kindly.

"Morganwaite killed Sarah and Hendrick Boone," Jones said. "He did it so he could marry Mrs. Boone and live in comfort on her money. He had been planning it even before I turned up. Mrs. Boone had a little property. The news I brought about the trust fund just gave him added incentive. I don't think there's any doubt that he would have married Mrs. Boone had his plan gone through. She was a timid, trusting soul, beaten down by years of living with her drunken husband. She wouldn't be hard for anyone as clever as Morganwaite."

"Well, how?" said the scarred man.

"Easy for him," said Jones. "He's quite a female impersonator. Must have been an old-time actor. He looks like one. First, he got rid of Sarah. On some pretext, he got her to go to that old house on Twelfth Street. He'd picked out the spot a long time ago. He shot her when he got her there—in the temple, close enough so it would look like suicide. Then he dressed himself in Sarah's clothes, painted some birthmarks on his arms, came down here and finished Hendrick Boone. Then, still pretending to be Sarah and laying a nice plain trail, he sent a note to Mrs. Boone and signed Sarah's name to it, asking Mrs. Boone to meet Sarah at the house on Twelfth."

"Huh!" said the scarred man. "You mean the old lady didn't even know her kid's writing?"

Jones held up the thick glasses. "Morganwaite thought of that, too. He stole Mrs. Boone's glasses. Look at 'em. They're an inch thick. Mrs. Boone couldn't read anything without 'em. Some neighbor read the note to her, or else the messenger did. Of course, she didn't question the writing. She went right down to the house on Twelfth. Morganwaite was waiting there for her. He hit her on the head as she came in, before she saw him, and left her there. The set-up was supposed to look as if Sarah had planned to kill her father and mother, but that, when she got to the point of actually doing for her mother, she had an attack of remorse and killed herself, instead.

"I was pretty sure of the set-up, but I didn't have any proof. So I went around and told Morganwaite Sarah wasn't dead—that she was here. Well, that upset his whole apple cart. Sarah knew he shot her, and, if she told, why there he'd be in the soup. So he came down to finish the job. This time he dressed up in Mrs. Boone's clothes to keep from being identified. He knew Mrs. Boone wouldn't be suspected, actually, because she was in a rest-home and would have an airtight alibi."

Jones looked around. "If you've got any more questions, we'll have to go somewhere where I can sit down. My feet are killing me."

Footprints on a Brain

D. L. CHAMPION

Chapter 1

THREE MEN AND A HALF

I WAS HALFWAY DOWN the hall when the commissioner came out of his office. On general principles I decided to keep out of the way and began a fast detour down the corridor that runs parallel to Centre Street—but he nailed me anyway.

"Symonds," he yelled. "Just the man I want. Come here."

I sighed, swung around and saluted.

The commissioner indicated a burly Irishman at his side. The man held a thick manila envelope under his arm.

"This is Detective-sergeant Carrigan of Chicago," said my chief. "Take him over to see Allhoff. Carrigan thinks he's got something."

The commissioner's tone implied that he, personally, didn't think Carrigan had anything at all. I saluted again.

"Yes, sir," I said. "This way, Sergeant."

Carrigan followed me out of the building into Centre Street. As I led the way to the ramshackle frame tenement opposite, he looked at me inquiringly.

"Who's this Allhoff?" he asked. "Why ain't he got his office in headquarters?"

"Well," I told him, "Allhoff's not exactly a member of the department."

"For God's sake," said Carrigan, mildly resentful. "What the hell's the chief sending me to him for? I got a murder case."

I didn't say anything to that. If Carrigan's murder case was so weak that it failed to interest the commissioner, Allhoff would make short shrift of it. If the commissioner, for reasons of politics or diplomacy, had refrained from telling this Irishman he had no case, Allhoff would certainly have no qualms about doing so. It was one of Allhoff's bad days, too. He'd been raising hell since breakfast.

I led the way up the rickety flight of stairs that ascended to Allhoff's tiny two-room combination office and living quarters. Carrigan followed me, his wonder increasing at every step. By the time we reached the door, he was completely bewildered.

The room, as usual, was in depressing disorder. A dressing-gown and a soiled pajama-coat were flung carelessly over the back of a chair. My battered old desk near the window was covered with disarrayed morning papers. Allhoff sat close up to the other desk, his narrow chest pressed against the wood. At his left a blackened coffee pot perked sullenly on an electric plate. Through the open door on his right, the unmade bed in the next room was evident.

The place looked like a fifteen-dollar-a-month slum tenement flat—which, as a matter of fact, it was.

Across the room, young Battersly, in uniform, stood by the window staring moodily into the street. His dark eyes smoldered. A single glance at him convinced me that Allhoff was in prime condition this morning.

"Inspector," I said to Allhoff, "this is Detective-sergeant Carrigan of Chicago. The commissioner told me to bring him over."

Carrigan, still somewhat confused by the layout, extended a meaty hand. "Glad to meet you, Inspector," he said.

Allhoff grunted. He poured some hellishly black coffee into a chipped, stained cup. He sipped it, and regarded Carrigan hostilely over the cup's edge. Carrigan stood there like a fool with his hand held out. A slow resentful flush came over his honest face. He dropped his hand and shifted his bulk uncomfortably beneath Allhoff's scrutiny.

It wasn't pleasant to have Allhoff stare at you. I knew that. His little seamed face was yellow as if it reflected the bad temper within him. His eyes held a savage bitterness, a dark brooding which had their roots deep down inside him.

Over at the window, young Battersly lifted his gaze from its unseeing contemplation of Centre Street and stared at the back of Allhoff's neck. His face was dark, his eyes sullen. I sighed, shook my head futilely and sat down at my desk. This was one hell of a place to work. Between Battersly and Allhoff I was going quietly nuts. Three times I'd asked the commissioner for a transfer. Three times I'd been told: "We need you there, Symonds. We need an old clear head to watch those two. You're the oil on the troubled waters." Well, damn it, let them change the oil. I was getting fed up.

Allhoff drained the cup and put it down. "Sit down, Carrigan," he said. "There—in that chair."

Carrigan removed the worn shirt from the indicated chair. He sat down, still clutching the manila envelope under his arm. It was apparent that he still resented Allhoff's manner. The amiability had left his face. There was a definite antagonism about him.

"Before you begin," said Allhoff, "you, Symonds, get me a scratch pad. Battersly, find my fountain pen."

His tone, as was customary, was dictatorial and insolent. Carrigan stared at him strangely. I took a pad from my desk and gave it to him. Battersly opened a closet door and rummaged in the pocket of a hanging vest for Allhoff's pen. Carrigan viewed these proceedings sourly.

"All right," said Allhoff. "Now what is it, Carrigan?"

Carrigan opened his mouth to speak when Allhoff interrupted him. "Here," he snapped with curling arrogance in his voice, "before you get going, hand me those cigarettes over there."

Carrigan looked around. An opened package lay on a typewriter stand less than three feet away from Allhoff's right arm. It was more than twice that distance from Carrigan over on the other side of the desk. Carrigan looked from the cigarettes back to Allhoff. Slowly his face became red as the Russian flag. The Irish in him which had been quietly seething since Allhoff had ignored his hand, boiled over now.

He got out of his chair and towered over Allhoff's anaemic frame like a giant.

"Damn it, Inspector!" he roared. "Get your own cigarettes! They're nearer to you than they are to me. You've been playing God ever since I came in here. You've treated me and these other two men like we were dirt. Maybe they'll stand for it. I won't. Get your own damn cigarettes. You're no cripple."

I nearly died at that. I heard the sharp intake of Battersly's breath behind me. I saw the little gleam of unholy joy that flashed in Allhoff's eyes. Battersly lit a cigarette with fingers that trembled. On Allhoff's face was an awful grimace that he meant to be a smile. His ugly teeth showed through his parted lips. His eyes were the eyes of a fanatic. Carrigan did not notice these things. He remained standing over Allhoff, glowering.

"Well," he bellowed again, "why don't you make a move? Why don't you get your own butts. You ain't a cripple. Are you?"

Allhoff's ghastly smile grew broader, more horrible. Slowly he pushed his chair away from the desk. When he spoke his voice was frozen honey.

"You have come to the crux of the matter, Sergeant," he said softly. "And I'm afraid I must correct you. I am a cripple."

Carrigan stared down at the chair in which Allhoff sat. He looked foolishly at the two stumps which ended Allhoff's body where his legs should have begun. I shot a swift glance at Battersly. His lips were compressed. His eyes were hot and tortured. Allhoff looked about the room, grinning like a fiend. Carrigan's wrath fell from him. Covered with confusion, he took the cigarettes from the stand and handed them to Allhoff.

"I'm sorry, Inspector," he blurted. "Sorry—er, I, er—I didn't know. I had no idea. I—"

Allhoff lifted a deprecating hand and waved him to silence. "We all make mistakes, Sergeant," he said. "Not your fault. No one's fault, excepting of course, the yellow rat who left me facing a machine-gun three years ago. It's an interesting story, Sergeant. Very interesting. It happened just three years ago next month. I was—"

Something cracked inside me. I couldn't stand any more of this. "Shut up, Allhoff!" I shouted. "Damn you, man! Shut up!"

Allhoff swiveled around in his chair and glared at me. "Symonds," he said, "I'll thank you to remember that you're a sergeant attached to the Nineteenth Precinct. My rank is that of deputy inspector."

That got me sore. "Deputy inspector of what?" I yelled. "You're not even a member of the department. What the hell right've you got to give me orders?"

That got him. His little eyes smoldered. For a tense silent moment, he fought his temper. Young Battersly looked on nervously. Carrigan sat quietly in his chair, a puzzled expression on his face.

"Listen," said Allhoff to me, and I knew his calm tone cost him an effort, "if you think you're not under my orders, ask the commissioner. If there's any doubt about it, I'll call him now." He reached for the telephone.

I threw up my hands. The commissioner would back him to the hilt, and I knew it. I could hear Battersly's knuckles drumming on my desk-top. I felt suddenly weary and despairing.

"All right, Allhoff," I told him. "I'll shut up. Go ahead. Have your psychopathic fling."

He swung around again and faced Carrigan. "Now, Sergeant," he said, "I was going to tell you how I lost my legs. Wasn't I?"

"Er—yeah," said Carrigan, obviously uncomfortable. "But I got a murder case, Inspector. I got a—"

Allhoff ignored him. He breathed deeply and sat back in his chair. A strange expression of feline pleasure was in his eyes.

"It was three years ago, Sergeant," he said again. "First week in August it was, and just as hot a day as today. You'll probably remember the Roseman mob. Well, it was the night we got Roseman and Kaylor."

Battersly's desk-drumming had stopped abruptly. I looked up to see him snatch his cap and jam it down over his eyes. He walked rapidly toward the door. Allhoff spoke to him as his hand was on the knob.

"Where are you going, Battersly?"

Battersly glared at him. He stood on the threshold like an animal in a trap. His lips moved convulsively. For a moment, I thought he was going to explode. Then his eyes fell on Carrigan. He took hold of himself again.

"Cigarettes," he said hoarsely. "I'm going down for cigarettes. I'll be right back."

"I've got plenty of cigarettes here," said Allhoff. "You can smoke mine. I want you to stay. I may need you."

You'll need him all right, I thought to myself. In about three minutes now you'll need him like a hophead needs a shot.

Silently Battersly recrossed the room. Allhoff turned again to Carrigan.

"We had a tip," he resumed. "Roseman and Kaylor, his right-hand man, were holed up in a rooming house on the West Side. We knew further, that they had a tommy gun trained on the front door. They were taking no chances."

Allhoff paused and refilled his cup from the blackened coffee pot. Battersly's eyes were riveted on his scrawny neck. A low feral growl came from Battersly's throat. He took a half-step forward. I put a hand on his arm.

"Steady, son," I said. But I was feeling sick myself.

Uneasily, Carrigan moved his bulk in the chair. "I remember Roseman, Inspector," he said. "He burned, a couple of years back. Now, listen, Inspector, I got a murder case here."

Allhoff sipped his coffee for a moment, then continued as if Carrigan had not spoken.

"We arranged a zero hour," he said and his voice was high with suppressed emotion. "We sent a man up the rear fire escape. His job was to effect an entrance through a window and, at any cost, to get the man behind the tommy-gun before we broke in the front door. Get that, Carrigan, *at any cost!*"

Allhoff made a nasty gurgling sound as he drained the coffee cup. His little eyes were glowing now. I watched him, fascinated. I had heard this damned story a hundred times, yet there was something repulsively attractive listening to him wallow in the slime of his own insane emotions.

"Well, Sergeant," said Allhoff, "to make it brief, the man we sent up the back way was yellow. Someone saw him, fired at him. He went to pieces. Instead of fighting it out and blasting the tommy operator, he ran up the stairs. At zero we broke down the door and charged in. I was at the head of my men, Carrigan—at the head, where I belonged. I got twenty bullets in my legs. Gangrene set in. They cut 'em off, Carrigan."

There was sweat on Allhoff's brow, there was a hellish glow on his face and madness in his eyes.

Carrigan, ill at ease, murmured something inadequate. "That's too bad, Inspector. Now about this murder case—"

"Wait a minute," snapped Allhoff. I tightened up. Now it was coming. Allhoff had said he might need Battersly. Well, this was the time. He needed him now. Needed him badly—to work off some of the accumulated bitterness that had seethed within him for three searing years.

He swung around in his chair, raised a trembling finger in Battersly's direction. His lips twitched. Now his crazy passion had reached its peak. Now he would shoot the works. I shuddered as I looked at him

But this time it didn't quite go off according to schedule. For once Battersly took the play away from him. I heard him inhale with a sound like a rasping saw. He leaned forward over my desk.

"All right, damn you!" he screamed in a voice that broke just two points this side of hysteria. "All right, tell him I did it! Tell him I went crazy for a minute and ran up the stairs leaving a machine-gun to cut off your legs. Go ahead and tell him! Tell him as you've told everyone else who ever came into this office."

He broke off to catch his breath. Then, before I could restrain him, he raced across the room and stood over Allhoff.

"But, tell him, too," he shrieked, "that if I was crazy for a minute that night, you've been insane ever since. Tell him that you've put me through hell for three years, that you're making me lose my mind and spirit as surely as I made you lose your legs. Tell him that, you grinning madman! God, I'll—"

He lifted his hand. I dashed across the room and grabbed him. Allhoff looked like a sneering skull.

"You're running true to type," he said bitterly. "After you cripple a man you find enough courage to lift your fist to him."

I felt the tenseness go out of Battersly's body. His muscles were limp beneath my fingers. Then he brushed me aside and walked out of the room. Allhoff made no attempt to stop him now.

As the door slammed Allhoff uttered a little feline sigh—almost the sigh of a woman surfeited with love. He turned to the dazed Carrigan. When he spoke all the passion had gone from his voice. His tone was crisp and businesslike.

"Now, Sergeant," he said evenly. "What was this you said about a murder case?"

Chapter 2

END OF A CHAPTER

CARRIGAN BEGAN TO TALK. I didn't listen to him. I was savagely wishing that I was pounding a nice quiet beat out on Staten Island. At least three times a week since I had drawn this assignment, I had been forced to witness this same ghastly scene. At every opportunity, Allhoff forced Battersly to pay for his lost legs.

It was inhuman and, if I knew anything about the minds of men, it was insane. Frankly, I believed that three years of hate and brooding had driven Allhoff, literally, crazy.

Officially, Allhoff no longer belonged on the force. After all, you couldn't have a deputy inspector minus a pair of legs. But Allhoff's brain was of more value to the commissioner than his body had ever been. He wasn't carried on the departmental roster, but through some circuitous bookkeeping the city paid him an inspector's salary.

The single condition Allhoff had laid down as the terms of his employment was that Battersly should be assigned as his assistant. With grim poetic justice the commissioner had acceded to his request.

Allhoff had rented this slum flat because it was close to headquarters. He rarely left it. He lived and worked here with his hate and bitterness. He, who had once been the Brummel of the department no longer cared about appearance. His clothes were soiled and dirty. The tenement in which he dwelt was always filthy.

I had been dragged down from a good desk job on the Heights to take care of his paper work. At least that was the ostensible reason. Actually, I was supposed to see that Allhoff and Battersly didn't kill each other. I had come up as a rookie with Allhoff and was one of the few men on the force who wasn't daunted by his superior attitude. That's why I was elected—and I'd been regretting it ever since.

It was a ghastly thing to sit here day after day, to watch Allhoff's cunning mind devise new methods of torturing the younger man. It was sickening. I'd rather stand in the basement of a precinct house and watch a couple of strong-arm dicks rubber-hose a murder suspect any day.

Besides, I'd never liked Allhoff, even in the old days. He was too damned smug and superior. He had a Sherlock Holmes complex. Granting his good mind, it annoyed me when he cloaked his simplest activity in unnecessary mystery merely to impress the rest of us. I suppose, too, that I resented his promotion over my head.

I was straightening up the papers on my desk, when I became aware of the fact that Allhoff was barking at me.

"Symonds," he snapped, "it's part of your job to clip all important police news for me each morning."

I swung around in my chair. "What's the squawk," I asked. "They were clipped and on your desk before you'd finished breakfast."

"Sure," he said sarcastically. "You just overlooked a little routine item that made the front page of every paper in town. Richard B. Hadley was found dead out on Long Island, early this morning. I suppose even you know who Hadley is?"

"Oh, that," I said. "What the hell do you want that for? It was cold suicide. Spectacular but cold. Both the papers and the Bayside cops agree on that."

"Carrigan doesn't," said Allhoff.

I looked up. So it was the Hadley affair that Carrigan had on his mind. No wonder the commissioner hadn't seemed particularly interested.

"Well," I said, "Carrigan knows more about it than Hadley himself, then. Hell, Hadley left a message saying he was killing himself. I got the whole story here."

I picked up the *Bulletin*.

"Hold it for a minute," said Allhoff. "Let's have it from the beginning, Carrigan. Tell me what you're doing here from Chicago."

"A couple of years ago I was assigned as Hadley's bodyguard in Chicago," said Carrigan. "He was in some trouble out there."

"You're damned right he was," I put in. "The plant of his only competitor in the whole middle west was bombed and fired. Five guys were killed. Hadley beat the rap, but every cop and newspaperman in the country is sure he was back of it."

"Shut up," said Allhoff. "Keep talking, Carrigan."

"Well," said Carrigan, "five months ago the medicos told Hadley he was a pretty sick man. He gave up all active management of his interests and moved out to a quiet place in Bayside to write his autobiography. Said he wanted to finish it before he died. He wanted me to come along with him. He was still leery about that guy whose plant was bombed. He had a lot of drag in Chi. So they let me come."

Allhoff wrote something down on his little pad. "See?" he said to me. "Get that?"

"So what?" I said impatiently. "It's still suicide. Hadley was a sick man— cancer. He came down to Long Island to write his book. That done, he shot himself. He always was a spectacular guy. All his life he'd made sensational gestures. If you doubt that, read the obits here. He'd promised his publishers something sensational in his book. All right, he gave it to them. That's the angle all the papers play up. In the last paragraph of the final chapter of his autobiography, he wrote this—" I picked up the *Bulletin* again and quoted: "I have lived my life as I have written of it. I shall not wait for

Death to come upon me slowly; to drag me through a vale of pain. Rather, I shall go forth to meet him. This is the end. *Deus Vult!*"

Allhoff grunted. "What's that last business?" he asked.

"I don't know," I told him. "Looks like Latin to me. Maybe it means: Dear Inspector Allhoff, the butler killed me."

"Keep those smart cracks for the precinct house," said Allhoff. "Go on, Carrigan."

"Well," said Carrigan. "We all left Chi and went out to the Long Island house."

"All?" said Allhoff. "Who?"

"Well, there was Nina Autrey. That's Hadley's daughter. Paul Autrey, her husband. And—"

"Wait a minute," said Allhoff. "This Paul Autrey was Hadley's partner as well as son-in-law, wasn't he?"

"Yeah," said Carrigan. "For the past ten years they worked together. Autrey is a ruthless, fighting, red-headed tough guy. Hadley cottoned to him right away. He's more like the old man's son than son-in-law."

"All right," said Allhoff. "Who else?"

"There was Rutledge, Hadley's secretary. A quiet little guy who's been his right hand for twenty years. And Parks—that's his valet—a nut on religion but otherwise O.K."

Allhoff was still scribbling on his pad. "Was that all?" he asked.

"Yeah," said Carrigan. "Except Weldon."

"Weldon?" said Allhoff. "I know that name. Utilities guy, isn't he? Worth dough."

"That's right. He's a fat bald-headed guy. Lousy with millions. I think he financed some of Hadley's deals."

"Why did he come along?"

"Just for the ride, I guess," said Carrigan. "Said he needed a rest. Wanted to get away from business."

Allhoff grunted again and proceeded to mark more hieroglyphics on his little pad. His manner irritated me.

"For Heaven's sake, Allhoff," I said. "What are you master-minding? Hadley was just that sort of a guy. He killed himself in a blaze of glory. Here, read the damned paper. It's obvious enough."

"Will you shut up," said Allhoff. "Go ahead, Carrigan. Tell me about last night."

I shrugged futilely. Allhoff was going moving-picture detective on me again.

"Well," said Carrigan, "a little after midnight everyone had gone to bed but Hadley and me. He told me to take the car and drive to town. Said he was going to work late on the book."

"What did he want in town?" asked Allhoff.

"A stamp and a package of razor blades."

"All right. What then?"

"I got a whole book of stamps out of a slot machine," said Carrigan slowly. "I got the razor blades. Then I went back. Hadley was typing like hell. He told me to go to bed. Said he'd have his book finished by morning. He seemed very pleased about it."

"So," said Allhoff, "you went to bed."

"I went to bed," said Carrigan. "Then the shot woke me. I jumped up, put on my bathrobe and raced into the library. Hadley had a hole in his skull and a gun in his hand."

"And the manuscript?"

"Was on the desk in front of him. The last chapter was written. Apparently, he had completed the book."

"Where is it now?"

Carrigan plucked the large manila envelope from under his arm. "Here," he said.

Allhoff took it and placed it on the desk. He nodded his head slowly and assumed an expression that he'd swiped from Warner Oland in the movies. I grinned at him.

"All right, Inspector," I said. "Who do I arrest?"

He didn't even yell at me, just held the pose of the master detective lost in thought.

"Listen," I said, nettled, to Carrigan. "Have you the slightest, foggiest reason for believing Hadley was murdered?"

Carrigan scratched his head. "Well, I'll tell you," he said slowly. "This may sound screwy to you, but I laid out my own dough for those stamps, for those razor blades. Hadley said he'd give it to me in the morning. He was awful fussy about little things like that. Whenever I laid out anything for him, he'd repay it to the penny. He never forgot. No matter how little it was."

I laughed in his face at that. "Screwy is the word," I said. "Old man Hadley, unofficially known as one of the biggest unindicted crooks that ever ran up a million bucks, postpones the most magnificent gesture of his life because he owes a big flatfoot a lousy thirty cents. Even you ought to get a laugh out of that, Allhoff."

Allhoff was staring at Carrigan. His little eyes gleamed as if there was a thought behind them that was forcing them out of their sockets. His thin nostrils quivered as he spoke.

"You're not as bright as you'd like to be, Symonds," he said. "Carrigan's right. Of course, he's got the wrong reason."

"If you're so damned superior," I snapped, "what's the right reason?"

"The razor blades," said Allhoff explosively. "Why in hell should a potential suicide be worrying about his beard?"

Carrigan sat upright in his chair. "Geez," he said. "I never thought of that."

"Listen," said Allhoff. "Did Hadley shave himself?"

"Yes," said Carrigan. "Either first thing in the morning or just before he went to bed at night."

Allhoff turned to me and bowed like Barrymore. "You see?" he said.

For a moment, I'd been startled. After a second's thought it seemed pretty thin.

"Wait a minute," I said. "Maybe he didn't want them for himself. Maybe he ordered them when he didn't know he was going to finish the book that night. Maybe—"

"Maybe you're a damned fool," said Allhoff. "Anyway, get out to that

Bayside house. See what you can see. Talk to everyone in the house. Look over Hadley's study carefully. Find me that stamp book. Look for that package of razor blades. See if one's missing. In the meantime, I'll look over this manuscript and ask Carrigan some questions."

"Listen," I said. "This is crazy. I—"

"Shut up," said Allhoff. "I'm thinking. Take Battersly with you."

I got up and walked to the door. "I don't know where Battersly is," I said testily.

"You know damned well where he is," said Allhoff. "He's downstairs in the corner saloon, drinking fifteen-cent rye and wishing to God that I had two legs."

I stood in the doorway and looked him in the eye. "Do you know what you are?" I said.

He grinned his mirthless, unholy grin at me. "Say it," he said. "Say it, and I'll have you fined a month's pay. Now what am I?"

I turned around and walked out of the room. I didn't say it until I was halfway down the stairs.

Allhoff was right again. Young Battersly was sitting at a table in Noonan's drinking straight rye. His black eyes were gloomy and morose. He paid no attention to me as I sat opposite him. He drained the drink and banged the empty glass on the table-top in signal for another.

I was looking at a beaten man. There was an air of utter hopelessness about him that gave me a vacant feeling at the pit of my stomach. The bartender brought him another drink. He gulped it like a man who was actually thirsty.

"Listen, kid," I said. "Why don't you quit?"

He shook his head miserably. "I can't quit," he said. "I can't."

"Why not?" I asked him. "I know it's a damn good job. Three thousand a year with a guaranteed pension's not bad at your age. But, hell, you're young. You can drive a truck or something. I wouldn't take the beating you take for ten times the money."

He lifted his head and looked at me with the eyes of an old man. "It's not the money, Sergeant," he said.

"My God!" I said. "What is it? Love?"

He shook his head again. "I'd quit in a minute if it was just the job," he said. "But it's not. It's more than that. I can't quit. See?" His expression was appealing—as if it were important that I understand him. "No matter what he does, no matter what he says, I got to take it. He's not altogether wrong. After all, what happened up there on West End Avenue was my fault. I got to pay for it. I got to stick with him till I can square it up."

"That's screwy," I told him. "How can you square up a thing like that?"

"You see?" he said. "I can't. That's just it. So I got to stay and take my beating."

He banged the empty glass on the table again.

"No," I said. "That's enough. We're going to Long Island. Allhoff's orders. Come on."

He sighed. "All right," he said. "Let's go."

He didn't ask where we were going or why. He didn't give a damn. He didn't give a damn about anything. He was completely licked. The trip to Bayside was like taking a train ride with a dead man.

Chapter 3

ALLHOFF SETS THE STAGE

IT WAS A LITTLE before two o'clock when Battersly and I got back to Allhoff's place. Carrigan drowsed in the chair where we had left him. Allhoff's dirty coffee pot was gurgling unenthusiastically, while Allhoff himself, still wearing his Charlie Chan expression, pored over the typewritten sheets of Hadley's biography. He had a pencil in his hand, and I noticed two pages that he had put to one side were annotated. He looked up when we came in.

"Well?" he said.

"Suicide," I said. "Cold."

"I don't want an opinion," he snapped. "Give me some facts."

"All right," I said. "I talked to everyone. They all swore that they were in bed when the shot was fired. I found out nothing that you probably haven't dug out of Carrigan by now. And if you're looking for a money motive, there isn't any."

"How do you know?"

"I talked to Rutledge, the secretary. He told me that Hadley's will provides him and Parks—that's the valet—with annuities. Autrey gets nothing. Apparently, he's got enough. Weldon gets nothing. The girl gets nothing. A Methodist charity gets it all. Maybe they killed him."

Allhoff ignored the last crack. He nodded his head slowly. "That's right enough about the will," he said. "I've already checked it with Hadley's lawyer. Had him on the phone. Where's that stamp book?"

I took it out of my pocket and handed it to him. "One stamp gone," I said. "He must have mailed a letter before he died—between the time Carrigan went to bed and when he shot himself."

"All right," said Allhoff. "What about the razor blades?"

"Well," I admitted, "the package had been opened. One blade had been used."

Allhoff pounded the desk. "I knew it!" he said explosively.

"I admit that's a point," I said. "But there are at least fifty things that might explain that. You can't go yelling murder just on that razor blade."

Allhoff waved his hand in the air like a hypnotist. "Shut up," he said. "I'm thinking. There's something screwy about this case. I can't just put my finger on it—but I feel it."

My God, he *felt* it! "Do you figure your psychic vibrations will name names?" I asked him.

He didn't even look at me. "Battersly," he said, "come here."

I threw up my hands and went to my desk. Battersly stood before Allhoff, avoiding his eyes.

"Now," said Allhoff, "what were you doing while Symonds was talking to all these people?"

"Well," said Battersly uneasily, "I was looking around. I—"

"What did you see?"

"Nothing much. When we got to the study, I found—"

"Wait a minute," said Allhoff. "Begin at the beginning. You're coming through the garden gate. There is a garden, isn't there? All right, you're coming through the gate. Start there. Tell me everything you saw and talk slowly."

I shook my head. Allhoff was getting positively infantile. I was certain he didn't have an idea in his head. He was simply trying to impress Carrigan.

Battersly screwed up his brow and concentrated.

"Well," he said at last, "there was the trees, and a car parked in the driveway. Then there was the birds. The birds squawking on the roof. Then there was—"

"What sort of birds?" asked Allhoff.

Battersly looked puzzled. "They was black," he said. "With sort of fan tails. They was making a hell of a noise."

"Chimney swallows," I said. "Maybe they killed Hadley."

Allhoff swung around in his chair and fixed me with his agate eyes. "Symonds," he said, "how'd you like to get back into uniform again and pound a beat in Staten Island?"

"It's been the dream of my life for more than two years," I said. "I'd love it. When do I start?"

He looked at me for a long time. Then that ugly smile split his lips. "I guess maybe you would," he said slowly. "So I suppose I'd better keep you here."

Battersly cleared his throat nervously. "Then," he went on, "we got to the porch—" He mumbled a lot more inconsequential detail, until at last Allhoff waved him to silence.

"That'll do," he said. "Now everybody keep quiet. I want to read some more."

Battersly crossed the room and sat down next to the window. Carrigan drowsed in his chair. I just sat there and got more and more irritated at Allhoff. I knew that he had an exaggerated opinion of his own mentality, that he delighted in acting the aloof and superior sleuth. But I'd never seen him go this far. He was playing it to the hilt today.

He made another mark on the manuscript with his pencil, lifted his head. "Carrigan," he said, "I want you to go out to Long Island. Stop in at the precinct house in Bayside and get a couple of men. I'll have the commissioner O.K. it. Bring everyone in the Hadley house here—to me. Now how long will it take you?"

Carrigan looked at his watch. "About two hours."

"All right. Get going."

Carrigan dragged his bulk out of the chair and waddled through the door.

"Allhoff," I said, "what are you trying to do? Hadley killed himself. You're arguing that he didn't merely because he happened to shave himself first. That'd be fine in a movie but it won't sound so good in the Grand Jury Room."

Allhoff picked up two pages of Hadley's book. "Look," he said. "I've picked out two very interesting spots in Hadley's life. Undoubtedly there are others."

"So what?" I said.

"First," said Allhoff, "it seems that years ago when Hadley was living on a ranch out West, he had a buggy accident. It broke his arm in two places. His right arm was shorter than his left all his life. The accident occurred while he was driving with a girl out in the country. The horse bolted when the whiffletree broke, releasing the surcingle."

"Allhoff," I said. "Why don't you stop? You've got no case and you know it. You're going to look like an awful fool when those people get here."

He ignored me. "The other item," he went on blandly, "was that Hadley went to the Senate once—in Nineteen Eight."

"Everybody knows that," I told him. "It's in all the papers this morning."

"He was elected by a plurality of the voters," said Allhoff. "That's what it says here."

"Well," I said, "how do you think a guy gets into the Senate. By buying a ticket?"

Allhoff looked at me and there was mockery in his gaze. He poured himself another cup of coffee.

"I suppose your mentality is typical of that in the Detective Bureau," he said, "so I shouldn't complain. You and Battersly go down and get some lunch. Hurry back. I'll need you."

"Delighted to get away even for a half-hour," I said. "Come on, kid."

Battersly and I walked to the door.

"You want us to bring you back a sandwich?" I called to Allhoff.

"Well," he said, deliberating, "I guess you'd better. Combination on rye. I don't feel like walking down the stairs myself. I don't—"

"All right," I said hastily. "All right. Come on, Battersly."

I took his arm and got him out of the room before Allhoff could elaborate on that theme.

When Battersly and I got back from lunch, we found Allhoff squinting through the barrel of a thirty-eight. He paid no attention to us. He lowered it and ran an oily rag over its blue steel. Battersly, as usual, did not speak. He walked across the room and stared with dark miserable eyes into Centre Street. I stared at Allhoff.

"What the hell are you doing there?" I asked.

He put the gun down and smiled unpleasantly. He unwrapped the sandwich I had laid on his desk and poured out some coffee.

"I'm strolling down the Boardwalk at Atlantic City," he said bitterly. "Occasionally, I'm breaking into a run. Sometimes, I skip gaily. Then—"

"Damn you!" I said. "Will you stop that?"

He glared up at me. "Well, what the hell do you think I'm doing? I'm cleaning a gun."

"For what?"

Allhoff bit into the sandwich, sipped the foul black brew from the chipped cup. That unholy gloating smile that I hated crawled over his face. He put down the cup.

"For two reasons," he said. "The first is that I expect to meet up with a murderer."

"You're pretty smug about it," I told him. "What's the other reason?"

"Stick around," said Allhoff. "You might find out."

I shrugged my shoulders and went over to my desk, Battersly still stared out the window. His lips were compressed and white. He hadn't missed that crack about the Boardwalk.

"Say," said Allhoff. "Got any carbon paper?"

I opened the desk drawer and took out a fresh package. Allhoff shook his head.

"Not that," he said. "I mean some that's been used."

"What sort of a tangent are you off on now?" I asked. "There's some in the waste basket if you want that."

"I want that," said Allhoff. "Give me all you've got."

I took a handful of smudged carbon paper from the basket and dropped it on his desk. I stood there, looking inquiringly at him for a moment. He didn't say anything. He opened the top drawer of his desk and took out the stamp book I had found at Hadley's place. Deliberately, he tore all the stamps from the book and thrust them in his vest pocket. He placed the empty book on the desk near the carbon paper.

Now he opened another drawer and took from it Hadley's manuscript. This, he also laid on the desk-top.

"That's one hell of an imposing array for the customers," I said. "All the exhibits of the case, plus a nicely cleaned thirty-eight and a diseased coffee pot."

I thought he'd growl at that, but he didn't.

"Battersly," he said. "Come here."

Battersly left the window, crossed the room and stood at my side. Allhoff looked at his watch.

"That mob'll be here with Carrigan any minute now," said Allhoff. "Now get this, both of you. I want you two guys in the bedroom there. Close the door and stay there. If curiosity overcomes your discretion, there are enough cracks in that panel for you to peep through. But no matter what happens, stay in there until I call you. Understand?"

"Yes, sir," said Battersly stiffly.

I grunted. Allhoff was being spectacular, superior and mysterious.

"What sort of voodoo is this?" I said.

"Shut up," he snapped. "If you had my brains, you might have my rank. I got where I am with my head. Despite the fact I have no—"

My God, here it was again. "All right," I said. "Anything you say. Come on, Battersly."

We went into the disreputable bedroom. I closed the door, selected a slanting crack that split the upper panel. I glued my eye to it.

In the other room, Allhoff carefully arranged the display on his desk. He pushed the thirty-eight to its edge and grouped the other exhibits in front of him. He drained the coffee cup again, and refilled it. It seemed to me that he looked even smugger than usual. There was a nasty sardonic glitter in his little eyes.

I had no idea what he was up to, but frankly, I considered that he was overplaying the hand. Whatever suspicion had crawled into his hateful mind, it was certain he had no evidence. If he had, he would order an arrest and dispense with all this mumbo-jumbo.

Battersly moved up beside me and put his face against the door. From below I heard the sound of scuffling footsteps on the creaking stairs.

"They're coming," I whispered. "I'd like to know what in hell he's going to say to them."

Battersly made a bitter sneering sound in his throat. "Probably going to tell 'em how he lost his legs," he said.

Chapter 4

"A BIRD TOLD ME"

TWO PLAINCLOTHESMEN USHERED IN the menage from Bayside. Paul Autrey, tall, slim and red-headed, entered first with Hadley's daughter, Nina, on his arm. Nina was thirty and brunette. Her face was pale, and her dark eyes sunken deep into her white cheeks. Rutledge and Parks came next. They wore the worried furtive air peculiar to the white-collar class when trouble arrives. Weldon, fat and well-to-do, brought up the rear with Carrigan.

Carrigan nodded to Allhoff who paid no attention to him. Carrigan's neck didn't get red this time. He was getting used to Allhoff. Weldon, on the other hand, was frankly hostile. He stood before Allhoff's desk and stared wonderingly around the shabby room. When his eyes fell on that filthy coffee pot he turned to one of the plainclothesmen.

"What's this?" he demanded testily. "Why have we been brought here? I understood that we were to go to headquarters. I—"

"Shut up," said Allhoff.

Weldon stared at him in utter amazement. Probably no one had told him to shut up for forty years. He made a little hissing sound as he exhaled. At the moment he was beyond speech.

"Sit down," said Allhoff. "Sit down, all of you. Carrigan, drag up some chairs."

Carrigan gathered up the furniture. They all sat down save Weldon who still stood there, his blue eyes blinking. He hadn't quite recovered yet. Allhoff waved a dismissing hand at the two dicks.

"You guys get out."

The dicks exchanged a dubious glance.

"But, Inspector," said one of them, "we ought to stay here. Our orders were—"

"Get out," said Allhoff. "Get out or I'll kick you out." He grinned ghoulishly and raised his voice. He wanted to be sure Battersly heard him on our side of the door. "That's a hot one. Isn't it? I'll kick you out."

I heard a crazy choking sob in Battersly's throat. On the other side of the door, Weldon had recovered.

"See here," he said angrily. "Why have we been brought here? Who are you? I'm damned if I see why all this fuss is being made, anyway. Hadley was a clear suicide. It was a grandiloquent gesture characteristic of the man. My God, he made that lucid enough in his manuscript."

Allhoff gave him his grade-A, first-class, nasty look. "Sit down," he said. "Sit down and shut up. That's all I'm asking of you for the moment."

But Weldon didn't sit down. He flushed and glowered at Allhoff. "I refuse to stay here. I refuse to be insulted. I'm leaving."

Allhoff grinned unpleasantly. "The hell you are," he said. "Try it and I'll have you held as a material witness."

Weldon sniffed and remained standing. Autrey frowned. But it was Nina Autrey who spoke.

"A material witness to what?" she asked in a thin tremulous voice.

"Murder," said Allhoff quietly.

Weldon sat down. Rutledge and Parks exchanged a nervous look. Nina Autrey clutched her husband's arm more tightly. There was a taut dramatic silence in the room, and I knew from Allhoff's expression he was loving it. But it still baffled me. I knew damned well he didn't have anything. Yet there was an inexplicable confidence about him.

"May I say something," said Autrey politely. "It seems apparent to everyone, including the Bayside police, that my father-in-law killed himself. Why do you say it was murder?"

Allhoff showed his teeth. "A little bird told me," he said.

"Will you stop clowning?" snapped Weldon.

"I'm not clowning," said Allhoff. "I repeat, a bird told me. And I'll know more when my messenger arrives from Buckley and Nunn."

"Buckley and Nunn," repeated Weldon. "You mean the publishers?"

"Hadley's publishers," said Allhoff. "And while we're waiting, I'd like to check on one point. Sergeant Carrigan told me this afternoon that none of you has ever read Hadley's manuscript, that he even refused to show it to his secretary. Is that right?"

I screwed up my brow and pushed my eye closer to the crack in the door. In the other room, Allhoff's inquiring gaze swept the faces of the visitors. Each of them in turn denied ever having seen the contents of Hadley's manuscript.

"Wait a minute," said Autrey. "What about this messenger from Buckley and Nunn?"

"What about that damned bird?" said Weldon. "What did you mean when you said a bird told you Hadley had been murdered?"

Allhoff sighed. "Well," he said, "while we're waiting, I may as well tell you about it."

"Tell me anything you like," snapped Weldon. "You'll never convince me Hadley was killed."

"No?" said Allhoff quietly. "The best authorities hold to the belief that beards are practically *de rigueur* in Heaven."

De rigueur? Well, I thought, he certainly is hitting on all six now, and where in hell did he ever pick that up?

"And yet," he went on leaning forward and glowering at Weldon. "Hadley shaved within an hour of his death."

"He'd been shaving himself at night regularly for years," put in Autrey. "Probably habit, that's all. There was no reason for anyone to kill him."

"What about the dough Rutledge and Parks get under his will?" asked Allhoff.

Parks squirmed in his chair. Rutledge opened his mouth and said nervously: "Mr. Hadley always shaved himself, Inspector. I assure you that Parks and myself—"

"Never mind," said Allhoff. "That's just a reason. It isn't the real reason."

"You needn't be so damned mysterious about it," said Weldon. "What the devil are you driving at?"

"This," said Allhoff. He lifted up the empty stamp book and the crumpled carbon paper. "See this?"

"What about it?" said Autrey.

"In a few minutes we'll know very definitely," said Allhoff. "As soon as Hadley's manuscript gets here from the publisher."

Nina Autrey uttered a little gasp. Carrigan stirred uneasily in his chair, then came out of his lethargy.

"What's it all about, Inspector?" he asked plaintively. "That's the Hadley script on your desk there."

"The hell it is," said Allhoff.

I moved back from my peep-hole and wiped my head with a handkerchief. "What, in the name of God," I demanded of Battersly, "is he doing now? He's had that script all day. What does he mean, it's not Hadley's?"

Battersly shrugged his shoulders. "I don't know what he's doing," he said. "But whatever it is, I hope he falls flat on his ugly face before he's through."

That was a sentiment I shared, but I kept my mouth shut and returned to my peep-hole.

"Now look here," Allhoff was saying. "I'll tell you why Hadley was killed. He was killed because of the sensational disclosures in his book—disclosures which would harm someone else." He picked up the thick manuscript from his desk. "This thing's as phoney as a Tammany magistrate."

"But—" Carrigan began, frowning.

"Shut up," said Allhoff. "I'm telling you what happened. The killer knew what was in that manuscript. He walked into Hadley's study last night. He shot Hadley through the head. He thrust the gun into the dead man's hand. He snatched the genuine manuscript from Hadley's desk and left this one in its place. He got back to bed before Carrigan arrived from his room on the lower floor."

It seemed to me that Nina Autrey's face was whiter than before. Parks shifted nervously in his seat.

Weldon cleared his throat. "How do you know that?" he asked in a matter-of-fact tone.

"First," said Allhoff, "there were the birds. Four chimney swallows were fluttering around on the roof of the Bayside house this morning. They were chattering frantically. That's an act chimney swallows usually resort to when their nest has been destroyed."

A little light began to seep into my brain. Apparently Weldon hadn't seen it yet.

"What's that got to do with it?" he asked.

"Well," said Allhoff, "it started me to thinking. The simplest explanation of anything that destroys the nest of a chimney swallow is that a fire has been lighted in the furnace. And if someone lit a fire in mid-July, it argues he was burning something."

Autrey laughed at that. It sounded as weak as the razor blades to me, personally.

"So," said Autrey, and it seemed to me that there was an undercurrent of relief in his tone, "someone was burning the original script, eh? That smoked out the birds. What are you going to do, Inspector? Put the swallows on the stand? The D.A.'ll have hysterics when you hand him this case."

I expected Allhoff to blow up then. He didn't like people who used mocking tones with him. He considered sarcasm strictly his own prerogative. However, he remained amazingly calm.

"Yes," he said with suspicious amiability, "I dare say he would if that was all I had to give him. But it isn't." He looked benignly around the room. "Whichever one of you mugs killed Hadley," he went on, "overlooked something that was right under your nose."

There was an aching silence then. I could hear Battersly's stertorous breathing in my ear, feel him tense beside me.

"Yeah," continued Allhoff. "You overlooked this." He lifted the empty stamp book and the carbon paper again. "You burned the original of Hadley's book all right. But it didn't occur to you that he had made a carbon copy. Carrigan bought Hadley a book of stamps early in the evening. This is the book and it's empty. My men salvaged this used carbon paper out of the basket in the study. After that it was a cinch. Undoubtedly, there was a copy, I reasoned from the carbon paper. Then the missing stamps indicated that Hadley had probably mailed it late on the night that he was killed. I phoned the publishers. The script had arrived in the afternoon mail. They hadn't even opened it. It's on its way over here now."

"And what," said Weldon, "do you expect to demonstrate with it?"

"Murder," said Allhoff. "The killer planned it all very neatly. He had some hack writer knock out this innocuous purported biography of Hadley. He stuck in that ingenious suicide paragraph at the end. What Hadley had written in the genuine script will undoubtedly incriminate the man who killed him. After that it should be easy enough to ferret out the hack who wrote it. His testimony'll clinch it."

"And," said Weldon, "suppose the script that the publishers send over is an exact copy of the one on your desk now."

Allhoff smiled thinly. "Then I shall feel like a damn fool," he said.

Again brooding silence fell over the room. What Allhoff had said sounded glib enough to me—too damn glib. It was smooth, logical, but still it seemed that there was something screwy about it somewhere.

"Say," whispered Battersly, "what's he talking about? He tore those stamps out of the book himself, didn't he? There was only one missing when we picked it up."

"Yeah. And that carbon paper came out of my own waste-paper basket, only half an hour ago."

"He's pulling a crazy bluff," said Battersly. "I don't know what it's all about, but he's going to look like an awful fool before it's over."

It certainly looked that way to me, too.

Chapter 5

WITHOUT LEG TO STAND ON

I PEEPED THROUGH the crack again. Allhoff was calmly pouring himself a cup of coffee. The others stared at him expectantly.

Knuckles cracked against the outer door. "Come in," said Allhoff.

A messenger boy walked in, carrying a thick brown envelope. "Inspector Allhoff?" he asked.

"Right," said Allhoff. "Give it to me."

He signed for the package, waved the kid away without tipping him. The kid slammed the door angrily and clattered down the stairs. Allhoff sighed and opened the envelope.

"This is the genuine manuscript," he announced. "You people will have to wait here while I read it."

There was a crackling silence for a moment, then Paul Autrey said: "Put up your hands!"

He had leaped from his chair as if catapulted by a steel spring. He snatched the blue thirty-eight that lay on Allhoff's desk, put his back against the wall and faced them all. The gun's sights drew a bead in the general direction of Allhoff's heart.

"God!" said Battersly. His hand jerked out to the knob of the door.

I remembered Allhoff's instructions. "Wait a minute," I whispered. "I don't think he's finished yet."

Battersly relaxed.

From the other room came the sound of Autrey's voice, tremulous, but determined. "I'm getting out of here, Inspector," he said. "Give me the key to this door. I'll lock it on the outside. That'll give me a five-minute start."

"Paul!" cried Nina Autrey. "For heaven's sake, Paul—" A sob shattered the words in her throat. She covered her face with her hands.

Allhoff unleashed one of his ghastly grins. "Changed your mind about the case I'll hand the D. A., Autrey?" he said mockingly.

Autrey, pale and grim, nodded. His calm, however, was the calm of utter desperation.

"I've changed it," he said. "You'll find it in the script. The complete story of how Hadley and I put the Juggers Company out of business four years ago. There's a murder rap attached to it. Hadley didn't care. He wouldn't have lived a year. Cancer. But I was damned if I was going to let him kill me, too. You called it right, Inspector. I had that phoney book written from facts that I supplied. But I'm not done yet. Give me that key."

Battersly strained beneath my grip. "We got to go in now," he said.

"Wait a minute," I told him.

"Give me that key," said Autrey again.

Allhoff shook his head. "I'm a policeman, Autrey," he said. "I'll give you no key. Instead, I'll give you—"

He jerked open his desk drawer with swift movement. Autrey saw the revolver there.

"Stop that!" he yelled. "Stop it, damn you! I'll—"

The thirty-eight in his hand jerked convulsively. Battersly swore as I let go his arm. He burst through the door like a battering ram, hurled himself across the room and flung his arms around Autrey's legs. The pair of them fell to the floor together.

I heard Nina Autrey scream. I saw her keel over in her chair in a dead faint. Weldon shouted an alarm. Carrigan sprang from his chair and groped for his gun. I raced across the room to Allhoff, but even as I did so, even with all this crazed excitement about me, I felt there was something wrong somewhere.

I put my hand on Allhoff's shoulder. "Are you all right?" I asked him. "Are you hurt?"

Allhoff reached for the coffee pot. "I'm O. K.," he said. I noticed that there was a little tremor of excitement in his voice.

Battersly was on his feet now. He had wrenched the thirty-eight from Autrey's fingers. He held the collar of Autrey's suit with his left hand. Rutledge and Parks had risen, were standing white-faced by their chairs. Weldon knelt at Nina Autrey's side, fanning her futilely with a handkerchief.

"Carrigan," said Allhoff, "take Autrey across the street. Have him booked for murder. I'll sign the complaint later."

"My God," said Carrigan slowly. He crossed the room and touched Autrey's arm. "Come along, Mr. Autrey."

He took his prisoner out the door. I lit a cigar and tried to think. I still had that damnable sensation of trying to recall something which had registered on my brain during that crazy ten seconds of bedlam.

Allhoff lifted his coffee cup and looked around the room.

"Get those people out of here," he said to Battersly. "Get 'em out."

Weldon, with the aid of Rutledge, dragged Nina Autrey to her feet. Battersly ushered them, with Parks, toward the door. I looked at Allhoff. He was beaming like a stock-company juvenile.

"Well," he said, sneeringly triumphant, "what did you think of that? I swung it, didn't I? Brains is what it took. Brains and cast-iron nerve. I—"

"I still don't get it," I said.

"It was simple enough," said Allhoff with a smirk that indicated it wasn't simple at all. "Those damned chimney swallows did give me the idea. Then, while reading this phoney script, I noticed those boners about the breaking surcingle and the Senatorial election."

"Listen," I said. "I admit you have a great mind. I grant you're God's own personal gift to the police department. And now will you come down to earth. Talk in one-syllable words and try to remember that I'm only mortal."

If I thought that would puncture him, I was wrong. His beam grew broader.

"All right," he said as if he really believed me. "First, take the surcingle. A surcingle is the girth strap that holds on the saddle. This hack writer of Autrey's had it confused with the trace. Hadley, who'd been born on a farm, would never have made a mistake like that. Of course, the error about the Senate was even worse than that."

"How so?" I asked.

"Hadley was senator in Nineteen Eight," said Allhoff. "Well, they didn't elect senators then. They were appointed by the State Legislatures. So that little paragraph about the popular vote and the electorate was ridiculous. Hadley never could have written that."

"All right," I said. "Keep talking."

"So," said Allhoff, "first, I decided the script was phoney. Then those birds gave me the idea that Hadley had been murdered, a switch made, and later the original manuscript had been destroyed. I thought if I could convince the killer that the publishers already had a copy of the book, he'd crack. I called Buckley and Nunn. As a matter of fact they had received a letter from Hadley—that's what he used that single stamp for. He told them he'd send the book along in a day or so. Then I arranged with them to send me over an envelope filled with blank paper by messenger. It arrived at a critical moment. And by God did I put it over? Boy, this'll kill the commissioner. It's a great day for me, Symonds."

"It's a great day for me, too," said Battersly.

I looked up at him surprised. There was a buoyant note in his voice that had never been there before. Allhoff's beam fell from him like a plummet. He scowled as he met Battersly's eye.

"What are you grinning about?" he demanded. "Anyone'd think you solved this murder."

Battersly laughed. I gave a little start. Then I realized that it was because I had never, in two long years, heard Battersly laugh before.

"In five minutes," said Battersly happily. "I'm writing out my resignation from the Police Department. I can do it now."

"What do you mean you can do it now?" asked Allhoff.

"I'm free," said Battersly simply. "You sent a man to prison today, Inspector. But you also let me out of a darker cell—one that I've been in for three damnable years."

Allhoff's death's-head grin spread itself over his thin lips. His little eyes glowed red.

"Do you mind telling me what in God's name you're talking about?"

"Sure," said Battersly. "Once I cost you your legs. I swore to myself I'd stick with you here until I squared it up. It didn't seem possible until today. But I did it. I just saved your life, Inspector. Autrey would have drilled you cold. We're even now and I'm through."

I was aware of a sudden elation. In the excitement of a moment ago, both Allhoff and myself had overlooked this point.

"Sure," I said. "Sure, Allhoff. The kid's right. He just saved your life. Autrey would have got you sure."

Allhoff nodded. "Sure," he said. "Sure."

I should have noticed his tone then. I should have remembered he was still wearing that grin, that he retained that wicked little flash in his eyes. But I wasn't paying much attention to Allhoff. I was too happy about Battersly. Besides I was still troubled about that crazy undefined stirring at the back of my memory.

I shook Battersly's hand. The brooding misery had gone out of his face. His eyes sparkled.

"I'm quitting tonight," he said. Then he added in a lower tone: "Thank God! Thank God!"

Allhoff laughed harshly. "Save your pious gratitude," he said. "You're not quitting."

We both looked at him. He wore that bitter sadistic expression which invariably accompanied his recital of the West End Avenue raid of three years ago.

"Now listen," said Allhoff, "you guys hate my guts. But that's no reason why you should think I'm a complete idiot."

Battersly stared at him. For some reason, I felt suddenly afraid.

"What now?" I said.

Now all his benignancy had completely vanished. There was frank hatred in his eyes as he glared at us.

"Do you think I'm fool enough to leave a loaded gun where a murderer could snatch it? A murderer that I had just sent to the chair? Do you think I'm fool enough to let a guy like Autrey blow my brains out?"

Then I got it. Then I knew what it was that had been bothering me. It was the sound of those shots Autrey had fired. They had made a flat crackling noise like a wet fire-cracker. It had not been the sharp staccato report of a thirty-eight.

My stomach was abruptly empty. I saw Battersly's hand tremble as he wiped it across his forehead.

"Wha-what do you mean?" he said.

"I put that gun there for Autrey to snatch. If he did it, it was a dead giveaway. It meant he'd actually read the original script when all of them had denied reading it. Furthermore, I figured he'd talk a trifle more freely, when he thought he could make a break for it. That thirty-eight was loaded with blanks. Are you such a lousy copper you can't tell the difference in sound between blank and ball ammunition. Hell, he fired two shots point-blank at me. Do you think I'm wearing bullet-proof underwear?"

Battersly's face was a dirty muddy gray. "You're lying," he said without conviction. "You're just saying that because I saved your life."

"All right," said Allhoff. "Have it your way. The gun was loaded with dumdums. He fired point-blank at my chest and I'm now in the morgue while the commissioner consults the records to see where the body goes."

Battersly's face was almost green now. There was moisture in his eyes. Allhoff took up the thirty-eight and swung the cylinder out. He took out three cartridge cases. There were no bullets in them.

Battersly stared at him for a moment. His facial muscles twitched palely. His eyes were blank and empty. In that instant I saw a man die as surely as if a bullet had pierced his heart. His lips moved slowly and a single short ugly word fell from them. He turned abruptly and walked out the door. Allhoff's savage laughter echoed in his ears.

I felt suddenly sick. I turned to Allhoff. Hateful words welled up inside me. I met his hard gaze, saw his bitter brittle lips. Then I knew that there were no words in all the world that could ever change him. I swung around and headed out for Noonan's.

Halfway down the stairs, I saw Battersly standing by the little window on the second landing. His back was toward me and his face was buried in his arms, against the windowsill. His shoulders moved convulsively, and I heard the horrible sound of a grown man sobbing. I raised my hand to touch his shoulder. I wanted to talk to him, to offer him what comfort I could.

But I forbore. I turned quietly and went on down to Centre Street. I felt like a weak-kneed coward, but I knew I never could have borne the look in his eyes had he turned around.

The Lady in the Lake

RAYMOND CHANDLER

Chapter 1

NOT FOR MISSING PERSONS

I WAS BREAKING a new pair of shoes in on my desk that morning when Violets M'Gee called me up. It was a dull hot damp August day and you couldn't keep your neck dry with a bath towel.

"How's the boy?" Violets began, as usual. "No business in a week, huh? There's a guy named Howard Melton over in the Avenant Building lost track of his wife. He's district manager for the Doreme Cosmetic Company. He don't want to give it to Missing Persons for some reason. The boss knows him a little. Better get over there, and take your shoes off before you go in. It's a pretty snooty outfit."

Violets M'Gee is a homicide dick in the sheriff's office, and if it wasn't for all the charity jobs he gives me, I might be able to make a living. This looked a little different, so I put my feet on the floor and swabbed the back of my neck again and went over there.

The Avenant Building is on Olive near Sixth and has a black-and-white rubber sidewalk out in front. The elevator girls wear gray silk Russian blouses and the kind of flop-over berets artists used to wear to keep the paint out of their hair. The Doreme Cosmetic Company was on the seventh floor and had a good piece of it. There was a big glass-walled reception room with flowers and Persian rugs and bits of nutty sculpture in glazed ware. A neat little blonde sat at a built-in switchboard off in the corner, out of harm's way. They had a receptionist at a big desk with flowers on it and a tilted sign reading: *MISS VAN DE GRAAF.* She wore Harold Lloyd cheaters and her hair was dragged back to where her forehead looked high enough to have snow on it.

She said Mr. Howard Melton was in conference, but she would take my card in to him when she had an opportunity, and what was my business, please? I said I didn't have a card, but the name was John Dalmas, from Mr. West.

"Who is Mr. West?" she inquired coldly. "Does Mr. Melton know him?"

"That's past me, sister. Not knowing Mr. Melton I would not know his friends."

"What is the nature of your business?"

"Personal."

"I see." She initialed three papers on her desk quickly, to keep from throwing her pen-set at me. I went and sat in a blue leather chair with chromium arms. It felt, looked, and smelled very much like a barber's chair.

In about half an hour a door opened beyond a bronze railing and two men came out backwards laughing. A third man held the door and echoed their laughter. They shook hands and the two men went away and the third man wiped the grin off his face in nothing flat and looked at Miss Van De Graaf. "Any calls?" he asked in a bossy voice.

She fluttered papers and said: "No, sir. A Mr.—Dalmas to see you—from a Mr.—West. His business is personal."

"Don't know him," the man barked. "I've got more insurance than I can pay for." He gave me a swift hard look and went into his room and slammed the door. Miss Van De Graaf smiled at me with delicate regret. I lit a cigarette and crossed my legs the other way. In another five minutes the door beyond the railing opened again and he came out with his hat on and sneered that he was going out for half an hour.

He came through a gate in the railing and started for the entrance and then did a nice cutback and came striding over to me. He stood looking down at me—a big man, two inches over six feet and built to proportion. He had a well massaged face that didn't hide the lines of dissipation. His eyes were black, hard, and tricky.

"You want to see me?"

I stood up, got out my billfold and gave him a card. He stared at the card and palmed it. His eyes became thoughtful.

"Who's Mr. West?"

"Search me."

He gave me a hard direct interested look. "You have the right idea," he said. "Let's go into my office."

The receptionist was so mad she was trying to initial three papers at once when we went past her through the railing.

The office beyond was long, dim, and quiet, but not cool. There was a large photo on the wall of a tough-looking old bird who had held lots of noses to lots of grindstones in his time. The big man went behind about eight hundred dollars' worth of desk and tilted himself back in a padded high-backed director's chair. He pushed a cigar humidor at me. I lit a cigar and he watched me light it with cool steady eyes.

"This is very confidential," he said.

"Uh-huh."

He read my card again and put it away in a gold-plated wallet. "Who sent you?"

"A friend in the sheriff's office."

"I'd have to know a little more about you than that."

I gave him a couple of names and numbers. He reached for his phone, asked for a line and dialed them himself. He got both the parties I had mentioned and talked. In four minutes he had hung up and tilted his chair again. We both wiped the backs of our necks.

"So far, so good," he said. "Now show me you're the man you say you are."

I got my billfold out and showed him a small photostat of my license. He seemed pleased. "How much do you charge?"

"Twenty-five bucks a day and expenses."

"That's too much. What is the nature of the expenses?"

"Gas and oil, maybe a bribe or two, meals and whiskey. Mostly whiskey."

"Don't you eat when you're not working?"

"Yeah—but not so well."

He grinned. His grin, like his eyes, had a stony cast to it. "I think maybe we'll get along," he said.

He opened a drawer and brought out a Scotch bottle. We had a drink. He put the bottle on the floor, wiped his lips, lit a monogrammed cigarette and inhaled comfortably. "Better make it fifteen a day," he said. "In times like these. And go easy on the liquor."

"I was just kidding you," I said. "A man you can't kid is a man you can't trust."

He grinned again. "It's a deal. First off though, your promise that in no circumstances you have anything to do with any cop friends you may happen to have."

"As long as you haven't murdered anybody it suits me."

He laughed. "Not yet. But I'm a pretty tough guy still. I want you to trace my wife and find out where she is and what she's doing, and without her knowing it.

"She disappeared eleven days ago—August twelfth,—from a cabin we have at Little Fawn Lake. That's a small lake owned by myself and two other men. It's three miles from Puma Point. Of course you know where that is."

"In the San Bernardino Mountains, about forty miles from San Bernardino."

"Yes." He flicked ash from his cigarette on the desk top and leaned over to blow it off. "Little Fawn Lake is only about three-eighths of a mile long. It has a small dam we built for real-estate development—just at the wrong time. There are four cabins up there. Mine, two belonging to my friends, neither of them occupied this summer, and a fourth on the near side of the lake as you come in. That one is occupied by a man named William Haines and his wife. He's a disabled veteran with a pension. He lives there rent free and looks after the place. My wife has been spending the summer up there and was to leave on the twelfth to come in to town for some social activity over the weekend. She never came."

I nodded. He opened a locked drawer and took out an envelope. He took a photo and a telegram from the envelope, and passed the telegram across the desk. It had been sent from El Paso, Texas, on August 15th at 9:18 A.M. It was addressed to Howard Melton, 715 Avenant Building, Los Angeles. It read—*Am crossing to get Mexican divorce. Will marry Lance. Good luck and good-bye. Julia.*

I put the yellow form down on the desk. "Julia is my wife's name," Melton said.

"Who's Lance?"

"Lancelot Goodwin. He used to be my confidential secretary up to a year ago. Then he came into some money and quit. I have known for a long time that he and Julia were a bit soft on each other, if I may put it that way."

"It's all right with me," I said.

He pushed the photo across the desk. It was a snapshot on glazed paper, showing a slim small blonde and a tall, lean, dark, handsome guy, about thirty-five, a shade too handsome. The blonde could have been anything from eighteen to forty. She was that type. She had a figure and didn't act stingy with it. She wore a swimsuit which didn't strain the imagination and the man wore trunks. They sat against a striped beach umbrella on the sand. I put the snapshot down on top of the telegram.

"That's all the exhibits," Melton said, "but not all the facts. Another drink?" He poured it and we drank it. He put the bottle down on the floor again and his telephone rang. He talked a moment, then jiggled the hook and told the operator to hold his calls for a while.

"So far there would be nothing much to it," he said. "But I met Lance Goodwin on the street last Friday. He said he hadn't seen Julia in months. I believed him, because Lance is a fellow without many inhibitions, and he doesn't scare. He'd be apt to tell me the truth about a thing like that. And I think he'll keep his mouth shut."

"Were there other fellows you thought of?"

"No. If there were any, I don't know them. My hunch is, Julia has been arrested and is in jail somewhere and has managed, by bribery or otherwise, to hide her identity."

"In jail for what?"

He hesitated a moment and then said very quietly: "Julia is a kleptomaniac. Not bad, and not all the time. Mostly when she is drinking too much. She has spells of that, too. Most of her tricks have been here in Los Angeles in the big stores where we have accounts. She's been caught a few times and been able to bluff out and have the stuff put on the bill. No scandal so far that I couldn't take care of. But in a strange town—" He stopped and frowned hard. "I have my job with the Doreme people to worry about," he said.

"She ever been printed?"

"How?"

"Had her fingerprints taken and filed?"

"Not that I know of." He looked worried at that.

"This Goodwin know about the sideline she worked?"

"I couldn't say. I hope not. He's never mentioned it, of course."

"I'd like his address."

"He's in the book. Has a bungalow over in the Chevy Chase district, near Glendale. Very secluded place. I've a hunch Lance is quite a chaser."

It looked like a very nice set-up, but I didn't say so out loud. I could see a little honest money coming my way for a change. "You've been up to this Little Fawn Lake since your wife disappeared, of course."

He looked surprised. "Well, no. I've had no reason to. Until I met Lance in front of the Athletic Club I supposed he and Julia were together some-where—perhaps even married already. Mexican divorces are quick."

"How about money? She have much with her?"

"I don't know. She has quite a lot of money of her own, inherited from her father. I guess she can get plenty of money."

"I see. How was she dressed—or would you know?"

He shook his head. "I hadn't seen her in two weeks. She wore rather dark clothes as a rule. Haines, this man up at the lake, might be able to tell you. I suppose he'll have to know she disappeared. I think he can be trusted to keep his mouth shut." Melton smiled wryly. "She had a small octagonal platinum wrist watch with a chain of large links. A birthday present. It had her name inside. She had a diamond and emerald ring and a plati-num wedding ring engraved inside: *Howard and Julia Melton. July 27th, 1926.*

"But you don't suspect foul play, do you?"

"No." His large cheekbones reddened a little. "I told you what I sus-pected."

"If she's in somebody's jailhouse, what do I do? Just report back and wait?"

"Of course. If she's not, keep her in sight until I can get there, wherever it is. I think I can handle the situation."

"Uh-huh. You look big enough. You said she left Little Fawn Lake on August twelfth. But you haven't been up there. You mean she did—or she was just supposed to—or you guess it from the date of the telegram?"

He hesitated, then nodded at me with approval. "Right. There's one more thing I forgot. She did leave on the twelfth. She never drove at night, so she drove down the mountain in the afternoon and stopped at the Olympia Hotel until train time. I know that because they called me up a week later and said her car was in their garage and did I want to call for it. I said I'd be over and get it when I had time."

"O.K. Mr. Melton. I think I'll run around and check over this Lancelot Goodwin a little first. He might happen not to have told you the truth."

He handed me the Other Cities phone book and I looked it up. Lancelot Goodwin lived at 3416 Chester Lane. I didn't know where that was, but I had a map in the car.

I said: "I'm going out there and snoop around. I'd better have a little money on account. Say a hundred bucks."

"Fifty should do to start," he said. He took out his gold-plated wallet and gave me two twenties and a ten. "I'll get you to sign a receipt—just as a matter of form."

He had a receipt book in his desk and wrote out what he wanted and I signed it. I put the two exhibits in my pocket and stood up. We shook hands.

I left him with the feeling that he was a guy who would not make many small mistakes, especially about money. As I went out the receptionist gave me the nasty eye. I worried about it almost as far as the elevator.

Chapter 2

THE SILENT HOUSE

M Y CAR WAS IN a lot across the street, so I took it north to Fifth and west to Flower and from there down to Glendale Boulevard and so on into Glendale. That made it about lunchtime, so I stopped and ate a sandwich.

Chevy Chase is a deep canyon in the foothills that separate Glendale from Pasadena. It is heavily wooded, and the streets branching off the main drag are apt to be pretty shut-in and dark. Chester Lane was one of them, and was dark enough to be in the middle of a redwood forest. Goodwin's house was at the deep end, a small English bungalow with a peaked roof and leaded windowpanes that wouldn't have let much light in, even if there had been any to let in. The house was set back in a fold of the hills, with a big oak tree practically on the front porch. It was a nice little place to have fun.

The garage at the side was shut up. I walked along a twisted path made of stepping-stones and pushed the bell. I could hear it ring somewhere in the rear with that sound bells seem to have in an empty house. I rang it twice more. Nobody came to the door. A mocking bird flew down on the small neat front lawn and poked a worm out of the sod and went away with it. Somebody started a car out of sight down the curve of the street. There was a brand-new house across the street with a *For Sale* sign stuck into the manure and grass seed in front of it. No other house was in sight.

I tried the bell one more time and did a snappy tattoo with the knocker, which was a ring held in the mouth of a lion. Then I left the front door and put an eye to the crack between the garage doors. There was a car in there, shining dimly in the faint light. I prowled around to the backyard and saw two more oak trees and a rubbish burner and three chairs around a green garden table under one of the trees. It looked so shady and cool and pleasant back there, I would have liked to stay. I went to the back door, which was half glass but had a spring lock. I tried knocking on it. I tried turning the knob, which was silly. It opened and I took a deep breath and walked in.

This Lancelot Goodwin ought to be willing to listen to a little reason, if he caught me. If he didn't, I wanted to glance around his effects. There was something about him—maybe just his first name—that worried me.

The back door opened on a porch with high narrow screens. From that another unlocked door, also with a spring lock, opened into a kitchen with gaudy tiles and an enclosed gas stove. There were a lot of empty bottles on the sink. There were two swing doors. I pushed the one towards the front of the house. It gave on an alcove dining-room with a buffet on which there were more liquor bottles, but not empty.

The living room was to my right under an arch. It was dark even in the middle of the day. It was nicely furnished, with built-in bookshelves and books that hadn't been bought in sets. There was a highboy radio in the corner, with a half-empty glass of amber fluid on top of it. And there was ice in the amber fluid. The radio made a faint humming sound and light glowed behind the dial. It was on, but the volume was down to nothing.

That was funny. I turned around and looked at the back corner of the room and saw something funnier.

A man was sitting in a deep brocade chair with slippered feet on a footstool that matched the chair. He wore an open-neck polo shirt and ice-cream pants and a white belt. His left hand rested easily on the wide arm of the chair and his right hand drooped languidly outside the other arm to the carpet, which was a solid dull rose. He was a lean, dark, handsome guy, rangily built. One of those lads who move fast and are much stronger than they look. His mouth was slightly open showing the edges of his teeth. His head was a little sideways, as though he had dozed off as he sat there, having himself a few drinks and listening to the radio.

There was a gun on the floor beside his right hand and there was a scorched red hole in the middle of his forehead.

Blood dripped very quietly from the end of his chin and fell on his white polo shirt.

For all of a minute—which in a spot like that can be as long as a chiropractor's thumb—I didn't move a muscle. If I drew a full breath, it was a secret. I just hung there, empty as a busted flush, and watched Mr. Lancelot Goodwin's blood form small pear-shaped globules on the end of his chin and then very slowly and casually drop and add themselves to the large patch of crimson that changed the whiteness of his polo shirt. It seemed to me that even in that time the blood dripped slower. I lifted a foot at last, dragged it out of the cement it was stuck in, took a step, and then hauled the other foot after it like a ball and chain. I moved across the dark and silent room.

His eyes glittered as I got close. I bent over to stare into them, to try and meet their look. It couldn't be done. It never can, with dead eyes. They are always pointed a little to one side or up or down. I touched his face. It was warm and slightly moist. That would be from his drink. He hadn't been dead more than twenty minutes.

I swung around hard, as if somebody were trying to sneak up behind me with a blackjack, but nobody was. The silence held. The room was full of it, brimming over with it. A bird chirped outdoors in a tree, but that only made the silence thicker. You could have cut slices of it and buttered them.

I started looking at other things in the room. There was a silver-framed photo lying on the floor, back up, in front of the plaster mantel. I went over and lifted it with a handkerchief and turned it. The glass was cracked neatly from corner to corner. The photo showed a slim light-haired lady with a dangerous smile. I took out the snapshot Howard Melton had given me and held it beside the photo. I was sure it was the same face, but the expression was different, and it was a very common type of face.

I took the photograph carefully into a nicely furnished bedroom and opened a drawer in a long-legged chest. I removed the photo from the frame, polished the frame off nicely with my handkerchief and tucked it under some shirts. Not very clever, but as clever as I felt.

Nothing seemed very pressing now. If the shot had been heard, and recognized as a shot, radio cops would have been there long ago. I took my photo into the bathroom and trimmed it close with my pocket knife and flushed the scraps down the toilet. I added the photo to what I had in my breast pocket and went back to the living room.

There was an empty glass on the low table beside the dead man's left hand. It would have his prints. On the other hand somebody else might have taken a sip out of it and left other prints. A woman of course. She would have been sitting on the arm of the chair, with a soft sweet smile on her face, and the gun down behind her back. It had to be a woman. A man couldn't have shot him in just that perfectly relaxed position. I gave a guess what woman it was—but I didn't like her leaving her photo on the floor. That was bad publicity.

I couldn't risk the glass. I wiped it off and did something I didn't enjoy. I made his hand hold it again, then put it back on the table. I did the same thing with the gun. When I let his hand fall—the trailing hand this time— it swung and swung, like a pendulum on a grandfather's clock. I went to the glass on the radio and wiped it off. That would make them think she was pretty wise, a different kind of woman altogether—if there are different kinds. I collected four cigarette stubs with lipstick about the shade called "carmeen," a blond shade. I took them to the bathroom and gave them to the city. I wiped off a few shiny fixtures with a towel, did the same for the front-door knob, and called it a day. I couldn't wipe over the whole damn house.

I stood and looked at Lancelot Goodwin a moment longer. The blood had stopped flowing. The last drop on his chin wasn't going to fall. It was going to hang there and get dark and shiny and as permanent as a wart.

I went back through the kitchen and porch, wiping a couple more doorknobs as I went, strolled around the side of the house and took a quick gander up and down the street. Nobody being in sight, I tied the job up with ribbon by ringing the front doorbell again and smearing the button and knob well while I did it. I went to my car, got in and drove away. This had all taken less than half an hour. I felt as if I had fought all the way through the Civil War.

Two thirds of the way back to town I stopped at the foot of Alesandro Street and tucked myself into a drugstore phone booth. I dialed Howard Melton's office number.

A chirpy voice said: "Doreme Cosmetic Company. Good afternoowun."

"Mr. Melton."

"I'll connect you with his secretary," sang the voice of the little blonde who had been off in the corner, out of harm's way.

"Miss Van De Graaf speaking." It was a nice drawl that could get charming or snooty with the change of a quartertone. "Who is calling Mr. Melton, please?"

"John Dalmas."

"Ah—does Mr. Melton know you, Mr.—ah—Dalmas?"

"Don't start that again," I said. "Ask him, girlie. I can get all the ritzing I need at the stamp window."

Her intaken breath almost hurt my eardrum.

There was a wait, a click, and Melton's burly businesslike voice said: "Yes? Melton talking. Yes?"

"I have to see you quick."

"What's that?" he barked.

"I said what you heard. There have been what the boys call developments. You know who you're talking to, don't you?"

"Oh—yes. Yes. Well, let me see. Let me look at my desk calendar."

"To hell with your desk calendar," I said. "This is serious. I have enough sense not to break in on your day, if it wasn't."

"Athletic Club—ten minutes," he said crisply. "Have me paged in the reading room."

"I'll be a little longer than that." I hung up before he could argue.

I was twenty minutes as a matter of fact.

The hop in the lobby of the Athletic Club scooted neatly into one of the old open-cage elevators they have there and was back in no time at all with a nod. He took me up to the fourth floor and showed me the reading room.

"Around to the left, sir."

The reading room was not built principally for reading. There were papers and magazines on a long mahogany table and leather bindings behind glass on the walls and a portrait of the club's founder in oil, with a hooded light over it. But mostly the place was little nooks and corners with enormous sloping high-backed leather chairs, and old boys snoozing in them peacefully, their faces violet with old age and high blood pressure.

I sneaked quietly around to the left. Melton sat there, in a private nook between shelves, with his back to the room, and the chair, high as it was, not high enough to hide his big dark head. He had another chair drawn up beside him. I slipped into it and gave him the eye.

"Keep your voice down," he said. "This place is for after-luncheon naps. Now what is it? When I employed you, it was to save me bother, not to add bother to what I already have."

"Yeah," I said, and put my face close to his. He smelled of highballs, but nicely. "She shot him."

His stiff eyebrows went up a little. His eyes got the stony look. His teeth clamped. He breathed softly and twisted one large hand on his knee and looked down at it.

"Go on," he said, in a voice the size of a marble.

I craned back over the top of the chair. The nearest old geezer was snoozling lightly and blowing the fuzz in his nostrils back and forth with each breath.

"I went out there to Goodwin's place. No answer. Tried the back door. Open. Walked in. Radio turned on, but muted. Two glasses with drinks.

Smashed photo on floor below mantel. Goodwin in chair shot dead at close range. Contact wound. Gun on floor by his right hand. Twenty-five automatic—a woman's gun. He sat there as if he had never known it. I wiped glasses, gun, doorknobs, put his prints where they should be, left."

Melton opened and shut his mouth. His teeth made a grating noise. He made fists of both hands. Then he looked at me steadily with hard black eyes.

"Photo," he said thickly.

I reached it out of my pocket and showed it to him, but I held on to it.

"Julia," he said. His breath made a queer sharp keening sound and his hand went limp. I slipped the photo back into my pocket. "What then?" he whispered.

"All. I may have been seen, but not going in or coming out. Trees in back. The place is well shaded. She have a gun like that?"

His head drooped and he held it in his hands. He held it still for a while, then pushed it up and spread his fingers on his face and spoke through them at the wall we were facing.

"Yes. But I never knew her to carry it. I suppose he ditched her, the dirty rat." He said it quietly without heat.

"You're quite a guy," he said. "It's a suicide now, eh?"

"Can't tell. Without a suspect they're apt to handle it that way. They'll test his hand with paraffin to see if he fired the gun. That's routine now. But it sometimes doesn't work, and without a suspect they may let it ride anyway. I don't get the photo angle."

"I don't either," he whispered, still talking between his fingers. "She must have got panicked up very suddenly."

"Uh-huh. You realize I've put my head in a bag, don't you? It's my license if I'm caught. Of course there's a bare chance it was suicide. But he doesn't seem the type. You've got to play ball, Melton."

He laughed grimly. Then he turned his head enough to look at me, but still kept his hands on his face. The gleam of his eyes shot through his fingers.

"Why did you fix it up?" he asked quietly.

"Damned if I know. I guess I took a dislike to him—from that photo. He didn't look worth what they'd do to her—and to you."

"Five hundred, as a bonus," he said.

I leaned back and gave him a stony stare. "I'm not trying to pressure you. I'm a fairly tough guy—but not in spots like this. Did you give me everything you had?"

He said nothing for a long minute. He stood up and looked along the room, put his hands in his pockets, jingled something, and sat down again.

"That's the wrong approach—both ways," he said. "I wasn't thinking of blackmail—or offering to pay it. It isn't enough money. These are hard times. You take an extra risk, I offer you an extra compensation. Suppose Julia had nothing to do with it. That might explain the photo being left. There were plenty of other women in Goodwin's life. But if the story comes out and I'm connected with it at all, the home offices will bounce me. I'm in a sensitive business, and it hasn't been doing too well. They might be glad of the excuse."

"That's different," I said. "I asked you, did you give me everything you had."

He looked at the floor. "No. I suppressed something. It didn't seem important then. And it hurts the position badly now. A few days ago, just after I met Goodwin downtown, the bank called me and said a Mr. Lancelot Goodwin was there to cash a check for one thousand dollars made out to cash by Julia Melton. I told them Mrs. Melton was out of town, but that I knew Mr. Goodwin very well and I saw no objection to cashing the check, if it was in order and he was properly identified. I couldn't say anything else—in the circumstances. I suppose they cashed it. I don't know."

"I thought Goodwin had dough."

Melton shrugged stiffly.

"A blackmailer of women, huh? And a sappy one at that, to be taking checks. I think I'll play with you on it, Melton. I hate like hell to see these newspaper ghouls go to town on a yarn like that. But if they get to you, I'm out—if I can get out."

He smiled for the first time. "I'll give you the five hundred right now," he said.

"Nothing doing. I'm hired to find her. If I find her, I get five hundred flat—all other bets off."

"You'll find me a good man to trust," he said.

"I want a note to this Haines up at your place at Little Fawn Lake. I want into your cabin. My only way to go at it is as if I'd never been to Chevy Chase."

He nodded and stood up. He went over to a desk and came back with a note on the club stationery.

Mr. William Haines
Little Fawn Lake

Dear Bill—
    Please allow bearer, Mr. John Dalmas, to view my cabin and assist him in all ways to look over the property.

                Sincerely,
                    Howard Melton

I folded the note and put it away with my other gatherings from the day. Melton put a hand on my shoulder. "I'll never forget this," he said. "Are you going up there now?"

"I think so."

"What do you expect to find?"

"Nothing. But I'd be a sap not to start where the trail starts."

"Of course. Haines is a good fellow, but a little surly. He has a pretty blond wife that rides him a lot. Good luck."

We shook hands. His hand felt clammy as a pickled fish.

Chapter 3

THE MAN WITH THE PEG LEG

I MADE SAN BERNARDINO in less than two hours and for once in its life it was almost as cool as Los Angeles, and not nearly so sticky. I took on a cup of coffee and bought a pint of rye and gassed up and started up the grade. It was overcast all the way to Bubbling Springs. Then it suddenly got dry and bright and cool air blew down the gorges, and I finally came to the big dam and looked along the level blue reaches of Puma Lake. Canoes paddled on it, and rowboats with outboard motors and speedboats churned up the water and made a lot of fuss over nothing. Jounced around in their wake, people who had paid two dollars for a fishing license wasted their time trying to catch a dime's worth of fish.

The road turned two ways from the dam. My way was the south shore. It skimmed along high among piled-up masses of granite. Hundred-foot yellow pines probed at the clear blue sky. In the open spaces grew bright green manzanita and what was left of the wild irises and white and purple lupine and bugle flowers and desert paint brush. The road dropped to the lake level and I began to pass flocks of camps and flocks of girls in shorts on bicycles, on moto-scooters, walking all over the highway, or just sitting under trees showing off their legs. I saw enough beef on the hoof to stock a cattle ranch.

Howard Melton had said to turn away from the lake at the old Redlands road, a mile short of Puma Point. It was a frayed asphalt ribbon that climbed into the surrounding mountains. Cabins were perched here and there on the slopes. The asphalt gave out and after a while a small narrow dirt road sneaked off to my right. A sign at its entrance said: *Private Road to Little Fawn Lake. No Trespassing.* I took it and crawled around big bare stones and past a little waterfall and through yellow pines and black oaks and silence. A squirrel sat on a branch and tore a fresh pine cone to pieces and sent the pieces fluttering down like confetti. He scolded at me and beat one paw angrily on the cone.

The narrow road swerved sharply around a big tree trunk and then there was a five-barred gate across it with another sign. This one said: *Private— No Admittance.*

I got out and opened the gate and drove through and closed it again. I wound through trees for another couple of hundred yards. Suddenly below me was a small oval lake that lay deep in trees and rocks and wild grass, like a drop of dew caught in a furled leaf. At the near end there was a yellow concrete dam with a rope handrail across the top and an old mill wheel at the side. Near that stood a small cabin of native wood covered with rough bark. It had two sheet-metal chimneys and smoke lisped from one of them. Somewhere an axe thudded.

Across the lake, the long way by the road and the short way over the dam, there was a large cabin close to the water and two others not so large, spaced at wide intervals. At the far end, opposite the dam, was what looked like a small pier and band pavilion. A warped wooden sign on it read: *Camp*

Kilkare. I couldn't see any sense in that, so I walked down a path to the bark-covered cabin and pounded on the door.

The sound of the axe stopped. A man's voice yelled from somewhere behind. I sat down on a big stone and rolled an unlit cigarette around in my fingers. The owner of the cabin came around its side with an axe in his hand. He was a thick-bodied man, not very tall, with a dark, rough, unshaven chin, steady brown eyes and grizzled hair that curled. He wore blue denim pants and a blue shirt open on a muscular brown neck. When he walked he seemed to give his right foot a little kick outwards with each step. It swung out from his body in a shallow arc. He walked slowly and came up to me, a cigarette dangling from his thick lips. He had a city voice.

"Yeah?"

"Mr. Haines?"

"That's me."

"I have a note for you." I took it out and gave it to him. He threw the axe to one side and looked squintingly at the note, then turned and went into the cabin. He came out wearing glasses, reading the note as he came.

"Oh yeah," he said. "From the boss." He studied the note again. "Mr. John Dalmas, huh? I'm Bill Haines. Glad to know you." We shook hands. He had a hand like a steel trap.

"You want to look around and see Melton's cabin, huh? What's the matter? He ain't selling, for God's sake?"

I lit my cigarette and flipped the match into the lake. "He has more than he needs here," I said.

"Land, sure. But it says the cabin—"

"He wanted me to look it over. It's a pretty nice cabin, he says."

He pointed. "That one over there, the big one. Milled redwood walls, celarex lined and then knotty pine inside. Composition shingle roof, stone foundations and porches, bathroom, shower and toilet. He's got a spring-filled reservoir back in the hill behind. I'll say it's a nice cabin."

I looked at the cabin, but I looked at Bill Haines more. His eyes had a glitter and there were pouches under his eyes, for all his weathered look.

"You wanta go over now? I'll get the keys."

"I'm kind of tired after the long drive up. I sure could use a drink, Haines."

He looked interested, but shook his head. "I'm sorry, Mr. Dalmas. I just finished up a quart." He licked his broad lips and smiled at me.

"What's the mill wheel for?"

"Movie stuff. They make a picture up here once in a while. That's another set down at the end. They made *Love Among the Pines* with that. The rest of the sets are tore down. I heard the picture flopped."

"Is that so? Would you join me in a drink?" I brought out my pint of rye.

"Never been heard to say no. Wait'll I get some glasses."

"Mrs. Haines away?"

He stared at me with sudden coldness. "Yeah," he said very slowly. "Why?"

"On account of the liquor."

He relaxed, but kept an eye on me for a moment longer. Then he turned and walked his stiff-legged walk back into the cabin. He came out with a couple of the little glasses they pack fancy cheese in. I opened my bottle and poured a couple of stiff ones and we sat holding them, Haines with his right leg almost straight out in front of him, the foot twisted a little outwards.

"I copped that in France," he said, and drank. "Old Pegleg Haines. Well, it got me a pension and it ain't hurt me with the ladies. Here's to crime." He finished his drink.

We set our glasses down and watched a bluejay go up a big pine, hopping from branch to branch without pausing to balance, like a man running upstairs.

"Cold and nice here, but lonely," Haines said. "Too damn lonely." He watched me with the corners of his eyes. He had something on his mind.

"Some people like that." I reached for the glasses and did my duty with them.

"Gets me. I been drinkin' too much account of it gets me. It gets me at night."

I didn't say anything. He put his second drink down in a swift hard gulp. I passed the bottle to him silently. He sipped his third drink, cocked his head on one side, and licked at his lip.

"Kind of funny what you said there—about Mrs. Haines bein' away."

"I just thought maybe we ought to take our bottle out of sight of the cabin."

"Uh-huh. You a friend of Melton's?"

"I know him. Not intimately."

Haines looked across at the big cabin. "That damn floozie!" he snarled suddenly, his face twisted.

I stared at him. "Lost me Beryl, the damn tart," he said bitterly. "Had to have even one-legged guys like me. Had to get me drunk and make me forget I had as cute a little wife as ever a guy had."

I waited, nerves taut.

"The hell with him, too! Leavin' that tramp up here all alone. I don't have to live in his goddam cabin. I can live anywheres I like. I got a pension. War pension."

"It's a nice place to live," I said. "Have a drink."

He did that, turned angry eyes on me. "It's a lousy place to live," he snarled. "When a guy's wife moves out on him and he don't know where she's at—maybe with some other guy." He clenched an iron left fist.

After a moment he unclenched it slowly and poured his glass half-full. The bottle was looking pretty peaked by this time. He put his big drink down in a lump.

"I don't know you from a mule's hind leg," he growled, "but what the hell? I'm sick of bein' alone. I been a sucker—but I ain't just human. She has looks—like Beryl. Same size, same hair, same walk as Beryl. Hell, they coulda been sisters. Only just enough different—if you get what I mean." He leered at me, a little drunk now.

I looked sympathetic.

"I'm over there to burn trash," he scowled, waving an arm. "She comes out on the back porch in pajamas like they was made of cellophane. With two drinks in her hands. Smiling at me, with them bedroom eyes. 'Have a drink, Bill.' Yeah. I had a drink. I had nineteen drinks. I guess you know what happened."

"It's happened to a lot of good men."

"Leaves her alone up here, the ———! While he plays around down in L.A. And Beryl walks out on me—two weeks come Friday."

I stiffened. I stiffened so hard that I could feel my muscles strain all over my body. Two weeks come Friday would be a week ago last Friday. That would be August twelfth—the day Mrs. Julia Melton was supposed to have left for El Paso, the day she had stopped over at the Olympia Hotel down at the foot of the mountains.

Haines put his empty glass down and reached into his buttoned shirt pocket. He passed me a dog-eared piece of paper. I unfolded it carefully. It was written in pencil.

I'd rather be dead than live with you any longer you lousy cheater—Beryl.

That was what it said.

"Wasn't the first time," Haines said, with a rough chuckle. "Just the first time I got caught." He laughed. Then he scowled again. I gave him back his note and he buttoned it up in the pocket. "What the hell am I tellin' you for?" he growled at me.

A bluejay scolded at a big speckled woodpecker and the woodpecker said, "Cr-racker!" just like a parrot.

"You're lonely," I said. "You need to get it off your chest. Have another drink. I've had my share. You were away that afternoon—when she left you?"

He nodded moodily and sat holding the bottle between his legs. "We had a spat and I drove on over to the north shore to a guy I know. I felt meaner than flea dirt. I had to get good and soused. I done that. I got home maybe two A.M.—plenty stinko. But I drive slow account of this trick pin. She's gone. Just the note left."

"That was a week ago last Friday, huh? And you haven't heard from her since?"

I was being a little too exact. He gave me a hard questioning glance, but it went away. He lifted the bottle and drank moodily and held it against the sun. "Boy, this is damn near a dead soldier," he said. "*She* scrammed too." He jerked a thumb towards the other side of the little lake.

"Maybe they had a fight."

"Maybe they went together."

He laughed raucously. "Mister, you don't know my little Beryl. She's a hell cat when she starts."

"Sounds as if they both are. Did Mrs. Haines have a car? I mean, you drove yours that day, didn't you?"

"We got two Fords. Mine has to have the foot throttle and brake pedal over on the left, under the good leg. She took her own."

I stood up and walked to the water and threw my cigarette stub into it. The water was dark blue and looked deep. The level was high from the spring flood and in a couple of places the water licked across the top of the dam.

I went back to Haines. He was draining the last of my whiskey down his throat. "Gotta get some more hooch," he said thickly. "Owe you a pint. You ain't drunk nothing."

"Plenty more where it came from," I said. "When you feel like it I'll go over and look at that cabin."

"Sure. We'll walk around the lake. You don't mind me soundin' off that way at you—about Beryl?"

"A guy sometimes has to talk his troubles to somebody," I said. "We could go across the dam. You wouldn't have to walk so far."

"Hell, no. I walk good, even if it don't look good. I ain't been around the lake in a month." He stood up and went into the cabin and came out with some keys. "Let's go."

We started towards the little wooden pier and pavilion at the far end of the lake. There was a path close to the water, winding in and out among big rough granite boulders. The dirt road was farther back and higher up. Haines walked slowly, kicking his right foot. He was moody, just drunk enough to be living in his own world. He hardly spoke. We reached the little pier and I walked out on it. Haines followed me, his foot thumping heavily on the planks. We reached the end, beyond the little open band pavilion, and leaned against a weathered dark-green railing.

"Any fish in here?" I asked.

"Sure. Rainbow trout, black bass. I ain't no fish eater myself. I guess there's too many of them."

I leaned out and looked down into the deep still water. There was a swirl down there and a greenish form moved under the pier. Haines leaned beside me. His eyes stared down into the depths of the water. The pier was solidly built and had an underwater flooring—wider than the pier itself—as if the lake had once been at a much lower level, and this underwater flooring had been a boat landing. A flat-bottomed boat dangled in the water on a frayed rope.

Haines took hold of my arm. I almost yelled. His fingers bit into my muscles like iron claws. I looked at him. He was bent over, staring like a loon, his face suddenly white and glistening. I looked down into the water.

Languidly, at the edge of the underwater flooring, something that looked vaguely like a human arm and hand in a dark sleeve waved out from under the submerged boarding, hesitated, waved back out of sight.

Haines straightened his body slowly and his eyes were suddenly sober and frightful. He turned from me without a word and walked back along the pier. He went to a pile of rocks and bent down and heaved. His panting breath came to me. He got a rock loose and his thick back straightened. He lifted the rock breast high. It must have weighed a hundred pounds. He walked steadily back out on the pier with it, game leg and all, reached the end railing and lifted the rock high above his head. He stood there a moment holding it, his neck muscles bulging above his blue shirt. His mouth made some vague distressful sound. Then his whole body gave a hard lurch and the big stone smashed down into the water.

It made a huge splash that went over both of us. It fell straight and true through the water and crashed on the edge of the submerged planking. The ripples widened swiftly and the water boiled. There was a dim sound of boards breaking under water. Waves rippled off into the distance and the water down there under our eyes began to clear. An old rotten plank suddenly popped up above the surface and sank back with a flat slap and floated off.

The depths cleared still more. In them something moved. It rose slowly, a long dark twisted something that rolled as it came up. It broke surface. I saw wool, sodden black now—a sweater, a pair of slacks. I saw shoes, and something that bulged shapeless and swollen over the edges of the shoes. I saw a wave of blond hair straighten out in the water and lie still for an instant.

The thing rolled then and an arm flapped in the water and the hand at the end of the arm was no decent human hand. The face came rolling up. A swollen, pulpy, gray-white mass of bloated flesh, without features, without eyes, without mouth. A thing that had once been a face. Haines looked down at it. Green stones showed below the neck that belonged to the face. Haines' right hand took hold of the railing and his knuckles went as white as snow under the hard brown skin.

"Beryl!" His voice seemed to come to me from a long way off, over a hill, through a thick growth of trees.

Chapter 4

THE LADY IN THE LAKE

A LARGE WHITE CARD in the window, printed in heavy block capitals, said: *Keep Tinchfield Constable.* Behind the window was a narrow counter with piles of dusty folders on it. The door was glass and lettered in black paint: *Chief of Police. Fire Chief. Town Constable. Chamber of Commerce. Enter.*

I entered and was in what was nothing but a small one-room pineboard shack with a potbellied stove in the corner, a littered rolltop desk, two hard chairs, and the counter. On the wall hung a large blueprint map of the district, a calendar, a thermometer. Beside the desk telephone numbers had been written laboriously on the wood in large deeply bitten figures.

A man sat tilted back at the desk in an antique swivel-chair, with a flat-brimmed Stetson on the back of his head and a huge spittoon beside his right foot. His large hairless hands were clasped comfortably on his stomach. He wore a pair of brown pants held by suspenders, a faded and much-washed tan shirt buttoned tight to his fat neck, no tie. What I could see of his hair was mousy brown except the temples, which were snow white. On his left breast there was a star. He sat more on his left hip than his right, because he wore a leather hip holster with a big black gun in it down inside his hip pocket.

I leaned on the counter and looked at him. He had large ears and friendly gray eyes and he looked as if a child could pick his pocket.

"Are you Mr. Tinchfield?"

"Yep. What can I do for you, son?"

"You're the law around here, I guess?"

"Yep. What law we got to have, I'm it—come election anyways. There's a couple good boys running against me and they might up and whip me." He sighed.

"Does your jurisdiction extend to Little Fawn Lake?"

"What was that, son?"

"Little Fawn Lake, back in the mountains. You cover that?"

"Yep. Guess I do. I'm deppity-sheriff. Wasn't no more room on the door." He eyed the door, without displeasure. "I'm all them things there. Melton's place, eh? Something botherin' there, son?"

"There's a dead woman in the lake."

"Well, I swan." He unclasped his hands and scratched his ear and stood up heavily. Standing up he was a big powerful man. His fat was just cheerfulness. "Dead, you said? Who is it?"

"Bill Haines—you know Bill Haines?"

"Yep. I know Bill." His voice hardened a little.

"It's Bill Haines' wife, Beryl. Looks like suicide. She's been in the water a long time, Sheriff. Not nice to look at. She left him ten days ago, he said. I guess that's when she did it."

Tinchfield bent over the spittoon and discharged a tangled mass of brown fiber into it. It fell with a soft plop. He worked his lips and wiped them with the back of his hand.

"Who are you, son?"

"My name is John Dalmas. I came up from Los Angeles with a note to Haines from Mr. Melton—to look at the property. Haines and I were walking around the lake and we went out on the little pier the movie people built there once. We saw something down in the water underneath. Haines threw a large rock in and the body came up. It's not nice to look at, Sheriff."

"Haines up there?"

"Yeah. I came down because he's pretty badly shaken."

"Ain't surprised at that, son." Tinchfield opened a drawer in his desk and took out a full pint of whiskey. He slipped it inside his shirt and buttoned the shirt again. "We'll get Doc Menzies," he said. "And Paul Loomis." He moved calmly around the end of the counter. The situation seemed to bother him slightly less than a fly.

We went out. Before going out he adjusted a clock card hanging inside the glass to read—*Back at 6 P.M.* He locked the door and got into a car that had a siren on it, two red spotlights, two amber foglights, a red-and-white fire plate, and various legends on the side which I didn't bother to read.

"You wait here, son. I'll be back in a frog squawk."

He swirled the car around in the street and went off down the road towards the lake and pulled up at a frame building opposite the stage depot. He went into this and came out with a tall thin man. The car came slowly swirling back and I fell in behind it. We went through the village, dodging girls in shorts and men in trunks, shorts and pants, most of them naked and brown from the waist up. Tinchfield stood on his horn, but didn't use his siren. That would have started a mob of cars after him. We went up a dusty hill and stopped at a cabin. Tinchfield honked his horn and yelled. A man in blue overalls opened the door.

"Get in, Paul."

The man in overalls nodded and ducked back into the cabin and came out with a dirty lion-hunter's hat on his head. We went back to the highway and along to the branch road and so over to the gate on the private road. The man in overalls got out and opened it and closed it after our cars had gone through.

When we came to the lake, smoke was no longer rising from the small cabin. We got out.

Doc Menzies was an angular yellow-faced man with bug eyes and nicotine-stained fingers. The man in blue overalls and the lion-hunter's hat was about thirty, dark, swarthy, lithe, and looked underfed.

We went to the edge of the lake and looked towards the pier. Bill Haines was sitting on the floor of the pier, stark naked, with his head in his hands. There was something beside him on the pier.

"We can ride a ways more," Tinchfield said. We got back into the cars and went on, stopped again, and all trooped down to the pier.

The thing that had been a woman lay on its face on the pier with a rope under the arms. Haines' clothes lay to one side. His artificial leg, gleaming with leather and metal, lay beside them. Without a word spoken Tinchfield slipped the bottle of whiskey out of his shirt and uncorked it and handed it to Haines.

"Drink hearty, Bill," he said casually.

There was a sickening horrible smell on the air. Haines didn't seem to notice it, nor Tinchfield and Menzies. Loomis got a blanket from the car and threw it over the body, then he and I backed away from it.

Haines drank from the bottle and looked up with dead eyes. He held the bottle down between his bare knee and his stump and began to talk. He spoke in a dead voice, without looking at anybody or anything. He spoke slowly and told everything he had told me. He said that after I went he had got the rope and stripped and gone into the water and got the thing out. When he had finished he stared at the wooden planks and became as motionless as a statue.

Tinchfield put a cut of tobacco in his mouth and chewed on it for a moment. Then he shut his teeth tight and leaned down and turned the body over carefully, as if he was afraid it would come apart in his hands. The late sun shone on the loose necklace of green stones I had noticed in the water. They were roughly carved and lusterless, like soapstone. A gilt chain joined them. Tinchfield straightened his broad back and blew his nose hard on a tan handkerchief.

"What you say, Doc?"

Menzies spoke in a tight high irritable voice. "What the hell do you want me to say?"

"Cause and time of death," Tinchfield said mildly.

"Don't be a damn fool, Jim," the doctor said nastily.

"Can't tell nothing, eh?"

"By looking at that? Good God!"

Tinchfield sighed and turned to me. "Where was it when you first seen it?"

I told him. He listened with his mouth motionless and his eyes blank. Then he began to chew again. "Funny place to be. No current here. If they was any, 'twould be towards the dam."

Bill Haines got to his foot, hopped over to his clothes and strapped his leg on. He dressed slowly, awkwardly, dragging his shirt over his wet skin. He spoke again without looking at anybody.

"She done it herself. Had to. Swum under the boards down there and breathed water in. Maybe got stuck. Had to. No other way."

"One other way, Bill," Tinchfield said mildly, looking at the sky.

Haines rummaged in his shirt and got out his dog-eared note. He gave it to Tinchfield. By mutual consent everybody moved some distance away from the body. Then Tinchfield went back to get his bottle of whiskey and put it away under his shirt. He joined us and read the note over and over.

"It don't have a date. You say this was a couple of weeks ago?"

"Two weeks come Friday."

"She left you once before, didn't she?"

"Yeah." Haines didn't look at him. "Two years ago. I got drunk and stayed with a chippy." He laughed wildly.

The sheriff calmly read the note once more. "Note left that time?" he inquired.

"I get it," Haines snarled. "I get it. You don't have to draw no pictures."

"Note looks middlin' old," Tinchfield said gently.

"I had it in my shirt ten days," Haines yelled. He laughed wildly again.

"What's amusing you, Bill?"

"You ever try to drag a person six feet under water?"

"Never did, Bill."

"I swim pretty good—for a guy with one leg. I don't swim that good."

Tinchfield sighed. "Now that don't mean anything, Bill. Could have been a rope used. She could have been weighted down with a stone, maybe two stones, head and foot. Then after she's under them boards the rope could be cut loose. Could be done, son."

"Sure. I done it," Haines said, and roared laughing. "Me—I done it to Beryl. Take me in, you——s ——s?!"

"I am to," Tinchfield said mildly. "For investigation. No charges yet, Bill. You could've done it. Don't tell me different. I ain't saying you did, though. I'm just sayin' you could."

Haines sobered as quickly as he had gone to pieces.

"Any insurance?" Tinchfield asked, looking at the sky.

Haines started. "Five thousand. That does it. That hangs me. O.K. Let's go."

Tinchfield turned slowly to Loomis. "Go back there in the cabin, Paul, and get a couple of blankets. Then we better all get some whiskey inside our nose."

Loomis turned and walked back along the path that skirted the lake toward the Haines cabin. The rest of us just stood. Haines looked down at his hard brown hands and clenched them. Without a word he swept his right fist up and hit himself a terrible blow in the face.

"You ————!" he said in a harsh whisper.

His nose began to bleed. He stood lax. The blood ran down his lip, down the side of his mouth to the point of his chin. It began to drip off his chin.

That reminded me of something I had almost forgotten.

Chapter 5

THE GOLDEN ANKLET

I TELEPHONED HOWARD MELTON at his Beverly Hills home an hour after dark. I called from the telephone company's little log-cabin office half a block from the main street of Puma Point, almost out of hearing of the .22s at the shooting gallery, the rattle of the ski balls, the tooting of fancy auto horns, and the whine of hillbilly music from the diningroom of the Indian Head Hotel.

When the operator got him she told me to take the call in the manager's office. I went in and shut the door and sat down at a small desk and answered the phone.

"Find anything up there?" Melton's voice asked. It had a thickish edge to it, a three-highball edge.

"Nothing I expected. But something has happened up here you won't like. Want it straight—or wrapped in Christmas paper?"

I could hear him cough. I didn't hear any other sounds from the room in which he was talking. "I'll take it straight," he said steadily.

"Bill Haines claims your wife made passes at him—and they scored. They got drunk together the very morning of the day she went away. Haines had a row with his wife about it afterwards, and then he went over to the north shore of Puma Lake to get drunk some more. He was gone until two A.M. I'm just telling you what he says, you understand."

I waited. Melton's voice said finally: "I heard you. Go on, Dalmas." It was a toneless voice, as flat as a piece of slate.

"When he got home both the women had gone. His wife Beryl had left a note saying she'd rather be dead than live with a lousy cheater anymore. He hasn't seen her since—until today."

Melton coughed again. The sound made a sharp noise in my ear. There were buzzes and crackles on the wire. An operator broke in and I asked her to go brush her hair. After the interruption, Melton said: "Haines told all this to you, a complete stranger?"

"I brought some liquor with me. He likes to drink and he was aching to talk to somebody. The liquor broke down the barriers. There's more. I said he didn't see his wife again until today. Today she came up out of your little lake. I'll let you guess what she looked like."

"Good God!" Melton cried.

"She was stuck down under that fat underwater boarding below the pier the movie people built. The constable here, Jim Tinchfield, didn't like it too well. He's taken Haines in. I think they've gone down to see the D.A. in San Bernardino and have an autopsy and so on."

"Tinchfield thinks Haines killed her?"

"He thinks it could have happened that way. He's not saying everything he thinks. Haines put on a swell brokenhearted act, but this Tinchfield is no fool. He may know a lot of things about Haines that I don't know."

"Did they search Haines' cabin?"

"Not while I was around. Maybe later."

"I see." He sounded tired now, spent.

"It's a nice dish for a county prosecutor close to election time," I said. "But it's not a nice dish for us. If I have to appear at an inquest, I'll have to state my business, on oath. That means telling what I was doing up here, to some extent, at least. And that means pulling you in."

"It seems," Melton's voice said flatly, "that I'm pulled in already. If my wife—" He broke off and swore. He didn't speak again for a long time. Wire noises came to me and a sharper crackling, thunder somewhere in the mountains along the lines.

I said at last: "Beryl Haines had a Ford of her own. Not Bill's. His was fixed up for his left leg to do the heavy work. The car is gone. And that note didn't sound like a suicide note to me."

"What do you plan to do now?"

"It looks as though I'm always being sidetracked on this job. I may come down tonight. Can I call you at your home?"

"Any time," he said. "I'll be home all evening and all night. Call me any time. I didn't think Haines was that sort of guy at all."

"But you knew your wife had drinking spells and you left her up here alone."

"My God," he said, as if he hadn't heard me. "A man with a wooden—"

"Oh let's skip that part of it," I growled. "It's dirty enough without. Good-bye."

I hung up and went back to the outer office and paid the girl for the call. Then I walked back to the main street and got into my car parked in front of the drugstore. The street was full of gaudy neon signs and noise and glitter. On the dry mountain air every sound seemed to carry a mile. I could hear people talking a block away. I got out of my car again and bought another pint at the drugstore and drove away from there.

When I got to the place back along the highway where the road turned off to Little Fawn Lake I pulled over to the side and thought. Then I started up the road into the mountains towards Melton's place.

The gate across the private road was shut and padlocked now. I tucked my car off to the side in some bushes and climbed over the gate and pussyfooted along the side of the road until the starlit glimmer of the lake suddenly bloomed at my feet. Haines' cabin was dark. The cabins on the other side of the lake were vague shadows against the slope. The old mill wheel beside the dam looked funny as hell up there all alone. I listened— didn't hear a sound. There are no night birds in the mountains.

I padded along to Haines' cabin and tried the door—locked. I went around to the back and found another locked door. I prowled around the cabin walking like a cat on a wet floor. I pushed on the one screenless window. That was locked also. I stopped and listened some more. The window was not very tight. Wood dries out in that air and shrinks. I tried my knife between the two sashes, which opened inwards, like small cottage windows. No dice. I leaned against the wall and looked at the hard shimmer of the lake and took a drink from my pint. That made me tough. I put the bottle away and picked up a big stone and smacked the window frame in without breaking the glass. I heaved up on the sill and climbed into the cabin.

A flash hit me in the face.

A calm voice said: "I'd rest right there, son. You must be all tired out."

The flash pinned me against the wall for a moment and then a light-switch clicked and a lamp went on. The flash died. Tinchfield sat there peacefully in a leather Morris chair beside a table over the edge of which a brown-fringed shawl dangled foolishly. Tinchfield wore the same clothes as he had worn that afternoon, with the addition of a brown wool windbreaker over his shirt. His hands were empty except for the flash. His jaws moved quietly.

"That movie outfit strung two miles of wire up here," he said reflectively. "Kind of nice for the folks. Well, what's on your mind, son—besides breakin' and enterin'?"

I picked out a chair and sat down and looked around the cabin. The room was a small square room with a double bed and a rag rug and a few modest pieces of furniture. An open door at the back showed the corner of a cook-stove.

"I had an idea," I said. "From where I sit now it looks lousy."

Tinchfield nodded and his eyes studied me without rancor. "I heard your car," he said. "I knew you was on the private road and comin' this way. You walk right nice, though. I didn't hear you walk worth a darn. I've been mighty curious about you, son."

"Why?"

"Ain't you kind of heavy under the left arm, son?"

I grinned at him. "Maybe I better talk," I said.

"Well, you don't have to bother a lot about pushin' in that winder. I'm a tolerant man. I figure you got a proper right to carry that six-gun, eh?"

I reached into my pocket and laid my open billfold on his thick knee. He lifted it and held it carefully to the lamplight, looking at the photostat license behind the celluloid window. He handed the billfold back to me.

"I kind of figured you was interested in Bill Haines," he said. "A private detective, eh? Well, you got a good hard build on you and your face don't tell a lot of stories. I'm kind of worried about Bill myself. You aim to search the cabin?"

"I did have the idea."

"It's all right by me, but there ain't really no necessity. I already pawed around considerable. Who hired you?"

"Howard Melton."

He chewed a moment in silence. "Might I ask to do what?"

"To find his wife. She skipped out on him a couple of weeks back."

Tinchfield took his flat-crowned Stetson off and rumpled his mousy hair.

He stood up and unlocked and opened the door. He sat down again and looked at me in silence.

"He's very anxious to avoid publicity," I said. "On account of a certain failing his wife has which might lose him his job." Tinchfield eyed me unblinkingly. The yellow lamplight made bronze out of one side of his face. "I don't mean liquor or Bill Haines," I added.

"None of that don't hardly explain your wantin' to search Bill's cabin," he said mildly.

"I'm just a great guy to poke around."

He didn't budge for a long minute, during which he was probably deciding whether or not I was kidding him, and if I was, whether he cared.

He said at length: "Would this interest you at all, son?" He took a folded piece of newspaper from the slanting pocket of his windbreaker and opened it up on the table under the lamp. I went over and looked. On the newspaper lay a thin gold chain with a tiny lock. The chain had been snipped through neatly by a pair of cutting-pliers. The lock was not unlocked. The chain was short, not more than four or five inches long and the lock was tiny and hardly any larger around than the chain itself. There was a little white powder on both chain and newspaper.

"Where would you guess I found that?" Tinchfield asked.

I moistened a finger and touched the white powder and tasted it. "In a sack of flour. That is, in the kitchen here. It's an anklet. Some women wear them and never take them off. Whoever took this one off didn't have the key."

Tinchfield looked at me benignly. He leaned back and patted one knee with a large hand and smiled remotely at the pineboard ceiling. I rolled a cigarette around in my fingers and sat down again.

Tinchfield refolded the piece of newspaper and put it back in his pocket. "Well, I guess that's all—unless you care to make a search in my presence."

"No," I said.

"It looks like me and you are goin' to do our thinkin' separate."

"Mrs. Haines had a car, Bill said. A Ford."

"Yep. A blue coupe. It's down the road a piece, hid in some rocks."

"That doesn't sound much like a planned murder."

"I don't figure anything was planned, son. Just come over him sudden. Maybe choked her, and he has awful powerful hands. There he is—stuck with a body to dispose of. He done it the best way he could think of and for a pegleg he done pretty damn well."

"The car sounds more like a suicide," I said. "A planned suicide. People have been known to commit suicide in such a way as to make a murder case stick against somebody they were mad at. She wouldn't take the car far away, because she had to walk back."

Tinchfield said: "Bill wouldn't neither. That car would be mighty awkward for him to drive, him bein' used to use his left foot."

"He showed me that note from Beryl before we found the body," I said. "And I was the one that walked out on the pier first."

"You and me could get along, son. Well, we'll see. Bill's a good feller at heart—except these veterans give themselves too many privileges in my opinion. Some of 'em did three weeks in a camp and act like they was wounded nine times. Bill must have been mighty sentimental about this piece of chain I found."

He got up and went to the open door. He spit his chaw out into the dark. "I'm a man sixty-two years of age," he said over his shoulder. "I've known folks to do all manner of funny things. I would say offhand that jumpin' into a cold lake with all your clothes on, and swimmin' hard to get down under that board, and then just dyin' there was a funny thing to do. On the other hand, since I'm tellin' you all my secrets and you ain't tellin' me nothing, I've had to speak to Bill a number of times for slapping his wife around when he was drunk. That ain't goin' to sound good to a jury. And if this here little chain come off Beryl Haines' leg, it's just about enough to set him in that nice new gas chamber they got up north. And you and me might as well mosey on home, son."

I stood up.

"And don't go smokin' that cigarette on the highway," he added. "It's contrary to the law up here."

I put the unlit cigarette back in my pocket and stepped out into the night. Tinchfield switched the lamp off and locked up the cabin and put the key in his pocket. "Where are you stayin', son?"

"I'm going down to the Olympia in San Bernardino."

"It's a nice place, but they don't have the climate we have up here. Too hot."

"I like it hot," I said.

We walked back to the road and Tinchfield turned to the right. "My car's up a piece toward the end of the lake. I'll say good night to you, son."

"Good night, Sheriff. I don't think he murdered her."

He was already walking off. He didn't turn. "Well, we'll see," he said quietly.

I went back to the gate and climbed it and found my car and started back down the narrow road past the waterfall. At the highway I turned west towards the dam and the grade to the valley.

On the way I decided that if the citizens around Puma Lake didn't keep Tinchfield constable, they would be making a very bad mistake.

Chapter 6

MELTON UPS THE ANTE

IT WAS PAST TEN THIRTY when I got to the bottom of the grade and parked in one of the diagonal slots in front of the Hotel Olympia in San Bernardino. I pulled an overnight bag out of the back of my car and had taken about four steps with it when a bellhop in braided pants and a white shirt and black bow tie had it out of my hand.

The clerk on duty was an egg-headed man with no interest in me. I signed the register.

The hop and I rode a four-by-four elevator to the second floor and walked a couple of blocks around corners. As we walked it got hotter and hotter.

The hop unlocked a door into a boy's-size room with one window on an airshaft.

The hop, who was tall, thin, yellow, and as cool as a slice of chicken in aspic, moved his gum around in his face, put my bag on a chair, opened the window and stood looking at me. He had eyes the color of a drink of water.

"Bring us up some ginger ale and glasses and ice," I said.

"Us?"

"That is, if you happen to be a drinking man."

"After eleven I reckon I might take a chance."

"It's now ten thirty-nine," I said. "If I give you a dime, will you say 'I sho'ly do thank you'?"

He grinned and snapped his gum.

He went out, leaving the door open. I took off my coat and unstrapped my holster. It was wearing grooves in my hide. I removed my tie, shirt, undershirt and walked around the room in the draft from the open door. The draft smelt of hot iron. I went into the bathroom sideways—it was that kind of bathroom—doused myself with cold water and was breathing more freely when the tall languid hop returned with a tray. He shut the door and I brought out my bottle. He mixed a couple of drinks and we drank. The perspiration started from the back of my neck down my spine, but I felt better all the same. I sat on the bed holding my glass and looking at the hop.

"How long can you stay?"

"Doing what?"

"Remembering."

"I ain't a damn bit of use at it."

"I have money to spend," I said, "in my own peculiar way." I took my wallet from my coat and spread bills along the bed.

"I beg yore pardon," the hop said. "You're a copper?"

"Private."

"I'm interested. This likker makes my mind work."

I gave him a dollar bill. "Try that on your mind. Can I call you Tex?"

"You done guessed it," he drawled, tucking the bill neatly into the watch pocket of his pants.

"Where were you on Friday the twelfth of August in the late afternoon?"

He sipped his drink and thought, shaking the ice very gently and drinking past his gum. "Here. Four-to-twelve shift," he answered finally.

"A lady named Mrs. George Atkins, a small, slim, pretty blonde, checked in and stayed until time for the night train east. She put her car in the hotel garage and I believe it is still there. I want the lad that checked her in. That wins another dollar." I separated it from my stake and laid it by itself on the bed.

"I sho'ly do thank you," the hop said, grinning. He finished his drink and left the room, closing the door quietly. I finished my drink and made another. Time passed. Finally the wall telephone rang. I wedged myself into a small space between the bathroom door and the bed and answered it.

"That was Sonny. Off at eight tonight. He can be reached, I reckon."

"How soon?"

"You want him over?"

"Yeah."

"Half an hour, if he's home. Another boy checked her out. A fellow we call Les. He's here."

"O.K. Shoot him up."

I finished my second drink and thought well enough of it to mix a third before the ice melted. I was stirring it when the knock came, and I opened to a small, wiry, carrot-headed, green-eyed rat with a tight little girlish mouth.

"Drink?"

"Sure," he said. He poured himself a large one and added a whisper of mixer. He put the mixture down in one swallow, tucked a cigarette between his lips and snapped a match alight while it was still coming up from his pocket. He blew smoke, fanned it with his hand, and stared at me coldly. I noticed, stitched over his pocket instead of a number, the word *Captain*.

"Thanks," I said. "That will be all."

"Huh?" His mouth twisted unpleasantly.

"Beat it."

"I thought you wanted to see me," he snarled.

"You're the night bell-captain?"

"Check."

"I wanted to buy you a drink. I wanted to give you a buck. Here. Thanks for coming up."

He took the dollar and hung there, smoke trailing from his nose, his eyes beady and mean. He turned then with a swift tight shrug and slipped out of the room soundlessly.

Ten minutes passed, then another knock, very light. When I opened, the lanky lad stood there grinning. I walked away from him and he slipped inside and came over beside the bed. He was still grinning.

"You didn't take to Les, huh?"

"No. Is he satisfied?"

"I reckon so. You know what captains are. Have to have their cut. Maybe you better call me Les, Mr. Dalmas."

"So you checked her out."

"Not if Mrs. George Atkins was her name, I didn't."

"I took the photo of Julia from my pocket and showed it to him. He looked at it carefully, for a long time. "She looked like that," he said. "She gave me four bits, and in this little town that gets you remembered. Mrs. Howard Melton was the name. There's been talk about her car. I guess we just don't have much to talk about here."

"Uh-huh. Where did she go from here?"

"She took a hack to the depot. You use nice likker, Mr. Dalmas."

"Excuse me. Help yourself." When he had I said: "Remember anything about her? She have any visitors?"

"No, sir. But I do recall something. She was addressed by a gentleman in the lobby. A tall good-lookin' jasper. She didn't seem pleased to see him."

"Ah." I took the other photo out of my pocket and showed it to him. He studied that carefully also.

"This don't look quite so much like her," he said. "But I'm sure it's the gentleman I spoke of."

"Ah."

He picked up both photos again and held them side by side. He looked a little puzzled. "Yes, sir. That's him all right," he said.

"You're an accommodating guy," I said. "You'd remember almost anything, wouldn't you?"

"I don't get you, sir."

"Take another drink. I owe you four bucks. That's five in all. It's not worth it. You hops are always trying to pull some gag."

He took a very small one and balanced it in his hand, his yellow face puckered. "I do the best I can," he said stiffly. He drank his drink, put the glass down silently and moved to the door. "You can keep your goddam money," he said. He took the dollar out of his watch pocket and threw it on the floor. "To hell with you, you————" he said softly.

He went out.

I picked up the two photos and held them side by side and scowled at them. After a long moment an icy finger touched my spine. It had touched it once before, very briefly, but I had shaken off the feeling. It came back now to stay.

I went to the tiny desk and got an envelope and put a five-dollar bill in it and sealed it and wrote "Les" on it. I put my clothes on and my bottle on my hip and picked up my overnight bag and left the room.

Down in the lobby the red-head jumped at me. Les stayed back by a pillar, his arms folded, silent. I went to the desk and asked for my bill.

"Anything wrong, sir?" The clerk looked troubled.

"I made a mistake in my schedule."

I paid the bill and walked out to my car and then turned and went back to the desk. I gave the clerk the envelope with the five in it. "Give this to the Texas boy, Les. He's mad at me, but he'll get over it."

I drove away from the Hotel Olympia, fast, and took the Foothill Boulevard this time.

I made Glendale before two A.M. and looked around for a place where I could phone. I found an all-night garage.

I got out dimes and nickels and dialed the operator and got Melton's number in Beverly Hills. His voice, when it finally came over the wire, didn't sound very sleepy.

"Sorry to call at this hour," I said, "but you told me to. I traced Mrs. Melton to San Bernardino and to the depot there."

"We knew that already," he said crossly.

"Well, it pays to be sure. Haines' cabin has been searched. Nothing much was found. If you thought he knew where Mrs. Melton—"

"I don't know what I thought," he broke in sharply. "After what you told me I thought the place ought to be searched. Is that all you have to report?"

"No." I hesitated a little. "I've had a bad dream. I dreamed there was a woman's bag in a chair in that Chester Lane house this morning. It was pretty dark in there from the trees and I forgot to remove it."

"What color bag?" His voice was as stiff as a clam shell.

"Dark blue—maybe black. The light was bad."

"You'd better go back and get it," he snapped.

"Why?"

"That's what I'm paying you five hundred dollars for—among other things."

"There's a limit to what I have to do for five hundred bucks—even if I had them."

He swore. "Listen, fella. I owe you a lot, but this is up to you and you can't let me down."

"Well, there might be a flock of cops on the front step. And then again the place might be as quiet as a pet flea. Either way I don't like it. I've had enough of that house."

There was a deep silence from Melton's end. I took a long breath and gave him some more. "What's more, I think you know where your wife is, Melton. Goodwin ran into her in the hotel in San Bernardino. He had a check of hers a few days ago. You met Goodwin on the street. You helped him get the check cashed, indirectly. I think you know. I think you just hired me to backtrack over her trail and see that it was properly covered."

There was more heavy silence from him. When he spoke again it was in a small chastened voice. "You win, Dalmas. Yeah—it was blackmail all right, on that check business. But I don't know where she is. That's straight. And that bag has to be got. How would seven hundred and fifty sound to you?"

"Better. When do I get it?"

"Tonight, if you'll take a check. I can't make better than eighty dollars in cash before tomorrow."

I hesitated again. I knew by the feel of my face that I was grinning. "O.K.," I said at last. "It's a deal. I'll get the bag—unless there's a flock of johns there."

"Where are you now?" He almost whistled with relief.

"Azusa. It'll take me about an hour to get there," I lied.

"Step on it," he said. "You'll find me a good guy to play ball with. You're in this pretty deep yourself, fella."

"I'm used to jams," I said, and hung up.

Chapter 7

A PAIR OF FALL GUYS

I DROVE BACK TO Chevy Chase Boulevard and along it to the foot of Chester Lane where I dimmed my lights and turned in. I drove quickly up around the curve to the new house across from Goodwin's place. There was no sign of a stake-out that I could spot. That was a chance I had to take, like another and worse one I was taking.

I drove into the driveway of the new house and got out and lifted up the unlocked swing-up garage door. I put my car inside, lowered the door and snaked back across the street as if Indians were after me. I used all the cover of Goodwin's trees to the backyard and put myself behind the biggest of them there. I sat down on the ground and allowed myself a sip from my pint of rye.

Time passed, with a deadly slowness. I expected company, but I didn't know how soon. It came sooner than I expected.

In about fifteen minutes a car came up Chester Lane and I caught a faint glimpse of it between the trees, along the side of the house. It was running without lights. I liked that. It stopped somewhere near and a door closed softly. A shadow moved without sound at the corner of the house. It was a small shadow, a foot shorter than Melton's would have been. He couldn't have driven from Beverly Hills in that time anyway.

Then the shadow was at the back door, the back door opened, and the shadow vanished through it into deeper darkness. The door closed silently. I got up on my feet and sneaked across the soft moist grass. I stepped silently into Mr. Goodwin's porch and from there into his kitchen. I stood still, listening hard. There was no sound, no light beyond me. I took the gun out from under my arm and squeezed the butt down at my side. I breathed shallowly, from the top of my lungs. Then a funny thing happened. A crack of light appeared suddenly under the swing door to the dining room. The shadow had turned the lights up. Careless shadow! I walked across the kitchen and pushed the swing door open and left it that way. The light poured into the alcove dining room from beyond the living room arch. I went that way, carelessly—much too carelessly. I stepped past the arch.

A voice almost at my elbow said: "Drop it—and keep on walking."

I looked at her. She was small, pretty after a fashion, and her gun pointed at my side very steadily.

"You're not clever," she said. "Are you?"

I opened my hand and let the gun fall. I walked four steps beyond it and turned.

"No," I said.

The woman said nothing more. She moved away, circling a little, leaving the gun on the floor. She circled until she faced me. I looked past her at the corner chair with the footstool. White buck shoes still rested on the footstool. Mr. Lance Goodwin still sat negligently in the chair, with his left hand on the wide brocaded arm and his right trailing to the small gun on the floor. The last blood drop had frozen on his chin. It looked black and hard and permanent. His face had a waxy look now.

I looked at the woman again. She wore well-pressed blue slacks and a double-breasted jacket and a small tilted hat. Her hair was long and curled in at the ends and it was a dark red color with glints of blue in the shadows—dyed. Red spots of hastily applied rouge burned on her cheeks too high up. She pointed her gun and smiled at me. It wasn't the nicest smile I had ever seen.

I said: "Good evening, Mrs. Melton. What a lot of guns you must own."

"Sit down in that chair behind you and clasp your hands behind your neck and keep them there. That's important. Don't get careless about it." She showed me her teeth to her gums.

I did as she suggested. The smile dropped from her face—a hard little face, even though pretty in a conventional sort of way. "Just wait," she said. "That's important, too. Maybe you could guess how important that is."

"This room smells of death," I said. "I suppose that's important, too."

"Just wait, smart boy."

"They don't hang women anymore in this state," I said. "But two cost more than one. A lot more. About fifteen years more. Think it over."

She said nothing. She stood firmly, pointing the gun. This was a heavier gun, but it didn't seem to bother her. Her ears were busy with the distance. She hardly heard me. The time passed, as it does, in spite of everything. My arms began to ache.

At last he came. Another car drifted quietly up the street outside and stopped and its door closed quietly. Silence for a moment, then the house door at the back opened. His steps were heavy. He came through the open swing door and into the lighted room. He stood silent, looking around it, a hard frown on his big face. He looked at the dead man in the chair, at the woman with her gun, last of all at me. He stooped and picked up my gun and dropped it into his side pocket. He came to me quietly, almost without recognition in his eyes, stepped behind me and felt my pockets. He took out the two photos and the telegram. He stepped away from me, near the woman. I put my arms down and rubbed them. They both stared at me quietly.

At last he said softly: "A gag, eh? First off I checked your call and found out it came from Glendale—not from Azusa. I don't know just why I did that, but I did. Then I made another call. The second call told me there wasn't any bag left in this room. Well?"

"What do you want me to say?"

"Why the trick work? What's it all about?" His voice was heavy, cold, but more thoughtful than menacing. The woman stood beside him, motionless, holding her gun.

"I took a chance," I said. "You took one too—coming here. I hardly thought it would work. The idea, such as it was, was that you would call her quickly about the bag. She would know there wasn't one. You would both know then that I was trying to pull something. You'd be very anxious to know what it was. You'd be pretty sure I wasn't working with any law, because I knew where you were and you could have been jumped there without any trouble at all. I wanted to bring the lady out of hiding—that's all. I took a long chance. If it didn't work, I had to think up a better way."

The woman made a contemptuous sound and said: "I'd like to know why you hired this snooper in the first place, Howie."

He ignored her. He looked at me steadily out of stony black eyes. I turned my head and gave him a quick hard wink. His mouth got rigid at once. The woman didn't see it. She was too far to the side.

"You need a fall-guy, Melton," I said. "Bad."

He turned his body a little so that his back was partly to the woman. His eyes ate my face. He lifted his eyebrows a little and half-nodded. He still thought I was for sale.

He did it nicely. He put a smile on his face and turned toward her and said, "How about getting out of here and talking it over in a safer place?" and while she was listening and her mind was on the question his big hand struck down sharply at her wrist. She yelped and the gun dropped. She reeled back and clenched both her fists and spit at him.

"Aw, go sit down and get wise to yourself," he said dryly.

He stooped and picked up her gun and dropped it into his other pocket. He smiled then, a large confident smile. He had forgotten something completely. I almost laughed—in spite of the spot I was in. The woman sat down in a chair behind him and leaned her head in her hands broodingly.

"You can tell me about it now," Melton said cheerfully. "Why I need a fall-guy, as you say."

"I lied to you over the phone a little. About Haines' cabin. There's a wise old country cop up there who went through it with a sifter. He found a gold anklet in the flour bag, cut through with pliers."

The woman let out a queer yelp. Melton didn't even bother to look at her. She was staring at me with all her eyes now.

"He might figure it out," I said, "and he might not. He doesn't know Mrs. Melton stayed over at the Hotel Olympia, for one thing, and that she met Goodwin there. If he knew that, he'd be wise in a second. That is, if he had photos to show the bell-hops, the way I had. The hop who checked Mrs. Melton out and remembered her on account of her leaving her car there without any instructions, remembered Goodwin, remembered him speaking to her. He said she was startled. He wasn't so sure about Mrs. Melton from the photos. But Goodwin didn't have to go by photos. He knew Mrs. Melton."

Melton opened his mouth a little in a queer grimace and grated the edges of his teeth together. The woman stood up noiselessly behind him and drifted back, inch by inch, into the dark back part of the room. I didn't look at her. Melton didn't seem to hear her move.

I said: "Goodwin trailed her into town. She must have come by bus or in a rent-car, because she left the other car in San Bernardino. He trailed her to her hideout without her knowing it, which was pretty smart, since she must have been on her guard, and then he jumped her. She stalled him for a while—I don't know with what story—and he must have had her watched every minute, because she didn't slip away from him. Then she couldn't stall him any longer and she gave him that check. That was just a retainer. He came back for more and she fixed him up permanently—over there in the chair. You didn't know that, or you would never have let me come out here this morning."

Melton smiled grimly. "Right, I didn't know that," he said. "Is that what I need a fall-guy for?"

I shook my head. "You don't seem to want to understand me," I said. "I told you Goodwin knew Mrs. Melton personally. That's not news, is it? What would Goodwin have on Mrs. Melton to blackmail her for? Nothing. He wasn't blackmailing Mrs. Melton. Mrs. Melton is dead. She has been dead for eleven days. She came up out of Little Fawn Lake today—in Beryl Haines' clothes. That's what you need a fall-guy for—and you have one, two of them, made to order."

The woman back in the shadows of the room stooped and picked something up and rushed. She panted as she rushed. Melton turned hard and his hands jerked at his pockets, but he hesitated just too long, looking at the gun she had snatched up from the floor beside Goodwin's dead hand, the gun that was the thing he had forgotten about.

"You———!" she said.

He still wasn't very scared. He made placating movements with his empty hands. "O.K., honey, we'll play it your way," he said softly. He had a long arm. He could reach her now. He had done it already when she held a gun. He tried it once more. He leaned towards her quickly and swept his hand. I put my feet under me and dived for his legs. It was a long dive—too long.

"I'd make a swell fall-guy, wouldn't I?" she said raspingly and stepped back. The gun banged three times.

He jumped at her with the slugs in him, and fell hard against her and carried her to the floor. She ought to have thought of that too. They crashed together, his big body pinning her down. She wailed and an arm waved up towards me holding the gun. I smacked it out of her hand. I grabbed at his pockets and got my gun out and jumped away from them. I sat down. The back of my neck felt like a piece of ice. I sat down and held the gun on my knee and waited.

His big hand reached out and took hold of the claw-shaped leg of a davenport and whitened on the wood. His body arched and rolled and the woman wailed again. His body rolled back and sagged and the hand let go of the davenport leg. The fingers uncurled quietly and lay limp on the nap of the carpet. There was a choking rattle—and silence.

She fought her way out from under him and got to her feet panting, glaring like an animal. She turned without a sound and ran. I didn't move. I just let her go.

I went over and bent down above the big sprawled man and held a finger hard against the side of his neck. I stood there silently, leaning down, feeling for a pulse, and listening. I straightened up slowly and listened some more. No sirens, no car, no noise. Just the dead stillness of the room. I put my gun back under my arm and put the light out and opened the front door and walked down the path to the sidewalk. Nothing moved on the street. A big car stood at the curb, beside the fire-plug, up at the dead-end beyond Goodwin's place. I crossed the street to the new house and got my car out of its garage and shut the garage up again and started for Puma Lake again.

Chapter 8

KEEP TINCHFIELD CONSTABLE

THE CABIN STOOD IN a hollow, in front of a growth of jackpines. A big barn-like garage with cordwood piled on one side was open to the morning sun and Tinchfield's car glistened inside it. There was a cleated walk down to the front door and smoke lisped from the chimney. It was not yet seven o'clock. I knocked.

Tinchfield opened the door himself. He wore an old gray roll-collar sweater and his khaki pants. He was fresh-shaved and as smooth as a baby.

"Well, step in, son," he said peacefully. "I see you go to work bright and early. So you didn't go down the hill last night, eh?"

I went past him into the cabin and sat in an old Boston rocker with a crocheted antimacassar over its back. I rocked in it and it gave out a homey squeak.

"Coffee's just about ready to pour," Tinchfield said genially. "Emma'll lay a plate for you. You got a kind of tuckered-out look, son."

"I went down the hill," I said. "I just came back up. That wasn't Beryl Haines in the lake yesterday."

Tinchfield said: "Well, I swan."

"You don't seem a hell of a lot surprised," I growled.

"I don't surprise right easy, son. Particularly before breakfast."

"It was Julia Melton," I said. "She was murdered—by Howard Melton and Beryl Haines. She was dressed in Beryl's clothes and put down under those boards, six feet under water, so that she would stay long enough not to look like Julia Melton. Both the women were blondes, of the same size and general appearance. Bill said they were enough alike to be sisters. Not twin sisters, probably."

"They was some alike," Tinchfield said, staring at me gravely. He raised his voice. "Emma!"

A stout woman in a print dress opened the inner door of the cabin. An enormous white apron was tied around what had once been her waist. A smell of coffee and frying bacon rushed out.

"Emma, this is Detective Dalmas from Los Angeles. Lay another plate and I'll pull the table out from the wall a ways. He's a mite tired and hungry."

The stout woman ducked her head and smiled and put silver on the table.

We sat down and ate bacon and eggs and hot cakes and drank coffee by the quart. Tinchfield ate like four men and his wife ate like a bird and kept hopping up and down like a bird to get more food.

We finished at last and Mrs. Tinchfield gathered up the dishes and shut herself in the kitchen. Tinchfield cut a large slice of plug and tucked it carefully into his face and I sat down in the Boston rocker again.

"Well, son," he said, "I guess I'm ready for the worst. I was a mite anxious about that there piece of gold chain bein' hid where it was, what with the lake so handy. But I'm a slow thinker. What makes you think Melton murdered his wife?"

"Because Beryl Haines is still alive, with her hair dyed red."

I told him my story, all of it, fact by fact, concealing nothing. He said nothing until I had finished.

"Well, son," he said then, "you done a mighty smart piece of detectin' work there—what with a little luck in a couple of places, like we all have to have. But you didn't have no business to be doin' it at all, did you?"

"No. But Melton took me for a ride and played me for a sucker. I'm a stubborn sort of guy."

"What for do you reckon Melton hired you?"

"He had to. It was a necessary part of his plan to have the body correctly identified in the end, perhaps not for some time, perhaps not until after it had been buried and the case closed. But he had to have it identified in the end in order to get his wife's money. That or wait for years to have the courts declare her legally dead. When it was correctly identified, he would have to show that he had made an effort to find her. If his wife was a kleptomaniac, as he said, he had a good excuse for hiring a private dick instead of going to the police. But he had to do something. Also there was the menace of Goodwin. He might have planned to kill Goodwin and frame me for it. He certainly didn't know Beryl had beat him to it, or he wouldn't have let me go to Goodwin's house.

"After that—and I was foolish enough to come up here before I had reported Goodwin's death to the Glendale police—he probably thought I could be handled with money. The murder itself was fairly simple, and there was an angle to it that Beryl didn't know or think about. She was probably in love with him. An underprivileged woman like that, with a drunken husband, would be apt to go for a guy like Melton.

"Melton couldn't have known the body would be found yesterday, because that was pure accident, but he would have kept me on the job and kept hinting around until it *was* found. He knew Haines would be suspected of murdering his wife and the note she left was worded to sound a bit unlike a real suicide note. Melton knew his wife and Haines were getting tight together up here and playing games.

"He and Beryl just waited for the right time, when Haines had gone off to the north shore on a big drunk. Beryl must have telephoned him from somewhere. You'll be able to check that. He could make it up here in three hours' hard driving. Julia was probably still drinking. Melton knocked her out, dressed her in Beryl's clothes and put her down in the lake. He was a big man and could do it alone, without much trouble. Beryl would be acting as lookout down the only road into the property. That gave him a chance to plant the anklet in the Haines cabin. Then he rushed back to town and Beryl put on Julia's clothes and took Julia's car and luggage and went to the hotel in San Bernardino.

"There she was unlucky enough to be seen and spoken to by Goodwin, who must have known something was wrong, by her clothes or her bags or perhaps hearing her spoken to as Mrs. Melton. So he followed her into town and you know the rest. The fact that Melton had her lay this trail shows two things, as I see it. One, that he intended to wait some time before having the body properly identified. It would be almost certain to be accepted as the body of Beryl Haines on Bill's say-so, especially as that put Bill in a very bad spot.

"The other thing is that *when* the body was identified as Julia Melton, then the false trail laid by Beryl would make it look as though she and Bill had committed the murder to collect her insurance. I think Melton made a bad mistake by planting that anklet where he did. He should have dropped it into the lake, tied to a bolt or something, and later on, accidentally on purpose, fished it out. Putting it in Haines' cabin and then asking me if Haines' cabin had been searched was a little too sloppy. But planned murders are always like that."

Tinchfield switched his chaw to the other side of his face and went to the door to spit. He stood in the open door with his big hands clasped behind him.

"He couldn't have pinned nothing on Beryl," he said over his shoulder. "Not without her talkin' a great deal, son. Did you think of that?"

"Sure. Once the police were looking for her and the case broke wide open in the papers—I mean the real case—he would have had to bump Beryl off and make it look like a suicide. I think it might have worked."

"You hadn't ought to have let that there murderin' woman get away, son. There's other things you hadn't ought to have done, but that one was bad."

"Who's case is this?" I growled. "Yours—or the Glendale police? Beryl will be caught all right. She's killed two men and she'll flop on the next trick she tries to pull. They always do. And there's collateral evidence to be dug up. That's police work—not mine. I thought you were running for re-election, against a couple of younger men. I didn't come back up here just for the mountain air."

He turned and looked at my slyly. "I kind of figured you thought old man Tinchfield might be soft enough to keep you out of jail, son." Then he laughed and slapped his leg. "Keep Tinchfield constable," he boomed at the big outdoors. "You're darn right they will. They'd be damn fools not to— after this. Let's us mosey on over to the office and call the 'cutor down in Berdoo." He sighed. "Just too dum smart that Melton was," he said. "I like simple folks."

"Me too," I said. "That's why I'm here."

They caught Beryl Haines on the California-Oregon line, doubling back south to Yreka in a rent-car. The highway patrol stopped her for a routine border fruit inspection, but she didn't know that. She pulled another gun. She still had Julia Melton's luggage and Julia Melton's clothes and Julia Melton's checkbook with nine blank checks in it traced from one of Julia Melton's genuine signatures. The check cashed by Goodwin proved to be another forgery.

Tinchfield and the county prosecutor went to bat for me with the Glendale police, but I got hell from them just the same. From Violets M'Gee I got the large and succulent razzberry, and from the late Howard Melton I got what was left of the fifty dollars he had advanced me. They kept Tinchfield constable, by a landslide.

Strangler's Kill

MERLE CONSTINER

Chapter 1

WITH THE SOLES OF YOUR FEET

A T THE AGE when most kids are pushing cast-iron trains across the
floor, I was taking down and assembling my old man's pistol and di-
agnosing the entrails of the mortise locks around the house. The older I got,
the more I fiddled with guns and tumblers until finally I worked myself up
to a sort of technical trouble-shooter for a small safe company. Then over-
production and a new efficiency system sneaked into the factory and canned
me. After six weeks of walking the streets and sleeping in alleys, I met the
Dean. I hate to think of what I might be doing right now if it hadn't been
for him. He said: "You got dangerous talent, son. Dangerous to society.
You join up with me and stay on the right side of the law."

Everybody you talked to, the grocery boy, the neighbors, the clerk at the
corner drug store, thought the Dean was a screwball and a crank. He was
so friendly and pleasant to strangers that if they ever found out he always
carried a shoulder gun about the size and weight of a plowshare, they would
have laughed it off and insisted he used it to crack nuts with.

Your impression when you met him was that he was about the most useless man in the world. The police and newspapers knew different.

We lived in an old brick rooming house in the slums and had three grimy
rooms on the ground floor where the Dean practiced fortune-telling with
the indirect sanction of the police commissioner. A tin sign tacked on the
front door read—

PEDOMANCY

**Fortunes Divined from the Soles of Your Feet
Learn the Secrets of Love, Hate, Riches**

**SPECIAL CONSULTATIONS IN:
LIBANOMANCY CATOPTROMANCY
RHABDOMANCY ALEUROMANCY**

FEE NEGLIGIBLE

Believe it or not, there is a branch of fortune-telling called pedomancy.
The fee was not only negligible but elastic. Sometimes, if the Dean got
miffed with a customer, he sky-rocketed it ridiculously high. Usually
though, the charge was small. Frequently there was none at all.

The whole set-up was merely a front. I don't mean that the Dean didn't
tell his fortunes conscientiously and accurately—he could read half a dozen
Eastern languages and owned a collection of sheepskin and papyri that
would have struck a museum curator blind. When he told a fortune he did
it as carefully as he'd play a game of chess. He'd make a little speech telling
the customer that it was all hokum and then get to work. His manner was
so frank that the toughest customer would usually break down and confide
in him. And let me tell you that all that stuff the Dean heard stayed buried
in his skull. No confidence ever slipped through his lips.

I finished dusting the reception room—a morning chore which I despised,
for the Dean was worse than an old maid with wiping his finger under the
mantel or across the table-top looking for dust—and went back for breakfast.

The Dean was seated at the table, an empty plate before him. My plate
was empty, too. And so were the coffee cups, and the bowls and platters
which customarily held cereals and bacon and eggs.

I grinned as I came through the door. He'd pulled this gag before and I
knew what it meant. The first time I had been surprised. He'd explained to
me how back in the eighteenth century there was a poet named Blake and
how when Blake loafed too long and the family bank account got too low,
Mrs. Blake set out the empty dishes and her old man got the idea and went
to work again.

"It's about time," I said.

"Sit down, Ben." The Dean nodded to a chair. "I want to talk to you."
He wouldn't be hurried. "I want to talk to you about arson and murder.
And it's a hard thing to believe, Ben, but the arson is worse than the murder." He pawed through his pockets and located the snipe of the thin Cuban
cigar which he always produced when he had a bit of heavy conversation
to get off. The average man, keyed up, looks tense. The Dean looked tired,
his shoulders drooped, the corners of his mouth relaxed.

"Arson?" I asked. "The firebug?"

"This is no firebug, Ben." He had a trick of speaking with his eyelids
closed. "This town is being terrorized by a series of fires that are caused by
no half-witted boy with a handful of oily waste and a craving to watch the
engines go by. These burnings are sane and vicious."

I knew what he meant. Every few weeks, for almost six months now, some building had collapsed in smoke and flames. Most of them had been groceries, delicatessens, or small tradesmen's shops.

There had been a death, too. Frederick Ortman, local manager of Solidarity Insurance, had been lured from his home and murdered. The police learned the details from his wife. The Ortmans had been asleep in their bedroom when, about four o'clock in the morning, they were awakened by the ringing of the bedside phone. Ortman, his wife recounted, spoke but two words—"Yes" and "Thanks." He then dressed in a frenzy of excitement. As her husband left the house, still wearing his bedroom slippers and leaving his lower plate on the shelf in the bathroom, he said: "It's all over now. I'll be back in an hour. We've got this thing whipped."

That morning at dawn the Acme Photographers went up in fire. Ortman's charred body was identified in the wreckage. There was a loop of scorched picture wire about the corpse's neck and the coroner's opinion was "murder by strangulation."

"This is no firebug," the Dean repeated. "This is just good old-fashioned crime of a very virulent and contagious type. It seems to be spreading. I feel the time has come, Ben, for us to dynamite these babies loose."

The Solidarity Insurance Company was locally owned, organized and financed. Fred Ortman had promoted the business on a shoe-string. The idea had taken hold and the town had gone for it strong. Business clubs agreed that the Solidarity had a big future. Then came the down-swing—first the fires, then Fred Ortman's murder. The fires continued, increased, and at present were riding a new high. Solidarity was in a bad way.

The manager's offices took up the entire third floor of the new black-glass-and-metal building. Lettered in gold across the double plate glass door panel, the company's slogan said

He Liveth Best Who Serveth Best
All Things Both Great And Small—
SOLIDARITY'S YOUR FRIEND

Inside, we could see a fleet of golden-oak desks, with their typewriters and wire baskets, manned by a none too busy crew of office workers.

We had a little difficulty in attaining the private sanctum of Hilliston Keith, Solidarity's new head man. I'd heard around town about Hilliston Keith. He'd been imported from Chicago to take over a dying business where Ortman had left it. Mr. Keith styled himself a "business doctor" and he was considered very high-pressure.

The Dean and I took in a load of the pseudo-manorial office furnishings. Stagy was the word for it. I saw the Dean wince. The room had been completely redecorated for Mr. Keith. The dark walnut wainscoting, the huge desk and the peach-bloom rug had been imported, along with Mr. Keith, from Chicago. So had the strawberry-and-cream blonde who sat so demurely on a silken hassock by Mr. Keith's ankle.

You know Hilliston Keith's type. The perpetual college man. He was fifty and had the mannerisms of an eighteen-year-old. His expensive tweed vest was studded with college emblems. I could make out, among others, two diamond-set fraternity pins and a little gold football. He ignored us as we entered. You would have thought we were just a couple of window-cleaners who had got lost in the building. He lighted a cigarette, whipped out the match and tossed it in the wastebasket.

The Dean bowed from the waist to acknowledge introductions which weren't forthcoming and said pleasantly: "Don't drop matches in the waste-basket. It's an unintelligent habit and very hazardous. You'd make a precarious assured, Mr. Keith." The blonde smiled. And she had a nice smile.

Little red veins stood out in Keith's face. He turned china-blue eyes on us and took out a memorandum from the desk drawer.

"The Dean," he read. His loose lips pursed with scorn. He turned to the girl and raised his eyebrows. "Dean of what and when?" he asked her in a theatrical voice. "No one seems to know. Livelihood, fortune-telling." The blonde perked up. "Hobby, amateur detective. Reference, the police commissioner himself." Keith wrinkled his nose. "Something smells. Whatever he's selling, we don't want any—do we Bitsey?"

"I do," the blonde said brightly. "This little girl does. She wants some."

"I came here to offer you a proposition, Mr. Keith," the Dean said amiably. "I intended to charge you ten thousand dollars to break up this arson ring that is wrecking your company. My proposition was satisfaction in six days or no pay. I've changed my mind. I don't like you and I don't like your insolvent company. Good day, sir."

Hilliston Keith lost his composure. "Get out of here!" he shouted. His voice creaked. "Get out of here, you meddling fourflushing charlatan!"

The blonde scrambled from the hassock and intercepted us at the door. She touched my elbow. "How do you tell these fortunes?" she asked. "I mean how? I mean cards or stars or crystal ball or what?"

I grinned. She was as hard as manganese but you couldn't help liking her. "You'd be surprised," I answered. "He can do it with rods and incense and flour and roosters. But our big play is reading the soles of your feet. Yes, I said reading the soles of your feet."

I knew it would floor her. And it did.

Out in the street, the Dean said: "A very profitable interview."

I gave him a cut with my right eye to see if he was kidding. He wasn't.

"We really have him softened up," the Dean chuckled. "We've got him plastic, boy, plastic. He's headed for twenty thousand and he doesn't suspect it. It's a great business. You'll learn to love it."

This was a sample of the Dean's own particular brand of guerrilla skirmishing. I couldn't for the life of me tell what he was talking about but one thing I knew, from past experience, was that when he started to forage he always brought in big game at top prices.

He popped a *non sequitur* at me before I could comment. "How about your gun, Ben? Have you got it with you?"

"Of course."

"Well, keep it handy. You may be needing it."

Chapter 2

THE FEEBLEWIT HAD BEEN AROUND

THERE WAS NO WAY of knowing just how many people in our town called the Dean friend, but the total would have been astounding. He developed his most casual acquaintances into deep friendships. He would do a favor whenever he could and save the return until he needed it. He had a hundred and one interests. He could milk a rattlesnake, fashion jewelry from Mexican coins, or load a pair of dice like an expert. Take his homemade camera, for instance, and you'll know what I mean. The Dean was sitting in a dentist's anteroom one afternoon waiting for his appointment and leafing through some boys' magazine when he came across directions on how to make your own camera for forty-seven cents. At home that night, he put one together. It was a good one, too. He took a picture of Mrs. Duffy, our landlady, setting out the milk bottles and won fifteen bucks in a big photo contest.

Nobody, not even me, knew what he did when he was away from the house. I found out by accident once that he was a professional piano-tuner. When I mentioned it to him, he said it got you into exclusive places like brokers' homes and backroom dancehalls.

We grabbed lunch at a cafeteria. The Dean bought a fresh copy of the *Journal,* turned to the editorial page, and indicated a paragraph. He seemed to be expecting it.

"Just off the press," he said. "Wait until Keith sees this."

It was a single paragraph winding up a long bitter editorial.

... should leave no stone unturned in our effort to curb this wave of incendiarism. Citizens in responsible positions appear to show little or no interest. It has come to us reliably, for instance, that only this morning, Dean Wardlow Rock, well known local investigator, and his assistant, Benton Matthews, driven by civic motives, offered their cooperation in point to a certain heavily involved insurance company and were emphatically discouraged.

I did a little mental arithmetic. It was impossible. The linotype operator must have had the copy at least an hour before our interview with Solidarity's new manager.

"That's right," the Dean remarked as I opened my mouth to inquire. "The newspaper had the information before our visit. As a matter of fact, I phoned it in to Hank Edwards, the city editor, before breakfast—while you were going over the reception room with your maidenly cheesecloth. I once helped Hank in a little libel fiasco."

I shook my head and frowned.

"You don't like it, eh? Hold on tight because unless I'm wrong it's due to get worse and worse."

How true.

We separated in front of the restaurant. I headed for the apartment. The Dean had mumbled something vague about getting a little air. Actually, he wasn't fooling me—and he knew it. When a case was in the making, he would disappear for a few hours and shoot a high-velocity charge of personality through his network of friends and admirers. He had dished out favors—now he was on the receiving end. He was about to put out the word to his informers.

I knew results would be immediate, for when the Dean stirred up action he didn't fool.

Mrs. Duffy, our landlady, was sitting in her bay window, shining her silver plate and keeping an eye cocked for me through her ribboned and rosetted curtains. As I entered the hall she opened her door a crack and beckoned. The customary gust of hundred-proof lilac perfume enfolded me.

"Mr. Matthews," she whispered in a stage voice, "there's two strangers"—anyone who didn't live in our house was a stranger—"in your reception room. Sitting there saying they want their fortunes told. I don't like their looks. If you should ask me I should say beware." The door closed as she withdrew.

Well, of course, I should have taken her advice. Her husband, Pat, had been a policeman for twenty years before he died, so Mrs. Duffy knew a thug when she saw one. It was the Mrs. Duffy atmosphere, the lilac perfume and the whispering and the cerise fingernails, that made me careless. If she were to tell you that arsenic was poisonous you'd discount it as Duffy whimsy.

I'm here to tell you I should have bewared. These two boys were poisonous. I could see, as soon as I stepped into the room, that the future was very dark and I didn't need the Dean with his thaumaturgics and grimoire to spell it out for me. One of the lads, short and chunky, and dressed in what sometimes is known as a symphony of browns, was stretched out on the Dean's priceless antebellum loveseat, sound asleep. He blinked and sat up as I entered.

The second man stood leaning against the fireplace. He was long and lank and his clothes were ill-fitting and wrinkled. He had a little bony vicious face set in jaundiced skin. His right ear was trimmed off close to his skull.

The gaunt man's elbow was resting on the mantel shelf and he was whiling away the time and tedium by drawing imaginary beads on various articles of furniture with a .45 Colt automatic. He swung the gun in a short efficient arc to cover the pit of my stomach and said: "Shut the door. There's a draft."

The chunky man in brown got to his feet, yawned, came over to me, and snapped a sudden backhand blow at my chin which knocked me to my knees.

"That's for waking me up."

"Get his gun, Herb," the gaunt man said. "And shut up."

I allowed him to take it. There was nothing else to do.

"My, my," Herb said clicking his tongue. "A bad man's gun—a bulldog. And it comes out so easy. Ain't this the guy, Dorf, that's supposed to be a wizard with one of these things?"

"I know a butcher shop when I see one," I said.

"Hold it, Loose Lip," the gaunt man said coldly to Herb. "I'll take care of this." He held a copy of the *Journal,* folded to the Dean's editorial, before my eyes. "This make sense to you?"

"Yes," I said. "It's true. We tried to get an in but they wouldn't have us. They gave us the bum's rush."

Dorf studied me with his deadly eyes. "I believe you," he said finally. "I believe you're telling the honest truth. That alters cases. You don't know nothing or they'd have bought it." Back of his bleak eyes, he was turning the thing over in his mind.

"What do we do?" the chunky man asked.

"We give this bimbo the beating of his life. Here and now. We send him to the hospital. We don't knock him off. We just learn him and his boss to stay in their own back yard."

Herb slipped a pair of brass knuckles on his hand and tiptoed to my side, like a dancer.

There was a boisterous thumping on the door and Mrs. Duffy's voice called: "I'm coming in, Mr. Matthews." Herb stuck his hand in his pocket and the gaunt man hung his hat over his gun-fist.

"Be good," Dorf said.

Mrs. Duffy minced into the room. She carried a tea tray covered with a piece of her fanciest linen. "And here's your bit of tay, Mr. Matthews," she said. I couldn't get the Irish dialect—her name before she married was Blugenheim. "I brought you some of them nice licorice muffins you're so crazy about." Licorice in any form gags me. "I just throwed a scrap of rag over them to keep them warm," she added.

She placed the tray on a table by my hand and smiled. "They's enough to go round. Help yourself and pass them to your fascinating friends."

"Scram," Herb said. "You're intrudin'. We're getting our fortunes told." She flounced out.

"Would you like a cup of tea and a licorice muffin," Dorf inquired with heavy sarcasm, "or shall we get on with our business?"

I said: "You've asked me. I've told you I don't know anything. You're way out of bounds. I don't like it and the Dean'll like it less. Anybody can make a mistake once so button up your coats and highball out of here before you get hurt."

Herb slapped splay-fingered at my cheek and I caught his thumb and snapped it for him. Dorf stepped in and they gave me my beating. It was a regular routine five-dollar beating that is the stock-in-trade of any poolroom thug. They started it off with a blackjack behind my ear to get me groggy and then went to work.

The Dean was pouring brandy down my throat and Mrs. Duffy was washing a cut in my scalp. "Where are they?" I asked weakly.

"Gone," the Dean said. "But not forgotten."

Mrs. Duffy fluttered. "Why didn't you use the pistol?"

I sat up. "What pistol?"

She lifted the cloth from the tray. Beneath, glinting blue steel, lay a Police Positive—Pat Duffy's old service gun. My vision blurred.

Mrs. Duffy's voice came to me. "You're just too tender-hearted. You knew it was there all the time, Mr. Matthews, you can't fool me. You'll have

to learn to assert yourself a little, that's what's wrong with you. There are
some very unpleasant people in this world. There are some very nice ones,
too, of course, take for instance—My, I almost forgot!"

It was then she told us about our other visitor—the old lady.

An old lady, very quaint, had called on us early that morning. She wore
a lot of old-fashioned lace and artificial flowers and things and was very
sociable and Mrs. Duffy took to her right away. She left us a message but
it was so mixed up a person couldn't remember it. Mrs. Duffy made a val-
iant effort. It didn't make sense, she insisted. Something about five diamonds in the north and five diamonds in the south.

We were to find out later that this cryptic information was really very
simple and very important. We struggled with it a little while and gave it
up. Had we spiked it then for what it so transparently was, we could have
put a stop that very night to the wave of fire and murder that was flooding
our town.

The phone call from Huey, the pawnbroker, came through that night after
supper. I was still a little fuzzy from my mauling. The pawnbroker rang to
pass along a hot tip. He had a customer in his shop, he said, whom the
Dean would like to talk to. Something to do with the Ortman kill. Come
right away. This customer was a nut. Huey would try to hold him until we
arrived.

"This lad Huey," the Dean said eight minutes later as we piled into a cab
and headed for the waterfront, "is a real friend. He has a brain as big as a
watermelon. If he says he'll hold him, he will. But maybe we'd better hurry."
He leaned forward. "How about a little more speed, driver?"

I've seen tenderloins and tenderloins—in fact I was raised in one—but
Huey's neighborhood was tough enough even for me. There was the smell
of brackish seawater and the musty ammoniac odor of decaying fruit from
the warehouses. The streets were bright with the lights of poolrooms and
taverns and the alleys were as dark as the mouth of Hades. Huey's pawnshop was a narrow one-story frame matchbox wedged between a cement-
block bowling alley and a crumbling brick flophouse. The windows were
curtained tight with sleazy black chintz. Huey's was temporarily closed.

The pawnbroker let us in. He was little and quick and bright in his movements like an English sparrow, the bird that can make a plump living in any
gutter in the country. He nodded silently and waggled his thumb toward
the interior of the store.

A grimy, unshaven man in a tattered olive-drab overcoat stood draped
against the glass showcase, an old-fashioned stereoscope glued to his face.

"O.K.," he said suddenly. "Change her."

Huey picked up the top card from a stack of photographic slides on the
counter and made the change. "This here is Niagara Falls froze over in winter."

"What in the world is this?" the Dean asked.

The pawnbroker smiled mirthlessly. "You tell me. This guy's a hobo and
a feeblewit. I been showing him scenes to keep him on ice for you." Huey
talked before the man in the tattered overcoat as though he were a child.
"He's got Fred Ortman's wallet and driving license. He showed it to me. He

came in to hock it but he won't let loose of it—he keeps switching the price."

"O.K.," the bum commanded. "Change her."

Huey slipped in a new slide. "This here is called *The Doctor's Vigil.* . . . Well, that's how it stands. Maybe you can do something with him."

The Dean touched the man on the shoulder. He blinked at us with bleary red-rimmed eyes. Without a word, he took the leather from his pocket and held it guardedly for our inspection. It was the wallet, all right—the one that police testimony reported burned. It was thick, with gold corners. The smooth ostrich hide was probably loaded with thumbprints.

"How much?" the Dean asked curtly.

The bum showed brown-streaked gums. "No dice. I'm keeping it. I've changed my mind. I ain't letting loose of it."

Huey grunted.

I said: "The gentleman does not desire to hypothecate."

"Put it this way," the Dean said. "Let Huey keep it tonight. Here in the shop. He's got a burglar-proof set-up and a good strong safe. How does that sound? Tomorrow, we'll do business."

The man grimaced angrily. "You fellows quit picking on me. Here's what I say—let Huey keep it tonight, he's got a yegg-proof set-up and a good safe. Tomorrow we'll do business. How does that sound?"

I think we all blinked. It was that easy.

"May I ask," the Dean inquired, "how you happened to get it?"

"Between the eyes."

Huey cut in: "He keeps saying that."

"Tell me about it," the Dean said soothingly. "Tell me how come."

"Oh. You wanna know how come. I was traveling into town on a string of gondolas and when we pass under Cherry Street some guy leans out over the bridge and lets it go. It sails down and socks me between the eyes."

"Did you see this man?"

"Oh sure. They's a light on the bridge—"

"Can you describe him?"

"No boss. I can't even describe nobody."

"Listen," the Dean pleaded. "Think. Was he tall? Short? Thin? Heavy? Was he light-complected or dark?"

The bum smiled helplessly. "That there stuff's too much for me. I can't describe him but I can tell you who he was—if that'll be any help. He was Sprigsey O'Hare."

"Sprigsey O'Hare! Are you sure?"

The hobo's stubbled, repellent face set in coarse malicious lines. "Sure I'm sure. I know them all. Big and little, in and out. I'm Daddy Melton and I been around. Yessir, you're talking to Daddy Melton, gents. Now if you'll so kindly open that door I'll be going."

We took the wallet back under Huey's jeweler's light and dusted it. Believe it or not, there wasn't a fingerprint on it. Not one. The leather had been rubbed down and cleaned with what smelled like tan shoe polish. And our hobo had been deft enough to get it out of his pocket and lay it on the counter without leaving so much as a smudge. Daddy Melton might have been a feeblewit but it looked like he was telling the truth when he said he had been around.

"Lock it up, Huey," the Dean said. "We're through with it. Tomorrow, notify the police but leave out the O'Hare angle. Daddy Melton won't be back—it looks as though you scared him when you called us in."

Chapter 3

MURDER IN FOUR SUITS

THREE POLICE CARS and an ambulance were parked at the curb before our rooming house. Gawkers congested the entranceway, stretched over the iron-pipe banister in their effort to peer into our windows. Something was causing a lot of excitement in our apartment.

A harness cop passed us into our living quarters. A circle of detectives stood in the center of the reception room, gazing at the floor. At their feet, surrounded by a ring of polished shoes, lay a pathetic huddle of wine silk and faded lace. I knew, and the Dean knew, that our visitor had returned. The old lady had come back and now she lay contorted in violent death.

"It'll get worse," the Dean had warned me. I looked away, a little sick.

There was a lot of bustle going on. The Dean was taking casual invoice of those present. Some of the police force were friendly to us—and some were pretty much the opposite. I suppose that's the position all private investigators are in. The Dean's drag with the commissioner both helped and hurt us.

Captain Kunkle was in charge and Kunkle was sociable enough if it didn't cost him pennies in prestige. Malloy wasn't in sight.

The M. E. said loudly: "Well, brethren, it's death by strangulation—or so it appears without autopsy. A loop of picture wire about her throat. Knotted in the back with the same twist that we found in that Ortman business."

Mrs. Duffy, seeing a light beneath our door and getting no response to our knock, had entered and discovered the body. She had called the police and retired to the seclusion of her boudoir.

Captain Kunkle, pressed and starched and powdered and heavily lotioned, prowled the room. He would take a step and stop, frown, wink, and shake his head. He was cerebrating for the benefit of his subordinates. Suddenly he wheeled and came to a caisson halt before the Dean.

"Spent the evening out, eh, Rock?"

"That's right." The Dean got his little Cuban cigar going.

"Doing what, may I ask?"

"Pricing a second-hand billfold."

There was a laugh. The captain flinched. "Jokes later, Rock. Please. We're in the presence of death. All we want is your help. You must know something helpful. Who is this party?"

"Never saw her before, Captain. No identification in her pocketbook?"

"No pocketbook, Rock. Strange thing."

The Dean said: "She's a complete stranger to me. I don't know a thing, but if you're interested I can tell you what I think. It's my conviction that this, in some way that is completely obscure to me, ties directly with this arson wave. Of course, I may be entirely wrong. She may have come here for a reading and walked in on a cat—but I doubt it. The missing pocket-book suggests that she was robbed. If it wasn't robbery and murder, your guess as to why it was done here in my living room is as good as mine."

The exultant voice of Lieutenant Malloy rasped from the bedroom: "Come here a minute, Captain."

I thought the Dean was going juramentado when we got a look at our bedroom. Clothes were thrown from the dresser and closet and lay strewn about the floor. The Dean's expensive, specially built mattress was slit from end to end.

"Who did this?" the Dean asked coldly. "You, Lieutenant?"

They say there never was a man who hadn't at least one mortal enemy. Malloy was the Dean's. Which was too bad, in a way, because in my estimation Malloy was the best man on the force. I think the Dean resented Malloy because he was so efficient and had the added advantage of the police system to aid him in getting results. And Malloy—everything the Dean said or did brushed him the wrong way. He knew the Dean had a much better brain and knew the commissioner realized it.

"Everything was this way when we got here," Malloy sneered. "Maybe you keep it this way. Maybe the old lady tore it up."

We waited. There was a crafty and satisfied look in Malloy's eyes. "Me, I've been browsing in your private, and I mean private, library. Get me, Rock?"

The Dean said woodenly: "No, I don't. And I wish I did."

The captain puffed out his breath and glared. "What's all this horseplay, Lieutenant?"

Malloy drew down the corners of his mouth. "We got him where we want him, Captain. Salted and peppered and ready to serve." With a flourish, he laid three leather-bound books on the dresser. "I found these in that tin steamer trunk under the bed. Take a look at them."

One by one, Captain Kunkle picked up the volumes and inspected them. The first was entitled *Spanish Garrote, The Art of Instant Suffocation*, the second was called *The Bola*. The third book, no bigger than a sweet-girl-graduate's diary, was the deadliest of the three. Kunkle glanced down the yellowed table of contents. "*Mm.* Why this is terrible. It's horrible. This is a kind of handbook for stranglers. Just listen to this: *The Science of Throttling. London, 1821. Thuggee—The Brotherhood of Kali—The Silken Scarf—The Bowstring—*" He closed the book with distaste and snapped the covers with his thumbnail. "I never saw the like. There should be a law. Rock, are these your books?"

The Dean said: "No. But I wish to heaven they were. The last one, by the way, Malloy, is worth a hatful of dollars. I imagine if you'll call the City Museum you'll learn that all three were stolen from their rare-book collection."—Malloy reached for the phone.—"They were left here in a not too subtle attempt to frame me for this promiscuous choking."

Malloy finished his conversation and slammed down the receiver. "He's right. They were stolen and not reported to us. There's a reward."

Half an hour later, after the tumult and the shouting had died and we were alone again, Mrs. Duffy paid us a short, snappy visit. She had the old lady's pocketbook, a big shiny patent-leather one, under her arm.

She told us about it. "I seen the streak of light and opened the door and there she lay, poor thing, as pretty as a bride in her nice silk dress. Well, I stood and looked and all at once it come over me that she had been slew. I said, 'Seraphina, that nice old lady's been foul kilt right here under your own rooftree.' So I called the officers."

The Dean started to ask a question but she waved him to silence. "First I picked up the pocketbook. Pat always claimed that officers brought strangers in the house—reporters and such. So I picked it up and took it to my room. Did I do right?"

The Dean patted her reassuringly on the shoulder. "You certainly did, Seraphina—if I may call you by what has hitherto been a concealed delight. Now go to bed and get a good sleep."

The pocketbook contained thirty-seven cents, a big brass door key, a tatting shuttle, and a newspaper clipping.

"Nothing here," I said. "We'd better turn this stuff back where it belongs."

The Dean said: "She was bringing us something. I've been sure of that all along. Was it this brass key, Ben?"

"I hardly think so."

"I agree. Then it must have been this news item." We held the clipping between us and examined it. It was torn from a column in the *Journal* and carried the masthead *Bridge Puzzlers*.

The clipping read—

'Populor' sends us this problem. What is the correct bidding for hands North and South? Solutions should be in the office of the Editor of this column not later than midnight, Thursday. Address communications, this department, care of the *Journal.*

So get out your thinking caps, fans, and see what you can do. Here it is. This week's Puzzler:

```
                          NORTH
                          S—K9385Q
                          H—(None)
                          D—KA45
                          C—287
                                                      EAST
          WEST                                        S—(None)
          S—J1064                                     H—843
          H—QJ109                                     D—Q10
          D—(None)                                    C—57AJQ867
          C—K10934
                          SOUTH
                          S—2A7
                          H—K25A67
                          D—253J
                          C—(None)
```

"I don't like it," the Dean said. "I don't like it a bit." He clipped a pair of spectacles on the bridge of his nose and settled back in his favorite broken-down morris. I opened a couple of bottles of ale and brought out a platter of cold crackling bread.

"It's a cipher and a very simple one," the Dean observed. "You can almost read it by sight. It was evidently chosen for persons who weren't particularly bright—like our friends Herb and Dorf—who would have difficulty in re-membering a complicated key. Before we tackle it, let's do some recon-structing."

He closed his eyes. "I think our elderly visitor was a bridge addict who followed this column in the paper. I imagine she has encountered these messages before this—for I am sure they have appeared in the past. The first few times she was no doubt astounded and confused at the unorthodox presentation—it is likely that the hands presented no problem at all. In any event, it is certain that no bridge problem was ever set up in such a man-ner—note how the suit sequences are jumbled numerically. This is so symp-tomatic as to preclude the possibility of mere typographer's error."

I had noticed this myself. The proper arrangement for Spades in North's hand should have been KQ9853—from the highest to the lowest—instead of K9385Q.

"To get back to our old lady," the Dean continued. "At first she was bewildered. Then she must have begun to wonder. Maybe she was a bit of a cryptographer herself—many recluses are. In any event, it is evident she was disturbed to find a five of diamonds in the hands of both North and South, two club sevens in East's hand as well as other duplications. I think we can take it for granted that she broke this message down and smelled a rat. Why she came to see us, we can only conjecture. Possibly because of our previous newspaper publicity. We can say that she solved the message and that her murderers, finding it out, trailed her here and killed her."

Subsequent events proved the Dean correct in his logic. The old lady had made a disastrous blunder.

"A deck of playing cards," the Dean explained, "offers many methods of communication. This particular system is all right if the entire deck is used helter-skelter. It seems to me to be a little limited to selection used in suit sequence." He touched his ale to his tongue. "However and however."

He was way over my head. My jaw dropped when he said placidly: "I'm going to let you solve this for us, Ben."

"Listen," I said. "This is no time for monkey business. Me solve a cipher? I can hardly figure out the directions on a box of aspirin."

"You've been to school, haven't you?"

"Through the sixth grade."

"Quite sufficient. A first-grader could break it down—if he could count to fifty-two."

"Nuts," I said, "You're taking me for a ride!"

"Take a pencil and paper," the Dean advised. I did. "Now, Ben, how many letters in the alphabet?"

"Twenty-six."

"So far, so good. Two times twenty-six are—?"

"Fifty-two." I grinned. I was beginning to see the light. "Then a deck of cards equals a double alphabet?"

"That's right. Two suits equal one complete alphabet—the four suits equal two. The next thing is the suit order. I imagine we can take the customary bridge rating as given here—spades and hearts will be the first group, diamonds and clubs the second."

He developed the probability. "We'd better check into that. The ace of diamonds would be the first letter in the second alphabet, or "a". The five of diamonds would then be "e". And that's the card that bothered the old lady because of its duplication. Check. The overuse of "e" is characteristic of the novice cryptographer. All right. Get to work. You take over from here."

Well, it's hard to believe but I broke it down in seventeen minutes. First, I made a list like this. I put the two suits, spades and hearts together, to form one alphabet, running from the ace of spades to the king of hearts. Then I ran off the diamonds and clubs to match.

Spades—

A	2	3	4	5	6	7	8	9	10	J	Q	K
A	B	C	D	E	F	G	H	I	J	K	L	M

Hearts—

A	2	3	4	5	6	7	8	9	10	J	Q	K
N	O	P	Q	R	S	T	U	V	W	X	Y	Z

Diamonds—

A	2	3	4	5	6	7	8	9	10	J	Q	K
A	B	C	D	E	F	G	H	I	J	K	L	M

Clubs—

A	2	3	4	5	6	7	8	9	10	J	Q	K
N	O	P	Q	R	S	T	U	V	W	X	Y	Z

And then I substituted in the original problem and managed to get this—

MICHEL
MADE
OUT

(Blank)		(Blank)
KJFD	BAG	UQP
YXWV	ZORN ST	LJHFG
ZWVPQ	BECK	RSAXY

The Dean inspected it. "There you are," he said. "East and West are blank—catch-alls for unused letters. The message is 'Michel made out. Bag Mr. Beck on Zorn Street.' This paper clipping was our visitor's death warrant."

"What does it mean?" I asked.

"It means more devilishness. Probably more fire."

I started for my coat. "Zorn Street, eh?" He stayed me with his hand. "We're too late, Ben. I'm sure of that. They've got the wind up. It was this clipping that was the object of so strenuous a search here in our bedroom. Yes, Mr. Beck's delicatessen—or grocery— or whatever it is, has gone up in flames some time ago. These people are desperate. They know we're hot after them. Just relax a bit before we do anything."

For a few minutes, he was silent. "What irritates me," he said abruptly, "is the nature of the whole affair. It's essentially transparent but I can't seem to unveil it. Believe me, Ben, we're dealing with one mind—a criminal mind which has put a new twist to an old racket. Let's see what we know about our quarry. We know, first of all, that his financial returns are so great as to cause him to kill to protect them. To kill at the slightest excuse whenever, and as often, as he feels his profits are in jeopardy. Secondly, in choosing his cipher he gravitated to the bridge column in the newspaper. Not the want ads, for instance, but the bridge column. Dorf and Herb would grav-itate to spit-in-the-ocean and red-dog. Thirdly, and most important, I think our criminal mind has had legitimate business training. I can't explain it to you but the imprint is there, a pattern of routine and systematic attention to detail. Yes, Ben, when we spear him our fish will turn out to be a man of ledgers and accounts."

"What about this Michel?" I asked. "Who is he? And what do we do about it?"

"Building on the theory of an arson ring, we can suppose Michel to be the fixer—the go-between who makes the arrangements. Who he is, I can't tell you at this moment. Forget him, Ben. His days are numbered." The Dean smiled. "You forget him. I won't. In fact, he's number one boy on my list."

The phone buzzed and I answered. "Your offer is accepted!" a voice shouted into my ear. "You're hired. Get on the case. Now!"

I cupped my hand over the mouthpiece. "Our offer is accepted," I told the Dean. "It's Hilliston Keith. He says we're hired."

"Tell him it's twenty thousand now," the Dean said.

"We've made new terms," I relayed. "Twenty thousand or no soap." I could clearly hear Keith's breathing, a sort of fluttery sputter. Finally, he said: "Accepted. Call Mr. Rock."

I nodded and the Dean shared the receiver with me. "I'm rather busy," the Dean explained. "So you had better let me do the talking, Mr. Keith. Has the Solidarity in its employ an ex-convict by the name of Sprigsey O'Hare. Or don't you know? He might be using another name, you under-stand."

"I know the man you mean," Keith said slowly. "Or rather I know of him. He worked for Ortman until Ortman canned him—about three days before Ortman's murder. The police have been all over that field without result. O'Hare has vanished. Information indicates he is an itinerant somewhere in the Middle West following the sugar-beet crop. I really don't see—"

The Dean closed his eyes in admiration. "There's genius behind this. A blocker in the beet fields. Who would ever think of that! That's about all. By the way, how much was Beck insured for?"

"Fifty thousand, building and stock. That's what I called you about." Keith gasped. "Wait a minute. Where did you hear about it? It just hap-pened."

The Dean chuckled. "I read it in this morning's paper. Don't tell me you passed it up? One thing more. Is Miss Bitsey about?"

Keith coughed. "Why, yes she is. By a remarkable accident, by a strange—" The blonde's tiny voice chirruped: "It's me. It's this little girl. Mr. Rock, I wanted to ask you this morning—do precious stones vibrate in harmony with their zodiacal signs. I mean, is the amethyst under the power of Sagittarius and can it make you go to sleep or get rid of a hangover, like a man I met on the train said?"

"So the ancient lapidists affirmed," the Dean said gravely. "Now, my dear, you can help me if you will. I am casting Mr. Keith's horoscope for him—without his knowledge, as a sort of surprise. Can you tell me if he has a middle name?"

"Why, yes," she said. "He does have. Now how shall I say it? You know about the two Irishmen?"

The Dean waggled his head. "The girl's good," he whispered to me, and into the phone. "Patrick?"

"No. The other."

"Michael?"

"That's right."

The blonde was rattling away, talking a mile a minute about astral spheres and planetary influences as the Dean eased the receiver down on the bracket. "I like that whelp," he mused. "I don't know why, but I do. . . . Tell me, Ben, what do you know about the name Michael?"

"Only that it's as Irish as the shamrock," I retorted.

"Wrong on all counts. A common fallacy. No, it's not Irish but Latin. It is from the Hebrew *Mikael* which, I believe, means: Who is like God? It is a very popular name and found in many languages. In Italian it is Michele, in Spanish it is Miguel. In French it is Michel."

The brick building had been gutted from basement to eaves. Its front wall had collapsed into the cobblestone street, throwing hot bricks and fragments of plaster as far as the mailbox half a block away. By the time we arrived, the department had checked it as safe. Workers had cleared the debris from the car tracks. Though it was after midnight, a handful of owlish slum children stood about, staring at the wreckage. The wet ashes gave off a strong, sickening smell. In the gutter lay a shattered wooden sign:

JOHN BECK—FURS

The Dean tapped the sign with his toe. "Furs. The racket is expanding. It'll have to be scotched and soon."

A mangy cat stepped daintily around the puddles and sniffed at the burnt timbers.

"She smells her nieces and her sisters and her cousins and her aunts," I said. "Many a cat pelt went up in that blaze."

One of the children, a little undernourished kid with tufts of cornsilk hair at his ragged collar, turned a pale, wrinkled face in our direction. He couldn't have been over nine but he spoke with the hostility of a tired, old man.

"Get wise to yourself," he slurred. "Beck's skins were all Grade-A. You uptown mugs get in my hair." I grinned. I knew how he felt. I had been a slum kid myself.

The Dean edged into the conversation. He showed a friendly, toothy grin and waved a big paw. He was putting on the harmless-crackpot act. "I hesitate to interrupt—but isn't that a kitchen range I see there in the wreckage?"

The boy watched him warily.

The Dean went on: "B'Jove, it is! So Mr. Beck lived in his store. Now he is homeless!"

"He'll get by," the kid burst out. "We get by down here. We got a good friend."

The Dean raised his eyebrows. "And who might Mr. Beck's friend be?"

A tiny five-year-old came to life. "Johnny Carter, he's our friend. He helps poor people. He gives kids candy at his drugstore."

The older boy cuffed the youngster. "Button your lip," he said.

The Dean passed out seven quarters to seven unresponsive palms—and we withdrew.

We returned to our apartment and hit the hay. For a long time, I lay in the dark, thinking. I was stiff and aching and frustrated. It had been a big day and as far as I could see nothing had been accomplished. A couple of red-hots had worked me over, a bum had taken us for a ride, an old lady had been murdered on our broadloom and a man named Beck had burned down his store because a man named Michel had told him to. I tried to disabuse my mind of the confusion by concentrating on the twenty thousand.

The Dean's rumbling baritone came to me from the bed in his corner of the room. "A guardsman's uniform, Ben. Red pants, silver-plated sword and a bearskin shako." He sighed. "That would do the trick."

"Listen," I said. "I can stand just so much."

He paid no attention. "Oh well, I guess we'll have to fall back on my old reliable—the country-garden nosegay."

I heard him roll over and a second later came the soft, controlled breathing that told me he was asleep.

Chapter 4

POOR MAN'S BLACKMAIL

I STARTED OFF the next morning bull-mad. We had a long talk at breakfast and the Dean explained to me the nature of the crime we were tackling. I remembered that yesterday he had said, "arson and murder—and the arson is worse than the murder." Now I knew what he meant and agreed with him.

Shopkeepers were falling into the clutches of a new racket. Or rather a new combination of two old rackets—an arson-blackmail ring. From various sources, for some time, little bits of information had come to the Dean suggesting the existence of such a syndicate. Now he was convinced.

"Indescribably vicious, Ben," he said. "It's hard to believe. The usurer's racket—from which this borrows its method, I might add—is naive by comparison." His eyes smoldered beneath their shaggy brows. "Today we wind this case up."

I stared at him. "You know the strangler?"

"The strangler! Yes, I know the strangler. I could leave this room, find him and shoot him down in thirty minutes flat." Worry creased his brow. "But that wouldn't stop the burning and killing. It's the brain behind this ugly business we must smash. We'll have to depend on my country-garden nosegay."

I let that one pass.

He went on: "Their *modus operandi* is cruel and direct. Their prey is the small merchant, none too thriving, timid, without influence. A mark is selected and approached by the contact man—Michel, we can say—who implants the idea of insurance fraud, offers the services of arsonists to do the job, and guarantees immunity from suspicion. If the shopkeeper is interested, his goose is cooked. If his character and honesty outweigh his cupidity, the syndicate follows up with strong-arm intimidation. The merchant is bound to lose. He can't even level. His store is burned. The insurance is collected in its entirety by the syndicate."

The Dean talked on. He was a little white around the corners of the mouth.

"This is just a beginning," he said. "The victim, guilty of crime, is ensnared in a net of blackmail. From then on, though his family go hungry, he must pay to keep himself from jail. I have heard, in a roundabout way, of an Italian family living down by the river whose four boys turn over their weekly paychecks to save their father from imprisonment and disgrace."

I said: "Poor man's blackmail!"

"Yes," the Dean agreed. "And it's pretty beastly."

A city directory revealed to us that John Charles Carter ran a drugstore at the corner of Elm and Water Streets. Mrs. Sprigsey O'Hare was a little more difficult to locate. A call to the commissioner, himself, informed us, after a lot of fuss and feathers, that she was living under the name of Celadine La Varre at the Hotel Lord Ashton on West Third.

"The *Journal* first," the Dean said. "I've had a growing premonition."

In the cab on the way downtown, he clammed up. "We know," I observed, "that the editor of the bridge column is intentionally or accidently involved. He was involved in that cipher. You can't get around it."

The Dean grunted. "We'll see."

"Take it this way," I insisted. "Those notices were messages. They had to appear on certain days—definite days. That presupposes connivance. You can't get around that. This bridge editor is in deep."

"Deep," the Dean rumbled. I didn't like the way he said it.

We were always welcome at the *Journal*'s office. Dean Wardlow Rock was news anytime. Today he was red-hot. The boys at the *Journal* respected him, and let me tell you they were a hard bunch of lads to fool.

Edwards greeted us with a scoff. "Murder in detective's parlor. Man bites dog—that's news."

The Dean shook hands. "No, Hank," he corrected. "Man bites dog—that's kynanthropy. Kynanthropy, as you no doubt were about to remark, is a form of ensorcellment closely related to lycanthropy, or wolf madness. The lycanthrope, or kynanthrope, is variously known as the werewolf or loup-garou."

Edwards laughed. "You should be working for the *Britannica*."

"I have," the Dean said amiably. "A little monograph on the hippogryph. . . . Tell me, Hank, is the bridge editor in?"

The city editor looked disturbed. "It isn't a he—it's a she." He paused, considered a moment, and came to a decision. "You're a friend, Dean. I'm going to blow my top to you. We have a funny situation here. Things have been happening that I don't understand and don't like. Our bridge editor is an aristocratic dame down on her luck—by the name of Arabella Trimble. We forward her mail and she sends in her copy. I've only seen her once in my life, yesterday, when she came in to get a confession off her chest. It seems that every three weeks or so, she'd receive a 'problem' in a plain envelope, containing instructions to publish on such-and-such a day. With each of these requests there was enclosed a twenty-dollar bill. She figured at first that it was some crank that liked to see his stuff in print—and boy there are plenty—so—"

"So she succumbed," the Dean finished. "Is that all?"

"No. She was all steamed up. Acting mysterious. Wanted a confidential detective."

"And you suggested me?"

"I might have. Come to think of it—"

"That," said the Dean to me, "was her death warrant." And to Edwards, "Did she leave any of these notes with you?"

"No, she didn't, Rock. She said they must have come from a woman because they were saturated with lavender sachet." He shrugged. "Maybe she made herself a little unethical dough but she caught herself in time. No harm done."

"No harm done!" The Dean glared. "Strangled on my carpet and he says no harm done. Call up the city morgue, Hank. You'll find your Arabella Trimble. Twelve hours murdered and still unidentified!"

The Sunshine Palette Flower Shoppe was the answer to our search for a florist. For a moment, we stood on the sidewalk and marveled. Along the curb were set a row of bright scarlet potted plants. The little store, with about eight feet of window space, was all dressed up like it was going to a children's party. A green-and-yellow awning about the size of a cigarette paper shaded the passersby. We stepped through the narrow doorway, around a gilded milk bucket crammed with jonquils, and pushed our way inside.

A male clerk, built along the lines of Peter Pan, was sprucing up a display of snaps by picking off the dead blossoms. He hesitated, as though he were caught in some guilty act, and trotted up to wait on us.

"And today it is what?" He V'd the muscles in his cheeks and showed us a couple of dimples.

"And today it is an old-fashioned bouquet," the Dean grunted. The clerk was off like a butterfly. "Hold on," the Dean ordered. "Now wait." The clerk was all arrested motion and attention. "This is a special kind of bouquet," the Dean explained. "A country-garden nosegay, you might say. It must have a touch of modesty—calendulas, possibly. And a rustic cabin-in-the-woods atmosphere. American heather ought to fix that up. There must be, too, a suggestion of sentimental sweet sixteen; maybe you can figure that one out yourself. Put them all together so that they spell innocent schoolgirl."

"Oh. They're for a schoolgirl?" The clerk was interested. "Then may I advise—"

"No, you may not. And they're for no schoolgirl. If this girl went to any school at all it was the correction home. Now shuffle them up. We're in a rush."

When they came in or how they came in, I couldn't tell you. All at once they were there. Standing a little to one side and behind us like a couple of wax dummies from a back-street sideshow. Dorf and Herb—a man without an ear and a man in a brown suit.

Their hands were in their pockets and their faces were tense. They were all ready to click. It gave me a jolt that frosted the back of my neck.

"I thought we told you not to pry," Dorf said hoarsely. He was trembling with suppressed fury, his sallow face livid to his ear stump. "See that old sedan out front? Get going."

The Dean seemed mildly interested. "Followed us from the newspaper office, eh? Just like you did the old lady."

Dorf's chunky companion blurted out: "That—that wasn't us."

"Reef it, Loose Lip," Dorf warned. And to us, "O.K. Single-foot it out of here."

The Dean shook his head regretfully. "Sorry, we must decline. You boys toddle back to your sandpile."

Bedlam broke loose. I went into a half-crouch. Dorf's heavy gun lifted a wisp of tweed from the shoulder of my coat and slammed the elfin clerk into a showcase of orchids. The retracting carriage of his automatic jammed. He cursed. Out of the corner of my eye I saw the Dean going into action with his Magnum, saw Herb's brown ensemble jerk and collapse.

The gaunt man pivoted and ran, behind the counter to the rear. I dashed after him. We sprinted through a back room littered with green waxpaper, tinfoil, unfolded cardboard boxes, around a work table, over a floral piece depicting two clasped hands, and out the back door. He was in the open all the way, I could have snapped him off like a clay pipe—but he was unarmed. He was home free and he knew it. When he hit the alley nothing short of a cordon could have caught him.

I chased him three blocks for the principle of the thing and then he slipped me.

Whistles were skirling and sirens were screaming toward the Sunshine Pallette Flower Shoppe. The cops arrived at the shambles. The Dean had left. He was lining up his double play. I caught a cab to West Third and told the driver to wait.

If the Hotel Lord Ashton had ever been clean, sanitary and respectable, its era of gentility must have faded out about the time of Custer's last stand. Despite dim corridors, fly-specked lightbulbs and musty carpet, it still attracted its modicum of guests. In a manner of speaking, it was a family hotel—but what a family. Of the four characters sitting around in the lobby as I passed through, I spotted two on parole and one dodging his fourth sentence. The other was probably wanted.

The day clerk, a small time grifter named Saracetti, was sprawled behind the desk trimming his fingernails. He was using a stag-handled shiv with an illegally long, sheepsfoot blade. We'd met here and there around the spots and didn't like each other.

"Your chief's in Three-thirty-three." Saracetti tried to be pleasant but he just couldn't put it over. He showed an edging of squirrel teeth between his lips. "What's little Celadine been getting into?"

Little Celadine. See what I mean? Family hotel.

"Forget it," I snapped.

I stopped on the second floor, took my hat and coat off, hung them out of sight in a broom closet, and knocked on the first door I came to. A nautical-looking bimbo with a tattooed forearm opened up, glanced at my shirt-sleeves.

"Hate to trouble you," I apologized. "I'm next door. Ran out of writing paper. Could you spare me a sheet of hotel stationery? Getting it at the desk is like pulling teeth. The way they dole it out you'd think it was black bread and we was in the Russian army."

He broke into a guffaw and brought me a mittful.

I took the paper with its printed letterhead and returned to my coat. Getting plenty of old time arm-movement into my Spencerian, I wrote—

Better scram for the day. Take the service stairs. There's a cop called Malloy prowling the lobby asking about you. Told him you were out. Did I do right?

I signed the day-clerk's name—*Saracetti*—and tacked on the T.N.T.— *P.S.:-He keeps asking do you know a hobo named Melton?* I walked to the elevator and pushed the bell. When the creaking cage lifted, I said to the boy: "Here's a buck. Deliver this to Three-thirty-three in exactly ten minutes."

It was like shooting fish. The Dean had said do it. Mine not to reason why. I put on my hat and coat and went up to Three-thirty-three.

Celadine La Varre, more intimately known as Mrs. Sprigsey O'Hare, peeped an inch of soft cheek around the corner of the jamb and let me in. I took a long, hard look. This was what Sprigsey had deserted for fields full of beets.

She was a little brunette, slim and tapered. From the dainty crown of her lacquer-black hair to the high instep of her continental pumps, she was as trim a bit of domestic porcelain as you'll find outside the New Jersey potteries. The frock she stood in had cost eight Cs if it had cost a penny. Her violet eyes, pollen-soft, were warm and inviting.

She reminded me of another waif I once knew who robbed the mission collection to get a pistol to shoot her sister.

My eyes popped a little when I noticed that she was wearing a bouquet of old-fashioned flowers. There was the American heather and there were the calendulas.

The Dean was sitting on a red-and-gold chair, grinning wolfishly. He introduced me. "Very pretty flowers, Miss La Varre," I commented.

"Aren't they too lovely!" She really meant it. "Mr. Rock brought them.

He says it's a country-garden nosegay. They're supposed to express my character. The calendulas are for modesty and the heather is for innocence, I believe."

"Very tastefully selected," I affirmed.

"Thank you, Ben," the Dean put in complacently. "As a matter of fact, I picked them out of the showcase and arranged them myself. I did it a little hurriedly—"

Celadine caressed them. "They're beautiful. And that nice thing you said about my being—what was it?—an unsophisticated country-garden girl."

This kind of stuff embarrasses me. I was irritated to see that the Dean was enjoying himself immensely.

"I get no credit for that observation," he remarked. "Everybody says so. It's all up and down the avenue." He coughed. "Now just a question or two more. You haven't heard from Sprigsey since Ortman's death?"

"Yes. But the police have been all over—"

"I know. But I want to find your husband for you. You want him back, don't you?"

Her eyes warmed wistfully. "We were happy as doves."

There was a knock on the door. The shabby uniformed arm of my elevator boy thrust in the letter. She slit the envelope and ran down the paper in a single sweeping glance. Her eyes flickered. There was fear in her face now. Unmistakable terror. The Dean leaned back in his chair and hummed military snatches from the *1812 Overture*.

Miss La Varre came over and kissed him on the forehead. "You boys had better leave now."

She unleashed about a million dollars' worth of smile.

On the main floor, we dog-legged around the desk, out through the coffee shop, and piled into our waiting cab. "Watch the servants' entrance," the Dean said. "She'll be bursting out like a ball of fire. That letter really rang the chime!"

"Did I carry it off?" I asked.

"Perfectly." The Dean became somber. "Ben, Miss La Varre has supplied the key." He lowered his voice. "That girl's a dominicide."

"And what's a dominicide?" I asked.

"You don't understand? Why that half solves the case." He sighed. "Oh, well. To tell the truth, I half suspected it. It seemed strange that— There she comes!"

Celadine La Varre came out of the servants' door carrying a patent-leather traveling bag. She came like she was being chased by bats and snakes. Her little heels flying, she ran across the sidewalk, leaped into a gray coupe parked at the curb, and ground the starter. She was off in a screech of gears, around the corner and out of sight.

"Let's move," I said to the cabbie. "Don't lose her and there's money in it for you."

The gray coupe went down Highland to Adams. At Adams she set her brakes, twisted suddenly to the left, cut under the viaduct and out Canal. We stayed on her tail in and out of the Italian neighborhood, in and out of the riverfront district, and headed for the wharves beyond the city limits.

So suddenly we almost bumped into it, the little car pulled up before a rambling three-story building. From where we stopped, a block away, the big sign read:

WAREHOUSE 29

An indefinable emanation from the Dean told me he was highly satisfied.

The cab driver said sententiously: "The end of the rainbow. And is that a screwy dame! She checks out of a hotel, bag and baggage, and checks into a warehouse. What do I do now?"

"You turn around, drive downtown and collect a well-earned bonus."

"Where next?" I asked.

"The Solidarity Insurance Company," the Dean decided. "It's about time we talked with our employer."

My first impression was that the scene hadn't changed. Hilliston Keith, still at his desk, fiddled with his fraternity pins. The blonde was still demurely on her hassock at his ankle. Then, with a shock, I noticed that Keith had aged ten years since we had seen him. The "business doctor" was showing strain.

"Rock," he said, "I'm glad you dropped in. I've been trying to get you on the phone. It looks as though our break has come. This affair is clearing up."

"It's been perfectly clear to me right along," the Dean remarked quietly.

"Here," said Keith, ignoring him, "is something that will interest you." He had a square of brown paper on the desk before him. It was the usual criminal's handicraft—printed letters, cut and pasted. It said—

DID JOHN BECK'S FURS BURN? GARAGE OF COTTAGE BACK OF FERRY STREET PIGYARD TEN TONIGHT—BRING ROCK & MATTHEWS

"Slipped under my door this morning," Keith supplied. "What do you make of it?"

"This case has been solved for two hours," the Dean commented. "However"—he studied the message—"academically interesting. Letters cut, not from a newspaper as is customary, but from an old mail-order catalogue." He touched the paper to his nose. "Faint smell of lavender sachet."

That touched the blonde off. "The lavender sachet is me. It's me that smells that way, Mr. Rock. I always use lavender sachet."

"And a very charming scent it is," the Dean endorsed gallantly.

"It's my lucky perfume. Shall I tell you about it? A gypsy out in Tulsa explained a dream I had and said I should always—"

Keith broke in. "This business ought to be investigated." He seemed at a loss for words. "Unfortunately I have an engagement this evening—so you'll have to go it alone. You and Matthews."

"An engagement?" the blonde asked. "With whom?"

"Why, with you, my dear." Keith smiled. "You remember now, don't you?"

"That's a lot of Creole gumbo," she retorted. "Since when did you start having unbreakable engagements with me?"

The Dean said suavely: "I get the idea, Mr. Keith. And that's what we're paid for." He added casually: "Ortman. What's his widow doing now? Ortman left her well fixed, I presume?"

Keith looked embarrassed. "No, he didn't. As a matter of fact, she had a pretty tough time getting by. So we took her on. She holds down a desk here. Sort of pasturage. We figured we owed it to her."

The Dean was actually startled. I knew that somewhere his calculations had sprung a leak.

"Are you telling me," he said slowly, "that Fred Ortman left no life insurance?"

Keith's discomfiture reached its climax. "It's terrible isn't it—the head of Solidarity and he wasn't insured himself. Don't let it go any farther. Please. He probably did it from spite. He and his wife weren't so pally."

The Dean sighed with relief. "Man, you really had me twisted. So that's it. That's all I want to know. That explains the tan shoe polish."

Chapter 5

SEVEN STICKS OF DYNAMITE

THE FRECKLED, WHISTLING CLERK behind the cigar counter of John Charles Carter's drug store was a gunsel if I ever saw one. He had a boyish shock of straw-colored hair, cut in a teddy-bear pompadour, and a happy-go-lucky lilt to his tenor voice but his eyes were as inhumanly bleak as a chicken hawk's. He was coked to the ears—and working in a drugstore. Already, as soon as I took a look at him, I began to get ideas about Johnny Carter, the benevolent druggist, the poor man's friend.

The Dean unsnapped the old-fashioned clip-purse he carried and selected a calling card from his assortment. He laid it with a flourish on the green felt dice board and bowed. "Mr. Carter?"

The boy was flabbergasted. "I'm not the boss," he blurted. "I just work here." He was sure enough flattered. The Dean had a manner about him. The card said, *Athelstane Berrymeadow—Fur Broker.*

"Wait a minute," the kid said. He disappeared through a curtain at the rear. A second later, he was back. "O.K. The boss'll see you."

Now, I'm no authority on prescription rooms, but I'm here to tell you that the set-up in the back of Carter's drugstore was the weirdest sight I'd beheld in many a day.

Every inch of the walls that wasn't shelved with rows of bottles and jars, was plastered with expensive anatomical charts, foreign importations, they looked like, and across the face of these charts were scribbled notes in pencil. The floor was littered with bright bits of yarn and scraps of dainty cloth.

John Charles Carter sat in the midst of this disorder—sewing. The druggist was a little fat man with down on his cheeks. You got the impression that he didn't have to shave. His eyes were frog-lidded and had long, curling lashes.

He took the gold thimble off his finger, dropped it into the sewing bag which hung from the arm of his chair, patted the tiny pink baby dress on his knee. Yes. Baby dress.

"The third I've finished this week," he said proudly. "It's my hobby, gentlemen. Making baby clothes—dresses, vesties, little flannel gowns—for underprivileged infants."

The Dean was hearty in his approval. "Now that's a real charity, isn't it?" He picked up a needle and a piece of thread, made several cumbersome attempts at threading the needle and gave it up.

John Charles Carter watched him with sudden interest. "The thread's a little large," he said. "So you must twist it into the needle's eye."

The Dean tried again.

"No," the druggist explained pettishly. "You're twisting against the lay. You must twist with the lay."

"The lay?" The Dean raised his eyebrows. "That's a new one on me."

"The lay of a rope or cable or thread is the direction in which the strands are twisted—also, the degrees of tightness or division between strands."

"My," the Dean observed. "I didn't realize there was so much to sewing. Wonder if my grandmother knew that."

"Probably not," the druggist said silkily. "But sailors know it—and hangmen."

"So I was thinking," the Dean said.

The room became deathly silent. Suddenly, for no understandable reason, the gruesome charts upon the walls gave me a sensation of freshly opened graves. There was something evil here, too evil to comprehend. The scraps of cloth upon the floor seemed like snippings from shrouds, the little toad-like man became a pall-maker.

"You wanted to see me about what?" the druggist asked. "About Beck's furs?" He spoke with open contempt. "They burned, you know, Mr. Rock."

"So you know me?"

"I know you both. I know you are too intelligent to be threatened. But I will say this—get out of town."

The Dean turned to me. "I brought you here for a reason, Ben," he said calmly. "This man is our strangler. He kills for profit and he kills for love. The time will come soon when you must shoot him down. Shoot him like a dog, with a clear conscience. You have heard the admission from his own lips."

We left John Charles Carter, strangler, rigid in his chair, the little pink baby dress across his plump knee. Outside, I burst into a torrent of invectives.

The Dean hushed me. "Please, Ben. I feel the same way. This method is best. We want that killer, and we'll get him, but more even than Carter we must have the man behind him. I've just had a hunch. Let's drop around to headquarters."

Lieutenant Malloy was standing by the battered Victorian fountain in the tiled rotunda of City Hall, watching the sluggish carp poke among the peanut shells. He pretended to observe us by accident but something in his breathing suggested that he had seen us coming and had taken a quick run to head us off. He looked up as we approached and gave a blink of surprise.

"Gaze, Ben," the Dean declaimed, "at our ichtholatrous friend. Now we know from what pastime comes that piscine look in his eye."

Malloy snorted. "Save it. It's being wasted here." He studied the Dean's rugged, intelligent face. "Last night, down at your place, you told us you didn't know the old lady." He smiled wickedly. "You remember—the one murdered in your living room? This morning you drop into the *Journal* office and tell them it's a crank that works for them."

The Dean nodded. "Substantially correct."

"You wouldn't be suppressing evidence, would you?"

The Dean started to wisecrack and thought better of it. "No." The urge conquered and he said: "Not much."

Malloy flushed. "I ought to shove you in the can. The both of you. You"— he fumbled for expression—"you fray my patience."

"I know we do," the Dean said seriously. "You have the same effect on me. We're too good for each other." He was being perfectly honest and I knew it. The next breath he was off again, lying like a sea-lawyer.

"I have a client that's up against a queer proposition. It's too involved to go into. That's why I'm here. I want to talk to you. I want to ask you a question. Do you know of a Frenchman, a gambler, first name Michel, who might be mixed up in an oil deal?"

Malloy thought it over. He was only half fooled but he was smart enough to take a chance. The Dean had come to the right man. Malloy had the well-earned rep of never having forgotten the face or photo of a wanted man.

He said: "At the convention out West eight years ago, I looked through some pictures. There was a guy wanted by Denver, named Michel André Cartier. He wasn't a gambler and he wasn't a con man. He was a druggist. An escaped murderer. He had nutty hobbies—knotting fishnets, making lace, and hanging around the fancywork booths at county fairs."

It was just like looking in the back of the book for the answers. John Charles Carter was Michel André Cartier—Michel, the fixer for the syndicate. That let's Keith out, I thought.

The Dean appeared discouraged. "I don't think I'll be able to use it," he said. "It hardly seems possible. This man, the man I want, followed a carnival pulling spikes with his teeth. Thanks just the same."

"Think of that!" Malloy retorted harshly. "Well, there's two thousand reward outstanding. Dead or alive. There's police widows and their children that could use a slice of two thousand."

The Dean nodded absently. He hardly seemed to hear.

I had observed a big deal negotiated—and barely realized it. Those boys really understood each other.

We polished off a double supper apiece in Gino's Kitchen, the first food we'd had since breakfast, and the Dean slept in his bent-wire chair for two hours. At nine o'clock he raised his eyelids and said: "Let's stroll down to the waterfront."

I'd been thinking about Hilliston Michael Keith and his anonymous tip. There was plenty about it I didn't like. Keith didn't like it either or he wouldn't have crawfished.

I got to my feet. "As you say, Cagliostro. And against my better judgment."

River fog shrouded Ferry Street, hung about the sparse lights in clouds of steamy mist, condensed on our wrists and foreheads. It was a neighborhood of junkyards, wrecked-car lots, coal and lumber yards. Rusty machinery and abandoned squatter's shacks loomed in the haze like crippled monsters from some prehistoric slime. In seven blocks we passed no one.

The Dean halted, hands deep in his coat pockets and pointed, African fashion, with his chin. "Here's our pig yard—pig iron," he said. He glanced over his shoulder. "There should be—and is—our cottage, facing us."

Why such a dwelling had been built in such a location, we wondered. A little four-room Cape Cod. When the painters and carpenters had finished it, it must have looked, in its poisonous surroundings like an apple-cheeked country lad fresh come to town. Now the city had claimed it. It was vacant, its windows were boarded, its plumbing, no doubt, long since looted, sold for brass, lead and iron. At the rear we could make out the silhouette of a squat, one-car garage.

We crossed the street, took a cinder path around the deserted house and hesitated before the garage door. We were twenty minutes early.

"Looks more like a shop than a garage," the Dean observed. "If it's a garage, where the deuce is the drive?" He flashed his pencil-light over the cinders. Over the sandy lawn, straight up from the curb, were deep wheel ruts. "There's been a car, though, Ben. Just one and recently." He made no attempt at concealment, nor at lowering his voice. I figured he knew what he was doing, that there was no danger.

The double doors were hasped with a dime-store padlock. I grinned. "This is very elementary, Mr. Rock," I said. "A child could spring it. You have been to school, haven't you? How many letters in the alphabet? I am going to let you solve this for us."

The Dean was irritated. "Don't clown around. Open it up. Let's get in."

I put my handkerchief over it while I unlocked it. The performance bugged his eyes. He could have opened it himself with a bent nail but you could never have convinced him.

"Ben," he said in awed tones, "that's sheer witchcraft. You just put your hand under that handkerchief and it opens."

"That's right," I said modestly. "I'm pretty good."

I didn't mention the fact that I unlocked it with a key. I always carry three standards—a cheap padlock key, an old-time trunk key, and an ordinary desk key. They're great time-savers if they happen to be the proper size.

We swung out the door and stepped into the dark.

I reached for the light switch on the wall and a great weight struck my wrist, almost breaking it.

"Leave that alone!" the Dean whispered. "Don't move." He took three plumber's candles from his pocket and lighted them, moving with the greatest caution. "This place is a charnal house," he said. "I can smell it."

Celadine La Varre's gray coupe bulked before us in the flickering candlelight. Slumped in the seat, her head on the steering wheel, was the girl from the Hotel Lord Ashton. Was this, I wondered, what my note had sent her to? She had been dead for some hours. Knifed—not strangled.

The Dean was unmoved and unsurprised. "She's come to the end of her crooked mile," he said softly. "She has been given what she gave her husband and now she is with him in those mythical beet fields."

"Sprigsey dead?" I gaped.

"For weeks."

"And you knew it?"

"And so did you, Ben. I myself told you that Celadine had slain her lord and master. That, of course, was the solution to the whole case. That exposes the identity of the man behind this ugly business."

"You know that, too?"

"Of course. And so should you. Anyway, you'll meet him face to face within the hour."

My wrist ached from the blow he had given me. "Hurt you a little, eh? Look here." The Dean pointed over his head.

Where the ceiling overhead light should have been there was a plug—with a wire running to a workbench in the corner. The wire disappeared behind a small, shiny radio. We broke the connection and took a look.

The walnut veneer cabinet was cleaned out. Inside were stacked seven sticks of dynamite, waiting for a contact spark. Very simple. You flick the light switch and it's all over.

The Dean examined the bench. He rubbed his finger on a brownish stain and touched it to the tip of his tongue. "This was their shop, Ben," he said. "All the tools and materials have been moved. It is here their chemist designed his fires."

The fog had lifted. We caught a stray cab by luck, and relaxed. "Listen, Dean," I said. "Did you ever hear of the old device known as the spring-gun alibi?"

"Oh, come now, Ben." He looked at me with amusement.

"It's a fact. A guy sets a guntrap, kills his victim, and all the time he's making a speech at a charity banquet. No evidence against him and a perfect alibi."

"Are you pointing a finger of suspicion towards Mr. Hilliston Keith?"

I let him figure it out for himself.

"Listen," I said at length, "tell me this. Did you know we were heading for that dynamite tonight?"

"There's no danger in dynamite, Ben," the Dean said smugly. "It can't possibly explode unless you detonate it."

"You're nuttier than a keg of peanut brittle," I flared. "I don't know why I left the security of my alleys and garbage cans to work for you."

Chapter 6

THE HOUSE ON THE ROOF

WAREHOUSE 29 WAS DARK and menacing. We obscured ourselves in the shadows of the wharves and gave the building the once over. There was no glimmer of light from its shuttered windows, no indication of a watchman at his rounds. After a few minutes' survey, we circled the rambling structure and approached from the rear.

A little prowling and we located the loading platforms. The Dean started up the steps toward the heavy corrugated shipping doors but I stopped him.

"Lesson two in breaking and entering," I whispered. "Expensive locks on doors, childish gadgets on windows." I flashed my light under the platform. It illumined the frame of a ventilator window.

Three seconds later, it was open. "Simple, isn't it?" I asked. I prayed it wasn't rigged up with an alarm.

"It's a squeeze," the Dean said. "But maybe I can make it." We wormed through and dropped to the floor.

We were in a huge basement storeroom. The cement floor was piled high to the ceiling with packing cases, barrels and crates. Narrow aisles, canyon-like, cut through the stacked merchandise in a rabbit warren of cross paths. We took a quick survey . . . canned goods, hardware, bolts of cloth, photographers supplies, china ware.

For the most part, the cases were nailed and banded and ready for shipping. Black lettering on the white pine showed us that they were headed for Central America.

The Dean nodded. "Well, Ben," he said softly, "here we have earned our fee from Solidarity. In this room is half a ship load of evidence—evidence of fraud. If this stuff can be identified—and there should be little difficulty—the merchandise, itself, will revert to the insurance company and outstanding unpaid claims will be voided."

"You mean these goods were looted from the insured stores before the fires?"

"Certainly. The racket appears to be worked on the European industrial plan of utilizing all by-products. Merely a sideline. They've Central America as a safe market."

A heavy plywood box blocked the path. It was about the size of an electric refrigerator and was tilted against an I-beam upright. The painted address on it was still wet. The address said: *Harley P. Reams, Beartrack, Wyoming.*

The Dean gazed at the box in fascinated silence. "It has to be," he said at last. "Think of that! Well, this is a surprise. An unlooked-for development." He turned to me and tapped the wooden case with a stubby forefinger. "Very valuable shipment, Ben. But incorrectly addressed." Wolfish wrinkles creased his eyes. "Want to take a look?" The cover was as yet unnailed. He lifted it.

I sensed something pretty shocking was coming but I wasn't braced for what I got. Inside the box, arms stiffly at his sides, lay the fat little body of Michel André Cartier. He was packed neatly and firmly in a bed of excelsior. He had been knifed, as had been Celadine La Varre, in the throat. With his round cheeks and long lashes and cruel, simpering mouth he looked like some diabolical doll on a toy-shop shelf.

Without a word, the Dean replaced the lid. He took a half-inch of blue crayon from his vest pocket and crossed out Mr. Reams of Beartrack. In swift strokes, he printed: *Lt. Bill Malloy, Police Headquarters, City Hall, City.* Down in one corner in bold heavy letters, he wrote, *PERISHABLE.*

"That's tampering with evidence," I exclaimed.

He grinned. "No didactics now, please, Ben. Let's go upstairs."

The ground floor and the second floor were the same. More boxes, numbered but unaddressed. The top floor was empty. And when I say empty, I
mean clean. Not a cobweb or a granule of dust.

"A clean floor leaves no footprints," the Dean remarked. "We'll explore
a little."

An iron stairway, bolted to the back wall, led us to the roof. In the center
of the roof, hidden from the street below by the brick facing which extended
from the walls six feet above the roofline, was a small, one-room cabin. It
lay in the moonlight like the superstructure on the deck of a boat. Yellow
light flowed from the unshaded window. From where we stood, we could
see gay wall paper and cretonne curtains, an army cot, a small safe and a
desk.

At the desk sat Dorf, the gaunt man, checking down a ledger's page with
a grimy thumb. By his elbow was a pile of currency that would have choked
a horse.

The pebbled tar roofing made noisy walking, but we made the door without flushing him. Even after we had stepped into the room, our guns in our
hands, it took him a split second to shake himself loose from his pipe dream.

He was speechless from surprise and anger. I slipped a cylinder gun—he
had evidently finished with automatics—from his belt at the small of his
back.

The Dean gazed at him pityingly. "You're an old-timer—a Westerner—
you carry your gun for a backhand draw. Old-timers have a sense of loyalty.
It's going to be hard to do business with you."

I put in: "This is the hooligan that gun-whipped me."

"Quiet, Ben," the Dean ordered gently. "Listen, old-timer. See that door?
Get out. We're through with you. Good-bye."

The gaunt man stood motionless. Terror grew in his eyes and little flecks
of foam gathered in the corners of his mouth.

"Go now," the Dean said kindly. "Good-bye."

"It's the old escaping-arrest gag," Dorf whispered hoarsely. "I been in
Mexico—I know how it works. I won't reach that door."

I watched the Dean. He was perfectly capable of a one-man execution
and I knew it. He had depths that couldn't be plumbed.

"I'll do business," Dorf said huskily. "Why not? I was a sucker to mix
with you in the first place. I didn't want any part of you but they told me
you could be handled. What do you want to know?"

The Dean took a little voile doll off the telephone and called police headquarters, asked for Malloy. He gave directions and hung up.

"I want to know what you were doing in this room. I know you don't live
here. I know who does."

A harried, cornered look pinched the gaunt man's face. "I said I'd do
business and I will. Here's the lay-out. There's the big boss, the guy that
lives in this dump. Carter works for him. Me and Herb worked for Carter.
The racket's smashed. I just dropped in—"

"To do a little farewell looting?" the Dean suggested. "I see. Figured on
going into the blackmail business for yourself."

He couldn't deny it. A briefcase on the cot was crammed with letters. The
top one said—

I am doing this against my will. Now I am in it, I can see no way of getting out. Have your truck in the alley at ten tonight and the furs will be ready to move.

John Beck

There was more of the same beastly stuff. Payments had been posted in the ledger.

I looked around.

In a waste basket under the table was an old mail-order catalog. Its pages had been sliced with a razor blade. "That's it," the Dean said. "He's really snared."

"Now, Dorf," he remarked, "you are in this up to your neck—but no murder. Right?"

"No killing, chief," Dorf said earnestly.

"You and Herb worked through Cartier, the druggist. You took care of the strong-arm intimidation. You set the fires. You made the collections. But no knifing or strangling. Right?"

"As I breathe—"

There were crunching footsteps on the pebbled roof outside and Lieutenant Malloy sauntered through the door. Behind him came Hilliston Keith and his esoteric blonde.

Hilliston Keith's flabby jowls were flushed with excitement. He elbowed the girl to one side and pushed his way to the forefront. "What's this all about, Rock? I demand to know. What do you mean, calling in the police without consulting me? Fortunately, I have some influence and was informed—"

"He tagged along," Malloy said drily.

The Dean picked up the mutilated mail-order catalog. "Here," he said to Keith, "is the source of your anonymous tip."

The manager seemed taken by a sudden seizure of spasmic goodfellowship. "That's earning the fee, old boy!" He patted the Dean's back, attempted to put a chummy arm around his shoulders.

"Don't fondle me," the Dean snapped. "And don't get the impression that I'm being retained by you. We're working for Solidarity. I don't like you, never did, and never will. In my opinion you're just another untrapped skunk—if you grasp my meaning."

The blonde put in pertly: "I can grasp your meaning, Mr. Rock. This little girl can. She's getting to feel the same way."

"Break it up," Malloy barked. "What is this anyway? What's it all about? Who's this earless guy?"

"Permit me to inform you," the Dean said with relish. "This man is Dorf. He's a touch-off man for the arson syndicate. The ring is run by one man— but more about the higher-up later. Under this higher-up was his killer-chemist, Michel André Cartier, the Colorado druggist."

The Dean went on. "Michel André Cartier, alias John Charles Carter, was the man you were after in the Ortman killing. He killed Arabella Trimble, trailed her on her second visit to my apartment and strangled her on my living room rug. For a newspaper clipping. It was Cartier who tore up my room—to attract the attention of the police to those books he stole from the rare book department of the City Museum which he left in my steamer trunk to frame me. This is a guess, of course, but I am certain the curator of the museum will recognize Cartier when he identifies him at the morgue."

"So Cartier is dead," Malloy said.

The Dean nodded. "Yes, Lieutenant, there are two murders not yet brought to the attention of the police. It is the manipulator of the racket, the big-shot himself, who is responsible for these. These are personal killings. Cartier has been knifed. Also a girl known as La Varre."

"Keep talking," Malloy said.

A gay, boyish tenor from the door behind our backs called out: "Hello there, Mr. Berrymeadow!"

It was the freckled, drugstore gunsel. At his shoulder, light licking along the fifteen-inch barrel of a sawed-off shotgun, was our old friend, Daddy Melton, the feeblewit hobo. It took an effort to recognize him. Professional-looking rimless glasses were clipped to his nose and his cheeks were rosy from barber-shop massage. He was wearing as good tweed as ever crossed the Western Ocean. He was right out of Dun and Bradstreet.

The Dean got out his Magnum and caught Melton in the arm as he tightened on the trigger. Melton meant to kill us all. You could tell by the cold glint behind those rimless glasses. Dorf chose this moment to make a break for the door—and blocked the full blast from the exploding shotgun with his chest. Lieutenant Malloy, standing erect and prim in model range stance, pumped three rhythmic slugs into Melton's heart that could be covered with a dollar watch.

It seemed like I had poured myself a cold cup of tea. The freckled gunsel refused to annoy. From the first, he had stood with his hands in the air. "No trouble," he kept saying. "If Michel is finished, deal me out."

Abruptly it was all over and there was a vacuum. The blonde said: "There's a fortune teller on Front Street, Mr. Rock. A gentleman called Yogi Shakun-something. He uses little lumps of dirt and a cloth marked in squares like a checkerboard."

"He's not a Yogi," the Dean explained calmly. "He must be an Arabian *fakir*. I know what you mean. He tosses the dirt over his shoulder and looks to see what square it falls on. Then he refers to a certain table and does his calculating. It's a very old form of divination. It's a form of geomancy. I've never seen a geomancer," he mused. "They're very rare."

Malloy picked up the phone and called in. He walked over to Daddy Melton. "So that's the answer," he said coldly.

"Yes," the Dean said. "It's Fred Ortman."

"Ortman?" Keith gasped. "It's impossible!"

"Tell us, Rock," Malloy said.

The Dean glanced at his watch. "I'll have to cut this short. I feel that I'm going to have an engagement. Well, it's not too cheerful. Ortman didn't like married life and Solidarity's salary. He met and became infatuated with the attractive Mrs. Sprigsey O'Hare. Her husband was an ex-convict. Together they worked out a scheme of arson-blackmail that Ben can explain to you later. Ortman gave Sprigsey a job at the company, gained his friendship. The new racket was so successful that Ortman decided to withdraw from his old environment and expand. Sprigsey was lured to the Acme Photographers and strangled by Cartier. This was, of course, the charred substitute body found in the fire. Sprigsey's murder cut down the split and got Sprigsey out of the way." The Dean paused.

"Ben and I entered the case and things began to get warm. They worked Ben over, killed the old lady. Ortman took his wallet to Huey to throw suspicion on the missing Sprigsey. He knew Huey was a friend of mine, figured he would call me in. He put on a good act. He fooled me.

"Ortman got the wind up when Celadine lammed to him from the hotel—and killed her. He and Michel had already sent Keith the note and planted the dynamite in the shop. They drove the body there in the gray coupe. Anything else?"

"Yes," Malloy said acidly. "There are still two bodies missing."

"Oh! Miss La Varre." He gave the Ferry Street location. "Now, about Cartier. He was killed because he was weakening. Somehow he had picked up a big scare and was hysterical." The Dean hesitated. "Dead or alive, he's worth money, Lieutenant. I'll make a trade. This is a blackmail case. Publicity—the wrong kind of publicity—can hurt a lot of innocent people." Malloy's eyes were blank. The Dean, however, seemed satisfied. "The body's in the basement." He told them about the illicit merchandise addressed to Central America.

"Pardon me if I get in on this," I said. "You've been saying all along you knew who was behind this. When did you find out?"

"Ben," the Dean said paternally, "I knew it was Ortman but I didn't know where he hid out. I knew it was Ortman ten minutes after he had left Huey's pawnshop. As soon as we had examined the wallet."

Malloy blinked.

I said: "But there were no fingerprints on the wallet. It had been rubbed with shoe polish."

"Now, look, Ben," the Dean explained. "Ortman's prints should have been on that leather plus Melton's. Two different sets. Ortman-Melton realized this and eliminated *all* prints. He gave himself away by being too careful. What about Sprigsey's prints, if Melton's story was true? Melton was Ortman, there was little doubt about that. Then whose body was found in the fire? Who was missing? Sprigsey."

"The lavender sachet?" I asked.

"An attempt to embroil Keith and his charming lady."

Hilliston Keith beamed. "When I clean up a job, I do it right. I'm a business doctor. Solidarity can never repay me—"

The Dean eyed him balefully. He bowed to the room at large and offered his arm to the blonde. She smiled that nice smile of hers and took it.

"You'll excuse us," the Dean said. "Ben can clear up the tag ends. We have to see a geomancer about some lumps of dirt."

Ding Dong Belle

HUGH B. CAVE

DETECTIVE LIEUTENANT MORONI was in a mood. "And you, Kane, you keep your nose out of this!" he snarled. His fat neck was red against the collar of his pink-and-white striped shirt, and his big face was puffed. "You hear?"

Kane grinned drunkenly through the amber sheen of his beer glass. "What intrigues me," he murmured, rolling his eyes at the buxom beauty in oils above Limpy's bar, "is that the gal was undraped at the time—or anyway, in a bathing suit. A bathing suit in the middle of winter, friend—"

"You keep out of this, Kane!"

"And playing Ping-Pong, of all things! Ping-Pong in a white bathing suit at midnight, in the middle of winter. Why that's—"

"It ain't Ping-Pong anymore," Limpy declared gravely. He was a little man who seldom smiled. He'd been pickpocket, cop, night-club owner, had lost half a knee in the war, and this quiet, high-class liquor trough on Stuart Street was Kane's favorite hangout. "They call it table tennis now," he declared. He poured Scotch and placed it beside Kane's beer. The beer was a chaser.

"And I'm warning you, keep out of this!" Moroni snarled again. "I had my fill of you when Moe Finch was in his prime, Kane. I got more to say now, and I'm tough!" He slapped his glass savagely on the bar and turned away.

"Dear, dear," Kane murmured. The phone was ringing and Limpy hobbled along back of the bar to answer it.

It *was* a queer case when you thought about it. Kane thought about it. The girl's name had been Dolores Trent before she married the Anderton bankroll, and as Dolores Trent she'd been on the covers of a lot of magazines. A lot of people had paid out nickels, dimes, and quarters just to take her home with them. She'd been framed and placed on mahogany bureaus. She'd been thumb-tacked to fraternity-house walls. She'd made old men young and young men reckless.

Day before yesterday at three o'clock in the morning, a newspaper photog named Hulett had found this gal's husband dead on the stairs in the Goodwin Building. He'd followed the dead man's blood up the stairs to the table tennis parlors on the floor above, and found Dolores Trent Anderton dead under one of the dark green tables—in a ravishing white bathing suit .

Kane wished he were back on the cops. This kind of case stirred the bloodhound in him. He gulped his Scotch and swayed a little and realized he was drunk. That was all right, too. As an agency dick he was seldom sober. He disliked being sober.

Limpy said: "For you, Kane."

It was a girl's voice and it called him Peter. The voice jarred him. He lowered his gaze quickly from the oil painting above the bar, because the painting was lewd and that sort of art was way out of line when you talked to a girl like Anne Finch. He'd been in love with Anne before she acquired the Finch. He'd been on the cops then, with a glorious future. The liquor had licked him with both the future and the girl.

He listened and said, scowling: "Moroni was just here. He must have figured you'd call me. He warned me to keep out of this."

The girl said: "Then I won't need to beg very hard, will I?" Her voice was low and cultured, as always. It was as soft and clean as Anne herself, but Kane caught the tremor in it. He guessed she was pale and desperate.

"Meaning?" he countered, not knowing what else to say.

"You've never turned down a Moroni challenge yet, Peter!"

"This is different," Kane muttered. "He's a lieutenant now."

"Then—you're afraid of him?"

That did it. Kane's mouth twitched and a dull red crept up his jaws. He was drunk—he'd been drunk for days—but there was a part of him the liquor never touched, and the girl had reached that part with a thrust that cut deep.

"Afraid of Moroni?" Kane snarled. "The hell I am! Where are you?"

She told him where she was.

"Wait there," he snapped.

Limpy said with a sigh: "Now look, Kane. Look what you done to my phone! Now how will I explain that to the telephone people?"

Kane poured a drink and downed it. It gagged him and he made a face. He slapped his last dollar bill on the bar to pay for it. "Tell 'em Superman was in," he leered, and went out.

She looked just the same. He hadn't seen her in six months, but she was the same girl with the same warm brown eyes and sensitive mouth and straight, slim body. The sight of her did things to him. He never could look at her without remembering the night three years ago she had told him she loved him, and always would love him, and never could marry him. Life with a perpetual souse, she had told him, was not her idea of security.

He'd been drunk that night. He'd spent the next two weeks in an alcoholic fog, and groped out of the fog at last to find her married to Captain of Detectives Moe Finch, his boss and best friend. Soon after that he'd quit the cops to go to the Beacon Agency as a private shamus. He and Finch were still friends, but there was a difference. Kane didn't try to define the difference—he just knew it existed.

She put her hands on his arms now and said, "You're drunk, Peter," and Kane said defensively, "I like to be drunk." They never talked of that other thing.

She drew him into the apartment and shut the door, steered him to a chair in the living room. She was worried. Her eyes had a hunted, desperate look and her hands shook as she reached for a cigarette. Kane lit it for her, stared at her and waited.

"It won't be the first time you've helped Moe out of a spot, Peter."

There was no answer to that. He just shrugged.

"This time," she said, "it means his career. Moroni's been waiting for a big, sensational job like this. You know."

Kane knew. He knew that the man she was married to was just a big, sober, hard-working cop with no flair for showmanship. When Moe Finch muffed a job, the papers tore him apart. When he cleaned up a city sin-spot or sent a killer to jail, the newspapers' silence was ear-splitting. Moe Finch had never learned to yell from the house-tops. He was good but not brilliant.

The newspapers were promoting Moroni for Moe Finch's job. Moroni the Mouth, the Great I Am. Moroni the swaggerer.

If Moroni solved the mystery of the girl in the bathing suit, he was in.

"Did Moe ask you to call me?" Kane demanded.

"No, Peter. He asked me not to." She took the cigarette from her lips and looked away from him, the lips trembling. "Moe says he's determined to sink or swim on his own, this time. You've held him together for three years. You've kept him up there. It can't go on, he says."

"He's a sap."

"Then you—you—"

"He's the biggest damn fool in the world," Kane growled, "with the biggest heart and the biggest conscience." He reached for a newspaper on the divan, and scanned the headlines. "What do you know about this case?"

"The girl, Dolores Anderton, used to be a model."

"I know that."

"Wednesday evening, she and her husband went slumming with another couple. That isn't in the papers because the other two, the William Singsens, were influential enough to hush it. The Singsens took Dolores and her husband home at one A.M., then went home themselves. That's all they know. At three, this newspaperman found the Andertons in the Goodwin Building, dead."

"How'd he happen to be in the building at that hour?"

"He has a studio there."

Kane studied his fingernails and wished he had a drink. His brain worked better when lubricated. The trouble was, he had to lubricate it often, because his system was pickled and the effect of each new drink quickly wore off. He was so sober now that it hurt.

He said: "These Singsens—who are they, pal?"

"William Singsen is one of the vice presidents of Anderton's machine-tool company. With Anderton dead, he'll move up."

"Anderton boozed a lot, didn't he?"

"Moe says he did."

Kane stood up. He had an idea this job was going to unravel him. It was a boat race. Moroni had the official oars and a long head-start, and Moroni, though still blessed with more bluster than brains, had learned a lot about rowing since the old days. It was going to be a hell of a hard job to scuttle Moroni's boat this time.

"I'll give it my old-time best, pal," Kane said. He reached for her hand and held it a moment, then looked into her eyes, pulled a deep breath into his chest and abruptly turned away. His best, he promised himself, would be good.

William Singsen's private secretary was a pert little chick with Jean Harlow hair and a way of using her eyes and voice that shrank a man down to size. Kane wished he had his old police badge to impress her with. Lacking it, he sat and munched his tongue while she phoned his name in to her employer.

He waited. The surroundings were magnificently modern and he was their only occupant. He stood up, said "May I?" and snaked a newspaper off the girl's desk. It was full of pictures.

That was the hell of this mess, the pictures. A newspaper photog had discovered the bodies and taken enough pictures of them to make him happy for life. They were good, too. They were sensational. They made this the biggest murder case in a decade.

He discovered something in the paper that Anne Finch had not told him. Both the girl and her wealthy husband had been shot with a thirty-eight. The same thirty-eight. The gun was missing.

Moroni had passed that out to the newsboys. "Detective Joseph Moroni, the sleuth of the city's police department, revealed this morning . . ."

Kane threw the paper aside with a snort. He smoked a cigarette, squashed it. His mouth was dry and he needed a drink. The liquor that was already in him was beginning to sour, and he had a headache. He looked at the clock and scowled at the pert little chick behind the desk. She ignored him.

Twenty minutes he'd waited. He was stewing. Then the inner sanctum door opened and he stood up, strode forward.

He stopped. He was face to face with the man who'd come out of there, and the man was Moroni. Moroni's face was a thundercloud.

They were Dempsey and Firpo, confronting each other. Moroni filled his barrel chest with air and let it out in a swift, noisy stream, jabbing a fat forefinger at Kane's face. "I told you to keep your nose out of this, Kane! By God, if you pull any tricks on me this time—"

Kane took out a handkerchief and elaborately wiped his face. "You spit too much." He tossed the handkerchief into a wastebasket beside the desk.

Moroni lurched about and strode back into the sanctum, slamming the door.

What was said in there, Kane couldn't know. The phone rang on the waiting room desk and the blonde answered it. She said, "Yes, Mr. Singsen," and hung up. She looked at Kane, her dark red lips faintly scornful.

"Mr. Singsen will be in conference the rest of the day," she said.

Kane glared at the sanctum door and slowly unclenched his fists. His knuckles were white. "Round one," he muttered.

Round one had gone to Moroni.

He wondered if Moroni had phoned Mrs. Singsen at her Chestnut Hill home and told her to throw him out, too. It was a pretentious place with an acre of winter-dead lawn and a driveway that curved between lanes of soldier-straight poplars. He punished the bell. A maid with a blank face and a large blank bosom opened the door and blinked at him.

Kane said unctuously: "I am Mr. Hadley. Mr. Singsen sent me with a message for Mrs. Singsen."

The maid thought it over. She let him in. She changed her mind about halting him in the hall and let him into the living room, which was almost too large for an Elks' convention. "Wait here, please," she said.

Kane prowled. He stopped beside a table on which lay a pair of gloves. They were a man's evening gloves and lay on a bright red rectangle of cardboard that bore the words, *Wop Willy Offers.*

He reached for the red cardboard and changed his mind when a door opened across the room. He turned. "Ah," he said. "Mrs. Singsen!"

She was no chicken, this Mrs. Singsen. She had several auxiliary chins and she wore a nondetachable life-preserver of blubber around her middle. The motif was nautical: embroidered anchors on a navy blue dress that hugged the hull-like armor-plate. She was designed to plow through heavy seas, this lady.

She frowned at him, fluttering her eyelids, and Kane said: "I'm investigating the Anderton affair, Mrs. Singsen. Your husband suggested that I come here and talk to you."

"Indeed!"

"He tells me that you two were out with the Andertons Wednesday evening, and—"

"One moment, Mr. Hadley," she said. Kane scowled at the broad of her back as she headed majestically for the hall.

He heard the dial-clicks of a telephone and guessed what she was doing. She'd been tipped off, then, that Peter Kane might come calling. Kane rolled the name Moroni under his tongue and in less refined surroundings would have expelled it vehemently. He stepped back to the table and snatched up the bright red oblong of cardboard. It was in his pocket when the woman cruised in from the hall.

She dropped anchor a few feet from the door, hipped her hands and delivered a broadside. "I have just spoken to my husband," she snapped. "*You* are without doubt the private detective we were warned about! You are Peter Kane!"

Kane sighed. With some ceremony he put his hat back on his head and headed for the door.

"And don't dare show your face here again!" the woman lashed. "Of all the underhanded, sneaky tricks—why, in all my life I—"

"Lady, lady," Kane growled, "you're not slumming now." With what dignity he could muster, he went past her and out.

The bright red folder was a menu, and was something special. The menu you usually got in Wop Willy's was a greasy typewritten sheet covered with fly-tracks as big as moose-prints. This was different.

Kane held it against the wheel of his car and studied it. It was Wednesday's menu. Wednesday had been Wop Willy's eleventh anniversary. Wop Willy's was a dump on a North End side street.

Kane slipped a pint bottle of rye from the glove compartment and shut his eyes while the whiskey gurgled down his throat. He looked at the last inch in the bottle and decided to save it, decided not to and killed it. He felt better. He thought of Mrs. Singsen and laughed, and that was a step in the right direction.

He drove downtown to the North End, parked his car and went into Wop Willy's where among other things you could buy the best spaghetti and meatballs in town.

A waiter smiled and said, "This way, Mr. Kane," and the checkroom girl smiled, too. Kane shook his head and said, "Willy." He went upstairs. He went along a hall up there, past the men's room to a door marked private, and knocked. A pleasant, cultured voice told him to come in.

Willy Sakarian was not a wop, he was a Greek with his B.A. from Harvard, but this was a wop district and Willy knew his business. He was small and swarthy, with beautiful teeth and beautiful blue eyes. He had the build of a sixteen-year-old girl, a handclasp gentle and soothing.

Willy had a gold mine here. He served cheap, noisy entertainment and the city's finest food. He lured the wealth that went slumming. He was grateful to Kane for a lot of ideas that had panned out and made him more money.

"You been reading the papers, Willy?" Kane asked him.

Willy nodded. As though by magic, a fifth of Scotch, a syphon of soda and two gleaming glasses appeared on his desk. He said while pouring: "The Andertons were here Wednesday night, Kane, with another couple. They came about eleven, left at one. Anderton himself was ugly drunk." He pushed a drink toward Kane's hand. "But if you hope I can tell you why they wound up the way they did, with that girl playing table tennis in a bathing suit—I can't."

"I was hoping you could."

"One thing did happen. Dolores Anderton had a drink with one of the boys in my band. I didn't like it, but it was her idea and what could I do? Her husband didn't like it, either. He never took his eyes off them. When she went back to her own table, he wouldn't speak to her. I was watching, I saw it. Soon after that, they left."

Kane rolled the Scotch under his tongue. His headache was gone and he was thinking better. "You speak to the boy in your band afterward?"

Willy shrugged. "Why should I?"

"Is he here now?"

Willy shook his head.

"Well," Kane said, "it may be nothing, but I got to start somewhere, and fast! Who is he?"

"Fred Patten. Nice kid, about twenty-five. He was down on his luck and asked for a job, three-four months ago. Said he could sing. I let him sing and never even heard him, he was so eloquent on the piano. He lives"— Willy pulled out a desk drawer and dipped into a neat row of file-cards— "at eighty Morris Street. No phone. Used to be a struggling artist. But wait a minute, Kane." Willy put down his drink, scowling. "Something else happened."

"Ah!"

"The Anderton woman used to be a model. You knew that, of course."

"I knew."

"Well, Carl Dolce was here Wednesday night, too. Carl Dolce, the photographer. She talked to him, and Anderton didn't like *that*."

"Hmm," Kane said. He stood up. "I'll look into that, Willy. Has Moroni been around here?"

"Not yet."

"You encourage me," Kane muttered. He had another drink, a quick one, standing, and put a hand on Willy's shoulder. "Thanks, pal. The more I know you, the better I hate Yale." He thought that was a dumb crack, but Willy found it funny and was still grinning when Kane closed the door.

Carl Dolce did covers for the magazines. Photographs of beautiful girls skiing, beautiful girls eating grapefruit, beautiful girls looking beautiful. He was a furtive, pop-eyed little man of unguessable age, with a prodigious reputation. His studio was the last word.

Kane hiked into the chrome and plastic reception room and leaned on the desk. He said to the pale young man there: "Like to see Mr. Dolce. Police business." That was cutting the corners pretty close, but Carl Dolce was known to be a difficult man to get close to, and time was precious.

The pale young man shook his head. He said Mr. Dolce was not in. He said he didn't know when Mr. Dolce would be in. He talked with a slight lisp and was very arty.

"Tell you what I want, then," Kane scowled. "Some of those pictures Dolce took of Dolores Trent before she was married."

The young man was perturbed. "I'm sorry, sir, but Mr. Dolce took all those pictures out of the files yesterday afternoon and—" He pulled up short. His face crimsoned and he seemed angry with himself. "You'll have to see Mr. Dolce," he said curtly, dropping the arty accents.

Kane said, "Sure." His eyes had a glitter in them and he wore a wolfish smile. "Just where does Dolce live?"

The young man glared, eloquently silent.

"O.K.," Kane said. He leaned across the desk and slid a phone book toward him, opened it and found the name without any trouble. "Carl Dolce," he read aloud, "three-four-one Riverway . . . Thanks, pal."

He didn't ask the pale young man if Moroni had been around. He was reasonably sure Moroni hadn't, and felt for the first time that he might have at least a Chinaman's chance of crossing the finish line first.

"We're in the stretch, fella," he told himself. "It's time to go all out!"

He drove hard out to Riverway. Three-four-one was a horseshoe-shaped apartment house of red brick and ivy, old and ornate. The apartment number was thirty-one, which meant third floor front. There was no response to Kane's steady pressure on the bell.

He tried the foyer door and it was unlocked, and his leather heels beat a tattoo on the tile floor to the elevator. So Carl Dolce had cleaned Dolores out of the files, had he? This was a lead. It was so hot it smoked.

But the door of Dolce's apartment was locked, and persistent knocking brought no answer. Kane curled his lips around an oath. He folded his fist around the knob and shook it savagely, swore again and went down the stairs. "If I were Moroni," he muttered, "the guy would be sitting on the steps waiting for me."

He kicked a long-handled broom leaning against the wall, and it fell with a clatter, and a voice in the hall said petulantly, "Hey!"

"Ah," Kane said, braking himself. "The janitor!"

The fellow was big enough to be two janitors, and had a face as empty of guile as a goldfish bowl. Kane picked up the broom and carefully replaced it. "You're just the man can help me," Kane declared.

"Huh?"

"I'm looking for Carl Dolce. It's important."

"Him," the janitor said. He rolled his eyes and gazed at the ceiling. "Him! You think *I* know where he is?"

"Well, you work here."

"Listen," the janitor said. He came closer and lowered his voice to a chummy halftone. "When I try to find him, he is never here. Yesterday I go up to his apartment no less than twenty times, to give a registered letter I sign for. I could leave it in his mailbox, sure, but he is funny, sometimes he does not look in his mailbox for days at a time. So all right. I go up there twenty times. I don't catch him. So then, at half past two o'clock this morning, when I am fast asleep, he knocks at my door downstairs to ask me will I burn some rubbish for him in the incinerator!"

Kane let his breath out slowly. "A very queer duck," he agreed. "And did you burn the rubbish?"

"The rubbish he gives me at half past two o'clock in the morning? No, not yet."

"Ah," Kane said. His hand slipped into his pocket, hungrily, and then he remembered, with a pang, that he had spent his last dollar in Limpy's. Liquor he decided ruefully, would be the ruin of him yet. "Friend," he said, his own voice confidential and cozy, "do you know *why* Mr. Carl Dolce sneaked down to your door at that unearthly hour?"

"Huh?"

"Yuh didn't peek at that rubbish, hey?"

"It was tied up," the janitor scowled.

"So! It was tied up. And you didn't untie it! Look, friend." Kane leaned closer, hypnotically staring. "You and I, we'll have a peek at that package,

right now!" His leer spoke volumes. "Mr. Dolce is a photographer, friend,
and photographers take some very interesting pictures!"

The janitor opened his eyes very wide. Kane had a mental picture of him
peering furtively into a penny-arcade peep box, turning the crank very
slowly to make his nickel last longer. They went downstairs. The big fellow
plucked a package from the incinerator and stared at it.

"You have to open it," Kane reminded him.

"Y-you open it!"

"Sure," Kane grinned. He snapped the string and peeled off layers of
newspaper. A very careless fellow, Mr. Carl Dolce. The pictures were intact,
not even ripped through once.

There were at least two dozen of them and they were warm. Kane pawed
through them, one by one—photographs of Dolores Trent in abbreviated
bathing suits, of Dolores Trent in sport clothes and evening gowns. Of Dolores Trent in nothing. Very alluring, very seductive, with the stamp of art
upon them. Especially upon those of Dolores Trent in nothing.

Kane shoved the pictures into his pocket and warped a scowl across his
face. A very severe scowl. He glared at the janitor, who looked back at him
puzzled and uneasy.

"These," declared Kane severely, "are not for the public eye. I'll take
them with me. Official business," he added, clearing his throat. "The word,
friend, is mum."

He went upstairs and out, the janitor too awed to stop him. He wondered
how to go about getting hold of Carl Dolce, and decided to return to the
apartment every hour until his efforts produced results. This was one lead
Moroni was not likely to stumble upon. Therefore he had nothing to fear
on that score.

Meanwhile, a few words with that piano-player might be of value.

Morris Street is an odd little thoroughfare in the heart of the old business
district. It is a dead-end lane of tenements. It is a dislocated wing of the red-
light sector, surrounded by aged, dignified, once pretentious office buildings. Number eighty was a three-decker tenement.

There was a barroom next door.

Kane counted the loose change in his pocket and found he had eighteen
cents. He hiked into the barroom and drank three nickel beers, placed the
remaining three pennies in a pile on the bar and haughtily walked out, leaving them there. He climbed the aged steps of number eighty.

The tenants' names were penciled under the bells beside the door, and
the name of the man he sought was under the top-most bell. Kane climbed
to the third floor and was thirsty again. He knocked. The impact of his fist
swung the door open.

He leaned over the sill and knocked again, on the open door, and got no
answer. He shrugged and walked in.

No one challenged him.

There were three rooms and they were in keeping with the house itself,
gloomy and gray. Yet they had a certain personality. This was supplied,
Kane realized, by the pictures on the walls, by a careful hand-painted spread
that was thrown over the studio couch. He was puzzled.

He remembered Wop Willy's words to the effect that Fred Patten was a struggling artist, and that explained it. The atmosphere was vaguely arty. But Fred Patten was not here.

The place smelled of cigar-smoke that had a familiar, choking reek. A sodden cigar-end lay on the edge of a table. Kane went back to the door and peered at the lock and realized why the door had opened when he knocked. The lock was broken.

"Moroni's been here," Kane decided. It was only a guess, but the cigar smell was strong, and Moroni was famous for his grisly taste in tobacco.

He looked around. On the table lay a Southern Air Lines folder designed to lure winter-weary northerners to the paradise isles of the West Indies. A sunburned female rode a surfboard on its cover. Inside, on the margin, someone had done some figuring with a pencil.

It seemed unimportant. Everything else in the place seemed unimportant. Kane tired of the arty atmosphere and went out. He was so thirsty that his throat made small whistling sounds when he breathed, but his pockets were empty and his credit in this part of town was not tall enough to reach the suds on a glass of beer, even.

He walked around the corner into Nason Street and hiked across to the Goodwin Building.

It had been quite a structure in its day. Now it was occupied by a couple of sign painters, a rubber stamp manufacturer, a rug repair plant and Jerry Verall's Table Tennis Parlors. The signs outside told him this. Another sign said,

Studio space for rent

Kane climbed the broad wooden stairs on which the body of Anderton had been discovered. Chalkmarks made by the cops were still in evidence. He tried the door of the table tennis parlors and found it locked.

He was disappointed. The idea of a gorgeous girl in a white bathing suit playing Ping-Pong at midnight in the middle of winter still intrigued him. The cops, he thought glumly, were always keeping him out of places he wanted to go. He scowled at the lettering on the door. It read:

City Table Tennis Center
Jerry Verall, Prop. Registered T.T.A.

"Hey!" Kane said softly, "Hey!"

He left the building and hiked down the street to a drugstore, thumbed through a telephone book and found the name and home phone number of Jerry Verall. The name itself had a familiar ring. He supposed he'd seen it on the sports pages, because table tennis was an up-and-coming pastime, getting a lot of publicity. He stepped into the booth and remembered again, ruefully, that he was broke.

"Brother," Kane said soberly to the clerk. "I find it necessary to make a few phone calls. I have no nickels. I have nothing to change into nickels.

But I have a watch, a very fine watch. You take the watch. You lend me three or four nickels with which to make phone calls. Can do?"

The clerk peered at the watch. He turned it over and read the engraving on the white gold case. "To Lieutenant Detective Peter Kane, for outstanding service. B. P. D."

"Gee!" the clerk said.

Kane made his phone calls. Three of them—the last to Willy Sakarian. He grinned at the clerk and walked out, as contented as though he had just wrapped himself around a fifth of the finest Scotch. He walked back to his car and drove to Wop Willy's, in the North End. It was now half past eight, and dark.

Kane went into Wop Willy's by way of the rear door, which was open. The door was open because Willy Sakarian had promised to open it. Kane climbed the stairs, went along past the men's room and entered Willy's office.

The slender Greek stared at him without smiling and said, shaking his head: "I'm sorry, fella. Moroni's here."

Those three nickel beers turned over in Kane's stomach. No other part of him moved except his fists. They curled into hard, white lumps.

"Five minutes after you phoned, Kane, the big slug walked in. He's downstairs with a couple of his men."

"Waiting?" Kane muttered.

"Waiting."

Kane walked the floor of Willy's office. He was sore now. He was sore with himself for having muffed the golden opportunity, sore with the croupier of his luck for having led him to believe he was winning. Losing was tough. Losing on the last throw of the dice was tougher. Losing when the future of an honest, sober, trusting pal like Moe Finch depended on you—when the swellest girl in the world had honored you with her faith—losing then was a numbing shock that twisted something deep inside you.

Kane felt the barb in that sensitive part of him that was never touched by the quantities of liquor he consumed. His lean face lost color and his eyes glittered. "Listen, Willy," he said. "You're doing me a favor!"

Willy listened. He didn't like it, and shook his head, scowling. He said: "Moroni will eat you up, Kane."

"You do what I say!"

"You want me to? You're sure of it?"

Kane pushed him toward the door.

Willy Sakarian went out, shaking his head. The door closed behind him and Kane went to work, hauling out the drawers of the desk, tossing papers around. In three minutes Kane had made a lot of progress. The office was a shambles, and he was snorting through the mess like a bull in a crystal-shop.

A snarling, guttural voice bellowed from the doorway, "All right, you! Hold it!" and Kane turned to see Moroni holding a gun on him.

Willy Sakarian was there at Moroni's elbow, and Willy was wringing his hands hysterically. "You see?" he wailed. "You see what he's done? He charged in on me and ordered me around! He said he was the police!"

"So you're the police now, Kane," Moroni snarled. He paced into the room, his big face oozing a leer of triumph. "This time, smart guy, you've gone too far!"

Kane stood stiff, defiantly glaring. He hoped the act was good because it was his last throw of the dice, his last chance. He didn't have to fake the trembling of his hands—that was genuine. Other things were genuine too. His disdain for the big dick who ploughed toward him. His determination to take a poke at that leering face, no matter what it cost.

He swung, and Moroni looked surprised. You had to belt that monkey-map more than once to change its shape. It was tough as granite. Kane swung again, awkwardly, and was knocked sprawling by an elbow to the side of his head.

He picked himself up, shook his head. His eyes were wild and he looked drunk, but at this stage of the proceedings he was more sober than he had been in weeks. He breathed hard and noisily, his hair hung in his eyes, but he was sober.

He said savagely: "You can afford to be tough, Moroni. You and your bodyguard!"

"Sure," Moroni sneered. He swung a fist and Kane drunkenly swayed away from it, in slow motion. Kane fell over a wastebasket and landed in a heap against the legs of the desk. Papers spilled out of his coat pocket.

Not papers. Photographs.

Moroni's eyes bugged. He pounced with surprising agility for one so big. He scooped up the pictures and pawed through them, the two cops crowding closer to peer over his shoulders. Willy Sakarian stood in the doorway, quiet now, sadly gazing at Kane.

Moroni stared at the undraped Dolores Trent and greedily sucked his lips. He said: "Well, well, Kane. You've been holding out on me!"

"You go to hell!" Kane snarled.

"Such language, Kane. Where did these come from?"

"Try and find out!"

Moroni pocketed the pictures and favored Kane with a thoughtful stare. "You shouldn't fight cops, Kane. People who fight cops get beat up all to hell. Legally, too." He grinned at his two henchmen. "You guys saw Kane slug me, didn't you?"

They nodded. Kane got to his feet and backed against the wall, breathing hard.

The two cops moved in on him with nightsticks, and Moroni said ominously: "I *have* seen guys go to the hospital for getting rough with the cops, Kane. They suffer from the damndest things, too—fractured skulls, busted ribs, kidney trouble—it's awful. But those pictures are hot. Where'd you get 'em?"

"You go to hell!"

The cops went to work on him, and there was very little Kane could do about it. He couldn't slug back, that would have left his head wide open to the rain of nightsticks. Kane crouched with his head under his arms, braced himself.

In the doorway, Willy Sakarian covered his beautiful blue eyes with his hands and uttered little moaning sounds.

Kane went to his knees, cursing. He called Moroni every name on the roster. He invented new names and snarled those. His arms felt like telephone poles, and he spat blood.

"The pictures, Kane," Moroni said patiently. "I want to know where they came from."

Kane rolled to the floor and glared up at him. He'd had enough. He'd put up a show, made it look good—more would be too much. "Carl Dolce took them," he groaned. "She used to work for him."

"That's better!"

"He was trying to destroy them. I got them away from him."

Moroni's leer was wolfish. He sucked air through his teeth, looked down at Kane and rubbed his big hands. "So why did you come barging in here to tear Willy's office apart?" he demanded.

"I had to know how hard-pressed Dolce was for dough. He owns a slice of this place. His papers are here."

Moroni's scowl was enormous. "Carl Dolce owns a piece of this dump? That's news to me, Kane!"

"A lot of things are news to you," Kane muttered, shielding his face.

Moroni could afford to take that lightly, and did. He grinned. "Go right ahead and snoop, Kane," he said. "Me, I'm a cop. I'll get my information from Dolce himself—the easy way." He patted the pocket that held the photographs. "Be good, Kane. I could be tough with you for all this, but I never kick a man that's down. Seldom, anyway." He put his heel against the end of Kane's tail, and shoved. "So long, sucker!"

Kane slowly stood up. He was a mess. His arms ached like ulcerated teeth and his head throbbed. He swayed to the desk and leaned there, and stared at Willy.

"You better go downstairs, Willy, and keep an eye open," he said.

Willy nodded. He went out.

Kane said softly, under his breath, "So long, Moroni!" and reached for the telephone.

It was a tense little gathering. Kelley of the *Post* was there, languidly filing his fingernails. Murchison of the *Telegram* perched on a corner of Moe Finch's desk and asked innumerable questions to which no one else paid any attention. Sisson and McArdle, veteran news-hounds from the city's other two papers, leaned forward on their chairs and tossed pennies against the wall.

Moe Finch kept his mouth shut and tried to look wise, which was not easy because Moe Finch had a face as wide-open and guileless as his heart.

The door opened and Kane walked in.

Kane was not alone. With him was a dark-haired, good-looking young man who was so scared it was pathetic. Kane had a hand on the young man's elbow, and after marching him across the threshold and pushing the door shut, Kane gave the young man a shove, toward Moe Finch's desk.

"You were right, Captain," Kane said. "Here he is."

Moe Finch looked at the young man. He looked at Kane. Not knowing what else to say, he said, "Ah!"

"Shall I tell the boys about it, Captain?" Kane murmured.

"Do," said Moe Finch.

Kane leaned against the desk. "Well, gentlemen." He paused to push his fingers through his hair. "Would one of you guys have a drink on you?"

One of them had, and Kane put a large dent in the contents of a pint of bottle. It was newspaperman's rye. It hit his stomach and exploded, and he clung to the desk for support. But when the first cruel dizziness had passed, he felt tons better.

He began over again. "Gentlemen, there were certain aspects to this case that led Moe—that led Captain Finch to some definite conclusions. First, Dolores Trent was wearing a bathing suit and was slain in a table tennis parlor at midnight. You boys made a lot of that, because it was unusual, it bordered on the fantastic. There could be only one explanation for it."

The newsmen held their collective breaths.

"Captain Finch figured out the reason for it," Kane said, leering. "But that wasn't enough. It didn't tell him who was responsible for the girl's presence in the table tennis parlor at that hour. So . . ." He rubbed his tongue with the back of his hand and gazed soulfully at the man with the pint. The pint was produced again, and Kane put a second large dent in it. "Bad cold," he said. After corking the bottle he placed it on the desk.

"So at Captain Finch's suggestion I found out from one Jerry Verall, head of the local T.T.A., the names of all those who have keys to the table tennis place. Sure enough, one of them—this lad here, Fred Patten—was an artist."

The newsmen stared at Fred Patten. The young man shuddered, clung to the desk with both hands.

"Investigations revealed," Kane continued, well-oiled now and thoroughly enjoying himself, "that Dolores Trent used to be very fond of this boy here. Last Wednesday night, while slumming with her husband and another couple, she had a chat with him at Wop Willy's. Investigation also revealed, gentlemen, a Southern Air Lines brochure in Mr. Patten's lodgings. The missing link!"

It made sense to no one but Kane. Even the eyes of Moe Finch were filled with question marks. But the newsmen were too intent upon Kane to be watching Moe Finch.

"At Captain Finch's direction," Kane declared, "I telephoned Southern Air Lines and talked to their advertising department. Sure enough, they had commissioned our struggling young artist, Mr. Patten, to paint a picture for them. What kind of picture, gentlemen? Why, one with glamor! One with romance! What else but a picture of a lovely young woman in a very yummy bathing suit, playing table tennis against a background of southern sun and palm trees!"

The gentlemen of the press needed no more. As one, they took in air. As one, they wolfed at Fred Patten, backed him into a corner. Kane elbowed them aside and held up a hand.

"I can tell it much more simply than he can, gentlemen. Much more briefly. Mr. Patten was given the assignment to paint the picture we've been talking about. Wednesday night, when Dolores Trent slummed at Wop Willy's, he told her about it. They'd been fond of each other, those two. Miss

Trent knew all about Patten's ambitions to be an artist. She offered to pose for his picture—to meet him later, if she could dodge her drunken husband.

"She did meet him. But her husband was not as dumb as she thought. He was wise. He followed her. And now, Patten, if you'd tell the boys what happened . . ."

The young man raised a sweat-drenched face and tried to look at the half-circle of wolves that hemmed him in. He was a very sick young man, numb with terror. But there was something clean and decent and desperate about him that softened the newsmen's faces even as they crowded him.

"She—she was wearing the bathing suit under her dress," he said. "We went over to Jerry Verall's place and she started to undress. There was nothing wrong about it. Some artists can fake a picture but I can't. I have to have a model. But he—her husband—rushed in while she was undressing. He was drunk and he had a gun."

Patten looked at his feet and swallowed a sob that was not for the benefit of the newsmen. "He called her a—he called her names, and shot her. I went crazy then. I grabbed him and we wrestled all over the place, and the gun went off and he fell. He wasn't dead. I suppose he was fatally wounded, but I didn't know. I just knew *she* was dead, and I was scared. I took the gun and ran. After I left, he must have crawled out and fallen down the stairs."

"And the gun?" said Kelley of the *Post.* "Where's that?"

"I threw it in the river."

The newsmen took notes furiously. Their pencils raced, and made a noise like hens scratching in a barnyard. Peter Kane plucked the almost empty pint off the desk, gazed owlishly at Moe Finch, and killed it.

Murchison, of the *Telegram,* said: "I don't get your angle in this, Kane. You're not a cop anymore. How come?"

"Captain Finch," Kane said solemnly, "is handicapped around here. He has to contend with the bullheaded blunderings of Moroni, and gets damned little cooperation. He asked me, as a favor, to do the roadwork for him. I'm unimportant. You can leave my name out of it."

"That right, Captain?"

"Why—ah—suit yourself," Moe Finch said.

"What do you think this kid will get, Captain?"

Kane answered that. He stepped up to Fred Patten and put a fatherly hand on the young man's arm. "I think he'll get a damned good lawyer," Kane said, "and if you boys are halfway human, you can win him the public's sympathy. He's a good kid and—"

There was a commotion in the hall. The door clattered open and into that room full of well-fed newspapermen surged Moroni. Moroni, the I Am.

The newsmen blocked Moroni's view of Kane, of Fred Patten. The Brain saw only Moe Finch and the press. He dragged a small, wasplike man into the room with him, flung the man forward. He and the man were handcuffed together.

"Boys," he said, flushed with pride, "take a good look at this guy! His name is Carl Dolce. You're looking at the man who murdered Dolores Trent!"

The silence was ear-splitting, but Moroni paid no attention. "Stick around, boys," he said, "and watch me slap a confession out of this guy!"

Carl Dolce was terrified. He squirmed against the desk and looked beseechingly at Moe Finch, rolled his large round eyes at the newsmen. "It isn't true!" he wailed. "Just because I got rid of some pictures that were in my files—I tell you it isn't true! I didn't have a thing to do with it! I just didn't want to have those pictures around if anyone questioned me, after what happened. Oh my God, I—"

"Shut up!" Moroni snarled. "I'll do the talking!"

Kelley of the *Post* snickered. Moroni gaped at him. The *Telegram*'s Mr. Murchison said, "Dear, dear, such a commotion!" in a voice as mocking as an echo. Moroni widened his eyes and looked confused.

With Kelley in the lead, the press filed past Moroni to the door. He yelled at them and they paid no attention. He turned red, waved his arm. The press walked out.

On the verge of apoplexy, Moroni swung on Moe Finch for an explanation, and saw Kane. He stopped short. Understanding rushed into his eyes, and up his fat neck rolled a wave of crimson.

"You!" Moroni choked.

"Me," Kane leered. "And this, Moroni, is Fred Patten. Fred's already confessed. And I wouldn't get rough with Fred if I were you, Moroni. The newspaper lads definitely won't like it." He plucked the empty pint off Moe Finch's desk, drained the last amber drop of its contents onto his tongue.

Moroni, red to the roots of his hair, unlocked the manacle that linked him to Carl Dolce. He clenched his fists and blocked Kane's path to the door.

"You think so?" Kane said gently. "It won't be as easy at last time, fella. I only take a beating like that when there's a need for it."

Moroni faltered. Kane leered at him, plucked the empty bottle off the desk and tenderly placed it in Moroni's hand. "You look," Kane said, "as if you need a drink. Have one, pal, on me."

You Slay Me, Baby

FREDERICK C. DAVIS

Chapter 1

THE HAUNTED LETTER

A T THIS UNHOLY HOUR of the morning, in Bill Brent's well-considered opinion, the *Recorder* plant was a dark and dreary hell-hole which no sane man would willingly enter. Brent, however, was inflicted with an ingrown sense of obligation. Having fled from the building for a few minutes' respite, he was dutifully trudging back, bearing a paper bag stuffed with four frosted doughnuts and a quart container of coffee, which he needed, though he felt an even stronger need for an equal quantity of ice cubes and rye.

Midway along the walk leading to the dim main entrance he paused. He never liked the looks of the place at high noon, when the advertising departments busily hummed. He always felt a definite aversion to it in the evening when the city room worked at fever pitch getting out the milk train editions. And he disliked it most heartily of all during these small hours following midnight when he alone must stick on the job in the thick of its hushed and deserted gloom. He paused to regard it warily, not merely because the entrance seemed as uninviting to him as the iron gate of a prison, but also because a shadow was now looming against it.

A man was standing there waiting, his back flat against the light shining vaguely through the panes, his face a black patch—and to Brent he seemed, somehow, faintly ominous.

He approached Brent with a long, reaching stride, keeping, Brent thought, his face shadowed. When he halted no more than three feet away, Brent could still see nothing of his features except a veiled glint in the whites of his eyes.

"If you're from the post office," he said, speaking in a throaty tone which Brent instinctively felt was disguised, "I've been expecting it."

"Have you?" Brent said.

"The party who sent it phoned ahead." The man's shoulders were peaked up now. "I'll sign for it."

"Sorry. Haven't got it," Brent said. "You might tell me, though, why you're pretending to be somebody on the *Recorder*'s staff."

The man stood tightly still and his hand slid back into his pocket—where, Brent hoped, he didn't have a gun. Brent was astonished when the man laughed—a laugh too tense to seem good-natured, as it was intended.

"This is rather embarrassing. I suppose I'd better come clean. I'm trying to get hold of a letter."

"A letter you sent to the *Recorder?*" Brent inquired.

"My—my wife wrote it to Lora Lorne. We had a bit of a disagreement and she asked Lora Lorne for advice." The man was choosing his words almost furtively. "We've patched it up now, though. Everything's lovely again, and it wouldn't do to have the letter made public now. I want to get that letter back—unread."

"Unread?" Brent said. This man, he surmised, was far more anxious about that than he wanted to appear. "I'll mention it to Miss Lorne. How will she recognize it?"

The faceless man hesitated, and Brent sensed the fear in him. "It's a plain white number ten envelope and the address is typed, but it's postmarked early this evening and it was sent special." He bent closer, anxiously intent. "Perhaps it's already been delivered."

"It hasn't been," Brent answered. "I'm sure of that." He had a clear-cut reason for being so certain. "When it comes—"

"Send it right back—unopened," the man urged. "Re-address it to—to the occupant of Room 404 at the Heights Hospital. You'll see that Miss Lorne does that? Returns it unopened?"

"Miss Lorne, as the whole world knows," Brent reminded him evasively, "is an extremely understanding and sympathetic woman."

"Tell her," the man said, still intent, still anxious, "that the contents must remain secret—absolutely must!"

He peered a challenge at Brent with eyes that Brent could not see, and suddenly he stepped past. As he strode swiftly away in the dim light shining from the door, back turned, Brent saw him as a man of ordinary stature and ordinary appearance, but one loaded with much more than an ordinary degree of purposefulness. There was something grim about him as he faded down the dark street—something desperate. Brent decided this unknown man's request was one to be earnestly considered.

"Why, sure, chum, sure," Brent said wryly, aloud. "Just leave it to me."

He pushed his two hundred pounds into the lobby and tramped up the iron stairs, carrying the doughnuts and the coffee. Only a few dim bulbs lighted his weary way. The offices below were empty and the big presses in the basement, their flood of news poured out, were at rest. Another hour or so would pass before the teletypes would resume their clatter, and even the cleaning women had called it a night. In this vast and stilly dungeon Bill Brent alone must remain to toil and mutter blasphemy.

He was parting the swinging doors of the news room when a burst of sound surged up the stairwell. It was a door banging open, followed by the *click-click* of leather heels crossing the foyer at a terrified pace.

"Cripes!" a frightened voice piped.

Brent started down to meet the noise. He was still en route when it echoed away. Reaching the lobby, he found it as silent as the grave—except for a quick gasping sound issuing from beneath the lowest flight of stairs.

A pair of scared eyes appeared, and then a whole boy. About fourteen, he had a face full of penny-colored freckles, a nondescript uniform and very little breath left.

"A goon chased me!" he blurted. "Out dere!"

He pointed in the general direction of the street. Brent looked through the glass of the entrance and saw nothing but somnolent quietude.

"If I hadn'ta got inside here, he'da grabbed me!" the boy insisted. "I t'ink he had a knife!" Two dirty hands were held up as if to measure a fish that had gotten away. "A knife as big as dat! Bigger!"

"You read too many comics," Brent said. "You should stick to the pulps. Anyway, he's gone now, if he ever was there. Why aren't you home and in bed, getting your growth?"

The boy probed into a small canvas bag suspended from one shoulder by a strap and produced a letter.

"I got a special delivery for Lora Lorne."

"Ah!" Brent sighed. "I'll take it."

"You? Say, you don't look like Lora Lorne to me, mister."

Brent hoped that that was obvious. Lora Lorne was the *Recorder*'s love oracle, its own Dorothy Dix or Beatrice Fairfax, who sweetly advised her immense family of readers concerning their philandering husbands, their faithless wives, their broken troths, their unrequited passions and practically anything else that might bother them, including stenographer's spread and the beautification of the bust. Her picture, printed every day above her column of intimately sympathetic expostulations, showed her to be a warm-hearted old soul with wise eyes in a kindly crinkled face, combs in her snowy hair, eyeglasses dangling from a reel pinned to her grandmotherly shoulder. Not in any respect did she resemble William Coleridge Brent, who wore size eleven brogans and a nose permanently flattened by a Princeton goal-post.

Noting this, the boy observed: "You ain't *nothin'* like her!"

"Ain't I!" Brent said sourly. "All the same, I'll take that letter—and shut up."

He snatched it away, made an indecipherable scrawl on the receipt and pushed the boy out of the lobby, leaving him to wonder what he had done to deserve such harsh treatment. Brent hoped he would never know. It was a closely guarded professional secret that Lora Lorne, as visualized by the thousands who anxiously sought her guidance in their amatory distress, simply did not exist except as a phoney name plus a copyrighted portrait which had graced the *Recorder*'s love column day in and day out, unchanged, for the past twenty-two years.

A long succession of female busybodies had masqueraded as the paper's seeress in *affaires de l'amour,* and it galled Brent to think that he was the first Lora Lorne ever to wear his pants long and externally. Rather than have it noised around that saccharine Miss Lorne and burly Bill Brent were one and the same these days, he would gladly have entered a bona fide jail.

Sourer than usual about it tonight, Brent waited to make sure that no monster with a machete was chasing the messenger, then tramped up the stairs again, still carrying the doughnuts and the coffee and now, also, the letter.

He wedged himself into a tiny cubicle in a remote corner of the news room. No bigger than a broom closet, it was crowded by a table heaped with letters, all addressed to Lora Lorne, like the one just received. Most of them ran to type; people as a whole, Brent had found, showed little originality in their tribulations, but seemed to get into the same damned messes over and over again, never learning better. He had come to consider it practically a godsend when someone managed to stumble into a reasonably unusual predicament. Having labored far into the wicked hours over a hundred run-of-the-mill heartbreaks, he hoped he was now about to be rewarded with a problem really worth losing sleep over.

Eyeing the special delivery letter which the unknown man had implored him to return unopened and unread, he shamelessly ripped it open and began to read it.

Darling Miss Lorne,
Now that my baby girl has come into the World, now that I *have* given her away, I'm heartbroken—and so terribly afraid for her!

You see, dear Miss Lorne, it isn't working out as you and I planned it. We *had* hoped for so wonderfully much, hadn't we? We wanted the baby to have a devoted mother, one who could give so much more time than I can to her care and upbringing, one who could give her every advantage in life that she would never have otherwise. So many women wrote to me after you printed my first letter in your wonderful column, all of them wanting to take the baby, and I was so careful to pick out the one I thought would make the very best mother for her. But I've made a horrible mistake and I'm so afraid—and now I want my baby back.

"Well, for God's sake!" Brent blurted aloud.

Glancing at the end of the letter, he saw a typical signature: "Hopeful." Manifestly it was from a young woman who had first appealed to Lora Lorne's fabulous wisdom a month or so ago. Brent had sweated his brain over Hopeful's plight, writing her fully a dozen long compassionate letters of guidance. Several times, in fact, he had devoted almost his entire column to her case.

She was young and married but her husband had left her; her health was none too good; she must work for a living. Within the past several days she had borne a child; she had no near relatives to bring up the baby for her and she rebelled at the mere thought of placing it in a charitable institution. While the baby was still unborn, Brent had practically bled himself white helping this girl to find a childless, intelligent, well-to-do woman to adopt it. And now, after all this travail, the dizzy dame wanted to call it off and get her kid back!

"Heaven help me!" Brent moaned. He resorted to the coffee, gnawed off a chunk of doughnut and resumed.

I'm frantic, Miss Lorne, really frantic. This woman who had taken my baby lied to me. She deceived me, Miss Lorne! She even gave me a false name and a false address, so that I can't even get in touch with her. She took my baby under false pretenses—stole her from me, really kidnapped her!

A woman who would do a heartless thing like that can't be trusted at all, Miss Lorne, and now I'm so terribly afraid the baby will be mistreated, cruelly mistreated. Please, won't you help me to get my darling baby girl back? I beseech you—

Suddenly the letter vanished. Everything around Brent was blacked out at the same instant. He stiffened in his chair, hearing the click of the light switch still faintly echoing in a portentous hush.

Peering over his shoulder, he saw a thin vertical flicker at the far side of the room. The lights were still burning at the top of the stairs, and the swinging door in between was just flapping to rest. Brent couldn't see the windowless wall, couldn't see anything against it—but he knew something was there. He heard it coming, rustling toward him.

He sprang up, jouncing the coffee container, hearing it plop wetly to the floor. Instinct urged him to protect the letter he still had in his hand. He groped for the table, intending to thrust it deep into the heap of correspondence and leave it there, buried. He moved fast, but the thing that was coming across the dark room toward him was moving even faster.

It was on him.

An arm hooked under his chin, snapping his head back. Before he could even squirm, he felt a sudden jolt and saw bright flashes like criss-crossing Roman candles. A dim glow swelled and burst like a soap bubble.

"It's a lie!" The words were a snaky hiss in Brent's ears. "You hear? It's false, a malicious lie!"

Then swift footfalls receded down an endless reverberating corridor, echoing long after they were gone.

Chapter 2

MURDER BY MAIL

B RENT SMELLED A nauseatingly sweet odor and gradually decided he was lying on his stomach on the floor. Scores of letters were scattered under and over him and his crooked nose was pressing upon one that reeked of heliotrope. He had acquired a horrible hangover, its pulsing pain concentrated behind his right ear.

He pushed himself dizzily to his knees in a pool of spilled coffee, hung there, then found his feet and propelled himself waveringly across the city room. He listened, heard nothing and thumbed the switch. It went off with a crack like a trench mortar and the blinding force of the light flattened him against the wall. Steadier after a minute, he pushed out.

From the start he felt his belated pursuit of his assailant was futile. The only sound in all the building was the muffled drumming inside his own punished cranium. An air of murky loneliness filled the halls and offices. Brent groped and tottered his way through a sort of vacuum until, abruptly, the sounds of an approach startled him to a standstill. He braced himself against the iron post at the base of the stairs as the street entrance swung open.

The man who strode across the lobby was Garrett, the *Recorder*'s hard-bitten city editor. Garrett seemed worried, but not about Brent's evident condition. He gave Brent one stern glance of his flint-gray eyes, jostled past and began climbing urgently toward the city room.

Brent doggedly followed him, blunt chin down. Brent had things to say to Garrett. He wished to point out that he was not an unreasonable man. If it was necessary for him to work twenty-four hours a day at times, he would do it, but he wished to add that when he came to getting his skull cracked into little bits, he drew the line. In a few words, he was quitting.

In advance he knew this speech would accomplish nothing. He couldn't quit, except under heavy penalty. Garrett would remind him of his iron-bound contract, would mention lawsuits and the blacklist. It was hopeless, and anyway Brent found no opportunity even to begin. Garrett had gone straight to the news desk and was impatiently spinning the telephone dial. He was not in a genial mood.

"Grandma," Garrett growled, "when I give you orders I damned well expect you at least to hear them."

"Meaning what?"

"I told you several days ago," Garrett said. "I told you last week. I also told you the week before that. In the clearest and most concise language possible I explained to you that you've got to get more variety into your column. Instead of following editorial instructions, you've been giving most of your space to just one case. For the last time—"

"Hopeful's?" Brent asked quickly.

"Hopeful's!" Garrett agreed with a snap. "Lay off it, Grandma! Kill it."

Brent narrowed one eye. "Why?"

"Because—" Garrett's face took on an angry flush. "Because, goddammit, I'm ordering you to!"

Brent considered this a suspicious evasion. His aching head told him that something strange lay behind this business of Hopeful and tonight it had somehow reached a crisis.

First an unknown man had been lying in wait outside the plant for Hopeful's latest letter, and in a vain attempt to get hold of it he had lied like a trooper. Next the same faceless man, undoubtedly, knife or no knife, had pursued the messenger who had delivered it. Then he had come prowling into the *Recorder* building after it, had peeked into the city room, and seen Brent sitting, back turned, devouring it. He had then forcibly applied a blunt instrument to a spot on Brent's head where it would best serve his purposes. On top of all this, Garrett had come charging into the news room at a most unaccustomed hour and for certain obscure reasons of his own was summarily demanding that Brent forget the whole affair.

Under the circumstances Brent definitely could not forget it. And besides, any city editor worth his salt ought never to feel so unfriendly toward anybody's new-born baby, because new-born babies were traditionally sure-fire human interest stuff.

"I can't kill it," Brent answered, eyeing Garrett as his suspicions soared. "Everybody's talking about it. Every time I go into a dog cart for a bowl of goulash, I even hear hardboiled truck drivers seriously discussing whether or not Hopeful should have given away her offspring. It's the most appealing case Lora Lorne has handled in years. Instead of ordering me to kill it you ought to be howling for me to play it up even bigger."

Garrett glared at him, continuing to struggle with the telephone, and said: "I don't trust it. I've got a feeling it's a phoney. Hopeful might blow up in our faces and ruin the rapture column for good and all. But never mind my reasons! If you write any more of your sob stuff about that dame and her brat it'll go into the scrap basket, and that's final. Scram, Grandma! I'm busy with a headache."

Intolerantly gesturing him away, Garrett kept spinning the telephone dial. Brent abandoned the issue, unable to understand Garrett's splenetic attitude toward the very young. How, he wondered, could a city editor in his right mind apply the word *phoney* to a tearful young mother and a brand-new baby girl? It was so paradoxical that Brent trudged back to his miserable cubbyhole, grimly intent on discovering for himself, if possible, why Garrett was attempting to deny the validity of one of nature's best-established manifestations.

As a starter he fumbled among the envelopes sent avalanching off the heaped table by his fall. He found the empty special-stamped envelope, but not the letter from Hopeful which it had contained. The letter had been spirited away over his unconscious body and by now, he sensed, it unquestionably had been destroyed. He was certain he would never see it again.

He pulled from his file cabinet a folder containing all the correspondence in Hopeful's pathetic case. In the beginning she had signed no other name to her letters. At first all of Lora Lorne's answers had been broadcast in the passion column for hundreds of thousands of readers to lap up, including Hopeful, for whom they were specifically intended. Later, in order to facilitate matters, Hopeful had identified herself as Mrs. Mira Rainey, 456 Forest Street. Keeping this information confidential, Brent had then written to her directly, though he had, naturally, avoided any personal contact with her.

Also included in the file folder were a variety of letters written by numerous women all eager to help Hopeful in her plight by adopting her baby when ready. Brent had forwarded the most promising appeals to Mrs. Rainey, adding Lora Lorne's own inspired comments, and Mrs. Rainey, in turn, had apparently made a selection and the necessary arrangements. Brent was hunting for a note recently sent to Lora Lorne by a woman who had written that she had been chosen as the foster mother of Hopeful's then unborn child.

Here it was, a rapturous missive:

Dear, dear Miss Lorne,
I'm the happiest woman in the world! Thanks to your column, where I first
learned of the priceless opportunity, I am to become the new mother of Hopeful's little baby! Rest assured that it will have all my love and every advantage
in an ideal home. Of course, the baby is to be known only as my very own. I'm
so indebted to you, Miss Lorne!
                                   Sincerely yours,
                                       "Grateful"

The source of this joyous outburst could never have been traced if its
sender hadn't supplied Brent with two clear-cut clues. Apparently in an
unguarded moment, she had written it on stationery imprinted with the
monogram EGF. Moreover, the flap of the envelope she had used bore the
name of Bay Terrace House, a swanky apartment building located near the
river. The initials plus the address gave Brent hope that a few simple inquiries would identify her as the woman now accused of bad faith and baby
stealing. As Lora Lorne, he felt responsible. As Bill Brent, he knew the
aroma of news when he smelled it. He got going.

Hurrying down the stairs, he was aware that Garrett had abandoned the
telephone and was following him. He ducked into his car and Garrett hustled into another. Starting off riverward, he noticed that Garrett's headlamps were glaring directly behind him. He drove straightaway and Garrett
tailed him. He turned corners and Garrett stuck close. Annoyed and puzzled, Brent stepped on the gas. When he veered to the curb behind a sedan
waiting near the entrance of Bay Terrace House he had gained a block on
Garrett, but Garrett was still coming.

"What the hell!" Brent protested.

He swung toward the doors and the breath left his lungs with a quick
whoof! Suddenly there was hair in his eyes and in his mouth. He couldn't
see anything, but in his arms, instinctively closed, he felt the warmth and
curvesome softness which could mean nothing on earth other than a young
woman's body.

She struggled to free herself of Brent, her breath a fast rushing sound.
He had no idea where she had come from so instantaneously, but she was
desperate to get herself gone with even greater alacrity. She was afraid,
Brent sensed—fleeing from something, terrified.

He was spun half around as she tore away. As if his brain were a camera
equipped with a flashgun, it registered an attractive action shot. The girl
was diving into the car parked in front of Brent's. She was hatless and both
pockets of her loose coat seemed heavily weighted. Her hair was wild in the
wind of her own movements. She had legs which won Brent's approval,
even though her white stockings and white oxfords did not set them off to
their best advantage. Her eyes gave him one glinting glance. Then she disappeared into the gloom inside her car and the picture went out of focus.

She whizzed away without switching on the lights. Her tires squealed at
the corner. That was all there was of her, and Brent regretted it.

She was gone, but Garrett had come even closer. He was parking behind

Brent's car. Still mystified, Brent strode to him and asked an indignant question.

"Why the hell are you haunting me, Garrett?"

Garrett attempted to brush past without answering, but Brent's hand fastened on his arm. He eyed Brent and countered, "Why are *you* here?"

"In the line of duty," Brent answered. "You don't live in a decent place like this, do you? I always thought you crawled back in a hole during the day."

Too anxious and preoccupied to take offense, Garrett answered: "My sister and my brother-in-law have an apartment here. He's clippering up from Rio and his plane was overdue from New York, but he's due to show up here any second now." Almost to himself Garrett added, "It's a special hurry-up trip because my sister has just had a baby."

Brent winced. "She's just had a what?"

Garrett scowled at him. "Surely, Miss Lorne," Garrett said with stringent sarcasm, "you know what a baby consists of. You're aware, surely, that a baby is a thing around the middle of which diapers are pinned. You yourself were once a baby, were you not?"

Brent inquired with a grimace, "Boy or girl?"

"Do you mean, which were you?"

Brent flushed angrily. Having to wear Lora Lorne's petticoats was humiliating enough without Garrett's flaunting them in his face. But he controlled his tone and answered, speaking very distinctly: "I mean which did your sister have?"

"A girl." Garrett still eyed him. "Why the hell are you staring at me? What's so startling about that? Women have babies every day, usually at the most inconvenient hours. Approximately half the time they have baby girls. My sister is no exception to the rule. Do you mind?"

"Yes," Brent muttered. "I mind very much. I have lately become allergic to new-born infants."

And new fire was kindled under his suspicions. Garrett's uneasiness had to mean that Brent was not far wrong in smelling a rat. Garrett turned away with guilty quickness, in fact, as a taxi appeared, swerving around the corner. He hurried after it as it stopped at the entrance of Bay Terrace House.

The man who hustled out of the cab was handsome in a gray-templed, sun-browned way despite the gauntness of his face. He was about to pick up two suitcases plastered with hotel labels when Garrett grabbed his hand.

"Mike!" Garrett boomed. "Just in time! Mike, old man, how are you?"

Mike answered the greeting unhappily. "Oh, hullo, hullo. I'm fine, thanks, except I was air-sick all the way up from Rio. Nerves upset. My liver's sluggish again. I've got to get an appointment with Dr. Hartwell first thing. My old indigestion's come back. I don't sleep well anymore, either. But otherwise I'm fine."

Urgently he trudged into the foyer as he spoke, with Garrett pacing at his one side and Brent, curiously, at his other.

Garrett said, frowning: "Meet my brother-in-law, Michael Farnam. He's just up from Brazil, where he's been busy these past nine months doing important things about industrial diamonds. This, Mike, is a minor employee of the paper whose name, if I remember rightly, is Brent. You may ignore him."

Farnam did so, after briefly squeezing Brent's hand, but he did it in a natural, charming way. Aside from his physical condition, which was probably not as bad as he imagined, he seemed too good a guy to be related to Garrett even by marriage. After all, too, he was understandably concerned about his wife and new-born daughter. He asked breathlessly of Garrett, "How's Elaine?"

Brent didn't hear Garrett's answer. A realization had pelted him squarely between the eyes. He had come to this building in search of a woman of suspicious character whose initials were E.G.F. and he was immediately connecting. The first initial of Garrett's sister Elaine, plus her maiden name of Garrett, plus her married name of Farnam—it checked! There might easily be another woman in the building whose initials were E.G.F., but certainly not another E.G.F. who had acquired a female infant within the past several days. Suddenly things were tying up with a neatness that had to be more than mere coincidence.

Brent was so struck by it that despite Garrett's forbidding frown he drifted after Mike Farnam into the automatic elevator. Suspecting skulduggery, Brent even trailed Farnam to the door of his apartment. There Garrett turned on Brent with a darker frown. Being a strict disciplinarian who had come out of the First World War a major at twenty-three, Garrett could pull off a scowl of truly formidable aspect.

"What the hell are you after, Brent?" he rasped. "A cigar? If so—"

"Good God!" Farnam blurted.

He had opened his apartment door. He had stopped short, clenching a grip in each hand. He was staring horrified into his living room.

"Good—God!" he said again.

Brent peered over Farnam's bent back and his whole framework snapped tight.

A man was crawling across the floor—or trying to crawl. Like a mortally wounded animal, he was flopping, writhing himself along. His arms wouldn't work properly and he was dragging his legs. A long streak on the rug showed that he had so far struggled a distance of ten feet from a dark, wet spot in the center of the room. His face was a ghastly smear of blood. The blood was trickling down from his matted hair. Staring at the crown of his head, all broken and pulpy, Brent wondered how he could move at all, how he could live. In a mad effort, blindly sensing that help was near, the terribly beaten man was snaking himself toward the open door.

Abruptly he rolled over, loosely, like an under-inflated inner tube, and an acrid cackling laugh broke from his throat. His smeared lips worked as Brent pushed past Garrett and Farnam and dropped to his knees beside the gasping man. He heard grating words in a mumbled whisper that scarcely reached his straining ears.

"Abigail! Had to come back—must stay with you. Don't do it! Abigail—it's a lie! Don't—Abigail—don't!"

Brent shook him gently. "Who's Abigail?" he asked, his tone low. "Where is she?"

The man's eyes fluttered open and turned unseeingly up at Brent—red-filmed eyes, glazing.

"Heights!" he choked out. "Heights!"

His arms stiffened up as if to ward off more murderous blows and then, with a cry of tortured terror rising thinly out of his lungs, he died.

Chapter 3

WHO IS ABIGAIL?

B RENT HAD NOT ALWAYS, God knows, worn the sweet false-face of Lora Lorne. Back in New York, centuries ago, he had been a full-fledged and completely male reporter living only a single life—and a glorious life of newshawking it seemed, now that he looked longingly back on it. It was his aggressive ability, in fact, that had induced Garrett to lure him away with a contract and an inflated salary. Even though Garrett had since condemned him to the passion columns as a punitive measure—Brent had merely missed a total of twenty-odd editions, all told, due to having been detained in various bars and boudoirs—he still had a newsman's instincts. They were perked up now, like a fighting cock's hackles, as he frowned down at the broken-headed victim of murder.

Garrett and Farnam had drifted in and were still incredulously staring.

"Who is that man?" Brent asked.

"Never saw him before—never!" Farnam blurted a breathless question of his own. "How did he get in here?"

Neither Brent nor Garrett offered a guess.

"Nobody has keys to this apartment except Elaine and me," Farnam went on quickly, "and of course the maid and the superintendent, but they wouldn't let a stranger in. Elaine's been at the hospital for days, ever since she had the baby, and I've been out of the country!"

It seemed reasonable but unanswerable. Brent, looking quickly about, discovered several red streaks on the back of a yellow leather chair. They were still wet. Fingers had left them there. They evidently meant that the murderer had stepped back, after shattering his victim's skull with repeated blows, and closed a sticky, steadying hand on the chair. Brent saw no ridge patterns. The prints were as smooth as if they'd been made by so many hot dogs, and they were thin. Either a man's slender hand had not pressed hard against the leather or it had been a woman.

A woman? Brent thought of the girl who had bumped the wind out of him when rushing anxiously from the building. Very likely her precipitate departure had begun in this room. Who was she? Brent recalled her legs with pleasant clarity, but not her face. He hadn't noticed that part of her.

Searching for further indications of her, he went quickly down a short hall. He found a door opening onto the service stairs from a kitchen that had apparently been unused for days. In a bedroom he paused, head lifted, sniffing a flowery fragrance hovering freshly in the air. Turning back, he encountered Mike Farnam. Having followed, Farnam was also noticing the scent.

"Nobody else here," Brent reported. "Whose perfume is that?"

Utterly bewildered, Farnam mumbled. "My wife's!"

"Sure?"

"It—it's her special favorite. She never uses any other. But it—it can't mean—"

"Just when did your wife have her baby?"

"Four days ago," Farnam said, pushing the words out. "She's still at the hospital, of course—will be there probably another week. She couldn't possibly have been here tonight! *No one* could have come in, considering the keys."

"But someone did come in," Brent reminded him. "Two people, in fact. One's scrammed and the others's staying longer than he expected, a little the worse for wear."

The maltreated corpse drew Brent back to the living room. Garrett was at the telephone—using it to call the Homicide Squad with, Brent thought, reluctance. News was Garrett's business, but he seemed to have little stomach for it when it sprang redly from the midst of his own family. The dead man had been beaten down in this room, certainly, but the weapon, whatever it may have been, Brent made sure, was nowhere in sight.

Brent tenderly fingered the lump behind his right ear. The clout he had received in Lora Lorne's sanctum sanctorum had been the forerunner of the murderous blows struck here. There was one other striking similarity. Having been conked down, Brent had heard his assailant asserting, "It's a lie!" and those very words had been among the last spoken by the man who now lay dead at Brent's feet. But, noting his slight build and short legs, Brent decided the corpse was not the man who had stolen the Lorne letter. The same words had, then, issued from two throats, no doubt for the same reason. And Brent surmised that both he and the murder victim had successively been bashed by the same vicious attacker.

Bending over him again, Brent probed into the corpse's pockets. His hand came up with an envelope. With a frown he saw it was empty. Whatever it contained had been removed. Had *two* letters been stolen tonight, Brent wondered. He couldn't be certain, but the envelope alone was enough to send a shock skipping along his nerves.

It was a plain white number ten. It bore a special delivery stamp. It was postmarked this city, four days ago, and it had been duly delivered to a street address in Chicago. The addressee's name was Victor Rainey.

"Rainey!" Brent blurted under his breath, snapping to his feet.

"Take it easy, Grandma," Garrett growled, and at the sound of that voice Brent's hand dove into his coat pocket with the envelope, unseen. "Remember you're on the rapture column, Grandma, not on news. My police reporter and I will cover this, and you'll confine yourself to Cupid's errant ways."

"Garrett," Brent retorted, "you're too hard-headed for your own good. This happens to be a particularly gory murder involving your brother-in-law and your own sister. Do a little remembering yourself. I came here for a reason."

Garrett asked, his scowl returning, "What was it, Miss Lorne?"

"Don't call me that name!" Brent gritted his teeth but erected his defenses. "I had a good reason and I still smell all sorts of skulduggery cooking behind the scenes. You don't want your own sister to simmer in such a ghastly stew, do you? You don't imagine that Captain Russo and the Homicide Squad will turn off the heat simply because she's related to you!"

"She had nothing to do with this," Garrett said, his stony eyes leveling. "A woman busy with an *accouchement* could have no hand in a killing. Neither could Mike."

"It's her rug that's all bloodied up," Brent pointed out. "It's her special perfume floating in the air here. It's her key that was the only one available. And it's her baby Lora Lorne is wondering about."

"What?" Garrett snapped. "Why?"

"I think you know what I mean, Garrett. Maybe it'll help to remind you that as a highly competent news sniffer-outer I've learned how to tell which facts will force their way into the headlines and which others can be clammed up. Well, I'm on the scent of something more complicated than simple obstetrics, and you can't sidetrack me. This is where I go back on the police trick unless you want to leave yourself wide open to get it where it will sting the worst."

Garrett actually sneered. "This is where you keep right on devoting yourself to the follies of Aphrodite, Grandma," he countered. "I can also issue a few warnings. If you should make this mess any worse than it already is, I'll make it so hot for you at the office that you'll be forced to quit. Then I'll sue the pants off you for breaking your contract and I'll blacklist you besides. Do you doubt that I can do it?"

Brent blanched. He didn't doubt it for one minute. Prudence demanded that he should not press the issue. Reorganizing his tactics, he retreated to the door. Garrett, however, strode after him, grabbed a handful of his coat and spoke with such vehemence that Brent shrank within himself.

"I mean that! This is one time when you'll behave or you'll play hell with yourself. You're asking for headaches compared with which the love column will seem like a bed of roses. Think it over, Miss Lorne. Good night, Miss Lorne."

He pushed Brent out. As the door slammed shut on him Brent said, "I'm scared to death," with an ominously confident smile.

He turned about and his smile waned. The narrow hallway was full of men who had just emerged from the elevator. They were the Homicide Squad and foremost among them was Captain Russo, regarding Brent with sad, lusterless eyes. Seeming to possess the instincts of a buzzard, Russo had appeared at the scene of the killing with his usual uncanny promptness. Even more uncanny was Russo's resemblance to a corpse. He was as gaunt-faced, as clammy-skinned, as imperturbable as any stiff he had ever smelled out.

"You again, Brent?" Russo said in his sepulchral tone. "Are you claiming squatter's rights on another cadaver?"

"By no means," Brent hastened to assure him. "You're more than welcome to it. I'm just an innocent bystander, as usual."

The captain said funereally: "I always wonder just how innocent, Brent."

Brent shuddered and escaped into the elevator. He sent it gliding down-

ward hoping he could escape from Lora Lorne's damnable apron strings—
a consummation devoutly to be wished—and doggedly convinced that this
time, considering Garrett as an anxious brother rather than a cold-blooded
city editor, he had Garrett where the hair grew shortest from a tender
area—particularly if he could snag a yarn that Garrett would want to keep
*un*published.

Driving through dark streets, he reflected elatedly that he had two leads
which Garrett didn't even suspect. One was the empty envelope addressed
to Victor Rainey, plus the similar envelope addressed to Lora Lorne. The
other was the dying man's words, words too faint to have reached Garrett's
ears; an unusual, old-fashioned name—*Abigail*—a word, *heights*. Taken together, did they mean that Rainey, in extremis, had gasped out an accusation
against a woman named Abigail who in some way was connected with the
Heights Hospital?

It seemed very likely to Brent, particularly when he recalled the shapely
white stockings and the trim white oxfords of the girl who had so anxiously
fled the building where Rainey had been brained.

It was a sizzling lead, Brent judged. Detouring in the hope of connecting
it with another, he returned to the *Recorder* plant. He ran up the iron stairs
into his cubicle and again tackled his file. In it he found a verification of his
growing suspicions—a letter addressed to Lora Lorne by Hopeful last week,
in which she had announced the imminence of her baby. "It's all arranged,"
she wrote, "and at any minute now I'll be rushing off to the hospital—the
Heights."

That word again!

Brent sped back down to his car and drove rapidly to the Heights Hospital, a small though impressive structure of white stone with an all-glass
entrance in modern style—a private concern, he knew, far beyond the
means of Mrs. Rainey, alias Hopeful. Pushing in, he heard the muted hustling of the staff setting about its manifold daily duties. Brent took a question straight to a cherub-cheeked woman at the admission desk.

"My friend Mrs. Rainey is a patient here, I understand," he said glibly.

"Oh, yes."

"She's just had a baby, I understand," Brent went on.

"Why, no!"

Brent stared and said, "What?"

"I said, no, Mrs. Rainey hasn't had a baby."

Blankly Brent repeated: "Mrs. Rainey has *not* had a baby?"

"Not at all," the woman at the desk assured him. "Mrs. Rainey just happens to be in a room on the maternity floor. You seem to have jumped to a
conclusion because of that. How amusing! Her trouble is really quite a different sort."

Brent reflected. As Lora Lorne, he was damned certain that Mrs. Rainey
had duly given birth. As Bill Brent he was being told authoritatively that
she had not done so. It was confusing, but the hospital ought to know. After
a numb silence he reverted to his primary lead.

"Is there someone named Abigail on the staff here?"

"Abigail isn't on our staff," the woman said. "Abigail is also a patient."

Taking a breath, Brent asked: "May I see her?"

"I think you may." The apple cheeks bunched, shiningly. "I'll call her special nurse."

When the nurse appeared Brent instantly regretted he was not in immediate need of hospitalization. The nurse was twenty-two or -three and she had natural red hair and sea-green eyes. She had a beautiful mouth. She was, in fact, beautiful all over. Beyond doubt she was one of the most luscious young women Brent had ever seen in or out of a nurse's uniform. She adorned it. She made it seem as svelte and breathtaking as a form-molded evening gown. It was dazzling. Brent goggled, wondering how many men there were in her life. At a moment's notice their number could be increased by one named William Coleridge Brent.

"I'm Nurse Olive Winslow," she said, and even her voice was beautiful. "You wish to see Abigail? Come with me."

Going with her was one of the easiest things Brent had ever done, but on the way he tried to put his mind back to the business at hand. His immediate purpose was not, regrettably, a delectable nurse, but someone whose name a murder victim had spoken with his last living breath. "Don't—Abigail—don't!" To Brent this had sounded like a frantic, tortured plea. In a delirium of pain, he believed, Victor Rainey had begged for mercy. "Don't do it—Abigail— don't!" What could this indicate, Brent asked himself, except that someone named Abigail had showered those murderous blows on Victor Rainey's head?

"There's Abigail," Nurse Winslow said.

Self-absorbed, Brent had followed her unaware of his surroundings. He had come into the maternity section, he realized, and he was facing a broad window in a partition. Nurse Winslow was pointing through the glass with a beautiful finger. She was indicating a crib in the nursery in which a very small infant was peacefully asleep.

"That's Abigail?" Brent blurted.

"Yes, indeed," Nurse Winslow said. "Isn't she a darling? Only four days old."

Reversing himself, Brent concluded on the spot that Abigail was not a murderess.

"What is Abigail's last name, please?" he asked thickly.

"Why, Farnam, of course."

Farnam! Brent heard it and stared through the pane, shocked and wondering if his tired eyes were tricking him. Was he imagining it, or did Abigail Farnam's baby face actually bear a resemblance to the face of the man named Rainey who had died at Brent's feet?

Chapter 4

DAMES ARE DANGEROUS

GAZING INTO THE immaculate crib in which the four-days-old Abigail innocently slumbered, Brent muttered: "I realize this isn't the visiting hour. I know I ought to come back later, but I have urgent news for Mrs. Farnam. Could I see her?"

Nurse Olive Winslow gave him a beautiful smile. "Dr. Hartwell and Dr. Marvin are with Mrs. Farnam just now. They just finished an emergency appendectomy on another patient, and dropped in to see how she's doing, and I don't think they'll stay with her long. You might wait here in the hall."

"Thanks," Brent sighed. "I've had a hard night, and that's very nice of you. You're very, very nice. You're so nice you'll tell me, won't you, off the record, whether Mrs. Rainey's husband called here last night?"

"I'm really not supposed to talk." Nurse Winslow's lovely smile faded into a lovely worried expression. "But he *was* here. He kicked up a frightful row, though I can't say what it was about. Seven or eight months ago he'd left her to shift for herself, and this was the first time she'd seen him since, and then he yelled and ranted at her and made such a fuss we had to put him out of the building. Aren't men terrible sometimes?"

Considering it in the light of Lora Lorne's wisdom, Brent agreed they were indeed. "Is Mrs. Rainey very sick?" he inquired.

"Not very." Observing her professional ethics, Nurse Winslow offered no specific clinical information. "Excuse me."

A door across the hall had opened. A brisk-mannered and darkly attractive woman of thirty-odd stepped out, followed by a younger man whose attitude toward her was markedly deferential. Both were carrying black instrument cases.

The woman spoke to Nurse Winslow in a crisp, low tone.

"Yes, Dr. Hartwell," the pretty girl answered her.

The young man said: "I'll be back later in the morning."

"Yes, Dr. Marvin."

Both physicians—the poised, self-possessed woman and the younger man who was evidently her associate—went down the corridor and Nurse Winslow informed Brent, "You may go in now."

Brent started in but stopped, gazing at the number painted on the door. It brought flashing back to his mind a recollection of a faceless man waiting outside the *Recorder* plant and a disguised voice urging that Lora Lorne must "return the letter to the occupant of Room 404 at the Heights Hospital." This was Room 404.

Stepping in, Brent was further astonished to find it was not a private room, but a semi-private, occupied by not just one woman, but two.

He gazed at them in perplexity as they lay in the two beds gazing back at him with, he thought, a certain wariness.

One of them was rather colorless and ordinary. Her hair was an intermediate shade of lackluster brown and her face was undistinguished except for her large, pleading blue eyes. The other was much more personable. She had finely chiseled features and her sherry-colored hair, neatly brushed, had evidently received the regular attention of an expensive beautician. Obviously she was a young woman of breeding, intelligence and social grace. Seeing a small, ornate bottle of perfume on the table beside her bed, Brent concluded that she was the young woman whom he desired to question.

"You're Mrs. Farnam?"

"Oh, no," she answered quickly. "I'm Mrs. Rainey."

"Mrs. Rainey?" Brent echoed.

"Yes." A neatly manicured hand indicated the other bed where the average-looking girl lay. "*She's* Mrs. Farnam. I'm Mrs. Farnam's maid."

Brent frowned a little at the nondescript girl and asked, "Mrs. Farnam?"

The big blue eyes flickered slightly and the unrouged mouth responded, "Yeh. Whaddaya want?"

Brent gazed from the unattractive one to the attractive one, and back again, and took thought. Something, he assured himself, was screwy here. In the first place, a woman and her maid were rarely hospitalized in the same room at the same time.

As far as he could make out the rest of it now, it added up to this: Mrs. Rainey had given birth to a baby girl, except that Mrs. Rainey had not. In a letter to Lora Lorne she had accused Mrs. Farnam, her employer, of kidnapping the child which she had not borne. And she had written this while lying in the same room with Mrs. Farnam, who was then herself recovering from the pangs of parturition, and even at this moment the anxious, sympathetic glances passing between them indicated they really were on the best of terms. Brent was unable to see, just yet, how anything as wacky as this could ever make sense.

"I've come here," he began, staring blankly at both women and feeling his way through the dark, "at the request of Lora Lorne."

Both women lifted their heads off their pillows and widely gazed at him.

"She received your letter, Mrs. Rainey," Brent added.

The attractive one asked quickly, "What letter?"

"The one you sent her last evening by special delivery."

"But I didn't send Lora Lorne any letter yesterday—or at any other time!"

"No?" Brent turned to the ordinary-looking one. "Did *you* send a special delivery letter to Lora Lorne yesterday, Mrs. Farnam?"

"Unh-uh, I didn't."

Brent was mulling this over when the door opened and Nurse Olive Winslow entered bearing a small florist's box tied with a pink ribbon. She gave Brent a lovely smile and carried the box to the farther bed in which her better-looking patient lay. "For you," she said, placing it on her patient's stomach. "It just came." Still smiling, Nurse Winslow then withdrew, leaving Brent still mulling.

He watched the long, well-enameled fingernails plucking at the pink bow. He saw the lid of the box lifted, the wax paper parted and heard a gasp. He saw rounded violet eyes staring into the box, a slender hand reaching slowly in, then darting back as if from something too vile to touch. Suddenly the cover was replaced, and two patrician hands held it down, trembling.

"Something wrong, Mrs. Rainey?" Brent asked.

"No—no, nothing!"

"I'm afraid there is," Brent insisted. "I have shocking news for you. I'll have to put it bluntly. Your husband is dead."

"Dead!" It was a screech. "My husband!"

Brent added gently, "Victor Rainey was murdered early this morning."

A strange series of expressions raced across the delicate face of the woman to whom Brent was speaking. They flickered on and off so rapidly he couldn't identify any of them, except the last one, which stayed—horrified consternation. At the same time the girl in the other bed went through a similar series of chaotic facial reactions and wound up by staring at Brent with tearful incredulity.

To her Brent added: "I also have to report that Mrs. Rainey's husband was found violently dead in your living room, Mrs. Farnam."

It was the first one, the personable one, who sat bolt upright in bed and gulped out, "Where did you say?" Then, without waiting for an answer, she again snatched the cover off the florist's box. Her hand dove into the waxed paper and came up holding a small envelope such as usually contained the felicitations of the gift's sender. Her eyes sped through the note inscribed on the card, and abruptly she was sent off into a hysterical outburst so vehement that Brent was overwhelmed.

"Who are you? What do you mean by coming here and saying such insane things? You must be crazy! It couldn't happen! It's impossible, do you hear? Go away! Get out, get out!"

Brent decided he had better. Nurse Winslow came running, her green eyes scolding Brent, but beautifully. He dodged along the corridor while other nurses rushed to her assistance. Room 404 was now full of vocal turmoil. Leaving it rapidly behind him, Brent felt that the news he had brought could not entirely be the cause of all that emotional upheaval. The fireworks had really been touched off by the fact that the contents of the florist's box, plus the message on the sender's card, had abruptly conveyed some terrible sort of meaning. Brent wondered what the hell the box contained, if not flowers.

He kept going in his car through still-dark streets. Swinging to the front of Bay Terrace House, he found the Homicide Squad's big limousine still parked. The knob of the Farnam apartment responded to his twist and he sidled in. The corpse was still present. Garrett and Mike Farnam, having not been permitted to leave, were sitting uncomfortably in the foyer. Captain Russo was now supervising the photographing of the blood marks on the yellow leather chair.

"Cat burglar," one of the squad was saying. "A heister, a three-time loser afraid of the Habitual Criminals Act. Otherwise why would he go prowling around with all his finger ridges eaten off with acid?"

It was a fair enough theory, except that it didn't account for Victor Rainey's penetration into an apartment to which he could not have had a key. Brent stood quietly aside, eyed forbiddingly by Garrett, vaguely by Farnam.

"They still don't know who he is!" Farnam said.

Evidently, then, Rainey had carried no means of identification except the empty envelope purloined by Brent. Brent began to think about the severe penalty for removing and concealing evidence.

"They think he was beaten with a gun," Farnam added. "They asked to see mine. I used to keep an automatic in the apartment, but I can't find it."

"Never mind," Brent said by way of heartening him. "Your wife's doing fine, and so is Abigail."

Farnam's face lighted up. "Did Elaine name the baby Abigail?" he chuckled. "That was sweet and thoughtful of her! I can't wait to see the kid. Must be a cute little dumpling, eh? I've wanted a baby of our own for years. I'm daffy about 'em!"

He would not continue to be daffy about this one, Brent mused, if he should happen to feel, as Brent did, that it resembled the corpse in the living-room.

A queasy expression passed over Mike Farnam's face. "My stomach's shaking up and down," he said. "My nerves feel like a mass of red-hot spaghetti. I've got to see Dr. Hartwell first thing in the morning."

Garrett gestured unsympathetically. "You're not one-tenth as sick as you think you are, Mike. You can imagine more things wrong with your insides than a quack could. Every time you feel a twinge somewhere you go rushing off to your doctor. You're perfectly healthy but you've been doing it for years. Your bills must be terrific."

Farnam nodded, admitting it, but added in a gone tone: "What can you expect of a constitution as sensitive as mine? It's terrible to need constant medical care, as I do. Perhaps Dr. Hartwell hasn't done everything possible for me. That's it! I'll change. Could you recommend another good doctor?"

"Nuts!" Garrett said. "No!"

Captain Russo was taking his lugubrious time over the cadaver, Brent noted, and nothing new was developing. Having interests elsewhere, Brent turned back to the door. He heard a quick click, the metallic ripple of a key sliding into the lock. The next instant the door opened a scant three inches. Through the crack Brent saw a face—the patrician features and the anxious violet eyes of the woman who was supposed to be confined to a maternity bed at the Heights Hospital!

She stared past his shoulder, then recoiled from him and instantly the door clamped shut.

Dazed by the unexpectedness of her face, Brent fumbled for the knob. Making sure that neither Garrett nor Farnam had noticed the incident, he sidled out and saw the elevator door closing. Gears ground as the car descended. Brent spun about, found the door of the fire stairs and loped out to the street just in time to glimpse a coupé skittering out of sight past the corner.

Brent propelled his own car after it. The streets were thick with pre-dawn darkness and there was no traffic—no car in sight except the one blocks ahead of him. The woman was driving like a female demon. Brent lost sight of her again as she skidded around another corner. Speeding past the front of the Heights Hospital without seeing her, he knew she had run into the alleyway leading to the parking space behind it. He shuttled through, but found the lot completely dark—every car at a standstill, lights out.

A flutter caught his eyes. It was an almost invisible motion against the hospital's rear stone wall. Brent heard the clatter of something falling to the cement pavement and a sound like a woman's wail, muted. He ran closer, his soles making quick sandpaper sounds. There was a basement entrance below the ground level and, directly above it, the rising black zigzag of a fire-escape. The counterbalanced ladder at the base of the fire-escape had been let down. The woman was pulling herself up it with breathless and desperate haste.

Brent slowed, knowing now where he could find her when he wanted her, which would be soon. Knowing also that in her hurry she had had no time to pick up the thing she had dropped, he looked for it. It was lying close beside the short flight of outside stairs descending to the basement. In the glow shining down from the windows, Brent saw it was a formidable Colt automatic, a .38. The dark stuff on its butt, crusty now but still slightly sticky too, must be blood—Victory Rainey's blood.

Galvanized by the discovery, Brent scarcely heard the snarl behind him. He removed the clip. While counting the nine cartridges that filled it to capacity he became aware that something like a stormy burst of wind was rushing at him.

A black gleaming shape was looming and advancing on him with a muffled roar. The swift sweep and the swelling sound of it expressed unswerving power. Instinctively Brent leaped backward to escape it. He stumbled into a void. First his upthrown arms, then his head, struck the basement stairs.

Next he was aware that he was on his hands and knees, crawling up them. His throbbing head lifted into darkness that was open and cool and silent. He realized now that he had almost been run down by a powerful car—deliberately. It had spurted out of line in the parking lot and had hurtled upon him, and he had escaped it by a narrow squeak. It was gone now, like Brent's patience.

Brent had an aching hunch that something else was also gone. Lighting paper matches, he speedily confirmed this suspicion. Like the two special delivery letters, the weapon that had killed Victor Rainey had been snatched into limbo.

Chapter 5

DEATH WITH FATHER

B RENT TRAMPED INTO the hospital through, appropriately enough, the emergency entrance. He pushed into Room 404 without knocking. He scowled at the two patients. The unlovely one gazed back at him in fright. The better-looking one had the bedclothes tucked closely under her chin and was giving a fairly good imitation of being sound asleep, except that her breathing was much too fast.

Letting her put on her act for the moment, Brent reached into the wastebasket between the beds and brought up the florist's carton and the pink ribbon. The address tag bore the typed name of Mrs. Elaine Farnam. The wax paper inside the box revealed a gun-shaped depression, and there were dark flakes adhering to it—dried blood particles. Brent also retrieved the card. It had been torn to bits. Roughly piecing them together, he made out the typed, unsigned message.

You carelessly left this in your apartment when you killed Rainey.

Brent gripped the bedcovers and tore them off clear to the foot of the bed. Its uncovered occupant squeaked in terror and sat up. Unlike the usual in-patient, she was wearing a dark suit, apricot-colored stockings and high-heeled suede pumps. She dragged the sheet over her again, Brent grimly allowing her.

"Now," Brent said. "As Lora Lorne's emissary, I'm going to get this thing straight. You're not Mrs. Rainey, as you said you were. Your looks, your perfume, the key you used a few minutes ago to open the door of your apartment—everything proves you're Elaine Farnam."

The blond Elaine Farnam, gulping at Brent, could not summon up a denial.

"And you," Brent added, turning upon the brownette in the next bed, "are actually Mrs. Rainey. Neither of you two entered this hospital under your own name. You entered under each other's. It's cockeyed as hell but it's beginning to jell."

The violet eyes of Elaine Farnam and the childlike blue eyes of Mira Rainey were focused fearfully on Brent.

"You, Mrs. Rainey, while passing yourself off as Mrs. Farnam, actually had a baby whose birth is now duly certified under the name of Abigail Farnam. As for you, Mrs. Farnam—you're in perfectly normal physical condition, personally concerned much less with giving life than with destroying it. Lora Lorne will be greatly disturbed to hear you're the prime suspect in a murder case."

Elaine Farnam now had a grip on herself. She gazed forthrightly at Brent. "What's Lora Lorne got to do with this?" she asked.

"Why," Brent said, "for at least the past month Mrs. Rainey has been writing frequently to Lora Lorne about her baby, and—"

"I never did!" said the young woman in the other bed, with flat emphasis.

Brent stared at her. "You *haven't* written letters to Lora Lorne about—"

"Not once, I never!"

Blinking, Brent turned back to Mrs. Farnam. "But *you* did. Miss Lorne received a letter from you a week ago saying how delighted you were to be chosen—"

"Don't be silly!" Elaine Farnam said. "Why should I? Don't forget, the city editor of the *Recorder* happens to be my brother and I happen to be one of the few who know who Lora Lorne really is, Mr. Brent."

Brent swallowed hard but, baffled as he was by these denials, he hastily abandoned the subject. Elaine Farnam, seizing upon his discomfiture, leaned pleadingly toward him.

"You must never mention this to my husband—never! You understand that, don't you?"

"I understand there's one hell of a lot of deceit being practiced here," Brent said.

"You've *got* to understand it," Elaine Farnam insisted, "because you've got to keep quiet about it. I'm sure you won't mention it to anyone once I've told you—"

Suddenly she was telling him in a rush of earnest words.

"You see, more than a year ago, I—I began to lose my husband's love. Miss Lorne would sympathize with me about that, of course! Mike was working in this city then, and somewhere he'd met—a girl. I still don't know where or how, or who she is. I only know she must be something very special, because he—he went off the deep end for her. Not that he wanted to. He fought against the attraction he felt for her, but it was so strong he couldn't control it. Suddenly there was 'another woman' in my life and my marriage was threatened and I was terribly afraid I was going to lose Mike."

Brent observed: "He doesn't exactly look like a heel."

"He's not at all!" Elaine Farnam staunchly rushed to her husband's defense. "Mike is always fair and honest. He told me what was happening. He couldn't help it and he was sincerely trying his best to do the decent thing. Both he and I wanted to be sensible and reasonable about it, to keep our marriage going if we could. When Mike went off to South America on business, I thought that might solve the problem by taking him out of this girl's reach, but it didn't. She wrote him often, and it went right on, becoming more and more dangerous. I desperately wanted to keep my husband—and that's when all this started."

"This baby business?" Brent said.

Elaine Farnam anxiously nodded. "Mike has always been crazy about babies, but somehow I'd never managed to give him one. I thought that if only I could, he'd never leave me then. It began to work out, in a special way. Mira Rainey has been my maid for the past eight months—she came to me shortly after Mike left for Rio, so he'd never seen her. Her husband had abandoned her and she was going to have a baby. Everything Hopeful wrote to Lora Lorne applies to Mira—even though Mira did *not* write those letters—and she couldn't give the baby a proper home or a proper upbringing, so she and I agreed that I would adopt her child and that Mike must never know the baby wasn't really my own.

"I thought I was all set, and so I wrote to Mike that a baby was coming along at last. He was delighted, never dreaming the truth. He was going to be in Rio for months and months longer, and I thought it would be a simple matter—the adoption arrangements, I mean. But I was wrong! I hadn't realized that legal adoption is a complicated, carefully handled, long drawn-out process. And besides, the adopting husband must sign the various papers along with his wife. Suddenly—after having told Mike month after month that I was about to have a baby—I discovered that my original plan was impossible to carry out, because above everything else Mike *had* to believe that the baby was really biologically his and mine."

Brent clucked, as Lora Lorne would have done.

"But Mike was so happy about it I had to keep up the pretense. Even to my friends! Whenever anyone dropped in at the apartment I had to sit with a blanket draped around me, so none of them would mention to Mike that I didn't look a bit changed. All the while I was desperately trying to find a way of working it out. And then I did find one—something so simple it seemed foolproof. It was that Mira would have her baby under my name."

Mrs. Rainey, in the other bed, verified this with a vigorous nod.

"So I made these arrangements and named the little girl Abigail because that was Mike's mother's name, and besides, it means 'a father's joy,' and—and the rest is obvious, isn't it?"

"Not quite," Brent said. "You couldn't have pulled it off without inside help."

Elaine Farnam nipped at her nails. "I appealed to our doctor, Dr. Jean Hartwell. Being a woman, she sympathized and fixed it, even though it was unethical. She put us both in this one room, each under the other's name, so that all the records would show it was Mrs. Farnam who had had the baby when it was really the other way around. It solved other problems, too. For example, our special nurse simply shows visitors to this door and they naturally don't know the difference. Mira and I are planning to leave the hospital at the same time, and then I'll simply take Abigail and she'll come back to work for me, and there'll never be any question. Not from Mike, above all! Mike must never know the truth—never!"

"If he should learn the truth," Brent said wisely, "he'd then know that you'd undertaken to hold him with lies and trickery, and it would send him straight into the arms of the other woman."

"You make it sound so awful!" Elaine Farnam protested. "It is deceit, but it's doing nothing but good. It's helping Mira, and the baby too—as long as Mira's my maid, they'll see a great deal of each other—and I'm sure Mike and I will be so happy with little Gail!"

"Your brother—my city editor—has been in on this secret from the very beginning, I suppose?"

"Yes, I had to confide in him. He became very upset when Lora Lorne began publishing those letters from Hopeful, because Hopeful's case so closely paralleled Mira's."

"It's closer than that," Brent answered grimly. "It *is* Mira Rainey's case, in every detail, including the date of the baby's birth and the name of this hospital. Those letters don't refer to anyone *but* Mrs. rainey. Yet you both say she didn't write them. Yet Lora Lorne received a note decorated with your monogram, Mrs. Farnam, and bearing your return address."

"Neither Mira nor I have ever written a single letter to Lora Lorne!" Elaine Farnam insisted anxiously. "I can't explain it, except by thinking that someone's deliberately trying to make trouble for me."

That suspicion, of course, accounted for Garrett's demand that Brent discontinue printing the letters signed Hopeful. He remembered the urgent whisper of the man who had conked him in the dark—"False—malicious lies!"—and he wondered coldly whether Garrett himself had resorted to a blackjack. As for the other letter monogrammed EGF, anyone could buy stationery so marked, and anyone could scrawl the words, "Bay Terrace House, City," on the back of an envelope. Thinking how he had fretted for weeks over Hopeful's case when all the letters involved were evidently forgeries, Brent muttered.

"Trouble?" he said, echoing Elaine Farnam. "I think so! There's one more troublesome deal worth mentioning—a murdered man. It's pretty clear to me that Victor Rainey was threatening to explode this careful plan of yours. He was going to yell his head off to Mike, which would have wrecked the works—and that's why he was silenced."

Elaine Farnam blurted: "You can't think I did that!"

"God knows, not actually being in childbed, you were physically capable of it. Moreover, Rainey came here last night, railed at his wife and promised to make plenty of hot trouble for you, Mrs. Farnam." Brent frowned at Mira

Rainey. "Your husband has deserted you and was in Chicago. Had you written him that you were going to give your baby away?"

"I cer'nly did not!" Mira Rainey answered. "I never even told him I was gonna *have* a baby. He'da thought I was askin' him to come back on account of it. I didn' want him comin' back just because he might think it was his duty. He'd left me flat and that was that. I never told him nothin' about any baby."

Mira Rainey's spunk, Brent felt, was of a higher order than her rhetoric. "But what brought him back here from Chicago immediately after you'd had the baby, then?"

"I dunno," Mrs. Rainey admitted. "All to once he come bargin' in here givin' me hell. He wasn't gonna have any kid of his raffled off, he says. He kept saying, 'Don't do it.' He says, 'Abigail—what a name! It stinks,' he says, 'and I'm gonna see you don't do it.'"

This, then, was the real meaning of the dying man's words. Rainey had not been protesting against the blows already struck. Instead, he had babbled his delirious disapproval of these secret maternal machinations.

Mrs. Rainey continued: "Vic says 'I'm gonna have this out with this guy Farnam right now,' and he kept on sayin' so many things so loud they hadda bounce him. But he never once mentioned how he found out about I had a baby."

"He meant it, Mrs. Farnam," Brent observed. "He did go to confront your husband, and he stayed inside your apartment, dead. Apparently he didn't live long enough to have it out with Mike. He was prevented—beaten down with the gun, the same bloody gun you dropped a few minutes ago at the bottom of the fire escape."

Elaine Farnam blurted: "I don't understand it! The way that gun was sent to me—and the message! I couldn't believe what you'd told us about Victor Rainey's having been killed in my livingroom. I was so upset. I had to see for myself, as soon as possible. That's why I slipped out of here—and I also had to get rid of that ghastly gun—but you surprised me at the door and chased me back so fast I didn't have a chance." Her violet eyes widened. "Will the police come here? Will they ask questions—questions that will bring this all out? Oh, they mustn't! Mike must never know!"

Brent wagged his head, thinking that the job of concealing Abigail's true parentage seemed almost impossible in the face of the fact that Mrs. Farnam had had the motive, the opportunity and evidently the means of silencing Rainey. Once the circumstances became known, her scheme would not only be revealed to Mike, but she would also stand accused of first degree murder. It seemed hopeless and tragic. Brent was still studying Mrs. Farnam dubiously when a knock sounded and a nurse came in carrying a basin of soapy water. Brent regretted to note that she was not Olive Winslow.

"Your husband and your brother have come, Mrs. Farnam," she said to Mrs. Rainey, and with a significant glance at Brent she added: "They'll be up as soon as I've finished giving you two girls your baths."

Brent rose but paused at the door for another question. "How many bottles of perfume do you own?"

Mrs. Farnam answered: "The one I have here is new. I had another with only a few drops in it, and I left that in my bedroom. Please, you won't mention any of this to Mike?"

"Don't worry about my talking," Brent said glumly. "Worry about getting nailed for murder. Then it will all come out regardless."

He left both Mrs. Farnam and Mrs. Rainey in a state of agitation. Turning to the elevator, he found Garrett pacing the waiting room, alone. Garrett lifted troubled gray eyes that became fiercely flinty at sight of Brent.

"You again!" and he ominously leveled a forefinger. "I warned you where to keep your nose, Grandma. You quit smelling around here or you'll get it caught in a rat trap."

"I know," Brent murmured. "Captain Russo apparently thinks Mike is in the clear or he wouldn't have let him go. How good is Mike's alibi? I mean, it's possible for a guy to fake his arrival at a certain time, of course."

"Not in this case," Garrett retorted. "Mike's movements can be traced minute by minute all the way back to Rio. Russo's already made sure he landed at the airport here too late to have had a finger in this murder pie. None of which is any of your business, Miss Lorne."

"You'd be surprised," Brent said. "You realize, of course, that you're a prime murder suspect yourself, Garrett?"

"What! Me?"

"Certainly," Brent answered, his spirits lifting with the thought. "You were in on this baby plot from the start. You've naturally been anxious as hell to protect your sister's secret and to keep it from Mike. She must have told you right away that Vic Rainey had come on the scene and was stirring up a stink. It would be easy for you to get a key to your sister's apartment— easy for you to get to Rainey before he got to Mike." Brent grinned. "I *like* this idea! I find it very pleasant to think of you frying for a killing."

"My God!" Garrett said.

"I must remember to discuss it with Captain Russo," Brent added thoughtfully. "Mike's supposed to be here with you. Where's he gone?"

Garrett sat again, making a vague gesture. "He wandered off somewhere, probably in search of Abigail. You can't expect a man who's just had a baby for the first time to act like a normal human being. But *you* haven't had a baby, Miss Lorne. I expect you to make yourself prudently and permanently scarce."

Brent turned about regardless and trudged in search of Mike Farnam. No one else was in the hall. A few rooms were unoccupied and Brent glanced through their doors as he passed. Abruptly he was standing stock still, staring into the gloom inside one of them.

Mike Farnam was in there and he was not alone. His arms were pressing around a luscious white-clad body. A fluff of copper-red hair was brushing his face. A pair of red lips were crushing his. It was as passionate a clinch as had ever wound up a two-hour movie. Suddenly aware of Brent, Farnam and the girl broke apart. He was struck with consternation, but Nurse Olive Winslow returned Brent's gaze with beautiful coolness.

"A fine thing!" Brent blurted. "Your wife lying in childbed practically in the next room! Your sweet little baby blissfully asleep in the nursery! And here you are, making love to this wench behind their backs! I must say this is one hell of a fine situation, Farnam!"

The sentiment Brent expressed was Lora Lorne's, but inside him there was a thoroughly masculine envy, strictly his own. He turned about, hot with jealous indignation, and went away from there.

Chapter 6

ALL'S FAIR

LEAVING THE HOSPITAL, Brent saw the Homicide Squad car stopping. Captain Russo was tracing a routine lead. As to what the captain might think when he discovered the dead man's wife reposing side by side with the woman in whose home the corpse was found, Brent hesitated to guess. He hurried on his way.

He strode into the *Recorder* building to find the business departments functioning and the teletypes clattering, but the news staff not yet on the job. The pile of mail on Lora Lorne's table had grown with the day and the sight of it made him faintly ill. He remained in his cubicle no longer than necessary to dig up the number ten envelope that had been delivered to him during the night.

Comparing it with the other envelope which he had stolen off the corpse, he found the letter *n,* occurring in both Lora Lorne's names and Rainey's, to be nicked, indicating that both envelopes had been addressed on the same typewriter.

In the *Recorder*'s morgue, Brent delved into a folder tabbed with Michael Farnam's name. It contained only two clippings. One concerned Farnam's departure for South America last year. The other was headlined "Burglars Surprised in Act." Farnam had captured one of the burglarous pair after a disrupting tussle, during which he was slightly injured, and the crook had been so incensed by these unfair tactics as to vow that his pal would return to hurt Farnam even worse. As a precaution, the item concluded, Farnam had promptly applied for and been granted a license to own a gun.

Brent was certain that Captain Russo, checking the records, would identify Farnam's missing gun as a .38 Colt automatic. Very shortly thereafter the captain would busily cook Elaine Farnam's goose to a brown turn, and Garrett would inevitably blame Brent for it.

Full of uneasy premonitions, Brent next made use of the telephone directory. He drove six blocks to the Medical Arts Building. On the tenth floor he opened a door bearing the names of Dr. Jean Hartwell and Dr. John Marvin. Behind the reception desk he was astonished to find Nurse Olive Winslow busily billing a list of patients for the month's services.

"You can't be twins," Brent observed. "There couldn't be two women like you. The nation's social structure couldn't stand the strain."

"I'm Dr. Hartwell's office nurse." Having taken a dislike to him, Miss Winslow did not give Brent one of her beautiful smiles. "I'm not usually at the hospital, but Mrs. Farnam's is an exceptional case. If you're here to see Dr. Hartwell, you're outside her office hours."

"I, too, am an exceptional case," Brent said.

He stepped into a corridor before Nurse Winslow could stop him, then into an office where Dr. Jean Hartwell sat at her desk. Jean Hartwell eyed him with brisk disapproval but he sat down nevertheless.

"It's a felony, isn't it?" Brent inquired.

"What?"

"I mean conspiring to circumvent the child adoption laws and to falsify the public records. As I further understand the law, a physician convicted of a felony in this state is ever afterward forbidden to practice medicine. Surely you considered that when you connived with Mrs. Farnam?"

Dr. Hartwell paled and her dark eyes grew more intense. She had a fine, strong face. She was, Brent felt, considerable for a woman. Though a bit older, she could, in her own way, stand right up alongside Elaine Farnam and even Olive Winslow. Brent could never bring himself to accuse her outright of illegal acts. His purpose was simply to verify the story Mrs. Farnam had told him at the hospital.

"I have nothing to say."

That, Brent thought, was straight, honest talk. She was neither denying it nor confessing. There was none of this overly feminine why-I-really-haven't-the-faintest-idea-what-you're-talking-about stuff. Fact was, Brent didn't need to hear any answer from Jean Hartwell. Judging her, he knew she had weighed the problem of Mrs. Farnam's false motherhood and then, with sympathetic courage, despite the risks, had gone ahead and arranged it.

But she was shaken. Brent's knowledge was too fraught with catastrophic consequences. Potentially it was enough to wreck her practice, ruin her reputation, rob her of her profession and even pack her off to prison.

"What do you want?"

"A man has been murdered," Brent said. "The murder is being investigated. The investigation is turning up facts. The facts in this case are threatening to play hell all around. The evidence says that while Mrs. Farnam was supposedly in confinement she actually was on the loose, doing a bit of murdering."

"Incredible!"

"But once the cops learn her true situation," Brent pointed out, "this whole thing is going to blow up in a lot of faces. You and Mrs. Rainey and Mrs. Farnam are confederates, which perhaps makes you technically a first-rank accomplice to the crime of homicide."

Dr. Hartwell was even paler now, but her fine strong face was set. "I have nothing to say to you or to anyone else."

"Well," Brent observed, "that rules out any further discussion of the matter."

He rose with wagging head. Whenever he talked with any woman in this case, it seemed, he must leave her steeped in anxiety. Regretting it, but seeing no help for it, he trudged out of Dr. Hartwell's office and, six steps later, found himself confronting young Dr. Marvin.

Having just stepped from another room, and apparently having overheard Brent's remarks, John Marvin's face was livid with anger. He grasped Brent's shoulder, pushed Brent through a doorway and shoved him hard against a wall.

"Whoever the hell you are," Dr. Marvin asserted hotly, "you're going to keep your damned mouth shut!"

"I feel—"

"Jean Hartwell's too swell a woman. Her work is too important to her and to me. She wouldn't want me to say this, but I can't let it ride, not by a long shot. I'm in this with her. Nobody's going to make trouble for us if I can help it."

The guy was plainly in love with Jean Hartwell and Brent couldn't blame him for that.

"I was only going to say—"

"Don't!" Dr. John Marvin's eyes were two fierce blazes. "You're the only outsider who's messed into this thing and if any trouble comes of it I'll be damned sure it's your doing. If you want to keep your skin whole you'll clam up and fade. This is the last time I'll mention it. After this I won't waste time talking—I'll act."

He swung Brent back into the hallway, gave him a push, then shut the connecting door, no doubt as a measure of self-control, in order to keep himself from doing violence to Brent then and there. Brent felt it would be unwise to attempt to explain that Dr. Marvin had misinterpreted his purposes. He kept going until he came to the little office where Olive Winslow was still making out the month's bills.

Brent went to her, leaned over her shoulder and punched the letter *n* on the typewriter she was using. The character impressed on the paper, he saw, was familiarly nicked. Stepping back, he took a good look at Olive Winslow's legs. He recognized them easily as the very nice legs he had seen fleeing from Bay Terrace House. As a final test he brought Miss Winslow to her feet and snugly wrapped his arms around her. That settled it. She also had the same soft and curvesome feel.

Olive Winslow briskly slapped Brent's face.

"I don't fool!" she said furiously.

"You certainly don't," Brent agreed, rubbing his smarting cheek. "You play for blood."

He turned to the hat tree in the corner. Miss Winslow's loose gray coat was hanging there. He quickly turned both its pockets inside out. The lining of the left pocket, he found, sniffing it, smelled faintly of Elaine Farnam's perfume. The lining of the right one was stained in several brown, crusty spots.

"The bottle and the gun," Brent said. "Proof that you were in the Farnam apartment when Rainey was murdered. Headquarters will be glad to hear they've found the guilty woman. It's too bad, but that closes the case."

Olive Winslow was struck breathless. She could make no move as Brent hurried out the door. An elevator carried him down to the lobby. Remembering one of Hopeful's letters that had informed Lora Lorne her name was Mira Rainey and her address 456 Forest Street, he turned to a phone booth, consulted the directory and looked up the address listed as that of Olive Winslow's home. He smiled wryly, when he discovered that Miss Winslow lived at 456 Forest Street.

Going out to his car, he sat watching the entrance of the building. After a short moment Olive Winslow appeared, her lovely legs flashing in a run. She halted uncertainly, lips parted, red hair blowing, and Brent opened the door.

"Get right in," he said. "I've been expecting you."

Miss Winslow slipped onto the seat beside him. She was more indignant than frightened. "Are you out of your mind?" she snapped. "I won't let you prattle all that nonsense to the police. It doesn't make sense!"

"You can't deny you've been trying to frame Elaine Farnam," Brent answered. "Who but a guilty woman would ever want to frame an innocent one?"

"An innocent one would want to frame a guilty one when the guilty one stands a good chance of getting away with it!" Olive Winslow blurted.

Brent frowned over this and decided to go back to fundamentals.

"You're the 'other woman' who's been such a worry to Elaine Farnam," he said. "She might have guessed. You're the type who makes any man's mouth water. The first second I laid eyes on you, my glands felt it right down to their toes. That same thing must have happened to Mike Farnam. Being a harmless sort of hypochondriac, he had a way of rushing to Dr. Hartwell's office every time he thought he felt bad somewhere, which was pretty often, and each time he went he was exposed to your attraction. Stronger men than Mike would have succumbed. Probably every one of Dr. Hartwell's male patients carries a torch for you, longs to be greeted by you in that office and runs up extravagant bills. Mike is the one you chose. He's a very good guy; he makes big money; his many little ailments aroused the possessive, maternal instincts in you, a nurse. Now that I've found out about you two, it seems inevitable."

"Who's denying it?" Olive Winslow said.

Brent eyed her skeptically. "Everything else logically follows. Your idea has been to get Elaine Farnam into the worst possible jam by framing her for a killing. Whether or not she actually gets nailed for it, you've meant to do your damnedest to expose her false motherhood, you witch—to win Mike away from his wife, the lucky dog."

"I didn't have to kill a man to manage that!" Miss Winslow retorted disgustedly.

"The evidence says you did," Brent answered. "As Mrs. Farnam's nurse at the hospital you could easily get hold of the keys—take them from her purse when she wasn't looking. That's how Rainey got into that apartment where his death would prove most embarrassing to her. Rainey wasn't fully dead when you began falsifying the evidence against her. You sprinkled a few drops of her perfume from the bottle she'd left on her dresser, making it seem she'd just been there, and later you chucked the bottle into a trash basket somewhere. You carried the weapon of murder away with you, then delivered it to Mrs. Farnam in that flower box, hoping she'd get caught with it in her possession. You couldn't have managed all that if you hadn't pulled off the killing yourself."

"Get it straight, get it straight!" Olive Winslow almost screeched. "Don't you see I'm the one who wanted Rainey to live—wanted it more than anybody else concerned? He was much more useful to me alive than he is now. The one who wanted most of all to shut him up was Elaine Farnam!"

This, Brent realized, was love and war and anything went. Olive Winslow considered herself Elaine Farnam's deadly enemy, and Mike was the prize of conquest. She was not one to pull her punches, and she couldn't feel ashamed of having punched her hardest, even below the belt. To be merciless and unscrupulous was all part of the emotional feminine game she was playing, a game never governed by any rules of sportsmanship.

"Look," she said earnestly. "I'll spell it out for you. I'm as nuts about Mike as any woman can be. From the very beginning I've meant to get the exclusive rights to him. When Elaine Farnam began playing right into my hands with this scheme of hers about the baby, I decided to make the most of it, damn her."

Brent let Olive Winslow talk.

"Mike had written me from Rio that his wife was going to have a baby, and so, he said, he'd have to do the honorable thing—call it off between us. I doubted it, though I didn't tell him so. Weeks and months went by, and I kept wondering why Elaine Farnam didn't come to see Dr. Hartwell about her condition. Finally Dr. Hartwell was called to see *her*. Something funny was up. I began to suspect Mike's wife was trying to put over a fast one and I was damned if I'd let her.

"Wanting to find out what was cooking, I just sat outside Bay Terrace House in my car and watched. Once Elaine Farnam came out wearing a big loose coat, but her profile didn't look right, especially when the wind blew. Then another girl showed herself, and there wasn't any doubt about *her* expectations. I followed her into a shop while she did some marketing and overheard remarks that told me she was Mrs. Farnam's maid. Then I *knew* what the scheme was."

"So then, in your ruthless female way," Brent said, "you set about wrecking the works."

"You bet I did!" Miss Winslow admitted without batting an eye. "I posed as a welfare worker—easy for a nurse—and asked questions in that neighborhood and found out all about Mira Rainey's situation. Then I began—"

"Writing letters to Lora Lorne, signing yourself Hopeful and pretending to be Mira Rainey," Brent went on. "You wanted to publicize the thing guardedly, without appearing to have any connection with it. You wanted people to talk about it, including Mike's friends. You even planned to call the printed letters to Mike's attention, subtly, after he got back from Rio, and let suspicion grow in his mind. Then, with that last forged letter—the special delivery, the one howling about kidnapping—you even hoped to bring the cops into it and expose the whole thing on the front pages of the entire country. You weren't giving Elaine Farnam a chance!"

"Not a ghost of a chance—and that's not all of it," Olive Winslow said with shameless candor. "I also got Victor Rainey's address out of Dr. Hartwell's file and told him the whole story in an anonymous letter. I thought it would bring him running, and it did. He barged into Room 404 at the Heights, raising all the hell I'd hoped he'd raise. I grabbed him on the way out. Having heard from Mike that he was due in town right away, I told Rainey how to connect with him. I even drove Rainey over to Bay Terrace House and waited in my car while he went up to have it out with Mike."

"A slight miscalculation there," Brent said. "Mike hadn't yet arrived. His connecting plane from New York was late."

"I didn't know that then," Olive Winslow continued. "I waited so long for Rainey to come back down that I got worried. I went up, which was taking a chance, because I didn't want Mike to know I was having anything to do with this blow-up. It would turn him against me too, if he knew I was engineering it, so I had to stay behind the scenes and be ready to comfort him when he came to me broken-hearted. I just went up on the chance that I might hear through the apartment door what was being said between Mike and Rainey. There wasn't a sound. The door wasn't locked, so I looked in, and there was Rainey with his head bashed in. He looked dead to me."

"He wasn't, very," Brent put in.

"Holy cats!" said Olive Winslow. "What could be plainer? In 404 Rainey had sounded off about having it out with Mike. What was more natural than to think it had thrown Elaine Farnam into a fancy panic? The way I figured it, Elaine had slipped out, had managed to reach the apartment first—using her own car, which she'd left in the parking space ever since entering the hospital—and she'd been waiting for him. She'd slammed Rainey down, to keep him from blabbing to Mike, then she'd beat it out by way of the service stairs. Well, it wasn't long dawning on me that the murder could be used as the best means of all for exposing Elaine Farnam's scheme about the baby."

"So you sprinkled her perfume about," Brent said, "and confiscated the gun."

"It was lying right there beside Rainey's body," Miss Winslow admitted, "and I had good use for it. The hotter I could make this mess for Elaine Farnam, the sooner she'd be shown up as a fake mother. It wasn't as good as if Rainey had given Mike the straight dope about the baby, but it would do. You see that, don't you? It should be perfectly clear now that I was the last person in the world who wanted Rainey to get killed."

Brent reflected that this dame was all woman, and as such was a dangerous character. According to her book, any tactics that promised to get her man, no matter how extreme, were thoroughly justified. She was emotionally incapable of feeling that anything she had done was wrong. Did she, then, also feel it unnecessary to lie about her actions? Brent wondered, peering at her.

"See here. Do you actually believe Elaine Farnam really killed that man?"

"Believe it?" By this question, strangely enough, Olive Winslow was shocked. "Certainly I believe it! Everything points to her. Who else could possibly have done it? How can any sensible person believe anything else? I'm absolutely certain Elaine Farnam is guilty as hell!"

"And when she's nailed for it," Brent mused, "it'll no doubt make you very happy."

"She'll be getting what she deserves—and I'll be getting Mike." Miss Winslow turned to slip out of the car. "That little scene you interrupted between Mike and me at the hospital this morning was just for old times' sake—or so Mike thinks. Now that he's assumed the responsibilities of fatherhood, it was all over between us, he said. That was farewell and good-bye—one last kiss. Little does he know! Will he be surprised—and pleasantly, I think!"

With the deep confidence and self-possession which only a triumphant woman can feel, Olive Winslow ran back into the building, leaving Brent shuddering and chilled.

Chapter 7

WHILE ABIGAIL SLEPT

B RENT TRUDGED DEJECTEDLY into the news room, avoiding Garrett's glare from the city desk in the far corner. Eight news men were now busily punching their typewriters. Among them Valerie Randall, the only girl police reporter in the fourth estate, who worked Brent's old trick these days under Garrett's fond tutelage, was fumbling with second-hand details about the corpse that by rights belonged to Brent. He took his woes into Lora Lorne's overcrowded cubbyhole and groaned with dismay when Garrett squeezed in, shoving the door shut.

"Don't try to blame me for this mess, Garrett," Brent said quickly. "*I* didn't kill Rainey. *I* didn't leave his dead body cluttering up your sister's parlor. My own personal relations with Abigail are above reproach."

"Like hell they are, Grandma," Garrett grated. "Russo is no dope. He's wondering how you happened to walk in on that cadaver and why you've been chasing in and out of hospitals ever since. When he found Elaine and Mrs. Rainey both in the same room, he just made a few remarks about strange coincidences and went thoughtfully on his way—but he'll be back. What it all adds up to is enough to freeze my blood."

"Is Mike suspicious?"

"Mike is curious about that wifely tie-up. He knows there's more to it than meets the eye. You're responsible for plenty of these complications, my dear Miss Lorne—the way you've been throwing your weight around. If Mike should find out the truth about Elaine—if their marriage should go on the rocks, they'll have you to thank. You, Lora Lorne, who's supposed to safeguard our happy homes, not wreck 'em!"

Having some degree of truth in it, the denunciation touched Brent's quick. "So far, anyway," he pointed out, "nobody in an official position has found out anything from me. If I can work it, they never will. But the problem's much bigger than that. If we can't manage to keep it under wraps, somehow, it'll splash out in such nationwide proportions that even you won't be able to keep it off the *Recorder*'s front page. What's more, Garrett, your sister may very likely get fitted for the chair."

"You're telling me?" Garrett growled. "You think Russo's not working around to that? Once he snags onto the facts Elaine will be minus a husband and a baby too, and she won't stand a chance against the homicide charges. All right, Grandma. You're the heart-throb specialist. Just how will you go about solving this little predicament? Just how, for God's sake?"

Brent came to his feet. "I've got ideas," he retorted. "But I want you to understand one thing. This isn't Lora Lorne on the job. It's Bill Brent, police reporter, successor to Val Randall. Is that clear?"

Garrett's jaw pointed a threat at Brent. "This is no time for horse-trading.

I just had a call from Mike. Russo's got him cornered right now. Russo's next move will be a showdown with Elaine and that'll be the payoff. Don't try to dicker with me until you've done something helpful—assuming you can think of something helpful to do."

Brent could. He caught up the telephone and the directory, urgently demanded the number of Dr. Hartwell's office and heard Nurse Olive Winslow answer.

"Please inform Jean Hartwell that all hell's due to pop," he said, "and she'd be wise to keep out of Room 404 for the duration. It's now the objective of hostile forces. The chief of the Homicide Squad may even bring along a police surgeon to examine those patients on his own hook. If you've any means of preventing that, you'd better grab it."

He disconnected and caught up his hat. Abandoning the comparatively minor items of international news piling up on his desk, Garrett went after him. Garrett was ominously quiet while Brent drove, and Brent devoted himself to thought. They strode together into the Heights Hospital and saw that Olive Winslow and Dr. John Marvin were just entering the doorway of Room 404.

Brent closed the door behind Garrett. Elaine Farnam and Mira Rainey watched him tensely, sensing that crucial developments were at hand. Dr. Marvin placed himself as if to balk any unfriendly approach to his patients, and Nurse Winslow looked beautifully, grimly pleased. This, Brent realized, was what she'd been hoping for. When all the loud noises had echoed away and the pieces were being picked up, she expected, Elaine Farnam would find her home and her marriage wrecked, at the very least, and Olive Winslow would go wandering happily down lover's lane, hand in hand with Mike.

"Mrs. Farnam," Brent said, "after Victor Rainey was bounced out of this room last night, did you warn Dr. Hartwell he was about to wreck the works?"

Elaine Farnam answered quickly: "I couldn't reach her on the phone, but when Dr. Marvin came in a few minutes later I told him. It worried him, but he said he couldn't see how any of us could do anything about it."

Brent's gaze turned sharply and John Marvin flushed with indignation.

"You're looking at me," Marvin said in a brittle tone, "as if you suspect me of every crime on the calendar. Well, it's too late for that sort of bungling. I'm going to talk and talk straight. If we've all got to get hurt, I'll see to it that the right one gets hurt the worst." Deliberately he pointed at Olive Winslow. "There's your killer."

Miss Winslow stiffened. "Don't be silly!" she retorted. "I've already explained myself, and I'm in the clear."

"She has," Brent admitted, "but is she?"

John Marvin's lips curved in an acrid smile. "She most certainly is not. She's a conscienceless little schemer, an expert liar and completely treacherous to Dr. Hartwell and everyone else concerned, except herself. I can tell you exactly how she maneuvered the whole thing."

Brent silenced Olive Winslow with a gesture and urged, "O.K., tell us."

"She's the one who brought Victor Rainey here, of course, and she promptly took him to the Farnam apartment," John Marvin continued, his eyes fiery upon her. "But after his first explosion Rainey began to cool off. I saw her leaving the hospital with him and heard him saying, 'Oh, the hell with it. Let it go, let it go.'"

"John Marvin," Olive Winslow said, her fists clenched, "that's an outright lie! He said nothing of the sort!"

"But he did," Marvin insisted, "and his change of heart was knocking the props from under your slick little scheme to expose Mrs. Farnam to her husband. You weren't aware that I followed you, were you? I saw you and Rainey go into Bay Terrace House together, bound for the Farnam apartment."

"Another lie!" Olive Winslow asserted furiously. "He went in alone!"

"You went up together," Marvin insisted, "and it's very easy to picture what happened next. Rainey didn't want to see Mike Farnam. He wanted to call the whole deal off, wash his hands of it. Without Rainey's help you'd be left out on a limb, so you tried to force him to wait and talk to Mike."

"Force him?" Olive Winslow answered scathingly. "How could I do that!"

"With a gun," John Marvin said. "Last year, after Mike got hurt capturing that burglar, he came to Dr. Hartwell for treatment and he said he was buying a gun—and besides, it was in the papers. You knew the gun was somewhere in that apartment, so you got it and tried to hold Rainey there. Rainey'd had a bellyfull by then. He tried to take the gun away from you. You lost your wits and hit him over the head with it and kept on hitting him. There's your answer, gentlemen. Little Olive overplayed her hand. No matter how the rest of us may come out of this, she's not going to wind up owning Mike after all."

Olive Winslow was now too furious to speak. Elaine Farnam was gazing at her open-mouthed, and Garrett was scowling his darkest. Brent weighed Marvin's charges and nodded.

"That's good," he said. "But it's not quite good enough. It's a bad fit in places, and it leaves things out."

"Nevertheless," John Marvin asserted tersely, "I imagine the police will be satisfied with it."

"But I'm not," Brent said, "and I happen to be in a better position to judge. For example, that letter Olive wrote to Rainey, which he brought back from Chicago with him, the one stolen off his dying body. Olive had no reason in the world for removing it. Quite the contrary. The letter told the inside story about Mrs. Farnam's little Abigail. If found on Rainey's corpse, Olive would have loved it. The letter was taken away in order to keep all this baby business dark. That lets Olive out. At the same time it lets in Jean Hartwell, Elaine Farnam, my pal Garrett—and you, Dr. Marvin."

Marvin's face went white. "You can be damned sure Jean Hartwell didn't do it!" he snapped. "As for Elaine Farnam, you've only to look at her—"

"You've only to look at the evidence," Brent corrected him, "to see that no woman could have committed that murder. A woman facing Rainey in that apartment, with so tremendously much at stake, would have been overwhelmed with emotion. With a fully loaded gun in her hand, would she have stopped to think she mustn't make too much noise? Certainly not.

Without thinking at all, but feeling to the utmost of her capacity to feel, she'd have pulled the trigger—pulled it again and again. But that didn't happen. The careful way was taken. The loaded gun was used silently, as a club, and the letter was remembered. Behind the murder of Rainey there was a thoughtful mind—a mind thinking all the while of protecting its interests—a man's mind."

John Marvin's lips were curling scornfully.

"That's only the beginning of the evidence," Brent went on. "You've admitted you knew Olive Winslow's purpose was to wreck Elaine Farnam's scheme. You probably saw her typing the special delivery letter to Lora Lorne, but you couldn't stop her from mailing it, so you tried to get it back before anyone could read it. Being Dr. Hartwell's associate, you also knew there was a gun in the Farnam apartment. Coming here to this room several times a day, you were able to get Mrs. Farnam's keys out of her purse when you needed them, without being seen. You clubbed me with the gun, in order to get Lora Lorne's letter back, and later you beat Vic Rainey to death with it."

Dr. Marvin pressed back against Elaine Farnam's bed and his teeth shone between drawn lips.

"Mrs. Farnam had told you Rainey was bound for her apartment to spill the works to Mike. To you that meant disaster. It would plunge Jean Hartwell, the woman you're crazy about, into the worst possible trouble. Not only that, but you as her accomplice in this baby business, would go through the same wringer. You saw that both of you were in grave danger of disgrace, of losing your careers and your profession. So you got into the Farnam apartment first, and then Rainey appeared at the door. If you tried to reason with him, it didn't work. Thoughtfully and carefully, in a way allowing you to get away without raising an alarm, you killed him."

"I'm very much afraid you've no way of proving any of this hogwash," John Marvin said.

"You forget those finger-streaks you left on the yellow leather chair," Brent said. "They show no ridge patterns. Thinking you had to be careful not to leave any fingerprints on the doorknobs or on the gun, you'd put on rubber gloves—a surgeon's gloves."

Dr. Marvin's whole body snapped tight. The door was opening. Mike Farnam appeared first, and Captain Russo followed him.

Sight of Russo's cadaverous face wrung a groan from Brent. He had the whole story now, and he couldn't tell it. To use the facts to pin Rainey's murder on John Marvin would mean that he must also expose the truth about Abigail, not only to the cops but also to Mike. Garrett was glowering at him, warning him, and Brent felt keenly the sharp points of his dilemma. He threw his brain into high and hoped desperately it would reach a safe solution.

"Well?" Captain Russo said in a tone that seemed to float out of a grave. "All this meddling of yours must add up to something by now, Brent. Surely you've solved my case for me by this time. Well?"

Brent's mind groped. Gazing at John Marvin's drawn face, he realized that Marvin was also fearful that the truth would flood out now—fearful not for himself, but for Jean Hartwell. Marvin had committed a murder largely for Jean Hartwell's sake, and the facts would condemn her—undo all his desperate work. Everyone's purposes were at stake—even Olive Winslow's, now that her part in it might be revealed to Mike Farnam.

"It's clear enough," Brent began, his words racing with his mental gyrations. "There'll be denials, of course, but it's such old stuff you won't be able to question it, Russo. The old stuff about two men being nuts about the same woman. There she stands. Who can blame them?"

His fingers indicated Olive Winslow, and astonishment held everybody silent.

"Working with Nurse Winslow day in and day out, Dr. Marvin couldn't help going tail over tincup for her. Miss Winslow, though, preferred a guy named Rainey. When Rainey came back to town last night, incidentally to see his sick wife but chiefly to renew relations with Miss Winslow, Dr. Marvin's jealousy drove him berserk. He found out that Miss Winslow had snitched Mrs. Farnam's keys, and that she and Rainey were going to hold an amorous rendezvous in that conveniently empty apartment. The rest is just the same as it's happened thousands of times in the past. Man kills rival over woman in love nest. Consult your local newspaper files."

Mike Farnam was staring scandalized at Olive Winslow. Brent saw that, thank God, he was impressed. "Is that true?" he blurted at her. "In Heaven's name, is it?"

Miss Winslow was stunned. "It's a filthy lie!" she screeched. "Me and Vic Rainey? It's crazy!"

She was right about that, Brent reflected; but the false crime picture he'd painted was so familiar it was carrying conviction. Dr. John Marvin was smiling tightly.

"That's the setup, Captain Russo," he said. "I don't see any hope of denying it, so I must admit it's exactly right. I killed Rainey in the Farnam apartment last night while he was waiting there for Olive to join him. A sordid mess, isn't it? Unfortunately that's the way life goes—and death too."

Nurse Winslow blurted out more high-pitched denials, but nobody heard them distinctly. Mike Farnam was staring at her, too revolted to speak when Dr. Marvin, with a sudden snap of his body, vaulted Elaine Farnam's bed. He landed at the window. In another instant he was scrambling out on the fire escape. Wild eyes turned back, he clambered down.

"Why doesn't somebody stop him?" Russo complained hollowly.

The captain scurried after Marvin, seeming to creak in every joint, like a skeleton. He squirmed onto the fire escape platform, his service gun gripped in a bony hand. Brent dove for the door. It was the longer way around, but he gambled on reaching the alley leading to the parking space before Marvin could dodge into the street. When he reached the mouth of it, he saw nothing of Marvin. There was a single muffled, blasting report.

Heels pounding, Brent came into the parking lot to find Captain Russo standing morosely at the head of the short flight of cement stairs leading to the basement door. John Marvin was lying at the base of them, loose as a bundle of old clothes, blood trickling from his open mouth, the back of his head blown out, Farnam's automatic lying beside his lax hand.

"He made it easy for you, Russo," Brent said, knowing that Marvin had really made it easy, instead, for Jean Hartwell and Elaine Farnam. "You'll never have to try him. But understand one thing. Those two patients upstairs are completely outside the case. Both of them—and Mrs. Farnam's little Abigail, too."

The captain looked sadly at Brent. "Who am I to go prowling around a nursery?" Russo said. "Healthy babies aren't nearly dead enough to interest me."

Brent was breathless when he hurried into the *Recorder* news room. With typewriters clattering and teletypes clicking, the busy night was at its height. Leaning over the city desk, Brent talked while Garrett's blue pencil skipped over pages of copy.

"Everybody's happy," Brent reported, grinning, "except our Olive, who's up a tall tree. She's denying that extemporaneous explanation I cooked up, but it's not doing her any good because she can't defend herself with the truth. She can't because it would turn Mike against her even more. Being the woman she is, she still thinks she might snag him sometime, so she's clamming—but she really hasn't got a chance. Dr. Hartwell's protected, Mike and Elaine are talking about a second honeymoon and their little Abigail still slumbers peacefully. O.K., Garrett. Tell Val Randall to vacate my desk. I'm back on the police trick, of course."

Garrett's pencil poised. "Just a minute, Grandma," he said evenly. "We're all grateful as hell, personally, but the real story you dug up is one that can never see print. I can't value a reporter highly because he produces stuff I can't publish. On the contrary, you've proved your skill as a solver of marital problems. As Lora Lorne nobody could ever replace you. Back on the job, Grandma."

Brent was aghast. "What! After getting myself bashed on the head, after being practically ironed out by a murderer in a high-powered car— Good lord, Garrett, where's your appreciation? You can't mean it!"

"But Miss Lorne," Garrett said implacably. "What would the paper do without you now? Besides, I've got a gigantic idea! A contest based on this case! A prize for the best letter on the subject, 'What Would *You* Do About the Other Man?' Swell stuff and exactly your dish!"

The enormity of it stunned Brent. He trudged morosely back into his cubbyhole and slumped in his chair. Automatically he plucked a letter from the mound on the table. His dulled eyes swam over words written in passionate red ink on lingerie-pink paper.

Dear Miss Lorne,
You've been so wonderfully sympathetic with Hopeful, I must turn to you for guidance in my own trouble. My husband has left me, and I'm in terrible circumstances, and very soon now I too am going to have a baby—

"Sometimes I wish to God women were salmon!" Bill Brent moaned. "God forbid!"

Sleep No More My Lovely

G. T. FLEMING–ROBERTS

W ITH THE CAR in the drive and Weaver out in the car, Bill came
back to the porch where Maude was waving good night. He was pale
with fury, and the blue circles of worry had deepened beneath his eyes.
Maude felt a little pale herself, and very, very tired. Bill took her two arms
just above the elbows, gripped them tightly.

"Don't bother with the dishes, will you?" he whispered. "Go right to bed.
And it—you were wonderful."

He kissed her as though he were going to the end of the earth instead of
to take Weaver to the bus line.

Maude stepped back out of the night and the damp. She closed the door,
crossed the living room with its company clutter to snuff out a cigarette that
was sending a thin twist of smoke to the ceiling. She sank into the lounge
chair and slipped off her shoes. From the lounge chair she could see into
the dining room where the banjo clock ticked upon the wall. It was ten-
thirty.

When Maude had faintly protested Weaver's departure, Weaver had said
that he believed in early to bed and early to rise. Had said that proudly as
though it were something he had invented, like Edison the electric light.
Weaver had wealth to prove his wisdom, but Maude had wondered—without much concern—how healthy he was.

She had never seen anybody eat like Weaver. She thought dismally of the
standing rib roast that had cost many precious ration points, remembered
what she had planned to do with the leftovers. There were no leftovers,
thanks to Weaver's bottomless, possibly nonexistent stomach.

Weaver had enjoyed himself. He had enjoyed the food, and, Maude thought, he had enjoyed a secret knowledge of why Bill Carrick had asked him to dinner. Even when he was putting away great slabs of beef, Weaver must have made up his mind not to let Bill have the money that was so desperately needed.

Weaver had paid for his bread in platitudes. . . . "The trouble with young married folk today is that they refuse to start small and grow. . . ." True, perhaps, but hardly applicable to the Carricks. Bill had no way of knowing that the business in which he had invested everything would be worth nothing at all during wartime. Maude, never a yes-ma'm, had pointed this out to Weaver in a nice way. For that, too, Weaver had an answer—"Foresight to keep ahead of the ever-changing pattern of the world today . . ."

To give Bill a chance to ask Weaver for the loan, Maude had spent more time than usual upstairs tucking Joe into bed. Though she had not heard Weaver's answer, it had been plainly written on Bill's face when she had come down. It wasn't a lot of money that they needed—enough for the mortgage payment, enough to keep Bill's insurance in force for another six months and to pay a portion of the tax on last year's income. Weaver could easily have managed it, and inasmuch as Bill was now working for Weaver, repayment could have been made in small installments from Bill's salary check.

A tired child's whimper intruded on the clock-tick stillness of the room. Maude got out of the chair and went half way up the stairs to listen. Joe was turning over, grunting, thumping the bedhead with small fists. Then all was quiet. Maude went up the steps anyway and into Joe's room to look down in the little bed. Joe was on his back, his hands beneath his curly head. He didn't look at all like the little boy who had scattered half a package of soap flakes all over the living room carpet a scant quarter hour before Bill and Weaver were due to arrive from the office.

"Joey," she thought, "I'll bet Mr. Weaver didn't approve of you either. You're such a little pig. And then according to Weaver standards we probably can't afford you, dear."

She smiled a little, pitying Weaver.

Unaccountably the *ping* of the banjo clock striking the quarter hour recalled to Maude's mind a picture of Bill bending over Joe's crib on the night before. Joe had been asleep and Bill had clenched the top of the protective rail.

"There isn't anything your old man wouldn't do for you, kid," Bill had whispered. "Not anything."

Something within Maude drew into a tight, cold knot that was gone as suddenly as it had come. She drew a short breath, then turned on tiptoe, left the room, walked down the carpeted steps. She looked at the clock in the dining room—fourteen minutes of eleven.

It shouldn't have taken Bill more than ten minutes to deliver Mr. Weaver to the bus stop. Fifteen at the outside if there was mist along the Cold Springs Road. It wasn't the safest road to travel this time of year with the steep bluffs and the fog that rose from White River at flood stage. She put all that aside and decided sanely that Bill had probably waited with Weaver for the bus and used those minutes to appeal again for the loan.

She counted dragging minutes. On the stroke of eleven, the car turned into the drive and went on back to the garage. Then Bill's footsteps crunched along the gravel and up onto the porch. He opened the door, turned to close it, scarcely looking at her.

"I thought you'd be in bed," he said.

"I was waiting for you, Bill."

He uttered a short laugh. "To hear the news? It was no go, that's all."

He walked out into the dining room, paused a moment, his hand on the white wood frame of the cased opening.

He said: "There any cocktails left, Maude?" still without looking at her. "We might as well get something out of this. Even a headache."

"Uh-huh. Not any for me, though."

"I know. You've got a headache. Me too."

She watched him go back toward the kitchen, his thin shoulders wearing a dejected stoop. His hair, she thought, is only a little darker than Joe's, and curly now with the damp. She listened to him out there in the kitchen, heard the trembling clink of the bottle of ready-mixed cocktails on the glass. He had one out there and brought another brim-full into the living room.

She said: "Was the bus late? Did you wait with Weaver for it?"

He laughed recklessly. "Wait with him? I wouldn't have cared if he had to walk home. No, I dumped him right there at the bench." And then he seemed to read what was going through her mind and explained hastily: "I had a little trouble with the car coming up the hill. It ought to be fixed. That's another thing . . ."

He sipped his drink, winked at her over the rim.

"We'll find a way," he assured her.

"Of course. Bill, had you thought of asking Rick Thomas—" She checked herself, knowing now she had said just the wrong thing. Rick Thomas was second in charge of the oil agency Weaver operated, and it was Rick's influence that had got Bill the job. More than that, in these days of adversity Bill never let Maude forget that she could have married Rick Thomas.

Bill's lips thinned and curled and his proud crooked brows rode high on his forehead. She thought suddenly of Rick who was dark and sardonic and never boyish like Bill was, who never could have been to her what Bill was, though Bill never fully seemed to understand that.

She said: "Let's skip it, huh?"

"No," he said, "let's not skip it." He was tired and feeling the cocktails. "Let's thrash that subject out right now."

"Bill, don't be absurd. Don't . . ."

Car lights threw fuzzy cones of light into the Carrick drive and through the windows. A door slammed and footsteps scurried on the gravel.

"Rick's still a bachelor," Bill said, "waiting to catch you on the second bounce. You'd be better off—you and Joe—"

"Bill, there's somebody at the door."

The rat-a-tat of knuckles dancing on the door to the accompaniment of the electric door chime announced their visitor. Maude slid into her pumps and stood up.

"It's Nels," she said. No one but Nelson Starr knocked and rang at the same time. Nels and Ruth lived three houses down the road, and Nels was auditor at the Weaver oil agency where Bill worked.

Before Maude could reach the door, Nels had it open, had thrust head, shoulder and knee into the room. He said breathlessly: "Your light was on— and I thought you'd want to know. You and Bill."

Bill waved his cocktail glass. "What's wrong? A blackout?"

Nels came all the way in, the loose pink flesh of his rounded cheeks quaking with every heavy step. Blunt thumbs were hooked in the sagging pockets of his topcoat. Then he remembered his hat, took it off, and his flat bald head looked damp.

"I wish it was," he said. "An air raid would be easier to take." He shook his head, shuddered like taking bitter medicine. "No, it's Weaver. He's been mugged. No, that's not quite right. This was with a paving brick. In the head."

"Weaver?" Maude and Bill said. Bill put his cocktail glass down slowly on the table but without taking his eyes off Nels' pale moon face. He asked: "Where? When?"

"Down there." Nels jerked his head. "The bus stop. When I drove by, there were the police. I stopped to see. It was Weaver."

"You mean," Bill said quietly, "he's dead."

"Sure. With a brick, I told you. Robbed I guess." Nels' mud-brown eyes saw Bill's glass and became eager. He moistened thick lips. "I hope that's not the dregs. I need a bracer. Old Weaver's got me down, I guess."

Bill said it wasn't the dregs. Nels took his coat off on his way back to the closet at the right of the front door. It was a small closet, crowded. Nels' coat fell off the hook and Bill hastened to find a hanger for it.

"Let it go, Bill," Nels said. "That old coat. Four seasons now."

But Bill was in the closet, hanging up Nels' coat, and Maude hurried out into the kitchen to get a glass and the bottle of cocktails. When she returned, Nels was in the lounge chair, fat knees spread, suit coat open, the tiny twenty-year-old gold football on his watch chain blinking bright with every breath he drew.

"Thanks, Maude. I tell you, this is a life saver." Nels took the glass and Maude sat down on the footstool beside Nels' chair. Bill stood with his fingers thrust stiffly into his hip pockets.

Bill said: "Weaver was here tonight for dinner. I drove him to the bus stop."

Nels drank deeply. "He was?" His black eyebrows arched. "You didn't wait with him for the bus. . . ." He broke off, laughed shortly. "I'm not asking, of course. The police will, though."

Maude drew a quick breath, looked at Bill. Bill's blue eyes were moody, space-staring.

Nels said: "I hope they won't be nasty. The cops. No reason why they should. Things like this are on the up-grade. Young toughs. It's the war. Weaver had quite a bit of cash on him. Took it out of the safe this afternoon, and I don't think he made a trip to the bank."

"The police will have to know, I suppose," Maude said, "about Mr. Weaver having dinner with us?"

Bill laughed. "I like the way you put that, Maude. They *will* know."

"Sure," Nels agreed. "Maude, you're so naive. Not that you've anything to worry about. Not with a place like this. No motive."

No motive that Nels knew about, Maude thought. And no alibi either. She gave Bill's rugged profile a quick, searching glance. Why did something go wrong with the car tonight, of all times? If anything *had* gone wrong. On the hill, Bill had said. Why, their car breezed up hills in fourth gear! It was nearly new—swift, silent, and powerful. But perhaps tonight because of the fog and the damp . . .

Bill turned his head toward her as he said distinctly: "It'll be nice for Rick Thomas. He'll be top man now. I don't think the central office would move in a man from outside to take Weaver's place."

"Not with things as they are today," Nels agreed. "It'll be nice for all of us for that matter. A step up." He slid a glance at Maude to see how she was taking this sort of talk. "Maude, you don't know Weaver. Does she, Bill?"

Bill smiled crookedly. "I guess she does."

"Oh, I'm not going to wear a mourning band. But *murder* . . ." A shudder twisted Maude's shoulders, and deep within she felt that unaccountable, cold, tight knot.

"Not murder," Nels said as he put down his glass and prepared to leave. "Mugging. Only with a brick. A lot of young toughs around. It's the war."

That was the way they left it for the night. After Nels was gone, Maude and Bill went upstairs. They never talked, getting ready for bed, because they might wake Joe. When the lights were out, Maude lay on her back in her bed, unable to relax. Against the dark curtain of her thoughts she could still see Bill bending over Joe's crib and saying: "There isn't anything your old man wouldn't do for you, kid. Not anything."

"Bill," she whispered after thirty minutes had been chimed away by the clock downstairs, "Bill, what was wrong with the car?"

"Uh—vapor-lock," he mumbled. "I guess. How the hell would I know?"

She lay there for hours in the blind, defenseless night, just waiting for the morning—

In the morning she was feeding Joe in the kitchen when the door bell chimed. Bill's electric shaver was going in the bathroom and he wouldn't have heard the bell. Maude took a quick knot in the cord of her housecoat and hurried into the living room. Through the picture window she could see a portion of the winding drive and a black coupe standing there. The car had a big blue shield painted on the door.

She stopped half way to the door, one hand on the back of the wing chair. "Bill," she called above the whine of his shaver. "Oh, Bill!"

He didn't answer, and the doorbell chimed again. She hurried to the door, and her lower lip was in her teeth as she twisted off the bolt and wrenched the knob.

"Oh, good morning!" she said, almost as though she had invited them to breakfast.

"Good morning," one of them said. "Mrs. Carrick? Hope we didn't get you out of bed."

"No, no," she said, forced a smile. "I have a young son who's quite an alarm clock."

There were two of them, a policeman in uniform and a detective in a gray suit with a white carnation in his buttonhole. She saw the carnation before she saw his face. It was a long, heavy-featured face with gray eyes deeply set in a nest of wrinkles. The wrinkles, she decided immediately, were not from laughing. She was surprised that he took off his hat when he came into the living room.

Out in the kitchen, Joe was yelling: "Dinny-dinny-dinny!" which meant anything from breakfast to dinner but was always quite imperative.

"You go right ahead, Mrs. Carrick," the detective said. "We would like to speak with Mr. Carrick for a moment, though."

She smiled them into chairs and they both sat down stiffly, very much on edge. She went to the foot of the stairs. Bill had stopped the shaver and the very silence upstairs told her he was listening behind the bathroom door.

"Bill," she called. "Two gentlemen to see you."

He showed himself in maroon dressing gown and scuffs, sleep still in his hair and eyes. Maude went through the dining room into the kitchen and there got Joe his silver cup of milk. She put the cup down on the trap of his high-chair and this morning she didn't care if Joe threw milk all over the kitchen. She went quietly back through the swinging door to stand flat against the wall of the dining room and listen.

"Weaver lived a pretty lonely life," Bill was saying easily. "My wife and I thought he'd enjoy a good home-cooked meal."

"I see." The gray-eyed detective apparently spoke for the law. "What time did Mr. Weaver leave?"

"I think it was about twenty-five to twenty-eight minutes after ten," Bill said. "I drove him to the bus stop. I couldn't very well take him all the way home. I've only got an 'A' card."

"But you didn't wait with him for the bus?"

"No," Bill said readily. "He wouldn't permit it. I left him sitting there on the bench."

"He's your employer, isn't he, Mr. Carrick?"

Bill said: "That's right. And I left him there on the bench in the fog waiting for the bus. I couldn't help it. He insisted that I get right home. My wife had been having a little trouble with the baby."

Maude could hear the hammer of her heart. Bill was lying. He had to lie. He couldn't tell them that they had tried to borrow money from Weaver. He wouldn't dare.

"I see," the detective said. "Pretty thoughtful old fellow Weaver must have been. What time you get home, Mr. Carrick?"

Bill hesitated perceptibly. "Not until about eleven. I had a flat tire about two hundred yards from the house."

A flat tire, was it? Not motor trouble coming up the hill. Bill, Bill, why lie about a thing like that? Bill what were you doing those fifteen extra minutes?

Maude stood there, wrapping her sash about one finger, gnawing on her lower lip. Bill was getting rid of them now. The gray-eyed detective was saying something about establishing the time of death pretty definitely. Then he thanked Bill curtly and Maude heard the closing of the door and the after-silence.

Finally Bill came shuffling out of the living room and into the dining room where the sight of Maude gave him a start.

He said: "Well . . ." and then went on out into the kitchen to pull Joe's ear. Joe grinned at him and said: "Bad Daddy."

"Well, it's bad Joe, if I know anything about it! Look at that milk all over everything." Bill went for a rag to mop the milk off the floor.

"Just coffee for me this morning, Maude. Then I'll scoot. If you don't have to go for groceries or anything, I'll take the car to the bus line."

She went to the stove to put the coffee maker on.

"Why did you lie about the car?" she asked flatly, her back to him.

He uttered a strained laugh. "So you were eavesdropping, darling. Why, I didn't want to worry you about the tire, that's all. A flat tire can be a pretty serious thing these days, you know."

She knew just how serious it could be, especially in a murder investigation, a few minutes after Bill had left for work. She carried Joe out to the road to see if the postman had left any mail in the box, and looking off the brow of the hill she saw their car parked along the side of the road, and there was Bill squatting down beside a wheel, changing a tire. To make his story stick with the police, in case they checked the car. Last night, it had been neither tire nor motor trouble that had delayed Bill. Something else— something he was keeping from her and from the police.

Bill was late getting home that night. He came in the door with his hat on, as always, and when Joe toddled to meet him he picked Joe up so that Joe could have the pleasure of removing his hat and mussing his hair. Bill put Joe down, looked across the room at Maude. He frowned a little.

"What's the matter?" he asked.

She shook her head. "Nothing. Joe's been fed. I'm waiting dinner."

He said: "You look pretty well pooped. Did Ruth Starr telephone?"

"No."

"Then you haven't heard." He took off his coat. "They made an arrest. I thought maybe Ruth had told you."

"Not—not Nels?"

"No. Rick Thomas."

"Rick. . . ." Her lower lip was suddenly quivering and she nipped it hard in her teeth. Her two hands closed on the chair arms tight, tight. Bill was watching her, studying her face. That crooked bitter smile twisted at his lips. He turned abruptly to the closet to hang up his coat.

He said from the closet: "I didn't expect it to be quite such a shock." His voice was hoarse and ugly.

She said: "No, Bill. You don't understand."

Joe, sensing the tension, started to whimper, took wobbling steps toward Maude, fell over a stuffed horse, and broke into a wail. Maude ran to pick Joe up.

"I guess I understand pretty well," Bill said. He came out of the closet, strode to the foot of the steps, went on up and into the bedroom.   For a long time Maude sat there with Joe in her arms, whispering absently into the boy's ear. Bill didn't understand. It wasn't that she cared a damn what happened to Rick Thomas. That wasn't it. It was the murder, and Bill's being late after taking Weaver to the bus. It was Bill lying about the car, and Bill changing the tire in the road this morning. It was Bill's foolish, groundless jealousy of Rick Thomas. It was the ugly, gnawing suspicion that came as a cold knot inside her.

That night there was no sleep for her either, and none for Bill. She heard him tossing and counted the strokes of the banjo clock, hour after hour.

"He killed Weaver. He killed him," kept running through her mind. "For Joe and for me, he killed him. He thought it was for Joe and me. Bill, oh Bill! Why? Why?"

And once in a while, another thought intruded. As long as she could remember that it was poor Bill in the bed next to her, she could somehow bear it. But when she thought it was a murderer, the fearsome shadows of the night crowded close about her—tangible things to be beaten off with clenched fists. She had to clutch the sheet to keep from striking back, had to bite her lips to keep from screaming. But it wasn't until two days later that she was absolutely sure. . . .

First, there was the receipt from the insurance company. It came in the mail shortly after Bill had left for the office, and it was a perfectly clear indication that Bill had got money from some place. Second, there was the telephone conversation she had with Ruth Starr. Or rather the monologue she listened to.

"Isn't it awful the way our men are having to work? I just told Nels last night that if the home office couldn't give him some more help he'd have to find another job. I don't see a thing of him anymore. Not a thing, with Weaver and Rick Thomas both out of the office. I was just thinking, Maude, how you'd feel right now if you had married Rick instead of Bill. Can you imagine, dearie? *Can* you imagine?"

"Yes," Maude said faintly. Yes, she could imagine.

"Of course, it was perfectly obvious it had to be someone in the office. You see Weaver had taken a thousand dollars in cash from the safe and was carrying it with him. The old miser was putting cash away in his safety deposit vault I suppose. And unless you knew he'd taken money from the office safe, you'd never suspect him of having a lot of money on his person. You know the way Weaver dressed. My dear, I always said to Nels that Weaver looked like a perfect pauper."

"Did they find the money?" Maude asked breathlessly.

"Of course. Well, part of it anyway. On Rick's person."

Part of it, Maude thought. The thousand dollars minus enough for the insurance payment, the mortgage, and an installment on Bill's income tax.

"I suppose he'd gambled on the stock market or was keeping some woman," Ruth speculated, "though that won't come out until the trial. But of course that wasn't what really caught Rick. Not the money. It was the hairs."

"Hairs?"

"Yes. Weaver had tried to defend himself. My dear, didn't Bill tell you about the hairs? They were clenched in Weaver's hand—hairs from the head of Rick Thomas. I said to Nels: 'That's one crime they could never pin on you, Nels.'"

Maude got rid of Ruth as soon as she could. There was always the excuse that Joe was into some devilment. And then with her heart beating up in her throat, threatening to choke her, she ran up the steps and into their room—hers and Bill's. Hers and the murderer's! She had noticed the comb absently that morning when she had been tidying up Bill's dresser drawer and had thought nothing of it. Now she opened the drawer with hands that shook the brass pulls and lifted the top of the leather collar box that had belonged to Bill's father and which Bill kept for some sentimental reason. There in the bottom of the box, hidden beneath some old handkerchiefs. It was a pocket comb of black rubber with a little silver clip. She remembered now. Rick Thomas had always carried such a comb. One of the things she hadn't liked about Rick was his habit of always running that comb through his sleek dark hair.

Now she knew. Bill hadn't just killed Weaver. He'd killed Weaver and planted the hairs from Rick Thomas's comb in Weaver's hand. He'd framed Rick because he hated Rick.

"Bill!" she moaned softly and sank down on the edge of the bed. "Bill!"

He was curiously light-hearted when he got home that night, Bill was. Or was that light-heartedness faked? She detected beneath his gaiety, beneath his efforts to make everything between them the same as before, a certain uneasiness. And after dinner when the phone rang, he came awfully close to knocking her off her feet beating her to it.

He said: "Joe's crying, Maude. You'd better go see what's wrong with him. Listen, don't you hear him?"

She didn't hear Joe crying. Joe was asleep upstairs. But Bill wanted her out of the room. She went up the steps, opened Joe's door, then stood there, listening. Downstairs, Bill's whisper just barely reached her ears:

"Tonight. The bluff. Two sharp."

She went on into Joe's room, dropped down beside the crib and wept. That was where Bill found her. He picked her up bodily, gathered her into his arms. She stiffened against his embrace, but he held her tight. She had never fully realized the strength in those lean arms of his. The strength to kill.

"Sweetheart, does Rick Thomas mean so much?" he whispered.

She didn't answer. She couldn't trust herself to speak. Because if she said anything at all it would be to accuse him of killing. And if he knew that she knew—what then? There was much less about him that was poor Bill and much more that was murderer.

He said: "You've got to get some sleep. You haven't slept since Weaver was killed. How's for getting to bed while I run downstairs and fix some hot milk with a dot of rum in it—remember?" He laughed. "Like after Joe was born and you couldn't sleep?"

"All right," she murmured, then crossed to the bedroom to go through the motions of undressing herself while he was downstairs fixing the milk. He wanted her to sleep. Perhaps he'd put into the drink some of those sleeping tablets the doctor had given her—one for a sound sleep and a hang-over, four for a sleep without an awakening.

She was in bed when he brought the milk and rum. She took it in both hands to steady it, touched the drink to her lips.

"Good?" he asked, beaming down at her.

"Too hot. I'll drink it later." She put the glass down on the nightstand. Was that a faint shadow of suspicion on his face?

"Hot or cold, just so you drink it." He yawned—it was so obviously a fake—and began to undress.

She insisted on him turning out the lights, and in darkness picked up her glass, clinked its edge against her teeth. She swallowed nothing, kept swallowing and clinking the glass on her teeth.

"Good?" he asked out of the darkness.

"Uh-huh. Fine, Bill. Thanks. I'm getting drowsy already."

He yawned again, turned over, and lay still. She put the glass down on the nightstand, the drink untasted, pulled up the covers. But she didn't relax and she didn't close her eyes. She listened to the ticking of the clock and the strike of the hours, the halves, the quarters.

She kept track of the hours. One o'clock, a quarter after, half past.

A cautious stirring in the next bed. Bill was getting up now, moving through the darkness. She heard the metallic clink of his belt buckle as he reached for trousers. She closed her eyes tight against the darkness, against the thing to come. And then Bill was bending over her. She knew it. He was over and above her. She thought he must have heard the beating of her heart. He moved away silently in his stocking feet, cautiously took his shoes from beneath the bed, stole from the room.

She didn't move until she heard the opening and closing of the front door. Then she bounded from the bed, pattered to the window to look out across the lawn and the curving drive. She saw the lank silhouette of him crossing the lawn. He went through the gateway in the privet hedge, was lost against the blacktop pavement of the road.

Without light she found her slippers and housecoat, put them on breathlessly.

"Joey," she whispered softly toward the room across the hall. "Don't waken, Joey. Don't stir." And then she hurried into the hall and down the stairs, across the living room and through the door. Because she *had* to know what he was doing across the road in the darkness of the park. He had said something about "the bluff" on the telephone. Did that mean the bluff in the park, overlooking the river?

She crossed the road, went between the fieldstone gate posts into the grove beyond. It was incredibly dark. She kept on the path, walking toward the river, stopped only when she saw the figures of two men standing near the lip of the bluff with the sky and the glow of the city behind them. She heard a crisp rattle as of paper and something passed between the two men. Money. Money, of course. Somebody was blackmailing Bill. Somebody knew all that she knew.

She whirled around. Something caught the skirt of her housecoat, held it fast. She groped with her hands, discovered that she had been standing near a picnic bench. Her skirt was caught on the bench somewhere. She jerked once, twice. Cloth ripped with a jagged sound.

"What's that?" a voice said hoarsely.

She pulled free from the bench, leaving part of the skirt of her robe behind. Near the edge of the bluff was the sound of a swift exchange of blows. Maude broke into a run. But behind her someone else was running and so much faster than she. She felt the pelt of feet up from the earth, heard the gasping breath. Then came the hands that snatched her from behind, caught her neckline, reached for her throat. She wheeled, struck out with her fist.

"Don't touch me, you—you murderer!"

"That settles it. That settles *you!*"

Blunt thumbs gouged into her throat, cut off that last quick drawn breath. She kicked with all she had. Only for Joe was she fighting now.

A blazing beam of light cut a clean swath through the dark. Against the light was the figure of a man running. The fingers at her throat relaxed.

"Drop, Mrs. Carrick. Get down. He may have a gun!"

She dropped only because another pair of arms was about her, tumbling her into the damp grass, a body sheltering hers against a flurry of gun fire. Then silence.

Somebody said: "That did it. You all right, Mrs. Carrick?"

"Answer Lieutenant Crane, sweetheart. You *are* all right, aren't you?"

And that voice came from the body sheltering her. Bill's voice. The beam of light showed her Bill's angular features, his worried eyes, the blackening bruise on the side of his head. The light showed her the gleam of police shields, the heavy face of the gray-eyed detective. And not two yards from her another man lay on the grass. There was some blood, some audible breathing, and the cold glint of steel handcuffs. She saw the moon-round face briefly—the face of Nels Starr.

Later, Bill said he knew he'd had a hangdog look ever since the night that Nels Starr had murdered Weaver.

"Because that night I almost did a terrible thing," he said gravely. "After I'd dumped Weaver, I drove back up to the top of the hill and turned the car across the road. I sat there for those fifteen minutes, trying to nerve myself up to drive straight ahead."

"Bill!"

He nodded gravely. "While the insurance was still in force. The bluff was steep and the river flooded. I thought it would be quick. But I didn't have the nerve. Of course I couldn't tell you about it, so I made up the story about the motor going bad. When the cops questioned me, it had to be something besides the motor in case they checked. So I told the one about the tire."

She nodded. "Then you had to change the tire, just in case they checked."

"That's right. But that wasn't the end of my crime. The night Weaver was killed, when Nels came to tell us about it, that comb dropped out of Nels' pocket when I hung up his coat. I got to wondering why Nels who was bald would have a comb. So I kept it and didn't say anything about it.

"I knew what Nels was scheming. With Weaver gone and Rick out of the way, Nels would be top man at the office with a ten-thousand-dollar a year salary. And then he'd been embezzling money. He had to get rid of Weaver to cover himself. I finally took all that to the police and we arranged this trap tonight. I was to go on as though I was blackmailing Nels, see, while the cops were hiding beneath the bluff."

"And they'll free Rick?" she asked. "Not that it matters to me."

"Sure. They never seriously suspected him. They could tell by the hairs that they hadn't been pulled out. They were dead hairs with no oil sacks at the end. The hairs constituted a plant, just like the stolen money found in Rick's possession. Rick's arrest was just to give the killer a little more rope. Actually, Lieutenant Crane suspected Nels and me."

"But how did you pay the insurance?"

He grinned sheepishly. "That's just one crime I went through with. I stole our movie projector and sold it. Now we can't show the pictures we took of Joe. Not until after the war anyway."

I'll Slay You in My Dreams

BRUNO FISCHER

Chapter 1

THE LETTER

T HE MAN ACTED QUEER from the first, but everything he did and said made sense. That's what I want to get straight—it could have happened to anybody. I'm no dumber than the next fellow. It's only that I had the tough luck to be hitching in that direction at that time.

At twilight I had only twenty miles to go to reach Coast City, and I was worried about getting a lift before dark. Then this swanky coupe came along. When it slowed as it approached me, I thought I was set.

The car didn't quite stop. As I moved toward it, it abruptly picked up speed. The mudguard missed me by a hair.

I figured that it was my fault. My good suit was in my bag. For hitching I wore unpressed Army pants and a faded windbreaker, and I hadn't had a chance to shave since the day before. Probably I hadn't looked prepossessing enough to be given a lift, with darkness coming on. But as I stood there looking after the car, it began to roll slowly, as if the driver were trying to make up his mind about me. Apparently he did, for the coupe soon came to a complete stop.

I broke into a run. The driver was waiting for me. He had the right door open, but his arm barred me from entering. He was a heavy-set, middle-aged man, with a florid face in which the skin sagged loosely. Through shell-rimmed glasses, he peered suspiciously at me in the gloom.

"I don't make a habit of picking up strangers," he said fussily. His eyes dropped to my battered straw bag. "I assume you don't live in Coast City."

"No, sir. I've just been discharged from the Army. I heard there were good jobs in Coast City shipyards."

His arm still blocked me. "Why were you discharged?"

It was none of his business. All I wanted was a lift, and he was acting as if he were interviewing me. I explained: "I'd had rheumatic fever as a kid, and it came back."

At last he seemed satisfied. "You look like a clean-cut boy," he conceded and removed his arm from the door.

It wasn't until I was sitting beside him in the car that I got a whiff of his breath. He smelled pretty drunk, but he didn't look it or act it. Seemed to hold his liquor like a real gentleman as they used to say in books.

For a while, we drove in silence. Then he mumbled: "She can't mean it. If she'd only let me explain."

"What's that, sir?" I asked.

He glanced sideways at me, somewhat vacantly, so I realized that he hadn't been speaking to me. He said: "What's your name, son?"

"Elliot Tucker."

"Have you come far?"

"From Trevan," I said.

"That's pretty far."

"Only four hundred miles," I told him. "It's a small place with no industry and little work, so yesterday morning I left to hitch to Coast City."

"Relatives?" he asked.

"Just my mother. If I get a good job, I'll send for her and—"

I stopped. Men who gave you lifts generally did so because they wanted company and conversation. They often asked personal questions, and that was all right, but this guy was different. I had a feeling that he was intensely concerned with my answers.

"I'm Howard Cobb," he said suddenly.

He said it as if I should be impressed. I wasn't. I just sat there.

Howard Cobb laughed. "I suppose you've never heard of the Coast City Cobbs?"

"No, sir."

"Naturally not," he said. "You're a stranger."

It seemed to me that he was leading up to something, but suddenly he became silent again. In a little while he turned the car off the highway.

It was dark now, but I could distinguish empty stretches of sand on either side of me. The road wasn't much, hardly wide enough for two cars to pass each other. There were no houses.

"Is this a short cut?" I asked.

"I have to stop off at my cabin for a minute," he said. "You don't mind, do you?"

"Not if I get to Coast City tonight."

He laughed again, a dry, thin sound. "You'll get there."

Now I could smell the wet, salt smell of the ocean, and I heard the dull rumble of breakers. Tall pines grew here, and amid them stood a rambling log cabin. Howard Cobb stopped the car.

"How about a drink?" he invited.

I'd have preferred supper, but a drink was welcome. He unlocked the door and put a light on in the hall and then in the living room.

The place might have been a cabin to Howard Cobb, but it was a palace to me. The living room in which I found himself wasn't much smaller than a barn and furnished in a way I'd seen only in the movies. Howard Cobb was money, all right.

He opened a liquor cabinet and poured two Scotch and sodas. With the glass in his hand, he crossed the room and brooded at the photo of a woman in a silver frame on top of the grand piano.

"She will," he said thickly. "If she'll listen."

I felt embarrassed.

Cobb turned to me. The folds of his fleshy face seemed to hang more loosely, and his wide shoulders drooped. "That's Clare, my wife."

"She's attractive," I muttered politely, though she wasn't, particularly.

Glumly, he nodded. "She kicked me out of the house."

I wished he'd stop it and drive me on to the city. I drained my drink and put it down with a thud to let him know I wanted to go. Through his glasses his pale eyes appraised me intently.

"How would you like to earn a thousand dollars, son?" he asked.

"A thousand dollars a year or a month or what?" I said.

"For a few hours' work tonight."

I stared at him. Anybody who made that sort of offer couldn't be honest—not even a rich man—or couldn't be sober.

"Oh, it's nothing shady," he said quickly. "It's like this. My wife and I quarreled and now she refuses to see me. When I enter the house, she locks herself in her room. When I phone, she hangs up before I can say a word. It's all a silly misunderstanding. I'm sure I can patch it up if I have five minutes with her. I want you to bring her here."

"Me?" I said.

Eagerly, he came forward and placed his untouched drink next to mine. "We have to be subtle, of course. Clare loves me, that I'm sure of. If she heard that I was here, injured, she'd come at once. And that would give me my chance to explain."

He didn't sound drunk or crazy now. A man in love would do something like that.

"You think I won't pay you the money?" he said. "Here." He took out a roll of bills which dazzled me. I saw a hundred-dollar bill on top, but what he peeled off were five twenties. "Here's a hundred dollars in advance. You'll get the rest when you bring Clare here."

I took the money from his outstretched hand. Why not? He could afford it and what I had to do to earn it wasn't in any way crooked. Even if he didn't shell out the rest of the money, this hundred dollars would be the easiest I had ever made.

"Will she believe me?" I asked.

Cobb thought that over and scowled. "She might suspect a trick." His fingers snapped. "I have it. Sit down at that desk and write a letter to her. Say that I fell outside of my cabin and injured my spine. Sign the letter 'Dr. H. L. Davidson.' He's my physician."

I went to the oak desk and found paper and a pen. With the pen in my hand, I hesitated. "This will be forgery, sir."

"Nonsense. You're not imitating Dr. Davidson's handwriting."

No, but I would be signing the doctor's name. I didn't like it. Then I looked at the money still clenched in my left hand and that decided me. After all, she was his wife.

I said: "Do I write 'Dear Clare,' or 'Dear Mrs. Cobb'?"

"'My dear Mrs. Cobb.'" I wrote as he dictated the letter. Then he told me the address which I wrote down on the back of the letter.

"You'll have to use my car, of course," he said. "It's the only way you can get to the city."

Nodding, I stuck the letter into my pocket and walked over to the piano. The woman whose photo stood on the piano was a brunette who might have been thirty, but no more. Her husband was a good twenty years older. She wasn't bad looking, except that her face was too plump for my taste.

Howard Cobb came up behind me. "Don't you trust me?" he said softly.

"I want to make sure I'll give the note to the right person."

"That's what I mean," he said. His mouth smiled, but his eyes didn't. They kept studying me. "Do you think my scheme is farfetched?"

I shrugged. "It's your money, sir. I hand her the letter, and either she comes or she doesn't."

"You understand that you are to drive her back?"

"Of course," I said. "I'd have to return your car anyway." Suddenly I frowned. "Talking about trust, aren't you trusting me too far with your expensive car? You don't know me. I might never come back with it."

"I think you will. Nine hundred dollars in cash is more than you can get for a stolen car. And you look honest." He made an impatient gesture toward the door. "You'd better go. It's getting late."

When I was in the hall, I glanced back. Howard Cobb was avidly gulping down the drink he hadn't touched before.

All the way to Coast City I was uneasy. One thousand dollars was too much for the job. Even if I didn't get more than the one hundred I had already received, it was too much. I would have considered myself overpaid for twenty bucks.

After a traffic cop gave me directions, I had no trouble finding the Cobb house. It occupied an entire block in the swellest section of town—final proof that the Cobbs were very rich. You could expect anything from the wealthy. They didn't know the value of money. A thousand dollars meant nothing to them. Besides, Howard Cobb was probably drunker than he seemed, and he was in love with his wife. Add that up and the whole thing was reasonable.

For the first time in my life I came face to face with a butler at a door. He looked at my clothes in haughty astonishment, making me feel socially unclean.

"I have a message for Mrs. Cobb," I said quickly. "Mr. Cobb is hurt."

Gingerly he took the letter from me and was about to close the door in my face. When I told him I was to receive an answer, he reluctantly permitted me to wait in the foyer and somberly walked up a curving staircase.

In a matter of seconds a woman came flying down those stairs. Though at the moment she was wildly distraught, there was no doubt that she was the woman whose photo stood on the piano in the cabin.

"What happened to Howard?" Mrs. Cobb cried. "Did you see him?"

"No, ma'm," I said. "I was passing the cabin when a man came out and said that Mr. Cobb was injured and asked me to drive to town and take you there. He said he didn't want to leave Mr. Cobb and he couldn't move him."

"Was that Dr. Davidson?"

"That's what he said his name was."

My letter was a crumpled ball in her hand. She was taking the news very hard, and I felt like a heel. It was a dirty trick.

The butler appeared with her coat. "Shall I call the car, madam?"

She glanced at the paper ball in her hand and shook her head. "Dr. Davidson said this young man would drive me. It will take less time."

"Yes, madam." The butler looked narrowly at me. "Do you think, madam, you ought to go alone with—a stranger?"

I suppose what bothered him mostly was the stubble on my chin, though my clothes didn't help any.

"Nonsense, Willow." Mrs. Cobb's eyes were on me and at the same time had a worried, faraway look. "You can see he's a nice young man. My coat."

She dropped the paper ball on a table, got into the coat the butler held for her and went out to the coupe with me.

Chapter 2

THE NIGHTMARE

FOR A WHILE Mrs. Cobb didn't say anything as we drove. She sat forward in the seat, her hands working convulsively on her knees. There was no doubt she loved her husband. They'd be reconciled in the cabin, and Howard Cobb would be so grateful that he wouldn't hesitate to fork over the remaining nine hundred dollars. This was my lucky night.

She spoke for the first time when we were almost there. "Why didn't Dr. Davidson telephone me instead of sending you?"

"What?" I said. "Oh, the telephone." I hadn't known there was a telephone in the cabin. Why hadn't Cobb thought of that question? "Dr. Davidson said it was out of order."

She gave me a sharp, sidelong glance. "Then how did my husband call Dr. Davidson?"

"I don't know, ma'm. Maybe the doctor was there when it happened. He didn't tell me anything except to deliver this letter and drive you back."

She didn't press the matter. I suppose she was too worried over her husband to think about details. Anyway, we were practically there by then.

She slammed out of the car the moment I brought it to a stop. As she ran, I tagged after her a little distance behind. She left the front door open. I was in the hall when it struck me that it would be better if I waited outside. Howard Cobb wouldn't want an audience.

Then I saw that the living room was empty. Mrs. Cobb had already crossed to a door on the other side. Apparently Howard Cobb was waiting in one of the other rooms. I sat down to wait for my money at the desk where I had written the letter.

Doors slammed in other parts of the house. I heard feet out in the hall. Then Mrs. Cobb was back in the living room, standing just inside the doorway with her hands tightly clasped.

"There's nobody here," she said.

"Are you sure?" I asked. "Did you look everywhere?"

"He's injured. Where would he be but in one of the bedrooms?"

I thought I had the answer to that. The idiot had got himself cockeyed drunk while waiting and had wandered out of the house. He'd be back, though. I was sure of that.

Her eyes were frightened as she waited for an answer. With a shock, I realized that she was afraid of me.

"Perhaps Dr. Davidson managed to get him to a hospital after all," I said.

She relaxed at that. "Then Dr. Davidson must have left a message at my house. I'll phone—"

"The phone's dead," I reminded her. "Dr. Davidson knew I was driving you here. He'll come back for you or send somebody to tell you where your husband is. I think we'd be better off waiting a little while."

"He would have left a note," she argued distractedly.

I was anxious to keep her here until Cobb returned. That was my only chance to collect all of the thousand dollars. I said: "Anyway, there's no harm waiting a couple of minutes."

"No harm?" she muttered and kept looking at me through wide, scared eyes.

To show her that I was harmless, I took up the pen, drew a sheet of paper to me and casually started to make a sketch.

When I looked up again, Mrs. Cobb was pouring herself a stiff drink. She drank the stuff straight and the glass shook in her hand. Silently, I cursed Cobb. I wouldn't be able to keep her here much longer.

After a minute I felt her standing beside the desk. "Oh, you're an artist," she said indifferently. Her eyes remained distant and preoccupied.

On the paper was a rapid ink sketch of her face. "I'm not very good," I said with a dry laugh and stuck the sketch into my pocket. "It's just a hobby."

I doubt if she heard me. She had turned to a window and stood tense, listening to the voice of the ocean. There was nothing else to hear. Abruptly, with quick, agitated strides, she went out to the hall. Then I heard the thin whirring of a phone being dialed.

I felt like a criminal being caught red-handed. What was I to do now?

The hell with Howard Cobb, I thought, and went out to the hall. Mrs. Cobb was bent over the phone, whispering: "Dr. Davidson? Did you—"

"I can explain, Mrs. Cobb," I said.

Her dark eyes tilted up at me in terror. The hand-set fell from her fingers. She cowered back. It wasn't a nice feeling to have a woman mortally afraid of you.

"The phone isn't out of order," she said, in a voice so hoarse that I could hardly distinguish the words. "Dr. Davidson is home. You tricked me into coming here."

"Don't be afraid of me, please. Your husband—"

She never let me finish. In panic she darted toward the door. Weakly, I put out a hand. It was so important that she let me explain. My fingers brushed her arm. She screamed and plunged past me.

"Damn Cobb!" I said aloud. It wasn't worth a hundred dollars, or a thousand, to have any woman look at me the way she had. At the least, she would drive off in the car and leave me stranded here.

I didn't hear the car motor spring to life. I waited, and there was nothing but the relentless rumbling of the waves breaking on the shore. In her terror, she must have run wildly into the darkness, forgetting about the car. Or maybe she was crouching somewhere out there, waiting for me to leave.

I went outside. The night was black except for the area around the lighted windows.

"Mrs. Cobb," I called. "If you'll only listen to me—"

A step sounded behind me. *She's come back,* I thought, puzzled, and started to turn.

I felt nothing. The night closed in on me and entered my brain, and then I knew nothing.

Slowly I pulled myself up into consciousness. I had been drifting in a state between sleeping and waking, and now I thought I lay in my bed at home trying to remember the bad dream I had had. It was something obscurely absurd about earning a thousand dollars in a couple of hours by luring a woman to meet her husband.

I opened my eyes, but the darkness remained. It was still night. My stomach was queasy, my limbs were stiff, and my head throbbed. I decided to get out of bed and go to the bathroom for a drink of water. That was when I learned that I couldn't move.

My limbs were weirdly rigid and numb, and there was something wrong with my tongue. My mouth was distended in a kind of frozen, silent scream, my tongue was fixed against my palate and tasted vile. And I heard the ocean.

Then I was fully awake, and truth came with a sickening rush. I wasn't at home. I was lying on a hard wooden floor, and I was bound and gagged.

It hadn't been a dream. All that business with Mr. and Mrs. Cobb had happened. Tentatively, I lifted my throbbing head. Fire stabbed the back of my skull and I sank back. That last instant of awareness outside the cabin ... I must have been knocked out. Then I'd been dragged back into the cabin and my arms and legs had been tied and a gag shoved into my mouth and the lights turned out.

But by whom? Howard Cobb? Why would he do that to me? And what had happened to Mrs. Cobb? I hadn't heard a sound out of her after she had fled from me. Maybe she was the one who had socked me. That was as reasonable as anything else.

In frenzied revolt against the unfairness of what had been done to me, I started to struggle. That only made my head hurt more. I subsided. Whoever had tied me had done the job very well, though strangely, I couldn't feel the ropes.

My fingers were free. I stretched them, groping, and felt the material of a Turkish towel around my arms, under the ropes. Was somebody stark, raving mad? The only explanation I could find for the towel was to prevent the tight ropes from digging into my flesh.

I laughed at that notion, or tried to. One can't laugh against a gag. Why would the person who had knocked me out be so solicitous of my comfort as to see to it that the ropes didn't hurt me?

Maybe I was still dreaming. Maybe I was really home in bed at this very moment and deep in a nightmare.

It wasn't many hours before grayness appeared in front of my eyes. Dawn was breaking. I'd lost consciousness around ten o'clock last night. Unless my sense of time had become completely cockeyed, that meant I'd been out cold for several hours, at least.

In bewilderment I stared up at the ceiling. The cabin ceiling, I was sure, had been beamed and paneled. What I saw above me was the underside of a tin shed roof.

Risking the pain of movement, I lifted my head. I wasn't in the cabin. This was a small shack, completely unfurnished. Inches of grime covered the plank floors. There were two doors, one leading outside and the second to another room or perhaps a closet. The two windows were both tightly shuttered. What light and air trickled in came through cracks in the siding.

Was this an outhouse of the cabin? One thing was plain—I was still very close to the ocean. The breaking of waves on the beach made an endless rumble in my ears.

Hours later I decided that I had been left here to die. There was no reason for it. I was nobody, I had nothing valuable, I was nobody's enemy. There were no answers to questions, only facts like this. Enough air came through the cracks to keep me from suffocating, but death would come even harder than that. I would die of thirst. Already my tongue seemed to swell against the gag. And my stomach twisted with hunger. My last meal had been lunch the day before.

From then on nothing mattered but thirst and hunger. The pain of the blow subsided, but that didn't atone for lack of drink and food. Nobody would find me here. Probably nobody had looked into this shack in years.

How long before I would die? How great the agony? Please God, make it come quickly.

It never grew lighter in the shack than that dismal grayness. Eventually it deepened and gave way to blackness, and it was again night. I thought that if I could sleep it would make it easier for me. I shut my eyes.

A cool breeze swept over me. Instantly I was alert. The door was open. Somebody was in the shack with me.

I could see nothing. I could hear no more than the creaking of a plank. Then somebody was breathing close to me. A hand fumbled on my body. I was pushed on my side and something hard and cold touched the back of my hand. It was the flat side of a knife. Whoever had knocked me out and tied me up had returned to kill me.

Now that I would die quickly and cleanly, I wanted desperately to live. I tried to plead with him against the gag. I squirmed away from the cold steel.

The knife moved up along my windbreaker sleeve and then down, over the towel and through the ropes which bound my wrists. I was free, except for my legs.

I didn't dare move. My arms were too stiff, and besides, he had the knife and probably another weapon. Now he was going away from me. A plank creaked again. Softly the door closed, and the silence that was louder than the clamor of breakers was back.

Slowly, I sat up, removed the gag from my mouth and rubbed the agonizing numbness from my arms. Somebody had made me a prisoner here and somebody else had freed me. Maybe the same person. But why slug me and tie me up in the first place? And why hadn't my rescuer wanted me to see him—or perhaps her? There was no logic in a nightmare.

The rope around my ankles wasn't easy to untie. Another Turkish towel was around my legs and the knots had become imbedded in it. When at last I rose to my feet, I tottered like an infant learning to stand. I stumbled in the direction of the door.

Light glowed dully outside the shack. It couldn't have been on when my rescuer had entered because I would have seen it through the open door. Blinking, I rubbed my eyes, though the light was far from blinding. It came from the dimmed headlights of a car parked only a few feet away.

"Who are you?" I asked. "What do you want?"

Nobody answered. Now that I was outside, I could smell the ocean as well as hear it. I had a sense of being terribly alone, though my rescuer had to be nearby.

I walked around the hood of the car. The dashboard light showed me that nobody was in the coupe.

Coupe! I stepped back, sweeping my eyes over the graceful length of the car. This was Howard Cobb's coupe. I had driven it for at least twenty miles to Coast City and back. So Cobb was the one who had freed me—or maybe Mrs. Cobb. Then why all this mumbo-jumbo about not letting me see who my rescuer was?

I got behind the wheel. The key was in the ignition lock. The motor turned over sweetly, everything was in order. It struck me that it was as if the car had been placed here at my disposal, with the lights on to show me where it was. That was absurd, of course. Cobb, or whoever it was, had parked the car here and gone to the cabin.

I switched on the brights and weaved the car back and forth across the narrow road, so that the headlights covered the area beyond the shack. Then I turned the car and searched the other side of the road. There was no structure of any kind visible. Nothing but a stretch of endless desolation. I headed the coupe away from the ocean.

This was not the firm concrete road which led to the cabin. It was crumbling tar, broken by murderous ruts. Where was I? At the moment, though, I couldn't really care about anything but food and water.

Soon, I was sure, this outrageous caricature of a road would get me to the Coast City highway. It didn't. I reached a better road, but one that seemed fiendishly to avoid stores, houses, any sign of life. My thirst became a kind of madness, and I was back in the nightmare on a road that had no end.

Presently, I came to a tiny village with only one street, and a lunchwagon. I stumbled in. The smell of frying food made me fight nausea, and I spilled half the contents of that first glass of water over my shirt as I gulped it down. Thirty minutes later, having eaten and drunk my fill, I felt as if I had just recovered from a long illness.

Over a cigarette, I asked the counterman how I could get to Coast City. His directions puzzled me.

"Look," I said, "I'm north of the city and you're telling me to drive north."

"Brother, you're really lost," he said. You're a good thirty miles south of Coast City."

The cigarette turned to straw in my mouth. While unconscious, I'd been transported forty miles from the cabin where I'd been knocked out, then left in the shack for twenty-four hours, then released and provided with transportation to get back. Who was stark, raving mad?

I took out my wallet to pay my check. Before closing it, I counted my money. One hundred and sixty-three dollars—what remained of the money I had left home with, and the five twenties Howard Cobb had given me. Whatever else had been done to me, my wallet certainly hadn't been lifted. Somebody hadn't been interested in money.

But something else of mine was gone. My valise hadn't been in the shack and it wasn't in the car. When I left the lunchwagon, I tried the ignition key in the coupe trunk. It worked. No valise. I didn't think that anybody who had transported me forty miles to get me away from the shack would have carelessly left my valise behind. On the other hand, why steal it? All it contained was some clothes and a few personal belongings.

Chapter 3

THE AWAKENING

I T WAS CLOSE to midnight when I reached Coast City. I not only had a car to return and a bag to get back, I was, by God, going to get an explanation. I had no taste for being pushed around, especially by rich people who thought they could buy anything for a hundred bucks.

Lights were on in the Cobb house and the butler was up. He wasn't surprised to see me. "Mr. Cobb is expecting you," he said stiffly.

Just like that. I'd been plenty sore before. Now I felt myself tremble with rage. With my hands clenched, I followed the butler into a sitting room.

Two men were in there. One was tall and slender and somewhere in his thirties. He would have been smooth-looking if not for the lines of strain around his eyes and mouth. The second was a bear of a man, looking as angry as I felt. I had never seen either of them before.

"So you came?" the younger man said tightly.

"You're damn right I came," I said. "Where's Mr. Cobb?"

"I'm Howard Cobb," he told me.

I wasn't interested in any of Howard Cobb's relatives who had the same name. I said: "I mean Clare Cobb's husband."

The younger man opened and closed his hands convulsively. His eyes were bloodshot. "Don't be wise. I'm Clare's husband. I'm the only Howard Cobb there is."

I couldn't seem to extricate myself from the nightmare.

"You can't be," I protested. "Howard Cobb is a short, thick-set man who wears glasses. And he's older."

"Cut it out," the younger man said testily. "You spoke to me twice over the phone today. The second time I told you I'd have the twenty-five thousand dollars waiting for you. You offered to come here. You were pretty cocky. The butler had seen you last night, so we knew what you looked like, but you thought your threat to kill my wife would keep me from going to the police. Well, now that you're here—"

"Just a moment," I broke in. "I don't know what you're talking about, except that I couldn't possibly have phoned you."

The bear-like man spoke for the first time. "This is getting us nowhere. You admit you have Mrs. Cobb?"

"I what?" I stared from one to the other. "Didn't Mrs. Cobb come home last night?"

"Do you mean to say you released her?" the younger man asked eagerly.

I thought I had it then. These men were impostors. They had taken possession of this house and the butler was in on the hoax with them.

I asked the older man: "Who are you supposed to be?"

"You should know," he replied. "You sign my name to letters. I'm Dr. Davidson."

I didn't believe him. If the younger man wasn't Howard Cobb, then this one wasn't Dr. Davidson. I turned to the door.

"Wait," the younger man called. "I've the money ready. Tell me where my wife is and it's yours."

I kept going. I'd been played for a sucker once by an offer of money. This was a matter for the police.

"All right, Lieutenant Kearny," the younger man said wearily.

Two strange men plunged into the room. One grabbed my arm and the other leveled an automatic pistol at me.

"It didn't work," the man who called himself Howard Cobb said bitterly. "Something made him suspicious."

I stared at the sour, rugged features of the man with the gun. "Lieutenant?" I said. "Are you a cop?"

"What do you think?" The lieutenant stuck out his jaw at me. "You sure played this dumb."

There could be two impostors—but four? And that wasn't counting the butler. The two detectives looked genuine.

I said tightly: "Was Mrs. Cobb really kidnapped?"

"You answer that."

"But I don't know," I said.

"Where's that butler?" Lieutenant Kearny turned his head and the butler stepped into the room. "Is this the man who drove away with Mrs. Cobb last night?"

"It certainly is." The butler's eyes flashed hatred. "I warned Mrs. Cobb, but she was considerably upset by the note and would not listen to me."

"That's true," I admitted, "but—"

The lieutenant stuck a sheet of crumpled paper in front of my face. "Did you write this?"

It was the letter I had written in the cabin, to which I had signed Dr. Davidson's name. Dully, I nodded.

"And did you phone Mr. Cobb twice this afternoon, each time demanding twenty-five thousand dollars ransom for Mrs. Cobb?"

"No, sir," I said firmly. "Even if I had wanted to do such a thing, I couldn't. I—"

The lieutenant cut me short. "Mr. Cobb, was it his voice you heard on the phone?"

Cobb scowled at me. "I'm sorry, Lieutenant. The voice sounded distant, as if disguised. He was perfectly willing to come here for the money. He said his accomplice would kill Clare if anything happened to him. He said he would be here between eleven and twelve tonight. What more do you want?" His voice went shrill. "Make him tell! Torture him! You've got to get Clare back alive!"

The fingers of the detective who held my arm tightened. On a wall there was a mirror, and for a moment I didn't recognize myself in it. The stubble on my cheeks, the wild look in my eyes, made me appear like what they thought I was—the worst kind of criminal, a kidnapper.

"Listen!" I said urgently. "The guy who said he was Howard Cobb used me as a dupe to kidnap Mrs. Cobb. Give me a chance to tell what happened."

"Go on," Lieutenant Kearny said quietly.

They listened to me in silence. I left nothing out. When I finished, their faces remained hard, merciless. They didn't believe me. I had trouble believing myself.

Dr. Davidson yanked up my right arm and pushed up the sleeve of my windbreaker and then of my shirt. His mouth went crooked as his thick fingers ran over my smooth skin. "So you say your wrists were tightly bound for many hours?"

"I forgot to tell you about the towels," I said. "There were two heavy Turkish towels, one wrapped about my arms and one about my legs, so that the ropes would leave no marks."

With a snort of disgust, Dr. Davidson threw my arm from him.

"Why not leave marks?" Lieutenant Kearny asked, as if he didn't care what I answered.

"So I could be framed, of course, by the guy who claimed to be Howard Cobb," I replied hotly. "Isn't it plain that he used me to kidnap Mrs. Cobb and then fixed it so I couldn't prove that I hadn't done it? Besides, how did I get hold of Mr. Cobb's car? It's outside now."

"What's this about my car?" Cobb said. "Both my cars are in the garage."

Of course, I thought. It wouldn't have been one of Cobb's cars. The nightmare had dissolved. Looking back, everything the man with glasses had done fitted into a pattern.

The lieutenant moved away from me and consulted in whispers with Cobb and Dr. Davidson. Even the detective who held my arm seemed to be ignoring me. I had a sense of having reached an end, of my fate having been decided. If they'd only believe me enough to look for that other man! My description wasn't enough. If I could show them—

"Listen!" I cried excitedly. "I'm pretty good at sketching. Give me paper and pencil and I'll make a drawing of the man who said he was Howard Cobb. Maybe he's a well-known criminal and you'll recognize him."

The lieutenant wasn't impressed, but he asked the butler to fetch pencil and paper. I sat down at the table. I'm not much of an artist and ordinarily it would have been difficult for me to sketch somebody from memory, but I would never forget that face. When I was finished, I thought it was a rather good likeness.

The four men stood around the table and stared down at my sketch. Hopefully, I looked from face to face. There was no recognition anywhere.

"He's sparring for time, Lieutenant," Dr. Davidson growled. "It's obvious this man never existed."

"He did!" I felt trapped. Walls were closing in on me. "Why don't you come to the shack where I was held prisoner? You'll see the ropes that tied me. Maybe there'll be other clues."

"That's what I've been thinking," Lieutenant Kearny said quietly. "Let's go."

A third detective was behind the wheel of a black sedan. The lieutenant sat in front with him while I was in the back seat with the detective who had held my arm in the house. Now he had handcuffs linked to his wrist and mine.

His name, I learned, was Sergeant Donlin. He had a round face and pleasant, round eyes. Unlike the lieutenant, he was capable of smiling.

"Why don't you get wise, son?" he told me confidentially. "They hang kidnappers these days. Tell us where Mrs. Cobb is and you'll get off easy."

"I told you what happened."

Sergeant Donlin shook his head. "It doesn't fit. To begin with, why all that hipper-dipper to kidnap a woman? It's not so hard to snatch somebody. And why frame somebody else for it before the whole purpose of the thing—collecting the ransom—has been completed? Cobb has to be convinced that a certain person kidnapped his wife before he'll pay out money. If Cobb thinks it was you, why should he fork up to anybody else?"

He was right. All that had happened didn't add up to kidnapping—except for one thing.

"But somebody did phone Mr. Cobb and demand ransom for Mrs. Cobb's return," I pointed out.

"That's what I mean. Your story is screwy. Now why don't you confess, son?"

The car stopped. We had reached the village where I had eaten and the driver turned to me for further instructions. I leaned forward in the seat, trying to work it out. Twice we took the wrong road and had to go back when the ocean stopped us. The cops got fidgety. They seemed to suspect a trick. I knew the third road was the right one as soon as we got on it. No other could be quite that bad.

The shack appeared in our headlights. Howard Cobb and Dr. Davidson had been following us in another car and they pulled up behind. The door of the shack was still open, the way I had left it. I started forward, but the handcuffs which attached me to Sergeant Donlin jerked me back. All three cops had flashlights. Lieutenant Kearny and the driver entered first.

The first thing I saw when I followed with Donlin was my straw bag near one wall. And there was nothing else in the shack. The ropes and towels had been removed.

My legs turned watery. Nothing had been overlooked. The walls closing in on me were all set to crush me.

"Well?" Lieutenant Kearny snapped fiercely.

Weakly, I said: "He came back. He removed the ropes and the towels. And he brought my bag. It wasn't here when I left. He—he . . ." I fought for air. "Don't you see how he's framed me?"

Nobody answered me. The lieutenant meandered across the room to that second door. He turned the knob, but the door stuck. He pulled his weight back and the door flew open.

"Here she is!" he yelled.

They all pushed forward. I tried to, also, but Sergeant Donlin held me back. I saw that it was the door to a small closet, and the converging beams of the flashlight showed me the oddly contorted body of a woman.

"Clare!" Howard Cobb cried and flung himself toward the closet.

Roughly, Dr. Davidson blocked his way. "Give me a hand with her, Lieutenant. I'm afraid we'll have to work quickly."

She wasn't wearing her coat, though I saw it in a crumpled pile in the closet. Her face was completely covered with a Turkish towel, and what I could see of her body seemed to consist of rolls of flesh, like tires of varying sizes placed together so as to form the shape of a woman.

"God!" Dr. Davidson said hoarsely. "She's been tied with wires. Wires all over her body tightened into her flesh. And she's—"

His strong fingers worked frantically to remove the towel from her face. That, too, was secured with wires. It seemed to take him forever. Then the towel was off and her face–

"No!" Howard Cobb shrieked. "Clare!"

Awkwardly, Dr. Davidson pushed his big body upright. I felt myself cringe under the look he gave me. "She's been dead for some time," he said tonelessly. "I should say, offhand, that she suffocated—the towel, the wires, the lack of air in the closet."

That was when Howard Cobb hurled himself at me. His hands were on my throat when the cops pulled him off. They pulled him off me reluctantly.

Chapter 4

THE DEAD ACCOMPLICE

ALL THE REST of that night and most of the next day they shouted at me and nagged me and bullied me. In the late afternoon I was permitted some rest, and at once I fell into a sleep of utter exhaustion. After a few hours I was yanked out of my cell and deposited in an office where Lieutenant Kearny and the district attorney were waiting.

The D.A. was a kindly-looking man. He offered me a comfortable leather chair and held a light for a cigarette he had given me. New tactics, I thought dully, to make me confess. On the desk I saw my Army discharge paper which had been in my bag and the sketch I had made of Mrs. Cobb and the letter I had written in the cabin.

"We all make mistakes, Tucker," the D.A. said amiably. "This seems to be your first one. I have ascertained that you had an excellent record in the Army. I had a number of your home-town authorities on the phone. Some of them know you and think highly of you. If you were the criminal type, I'd slap a murder indictment on you and see that you hang. But in your case, if you meet me halfway—"

"Whoever murdered Mrs. Cobb," I broke in, "deserves to hang."

Lieutenant Kearny started angrily to his feet. The D.A. waved him silent.

"I'll tell you precisely what happened," the D.A. said to me. "You must have planned this job right after you left the Army hospital. You said you'd never been in Coast City before. I doubt that—you knew too much. You knew that the Mintons were the richest family in Coast City, and you knew of the Cobbs' summer cabin and that nobody would be using it at this time of the year."

"Minton?" I said. "Are they the ones who own the shipyards in Coast City? Everybody's heard of them. But what have they got to do with Mrs. Cobb?"

"Come now, Tucker. I'm sure you were aware that Mrs. Cobb's maiden name was Clare Minton. You planned carefully. After your discharge from the Army, you returned to Coast City, ostensibly to look for a job. On the way you stole a car. We've traced the owner, a highly respected citizen living on the route you must have taken from Trevan."

"The man with the glasses stole it," I maintained. "Then he drove along looking for a sucker. He studied me before picking me up and asked personal questions before he decided that I had the makings of a fall-guy."

The D.A. went on, as if I hadn't said anything: "The Cobb ocean-front cabin is easy to break into. You thought you were clever. You wrote the letter with paper and pen you found there, and made a sketch of Mrs. Cobb from the photo on the piano to be sure you abducted the right woman."

"And took her to the cabin where the butler knew we were going," I said dryly.

"For a short while, yes. She would have become suspicious if you had driven her anywhere else, and you couldn't afford a row on the highway or any road on which cars passed. The cabin was isolated. There you could render her helpless without fear of interruption. You took your time when you reached the cabin, but when Mrs. Cobb saw that nobody else was there, she started to phone Dr. Davidson to check up on the letter. You pulled her away from the phone, tied her with the wire, gagged her with the towel, and transported her to the shack."

I opened my mouth to interrupt again, but I was too tired, too overwhelmed with a sense of futility.

"I doubt if you intended to kill Mrs. Cobb," the D.A.'s voice purred on. "There would have been easier and less brutal ways. She died because you're not a criminal. Everything you did smacks of the amateur. A professional would have known that she could not survive the towel and the wires and the airless closet. A professional wouldn't have been so confident that he had Howard Cobb so scared into helplessness that the ransom could be boldly collected at the house."

Bitterly, I laughed. "Everything that doesn't make sense you explain by saying that I'm young and stupid and an amateur. Why would I take the police to the shack to show them the body of Mrs. Cobb?"

The D.A. frowned, but Lieutenant Kearny had the answer to that one. "You figured the jig was up when Mr. Cobb handed you over to the police. You tried to get out from under. You had a cock-and-bull story prepared. You figured if you showed us Mrs. Cobb, we'd believe you."

"In that case Mrs. Cobb would have accused me of having kidnapped her," I pointed out.

"Only she wasn't in a position to accuse anybody." The lieutenant turned his sour face to the D.A. "That's one thing I disagree with you about. He deliberately murdered Mrs. Cobb."

It was plain that the D.A. thought so, too, but he was trying to give me enough rope to hang myself—literally. "Let's assume it was an accident," he purred. "This is your one chance, Tucker." His manner was urgently ingratiating. "It was an accident, wasn't it?"

I leaned against the back of the chair and closed my eyes. All of me, including my throat, was so tired that I had to push my voice out. "It was murder," I said. "I know enough law to know that however she died the kidnapper is legally guilty of murder."

Lieutenant Kearny pounced. "And you admit you kidnapped her. You wrote that letter. You called for her."

That was it. Whichever way you looked at it, I had tricked her into coming to the cabin, I had brought her to her death. I hadn't known what I was doing, but I had done it.

The door opened. A voice said excitedly: "I think I located the accomplice."

I opened my eyes and there was Sergeant Donlin with my sketch of the guilty man in his hand.

"Ah!" The D.A. rocked gently in his chair. "I considered the probability that there was somebody in this with Tucker. The sketch Tucker voluntarily made for us bears the stamp of the amateur criminal, the attempt to immediately shunt off the guilt on his accomplice."

"I've been showing this drawing around," Donlin said. "There's a bartender on the east side who says the guy comes to his joint for drinks. Then a stoolie knew him. The guy's name is Augie Brill. He's new in Coast City, but the stoolie knew him in Chicago where Augie Brill was an all-around bad guy. My idea is Brill is hiding out from the Chicago cops. We'll check."

The sergeant's words were like a cold shower reviving me. I sat up. "Let me get my hands on him. I'll make him tell me the truth. Where is he?"

"We located his place," Donlin said, speaking to the lieutenant. "Brill lives over a grocery store on the east side. His door was locked when we got there. I've got men posted. They'll pick him up when he comes home."

"*If* he comes home," the lieutenant growled. "Maybe he took a powder. Maybe he's up there asleep. Why didn't you go in?"

"Well, I figured—"

"I'll do the figuring." Lieutenant Kearny strode to the door and turned. "Bring Tucker along. I like confronting criminals with each other. Sometimes it produces interesting results."

Donlin snapped handcuffs on my wrist and on his. The D.A. stood up and wished the detectives good luck. By good luck he wasn't thinking of the same thing I was. He was after a closed case—I was after my life.

We drove to a shabby part of the city near the shipyards. The moldering, wooden building consisted of a small grocery store and a single story above it. From the car I could see a dim light in one of the two windows over the store.

A man in overalls and cap came over to our car. He was obviously a detective.

"So he came home?" Lieutenant Kearny said, gesturing toward the lighted window.

"That's a funny thing. Nobody came or went. That light's been on all day, but it's so far back that I didn't see it till it got dark. Guess he left last night and forgot to put the light out."

"Maybe," the lieutenant snapped. "We'll see."

I don't know where the other detectives came from, but there were five, including Kearny and Donlin, when we went up the rickety stairs. The door was locked. The lieutenant barked an order, and a beefy detective hurled himself against the door and snapped the lock.

Augie Brill was inside. His stocky body lay face down under the light of a floor lamp. His shell-rimmed glasses had fallen off and were just beyond the reach of the fingers of one outstretched hand. The hilt of a carving knife protruded from his back.

"That's why the light's still on," Lieutenant Kearny muttered. "He was murdered last night." He swung toward me in cold rage. "Smart lad, aren't you? You drew that picture of Brill last night because you knew he was already dead."

I sat crushed and silent in that room while the homicide squad moved about its job. Sergeant Donlin remained linked to me by the handcuffs. He was a good guy. He kept feeding me cigarettes and didn't nag me the way Lieutenant Kearny or almost any other cop would have done.

The body of Augie Brill had been removed to the bedroom. Before that, through the open door, I had seen a suitcase sitting on the bed. It was open and half-full, as if somebody had been interrupted while packing.

After a while, the medical examiner came out wiping his hands. He told the lieutenant that Augie Brill had been dead for approximately twenty-four hours.

"That would make it ten o'clock last night," Lieutenant Kearny commented happily. He practically beamed down at me. "That's the time you claim Brill released you in the shack."

"I didn't say it was Brill. I didn't see who it was." I roused myself. This was terribly important. I looked at the medical examiner. "Can you be sure of the exact time of death, sir? I mean, it was many hours ago, and I understand that the longer the interval since death the harder it is to tell."

"I said *approximately* twenty-four hours," the M.E. pointed out.

"Could it be less?" I persisted. "Could Brill have been murdered, say, twenty hours ago?"

The lieutenant watched me narrowly, but he didn't try to stop my questions. At my side, Sergeant Donlin smiled.

"Certainly," the M.E. said. "Twenty hours ago or twenty-eight hours ago. The window was open and the room temperature varied. Even after the post-mortem, I doubt if I'll be able to be more definite."

"Good enough, Doc," Lieutenant Kearny snapped. "Still trying to be wise, Tucker? If it could be shown that Augie Brill was murdered after midnight, that would let you out because that was when we nabbed you. It can't be shown. Anyway, it didn't happen that way. Before going to the Cobb house for the ransom, you stopped off here to stick a knife in Brill. He was packing his bag as if he intended to leave as soon as he got his share. But you wanted the whole twenty-five grand for yourself, so you liquidated him."

Angry, desperate words poured from my mouth, but Lieutenant Kearny wasn't interested. He had his case. "Take him away, Donlin," he ordered, and turned from me. I felt the steel cuff tug gently at my wrist as the sergeant rose to his feet.

Our shoulders touching, Sergeant Donlin and I walked down those dim, narrow stairs. They wouldn't listen to me, wouldn't believe me. I was being taken to my death. Rage completely possessed me. I swung my free fist at Donlin's jaw.

Chapter 5

THE TRAP

THE SERGEANT BOUNCED BACK from the banister and put the heel of his hand hard against my chest. I tried to hit him again, but he jerked the handcuffs and got me off balance. I tottered on the edge of a step.

"Don't be a sap," he said harshly. "I can bring a dozen cops here in no time by yelling. Or I can get out my gun."

I sagged against the wall. "I'm sorry," I murmured. I had nothing against him personally. He was the best of the lot.

"That's better," Donlin said.

We continued down the stairs. A police sedan waited at the curb. The driver leaned against the mudguard. "Take a walk around the block, Shapiro," Donlin told him, and then we got into the back seat.

Dully, I wondered what the sergeant was up to now. More fatherly advice, probably, aimed to get me to confess so that the road would be cleared to the gallows. The hell with him! They'd hang me, but not with my help.

Donlin rubbed his jaw and looked sideways at me in the dimness of the parked car. "You're mighty sore, son, aren't you?"

"I said I was sorry," I replied testily. "If I had to hit somebody, why wasn't it Kearny?"

He grinned at that and handed me another smoke. After we both had lit our cigarettes, he said musingly: "You know, Tucker, I have a boy just about your age. He's in the Navy. Petty officer. He's a good boy. Clean-cut, like you. Eyes like yours—decent, honest."

"Stop the oil," I said bitterly. "You think I'm a kidnapper and a murderer."

"Do I?" He flicked ash from his cigarette. "Get something straight, son. Mrs. Cobb came from important people in this town. The D.A. has to wrap up her killer quick. Good politics. Lieutenant Kearny is in line for a captaincy. It won't hurt him any if he closes this case successfully. Me, I've been on the force nineteen years. I'll never be more than a sergeant. My eyes aren't clouded by ambition."

I stared at him. "You mean you don't think I did it?"

He didn't answer that directly. "I saw the reports the D.A. got on you by phone. You have a fine record in the Army and in civilian life. Criminals don't just happen overnight—not the kind that plan a hellish crime like this in advance. I think I can judge character. And you're not stupid—you're a bright lad. If you were kidnapping Mrs. Cobb, you wouldn't show your face to the butler. Not even a halfwit would come openly to the house to collect the ransom. Too many other things besides, such as the way Mrs. Cobb was tied."

"That was deliberate murder," I said.

"Uh-huh. Not kidnapping—murder! Which makes sense in only one way."

"Don't you think I know that?" I said. Through the car window I saw the driver returning to the car. "If Mrs. Cobb was a Minton, she must have been pretty rich in her own right. So what? Everything you police have points my way and nothing any other way."

"Not if it wasn't kidnapping," Donlin said.

The driver poked his head in the window. "O.K. now, Sarge?"

"O.K., Shapiro."

As we drove, Sergeant Donlin had no more to say. Actually, he hadn't committed himself to anything. Maybe he would be able to do something, but I couldn't see what. The thing had been too carefully planned, and I was on my way back to jail.

Suddenly I sat up. The neighborhood was familiar. I had been here twice before. The car swung up the Cobb driveway.

"We'll be quite a while," Donlin told the driver as we got out.

We went up the flagstone walk to the house. At the foot of the porch-steps Donlin stopped and unlocked the handcuffs.

"What will happen to you if I escape?" I said.

Shrugging, he dropped the handcuffs into his pocket. "I'll be broken, maybe. But you won't try, son. Not if I put you on your honor."

"No," I said, "I won't."

We went up to the door. As he rang the bell, he looked at me with a kindly smile. "It's a long chance, son. I can't promise anything."

"I don't understand," I said. "What—"

The door opened. The butler looked surprised to see me there. He said that Mr. Cobb was in the library.

Howard Cobb and Dr. Davidson were drinking highballs and listening to the radio. They jumped up to their feet and stared at me.

"What's this?" Dr. Davidson demanded. "I thought this young man was in prison."

Sergeant Donlin moved into the room with his hat in his hands. "Have you heard the latest developments?"

Cobb nodded, not taking his eyes off me. "We heard it on the radio. It seems that Tucker actually had an accomplice, a man named Brill. He was found murdered, and Tucker murdered him."

"Did the radio say that Tucker murdered Augie Brill?" Donlin asked, in a puzzled tone.

"Definitely. Besides, isn't it obvious?"

"No," Donlin said. "It's only obvious that we were intended to see it that way. The fact is, Augie Brill was seen going up to his apartment at one o'clock this morning."

I couldn't follow the sergeant. What he said wasn't true. If there had been such a witness, Lieutenant Kearny would not have assumed my guilt.

"I see," Dr. Davidson said slowly. "Tucker was in the hands of the police since midnight last night, so he couldn't have—"

"But that's impossible!" Cobb exclaimed. He glanced away and then back. "I mean, it doesn't change anything, does it? Tucker still murdered my wife."

Donlin smiled without mirth. "Do you think, Mr. Cobb, we would let Tucker walk around free like this if we thought he did?"

Cobb walked stiffly around the big library desk and dropped into the leather chair. "Stop talking in riddles, Sergeant," he said.

"There's no riddle, Mr. Cobb." Donlin turned to me. "Tell him how it was son."

I was completely bewildered. Where would this get me? Cobb would merely say I was lying, and that would be the end of it. But Donlin's gentle smile urged me on. Maybe he knew what he was doing.

"All along it was a crazy kidnapping," I said. "The only way the district attorney and Lieutenant Kearny could explain it as a kidnapping was by saying that I was a stupid amateur. I knew better because I was on the inside. I knew that I was the fall-guy for Mrs. Cobb's murder. But why murder her like that? It was much too complicated. I didn't really get it until a little while ago when I learned that Augie Brill had been murdered last night—it seemed likely a few hours after midnight. In a way I was responsible for his murder because I had drawn a sketch of him."

I paused for breath. "You're doing fine," Donlin encouraged me.

"I think Brill's job was over when he tricked me into bringing Mrs. Cobb to the cabin," I continued. "Murder itself could be handled by the man who had hired him. I might describe him, but descriptions at best are vague. Brill was about to leave town, not hurrying much because he believed himself safe. Then the man who had hired Brill saw me make a sketch of Brill, a rather accurate one, if I do say so, and Brill became a menace to him. Since Brill was a criminal, his photo would be on record. He'd be identified, captured. And to save his own neck, Brill would accuse the real murderer."

Dr. Davidson scowled at me. "Only Cobb and I, besides the policemen, saw you make that sketch."

"That's right, sir," I said. "You or Mr. Cobb. I learned something else—that Mrs. Cobb was the only one who had the money in the family. I'm pretty sure Mr. Cobb hadn't a cent of his own."

Donlin said: "You're dead right, son. Not a red cent."

At the desk, Howard Cobb cupped his chin in his hands. He said nothing, but the corners of his mouth twitched.

"Probably Mr. Cobb is quite a man with the ladies," I went on. "He's quite handsome. Isn't that right, Dr. Davidson?"

The doctor stood with his hands clasped behind his back and looked at the floor. His silence was answer enough.

"That's it, then," I said. "It couldn't be any other way. If it wasn't kidnapping, it had to be murder—and who but Mr. Cobb would murder her in that way and get a sucker like me to take the rap? If Mrs. Cobb were found murdered, he'd at once be suspected. Don't you see, nobody but Mr. Cobb would murder his wife that way, and Mr. Cobb couldn't murder his wife any other way and hope to get away with it."

I had finished, but what had I accomplished? Cobb sat back in his chair and laughed.

"Sergeant, I'm surprised that you should annoy me with such nonsense," he said. "I shall certainly make a vigorous complaint to your superiors."

Donlin shifted his hat over one hand. "Would I come here if I didn't have evidence? A man was seen going up to Brill's place after Brill went up. You're pretty well known in Coast City, Mr. Cobb. You were recognized."

Though Cobb didn't move, he gave an impression of jumping inside his skin. That was another of the sergeant's lies, but it was so close to the truth that Cobb couldn't know it wasn't true.

"I was with you and the other policemen most of last night," Cobb protested.

"Till two o'clock. It was after two when you were seen going up to Brill's place. Then there are the fingerprints."

The third lie, but again it could have happened. I saw now what Donlin was doing. It was an old police trick. A murderer's nerves start to fray the instant he begins to contemplate the crime.

A wild look came into Cobb's eyes. "But I—" he started, and caught himself.

"You mean you were careful?" Donlin said. "But you can't be careful enough when you murder somebody. Take the wire you used to tie up your wife. Thin stuff, you thought, but it's thick for wire. Police science does wonderful things, Mr. Cobb. A wire will hold fingerprints—tiny bits of prints, but lots of them and they can be put together. Remember last year when we got everybody in town to file their fingerprints as identification in case Coast City was bombed? Yours, too, Mr. Cobb, and they match the prints on the wire."

Police third-degree consists chiefly of bluff combined with what is known, and Donlin was giving it to Cobb right here in his own home. Cobb seemed to shrivel behind his desk.

"But I—I was right there when we found Clare. I touched the wire."

"Dr. Davidson pushed you away before you could reach the body and you were never near it again," Donlin pointed out. "Right, Doc?"

Dr. Davidson nodded heavily. "Lieutenant Kearny undid those wires. There's only one way Cobb's prints could have got on them, and that was before we arrived." He turned to Cobb. "If ever a man deserved to hang, it's you."

I think it was that last sentence that did it. Cobb pulled open a desk drawer, and leaped to his feet with a small revolver in his hand.

"I'm getting out of here!" he croaked. Sweat glistened on his brow, his tongue flicked over his lips. "I'll shoot if anybody moves." And he started to back toward a window.

There was no sound then. I looked at Donlin. His hat dropped from his right hand, and his fist held an automatic. Calmly, expertly, he put a bullet into Cobb's gun hand.

Cobb slumped to the floor and sat there, whimpering like a hurt kitten.

Donlin swept up the revolver and stepped back. "Better fix him up, Doc, so we can get him to jail. Sorry I had to do it this way, but I knew he had a gun permit and I hoped he'd pull the gun. That's as good as a confession."

I stepped to Donlin's side and touched his arm. "Thanks, Sergeant."

He grinned at me. "That's what we cops get paid for," he said.

No Minimum For Murder

JULIUS LONG

CLARENCE DARROW MORT, the famous criminal lawyer, and four other lawyers were seated around a back table at Milligan's saloon. The subject under discussion was murder. Mort held the floor by common consent, for he had that day secured the acquittal of his hundredth client, a garage mechanic accused of liquidating his wife with a Stillson wrench, a tire iron and a cold chisel.

"The verdict was just," said Mort.

"You can't be serious," said Walter Price, a corporation lawyer. "Sam Anderson had an airtight case against that mechanic. I don't see how he missed. Evidently he's not the district attorney I thought he was."

"Don't blame Sam. He failed to get a conviction for a damn good reason. He couldn't prove motive. That mechanic had always got along with his wife—there simply wasn't any reason shown for him to kill her."

"Oh, he did it, all right," commented Harry Sylvester, a young and rising criminal lawyer. "Why else would he have taken those garage tools home with him that particular night?"

Mort shrugged. "On the other hand, why should he have taken them home to kill his wife? What was his motive in killing her?"

"Why didn't the judge throw out the case if the D.A. didn't prove any motive?" It was a new voice, that of Ned Dumont, whose practice was limited to divorce cases. Mort eyed him as if he were a backward child.

"Ned, it's plain to see that you've let your criminal law grow rusty. If I had moved for a dismissal on the ground that no motive was shown, Sam Anderson would have made a fool out of me by citing the case of Liggins vs. U.S., 297 Federal, page 881. The case is fresh in my mind because I double-checked the motive angle. It holds that proof of motive is not an essential element of homicide."

Ned Dumont reddened. Mort quickly attempted to pour balm on his wounded vanity. "I doubt if anybody here but Harry had the right slant on motive. Anyway, you were really right in lending it that much importance. Though a conviction for murder can be legally obtained without a showing of the motive, it is practically impossible to get a jury to convict unless motive is proved."

"And you've got to come up with a strong motive," added Harry Sylvester, "not just a petty, insignificant one."

Mort nodded. "Many a murderer has gone scot-free because a jury was incapable of appreciating that any human being could commit such a vile deed upon such a trivial motive. Just as there is no motive powerful enough to make some men kill, others need only the slightest pettiest provocation. When it comes to motive for murder, there is no minimum requirement."

"I wish you would tell me," said a thick voice from the far side of the table, "just what the hell you are talking about."

It was Al Carter. These days Carter rarely drew a sober breath. He had a complete lack of ambition and a rich wife, and he had acquired them in the order named.

Mort looked across the table and smiled indulgently.

"Sure, Al. What I mean is that a jury is inclined to misjudge human behavior. It is pathetically optimistic. It simply refuses to believe in the inherent pettiness of the human race. Never try to tell it that a man would commit murder for a few dollars. A few hundreds of dollars maybe, and thousands, yes. Perhaps the jurors are judging the accused by themselves."

"Perhaps," said Sylvester, "they dare not commit themselves. To admit that others could kill for a paltry prize would be to admit that they can understand such an act."

Mort nodded approvingly. "I see that I have one understanding listener. You can appreciate my point when I say that there is absolutely no minimum motive for the committing of a murder even in second degree. To illustrate, I one time freed a lady accused of having shot her husband. This time, too, no motive was shown. When we had left the courtroom and got back to my office, I said: 'Of course it's none of my business, but I have a certain professional curiosity which I hope you will pardon. Whatever made you kill that man?'

"She wouldn't tell me then, but months afterwards she did. 'I killed him,' she said, 'because of the way he ate corn on the cob. He got it all over his fingers, and he would end up with butter clear to his ears. I stood it for fifteen years, then I could stand it no longer.'"

From the far side of the table came a grunt. "I still wish you would tell me what you're talking about!"

There was quiet laughter in which Mort did not share. He eyed Carter coldly.

"You're a sight, Al. I'm a firm believer in a man's right to ruin himself, but you're abusing the privilege."

Carter stared with glazed eyes. He hiccuped.

"Listen to who's talking! The one and only Clarence Darrow Mort! The guy who can go on a month's bender with a dozen clients in the clink! And you're telling me I'm drinking too much!"

Mort became pale. This was a sure sign that his temper had flared almost beyond control. But he did master it this time. He rose abruptly from the table and strode from the saloon.

There was a round of silence at the back table, then Harry Sylvester ordered a round of beers. Carter sipped his own, then looked around pleadingly.

"You don't blame me, do you, for sounding off? Hell, he may be a hotshot criminal lawyer, but he's a souse just the same. Isn't that right, fellows?"

"Sure," replied Sylvester. "That's right, but that's not what got his goat. He couldn't stand your calling him Clarence Darrow Mort. Remind him he was named after Darrow, and he'll be your enemy for life."

"It does seem," conceded Carter, "that I did hear of that. It was his father, wasn't it, who named him after Darrow?"

"It was. And Mort is convinced that it was that circumstance that ruined his life. If he hadn't been named after Darrow, he says, he never would have been hoodwinked into a profession which he loathes. The name determined his destiny."

"Well, what's he got to beef about? Isn't he the tops? He's even been written up in *Time-Week*. Most of the lawyers I know would give their right arms to be in his shoes!"

"So would Mort," said Walter Price. "I mean he would give his right arm rather than step out of his own shoes. He can't fool me. The way he acts about being a lawyer is just an act. If he's soured on the profession, why does he have the biggest law library in town?"

The others exchanged thoughtful glances.

"You may have something there," conceded Sylvester. "Come to think about it, he's the only lawyer in town who has every series of the *National Reporter System*. Most of us think we're flying if we keep up with the *Northeastern*. Old Judge Crawford once got drunk and let a salesman sell him the *Atlantics*, but none of us at this table would think of such extravagance."

Price nodded. "And he cuts the books, too. Ask any judge. The reason he gets away with so much is that the judges are afraid he may be right." He lowered his voice. "Besides that, I don't think he really drinks as much as he pretends."

At this there was an uproar of protest.

"It's all right maybe to talk about C.D. a little behind his back," said Sylvester, "but that's going too far!"

The taxicab that picked up C. D. Mort outside Milligan's moved at his request to the south and nightclub infested side of town. Mort had designated the Lucky Club, owned by Lucky Page, whom Mort cordially despised. Page, however, possessed one virtue which Mort could at this moment appreciate. Page would honor his checks.

Mort was stony broke. He did not have cab fare. He did not have change for a quarter. His colleagues back at Milligan's would have been astounded if they had been told that his sudden exit had been prompted by expedience rather than indignation. He had chosen to make an incident of Al Carter's drunken remark for the practical reason that he could not stand a round of drinks, and it was his turn next.

Mort made money. His fees were not so fabulous as rumored, but they were more than sufficient to support a first-class spendthrift. Mort was no spendthrift. He was merely a man through whose fingers money flowed like water. Every time he would pocket a sizable fee he would tell himself that this time he would salt it away. His resolve would endure perhaps three weeks, then the bank would send him a polite note, and he would be confounded.

His financial problems were complicated by his propensity to take on charity cases at a time when bills were due. The mere maintenance of his law library cost him thousands, and he would spend unstintingly upon detectives and expert testimony for a client who would never pay a fee. The garage mechanic he had that day freed was a case in point. The nominal retainer had long since been spent, and there would be no more.

Mort leaned back in the cab and felt sorry for himself. This last trial had taken only four days, but, as always at the end of a murder case, his nerves were exhausted. There was nothing he could do about it. He knew that by midnight he would consume a dozen doubles, but the liquor would not even give him a lift. Even benzedrine sulphate tablets would not help—they would only keep him awake all night.

But he was going to tank up anyway. Lucky Page could be counted on to cash his check, for Lucky had once, through a clerical oversight, caused his arrest in the matter of an old one. Since then Lucky had been outdoing himself to prove his good will. He had almost begged Mort to cash another check, not a good one, but one that was sure to bounce.

Mort was about to gratify his whim.

The cab deposited him in front of the Lucky Club, and he took the driver inside with him by express invitation, for he was not a man to bring out the cynicism in others.

"Well!" said Lucky Page. "Look who's here! Congratulations on getting that guy off today! Nobody but you could have done it!"

"Thanks," said Mort. "I would like to cash a check."

Lucky beamed. "Come right into my office. I'll be delighted."

Mort left the cab driver, slightly impressed now by the warmth of Lucky's welcome of his fare. All the way to Lucky's office Mort had been trying to make up his mind how much to stick him. To give a rubber check for only thirty or forty dollars would be in awkward taste. It was a situation which he could in decency place no man, even a heel like Lucky. A sensible sum would be one hundred dollars. But then Lucky's overtures had left the door open even wider. By the time Mort reached the office he had settled on two-fifty.

"You've been quite a stranger," said Lucky. He was a fat man in the nightclub tradition, a little bald to boot. He got out a blank check, and Mort filled it in. He handed it over to Lucky without daring to look at him.

Lucky seemed in ecstasy as he opened his safe. He took out a tiny packet of bills held together by a paper clip. He tossed them to the desk at which Mort sat.

"There's five bills there. Your check was for only half that, but you can pay me back when you feel like it. Maybe you'll want to get your feet wet at the tables."

"Thanks, but I'm keeping them dry," replied Mort. He had no objection to owing Lucky two-fifty or even five hundred, but he did not care to owe him twenty or thirty thousand. It was rumored that the man who had wired Lucky's tables had formerly held the chair for higher electrical engineering at a famous university and that his fee had been a percentage of the first year's take. He had, as a consequence, been able to retire from his chair to spend the remainder of his days in a thirty-room bungalow with as many baths, a swimming pool and four tennis courts.

Lucky remained on, for he was a man of ambitions. Mort sensed that Lucky desired to cultivate him, for in his racket he never knew when he would need the services of the city's ranking criminal lawyer.

"Come in and watch the fun anyway," invited Page. "We got an extra special crowd here tonight. There's one dame never been here before. She said her name was Smith, but I told the boys to let her in. Class! She's got it all over. But not much else. And is she throwing the dough! She's gone through her third stack of blue chips already!"

"I'll take a look later," said Mort without interest. "I want to pay my driver."

He went back out front, cashed one of the bills, bought his driver a drink and paid him off. Then he drank three double bourbons as fast as he could put them down. The liquor burned, but that was the only effect he got. After a while he went into the gambling room.

It was a dressed-up crowd. Mort spied the woman in the backless evening gown and guessed at once that it was she whom Page had raved about. Mort walked over to the woman and watched over her bare shoulder as she played roulette.

He watched her lose a stack of blue chips on No. 13 and said: "Mimi, even you can't afford to lose like that."

"Gambling is no fun," she replied without turning, "unless you play for more than you can afford to lose."

"But you're playing such long odds. Why don't you play a color instead of a number?"

"The hell with the red and the black. They're good only for the title of a novel."

She put another stack on 13. Mort knew that if the croupier let her win he would never turn another wheel for Lucky Page. He could have stayed there making money on the other color, but he had no desire to capitalize on the misfortune of a beautiful woman. And Mimi Carter was beautiful. Just thinking about Al Carter slopping over the table back at Milligan's made Mort feel sorry for her. He let go of her back and moved away.

He felt depressed. To think about Mimi coming here under the name of Smith and trying to kid herself into thinking she was having a thrilling time was bad enough. But there was something more. It was deeper down. You couldn't put your finger on it, but you could feel it just the same. Mort walked back to the bar. He began to drink doubles again and this time with some seriousness.

He was fairly well paralyzed when Phil Sinton, Lucky's manager, came up beside him.

"Lucky wants to see you in his office. It's important."

"Then tell Lucky to come here. I don't dare get off this bar stool, and I'm not joking."

Sinton looked at his eyes. He walked away. When he returned, Lucky was with him. He stared into Mort's face.

"My god, you *are* tanked! And I need you like I never needed anyone before!"

Mort had never been so drunk that he was incapable of precise, clear speech.

"What have you, Lucky?"

"A suicide. That girl I told you about. She's shot herself."

It was unnecessary for Lucky to draw a diagram. A suicide in his gambling club would close it as sure as God made little green apples. Hell would break loose in all the papers. Every one-lung reform league would take a new transfusion, and the heat would be on.

But Mort was not thinking about the imminent threat to the security of Lucky Page's club. He was thinking about how lovely Mimi Carter had looked in that backless evening gown. Mort thought it very probable that Mimi was about the most beautiful woman in the world.

"Mimi is dead," he said thickly. For the first time in many years tears that were not theatrically forced welled in Mort's eyes. Page eyed him in bafflement, then his eyes lighted.

"So you knew her, C.D.?"

"Yes. I nearly married her. But we had only one thing in common. We both agreed that she was goo good for me."

"So it's like that. Well, at least you can tell me who she is."

"She's Mimi Carter. Her husband is Al Carter."

"Al—" Page stared. "Why, Al's here now! He's sleeping one off in the private room adjoining my office!" Ideas seemed to stagger him. "And this girl, his wife, she shot herself right next door!"

Mort turned slowly. "She shot herself where?"

"Just where I told you—in my office. This girl went in there to cash a check. Phil Sinton, my manager, was handling it. He left her in there for a moment, and when he came back she was lying on the floor in front of my desk. There was an automatic on the floor beside her. Right away I figured she'd done it on account of how much dough she lost. But now—"

Mort slid from his bar stool. Page grasped his arm, for he thought he was going to fall. Mort shook off his grip.

"Let me of me, Lucky. I sober up fast." He moved slowly but with amazing steadiness, and Page followed. They found Phil Sinton seated coolly upon the edge of Page's desk. He was smoking a cigarette, and a foot dangled over Mimi Carter's head.

Mort knew that he was in no condition to look at her honestly. He stared for a moment at the small automatic pistol lying a few inches from her slim, outflung hand, then he looked around until his eyes came to rest upon a door.

"Carter in there?"

Page nodded. "Go get him, Phil. This woman is his wife."

Phil Sinton's eyes widened, but only for an instant. He crossed to the door, opened it, and went inside. He closed the door behind him. Mort forced himself to look at Mimi.

"She never did this, Lucky."

"Well, she lost a lot of money. About fifteen grand."

"She had a lot more. At least a million."

"The hell you say! Who gets the dough now, Al?"

"Yes."

Page stared. "Hell, it looks like—"

"Sure, it does. Al could have done it. He could have been less drunk than he seemed. But someone else also could have done it. Who else had anything to do with her tonight?"

"I'll have Phil find out as soon as he's through with Carter."

The inner door opened, and Sinton appeared, virtually holding Carter in a standing position. Carter looked terrible. Evidently he had not been told about Mimi. He stared with glazed eyes when Sinton led him around the desk and he could see.

"Mimi! My God! What's happened to her?"

"We really aren't sure," said Mort. "She may have committed suicide. Or someone may have killed her. You had about the best opportunity to do that."

Carter looked as if he were going to be very sick.

"C.D.—you can't mean that! You can't!"

"I'm only offering the suggestion. Of course, at first blush the motive appears to be clear. By Mimi's death you inherit about a million dollars. But, on second thought, you didn't have to kill her to get at the money. You were doing all right as it was."

Carter reddened, then he turned a sickly green. He shook off Sinton and subsided into a chair.

"Don't think I didn't get the insult, C.D., because I did. But I'll let it go. I'm thinking that I need you too much to start a fight with you right now. That's because it happens that I had plenty of motive to kill Mimi. Take a look at this."

Carter reached into his inside coat packet and handed over some folded papers. Mort accepted them, looked them over with growing interest, then whistled softly.

"So Mimi's divorcing you! When were you served these papers, Al?"

"Right after you left Milligan's. Can you imagine Ned Dumont pulling a trick like that on me? It was bad enough, his taking Mimi's case against me, but to top it all off, he phoned the sheriff's office from Milligan's and had a deputy come over. Well, at least I got in one good punch before Harry and the others could stop me!"

"You mean you slugged Ned?"

"A honey! And now you're going to tell me that that adds in with everything else against me. It shows how mad I was. It shows I might have been mad enough to come here and kill Mimi. But, honest, C.D., I didn't have the slightest idea that Mimi would be here. Lucky will tell you she's never been here before."

"That's right," said Lucky. "I told you that."

Mort coolly handed back the papers.

"It does look bad for you, Al. If you're guilty, I hope you burn."

Carter's eyes widened.

"But you don't understand! I want you to take my case. I'm enough of a lawyer to know I need you."

"Not a chance, Al. Whether you killed Mimi or not, I still think you're a heel, running around with other women the way it alleges in the divorce petition. And to think Mimi turned me down because she thought I drank too much!"

Carter glared angrily. "I'd forgot, you gave her a rush once. It couldn't be you decided to frame me, could it?"

Mort took a step toward Carter, then controlled his temper. He turned on his heel, was about to leave.

Lucky Page said quickly: "Don't go, C.D. I want you to work for me. If somebody doesn't crack this case before the cops spread it all over the papers, the heat will be on. I'll pay you enough to make it interesting."

Mort studied him. "Let's see the color of your money."

Page went to his safe and opened it. He came back with a single bill.

"Here's a grand. Added to the five hundred I loaned you, that makes fifteen hundred. I'll give you back your check."

"And also a small bag of peanuts!" Mort sneered. He started for the door, ignoring the outstretched bill.

"Wait a minute. How much do you want?"

"Ten on the line, ten more if I crack this thing before the papers get it."

Page gave him an instant's murderous look, then returned to the safe and added nine bills to the one he had offered. He handed them all to Mort, who casually pocketed them, and then turned to Sinton.

"You find out who talked to Mimi here tonight."

Sinton looked to Page, who nodded. "Do anything Mr. Mort says."

Sinton left the room. A little white, Mort walked to the body, stooped and forced his gaze upon the bullet wound. It lingered there perhaps a minute, then he rose. He was a shade whiter as he turned to Carter.

"There are burns, Al. Not just powder marks and blackening, but burns. Whoever shot her held the gun within three or four inches of her face. That means it had to be someone she knew and trusted."

"O.K., she knew me, but she didn't trust me much any more. Hadn't she just filed suit for divorce?"

"Sure. But a certain amount of intimacy always lingers between divorcés. She would have let you come that close and thought nothing about it. There's nothing in the divorce petition to indicate that you ever gave her any personal injury."

"Well, I never did. Say, what about giving me a paraffin test? That will prove I haven't even fired a gun all day!"

Mort shook his head. "No, Al. Take a look at that gun. It's a new automatic. The cartridge cases fit it too snugly to permit the escape of gases carrying nitrate. The dermal nitrate test is not infallible."

"Well, I want to be tested anyway. I want the police to do it." He faced Page. "If you won't call them, I will."

Page glowered. "Make a move for that phone and see what happens."

Mort shook his head at Page. He faced Carter. "Call the cops if you like,

Al, but it may not go so well with you. If you didn't kill Mimi, you'd better give me a head start before the cops give you the old third-degree."

Carter eyed him sullenly, but he did not rise from his chair. The door opened. Mort saw Carter start and sit forward, then he turned to see why. Phil Sinton had ushered Ned Dumont into the room. Dumont stopped short at the sight of Mimi's body.

"My God! What happened to her?"

"She's been shot. What do you know about it?"

"Why, why, nothing!" Dumont's eyes shifted to Carter. "He did this! He did this, I'll bet my last dollar! She was divorcing him! He lost his temper when he was served the papers tonight, and he socked me. Then he came out here and murdered poor Mimi!"

"The hell I did!" said Carter. He got up from his chair, tottered slightly, but managed to stay on his feet. "I socked you all right, and I'll gladly sock you again. But I didn't kill Mimi. You might tell us what the hell you're doing here!"

"Yes," said Mort. "What are you doing here?"

"I came out to tell Mimi that the papers had been served. That's all. I merely spoke to her." He nodded to Sinton. "This man will tell you that."

"Sure," said Sinton. "I saw him myself. He just talked to the woman a little bit, then he went over and got into a poker game."

Dumont looked around with satisfaction. Carter's scowl did not diminish. Mort turned to Sinton. "Did Mimi talk to anyone else?"

"Yes. There was another gal about her own age. A looker, too. One of the boys spotted her being friendly with this one. He's looking for her now."

Dumont eyed Mort with curiosity. "What's going on here? Haven't the police been notified?"

"No. This is no affair of yours, Ned. Suppose you let us handle it."

"I'll do nothing of the kind! Mimi was a valued client! I'm calling the police!"

He went over to the phone on the desk and dialed. Page made a move toward him, but Mort stopped him with a look. When Dumont had put down the phone, Page said: "It's all yours, C.D. You'll have to work fast."

Made made no comment. The door opened suddenly.

A croupier ushered a beautifully gowned woman into the room. She was young, as had been Mimi, and very nearly as attractive. She wore a look of mingled indignation and curiosity. She saw Mimi, clapped a hand silently to her mouth.

"Hello, Nadine," said Carter. "Isn't this terrible? They think I did it on account of the divorce."

The girl stared from one to the other. Finally she said: "But there wasn't going to be any divorce, Al. Mimi told me she had decided that was what you wanted. She said she was going to withdraw the suit."

Carter stared. "When did she tell you that?"

"Just a little while ago. She had a lot of satisfaction doing it."

Mort said quietly: "I believe you're Nadine Gray. I also believe that you're the woman mentioned as correspondent in Mimi's divorce case. Am I right?"

"You are. Al and I have been in love for months. We told Mimi at the start."

"That was very noble of both of you," said Mort. "Now suppose you tell me where you've been since you talked to Mimi."

Nadine Gray looked to Al. He spoke up angrily.

"What are you trying to do, C.D.? Frame Nadine?"

"She had a good enough motive, Al. She wanted you to be free to marry her, and only by killing Mimi could she accomplish that."

Neither Al nor Nadine spoke a word. Lucky Page pointed out: "This job was done with a woman's gun, all right."

"And it could have been done by Mimi herself!" snapped Carter.

"Do you really think Mimi would pull a suicide?" Mort asked. Carter dropped his eyes. Mort turned to Page. "You could have done this yourself. So could Sinton. Have you both got an alibi ready?"

Page scowled deeply while Sinton eyed the lawyer imperturbably. "Sinton's got a perfect alibi," said Page. "He was dealing faro. I had to supervise the room. That's why I couldn't wait when Mimi Carter wanted to cash a check. I showed her to my office and came right back. A dozen guys can testify to that. Besides, what motive did I have for killing her?"

"She might have complained about her losses, threatened to start trouble."

"And you seriously think I'd commit a murder in my own club over something like that?"

"No. I'm just considering all the possibilities."

Mort faced Dumont. "You, Ned—you had a motive. I've seen that trick form contract you have for your wealthy divorce clients. A divorce for Mimi would have netted you at least two thousand dollars. That's just about what her dropping her suit cost you. With Mimi dead you could collect the full amount from her estate."

Dumont turned slightly purple. "Why, you cheap shyster! Do you think I'd kill Mimi or anyone else for a lousy two thousand dollars? Why, my practice nets me a fifty grand a year!"

"I don't doubt that. But, as you heard me say at Milligan's, there's no limit to human pettiness, no minimum motive requirement for murder. So I'm not ruling you out. Of course, if you were in a card game, you'd have an alibi."

Dumont was no longer purple, only red. "I didn't stay in the game very long. I moved around."

Carter said quickly: "I think he's the man, C.D. Anyone petty enough to take a case against a pal wouldn't stop at anything!"

Dumont forced a laugh. "Prove it! Prove I did it!"

Mort regarded him a trifle coolly. "Oh, proving the murderer's guilt will be easy enough. I was merely trying to establish motives before I put you all to the test."

Page stepped forward. "Damn it, Mort, have you been playing with all of us, making us sit on pins and needles until you got ready to show off? If you can clinch this case before the cops get here, for crying out loud, do it!"

"Easily done. Notice, folks, the little automatic with which Mimi was shot. You will notice that it has a tiny grip. The grip is so tiny that it fits a woman's hand, but a man can get only two fingers around it. When it goes off it kicks up violently, causing the imprint of the front strap to remain for several hours on the skin of the fingers. So, if you good people will simply hold up your hands. . . ."

"That won't be necessary!" There was no alcoholic sluggishness in Al Carter's voice now. Nor was there any clumsiness in the quick scoop of his nimble fingers as they picked up the gun from the floor.

"I'm going out of here. Don't anybody try to stop me!"

Nobody did, as he moved to the door. He reached behind him, drew the door open.

"You, Clarence Darrow Mort, have won your last murder case. You're responsible for showing me up—and you're about to get your reward for your smartness. Here goes, C.D.!"

The shot roared deafeningly. Then Carter settled quietly upon the floor.

Phil Sinton had drawn and fired so fast that by the time Carter had seen him it was too late. He growled: "Imagine that little punk thinking he could do a job like that right under my nose!"

"Nice work, Phil." Page crossed to his safe, got out another sheaf of bills, which he handed to Mort. "There it is, less the five hundred I gave you. And here's your check. It was a quick way to earn twenty grand, but you did earn it. This takes a load off my mind. By the way, before the meat wagon comes for Carter, show me those marks on his fingers you talked about."

"I doubt very much if there are any such marks," Mort yawned. "I'm afraid I cashed in on my prestige with poor Al. You see, he did have a profound respect for my knowledge of criminal lore. First off, I convinced him that I was an authority on the dermal nitrate test for he knew well enough that I was right. On top of that, he knew I'd tried a hundred murder cases, so when I told him the little gun would leave tell-tale marks he didn't wait to find out."

Page exchanged a quick glance with Sinton. Neither had a word to say. But Ned Dumont said: "Well, Al's being the murderer didn't illustrate your little theory that there's no minimum requirement for murder. Al had a million good reasons to kill Mimi besides Nadine here."

"True, he stood to gain a million dollars and thus insure the love of the fair Nadine—so long as the million lasted. All this would point the finger of guilt directly toward him. But tonight he had heard me expounding my theory of motive for murder. He counted on me to raise in the mind of a jury the possibility that someone else, with a horribly petty motive, might have committed the crime.

"Actually his crime illustrates my theory that no motive for murder can be too trifling. As Einstein says, all things are relative. A woman like Mimi was so wonderful that killing her for a mere million dollars is an act of ghastly pettiness."

Mort faced Nadine Gray.

"Al Carter didn't have as logical a motive for killing Mimi as he would have had if he had killed a dozen of you for a dime!"

A Ghoul and His Money

C. M. KORNBLUTH

I T WAS THE FIRST TIME in twenty years of handling pottery that I've ever dropped a piece. It smashed to bits on the tile floor, and a twenty-dollar gold piece rolled out.

My assistant, Mr. Linehan, picked it up and said, with his customary, ill-advised sense of humor: "Maybe we ought to smash the rest of them, eh, Doc?"

I reminded him coolly that my title was "Doctor," took the eagle from him and put it in my pocket. We began to assemble the fragments of the piece that had broken. It proved to be a quart jug, one-eared, of a raw-earth color fired with a peculiar transparent crackle-glaze over the bisque body. When I picked up the piece inked with the catalog number I looked in my ledger.

"American Ceramics Gallery," said the page. "#6684503, gift of Hannes Schlectman, Reading, Pa. 3/5/39—thrown and fired *circa* 1920, maker unknown, insured $10."

Mr. Linehan showed me a circular groove in the base of the jug where the coin had been hidden and suggested, only half humorously, I fear, that we split the value of the coin between us and say nothing of the affair.

I assured him that I would, of course, make a full report of the affair to my immediate superior, the Curator of Ceramics, and turn the eagle over to him. Mr. Linehan was visibly disappointed as I left for the Curator's office.

The Curator looked up the piece in his own files and marveled that so ordinary a piece had been accorded a place in the museum, even The American Gallery. I hotly resented this slur on my department, and I regret to say that there were words between us which culminated in my ejection from his office at the hands of his secretary.

There was a subsequent exchange of formal memoranda between us and within the week he hailed me up before the Board of Museum Trustees' regular meeting.

I stated my grievance frankly, though as temperately as possible, to the trustees, who seemed to be having a difficult time controlling their tempers. One actually held a newspaper before his face, and I observed the paper shake as though he were trembling with the effort of repressing harsh words against the shockingly unprofessional conduct of my colleague.

The chairman gravely promised me that the matter would receive their immediate attention, and asked me to withdraw while it was discussed. Waiting in the anteroom I heard some laughter within. Doubtless one of them had told some humorous anecdote to relieve the tension of my hearing.

I was summoned to enter, and was informed that I had been granted a month's vacation with pay. It was slyly pointed out that the Curator was due to retire within the month, and that thus a difficult situation would be relieved without the necessity of censuring him publicly.

I determined to spend my vacation in the field. Mr. Linehan coarsely suggested that I investigate the contents as well as the composition of some American jugs. I of course treated the remark with the contempt it deserved and made ready for my expedition.

In the course of preparations I realized that I had not yet turned over the gold piece, and in fact that no one had officially required me to do so. I had a jeweler braze a small loop to it, and hung it on my watch chain beside my Phi Beta Kappa key.

A fragment of the broken vase which I had retained excited my curiosity. I easily recognized the clay as a refined seaboard kaolin of the East Coast, and careful analysis and tabulation of the impurities convinced me that it was native to central Pennsylvania. The glaze, as I have said, was unfamiliar.

I determined to spend my month in the field investigating the origin of the piece. It would result at the least in a fascinating paper to read at one of my "Little Talks on Pots" which have been received with so much enthusiasm by habitués of the museum.

There is no need for me to itemize the hardships of the journey. Suffice it to say that for three whole days together I subsisted entirely on hamburger sandwiches and cups of dubious coffee consumed in roadside cafes, with truck chauffeurs and salesmen for my sole companions.

Professor Schroon of Witterburg College, a small but venerable institution on the outskirts of Reading, finally was able to identify the clay for me. He localized it to a long stratum parallel to the Wappaconsie River. On his maps it was evident that the only considerable settlement on that small stream was the town of Vleetsburg, rejoicing in a population of one thousand.

Despite his urging that I stay the night I promptly set off for Vleetsburg itself. Truth to tell, Professor Schroon's views on the influence of Delft blue-tile ware in American ceramics were most unsound, and I feared that if I had stayed so long as another hour we should have arrived at a difference of opinion and that possibly unfortunate words would have been exchanged.

I arrived at Vleetsburg by nightfall and registered at the Commercial House, a ramshackle institution whose rates were most disproportionate to its lack of comfort. After an uncomfortable night I breakfasted on my usual dry toast and glass of warm water. Refreshed, I set out for the local library.

I introduced myself to Miss Kretzl, the librarian, and was gratified to note her respect for scholarship as exemplified by my doctorate. She was a charming person, though decidedly mature, and informed me that she had several times visited New York and the museums to which I was attached.

When I mentioned the quart jug she instantly informed me that beyond doubt it had been the work of the late Miss Henderson of that town. "At least," Miss Kretzl added significantly, "she *called* herself Miss."

To my natural question she replied, with some relish, that Miss Henderson had been married to a man named Hobbet who had abused and finally deserted her after a final, terrible beating which had caused his wife to lose an expected child. Mrs. Hobbet had then resumed her maiden name and— here Miss Kretzl leaned across her desk and whispered piercingly, with dismay in her voice—had gone to *work*.

I myself, of course, am liberal about such matters and believe that women are quite capable of labor nearly equal to that of men, though in their proper sphere, of course. But I did not betray my advanced views to the librarian, heeding the adage, "When in Rome do as the Romans."

She continued—the woman had pursued ceramic work as a hobby, there being the clay bank of the Wappaconsie to hand, and had moved to a tumbledown house left her by a relation and set it up as a pottery shed, building kilns fed with the local natural gas.

Miss Henderson, as she now called herself, worked far into the night, even on the Sabbath, making decorative and practical pieces. She sold no work in town, since the villagers disapproved of her unladylike toil, but eventually secured small, regular orders from stores in Philadelphia and New York and from a large establishment in Chicago. She lived simply and alone, worked hard every day, and died at last in 1930 of cancer, at the age of fifty-one.

I eagerly asked directions to her pottery shed and was given them. It lay well out of town to the south, on a small road which was minutely described to me.

I was about to take my leave when a gentleman came to the desk. He wore a police officer's badge in the shape of a star and carried with some ostentation a large firearm of the type which I believed is called a revolver. His nose was remarkably large and red. "Emmy," he said to Miss Kretzl, "who's the stranger?"

I was introduced to him, or rather, vice versa, the librarian seeming to believe that my academic attainments outweighed the considerable age of the constable.

He was Marshal Cuppy, for thirty years the sole keeper of the peace in

Vleetsburg, and though I regret to say it he was a tedious old bore. His attention was called to the gold eagle on my watch chain—next to the "doo-dad" as he called my Phi Beta Kappa key!

He was reminded by it of a long, dull anecdote which certainly reflected on him discreditably. With many chuckles and snorts which carried the un-mistakable odor of alcohol, he informed me that there had been a bank robbery in Vleetsburg during the spring of 1919, a completely successful robbery, since he had been on a fishing trip at the time. A large sum in gold eagles and double eagles had been abstracted by two masked bandits at the time the bank opened in the morning, and the bandits had utterly disap-peared, leaving not a trace behind to indicate their identity or whereabouts. Mr. Cuppy spoke at great length on the audacity and cleverness of the ban-dits, whom he seemed to admire rather than otherwise.

He informed me, as though it were the greatest joke in the world, that the Farmers' and Drovers' Bank had afterwards failed and been supplanted by a branch of the First National Bank of Pittsburgh.

I at length was able to make my adieux to Mr. Cuppy and Miss Kretzl, who warmly expressed the hope that I would return to her should I require any further information. I thanked her and set off for Miss Henderson's pottery shed.

It was indeed in wretched condition. I was dismayed to behold its per-forated roof and peeling boards, but discomfort is no stranger to a scholar on the trail, so I plunged boldly into the debris.

There was a large room in fair preservation. It had been boarded up and only recently had the boards failed in their guardianship. Its principal fea-ture was a long work-bench, dusty with plaster and surmounted by several large bats. Perhaps I should explain that a bat is the heavy plaster disc used by potters as a base for flat work and plaques.

There was a great tub of long-dried raw clay, of an interesting, friable consistency, a pair of potter's wheels once powered by an electric motor now removed, a shelf of trays containing dried slips of various colors and several pots and jars of glaze. I sampled them all, slipping a bit of each into one of the envelopes I had brought.

In an out-building were three large refractory kilns of amateurish appear-ance. One was obviously of a later construction than the other two. I at-tempted to open them, and the newer one and one of the older pair I was able to open with little trouble.

The other, older kiln appeared to have been sealed with a high-tempera-ture cement of the toughest grade. Breathless with excitement I attacked the cement with a sledge hammer which once had been used to set seggers, no doubt. I hoped against hope that sealed within I should find a long-neglected sample of the potter's art intact.

The cement gave way at last. I was chagrined to discover that the kiln contained nothing but a quantity of organic ash, not unlike the bone-ash slip used by potters of the Soong dynasty in conjunction with their lapis-lazuli pigment. Though cast down, I sampled the ash and, seeing little more that could be done, left the shed.

I lunched at the Commercial House and inquired the way to the local high school. At that unpretenious institution I sent in my card to the principal, who welcomed me enthusiastically and inquired as to whether he could be of any service to me. I secured his permission to use the chemical apparatus and reagents of his science department and, in the school's one laboratory, performed my analyses of the samples I had taken from Miss Henderson's shed.

They proved to consist of various native oxides and sulfates, meticulously ground and purified, equal in quality to the very best commercial glazes. I analyzed the ash I had found in the sealed kiln and recognized its formula with considerable surprise.

Returning to the principal, I set about questioning him tactfully on local history. The bank robbery had been "before his time," that is, he had been attending college in New York pursuing the degree of M. Sc. in Education when it occurred. However, he distinctly recalled the seven days' wonder it had aroused in the town, which had been communicated to him by letters from his family and friends.

Not the least mysterious feature of the robbery had been the subsequent disappearance, after the lapse of a month, of a young man named Bevan who had been the teller in charge at the time the bank had been robbed. There had been no thought of his complicity whatsoever, and his family had placed classified advertisements in various newspapers of the larger cities assuring him that he was under no suspicion, imploring him to return.

He never did, and it was evidently believed that he had simply abandoned his family and the town in an adventurous fling from which he had been ashamed to come back.

I jestingly remarked that there seemed to be a good deal of abandonment for so small a town, citing the reprehensible behavior of Mr. Hobbet. To my surprise the principal took my humorous comment ill, and I left in an atmosphere of some strain.

As I strolled down the central street of the town, noting with some amusement that it was called Broadway, which of course it did not resemble in the slightest respect, I was accosted by a curious and ragged individual. He assured me that he was destitute and asked of me a small loan with which to purchase a meal.

I replied that it would be false charity of me to do as he wished, and that for his own good I felt called upon to advise that he seek some honest employment, no matter how humble or arduous, explaining that bread won by labor is the best.

He protested that he was unable to secure employment, that he was indeed a skilled bank teller.

"A teller?" said I, astonished.

He explained that he had been chief teller at the Farmers' and Drovers' Bank which had failed after the robbery, and that he had not been able to occupy a position with the branch bank that succeeded it, since it had brought its own personnel from Pittsburgh.

I took him into the nearest restaurant, an establishment called The Busy Bee which appeared to specialize in the hamburger sandwich and the exotic dish of chile con carne. The mendicant consumed at my bounty no less than three of the former and two bowls of the latter, together with two cups of hot coffee. I ordered him a portion of apple pie, and as he toyed with that I artfully began to question him.

He remarked that he had known young Bevan well, and ventured the opinion that he had been afraid to stay in the town, having been the only one to see the bandits face to face and fearing lest they seek to harm him.

I remonstrated that I understood the bandits to have been masked.

"You can't mask a man's walk or build," said the old fellow. "Bevan was pretty sure he recognized one of 'em, and he told the law about it. Then he left town, I figure."

"Good Heavens!" I cried. Seldom though I resort to an oath, I was profoundly shocked. "Why was nothing done about it? Who was the man whom Mr. Bevan recognized?"

The fellow laughed in a manner I can only describe as cynical. " I see you don't know small towns," he said. "The man Bevan recognized was Joe Hobbet, a fellow who lived in this town and then left after kicking the blazes out of his wife. I guess I'm the only one Bevan told besides the law, and I figured if the law didn't find him I couldn't. You're the only man who's given a damn about it in twenty years. Thanks for the feed, mister."

Hr arose and left me to ponder. I ordered a cup of weak tea with milk and sat considering the information which had been imparted to me. I could make little of it, and left for the Commercial House. I informed the clerk that I wished to take a short nap before dining and desired not to disturbed. He grinned broadly, for some reason or other, and assented.

In my room I removed my jacket, shoes and vest and reclined on the bed, composing myself for slumber. The twinkle of sunlight on a bit of metal caught my eye. It was the gold-piece hanging from my vest, which in turn hung from the old, painted-over gas fixture by the door.

The gold-piece slowly dimmed before my eyes. It appeared to be growing dark rather early. I tried to rise from the bed to take my watch from the vest, and was dismayed at a curious lassitude which overcame me. I was almost unable to move.

Then and only then did I notice a very faint hissing sound which I had hitherto ignored. I remembered that the region abounded in odorless natural gas. I lurched to my feet in what seemed like total darkness and staggered to the window. I had not the dexterity to rotate the small lock which held it shut. I drove my head at the pane, which shattered to bits, and hung over the sill desperately gulping at the pure outside air.

After recovering my strength and sight I held my breath and crossed the room, turning off the tap of the gas jet and flinging open the door. The one bell-boy of the establishment ran in and as promptly ran out. From the corridor he cried: "Don't do it, mister! Things ain't as bad as they seem and you only got one life!"

"Don't be ridiculous, young man!" I snapped at him. "I have no intention whatsoever of taking my life. Call the manager. At *once,* if you please!"

He retreated down the rickety stairs and returned with the manager, whose principle interest in the matter seemed to be the cost of replacing the broken pane of glass. However, I demanded an instant investigation, which he reluctantly commenced.

It was seen that somebody had cleared the hole of the painted-over gas jet with a nail or similar instrument and had scratched away the paint from the tap, then turning it open. However, the gas supply for illuminating purposes was shut off at a main which rose to a standpipe at the rear of the building.

We hastened to that point and found that the rusty old valve had been forced open very recently, as chips of ferrous oxide still were scattered on the ground.

Mr. Cuppy, the town marshal, appeared at this point, summoned by an excited small boy. He was surprised to find me alive, as the lad had informed him that I had been slaughtered in my bed with a butcher's knife.

After a great deal of reflection and surveying the ground, first downstairs, then in my room, and then outside again, he delivered his opinion. He believed that some person had "snuck" into my room, an easy enough matter, had worked on the gas light, gone back of the building and bided his time until he knew me to be resting in my room. He had then forced the main valve open and departed hastily, possibly expecting an explosion to ensue if I were not already asphyxiated.

Mr. Cuppy found neither footprints not fingerprints anywhere on the assassin's field of operations, but assured me he had a "theery" as to the identity of the malefactor. He promised to leave no stone unturned, and departed for the restaurant surrounded by an excited knot of citizens and small boys.

Save for a slight headache I was thoroughly recovered from my exposure. I returned to my room and donned my vest, my jacket and my shoes, which, I regret to say, I had forgotten to put on before descending to the street. I was surprised to find the gold-piece gone from my chain.

"Good riddance!" thought I. "It has brought me nothing but trouble and disorder." Therefore, polishing my Phi Beta Kappa key until it shone as if it would outdo the missing ornament, I descended to the dining room of the Commercial House to sup upon my usual dry toast and omelette, washed down by a refreshing cup of weak tea.

A postprandial stroll found me in the vicinity of Miss Henderson's pottery shed as the sun was going down. I went within and waited for possibly ten minutes before hearing a heavy foot stumbling on the shed's entrance.

"You are late, Mr. Cuppy," said I coolly.

The man had an electric torch which he rudely turned full in my eyes. "How'd ye know 'twas me?" he demanded.

"Tut, sir!" I chided him. "It's futile for a layman to match wits with the trained intellect of a scholar. It was the veriest child's play to assemble those facts which have come to my attention."

"You ain't playin' with children now," he said grimly. "Tell me right quick where the stuff is, mister, or I'll fill ye with lead."

"Please," I remonstrated. "I shall be happy to tell you. But first I should like to know how you ensured the silence of Miss Henderson, or rather, Mrs. Hobbet? I cannot understand her complicity in the murder of Mr. Bevan."

"You're crazier'n hell," he said disgustedly. "She never knew the first damn' thing about Bevan. I killed him and buried him in Miller's Creek fork myself after Hobbet skipped with the gold."

"One moment," I said, my senses in a whirl. "Do I understand you to say that Mr. Bevan was *buried?* And that Mr. Hobbet—who, of course, 'hid out' here with the loot after you and he had robbed the bank—ran away with the gold?"

"That's right, mister," said he. I heard a click, no doubt connected with the fire-arm he carried. "And I'm giving you thirty seconds to tell me where the gold is before I shoot. Nothing but gold could bring a man to a town like this. And that eagle I lifted from your vest was Philly 1915 like the rest of 'em."

"Mrs. Hobbet," said I thoughtfully, "must have been a remarkable woman, and her husband must have treated her with almost incredible brutality. Mr. Cuppy, your accomplice did not run away with your gold. He is still here, or rather, his ashes are.

"His wife, terrorized into concealing him, finally rallied her courage to kill him, dismember his body and incinerate the parts in a kiln which she later sealed. I have analyzed the ashes which I found there; they are unquestionably the residue of a human body."

"The gold," he said grimly.

"Yes, the gold. Mrs. Hobbet was a remarkable woman, with a remarkable sense of values. She refused to return the gold to the bank, and so to the town which despised her instead of sympathizing and proffering assistance. It pleased her to embed each coin in a piece of pottery. Why not? She earned an adequate living and her work was her pleasure.

"Perhaps, too, she was the possessor of an unusual sense of humor. The gold is scattered over the face of the earth by now, Mr. Cuppy. No conceivable power could assemble it in one place again. Is that what you wished to know?"

He cursed horribly and continuously for a full minute. Then, in a voice trembling with rage, he snarled: "Say your prayers, mister. I couldn't gas you today, but I'm going to shoot you tonight."

"I should like a drink of that grog on the shelf, if you please," I requested. "It might make my passing less difficult."

Keeping one eye and his weapon on me he directed the electric torch to the shelf I had indicated. It picked out the tall clay bottle labeled "Grog" in large letters. I had not been mistaken in judging his red-nosed appearance.

"I didn't know ol' Miz Henderson was a drinkin' woman," he commented. "I figger I'll just sample this—mebbe I need it more'n you." He pulled the cork, glancing sharply at me and settling the gun in his hand. He tilted back the bottle and took a great swallow.

There are two liquids called "grog". One is a concoction of rum and water favored by nautical persons, the other is a suspension of burnt clay used to counteract warpage in the firing of pottery. It was of course the latter that Mr. Cuppy swallowed, for Miss Henderson had been no drinking woman after all.

He choked noisily in astonishment. On his first spasm I seized one of the heavy plaster bats and hurled it at his hand. His gun exploded, missing me by a considerable margin. A second bat struck him in the face, and then I was upon him with a third held in my two hands.

I beat him to the floor with it and pounded him mercilessly, old as he was. After about a dozen blows on his head and neck one apparently struck some significant spot, for he went quite limp. I removed his weapon from his hand and studied it by the light of his electric torch. By the time I had mastered its principles—unfortunately firing one bullet through the dilapidated roof—he had come to.

I marched him to the town jail, the keys of which he carried on his person, and locked him in the one cell. To the bewilderment of the citizens of Vleetsburg, who finally decided that I was federal officer of some sort, I called the state police, who appeared within the hour.

By the light of their automobile headlamps they enthusiastically dug up the nearby fork of Millers' Creek, enlisting the aid of several townspeople. It was one of the latter whose spade struck the skull of the late Mr. Bevan.

One of the state troopers appropriated what was left of the boots and tenderly brushed away the soil, then applying a fine, white powder of talc. Some fingerprints appeared distinctly. They were Mr. Cuppy's. But when we returned to the town jail we learned the consequences of our heedlessness, for Mr. Cuppy, unwatched, had hanged himself to the barred door by his suspenders.

I was given the privilege of an interview with the Lieutenant Governor shortly after, who presented me with a handsomely engraved badge attesting to my membership—in a purely honorary capacity, of course— in the State Police of Pennsylvania.

I took good care to place the badge well down in my suitcase when I started back for New York and the museum. If my assistant, Mr. Linehan, should see the thing I'd never hear the last of it. He has a decidedly ill-advised sense of humor most inappropriate in one pursuing the scholar's vocation.

Cold Storage

ROBERT TURNER

SHE WAS STILL very beautiful. Lee Nolan had to give her that. Five years had passed over her like a day and her long, cascading blond hair was still the color of sun-ripened wheat; her long legs still had the supple grace of a dancer's. Nolan looked at the filmy black negligee contrasting with the white smoothness of her flesh. She was blindingly lovely, no question.

"It's funny, Rita," he said to her. "Look. It's a joke. I'm laughing." He wasn't really. His long thin mouth twitched at the corners, momentarily. But it wasn't a laugh. It wasn't even a smile. He took a dull black .32 police special from his pocket, showed it to her. "See, Rita, I came up here to kill you like I said I would five years ago. Remember?"

Nolan remembered. Just mentioning it brought it all flashing back through his mind in kaleidoscopic pattern. It had been a nightmare of a day in the courtroom. He could still hear the judge's sepulchral tones doling out the manslaughter sentence. He could still feel the bite of the handcuffs as they led him up the aisle. He could see the blurred faces of spectators ogling him. And up front, at the rail, was Rita—laughing at him, laughing fit to bust.

It had made him a little insane. He'd wrenched toward her, screaming names and promising to kill her when he got out, before they shut him up and dragged him away. And all she'd done was laugh louder, longer. That was the last thing he saw, that beautiful, green-eyed, laughing, cruel face of hers, and it had stayed in his mind for five years.

Now, Nolan put the gun slowly back into his pocket. He said: "Of course I really wasn't going to kill you, Rita. Five years was enough. I wouldn't want it for life. I was just going to scare you. Try to. Try to scare you into giving me a divorce. But I can't even do that. You've cheated me out of that, haven't you?"

She didn't answer him. She just kept staring at him. The expression on her face didn't change. Her lips stayed loosely parted, the full, perfectly carved lips that he had once thought so beautiful, that he had once kissed. She just lay there on that expensive rug, so still, so dead, so lovely, even with the blood spread from the bullet hole like a crimson corsage on her right side.

Slowly, he turned and looked around the huge, dropped living room of Rita's apartment. He saw that the furniture was all pushed over to one wall, where the rug had been partly rolled. All the shelves and the fireplace mantle had been emptied of knickknacks. Bookcases were stripped. Packing barrels stood in a corner, filled with china, ready for moving.

"You *were* scared, though, weren't you, Rita?" Nolan whispered into the empty room. "You knew I was out and you were going to move. You were afraid I'd keep my promise. You did give me that much satisfaction. . . . Only somebody stopped you from running away. Somebody hated you more than I do."

A mirror was standing on the floor, leaning against a wall and tilted at an angle, and looking down into it, Lee Nolan saw a rather distorted full-length reflection of himself. It wasn't a nice thing to see. The angle emphasized his tall leanness. It made his cheeks thinner, more hollowed, and his eyes seemed more deeply sunken. The cheap gray felt hat he wore was pulled too low in front. He looked pretty grim, pretty ruthless. Well, that was the way he'd felt when he'd come up here. He'd been determined to make Rita give him a divorce, if he had to threaten her, beat her, hound her day and night. He had wanted it badly enough before. It had become even more important now.

The funny part was, now he was free of her. He didn't need any divorce. Rita was dead. But in the vicious, twisted way that was typically Rita, even in death, she had double-crossed him because though he was free of her, he wasn't free—period. At least not for long. They'd nail him for this sure as thunder. The police would remember that threat he'd made the day they'd marched him off to prison. Whoever had killed Rita had planned it that way, figured him for the fall guy.

Sweat came out on Nolan's lip and forehead and made his shirt stick clammily to his spine. He turned quickly and started for the door, then stopped in midstride. Cold reason suddenly replaced his panic, and he saw that he was acting like an idiot. He didn't have a chance of getting away. The minute the murder was discovered, they'd have an eight-state alarm out for him. They'd get him, too. And running was admitting guilt, in the eyes of the law.

He moved swiftly across the room to a table and Rita's ostrich-skin bag, lying on it. He went through it quickly, extracting a small gilt-edged leather address book and a business card. The card was for a moving company. Nolan tried the phone, holding it with his handkerchief, and found it was still connected. He called the moving company. Pretending he was the super of the apartment, double-checking, he found out that they weren't coming for Rita's furniture until five o'clock. It was now a little past three. Chances were he had a couple of hours before the murder was discovered.

Nolan walked over to a window and stood looking down onto the street, tapping the address book against his teeth, thinking. Outside, it had clouded over heavily, and in the distance, thunder rumbled. A few heavy raindrops were starting to fall. A couple of them splashed on the window glass. People on the street and across in the park were starting to scurry for cover.

Knowing Rita as he did, Nolan thought it shouldn't be too hard figuring out why she was killed and by whom. He assumed that she had been keeping company with other men while he was in prison. She must have double-crossed at least one of them, made him crazy with jealousy—because that was Rita's way with men. She thrived on jealousy. It was the weapon she had used on him, Nolan. It was the reason he had finally decided to try to divorce her, because he knew that she was constantly two-timing him even though he could never actually catch her at it. Even though he had stopped loving her, having learned the kind of woman she really was, he couldn't stand being made a fool of.

But Rita had laughed at the idea of a divorce. Nolan had a rich uncle whom Rita had played up to on a visit when they were first married. The old gent had never forgotten her. When he died, he had left them a joint legacy of a hundred thousand dollars, in the form of a five-hundred-dollar per month endowment, which was to be immediately canceled and the balance of the legacy turned over to charity if their marriage ever broke up. Rita liked her share of that legacy. She didn't mean to give it up, even if Nolan were so foolish.

Nolan had tried every way to force a divorce. The money meant nothing to him without his happiness, and he could never be happy married to Rita. But she had been smart. He was never able to get anything on her.

One night at a party he'd had too much to drink. He'd gotten into a fight with a man with whom Rita had been flirting all night. Nolan had hit him. Falling, the man's head had cracked against a stone fireplace. He had died and Nolan was brought to trial. Which was fine for Rita.

Looking out the window, thinking over all that, now, Nolan decided that Rita's killer must be one of the men she was currently carrying on with. He thumbed through the little address book he had taken from her bag. Most of the names were familiar to him. Men who moved in their set, whom he had known before he was sent away. He isolated a half dozen of these as the most likely suspects because from time to time in the subtly taunting letters Rita had written him in prison, she had mentioned them most. She had gone to dinner with them, or to the theater or the opera.

A man named Dayton Lido was the first on the list, in Nolan's mind. Nolan remembered him well—a wealthy middle-aged sportsman, well-preserved, tanned, and gray-templed. Lido had been a persistent, off-the-record suitor of Rita's for years. He had even worked with Nolan once to try and persuade Rita to divorce him so that he, Lido, could marry her. He was a blustering, strong-willed and hot-tempered man. He was a man who might easily be brought to violence by a woman of Rita's type. There were others but Nolan had an awful strong hunch about Dayton Lido.

The question was to prove something. He couldn't just tell the police: "Look, there are ten other men who could have killed her." The police didn't like to play games. Peculiar people, the police. They liked things easy, cut and dried, for them. They liked nice ripe suspects like Lee Nolan.

A sudden thought lanced into Nolan's mind. Since the crime was still undiscovered, there was only one other person who knew that Rita was dead. If he could work some kind of a trap out of that guilty knowledge. . . .

Nolan paced the room, his eyes avoiding the corpse of Rita, his mind threading ideas in and out like the fast nimble fingers of a woman, knitting. Outside, the thunder rolled in over the city in deafening waves. It got black as Judgment Day and the room filled with long shadows. Rain rattled against the window in huge drops. Finally Nolan evolved a scheme. It was a little desperate, a little fanciful—but there wasn't much time. He had to do something and he had to do it as quickly as possible.

Again Nolan picked up the phone, and this time he dialed the office of Wynn Andrews, the attorney who handled his uncle's estate and had defended Nolan at the manslaughter trial.

"Wynn," Nolan said. "This is Lee—Lee Nolan."

"It's great to hear you, old man," the lawyer's deep voice cut in. "Come on downtown and have a drink. We've got a lot of things to talk over. Where are you?"

"At Rita's flat. Listen, Wynn, I can't waste any time. Listen to what I have to say carefully and please believe me. I have only a little time. You're the only one can help me. I want you to do something for me."

"Sure," Andrews said. "But what are you doing up there? I thought Rita was moving today."

"She's not," Nolan interrupted. "Rita—Rita's dead, Wynn."

There was the sound of breath being sucked in at the other end of the wire, then silence for a few seconds. "Rita's *what*?" Andrews exploded, finally. "What are you talking about, Lee?"

"Shut up!" Nolan said sharply. Quickly, then, without dramatics, he told Andrews the whole story. When he finished, he pleaded: "That's the truth, Wynn. I know it looks bad, and that you'll probably recommend that I go right to the police. But you don't know what it's like up—where I was. I can't take any chances. My only hope, the way things are set up against me, is to nail the real killer. I've got an idea how to do that."

He outlined his plan, then. He was going to give Andrews a list of possible suspects. Andrews was going to have the girl in his office call each of them on the phone. She would talk in a hoarse whisper, pretend she was Rita Nolan, tell each of the men that she was in trouble and had to see him right away, for him to come to her apartment.

"That's fantastic," Andrews boomed when Nolan finished. "Your theory is that the guilty man won't show up. It won't work. He'll see through it and he'll come, too. Then where will you be? Besides, we might not be able to contact all of these men immediately."

"That's a chance I'll have to take," Nolan told him. "And I don't think the guilty man will show. He'll get panicky. He won't know what to think. He'll suspect a trap all right, but he won't be sure whether it involves his coming or staying away."

Andrews pleaded with Nolan to go to the police and see the thing through the proper channels and let justice take its course. But Nolan remained adamant. Finally, Andrews gave in, said he'd put the plan into action right away.

Nolan hung up and stood by the phone, his nerves tightening, the tips of his fingers beginning to tingle. He took the .32 from his pocket, broke it open, made certain there was a cartridge in the firing chamber, flicked off the safety. There was nothing to do now but wait.

When the men on the list Nolan had given Andrews started to arrive, Nolan planned to just tell them that Rita wasn't there, that there must have been some mistake. If the killer did show up, Nolan felt he would be able to tell something by the man's guilty actions or undue suspicions. If he didn't show up, Nolan would know by that fact who the guilty man was.

He didn't have long to wait. In about twenty minutes, the doorbell rang. Nolan moved slowly to answer, his legs feeling weak in the knees. He kept one hand on the gun in his pocket, swung open the door. A gasp of surprise broke from his lips. The man at the door was Wynn Andrews.

The lawyer was a big man and was handsome in the way of a slightly aged matinee idol, with his wide-set eyes and dappled temples. He flashed a set of large, perfect white teeth.

Wynn Andrews had the poise and clear baritone voice of an actor, too. He always made a fine and impressive courtroom appearance. Lee Nolan was not impressed, though, right now. He was just startled.

"Don't get excited, Lee, old boy," Andrews boomed. "Let me in. I have great news for you. You're all set. You have nothing to worry about. We've got the real killer."

He pushed past Nolan and walked into the living room, flicked on a wall switch. "Lord!" he said, "how can you stand the gloom in here with—with *that*? Let's have a little light."

Nolan stood there gaping at him, trying to figure it out. "You've got the killer, Wynn?" he finally managed. "What do you mean?"

Andrews laughed, throatily, teetered on his toes, both hands thrust deep into the pockets of his jacket.

"It's simple." He pulled his left hand from a pocket, waved it airily. "I've saved you the trouble of going to all that fol-de-rol you outlined over the phone." He snorted disdainfully. "A silly idea, anyhow." He tapped a finger to his temple dramatically. "The legal mind works along much simpler, more astute lines. The crime was very obvious. I'm surprised you didn't figure it out yourself, Lee."

Nolan put his hand up over his eyes. He felt very tired. He didn't seem able to think at all anymore. The shock of coming here and finding Rita dead—the threat to his own safety that derived from that—had done him in.

"Go ahead, Wynn," he said softly. "I don't have the slightest idea what you're talking about. *You* tell *me*. But you've loused up my plan, so you'd better make it good."

"It's good," Andrews said. "It's perfect, Lee. You see, the killer knew you were getting out of prison and would arrive in town today. It was a chance for him to commit the perfect murder, knowing you'd be blamed for it. He figured it this way: When the moving men came, they'd discover the crime and notify the police. You would be picked up and that would be that. He didn't figure on your coming here first thing. And if you did, he didn't figure on your staying and playing games, trying to figure out who he was."

"That sounds all right," Nolan told him. "I'll buy that, so far. Get to the point. Who?"

Andrews held up a finely manicured hand toward Nolan. "Don't be hasty, Lee. Let me tell it my way. . . . The killer, though, rather than have you go to prison again, go through all the long drudgery of a trial, during which you might stumble upon some way to clear yourself, would have much preferred that you be killed, also. It would be much, much simpler all around, that way. But that was difficult to arrange. No opportunity presented itself. Until suddenly, you—yourself—presented it."

All the time Wynn Andrews was talking, Nolan had been watching his face. He gradually began to notice that although Andrews was smiling, held control of his voice and appeared on the surface completely at ease, the lawyer's face was much more florid than usual. He saw that Andrews' eyes, too, seemed to hold a hard, agate-like sheen. Little pearls of perspiration showed along his lined forehead. A vein worked like a little fat blue grub in his temple.

A ringing came into Nolan's ears and a small hollowness formed in his stomach. A stirring, a feeling of foreboding and impending trouble burst through his subconscious and he opened his mouth to speak but no words came out.

Wynn Andrews broke off his speech suddenly, said in clipped hard tones: "Put both your hands up behind your neck, Lee Nolan!"

For the first time, Nolan's eyes moved from Andrews' face down to the lawyer's hands. They were both out of his pockets now. The fingers of one were splayed against his side. The other held a snub-nosed automatic aimed straight at Nolan's belt.

In Nolan's brain thoughts were like a big top with fancy designs painted all over it, which were all a blur while it was spinning. But abruptly the top stoped and the design was dead clear.

"You killed Rita," Nolan said in a low, slatey voice, "for the money in my uncle's estate. With Rita dead, with me executed for the crime, you'd have the sole handling of the estate. You could do what you wanted with it."

"Precisely," Andrews admitted. "They must've taught you how to think a little, up there. And you see, Lee, I've been using a little of that legacy from time to time." He moved his free hand from his side in a quick gesture. "Investments, that sort of thing. Rita was beginning to press me for an accounting. I was glad they let you out, Lee. By the way, you could have demanded that accounting too, even though you were in prison—if you'd happened to think about it. . . . So, I'm rather happy that you called me, set yourself up. This way, I can stage a little murder-suicide scene and—"

He never finished. Lee Nolan hurled himself toward Wynn Andrews in a long, low flying tackle, yanking the .32 from his pocket. The automatic made a baby thunderclap in the room. White hot pain exploded along the top of Nolan's head and he felt himself hit the floor a few inches short of Andrews' feet. But the bullet had only creased his scalp. He was still conscious, though momentarily paralyzed. He couldn't move a muscle. As though from a great distance, he heard Andrews' cursing. He watched Andrews kick the .32 across the floor. He lay there waiting for the shock of the second bullet, the one that would bring death. It didn't come.

Instead, the ringing of a bell filled the room. The sound hammered through the silence, insistent, jarring. Nolan watched Andrews' feet move away from in front of his face, across the floor. Like something in a dream, he heard Andrews' voice speaking. The ringing had been the telephone, Nolan realized, vaguely. He heard Andrews say:

"The moving men got here early? . . . No, no, they'll have to wait. We— I'm not quite ready for them, yet. Have them wait downstairs about ten minutes. At least ten minutes. You understand?"

Andrews hung up, then. His footsteps pounded across the floor toward Nolan. Strength was coming back to Nolan's muscles now. He felt as though he could move a little, but he didn't. Andrews still had that gun. Nolan lay very still, gathering his strength. He kept his eyes closed. Suddenly he felt Andrews' foot boot him in the ribs, roll him over. He suppressed a moan and fought against the flood of pain. Andrews kept kicking him, rolling him over the rug until suddenly he was on the bare floor, near the furniture lined up against the far wall.

Nolan slitted one eye open, then. He saw that Andrews, ignoring him, thinking him unconscious, was squatted down by the rug. He had set the automatic down on the floor next to the .32. The lawyer was rolling up the rug with Rita's dead body right in the center of it.

"I've got to hide the corpses," Andrews muttered, "until the moving men leave. I'll tell them to leave the rugs. Then I'll have time to set the scene."

Slowly, inch by inch, Nolan moved his tired body across the floor toward the guns. For a few moments Andrews was so engrossed with his task, he didn't notice. But at the last moment, when Nolan was just a few feet from his goal, Andrews finished rolling up the corpse in the carpet and wheeled around. With a cry of rage, he leaped toward the automatic.

Nolan couldn't beat him, slithering across the floor, the way he was. He couldn't reach the weapon before Andrews. But he could reach the lawyer. He grabbed one of Andrews' thick ankles and yanked with the last of his remaining strength. Caught in midstride, off balance, the other man's feet went out from under him. He fell with a thud that shook the packed china in its barrels.

While the big man sprawled still for a moment, all breath knocked out of him, gasping like a gaffed fish, Nolan scuttled crabwise toward the guns on the floor. He got a grip on the .32 and swung it once, solidly against Andrews' dark head.

Nolan dragged himself to a wall, then, propped against it and sat waiting out the moving men, holding the .32 trained on Andrews. There would be a lot of explanations, Nolan knew, a lot of red tape to go through in the next few hours, but he was all set. There was plenty of evidence against Andrews—the call a few minutes ago, his fingerprints on the murder weapon and on the backing of the rolled-up rug, a nitrate test, and the estate accounting. But after those few hours, Nolan would be a free man, again. Really free, this time.

Death Comes Gift-Wrapped

WILLIAM P. McGIVERN

S ERGEANT BURT MORAN was a tall man with hard flat features and eyes that were cold and dull, like those of a snake. He was that comparatively rare thing among cops, a man equally hated by crooks and by his fellow officers. Operators on both sides of the law forgot their differences and came to agreement on one point at least: that Moran was a heel by any or all standards.

Moran was a bully who shook down petty crooks for a few bucks whenever he got the chance. But he left the big boys alone. He lacked the imagination to serve them and, consequently, he never got in on the important payoff. There would have been some dignity in being a big grafter, but Moran grubbed for his few extra dollars the hard way, the cheap way, the way that earned him nothing else but contempt.

There was a streak of savage brutality in him that caused the underworld to mingle their contempt with a certain fear. Moran had killed six men in the line of duty, three of whom were unarmed at the time, and another who had died after Moran had worked him over with a sap for fourteen hours. The story of the men he'd killed wasn't told because a corpse is an unsatisfactory witness. Moran knew this. He knew all about killing.

Now, at two o'clock in the morning, in the cheap room of a cheap hotel, Moran was going to learn about murder. He had to commit a murder because of something new in his life, something that he had always sneered at in the lives of other men.

Moran was in love. And he had learned that love, like anything else, costs money.

He stood just inside the doorway of the room and watched the scrawny, thin-faced man who was staring at him from the bed. The man was Dinny Nelson, a small-time bookie who, Moran knew, carried all his assets in a hip wallet.

Dinny brushed a hand over his sleep-dulled features and said, "What's the pitch, Moran? You got no right busting in here."

Moran drew his gun and leveled it at Dinny. He knew what would happen with crystal clarity, not only to Dinny and the portions of his body hit by the heavy slugs, but after that, to Dinny's corpse, to the police department and to himself, Moran. It was an old story to him. He had killed six men in the line of duty and he knew the way everything worked. No one would doubt his story.

Dinny saw his fate in Moran's face. He began to beg in a cracked voice. "No, no, you can't," he said. "There's no reason to kill me—I ain't done nothing. Don't."

Moran fired three shots and there were very loud in the small, thin-walled room. Dinny's body jack-knifed with the impact of the slugs, rolled from the bed to the floor. He didn't live long. Moran watched expressionlessly as Dinny's limbs twisted spasmodically, then became rigid and still. Underneath Dinny's body the roses in the faded pattern of the rug bloomed again, bright and scarlet.

There was two thousand, three hundred and thirty dollars in Dinny's wallet. Moran left thirty. The money made a comfortable bulge against his leg as he sauntered to the phone. . . .

While the coroner did his work and two lab technicians went over the room, Moran told his story to Lieutenant Bill Pickerton, his immediate superior at Homicide.

"Tonight I seen him taking bets in the lobby," Moran said. "This was eleven. I started across to him but he seen me and ducked into the bar and then out to the street. So I drifted away. Around two I came back, came right up here to his room. I told him to get dressed but the fool went for me. I had to shoot him."

Lieutenant Pickerton rubbed his long jaw. "This stinks worse than your usual stuff, Moran. You could have handled him with your fists. He doesn't have a gun."

Moran shrugged. "Why should I risk getting beat over the head with a chair or something?"

Pickerton looked at him with active dislike. "Okay, turn in a written report tomorrow morning. The old man won't like this, you know."

"To hell with the old man," Moran said. "He wants us to bring 'em in with a butterfly net, I suppose."

"All right," Pickerton said. He paid no more attention to Moran, but studied the body and the room with alert, careful eyes.

Downstairs, Moran hailed a cab and gave the driver the address of the Diamond Club. He stared out the window at the dark streets of the Loop, his impassive face hiding the mirth inside him.

When Moran had realized that a nightclub singer couldn't be impressed by a cop's salary, he had looked around in his dull, unimaginative fashion for a way to get some money. Nothing had occurred to him for quite a while. Then the idea came, the idea that a cop could literally get away with murder.

After he got that much, the rest was easy. He had picked Dinny because he wasn't big-time, but big enough as far as money went. Now it was all over and he had the money. There would be a routine investigation of course, but there was no one to come forward with Dinny's version of what had happened. Therefore, the department would have to accept Moran's story. They might raise hell with him, threaten him some, but that didn't matter.

Moran's hand touched the unfamiliar bulge of money in his pocket and a rare smile touched the corner of his mouth. It didn't matter at all.

He paid off the driver in front of the Diamond Club on Randolph street and walked past the headwaiter with a familiar smile. The headwaiter smiled cordially, for Moran's visits to the club had been frequent over the past two months, dating from the time Cherry Angela had joined the show.

Moran found a corner table and watched the girl singing at the mike. This was Cherry Angela. The blue spot molded her silver evening dress to her slim, pliant body, revealing all the curving outlines. She wore her platinum hair loose, falling in soft waves to her shoulders, and her eyes and features were mocking as she sang an old, old story about a man and a woman.

Moran forgot everything watching the girl. And there was an expression of sullen hunger on his face.

She came to his table after the number and sat down with lithe grace. "Hi, copper," she said, and her voice was amused. "Like my song?"

"I liked it," Moran said.

Her lean face was mocking. "I should do a back-flip from sheer happiness, I suppose. Would a beer strain your budget?"

"Go ahead," Moran said, flushing. "I've spent plenty on you, baby."

"You tired of it?" she said lightly.

Moran put his hands under the table so she wouldn't see their trembling. She was in his blood like nothing else had ever been in his life. But he got nothing from her but mockery, or sarcasm that shriveled him up inside.

He knew that she let him hang around for laughs, enjoying the spectacle of a forty-year-old flatfoot behaving like an adolescent before her charms. For just a second then he wanted to tell her what he had done tonight, and about the money in his pocket. He wanted to see her expression change, wanted to see respect for him in her eyes.

But he resisted that impulse. Fools bragged. And got caught. Moran wasn't getting caught.

Someday he'd have her where he wanted. Helpless, crawling. That was what he wanted. It was a strange kind of love that had driven Moran to murder.

He took her home that night but she left him at the doorway of her apartment. Sometimes, if he'd spent a lot of money, she let him come up for a nightcap, but tonight she was tired.

Leaving her, Moran walked the five miles to his own apartment, hoping to tire himself out so that he could sleep without tormenting himself with visions of what she might be doing, or who she might be with.

But once in bed, he knew the walk hadn't helped. He was wide awake and strangely nervous. After half an hour of tossing he sat up and snapped on the bed lamp. It was five thirty in the morning, and he had a report to make on the murder in about four hours. He needed sleep, he needed to be rested when he told his story, and thinking about that made sleep impossible.

He picked the evening paper from the floor, glanced over the news. There was a murder on page one, not his, but somebody else's. He thought about his murder then and realized with a slight shock of fear that it had been on his mind all the time. It was the thing keeping him from sleep. Not Cherry Angela.

He frowned and stared out the window at the gray dawn. What was his trouble? This killing tonight was just like the others. And they hadn't bothered him. There must be a difference somewhere, he decided. It came to him after a while. The others had been killings. This one was murder. And the difference was that murder made you think.

Moran lay back in the bed, but he didn't go to sleep. He kept thinking.

At ten after eleven Moran had finished his report. He read it over twice, frowning with concentration, then took it down to Lieutenant Bill Pickerton's office.

There was someone with Pickerton, a young man with mild eyes and neatly combed hair. He was sitting beside Pickerton's desk, and the two men were talking baseball.

Pickerton nodded to Moran, said, "This is Don Linton from the commissioner's office, Moran."

Moran shook hands with Linton and put his report before Pickerton. Pickerton handed it to Linton. Linton said, "Excuse me," put on rimless glasses and bent his head to the report.

Moran lit a cigarette and dropped the match in Pickerton's ashtray. He guessed that Linton was here to look into the Dinny Nelson killing. His eyes were hot from his sleepless night and he was irritable.

"Is that all you want?" he asked Pickerton.

Linton answered. He said, "No. I've got a few questions. Have a chair, Sergeant."

Pickerton remained silent.

Moran sat down, trying to control the heavy pounding of his heart. They had nothing on him. It was his word, the word of a cop, and it was the only word they'd get.

"Okay, this seems clear," Linton said. He put his glasses away, studied Moran directly. "I'm from the commissioner's office, Moran. The commissioner wants me to ascertain that the shooting of Dinny Nelson was justified. Let's start with this. You're a homicide sergeant, assigned to roving duty in the Loop. Why did you make it your business to go to Nelson's room to arrest him on a gambling charge?"

Moran was ready for that one. He explained that he'd seen Dinny taking bets in the hotel lobby, that it seemed a pretty flagrant violation, so he'd decided to pick him up, even though it wasn't his beat.

Moran's voice was steady as he talked. All of this was true. He *had* seen Dinny taking a bet, had tried to pick him up, and Dinny had given him the slip. On that ground Moran felt confident.

"Okay," Linton said casually. "Now according to our information Dinny Nelson usually carried a sizable amount of cash with him. But there was just thirty dollars on his body after you shot him. Got any ideas about that, Sergeant?"

"No," Moran said.

There was silence. Pickerton and Linton exchanged a glance. Then Linton put his fingertips together precisely and looked at Moran. "Did you leave the hotel room at any time after the shooting? I mean did you step out and leave the body alone?"

"No," Moran said. He wondered what Linton was getting at.

"You see, there was a bellhop on the floor at the time. He had brought some aspirin up to a woman. He has a record for theft and it occurred to us that if you left the room for any length of time, he might have slipped in, stolen the money and left before you returned."

"I didn't leave the room," Moran said. He felt scared. They might be telling the truth, but he doubted it. They were setting a trap, leaving an opening for him to dive into. A man guilty and scared would grab any out. Crooks who got caught got scared. They started lying, blundered, and hung themselves talking. That wouldn't happen to him. They had his story.

Linton asked him then why he hadn't subdued Dinny with his fists. That was better. That was the sort of stuff he expected. Half an hour later Linton said he had enough, and Moran walked to the door. He was sweating. He was glad to get out. Linton might look like a law student, but his mind was sharp, strong like a trap.

As he reached the door, Linton said, "By the way, you know Cherry Angela, don't you?"

Moran's hand froze on the knob. He turned and his body was stiff and tense. "Yeah," he said. His voice wasn't steady.

Linton looked pleasantly interested, that was all. "I've heard her sing," he said. "And I heard you were a friend of hers." He said nothing else, volunteered no other information, but continued to watch Moran with a polite expression.

Moran stood uncertainly for a moment, then nodded quickly to the two men and went out to the elevators. Waiting for a car, he wondered how Linton knew he was a friend of Cherry's. They must already have done some checking into his activities. Moran lit a cigarette and wasn't surprised to notice that his fingers were trembling. . . .

That day was hell. He couldn't sleep, and food tasted like sawdust. Also, he kept thinking, turning everything over in his mind a thousand times. That made him tense and jumpy.

That night Moran went to the Diamond Club for Cherry's early show. When he walked through the archway he saw her sitting at a corner table with a man. There was a champagne bottle beside them in an ice bucket and they were talking very seriously. Moran felt a bitter anger and unconsciously his hands balled into fists.

He started toward their table, moving deliberately. This is the time for a showdown, he thought. I'll chase that punk out of here and have it out with her.

Then he recognized the young man with her, and the shock of that recognition sent a cold tremor through his body.

It was Linton, the investigator from the commissioner's office.

Moran's face felt hot and stiff. He turned clumsily, hoping they hadn't seen him, and went back across the room, forcing himself to walk casually.

But splintered thoughts were flicking into his mind with frightening intensity. What was Linton doing here? What was Cherry telling him? More important, what was Linton asking her?

Ignoring the headwaiter's puzzled smile, Moran hurried out of the club. He walked a block quickly before his heart stopped hammering and he was able to think. He knew he had behaved foolishly. He should have gone to her table, said hello and sat down. Any change in his normal routine would look suspicious now.

Lighting a cigarette, he realized that he must see Cherry tonight, find out what Linton had been after. He retraced his steps until he came to a doorway about fifty feet from the entrance of the Diamond Club. There he stopped and prepared to wait. For he had to be sure that Linton was gone before going in to see Cherry.

It was a long wait.

The last show ended, noisy customers streamed out, but still Linton had not appeared. Moran's throat was dry from too many cigarettes, and his eyes burned from lack of sleep. But he waited, a deep shadow in the doorway.

Then Linton appeared and Moran cursed bitterly under his breath. For Cherry was with him, bundled up in furs and chattering so that her voice carried along the street to him.

The doorman went out in the street to hail them a cab. There were plenty of cabs out and that was a break. Linton and Cherry climbed into one, and Moran hurried down the block from the club and caught the next cruiser. He told the driver to follow Linton's cab and it led them to Cherry's apartment.

Moran ordered his driver to stop half a block away. He watched while Cherry and Linton got out and went into her building. But their cab waited and in a few seconds Linton appeared again and drove away.

Moran let out a relieved sigh. He paid off his cab and walked slowly along the darkened street until he came abreast of Cherry's entrance. For a second he hesitated, wetting his lower lip uncertainly. It was stupid for him to barge in on Cherry now. It would look as if he were afraid, guilty.

But he felt he had to know what Linton had wanted. That was the only way he could release the tight, aching feeling in his stomach. He made up his mind and turned into her entrance.

She opened the door in answer to his knock, her eyes widening with surprise. "Well, it's a small world," she said. "I just left one of your buddies."

"I know," Moran said, and stepped inside. She had changed into a green robe and as she turned he saw the flash of her legs, slim, smooth and bare. But they didn't distract him now.

"What did he want?" he said watching her closely.

"The copper?" She shrugged and went to a table for a cigarette. "What does any copper want? Information."

He walked to her side and suddenly all the twisted feeling he had for her crystalized to hatred. She was so cool, so bored and indifferent, while he was ready to crack in pieces from the pressure inside him.

Raising his thick hand he struck the cigarette from her mouth with brutal force. She staggered, face whitening with shock and anger. But he caught her shoulders and jerked her close to him.

"Now," he said, in a low hard voice. "You talk, baby. What did that guy want?"

"You're hurting me," she said, breathing angrily. "He wanted to know about you. Now let me go."

The tight ache crept back inside Moran. He released her and let his hands fall to his sides.

"What did you tell him?" he asked hoarsely.

She turned from him and sat down on the couch. "I didn't tell him anything," she said, rubbing her bruised shoulders. "Now you can get the hell out of here. No guy pushes me around, Moran."

"Forget that," Moran said. "I didn't mean to get rough. But I'm in a jam, baby. I had to shoot a guy last night and the old women in the commissioner's office are on my tail. They're trying to frame me, and that's why that guy Linton was snooping around you."

Cherry's lean face was interested. She said, "Did you kill the guy, Moran?"

"I shot him. He went for me and I shot him, that's all."

"Oh," she said. She smiled. "You wouldn't do anything original, I guess. Nothing that might put an extra buck in your pocket."

"I get along on my pay," Moran said.

"And your friends have to, too," she said. "That's why you haven't got any, I suppose."

"I didn't get anything out of shooting the guy," Moran said. That was smart. Not talking, not bragging. Guys talked to dames, then the dames talked. That wasn't for Moran.

Cherry grinned ruefully and leaned back against the fat pillows on the couch. There was one light in the room, a lamp on an end table that caught lights in her loose blond hair and accentuated the soft curves of her body. Yawning, she put her legs onto the couch. The green robe parted revealing her slim calves in the soft light. She didn't seem to notice.

She was smiling, but there was a hard light in her eyes. "Tell me, Moran," she said, "how does it feel to kill a man?"

Moran swallowed heavily. He couldn't wrench his eyes from her long bare legs, or stop the sudden drumming in his temples.

When he spoke, his voice was dry. "It's like anything else you do, like smoking a cigarette or buying a paper, that's all."

She sighed. "You're such a clod, Moran. You're like a big heap of dough that's turning sour."

He came closer to her. "I could be different with you," he said. "You drive me crazy, baby."

She laughed with real amusement. "In the Casanova role you're a riot."

"Damn you," he said hoarsely.

She laughed again and sat up, putting her feet on the floor. "Let's break this up," she said. "You're a jerk and always will be, Moran. I might have liked you a little if you were smart, or if you had a spare buck to spend on a girl, but as you stand you're hopeless. So beat it, will you? And stop hanging around the club."

"Now wait," Moran said. His anger broke, melted away. "You don't mean that. I'll go, but let me see you again."

Her voice was hard. "No. You're all through. Beat it."

Moran stood beside her, reached for her hand. "What would you think if I was smart, if I did have a little dough?"

"I don't want to play twenty questions," she said coldly.

"This is no gag," he said. When he saw interest in her face, he slid on the couch beside her and began speaking rapidly, the words spilling out in a rush. "I got a little dough," he said. "I got it from Dinny Nelson last night. He was the guy I shot. I blew him out like a candle, then took his bundle. It's all yours, baby, for anything you want. But we got to play it quiet until I get a clean bill from the commissioner's office. You see that, don't you?"

"Are you on the stuff?" she said. "Is this story coming out of a pipe?"

"No, no, it's on the level," he said. "I did it for you, baby. I shot hell out of him and got the dough. And I'm in the clear."

"Let's see the dough," she said skeptically.

He took the roll from his pocket. He had kept it on him because there was no safer place. Now he spread it in her lap and watched her face. She fingered the money gently and gradually a little smile pulled at her lips. "I might change my ideas about you," she said at last.

"Sure you will," Moran said eagerly. "I'm okay, baby. You'll see."

"I kind of want to find out," she said, grinning at him. "Want to excuse baby a minute?"

He watched her as she walked to the bedroom door. Something tightened in him as he saw the way her shoulders tapered gracefully to her slender waist, and the way her hips moved under the silken robe. She turned at the doorway and winked at him, and he saw the gleam of her long legs before she disappeared.

It was worth it. Moran thought exultantly. He felt happy for the first time since the murder. This was going to make it all right, and the tight ache inside him melted and he knew it was gone for good.

He lit a cigarette and leaned back against the cushions, closing his eyes. Linton could go to hell, and so could Pickerton. They had nothing on him, now or ever.

He opened his eyes when he heard the click of the doorknob. Straightening up, he crushed out the cigarette and got to his feet, a grin on his face.

The bedroom swung open and Moran's heart lurched sickeningly.

Lieutenant Pickerton walked into the room, a gun in his hand. The gun was pointed at Moran's stomach.

"You're all through," he said.

Moran stood still, the grin pasted on his face, his mind frozen in the paralysis of panic. He tried to speak but no words came out, and the noise he made was like the grunt of an animal.

There was the sound of a key in the front door and then Linton came in, gun in hand.

He glanced at Pickerton. "You get it all?"

"The works," Pickerton nodded.

Linton came to Moran's side, deftly slipped the gun from his shoulder holster. "You're under arrest for the murder of Dinny Nelson," he said formally. "Anything you say may be used against you. As you know," he added dryly.

"Yeah, I know," Moran said numbly. Linton's words, the old familiar words, released him from paralysis.

Cherry appeared in the bedroom doorway, stepped around Pickerton and entered the room. She picked up a cigarette and smiled. Her fingers moved to the mark on her cheek where he had struck her.

Then she looked at Moran. "They wanted me to get you to talk," she said. "I wasn't going to, because I'm no informer. I might even have warned you that Pickerton was hiding in the bedroom, but after you hit me, I had to pay you back."

"That was just one of the stupid things you did," Pickerton said. He shook his head disgustedly. "What made you think you were smart enough to get away with murder? Your speed is the little stuff, Moran."

Moran wet his lips. "What did I do wrong?" he asked. He didn't know what was happening to him but he felt weak and drained.

Pickerton glanced at Linton. "You tell him," he said.

"We had nothing on you," Linton said, "except your bad record, and the fact that Dinny's money had been taken. But you acted from the start in a suspicious manner. During our first talk you were nervous, sweating. Later you came to the Diamond Club, but when you saw me with Cherry, you turned and got out. We saw you, of course.

"Pickerton came here to Cherry's apartment because we knew you'd come here. A smart man wouldn't have. I took Cherry home, drove off. You immediately barged into the building and I came back and followed you up here."

He glanced at Cherry, then back at Moran. "You were too nervous to be subtle with her, or to go easy. You pushed her around and that did what we hadn't been able to do, convinced her to help us. She played you like a sucker. You spilled everything to her, which is the thing only a fool would have done. Fortunately for us, Moran, you're a fool." His face became curious. "A cop should have known better. Didn't you stop to think at all?"

"I was thinking about the murder," Moran said slowly. "It was on my mind. That left no room for any thinking about the smart thing to do."

Pickerton took his arm and started him toward the door.

Linton walked over and shook hands with Cherry. "Thanks for the help," he said. He hesitated, then smiled. "I'd like to see you sometime when I'm off duty."

Cherry pulled the robe tight around her slim waist. "Any old time—just any old time."

Linton grinned. "I'll call you."

He took Moran's other arm and the three men went out the door.

Moran walked like a dead man.

A Dish of Homicide

HANK SEARLS

Chapter 1

DEADLY COPPERHEAD

I WAS SITTING at my desk, wondering about the office rent, when the door opened and in walked the most beautiful assemblage of female parts that had ever shrugged into a mink coat. She had hair the color of burnished copper and dead white skin and her eyes were as green and as hard as emeralds.

Suavely, as in a movie, I stood up, knocking over my chair. She's come to the wrong office, I thought. The theatrical producer is three doors down.

"Good morning," I said. It was three P.M.

She laughed. "Relax, buster. Are you Mike Blair?"

"Unless you're from the finance company."

She eased into one of the finance company's chairs. "I've heard of you," she said. Her voice was low and husky. It was a voice that had been around. "You worked for a friend of mine . . . a former friend . . . when she was getting a divorce. Sugar Lynn."

I remembered Sugar, and it hadn't been strictly what you'd call work, but I nodded. "Oh, yeah. Sugar. The little singer. She divorced her husband to marry Howard Morrison, the cowboy star. I wonder if she did?"

"No."

I shook my head. "Too bad. Are you in the show business too?"

"Off and on. Right now, off. When I found that I needed some—well, confidential work done, I remembered that Sugar had come to you."

"I have always considered Sugar among my most satisfied clients."

She lit a long cigarette and looked at me lazily, taking a slow drag.

"I'll bet," she said finally. "Well, this is a different kind of work."

I went to my office safe. I opened it and took out the bottle of scotch that I must have been saving for the first beautiful redhead that came to visit me in a mink coat. I poured Beautiful a drink.

"Is your name confidential, too?" I asked, handing her the glass.

"Dawn Sherril."

"Very pretty. Miss or Mrs.?"

"Mrs., right now."

"Oh," I said. I sat down at my typewriter. "My secretary has the day off," I lied, "so if you'll just give me your husband's address and the address of the other woman, I'll start tailing them tomorrow. The price will be twenty-five dollars a day, and expenses, but you can tack that on the divorce—"

"I don't want him tailed."

I swung away from the typewriter.

"You want him shot? You want his girl friend murdered? Name it. Special on murders this week."

She gazed at me coolly, lying back in the chair, her cigarette held carelessly.

"You know," she said slowly, "for a guy who's supposed to know how to keep his mouth shut, you sure do a lot of talking."

"I'm sorry. Go ahead."

She reached into a handbag that must have cost a hundred dollars and pulled out a newspaper clipping. She tossed it on the desk.

It was from the column of an Eastern newspaperman.

Dawn Sherril, the former New York nightclub warbler, is singing the blues to a certain guy in the West, and may earn a lifetime contract.

"Well," I said. "What's wrong with that? Who's the lucky guy?"

She hesitated. "I don't think you have to know."

"Look, when I work on a case, I know everything my client knows, or no go."

She thought for a while. "Howard Morrison."

"Howard Morrison? The same guy Sugar—"

"That's right. Any objections?" she asked me.

I shook my head. "He must like married women," I said.

"Maybe he figures there are less complications."

"Maybe he's nuts, too. Every kid in the country pays a dime a Saturday to watch him shoot up the screen. One piece of bad publicity and he's all through."

"There won't be any bad publicity. That's what you're going to prevent."

"Go on, you interest me."

"My husband saw the clipping and he's flying out from New York."

"I see. And what do you want me to do? Shoot down the plane?"

Her eyes flashed green flame and I shut up.

"No, comedian. I want you to pass as the guy I'm going around with, while my husband's here. At my expense, of course. And I think I can afford the twenty-five a day, besides."

"Dawn, daughter, you just hired yourself a private escort. Would it be too much to ask why you need to hire somebody?"

Her eyes dropped.

"My husband is a bum. He's done time for blackmail, and he has a lot on me. I worked with him once. I was just a kid, and in love." Her eyes melted into tears. It was very effective. Then I remembered acting was her racket and that she was probably just rehearsing. "I finally left him because he wouldn't go straight. But he'd never give me a divorce, probably because he was waiting for me to snag somebody with money so he could blackmail me."

I looked at the mink coat.

"And you finally snagged somebody, as you put it?"

She nodded.

"Nice going," I said. "But where do I come in?"

"I want you to convince him that you're the man the column mentioned, that you haven't any money, and that you don't care about my past. If he thinks there's nothing in it for him, if he thinks we'll get married sooner or later anyway, he may let me have a divorce for a couple of hundred. If he knew who I actually was going to marry, he'd be after him for thousands. Besides," she added, "I'm not too sure Howard would marry me if he knew I'd been tied up with a blackmailer."

I looked at her in admiration.

"I'll be damned. Who would have thought a girl as beautiful as you could have figured all that out? Of course, Mr. Sherril will find you've tricked him after you marry Morrison, and he'll be on you like a leech."

She smiled sweetly. "After I marry Morrison, Morrison will be too busy to care."

I looked her over and nodded. "I guess he will," I said thoughtfully. "I guess he will."

We stood on the ramp at the airport and Dawn shivered in the cold. The mink coat was back in my office, with a diamond ring the size of a pea, but she still looked like a million dollars.

The huge airliner taxied up under the lights, swung in a circle, and stopped. Its engines coughed and died. A few passengers got out and one headed our way. I began to feel uncomfortable.

You can tell them a mile away—the born crooks and the crumbs. You can spot them by their eyes. Their eyes are cold and blank, and their faces are deadpan. This one was big and had blond, wavy hair, and I could see that he was the kind of guy a girl might turn crooked for, if she hadn't been around. He walked up and nodded coolly.

"Well, Dawn, we meet again. The California climate agreeing with you?"

Dawn shrugged.

"And who is this joker?" asked Sherril.

"Mike Blair, the man I'm going to marry."

Sherril looked me over critically. I was glad, for our purposes, that my overcoat was four years old and I was wearing a five o'clock shadow.

"This is the guy you want to marry?" Sherril asked sullenly. There was disappointment all over his face.

Dawn nodded. "And what's wrong with him?"

I began to feel like a used car.

Sherril shook his head. "Let's go get a drink. If Joe Blow can afford one."

I was disliking Mr. Sherril more every minute.

"The name is Blair," I said. "Mike Blair." I flagged a taxi and told the driver to take us to the Hi Hat Club. . . .

The place was crowded, but the headwaiter stared at Dawn and then gave us a table next to the dance floor. We ordered a round of drinks. Then Sherril sat back and cased the place.

"What do you do for a living, Blair?" he asked finally, still looking around.

"I'm in the oil business," I said, just to get him excited.

His face lit up and he glanced at me with new interest.

"Is that so? That's a good racket."

"Things are slow right now. My boss has a nice station, right on Route 40, but people aren't traveling much anymore."

His face fell and he looked at me suspiciously. I stared back blankly.

"And you want to marry my wife?"

"Yes, Mr. Sherril, I do."

"How the hell do you expect to support her working in a gas station?"

"Dawn is willing to struggle along until I get started."

Sherril regarded her closely. "What's the angle? You don't want to marry this guy for his looks. What's he gonna do, inherit a million clams?"

Dawn went into her act. I had to admire the way she did it. Her eyes turned starry and her face softened.

"You wouldn't understand, Pete. I didn't understand about love before, either. When it hits you, things like money don't matter any more. I love him, Pete, and I'm going to marry him."

It was pure ham, and she was playing to a tough house, but she got it across. Sherril looked thoughtful.

"I don't know about that. I don't know. There's the little matter of getting a divorce, for one thing. And there's something else. . . ."

"Dawn told me she worked with you in a confidence game," I said. "And I don't care. I still want to marry her."

Sherril looked at me and shook his head sadly.

"That's your worry, Mac. As a wife, she makes a good singer. I don't suppose she told you that she gave the cops enough to send me up for three years?"

There was a long silence. Then the lights dimmed and the band began to play softly.

Sherril went on, his voice low across the table. "Just the same, I don't want a divorce."

"Why?" I asked.

"I think I'll just let her sweat it out. I spent three years in the jug on account of her . . . she can spend the rest of her life married to a jailbird."

A spotlight shone on the dance floor and I started suddenly as a slender figure floated out from the wings. She was dressed in a flimsy strapless gown that made you hold your breath for her, and she was singing in a low, haunting voice that sent shivers up and down your back.

It was Sugar Lynn, her soft raven hair shimmering in the glow of the spotlight. I hadn't been to the Hi Hat since the recession hit the detective business—it had been over a year—but she was just as provokingly beautiful as ever.

She glided over to our table, looked coldly at Dawn and myself, and moved away, putting everything she had into her quiet, throaty voice. I heard Sherril draw in his breath.

"Who's that?" he asked. Neither of us answered him.

Sugar got a big hand when her song was over, and disappeared into the wings. In a moment she was out, standing at our table. Dawn looked up at her. When their eyes met, the temperature in the room dropped ten degrees.

"Sugar," said Dawn. "It's so nice to see you. You know Mike, of course."

"Of course," Sugar said coldly. "I see him all the time. Every couple of years."

I looked at my fingers and tried to think of something brilliant to say. I decided to skip it.

"I just thought I'd tell you that Howard has a reservation here tonight, Dawn, dear." Sugar's voice was dripping honey. In case you wanted to unload any of your surplus cargo."

Dawn's green eyes never wavered. "Thank you, Sugar," she said. "It won't be necessary. Don't you have to mingle with the other guests?"

For a moment Sugar's face was naked with hate, and then she smiled and drifted off.

"Who's Howard?" asked Sherril.

"A mutual acquaintance," said Dawn absently.

Sherril looked at her doubtfully and then turned back to me. "As I was saying, I don't want a divorce."

"How much don't you want a divorce?" asked Dawn.

Sherril swished his drink absently around in the glass. "Oh, I'd say about three thousand dollars' worth."

"Mike hasn't got that kind of money." She gathered up her handbag and turned to me. "Let's go, darling. We're wasting our time with him."

I nodded and got up, saw that Sherril was hesitating.

"Wait a minute," said Sherril. "Isn't there somewhere we can go to talk this over?"

"Not to talk three thousand dollars over, there isn't," said Dawn.

"Well, maybe the price is a little high for a grease monkey. Maybe we can work out a deal."

"We'll go out to my place," said Dawn sweetly.

I paid the check and the three of us started for the door. As we walked across the dance floor, I saw a commotion by the hatcheck counter. Somebody had just come in, somebody important, and the headwaiter and the hatcheck girl were breaking their necks to take care of them.

He looked up and I recognized a face I'd seen on the billboards of neighborhood movies all over the country. He saw Dawn and started toward us, nodding hellos along the way.

"Dawn," the cowboy said. "Where have you—"

"Hello, Howard," said Dawn coldly. "We're just leaving. Sugar is here. Have a good time."

As we stepped outside, I saw that Sherril's face now was wearing a very puzzled frown.

"Where have I seen that face before? What's that guy's racket?"

Dawn shook her head. "Just somebody I met at a party once."

Chapter 2

COOLING OFF—FAST

WE TOOK A CAB out to the suburbs and stopped at a little house that looked like all the other little houses on the block. But it was modern and clean and new, and cost a lot of rent. We walked in and sat down.

"This is a nice set-up you have here," said Sherril. "You got a job, Dawn?"

She nodded. "I have a job. Eighty a week; most of it goes into the rent."

"Aren't you two lovebirds saving anything for getting married? Seems like I would, if I were you."

"Mike's got a little saved. A few hundred. That's all."

Sherril thought it over. "All right," he said. "I need money. I'll agree to a divorce for five hundred dollars."

I looked at Dawn and she nodded slightly.

"Two hundred now and three hundred when the divorce is final?" I asked.

"Okay. Let's have a drink on it."

Dawn went to the kitchen and a moment later her voice floated out. "Mike," she called. "Help me with the ice."

I went in and closed the door behind me.

She reached up behind a shelf and pulled down a package of bills. She counted out two hundred and added another fifty.

"Give him the two hundred," she said. "And get rid of him. I want to get back to the Hi Hat before that woman cuts my throat with Howard."

I brought the money out and handed it to Sherril. He counted it carefully and put it away.

"Okay, brother," he said. "I guess you'll marry her when the divorce is over. Don't say I didn't warn you."

I gave him his drink and waited until he'd finished it. "Now get out," I said. "You'll get the other three hundred when the divorce is through."

"Don't rush me, Sonny," he said. "Don't forget, she's still my wife. Maybe I don't feel like leaving her here with you."

I grabbed him by the lapel and lifted him out of the chair. "You heard me. I said get out and, brother, I really meant that!"

"Okay," he said. He started for the door and I relaxed. Suddenly he swung around and his fist lashed out at me. I started to duck. Then my head exploded in a symphony of light. . . .

I struggled up from the depths of oblivion. A buzzer was ringing impatiently in my ear. For a long while I stared at the unfamiliar furniture, trying to remember where I was. When I remembered, I grabbed the couch and lifted myself painfully. Sherril was gone. The buzzer kept droning. Then it stopped and sounded angrily three times.

I lurched to my feet and headed for the front door. I could hear footsteps retreating down the walk toward the street. There was a taxi in front of the house and someone was climbing into the front seat.

"Hey," I yelled. "Were you ringin'?"

The figure turned and started up the walk. "Yeah. Your cab's here."

"What cab?"

"The cab you phoned for, pal. It's here."

I stuck my head back into the room. "Dawn," I yelled. "Dawn."

There was no answer.

"I don't know who called you, but there's nobody home now. Did you see a big blond guy come out of here?" I rubbed my jaw.

"No, Mac. No big blond guy. And the next time your wife calls two cab companies and takes the first cab that shows up, paddle her for me, will you?" He spat in disgust and started down the walk. He jammed his cab into gear and was gone in an angry burst of noise.

I discovered suddenly that I was thirsty. I weaved through the living room to the kitchen door, my head still spinning. I opened the door and felt my heart turn over.

Dawn was crumpled in front of the refrigerator. An ice tray was clutched in her hand, and a bright red pool was spreading over the colored linoleum. I staggered over and squatted beside her. I lifted her head and looked at her eyes. Then I felt her pulse.

She was dead.

My head began to throb in waves and I felt sick. I sprinted through the house and out the front door, reaching for the gun in my shoulder holster. On the tiny front porch I stopped short.

The holster was empty. I groaned aloud and walked back into the house. On the way in I looked at the address. I picked up the phone in the living room and dialed the police.

A gruff, sleepy voice answered:

"Parkview Police."

"There's been a murder at 307 Melbourne. You better get out here."

The voice was suddenly wide-awake. "Who is this?"

I started to tell him and then changed my mind. "I'll be here when you get out," I said. "Probably."

I hung up and walked back into the kitchen, looking for my gun. I looked all over the kitchen and couldn't find it. I decided that Sherril had taken it with him. Then I saw the open kitchen window and the thought hit me that he might have thrown it out. I peered out and saw a tangled mass of shrubbery. There was no use even trying to find it at night.

And being found with a redhead who'd just been murdered was bad enough, but if she'd been murdered with my gun. . . . It didn't seem that cops would exactly see the picture my way. At any rate, sticking around seemed to be a good start toward spending the rest of the night in jail, while Sherril blew town for parts unknown.

If I was going, it was time to go. I stood for a moment undecided. Then I heard the wail of a siren far away in the night. It made up my mind. A moment later I was walking down the darkened street. I turned toward the lights of a neighborhood shopping district and ten minutes later I was on a bus toward town.

I didn't go to my apartment. I registered under a phony name for a room in a cheap hotel and got on the phone. When you make your living tailing husbands and tracing down runaway wives, you develop contacts at the airports and the train stations. I phoned my contacts and gave them descriptions of Sherril. Then I flopped down on the bed and lit a cigarette.

There didn't, at the moment, seem to be much more that I could do. I'd obviously been used as a fall guy by Sherril. He must have planned to murder his wife all the time, and just waiting until he could cash in on the marriage ties.

The motive? She'd sent him up for three years. That was the motive, and I'd been handy to frame. Whether he'd succeed would depend on whether the cops found my gun and whether I found Sherril. Until one or the other happened, there was nothing to do but wait.

It had been a hard night. My head throbbed and my bones ached and I felt a stubble on my chin and my nerves were tied up in knots. I ground out my cigarette and closed my eyes.

I opened them with a start.

The mink coat and the diamond ring!

I sat up suddenly. The coat and the ring were in my office, where they wouldn't hurt Dawn's act. "Tonight I'm poor but proud," she'd said, peeling off the coat and jerking off the ring. If the cops traced the gun, that's where the cops would be, right in my office. And a cop who doesn't believe that a private eye would murder a client for a diamond ring and a mink coat is a pretty rare cop indeed. . . .

I grabbed a taxi and headed for the financial district. On the way down I smoked three cigarettes. In front of the building, we stopped and I got out. I paid the driver and walked through the deserted lobby to the service elevator.

I rode myself up and walked down the dark hallway to my office. With relief I noticed that the light inside was out, and unlocked the door. I wouldn't have been surprised to find the whole homicide squad waiting for me. There was no one there. The mink coat was draped over a chair. I went to the safe and fumbled with the dial. I took out the ring and slipped it into my pocket and picked up the coat. Then I started for the door—and froze.

Far down the hall I heard the whine of the service elevator. It stopped and I heard voices. My heart sank miserably. I dodged back into the office and locked the door. I looked wildly around for a place to ditch the coat and ring. The office had never looked more barren. I thought of tossing them out the window and then decided that if they found them on the street, it would be worse.

Finally, I compromised by jamming the coat under my desk. I flipped on the desk light and spread papers around. I put an old report into my typewriter and began to pound the keys.

I heard the voices die down outside and the squeak of dry leather moving slowly up the hall. I continued to type. There was a whisper and then a knock.

"Who is it?" I asked, with what I hoped was the proper amount of surprise.

"Police," a voice answered.

I got up quickly and opened the door.

A tremendous plain clothesman with innocent blue eyes crammed himself into the office. A policeman in uniform followed. I'd never seen either of them before.

"Are you Michael Blair?" asked the giant.

"Yes, sir," I said. "What can I do for you?"

He swept the office with a glance. "Working late tonight, aren't you?"

"Yeah. Business is good."

He walked to my typewriter and read the report I'd been typing. I hoped it made sense. It seemed to satisfy him. He turned back to me.

"How long you been working here tonight?"

"I don't know. What time is it?"

"It's one A.M."

"I've been here all night."

"Maybe," said Blue-eyes. "We think different."

He began to walk around the office, lazily, but not missing anything. He moved back to the desk and I held my breath.

"Would it be too much to ask what you guys want?" I inquired, to divert his attention.

"Not at all," he said.

There was a long silence.

"What do you want?" I asked finally.

"There's been a little touch of murder going around. We seem to think you might know something about it."

"Sure," I said. "I probably murdered him. Who is it?"

"It's not a him. It's a her. And you probably did at that."

He kept moving closer to the desk, and I thought fast.

"You boys don't happen to have a search warrant, do you?"

He went on poking carelessly around in my waste-paper basket. Finally he looked up and smiled.

As a matter of fact, we do. Want to see it?"

I shook my head. "I'm not hiding anything. Tell me what you want and I'll help you look for it."

"I don't know what we want. We're just looking. Mind?"

"No," I said. "Go right ahead." I sat down behind my desk and felt the mink coat under my feet.

He walked to the safe and kicked it. "Do you mind opening this up?"

I looked at my fingernails. "I'll open it if you'll tell me what you're trying to prove."

The baby-blue eyes grew suddenly hard.

"You'll open it anyway. Or we'll cart it down to the station and have it opened, the hard way. And then you won't have a safe any more." He paused and smiled. "Not that you'll ever need one again, probably."

I didn't like the note of confidence in his voice, but I opened the safe. He looked through the papers inside.

"Nothing here on a Dawn Sherril, is there?"

"Who's that?"

"The girl you lent your gun to. She was carrying your name and address in her handbag. She shot herself through the heart and then opened the window and threw your gun out into the shrubbery."

"What gun?"

"The gun you have licensed in your name."

I took a deep breath. "Oh, yeah. I know. That gun. As a matter of fact, I just—"

"I know, buddy. You just sold it last week. Right?"

I nodded.

Blue-eyes laughed, without much mirth.

"I've been on the force seven years. Never found a murder gun yet that somebody hadn't just sold the week before. And they never seem to change the registration. Never even able to describe the man they say that they sold it to."

I sat down behind the desk again. The sweat was coming out on my forehead, and I wiped it with the back of my hand. I needed a drink, bad.

"I don't know what you're talking about."

Blue-eyes began to speak in a flat monotone, as if he were reciting.

"A girl was shot tonight. In her home. A girl named Dawn Sherril. She was shot with a gun we found in back in the shrubbery. The gun was registered to a private dick named Michael Blair. That's you. In her handbag was a name and address. The name was Michael Blair. That's you, remember—with this address.

"A neighborhood cab driver volunteered the information that he was called to Mrs. Sherril's home to pick her up. The cab company operator remembers the call. She says it was a woman's voice. The cab driver tells us that when he got to the address, it took ten minutes to get anybody to the door. The guy that came to the door needed a shave. You need a shave.

"The guy that came to the door had on a gray flannel suit. You have on a gray flannel suit. He had gray eyes. You have gray eyes. And the guy that came to the door said there was nobody home. But there was somebody home—Dawn Sherril. Only she didn't need a cab. She needed a hearse. Search him, Muller."

The cop moved over and began to frisk me, from the top down. When he got to my coat he opened it and grunted.

"You didn't sell the shoulder holster, did you?"

I shook my head. Things were looking bad, but there was no sense in admitting anything.

Muller emptied my pockets onto the desk and whistled.

"Look at that rock, boss."

The diamond shone like a living thing. The big detective picked it up carefully and looked inside.

"D. S. from H. M.," he read. "Dawn Sherril from . . . who's that cowboy joker she was supposed to be running around with? Howard Morrison."

He looked at me and smiled politely.

"You aren't too cagey, are you, Blair. I guess you got this at the hock shop?"

"Maybe."

He began to go through my desk drawers. "Let's see if you got anything else. Anybody who'd kill a dame for a diamond ring is pretty hard up."

He looked through the last drawer and started to turn away. Suddenly he wheeled and squatted, peering under the desk.

"Well, what do you know about this?" He pulled the coat out and held it at arm's length. "Yours, Blair?"

"Yeah," I said. "It's a disguise."

"Cute," said Blue-eyes. "Well, Muller, lip the cuffs on. We'll take him in and book him on suspicion of murder."

I figured the thing had finally gone far enough.

"Wait a minute," I said. "I'll tell you all I know about this case. I know

Dawn Sherril. She wanted me to pass as the guy she was going to marry, because her husband was due to fly in this evening—and she wanted a divorce to marry this Morrison joker. But she didn't want Morrison to know she'd been a blackmailer. Also, she didn't want Sherril to know she was in the chips, so she left her ring and coat here. The act seemed to work okay.

"Sherril wanted five hundred for giving her a divorce—but when he got it he slugged me, took my gun, and shot his wife. When I woke up, she was dead. I called the police. When I found out my gun was gone, I got scared, I guess. Also I wanted to find Sherril, and I figured you guys would slow me up. So I shoved off. I've got my contacts at the airport and train station looking for him now."

Blue-eyes smiled sweetly.

"What an imagination! The one-man police force out to trap a murderer and make the cops look silly. Just like in the detective stories. It's a great tale, Blair, but it's no soap. I don't believe you. I think things are tough in your racket, I think you knew this dame had a ring and a mink coat, I think you murdered her, got scared, tossed your gun away, called the police for an alibi in case we found the gun, and left. That's what I think."

"Look," I said. "At least check on Sherril. He came in on flight #307 from New York this afternoon—a big blond guy, flashy dresser, red tie, green suit."

The detective picked up my phone. He dialed Municipal Airport.

"Give me the airlines dispatcher," he said. There was a long wait. "This is Peterson, of the homicide squad," he said finally. "Find out if you had a passenger named Sherril on your evening flight from New York." There was a pause. "Okay," he said. "Thank you."

He turned back to me.

"No such name on the passenger list," he said. "Surprised?"

My heart sank. "Like I said, this guy is a convicted extortionist," I told him. "Those people don't use their right names. He's probably on parole and not supposed to leave New York."

"Yes," said Blue-eyes tolerantly. "Yes, indeed. Put the cuffs on him, Muller."

A picture flashed across my mind—a picture of myself languishing in a cell while the newspapers and a D.A. hungry for convictions built up a case against me, and a guy named Sherril bought himself an airtight alibi to prove that he'd never been out of the State of New York. I didn't like the picture—I didn't like it at all.

Muller was little for a cop. Little, but stocky, built like a barrel, with nothing to grab. I let him get close to me and then threw my arms about his neck and swung him around. He cursed and tried to jerk away. Blue-eyes whipped out a gun and lunged across the office. I hung on to the cop and backed toward the door.

When I felt the knob in the small of my back, I shoved the cop hard and he reeled toward the detective. I dodged through the door and slammed it. A shot roared from inside the office and a slug ricocheted down the hallway. I was three quarters of the way down the corridor when they untangled themselves and got to the door.

Another shot sang past my head and then I was in the elevator, slamming the gate. I pushed the button marked *garage* and cursed as the elevator whined slowly into motion. I heard Blue-eyes above me. A deafening report sounded in the shaft. A slug clanged on the roof of the elevator, and I ducked instinctively. I heard the sound of feet disappearing down the hallway as the two of them raced for the stairs.

It was the longest elevator ride I had ever taken. It seemed as if two hours passed before I finally came to the garage. I yanked open the gate and walked quickly through the empty spaces. Then I was out in the night. Across the street was a squad car, with the lights on and a bulky figure slouched over the wheel. I turned south, away from the car, and forced myself to saunter instead of run. At the first corner I turned west, and at the next I turned south again. A siren began to moan in the night and grew louder and louder, and then was past, a block away. It died away in the distance, and I flagged a cab. . . .

Chapter 3

DON'T TANK ME

THE CABBIE DROVE ME uptown and let me off at a neighborhood bar. I went in and ordered a shot of bourbon and a bottle of beer. While I was waiting, I phoned the airport and the train station. Neither of my contacts had seen Sherril, but the man at the airport said that the place was crawling with cops, and wanted to know if they were looking for him too. I said no, they were looking for a private eye named Blair, and hung up.

I went back to the bar and downed the shot. It saved my life. My nerves began to unknot and my head began to clear. I ordered another shot and started to think.

The fact that Sherril hadn't showed at the airport or the train station didn't indicate that he was still in town. He might have taken a bus, or more likely, decided to hitchhike to another town and take a plane to New York from there. I wondered if there were any way to get his address in New York. Dawn might have known it. Dawn might have told some friend where her husband lived. The trouble was that I only knew one friend of Dawn's— Howard Morrison—and she'd hardly have told him her husband's address.

Of course, there was Sugar. She wasn't exactly a friend of Dawn's, but they'd apparently been chummy once. The possibility that she'd know where Sherril lived in New York was a pretty slim one, but you have to start somewhere. I finished my second shot and paid the barkeep.

The Hi Hat Club was crowded, even though it was near closing time. I asked the headwaiter for Sugar. He gave me a cold stare and told me that she was in her dressing room and it was off-limits. I slipped him a fin. He decided that it was on-limits to friends of Sugar. I went back and knocked.

There was a long wait. Then the door opened and Sugar stood there in what might have passed for a negligee. She had a smile on her lips. When she saw who it was, her face fell.

"What do you want?" she asked icily.

I slid past her like a magazine salesman. "Just wanted to talk to you, Sugar."

She shrugged and pointed to a chaise lounge. "Make it short. I'm tired."

"I've got news for you," I said. "Good news for you."

She sat at her dressing table and began making up her face. "Yeah? I can hardly wait. Have you decided to take me out to a movie next month?"

"Dawn's been murdered."

I watched her face in the mirror. She was dabbing lipstick on her lower lip. Her face never changed and her hand never wavered.

"Really? Lynched?"

"I'm serious. She was shot tonight, just after she left here."

Sugar swung around on her stool. "By whom?"

"According to the police, me. Actually, her husband."

"You mean you're denying it? I'd be proud." She turned back to her mirror.

I looked at the back of my hands. "I'm in a bad spot, Sugar. Her husband got away. Unless I can find him they'll hang it on me."

"You're breaking my heart. What do you want me to do?"

"I thought Dawn might have told you where he lived in New York, when you two were so chummy."

"We two were never so chummy, as you put it. I've never seen her husband, and I don't know his address."

"You saw him tonight?"

"What do you mean?"

"He was the big blond guy sitting at our table."

She shot me a startled glance in the mirror. "That was her husband?"

I nodded. She started to say something and then changed her mind. "I don't know his address. Sorry."

I walked over to her and looked down at her.

"What were you going to say?"

She dropped her eyes. "Nothing."

I took a deep breath. "Look, Sugar. I'm in a hole. If you know anything about this thing, for Pete's sake, tell me about it."

"I don't know anything about it. Now I'd appreciate it if you'd get out and leave me alone."

"Something tells me, sister, that you know more than you're telling. I'm staying here until I find out what it is."

She looked up and her eyes were blazing. "I'll call the bouncer and he'll toss you out. Or else turn you over to the cops."

Something told me that she was waiting for a date and that she didn't want me around when he showed up. I decided to bluff it out.

"I don't think you'll call the bouncer. I'm staying."

She looked at me thoughtfully. "You're right, Mike. You're a stinker, but I'm not turning you in. Your boy Sherril is here now. Or he was ten minutes ago."

"What? He came back *here*?"

"He turned up a couple of hours ago. Tried to make a date with me. I turned him down and the last I saw of him he was sitting in the bar drowning his sorrows."

"Thanks, honey," I said. "Thanks a lot."

I was halfway to the door when it opened slowly. Howard Morrison stood there with a grin on his face. When he saw me, the grin faded. I brushed past him and out onto the dance floor. I walked swiftly across to the bar.

The bar was a modern one, slick, chromium plated, dark in spite of the violet fluorescent lighting behind the mirrors. It was still crowded.

At one end sat Sherril, alone, staring into his drink. I walked over and stood behind him in the crowd.

"We meet again," I said.

He turned slowly. His eyes were bleary and a shadow of fear crossed them when he saw me.

"Well," he said. "Dawn's dream man. What are you doing here? I thought you'd be busy."

"Where? In jail?"

He looked at me blankly.

"Come on," I said. "You and I are going to take a little trip to the station house."

He rose unsteadily. "You really have a taste for punishment, haven't you?" He cocked his fist and sighted at my chin, striking out blindly. I moved my head. I slapped him three times, hard, and he fell back against the bar, rubbing his jaw. I saw the bartender moving down with a dangerous look in his eyes.

"It's okay, buddy," I told him. "My friend's just a little tanked, that's all."

"You boys fight somewhere else," said the barkeep. "This is a respectable house."

"You heard what the man said," I told Sherril. I took him by the arm and shoved him to the door. "Come with me. I'll take care of you." I steered him past the doorman and pushed him into a cab.

"Drive around," I said to the driver. Then I shut the glass partition and turned to Sherril.

"Okay, Sherril," I said. "I'm taking you down to the station. First I want to talk to you."

He shook his head. "Nobody saw me slug you. You'll never prove a thing."

"I've been slugged before. But I never woke up and found my client murdered before. And I don't like the experience."

Some of the glaze left his eyes. "Murdered? What client? What are you, a lawyer? What are you talking about, anyway?"

"I'm a private detective. Your wife was my client. And after you slugged me you shot her—with my gun. Remember?"

"Dawn was shot?"

"Yeah. Surprised? You have my sympathy. It must be a terrific shock."

He was sober now, and I watched him carefully.

"Dawn shot," he repeated slowly. "Dawn shot." He shook his head. "And she still owed me three hundred dollars."

"You know," I said, "that's one of the things you're going to tell me. Why you murdered her before you got the whole five hundred, and why you came back to the Hi Hat Club—the one place the cops would be looking for you if they'd believed me."

"I didn't shoot her."

"You don't say."

"When I left Dawn's place, I came back and tried to get a date with that singer. She wouldn't go out with me. I've been in the bar ever since."

Somehow, in spite of myself, I began to believe him. It was illogical to think that somebody else might have done the job—nobody else would have had the motive. Just the same, Sherril hadn't left town, and if he'd planned to murder Dawn, he'd have been better off to wait until she'd had her divorce.

The germ of an idea entered my head, and the rusty wheels in my brain began to turn. It seemed incredible, but . . .

"All right. We'll say you left the place after you hit me. Did you see Dawn before you left?"

"No. She was in the kitchen."

Now for the sixty-four-dollar question.

"Did you call a cab?"

"No. I just left, quiet-like. I was sick of the whole set-up. I didn't want her yelling at me for hitting her boy friend. And speaking of hitting her boy friend, I've had about enough of this Sherlock Holmes stuff, and—"

I could sense from the set of his shoulders that I was about to be slugged again. This time he was sober, and it was no place for a brotherly tap. I needed time to think his story over, and I knew that if I lost him again, he'd leave town. I let him have it with everything I had. My fist crashed into his jaw. He groaned once and slumped to the floor of the cab. I glanced at the driver. He was busy weaving through the traffic. I slid the glass aside.

"Take us back to the Hi Hat Club."

Chapter 4

STRONG, SILENT SLAYER

WE DROVE UP in front of the nightclub. The doorman stepped up to the cab. "My friend passed out," I said. "Forgot his coat inside. I'd like to go back inside and get it."

I went through the revolving door, glanced at a broad back in the blue uniform of the Parkview Police, and turned right around and back out into the night. Sweat broke out on my brow and I took out a handkerchief.

"Say," I told the doorman, "I don't like to go through the dining room needing a shave. My buddy left his coat in one of the dressing rooms back stage. You got a back entrance?"

The doorman peered at me suspiciously and then jerked his thumb toward an alley.

This time I was more careful and luckier. I sneaked through the side door and found myself opposite Sugar's dressing room. I crept to the door and stooped to tie my shoe, with my ear a half inch from the crack.

It was quiet inside. I stood up and began to turn the doorknob slowly. I pushed the door open with my shoulder, a fraction of an inch at a time. Then I put my head to the crack.

The lights inside were lowered. On the couch were Sugar and Howard Morrison. They seemed to be getting along well together.

I opened the door and cleared my throat. "Sorry to break this up, but I'd like a few words with you, Morrison."

Morrison jumped up and stepped toward me.

"Who the hell are you? What are you doing here?" He had, I was glad to note, a genuine Texas drawl, even in real life. Sugar got up slowly, a dangerous look in her eyes.

"You know me, Morrison. I'm the guy you just got through trying to frame for murder."

"Blair," said Sugar. "If you aren't out of here in two minutes I'm calling the police."

"I'll call the police myself. First your cowboy and myself are going to have a little talk."

Morrison shrugged. "Let him have his fun, Sugar." He sat down on the couch.

"Morrison, I'm going to tell you what you did tonight. If I'm wrong, correct me. And when we get through our talk, I'm telling it to the cops."

He laughed. "Go on, you interest me. But don't take long. I'm busy."

"I know what you mean. All good clean fun, but no strings attached. Right?"

"I don't know what you're talking about."

"Yes you do. A wife in the background might hurt your box office appeal. Strong, silent type. A cowboy star. Never even kisses the heroine—or the kids up front start booing. Getting married wouldn't be good. But it would be better than a lot of bad publicity, just the same. If you get bad publicity, Momma won't let Junior go to the Saturday matinee. Right?"

"Look, buddy, I haven't got all night to listen to you rave."

I stepped toward him.

"You'll listen to me rave just as long as I want you to. See? Getting married would be bad, but running around with a married woman would be worse, if there was a scandal. Just the same, the clean-cut cowboy star picked Dawn Sherril."

I paused and lit a cigarette.

"The trouble was, Dawn has been brought up wrong. When you decided you were through with her, she wouldn't go away. She'd been tied up in a blackmail racket before, so what's she do? She says: 'Marry me, or I'll spread your name over every paper in the country.' Right?"

Morrison got up suddenly. His face was blazing. "Shut up. I'm not sitting here listening to this stuff any longer."

I grabbed his coat and shoved. He sat down on the couch.

"You decided to get at the source of your trouble by killing Dawn. But you knew that if she was found murdered, you'd be involved. Unless, of course, there was somebody else on the scene with a motive for murdering her. You had to work a frameup. How?"

I took a drag on the cigarette.

"You knew she was married. Her husband might be a good guy to frame. But you didn't know where he was. So what did you do? You advertised for him."

Morrison relaxed and shook his head. "Sugar," he said. "This guy's nuts. Plain nuts."

"You advertised for him," I repeated, "the best way you could have. You sent in an item to a gossip columnist. The item didn't mention you—just Dawn. It worked. Her husband showed up. When you saw us tonight, you knew one of the men with Dawn was her husband. You hadn't figured on there being a third party.

"After we left here, you asked Sugar who the men with Dawn were. She didn't know Sherril, but she knew me. She told you I was a private detective, but that didn't mean anything. You decided to go to Dawn's house and wait until I left."

I turned to Sugar. "He did ask you who we were, didn't he, Sugar?"

She shot a startled glance at Morrison. She shook her head slightly.

"And he did leave for a while, after we left, didn't he?"

Sugar walked to her dressing table. She ran her fingers through her hair nervously. "I don't know. I don't know. Why don't you leave him alone?"

I turned back to Morrison.

"When you got to Dawn's house, you sneaked up to the window. You watched for a long while, waiting for me to go. You had a gun. I imagine you intended to make it look like a double suicide, and kill both Dawn and Sherril. But for some reason, things didn't work out right. You saw me bring Sherril a drink, and tell him to get out, and then you saw him slug me. He left after that. You stood there, thinking it over, and while you did, Dawn came out of the kitchen.

"She saw me lying there, went to the window, and looked out. She didn't call after Sherril—she didn't want him back. As far as my getting slugged, that was none of her business—that's one of the things a private eye gets paid for. She didn't want Sherril back, so she locked the door. That's important, Morrison. She locked the door, went to the phone and called a cab to take her back here.

"Dawn was afraid of leaving you with Sugar for too long, and I can see why. Then she went to put the ice tray away."

Morrison was fidgeting now, and there were beads of sweat on his upper lip.

"Meanwhile, you were watching. Suddenly it hit you. You were better off than if I'd left and Sherril had stayed. There I was, out like a light, and Dawn was out of the room. Maybe I had a gun—Sugar had said I was a private detective. You went in. You searched me. I had a gun. Perfect. I was suitable for framing. So you shot Dawn and left."

Morrison laughed nervously. "Very clever. It just doesn't hold water, that's all. The only reason I left here was to go see myself in a neighborhood theater."

"What theater?"

He hesitated. "I don't remember. What's the difference. Your whole story's ridiculous. Now that we've—"

"Ridiculous? I don't think so. Not at all. How'd the murderer get in? Dawn would have locked the door. She didn't want her husband to come back. The murderer got in because he had a key. Who had a key? You had a key, Morrison, because you were paying the rent." I hoped my guess was right. "Guys who pay the rent always have keys."

"You're nuts." Morrison lit a cigarette. His hand trembled. Sugar looked at him cautiously.

"Maybe. But there's a cop out here, probably looking for me. I'm telling him what I just told you, and we'll see if he thinks I'm nuts."

I turned my back and walked to the door. I'd made plenty of mistakes during the day, but that was the biggest. Almost before I heard Sugar's scream, I realized what I'd forgotten: Morrison must have taken a gun of his own with him when he went to Dawn's. He still had it.

Sugar yelled: "Mike!" The gun roared behind me, and a crashing blow on my left shoulder sent me rolling across the dressing room. I lay there a moment, stunned, trying to see through a red haze. Far in the distance I could hear Sugar's voice.

"You've killed him. You've killed him, and you killed Dawn!"

"Shut up! When the cops get here, you're telling them it was self-defense. Understand?"

"You killed him. You killed him."

The red fog in front of my eyes lifted and I saw Morrison take Sugar by the shoulders and shake her.

"Calm down! Get hold of yourself! He attacked me and I had to shoot him. Understand?"

I disagreed, but attacking him seemed like a good idea. My left arm was beginning to feel as if it had been cut off at the shoulder, but everything else seemed as if it would work. I set myself and waited until Morrison let go of Sugar. Then I lunged across the room, aiming for his knees.

It was a beautiful tackle for a guy my age. Morrison crashed to the floor. His gun dropped and slid under the couch. I hung on to both of his legs with my good arm.

"Sugar," I grunted. "Get the cops, and hurry."

Morrison was powerful and had two arms that worked. I heard the door open and heard Sugar's high-heeled shoes tapping down the passageway. Then a smashing blow on the side of my head brought back the red mist. Dimly I remember holding on to a pair of squirming legs, and being dragged across the floor as if I was a limp old rag doll, toward the couch.

Then it seemed as if the roof fell in on my left shoulder. Just before the darkness engulfed me I heard a click, the click of a revolver being cocked. . . .

I looked up at the detective with the blue eyes. I was on the couch and the dressing room was crowded. I tried to sit up, and Blue-eyes put a huge hand on my chest.

"Look," I said. "Find Morrison. He's the guy you're looking for."

He smiled.

"Morrison's in the city jail. He's charged with one murder, and if it hadn't been for a cop named Shaughnessy and a girl named Sugar, we'd be charging him with two."

"Where are they?"

"Right here," said a voice with a pleasant Irish brogue. A red, beefy face looked down at me, and next to it floated a face like an angel's, a face with a pair of smoky gray eyes.

I reached into my pocket. "I don't know how to thank you, Shaughnessy, but here's a cigar, anyway."

I turned my head and looked at Sugar Lynn.

Sugar, I decided, I would thank later.

Safe as Any Sap

WILLIAM TENN

M E, I'D JUST as well have stayed out of the whole thing. When they made me a political columnist, I kissed the boys on the police beat good-bye, chucked the city editor under the chin and hoped he'd still be this side of the green grass the day they got the city washed clean of the Prohibition-style gangs the previous, corrupt administration had left behind.

I was through with corpses and cops, with bodies that hadn't quite made it to the morgue in one hunk, and with hoods who weren't quite complete in the head. I was through with murder.

I thought.

Don't blame me: a newly married guy likes to forget his past. He forgets his past can have a wonderful memory of its own.

"You're just being self-conscious, Frank," Louise laughed at me. "Nobody remembers Carlyle, the crime reporter, anymore. You've stopped drinking, you wear your pants with a noticeable crease and you have a shiny, brand-new wife. What's wrong in taking me to an old haunt like the Red Devil, even if it is a dive? I want to see that hatcheck girl you used to date."

"Only saw Ginnie when her boyfriend was patrolling his beat, just helped fill in her spare time. She was an occasionally valuable source of tips on this and that. No more."

Louise curled a mischievous grin out of sight. "No more?"

"That's what I said. Besides Regg makes the Red Devil his squirming ground. And he feels sorta unhappy over the way I suggested his name in the Daniels killing."

"That was over a month ago, before you'd started your column—why it was even before we were married. And we needn't get a table; we can just sit at the bar and peek inside."

So we went and just sat at the bar and peeked inside.

Louise leaned over and whispered, "That dumpy little brunette who took our coats—was *she* Ginnie?"

"No," I answered over my soda water. I still felt uncomfortable at the way the bartender was staring at me and shaking his head. He had welcomed me effusively and set out my regular—gin with just a dash of lemon. When I had ordered soda water instead, his face dropped like a man hearing a singing commercial in a church. "No, Ginnie is as blond as you. But not one-third as pretty," I added hastily. "She takes over for the heavy-spenders' part of the evening. That's her, now."

As the girl in the short satin skirt replaced her friend in the ornate niche of the hatcheck concession, Louise slipped off her red stool and moved toward her. I followed, glad to get away from the transparent soda water which only looked like gin. Behind us, people danced under bad lights to choppy music.

A large, impeccably dressed man detached himself from the group of large and small impeccably dressed men with whom he had been lounging near the entrance. He cut ahead of Louise to the checking counter. My wife stopped and waited patiently as he leaned over the counter, speaking to Ginnie in a rapid undertone.

I stopped too. My fingers curved into fists. I recognized that shiny bald head, that ugly face—loose and hard at the same time—leering out over the stiff white lawn of shirt-front. Mumbles Regg—and all his Regglets!

The sensible thing to do was to pluck Louise's sleeve and move back quietly to the bar. But I had to see how Ginnie fitted into Regg's affairs. I waited.

She evidently didn't. Fit into Regg's affairs, that is. She answered his mumbling suggestion with a slight shudder and a disgusted exclamation. She retreated from the counter to the patiently hanging rows of hats and coats.

Regg reached out, seized her arm and pulled her back to him. I heard my wife gasp as Ginnie's lipsticked mouth contorted in pain. Regg mumbled again, more insistently, more angrily. Ginnie was half-twisted on her side as he pulled her roughly against the hatcheck counter.

There were lots of people watching, lots of big, broad-shouldered men bigger than me, bigger even than Mumbles. But most of them knew the gangster's reputation. None of them seemed willing to risk their tuxedos.

So up stepped little Frankie.

I grabbed Mumbles's shoulder, feeling uncomfortably like a private who has volunteered to draw the enemy's fire—and is immediately astonished at the too-brave words he has heard issue from his own big mouth. I swung the large man around and down, so that I could get at him. Then I pumped my fists, fast, once solidly at the chest, once in solid cracking connection with his jaw.

His back slammed against the opposite wall.

I came up quickly to finish the job, reassured by the stupid daze in his eyes. Then I came to a halt. I took a long deep breath as the two women sounded off behind me.

"Oh, Frank!"

"Be careful!"

The bunch of darkly dressed men who had been lounging around the entrance were now lounging around me. Only, I knew they weren't lounging. They had quickly formed a tight little circle, closing me off from Regg. Maybe even from life; I didn't know.

Every one of the men, tall or short, thin or stout, had the same consciously vacant expression as they stared easily at me. Every one of them had a right hand inside a left breast pocket. And every breast pocket had a bulge.

I straightened my hands and rubbed the pain off my knuckles as Regg shook himself free of the wall. I had no plans at the moment, beyond standing still—very, very still.

Anyone who thinks I should have done something else, that those highly experienced assassins might have hesitated to shoot me in front of so many witnesses, has never been to the Red Devil, that's all. Though come to think of it, anyone who has never been inside the Red Devil is smart enough for all normal purposes. . . .

The gangster had recognized me. "Little Frankie Carlyle," he whispered, "the nosiest newshound of them all! Still nosy, Frankie? Don't you know a married guy shouldn't be so nosy?"

Perspiration began to roll down my forehead, piled up against my eyelids. It trickled past my eyes, making me blink.

"I thought you were going to settle down now, Frankie, and concentrate on Washington. I thought you weren't going to make me mad at you any more, like you did in the Daniels killing. I still haven't forgiven you for saying around that I carved Steve Daniels up and dumped him into that barrel of concrete. Steve Daniels was my friend, Frankie. And now you hurt my feelings again."

He grinned at me out of his terribly marked face. I stood there and sweated, trying not to hear his almost inaudible voice. I looked at the streak of powder on the top of his bald head. Around me, his friends watched imperturbably.

The mocking whisper flowed on, "Stand still, Frankie—I'm going to hit you."

I couldn't have moved right then if anyone had jabbed a nail into me. I saw his right hand flailing up; I heard Louise plunge forward and scream, "No! Don't!" I wondered vaguely why he didn't use a better grade of powder on his head to cover the shine, the stuff he had on hardly stuck at all

Then his open palm crashed into my mouth and my teeth seemed to bend. I staggered back, through the opening ring of gangsters. I crashed into Louise and carried her back with me.

After a while, I got to my feet and helped Louise up. I noticed there was blood going down my white dickey.

"That's all for now, little man." Mumbles' voice seemed to be floating against the brightly lit ceiling. He laughed. "Give my regards to the missus. I'll be seeing you." He turned and moved toward the bar, his hired hands trailing compactly.

Suddenly I felt there wasn't anything more important than killing him right there and then. The night club seemed to have dissolved away, leaving only Mumbles Regg and myself. Between us there was no empty space—the need for murder filled it completely. I surged forward.

Ginnie had slipped out of the concession booth. She was holding my right arm; my wife tugged at my left. Both of them were babbling incoherently, pleading with me to forget it, to keep still, to sit down. I saw their begging, beautiful faces and grew quiet. I allowed them to lead me to a chair in the shadows and seat me there.

"His lip—oh, his lip!" Ginnie cried. "Wait a minute, I'll be right back."

She slipped off, came back with a couple of gauze pads soaked in ice-water. Louise took one from her and applied it to my mouth with a touch of the expert that surprised me.

"I had two kid brothers who were always in trouble, darling," she reminded me. "I'm accustomed to this sort of thing."

"I'm sorry this had to happen, Mrs. Carlyle," Ginnie broke in. "Mumbles has been bothering me for a week. If Tony heard about it, he'd run amuck and get kicked off the police force. We're going to be married Tuesday."

"Congratulations." My wife smiled at her. "We'll come and dance at your wedding. Meanwhile, do you think you could get us out of here?"

Ginnie nodded and returned in a moment with our wraps. Despite the smart in my mouth and the pain in my soul, I was proud of Louise for knowing and remembering to tip Ginnie lavishly. We moved out, water seeping down my chin from the gauze pad. I felt the bump beginning on my cut lip.

In the taxi, my humiliation forced me into a corner. Louise chattered as if we had just emerged from a bridge party.

"So that was Ginnie. Nice girl. Only she isn't a real blonde, Frank. She bleaches her hair."

I grinned, though the effort agonized my lip. "Here, pussy. Pretty pussy," I said.

"I'm *not* being catty, darling. She does bleach her hair—I can tell. With her coloring, she'd make a very beautiful brunette; I think she's foolish."

"Tony Pirotti doesn't think so."

"She said he's a cop."

"That's right. He's studying to be a detective. His beat is near the Red Devil. If he knew Mumbles had laid his paws on Ginnie, Regg would be a brand-new corpse by tomorrow morning. Which is more than I can say for my capabilities," I added morosely.

Louise protested, told me very vividly that I was being silly. I leaned back against the seat as the streetlights whipped past the cab and enjoyed her voice.

All very well for Louise to say I was silly. I knew Regg. He wouldn't let the matter drop. And, neither could I. . . .

Tony Pirotti had discovered Steve Daniels's shoe sticking out of a barrel of concrete near the new south highway that was under construction a month ago. Since I was a friend of Ginnie's, Tony let me have a beat on the killing, and I was the first reporter to get to the morgue and the only one to see the body.

Everyone knew who had done the job, or at least ordered it, but there was no proof. Daniels had been Regg's chief lieutenant, handling the narcotics end of his vice empire. He had altered a few entries in the books, held back a few receipts. He had thought he was one clever fellow. He wasn't.

I couldn't say anything direct, of course, but with the help of the few facts Pirotti and some other policemen dug up, I pounded at Regg day after day with insinuation, unspoken accusation and involved hinting. There was investigation after publicized investigation, but nothing was found that could be pushed at a jury successfully.

The matter was dropped. For my efforts, I earned Regg's personal interest in my welfare and a crack at a column. Maybe I also earned Louise that way; I don't know.

But when I thought of Regg slapping me in front of my wife, of the personal museum he was reputed to keep containing souvenirs of all his killings—I knew I would have to find some way of settling the matter. Either that, or he'd come calling on me.

"There's one thing I can't understand," Louise marveled as the hotel elevator shot us up to our room. "Why nobody—*nobody*—stepped forward to lift a finger to help you or Ginnie. Everyone must have known that all those men were carrying guns."

"Everyone also knew that any interference would earn them a short life, but not a merry one." I unlocked the door. Louise rustled in, her head half-turned to me. "The Red Devil is that sort of place. A man was kicked to death in the alley outside last year."

"Then that's why you didn't want to take me. I thought it was because you were afraid of my meeting Ginnie. Tell me, if it's as bad as you say, how does a girl like Ginnie come to work there?" She moved into the other room.

I picked up the ringing telephone. "Ginnie can usually take care of herself," I called after her. "Besides, it pays well, she and Tony have a sizable nest-egg by now. He wanted her to quit right away, but she held out until after the wedding. Hello," to the phone. "Mr. Carlyle speaking."

"Mr. Carlyle," the clerk's voice said, "A Mr. Harlow Dexter to see you about an item for your column. Shall I send him up?"

"Sure, send him up." I dropped the telephone and went over to a mirror. I couldn't remember the guy, but since I'd been doing a political column, I'd become accustomed to people with first names like Harlow instead of Joe or Louie or Mac.

My upper lip was doing nicely, thank you. I felt it tenderly and wondered what it was about a guy getting away with a sock at you that made you burn.

I called into the other room. "Somebody by the name of Harlow Dexter coming up to see me about my column, honey."

"Don't stay up too long with him." She closed the door; I went to see him in.

There was something very familiar about him that I could not place. Mr. Harlow Dexter did not look like his name. He wore one of those light hats with a colored bandanna band that were already going out of general style.

He was dressed in light sport clothes and perforated shoes, like a movie-styled Californian. But his hard face was not tanned. It was white, very white.

"Seat?" I asked. "Sorry I can't offer you a drink; my wife's put her wedgie down as far as alcohol is concerned."

He nodded, looked around slowly and sat down with his hat on. I started to sit on a chair, wishing that I could remember what he reminded me of, when my legs got stiff and my knees went weak. I completed the motion and sat down very carefully.

This Harlow Dexter was carrying a gun. It was a sizable weapon—a .38 or .45—from the looks of the bulge in his coat pocket. He must be a Western hood at that: no one in this town let his criminal intention be that obvious. But he couldn't be a Regg yegg. Regg used much smoother characters. And their eyes were always straight and deadly, not wild and shifting like this boy's.

I leaned back in the chair and lit a cigarette. After I'd dropped the match in the ash stand beside me, I kept my hand there idly. The ash stand had a long metal base, it would make a useful weapon if necessary.

I hoped it wouldn't come to a scuffle. This man was about my height, but he had broad and terrifically powerful shoulders. Besides, he had a gun. And after what had happened tonight, I wasn't sure of anything, including myself.

He stopped looking around the room and stared over my shoulder. I tried desperately to catch whatever it was that was teasing my memory.

"Got your name from the hatcheck girl," he said suddenly in a rather high voice, still staring over my shoulder. "Saw the fight, saw what you took. Heard you and Regg. That right about you believing Regg killed Daniels?"

"Now, Mr. Dexter," I expostulated, getting a good grip on the ash stand handle. "I don't want to discuss the matter. I understood you had some political item, something I could use in my—"

"Drop that!" he screamed, tearing the gun out of his pocket. It was a .38 caliber revolver with a sawed-off barrel. I took my hand off the ashstand and placed it gently on the arm of my chair. "Don't try anything! Name ain't really Dexter. Name's Daniels, Harry Daniels."

Daniels! That was what my mind had been fumbling at: the resemblance between this wild-eyed person and the body in the morgue.

"I'm Steve Daniels's kid brother. I want to find out things. True Regg put the finger on him? True he used a knife on him first?" The voice was mad and wavering. Even the gun wobbled as it pointed at me. Again I debated the value of a fast rush, again decided against it. Those powerful shoulders were one factor; the knowledge that I was dealing with an extremely off-base mind was another. "Speak up, damn you! Don't care how scared you are of Regg!"

"Who's afraid of Regg?" I blustered. "It's common gossip that he killed your brother, though I wouldn't advise you personally—"

"That's all. Save the rest." Daniels rose and backed to the door, the gun wavering back and forth at me. "Sit easy for a while. Don't move."

He reached behind him with his free hand and turned the doorknob. Then he opened the door and moved out backwards. The moment the door slammed, I heard his feet running down the stairs.

I walked unsteadily to the telephone. Louise piled out of the other room and into my arms.

"I heard it all, Frank, I heard it all," she cried. "That lunatic! I didn't know what to do—afraid if I made a noise he'd shoot. What are you doing, having him stopped downstairs?"

I soothed her shoulder and kissed her. After that, we both felt better. "No sense in stopping him. He'll be out of the lobby in a few seconds. Besides, I'm not so sure I don't like the idea of that character trailing Mumbles. It's sort of poetic justice to have him wind Regg up. Probably will work the other way, though."

"Room service," I said into the phone. "Send up a crock of gin—no, better make that rye. A quart of rye. Don't bother about ice or glasses, just hurry. Room 311."

"Frank, do you think that's necessary? After all—"

"Yes, honey, I think it's necessary," I told her firmly. "There are times when a man most definitely needs a drink. Now let me think this thing out."

"I wish I'd never insisted we go to that nasty place. Frank, you don't have to justify yourself in my eyes. I know you aren't afraid of Regg. Honestly, I want you to stay out of trouble. I don't care who hits you or what you do, I love you as is."

"Sure, honey. Sure."

After I'd tipped the bellboy, I leaned against the wall and took a long swig out of the bottle. Three weeks since I'd tasted the stuff; it felt unusually strong.

So my wife was sweet, loyal, and considerate. Fine. I didn't have to justify myself in her eyes. But what about my own? I'd never just stood and taken anything before.

And who knew what a woman really thought of a man who practically curtsied to the guy who'd socked him, and who allowed himself to be toddled away without so much as raising a finger?

I tilted the bottle and swallowed the fire.

It was no good consoling myself with the thought that his bodyguard would have let daylight through in a dozen different directions if I'd tried to stop him, even tried to counter the blow. On that basis, any time Mumbles and I caromed off each other, I was to make like a punching bag. The idea somehow lacked zest.

I couldn't avoid him. He'd come looking for me—he'd said so. Mumbles might be interested in acquiring some part of my anatomy for his vaunted museum. They say he began carrying the cartridge that killed Little Ruby Green as a watchfob about a month after the D.A. lost interest in the case. There wasn't much danger then that he'd be picked up for questioning. Even if the police became suddenly inquisitive, he could always slip the gadget to one of his bully-boys.

I paused in the middle of a gurgle and lowered the bottle. Would it work? Why not? Only I needed a gimmick, a lever. Ginnie! I could do it that way!

Very regretfully, I deposited the rye on a table and got started. I looked at my wristwatch in the cab; Ginnie wouldn't be going off duty for two hours. Perfect.

I paid the cab driver about a block away from the Red Devil. Then I wedged into a drugstore telephone booth and called the nightclub, asked for Ginnie.

Yes, she could get relieved for ten minutes. What was it all about? Oh, all right, then, she wouldn't tell anybody; she'd be right over.

She came trotting into the drugstore, an old gabardine coat thrown over her back satin costume, her eyes small with anxiety. I gave her the pitch, assured her it would work.

"Think you can make up to Mumbles convincingly enough in a half hour or so?"

"Ye-es. The way he's been chasing me. But Frank—Mr. Carlyle, I mean—are you sure Tony won't get into any trouble? False arrest would be very bad for him. And if you haven't found out anything, he may have to arrest you on complaint of Mumbles. Besides, it's so dangerous."

"Don't worry. Just call Tony after Mumbles leaves. I hope you can get him. Give me the key to your place. It isn't far, is it?"

She fumbled in her purse. Her hair *was* dark at the roots. "No. About three blocks east. Same section, but not so ritzy. Nine seventy-two, eighth. After Mumbles gets interested, I tell him to go to my room and wait for me? Right?"

"Check. Say the door's unlocked. You always keep it unlocked."

"Please be careful," she called after me. "I wouldn't want Mrs. Carlyle to think I was responsible for anything."

Her room wasn't ritzy. It was drab as a dirty apron. Its only advantage was that it was close to the two most important things in Ginnie's life: her job at the Red Devil and Tony Pirotti's beat.

I let myself in, 123e sure the door was unlocked behind me and took the place in. Studio couch, two chairs, a dresser, and a gas range. Bathroom in the hall. Cheap store-bought cedar closets.

I crossed to the window as I heard the motor of a powerful car stop in the street. Mumbles Regg got out, whispered something to his friends inside.

This was faster work than I'd expected. But Ginnie was cuddlesome when she wanted to be. And I'd walked over: that had taken some time.

Mumbles put an additional fold into his gleaming white silk scarf and started for the street door. My knees felt as if they were going to fold any minute now. I licked the sore cut on my lip nervously.

"Aw," I said. "Who's afraid?" Then I grinned at myself.

I jerked the window shade down and went to a cedar closet. I tore a flimsy pink dress off a coat hanger and hefted the triangular piece of wood in my hands. Not heavy enough. I wished I'd brought the bottle along. I also wished I'd never drunk from that bottle. I wished I was home.

There were heavy steps approaching from the landing. I flattened myself against the wall near the door hinges.

Mumbles came in, exhaling a deep sigh of anticipation. The sigh became something like *"Gloosh,"* when I splintered the wooden hanger over his head.

Then, as he stumbled forward, holding his head with both hands, I slammed the door shut and flipped the bolt over. It meant I'd lose part of the jump; but I'd worked this item out—I couldn't stand to be interrupted while Mumbles and I were debating.

He was facing me when I turned around. The only sign of my blow was a thin line of red going past his left ear.

"Little Frankie again?" he snarled in a low voice. "Still wants to get hurt." His hand twitched toward a breast pocket.

I came at him so fast that my feet only touched the floor twice. I smashed one satisfying crack at his jaw. The force of my rush carried us both to the dresser in one pile of arms and legs and grunts. He drove an elbow into my ribs and brought a knee up sharp into me.

As I doubled, his huge right hand, balled into a murderous fist, came tearing around at my face. I twitched my head and the fist bounced off my eye. I butted him with my head. He grunted. He was soft.

I brought my fist back with every ounce of energy I had and hit him hard. He started to scream. I jabbed a fist wristdeep into his jaw. Then, as he started to slide to the floor, I went to work on his face. I must have hit him ten times before he lit. He was out colder than dry ice.

My lip had opened again; but then, so had my ego. My fists hurt, my back ached, my eye was a patch of numbness—but I felt fine.

I dropped to one knee and began to search him.

After a while I stood up, feeling sick. I'd found everything from brass knuckles to foreign picture postcards but no souvenir of Daniels or anyone else. Mumbles must have felt the case was still too hot to indulge his hobby.

He stirred and groaned. I put him back to sleep.

I was in a fine spot. If Tony Pirotti came sweeping in, he was likely to be very embarrassed. I didn't have a thing to show him, a shred of proof against Mumbles. And Mumbles could very easily prefer charges against me for assault and battery. Which, under the peculiar circumstances, wouldn't do Ginnie very much good. Or Louise. Or myself.

What time was it? I flipped my sleeve back. I had broken my watch in the scuffle. Mumbles was wearing a pocket watch. I bent over and pulled it out of his vest.

I put my fingernail under the cover of the watch and opened it. Then I let out a gulp. There, pasted to the inside of the watch cover, was a human ear. Daniels's body was missing it when they found him. An expert could identify it.

I turned the watch over. On the back, engraved into the gold, was a rather ornately lettered *Regg.*

There were shots downstairs, under the noise of a police siren. Feet made large from patrolling a beat were pounding up the stairs. I unlocked the door and leaned hazily against a wall. Tony Pirotti and another cop came in with drawn revolvers.

"This is good," Pirotti grinned as he snapped his handcuffs on Regg. "Well, well," he said with relish, after I had told my story and given him the grisly memento of Steve Daniels. "Headquarters will be awfully glad to see this guy. You've had quite a night."

I nodded. I felt as if I'd eaten two whole lobsters in one gulp. The room was beginning to quiver and melt.

"Hey, Joe," Tony called. "Get Mr. Carlyle home. I heard all about what happened at the Red Devil," he told me. "But here's something you don't know—we picked up another one of Regg's hoods, a new boy. Calls himself Harlow Dexter. Yeah, that one.

"The room clerk noticed he was carrying a gun and phoned us. We grabbed him as he left your hotel, holding him on a charge of—Hey, Joe, get this guy home! He's ready to pass out!"

As Joe began to lead me out, Mumbles woke up. He took it all in fast: me, the police, the watch in Tony Pirotti's hand. He began yelling—not mumbling anymore—but *yelling:* "This isn't over yet, Frankie! They won't make this rap stick. We have a date when I get out."

That's what I was worrying about, back in the hotel, with Louise bathing my cuts.

I said to myself: *What will happen to Louise, to me, to Ginnie, when Mumbles gets out!* Even in prison, Regg could still give an order to an outside hood. . . .

Maybe. But the law made a terrific mistake when Mumbles was booked and shoved into an overnight cell with a character named Harry Daniels, alias Harlow Dexter. There wasn't much left of Daniels's mind the next morning.

And not much of Mumbles's throat.

None but the Lethal Heart

WILLIAM C. GAULT

S HE WAS FROM Escradilo, Iowa, she said, and she'd been lonely in this big, mad town and she'd joined this—well, this club, sort of.

She sat in my office, telling me this. She didn't look lonely as if she was from Iowa nor the kind who'd join a friendship club. She was around thirty, fine and firm and blond. She was wearing a green faille suit which disguised nothing it shouldn't. I'd seen her convertible pull up at the curb below.

I said, "I'm surprised you considered a—an introduction club necessary, Miss Teague."

She smiled. "Shall I begin all over? I'm from Escradilo, Iowa, and—"

I smiled, too. "Okay. I'm sold. And now?"

"Well," she said, "there's a man." And she paused.

I waited.

"I mean, a man who—a man in whom I'm very greatly interested. I—"

Love comes to Lancaster Avenue, I thought. I said, "Was it a character reference or a credit reference you wanted, Miss Teague?"

Her chin came up and the blue eyes looked a little displeased. "I'm not interested in his credit."

"Which leaves his character." I fiddled with a pencil on my desk. "I'm a one-man agency, Miss Teague. There are large and very efficient organizations which are equipped to handle that kind of work much better than I can."

A silence, while she studied me. Then, "You're saying, in your oblique way, that the work's beneath you, Mr. Calvano?"

I took a breath. "N-no, it isn't that. I—"

"If it's money," she said, opened her purse. She put a pair of fifties on my desk.

I looked at them and at her. "How did you happen to come to me, Miss Teague?"

She met my gaze evenly, and there was a partial smile on her face. It could have been scorn. "I've been reading the papers."

I'd just had some ink. I'd helped send a shake-down artist to the clink, a very rough lad who'd been bothering one of our local starlets. But my name hadn't been mentioned enough to make me believe Miss Teague.

The two fifties were crisp and clean, though, and obviously legal tender.

I asked, "What's the man's name—and where does he live, Miss Teague?"

"Edmund Swallow," she told me, and gave me an address on Charnock Road.

I stopped writing. "There's a gambler by that name."

She nodded, watching me. "He's a gambler."

She'd come a long way from Escradilo, Iowa. I said, "The police would undoubtedly be glad to give you a complete character and credit report."

The chin lift again: "He has no record, excepting in the newspapers. Do you believe everything you read in the papers, Mr. Calvano?"

"Some papers," I admitted, and looked at the fifties again. Bait. I continued writing, and picked up the bills. I said, "It might not cost you this much." I wrote out a receipt.

Her address was Bolinger Drive, which was in the Palisades, I knew. I handed her the receipt, and she studied it.

"Calvin Calvano," she said. "Italian, Mr. Calvano?"

"And Irish," I added. "I'm from Boston, and my father was a great admirer of Mr. Coolidge." I smiled. "Before he became president."

She rose, and picked up her purse. I couldn't read anything in her face. "You'll report to me?"

I nodded. "Of course. Oh, one thing more. What was the name of this— this introduction club?"

Her face was bland. "The Sunset Social Club. It's over on Olympic."

I wrote it down, and now she was standing near the door. "You're not— laughing at me, are you, Mr. Calvano?"

I shook my head. "Of course not, Miss Teague. It's a lonely town."

"And a crazy one," she said. She smiled again, looked long at me, and left.

It wasn't a lonely town for well set-up blondes with '50 convertibles, though. No town is. Unless the blonde was inordinately shy. Or maybe particular.

The office was again as drab as it had been before she entered it. Three files, one empty, one half empty. My chair and two upholstered customers' chairs, a window to the north and one to the west, the drapes sunfaded.

I looked up the Sunset Social Club in the phone book and went down to the Coupe. The sun was trying to come through, but it was a dull day. . . .

It was a huge stucco building with a pillared porch, and a very small sign next to the door. Discreet, they were. I went through and into a long hall that seemed to run the length of the building.

There was a door to the right, at the head of the hall here and another modest sign. *Director,* this sign read.

I knocked and somebody said, "Come in." I went in.

Cutie, he was. Small and blond and round, with a cherub's face and a blue and silver bow tie. With a powder-blue gabardine suit, a too fleshy handclasp.

"Welcome to our club, Mr.—?" He showed his teeth.

"Calvano," I said. "Mr.—?"

"Darcy," he said, "Rupert Darcy. I'm the director here, Mr. Calvano. It's a big town, isn't it? And seemingly a cold one."

"Not according to the Chamber of Commerce, it isn't cold," I said. "I'm not a prospect, Mr. Darcy."

"Oh?" His full lips made the *O* as he said it. His eyes moved around my face. "A salesman?"

I shook my head. "I work for a credit firm." Which I did, at times, when things were dull. "It's about a man named Edmund Swallow."

Silence, and some rigidity in the round, smooth face. A smile then and, "You've come to the wrong place, Mr. Calvano."

"You don't know him?"

"I know him. We don't discuss our clients."

"You know a Miss Ellen Teague, too?"

He nodded. He pulled a cigarette case from his jacket pocket, opened it, and offered me one.

I shook my head. "They met here, eh?"

Nothing from him. He was tapping the cigarette.

"She told me they did," I said. "Phone her, if you want."

"There's still Mr. Swallow's privacy to be considered, Mr. Calvano." Then he frowned. "Calvano—you're the man who was in the papers. You're the detective who helped apprehend Solly Quirck."

"The same," I agreed.

He was frowning again. "Mr. Calvano, if there's something seriously wrong, if there's something—criminal—"

"Nothing," I said. "I can't always work on headline stuff, Mr. Darcy. Credit investigation pays the rent."

"Let's be frank with each other," he said. "If you'd wanted a credit report, you'd have gone to a credit bureau, to a retail establishment, to his bank. You wouldn't come here."

I'd already learned what I'd come to learn—they'd met here. She hadn't been lying about that. But some perversity in me made me toy with Rupert.

"I was thinking of—of collusion, as long as we're being frank, Mr. Darcy," I said quietly. "Some of these lovelorn ravens have pretty shoddy reputations and Miss Teague is obviously a lady of wealth. I—"

But I got no further. His little, round face was white and his light blue eyes were blazing. "Get out!" he almost screamed. "I won't stand for that kind of talk in here. You can check through the Chamber of Commerce, through the Better Business Bureau, through the Sepulveda National Bank, Mr. Calvano. But don't even whisper an accusation like that in—"

I heard no more. I was out on the porch, and going down the steps to the street.

I went down to Central Headquarters from there and down the hall to the office of Captain Rodriguez. He was in—and amiable, for a change.

"What's on your mind, Cal?" he wanted to know. He waved toward a chair.

"A guy named Swallow," I said, "Edmund Swallow." I sat down, and pulled out a cigarette. "Solvent, is he?"

Rodriguez nodded. "Always. If the cards aren't running, a great ladies' man."

"No record, though?"

"No convictions." Rodriguez yawned. "What's up?"

"Nothing of any importance. Quirck going to appeal?"

"He'd be wasting his time. He only got three years, and he'd go up in front of Judge Whittier next. He could do worse than three years." Another yawn. "What gives with Swallow?"

"Character reference for a client."

Rodriguez chuckled. "You kill me, Cal. What gives?"

"So help me, that's it."

"What's the client's name?"

"No," I said. "Be seeing you, Rod." I got up.

"Just when we were friends, again," he said. "And me with a dull day. I could help, maybe."

"You've got enough to do," I told him. "So long, Rod."

"So long," he said, and then his voice was a little stiffer. "Keep your nose clean, Cal."

I nodded and went out.

I cut over to Olympic and took Olympic all the way to the beach. Up the Coast Highway to Sunset, and the turning climb of Sunset into the Palisades.

Her place on Bolinger Drive was nothing fancy, but it wasn't stucco for a change. This is a stucco town. Hers was redwood, low and with some taste, a view of the water to the front and the mountains behind.

She'd changed from the green suit into denim shorts and a striped T-shirt under her denim jacket. She did all right by the T-shirt. She stood in the doorway, a drink in her hand. Behind her I could hear music. I could see through the entry hall into the living room. Cigarette smoke was in there, but she wasn't smoking.

"Well," she said. "Reporting already?"

"He's solvent," I told her, "and a ladies' man. And you *did* meet at the Sunset Social Club."

A small frown. "I told you we did. Did you think I was lying?"

"I had to check," I said. "It didn't make sense. Are we going to do all our talking out here?"

She smiled and said, "I'm sorry. Come in. Come in and have a drink."

We went through the entry hall into a low living room with a beamed ceiling and full-length windows comprising the seaside wall.

A man got up from a deep chair near the record player. He was as tall as I am, but thinner and a hell of a lot better-looking. He was wearing a Harris tweed jacket and fawn slacks and a white silk sport shirt. He wasn't wearing a smile.

"Mr. Calvano," she said, "this is Peter Lunt. Mr. Lunt's an agent who still has hopes for me."

I thought there was a trace of lipstick on his neck, but I could have been wrong. His handclasp was thin and strong. His smile was professional.

"The detective," he said. "I've been warning Ellen about this Swallow person."

His hair was dark and curly, his eyes a soft brown and he was tanned like a saddle. If I'd have been a girl, I'd have put some lipstick on his neck myself.

"I guess Swallow's all right," I said. "A gambler, but Miss Teague probably knows that by now. He's never been convicted of anything."

"I was thinking of her reputation," Peter Lunt said. "I was thinking of her reputation in the light of my ten percent. I'm sure she can take care of herself."

I agreed to that.

He looked at the watch on his wrist. "Well, I've an appointment for three-thirty. I'll be running along. Glad to have met you, Mr. Calvano."

Ellen went with him to the door. She still had the drink in her hand. I was still waiting for mine.

She came back into the living room and went over to a liquor cabinet. Her back was to me as she said, "Isn't he handsome?"

"Very."

"Smart, too. Does very well."

I said nothing.

"Rye, bourbon, scotch, Mr. Calvano?"

"Rye and water. I didn't know you were an actress. Childhood ambition?"

"I'm not. Peter doesn't know I'm not, or maybe he does, and it's part of his pitch. I think he likes me."

"But you prefer Mr. Swallow?"

Nothing from her for a moment. She finished pouring the drink and turned to face me. "I was lying about that." She came over to hand me the drink.

"Go on," I said.

"He's just another Solly Quirck, Edmund Swallow is. He—he knows some things about me, and he wants payment."

"Money?"

"Money or me."

"He put it that bluntly?"

"Of course not."

I sipped my drink. "And the Sunset Social Club. Did you throw that in for laughs?"

Silent, excepting for the Gershwin from the record player. She drained her drink. "You must think I'm an awful liar."

"You're a client," I said. "Level with me, huh, Miss Teague?"

"I belonged to the Sunset Social Club," she said. "I'm terribly interested in people. It's really amazing the variety of people I met there. Some of them are fun and *all* of them are real. Don't forget I'm from Iowa."

"All right," I said, "we'll get back to Edmund Swallow, one of the *real* people who belong to the Sunset Social Club. How much does he want?"

"Fifteen thousand dollars."

"And what can I do about that?"

"You can get something on him; that's what I'd hoped when I asked for the report." She took my empty glass and hers, and went back to the liquor cabinet. "You could watch him for a week or two, and I'll bet you'd get enough to *hang* him."

"Not for a hundred dollars and two drinks of rye," I said. "That kind of job costs money, Miss Teague."

"Don't worry about money," she said, and brought me a fresh drink. "The hundred was a retainer. I want you to stay with Mr. Swallow. A man who can handle Quirck shouldn't have any trouble with Edmund Swallow." She lifted her drink in a partial salute, and sipped it.

"Well," I said, "it's your money. You don't want to tell me just what it is he has on you, do you?"

"No."

I gulped the rest of my drink and stood up. "Maybe I could reason with Swallow. Maybe, if I flexed my muscles—"

Her voice was sharp. "That's just exactly what I don't want, Mr. Calvano. I'd have gone to the police if I thought muscles would do it. They have those and guns, too."

"All right," I said. "Adios."

I went back to the office from there, but there was no mail. I was about ready to leave when the phone rang. I couldn't miss that voice.

It was Rupert Darcy, and he sounded perturbed. "Mr. Calvano, I want to see you. I—it's very important, and I want to see you immediately."

"I'll be right over," I said. "You're at your office?"

"Yes. How soon—"

"As soon as I can make it."

"There's been a man parked across the street for the longest time," he went on, "and I—"

"What kind of a car?" I interrupted. "Can you see the license number?"

"Not the number, but it's a gray club coupe with whitewall tires." A pause. "A '49 or '50."

"I'll be right over" I said and hung up.

It wasn't the man across the street that interested me. It was the fact that Rupert sounded scared enough to talk. People in cars don't bother the innocent; Rupert had some sins to confess.

I made fairly good time. When I pulled up in front of the stucco building there was no gray club across the street. I went up onto the porch and into the hall. His door was closed, but I didn't stop to knock. I pushed in.

The room was empty.

It seemed that way, at first. It was quiet, with only the hum of the passing cars, outside. I moved past the love seat near his desk, and over toward the windows which faced on the porch. When I got past the desk, I saw him.

He was spread-eagled on the floor, one hand gripping the bottom of the drape, his open, blank eyes staring at the distant ceiling. There was a knife-handle protruding from his throat, blood staining the powder-blue gabardine suit.

I called Syd Mueller, first. Syd runs a personal loan service and I worked for him at times. And borrowed from him other times.

"I was checking a man named Edmund Swallow, and I was checking him for you. Got that?" I told him.

"Trouble again," he said in a tired voice.

I gave him Swallow's address, and hung up.

Then I phoned the law.

I went through Darcy's desk while I waited for the sound of the siren. Only copies of his ads were there.

Like this:

Widowed darling of 68 with five hundred a month and you'll have to be on your toes, you gallant old-timers. Because she's the neatest, sweetest bundle of American beauty . . .

After the prowl car, Doheney came. He's a sergeant in Homicide and he'd come to the department after I'd left. He took me out into the rear of the long hall.

"This Darcy phoned me," I told him, "and said that he'd read about me in the papers, and he needed a private investigator, but bad. He said there was a '49 or '50 gray coupe with white-wall tires parked across the street too long. I'd keep that part out of the papers, about the car, because they or he wouldn't know Darcy told me about it. I said I'd be right over, and I was."

"And found him like that?"

I nodded.

"You working on something right now?"

I shook my head.

"The captain says you were working on Edmund Swallow."

I shook my head again. "That was just a credit and character report. I'd finished it."

"For who?"

"Syd Mueller—you know, Pacific Personal Loans."

"The five-percent man," Doheney said, "five percent a month. You mean Swallow needs money that bad?"

"I've an agreement with Syd," I said. "He doesn't ask me my business and I don't nose into his."

Doheney gave me a long look. "Maybe you'd like to talk to the captain."

"If you think I should, I will." I took out a cigarette and lighted it, and gave him stare for stare. "I've known Rod a long time. We've worked together a lot. Why all the heat?"

"Maybe," Doheney said slowly, "I haven't just the proper regard for private operatives."

"That would be personal," I said. "A prospective client phones me. I come and find him dead. I phone the police. Nobody knows he phoned me. I could have walked out of here after I found him, and been clear."

"That's just it," he said. "Nobody knows but you if he phoned you, or if you came here without his phoning you. I never saw a private investigator yet who wouldn't have just breezed."

"You've been unlucky," I said, "until now. What do you want me to do, make up a story for you?"

"You already have, I figure. Stay here. I'll be back." He went down the hall to the director's office, again, and I figured he was going to phone Syd.

A couple reporters saw me, and came back, along with a photographer. "Cal," one of them said. "*You* again. You're doing all right, aren't you?"

I turned a smile on and off.

"What's the story, Cal?"

"We'd better wait for the sergeant," I said. "He'll have a statement for you."

A flash bulb popped, and then another photographer came hurrying down the hall. I gave him my profile.

"This part of the Solly Quirck business, Cal?"

I shook my head. "I'm an innocent bystander."

"You've been out of the papers for two days," he said. "What some guys won't do for publicity."

Now the sergeant was coming back along the hall, his face showing nothing. "Better get down and see the captain right away," he said. "I can have one of the men take you."

"My car's outside," I told him. "Thanks." I turned my back on him and went along the hall, wondering if he'd call me back. He didn't.

There was a crowd on the sidewalk outside. The police ambulance was there, and two department cars beside the squad car. I climbed into the coupe and swung out into the traffic. I was thinking of the widowed darling of sixty-eight all the way down to the captain's office.

Rodriguez didn't look any meaner than usual. "You give Sergeant Doheney some trouble?"

I sat down across the desk from him, and faced him squarely. "No. He opened up by telling me he didn't like private investigators, and wound up by practically calling me a liar. But I leveled with him."

Rodriguez had a sad, pock-marked face and my words didn't brighten it any. His voice was weary. "It could have been just a coincidence you were in to see me this afternoon and walked into a murder a couple hours later. I can't believe you're that busy."

"I got a lot of publicity lately," I said. "That always brings in business. This gent on Olympic told me he'd read my name in the paper."

Rodriguez clenched both hands on top of his desk. "You know, I think, Cal, that I've no loyalties outside of the department. If I thought somebody was playing me for a patsy, I'd get him, friend or not. I'd be awful rough on a man like that."

"I know those things," I said.

He nodded. "All right. Run along. We'll call you clear for now."

Traffic was still curb to curb. It was nearly six. I walked over to a nearby restaurant for supper.

Coincidence, the captain had said. It's happened enough so they've got a word for it. I didn't think it was one, this time. I had a feeling the death of Rupert Darcy had something to do with Edmund Swallow. Not that Darcy probably didn't have enemies enough. Some of these outfits were on the up and up; some of them were lucrative rackets.

It was hard to figure a guy like Darcy. He looked soft, but some of the boys who'd gone to the chair looked softer. If he was tied up with con men, I wouldn't have been surprised. But con men don't go in for the heavy stuff, and murder's on the heavy side.

And Ellen Teague—there wasn't anything soft about her nor any reason to think she wasn't playing me for fish. But why?

After dinner, I phoned her from a drugstore near the restaurant.

I said, "Rupert Darcy's just been murdered. Do you still want me to follow Swallow?"

"More than ever," she said. "Do you think Swallow did it?"

"The law almost thinks I did it," I told her. "I found him dead and reported it."

"They're not holding you? You didn't give them my name?"

"They're not holding me. And I didn't give them your name, *yet.*"

A silence. Then, "*Yet?*"

"That's right, not yet. Have you ever heard of Tehachapi?"

"N—no."

"You might, before this is through. It was a little too cute the way I walked in on Darcy."

A longer silence, and now her voice was just a whisper. "You've got to believe in me, Mr. Calvano. You'll have to go along with me. I desperately need your protection."

There was no use kidding myself. If she'd have been fifty and fat, I'd have told her to go to hell. I said, "You want to phone Swallow to see if he's home now? So I can pick him up if he's there."

"What shall I say to him?"

"Anything. Tell him you're having a hard job raising the money, but you're working on it." I gave her the number in the booth to call back.

I was watching through the glass sides of the booth as I waited, and I saw the man come in the door of the store. A very ordinary guy, thin, of medium height wearing a plain gray suit.

The only thing unusual about him was the gray club coupe he'd left at the curb.

The town, I told myself, is full of gray club coupes. And killers don't use the same car on two jobs. They ditch them after a murder. Only this gent probably hadn't known his car had been spotted. Too many people park on Olympic.

The phone rang, and Ellen said, "There's no answer. Maybe you'd better come up here. We'd better have a talk." Her voice was tired, defeated.

"Okay," I said. "Do you know anybody who drives a gray club coupe with whitewall tires? Skinny gent, average height?"

"No," she said. "You'd better come up here, Cal."

That was the first time she'd used my informal name. "I've a little business first," I said. "But I'll be there."

I looked up Swallow in the phone book and spent another nickel. A man's voice answered.

"Edmund Swallow?" I asked.

"Right," the voice said.

"How are you, Eddie," I said jovially. "Just got into town. Bet you don't know who it is."

"I'm holding my breath," he said.

"I'll give you a hint," I said. "T.P., Eddie. From Eau Claire, Eddie."

"I have never in my life been in Eau Claire, wherever that is, chum," the voice said. "Would you mind identifying yourself?"

"Tommy Parsons. You gone high hat, Eddie?"

"You've got the wrong Eddie, T.P.," the voice said. The line went dead.

Of course, he could have come home in the two minutes between her call and mine. He might have been taking a shower and just got to the phone by the time I called. Of course. . . .

I looked out at the thin guy, and he was moving my way now. I moved my .38 from its holster to my jacket pocket and stepped from the booth.

He kept coming at me, his hand in his pocket. I felt cold, but I kept moving his way, watching that hand. He pulled it out. There was a nickel in it, I could see.

"It's about time," he muttered, and went past me into the booth.

His coupe had regulation black tires . . .

The sun was down, but there was moonlight on the water as I drove out the Coast Highway. It was cold, and I turned on the car heater for a minute.

Traffic was thin. The bluffs to my right seemed to hang over the car threateningly. The coupe purred to herself, and I tried to make some sense out of the day.

Headlights came up from behind, moved alongside, and a gray club coupe with whitewall tires went by, making time. The way his motor was chugging, he must have had an overdrive.

It had Nevada plates. I watched the twin tail lights disappear around a bend. When I rounded the bend, it was almost out of sight.

I went past the San Vicente intersection, working forward in my mind from the first lie, which must certainly have been the Sunset Social Club, and looked for the way.

I ran them through my confused mind. Ellen and Rupert and Swallow and Peter Lunt and the man in the gray club coupe. Or *men*.

I thought there's only one way, that's to see Swallow. Then I was making the climb of Sunset, where it goes past the Santa Ynez Inn.

She was waiting in the doorway when my car stopped. She was wearing her third change of costume for the day, a strapless number of a pale green, misty material.

She handed me a drink as I came up onto the porch. "Time to let my hair down, Cal."

"I'll bet," I said.

We went into the living room. The record player was silent. She sat down on a love seat and I took an armless chair nearby. She said, "I remembered what Tehachapi is. It's the state women's prison, isn't it?"

I nodded.

"You're not an easy man to fool."

"Easy enough. I've been in a fog all day. That Sunset Social Club was a little thick, but the rest hangs together. Who killed Darcy?"

She stared at me. "You don't think I know about that? How corrupt do you think I—"

I lifted a hand. "You said you were going to let your hair down."

"All right." Her hand which held the drink was trembling. "I used to work with Edmund Swallow." She chewed her lip. "Promotional work, I suppose you'd call it."

"Confidence work might be better."

She looked at me and smiled. "Guilty. In any event, nothing I'd be proud to admit now. We were careful; at least I was. I invested mine. I'm pretty well fixed. Now Peter's come along and there's a very good chance he could wrangle me a fair contract. I'm no world beater, but I've been on the stage and done radio work. Edmund's put out about that."

"Why?"

"I suppose because Peter's so handsome. And because I've grown weary of dear Edmund. Anyway, he threatened to reveal enough of my—background to kill any deals." She looked at me. "He doesn't want money. He wants me to stick with him. I thought if he saw you around, following him, he might—well, think you're a—"

"A gun? A mug? A torpedo?"

She nodded. "I thought it would scare him. But now I don't want you to go near him. I realize now that Edmund could be dangerous."

"Tell me about the Sunset Social Club." I was being patient.

"It's surprising the people you meet there," she said tonelessly. "Lonely people and stupid people and gullible people. Quite a few of them very well off, willing to buy gold mine stock and oil stock. Even uranium stock." She looked at me quietly, stood up. "Another drink?"

"In a second. You say you don't want me to go near Swallow, because he might be dangerous. Why should you worry about that? Why should you worry about me?"

"I've grown quite attached to you, Calvin. You're not as smooth as Edmund nor as handsome as Peter, but you're more man than both of them. I'll get your drink."

I was tired enough to believe what I wanted to believe, and I didn't believe more than a fraction of that. But it had been a busy day.

Two hours later I had acquired some lipstick, too much rye, and we were listening to *Porgy and Bess.* I was bushed and half-drunk and all the events of the day kept running through my mind, and I remembered what the reporter had said in the hall.

Ellen's eyes were closed and her head was back. I looked at the clean line of her throat and said suddenly, "I'm going to see Swallow."

She came alive. Her eyes flashed open and her head turned swiftly toward me. "Don't. He's a moody man. He's never killed, to my knowledge, but I think he could."

"I've never met him," I said, "but I've seen him around and he doesn't frighten me a bit. Don't fret about him; I'll go easy."

She was gripping my arm. "Cal, leave him alone."

"All right," I said, and stood up. "It's been a full day."

"I'll . . . see you again?"

"I think you will. There's a little matter of Rupert Darcy's murder the police are going to investigate, and they'd like to involve me. They might even go to Swallow."

"Why should they?"

"Because," I said evenly, "when I first started to check Swallow, I checked him at headquarters. So they know I was working on him. Then, *I* find Darcy."

"You went to the police?"

"Naturally. It's bad business to work without them. I didn't give them your name, and I probably won't. But I won't be railroaded. Not for *anybody.*"

She was staring at me as though trying to read my mind.

"You told me Swallow wasn't home when you phoned. He was home when I phoned—two minutes later."

"I didn't call him. I lied about that. I'd decided by then to forget him."

"I wish I could. I must have a one-track mind." The room seemed unsteady and my vision of her was blurring. "What does a man have to do to earn his hundred bucks?"

"Cal!" Her face blurred, grew clear, and I saw her eyes were blazing in a white face. Then she started to swear.

"You never learned those words in Escradilo, Iowa," I said softly. "I'll be seeing you."

I went out, and the night air was cold, which helped. I got into the coupe and drove very carefully back to the ocean road. I took Olympic again to Sepulveda, and that to Charnock Road. I had the windows open, and my head was beginning to clear.

There was a light at the residence of Edmund Swallow. I parked a couple hundred feet past the house and walked back. Two houses down a party was going on. The driveway was crowded with cars and there were some at the curb.

I walked up onto the porch of the Swallow domain and pressed the button. Chimes, but no other response. I walked along the porch to the wide living room window, and looked in. Nobody in sight. A single table lamp was lighted. My eyes moved around the room and paused at the shadows near the end of the davenport. There were shoes there, the toes pointing upward, shoes that must contain feet, considering their position.

I went back to the front door. It was unlocked. I pushed in. The door opened directly into the living room.

A knife, again. The dead eyes of Edmund Swallow caught a bit of the lamp's gleam, shining at me without seeing.

She'd had a change of heart. She'd tried to keep me up there, give me an alibi, keep me out of it. Maybe. And if she had, she knew this was going to happen.

I could call the police and wait. Rodriguez would believe me—like hell. A man would need to believe in a double coincidence on the same day. I didn't think there were any men like that and I *knew* there weren't any on the police force.

I didn't believe it myself.

I called headquarters. "This is Helmuth Frontenac," I said, "and I've discovered the body of Edmund Swallow at Charnock Road. He's been stabbed to death." I wiped the phone and the doorknob; I hadn't touched anything else.

They were still raising hell at the party as I walked back to the coupe.

Round and round we go. And where now? Not home for Calvin Calvano. It's a small apartment, and there wouldn't be room for me with all the cops that would soon be there.

Somebody had set up a pattern and put me in the middle of it as the patsy. I didn't like being one of those any more than Rodriguez did.

This Darcy business had been incidental. He'd seen he was getting out of his depth. He'd learned something and phoned me as he couldn't afford to go to the law because of the publicity.

I was bone weary, but my mind was alive and I thought back to the reporter in the hall and knew he'd called it right. For anybody else I'd have played it differently, but she had all she needed.

I headed back that way—and then decided against it. There were some things I had to know first. I'd been working blind too long. I heard the siren as I turned back onto Sepulveda.

Hans Ehler's house was old and Spanish and huge. A tile roof and floor length windows and a mammoth lawn, complete with built-in sprinklers.

I went up the drive and parked in front of the four-car garage. There was a light on in the rear, and I knew it was Hans's study.

A very solid citizen. With a finger here and a finger there, an old resident who hobnobbed with senators and shot craps with sharpers. What went on in this town Hans Ehler knew, and we were friends.

At the side door I pressed the button. After a while I could see him coming along the hallway from the study. He had his pajamas on and an old bathrobe. His thin, gray hair was wet as though he'd just washed it, and his moon face was freshly shaven. He was a lot of man, about two-seventy, and not all of it fat.

"Cal," he said. "Come in, come in. What is it?"

"I want a bed for the night, Hans," I told him.

He closed the door quietly behind me. His voice was as quiet. "Hot, Cal?"

"Warm. I've been playing stooge."

He chuckled. "Not you. I know you, Cal."

"There's a blonde," I began.

"That makes it different. For blondes, it's sometimes fun to be a stooge. Nice build?"

"Very fine." We went into his study. I sat in the big chair near the bookcases and told him all about it.

When I'd finished, he said, "Solly Quirck owes Edmund Swallow thirty thousand dollars."

I wasn't surprised. This was a hangover from the Solly Quirck deal, just as the reporter had suggested. Somebody had wanted Swallow out of the way, and why not get rid of me at the same time? Solly was in the clink, but his allies weren't, and Solly was a man who lived by vengeance.

"How about Rupert Darcy?" I asked.

"Swallow worked with him from time to time. They didn't get along very well though." Hans smiled. "Rupert could be a hard man to get along with."

"But Swallow was no killer."

Hans shook his head. "You want me to put some men on it, Cal? You want me to call off Rodriguez for a while?"

"No," I said. "Some puppet master is pulling the strings, and I'd like his name, but it's got to be a personal thing with me."

Hans nodded slowly. "This blonde would know. It's probably someone very close to Solly, and someone who's otherwise clean. She should know."

"I didn't think Solly had any friends," I said. "He usually worked alone."

"And with people of prominence, people whose reputations mattered, who were building a reputation, or trying to."

That didn't click, then. I was tired. I yawned, and tried to stretch the ache out of my muscles.

"A hot bath," Hans said, "and a bed. We'll talk about it in the morning. . . ."

We had breakfast in the patio at ten o'clock. Hans said, "I've made some phone calls this morning. Nothing. Solly didn't have any friends who are admitting it."

"I'll go back to the blonde," I said. "They'll be watching for my car, Hans. You got one I can use?"

He nodded. "Take the sedan. And if they pick you up, phone me. I think you're all right, Cal."

"Thanks," I said. "I guess everybody thinks you're all right, Hans."

He chuckled. "And how wrong they are, eh?"

I didn't think so.

I was getting to know this Coast Highway. The water was calm, today, the air clear enough to see Palos Verdes, behind me.

The convertible was on the drive, in front of the double garage. I looked toward the doorway, expecting to see her there with a drink in her hand. But the doorway was closed.

After I'd pressed the button four times, she opened the door. She had a blue flannel robe over whatever was underneath.

"Late sleeper," I said, "I suppose I'll have to wait for breakfast."

"Cal, darling," she said, and put a hand on my arm. "Welcome home."

I came into the entry hall. "Edmund Swallow's dead," I told her.

Her face sagged. Her eyes met mine. "You didn't do it. You were here with me. I'll swear to that in court."

"Is it me you need or my gun?" I asked her.

Her face stiffened, and her eyes began to flame again.

"I'll bet you never even knew Edmund Swallow," I said. "I'll bet you're just a finger for one of Solly's boys."

"I knew Edmund Swallow. I worked with him."

"And tired of him. You'd just as soon see him dead, and so would Solly Quirck. If they could make it look like Calvano was the gun, so much the better. Two birds with one knife."

"But you were with me," she said hoarsely. "You're clear."

"Why was Darcy killed?"

"I—I don't know."

I gripped her shoulder hard enough to bring tears to her eyes. "Why was Darcy killed?"

"Cal—I—" She started to cry quietly.

"I've got all kinds of friends in this town," I told her. "I'm an awful hard man to frame. You'd better string with me."

Her mouth opened, and she said, "He was afraid of—of murder. He went along with it up to the time he heard we—up to the time he heard Swallow was going to die."

"And who's the killer?"

"I—I only know part of it. Honestly, Cal, I—"

The door chimes sounded, and she twisted in my grasp, looking frighteningly toward the doorway.

"Wait," I said. "Don't open it yet." I went to her bedroom window, the one that faced the street. There was a gray club coupe with whitewall tires parked in front. A '50. Peter Lunt stood on the front porch.

I hadn't seen that car in front yesterday, or hadn't noticed it, if it was in front. But I hadn't been club coupe conscious, then.

"It's Lunt," I called to Ellen. "Better let him in."

I thought of Hans saying, "—people who were building a reputation, or trying to." Lunt would know about those kind of people. Those were the kind he got his ten percent from. He wasn't well enough established to get the big shots, but he was smart enough to spot the comers.

As I came out of the bedroom, he came into the entry hall. His eyebrows lifted.

"The police are looking for a car like yours," I said. "I hope you're clear."

"Police? I don't quite understand."

"A car like yours was parked in front of the Sunset Social Club yesterday before Darcy was killed. I don't know if the police have the license number, but they've got a description, and they've probably got the number."

He smiled. "I imagine, if it was my number, they'd have bothered me by now. Try again."

He looked at Ellen and his smile was reassuring. As though to tell her there was no cause to worry; guys like Calvano could be handled with a minimum of effort. In carload lots.

"One of Solly's boys, aren't you?" I asked him.

Now, he turned to face me, and there was no smile on his face. Ellen gasped, but I didn't need that to know I'd hit the bull's-eye. His brown eyes were glittering and there was menace written all over his suddenly tight face.

Ellen's eyes went from me to him and back. She was about due to topple.

"You big, dumb—" he started to say.

He didn't finish. I caught him with a heavy right hand flush on the mouth, and he went stumbling back. He started to get to his feet, but I had him by the throat, dragged him into the living room.

Lunt was choking and sputtering when I propped him on the love seat. I slapped him, forward and back, and then put a stiff right hand under the heart.

I heard a thump behind me and knew Ellen had passed out. She didn't have the stomach for this. She liked her murder by remote control.

I worked on him for a while. When I got busy on his face, he started to scream, and then to babble. Soon some of his words made sense, and I went to the phone.

Rodriguez came in and sat down behind his desk. "He's admitted he's Solly's brother, but not much more." He paused. "Not yet. What the hell did you hit him with, Calvano?"

"My good right hand. I suppose by not calling me Cal you're telling me I'm a long ways from the clear."

"You didn't play it very straight."

"I came in here twice yesterday, once by my own volition. I phoned twice, yesterday, and once today. If I'd see you any more than that, people would say we're in love. What do you want me to do, pull the call box every hour?"

"Don't get lippy."

"I apologize. You are the law. I'm just a crummy private dick scrambling for nickels. Unlike the others, I believe in working *with* the department."

"You ought to run for Congress."

"Maybe I will. If Peter Lunt, alias Peter Quirck doesn't squeal, the girl will. She's not as hard as she looks."

Something like a smile came to Rodriquez's face. "She says you'll clear her. She says you know she's innocent. How about that?"

"She's a good kid," I said, "but she'll be better after a spell in Tehachapi. She knew all about it."

Now he smiled. "All right, Cal. Friends again, for the moment. I thought you might go to bat for her."

"She's just another blonde," I said.

But I knew she wasn't.

The Man From Limbo

JOHN D. MacDONALD

Chapter 1

AWAKE TO TERROR

H E SAT ON THE hotel bed, lying over so that his forehead was against
the back of his right hand, and his right hand clasped his knee. It was
warm, but he could not stop shivering. He wanted to fold himself smaller
and tighter, shrink down into darkness and nothingness.

"God," he said, "help me." It was prayer.

This time it was worse than all the other times. Deeper, blacker. The
doctor had said, "Dolph, you've got to do it. You've got to take the job."

Job for a psycho. Fear psychosis, they call it.

"You've got too much pride to hide in hospitals the rest of your life,
Dolph."

Have I?

The doctor had lined up the job. It sounded so simple. "You just take this
sample case and your routing and this literature. You go out on the road
and you go to jewelry stores and sell the Russell Line. Compacts, costume
jewelry. You have to make yourself do it. Do it for three months, Dolph,
and this will never come back again."

"Why did *I* have to get this way?"

"The war. It brought out . . ."

"But I was all right during the war. All right, I tell you. And for two years
afterward I was all right. Now I . . ."

. "You can do this. I know you can. Memorize sales talks."

For six weeks Dolph Regan had forced himself to do the job. Sometimes it was a full hour before he could force himself to enter a store. If the owner was too busy to talk, it was like a reprieve. He gave his sales talks woodenly, his body bathed in cool sweat. But he forced himself to do it. He forced himself to believe that it was becoming easier. He made sales—not many. But those he made were precious to him.

And yesterday it had blown up in his face. Here in Brasher, New York, a perfectly normal, grubby, upstate city of fifty thousand. Here in Brasher in a small average jewelry store called Dreifer's.

He was talking to Mr. Dreifer. Dreifer was listening without much interest, fingering one of the compacts. Dolph heard his own voice getting unaccountably louder. He tried to keep it down. A clerk began to stare at him, and two women customers. Dreifer startled, faintly alarmed, stared at him. Eight eyes, looking at him. Familiar roaring in his ears. Eyes pulsing at him, growing enormous, then shrinking to tiny dots, growing enormous again. The store was steadily shrinking. The walls were going to crush him.

He ran stumbling to the door, ran all the way to the hotel, leaving the car by a meter, leaving the sample case with Dreifer; ran with panic at his heels, wanting only to be alone behind a door that was sturdy . . . and locked.

That had been yesterday. Mid-morning. Now it was afternoon. He did not know if he had slept. He had not left the room. After six weeks this had happened again. He did not know what had set it off, what had triggered if. The doctor would question him closely. The doctor was trying to find a clue, a clue in the past.

There wasn't much that he could tell the doctor. Just that the name of the city had a tantalizing familiarity. Familiarity tinged with faint dread. Nothing much there.

"What are you afraid of?" he whispered.

Nothing. And everything.

Fear of people, with overtones of claustrophobia. Fear of failure.

A sound had been growing in the distance. It intruded on his attention and it took him long moments to identify it. Drums. Parade. He stood up, wavering with weakness, and went cautiously to the window, standing well back as he looked out. The street was three stories below. Sidewalks lined with people.

Now was the time to break out of the room, to go down there. Now he could be certain that they would not be looking at him, would not be wondering about him, nudging each other, smirking behind the concealing hand.

The drums grew louder. Don't wait too long. He fled from the room, went down the two flights at a half run, slowed to go across the lobby. He gave a quick glance from side to side. They did not notice him. He would play the old game, that he was invisible, the game that had put him to sleep during the nights of childhood.

He was tall enough to see over their heads. There was a bank near the hotel. He leaned against the front of it. A fife and drum corps. Tan-legged girl strutting out in front. Brief red skirt and gold halter, and high white shako. Baton with chrome glint in the sunlight, twirling first on one side of her and then the other, miraculously missing the knees that came high in the prancing strut. A girl that was good to look at.

Boom tah dah, dah, Boom tah dah dah, Boom tah dah dah. Then a blast of whistle and the harsh high skirl of the fifes.

Next a car. A huge convertible. Banners. Block for Mayor. Dolph bit his lip until his eyes watered. He had seen the posters without actually seeing them. He had been uneasy without knowing why.

Block. Sergeant Wally Block. Dolph Regan knuckled his eyes and stared at the big-shouldered man who sat smiling on the folded top of the convertible, his feet in the rear seat. No one else. Wally Block. Certainly! That was why the name was familiar. "When I get back to Brasher, boy, there's going to be . . ."

Wally Block, with his big, blunt, florid face, tiny blue eyes, neck and shoulders like a bull.

Wally was waving a pale, wide-brimmed felt hat at the crowd, turning from side to side. He looked toward the bank. Dolph instinctively lifted an arm. Wally froze for a long moment, staring over the heads of the crowd at Dolph.

Dolph grinned and clasped his hands high over his head like a fighter. As the car moved slowly along, Dolph ran down to the hotel entrance, pointing meaningfully at the door. He saw Wally's quick nod of comprehension.

The rest of the parade went by. Traffic started up again. The crowds began to drift away. Dolph stood and smiled to himself. He straightened his shoulders and stared boldly into the faces of the people around him. It was gone for this time, cured and gone. Just seeing Wally had been enough to do it.

At the door of Dreifer's there was a moment's hesitation, but he walked in, made himself smile at Mr. Dreifer. "Sorry about yesterday. I was sick."

"You didn't do those customers any good, fella. They run out as fast as you did."

"I'm sorry about that."

"You start shouting when you get sick? Funny sickness."

He retrieved his sample case and managed to make a small sale. The car was at the police garage where it had been towed. He paid his fine and the towing charge and drove back to the parking lot behind the hotel. For the first time in over twenty-four hours he realized how hungry he was.

He went to the desk clerk. "I'm Dolph Regan, Room 220. I'm expecting a phone call or a visit from Wallace Block. I'll be down in the grill room for a time. If anything should . . ."

"From Wallace Block? Certainly, Mr. Regan. Pardon me, but are you a friend of his?"

"In the army."

"He's going to do a lot for this town, Mr. Regan. He's waking the people up."

Dolph started to go downstairs, then fingered his stubbled chin. He went up and shaved quickly, showered, changed to a fresh shirt. He found that he could look at his long lean face in the mirror, at the black arch of brows, the firm jaw, and feel with confidence that this was the last time it would happen. The very last time.

And then he remembered that it was always this way. The swing of the pendulum. After the depths there came a brief time of elation. He shrugged it off and went down to order a special steak.

The second cup of coffee had just been served when the girl came and stood by his booth. "Mr. Regan?" she said. Her voice was low.

He got up awkwardly. "My name is Regan."

"I'm Jan Holland, Mr. Regan. Wally described you and the desk clerk told me where to find you."

"Please sit down. A drink?"

"Black coffee, please." She took off her gloves as Dolph signaled the waiter. She met his inquisitive stare with a frank, level-eyed smile. He decided that she was an extraordinarily pretty girl, very nearly a beautiful girl. Her hair was the shade of butter toffee under the pert hat with its tiny veil. The furs slung across the shoulder of the green fall suit appeared to be sable. Her face was broad through the cheekbones, her eyes set wide and gray, her mouth cool and fresh.

"I suppose I should explain, Mr. Regan. Wally sends regrets. He'll try to see you soon, possibly this evening. But with election the day after tomorrow. . . ."

She gave a pretty shrug, very expressive.

"It certainly was a surprise to me to see him sitting on that car, Miss Holland."

"No surprise to us, Mr. Regan. We've worked for a long time to find a man strong enough to knock over the local applecart. I'm a campaign worker and sort of secretary to Wally. He wants to know why you are in town."

"Working. I'm on the road, selling."

She tilted her head to one side. "He seemed to remember that you were an architect, Mr. Regan."

"I was. I guess, in a manner of speaking, I still am. This is a—sideline."

"I see," she said in a tone that meant she did not see at all.

"Does he have a good chance of winning?"

"We think so. We hope so. If you lived here, would you vote for him?"

"What an odd thing to say! Of course I would. My platoon sergeant? I was a replacement officer, green as grass. Most replacement officers in combat had a life expectancy of about three days. Wally taught me the tricks. He said he was tired of breaking in new lieutenants."

She bit her lip. "Sorry if I seem a little puzzled, Mr. Regan. Could there have been any bad feeling between you two, at the end?"

"What are you driving at?"

"Wally got me aside and gave me that grin of his and told me to come down here and find out if you were for him or against him. So I wondered . . ."

"He must have been joking, Miss Holland."

She made a face. "Maybe he's getting supersensitive. It's been a rough, dirty campaign. One little group has controlled Brasher for so long that until a week or so ago they still thought the Good Government League was a joke. We had a newspaper poll that woke them up. I've worked so hard I feel unreal, like I could be a million miles away. I've run so many doorbells my thumb aches. They're calling us a 'bunch of amateurs.' But we're getting results."

"Maybe I could help in some way," he said. He knew at once that it wasn't from any desire for good government for Brasher, but from an urge to become better acquainted with this girl.

"Would you, Dolph?" she said eagerly. She blushed. "Wally called you that and I . . ."

"I was wondering how I was going to start calling you Jan," he said quickly.

"Anyway, I was thinking that maybe at the banquet and rally tomorrow night you could sit at the speaker's table and say something about him, a sort of introduction or . . . Are you ill?"

He knew his smile was closer to a grimace. "No."

"You looked so odd for a moment."

"I don't think I'd better try to make a speech, Jan. I'm—no good at that sort of thing anymore. I might do more harm than good."

She frowned in thought. "How about a statement? You could write it out. Lieutenant's commendation for his platoon sergeant or something. We could get it in tomorrow's paper and maybe have it read over the air."

"I'd be glad to do that, Jan."

She glanced at her watch. "Could you come over to headquarters right now? There'll be somebody there who can take dictation. And Wally ought to be going back to headquarters a bit later."

"Glad to." They walked side by side in the gray dusk. She had a nice long-legged stride and seemed to know every third person they met.

Headquarters was a vacant store into which desks and chairs had been moved. Banners hung spotlighted across the front of the building. Workers were turning in reports, and over in one corner, under a sign which said Auto Pool, a group of men were arguing over a routine chart. Some of them stopped to wave at Jan.

A tall thin blond man in his thirties came over, smiling. "New recruit, Jan?"

"Bill, this is Dolph Regan. Dolph was Wally's lieutenant in the war. He's willing to give us a statement we can use."

"Glad to have you aboard, Regan. Eager beaver left out my last name. Holmes. Nice of you to help, but I don't want to overdo the war stuff. It's sort of old hat."

"I wasn't thinking of any valor and clenched teeth sort of thing, Mr. Holmes. Just how you get to know a guy by sharing a hole in the real estate with him."

"That ought to be just what we need, then. Jan, go take Betty off that Martinson speech and have her take this down. I'll check it later. Glad to meet you, Regan."

He hurried away. Betty was a little girl who looked remarkably like an owl. Chairs were scarce, so Dolph sat beside Jan on a desk top while Betty sat with the notebook braced against her knee.

Jan made alert suggestions and between them they got it into shape. Betty read it to Bill Holmes from her notes, and he liked it. Betty was almost through typing it when the atmosphere of the crowded room changed. Dolph looked toward the door and saw Wally coming in, looking, as always, a bit larger than life size. Wally seemed confident, happy. His big voice filled the room.

"Amateurs, are we? I think we're going to show 'em."

He spotted Dolph and came over, without haste. His small eyes twinkled. "The Lieutenant! Damn your eyes, Dolph! I nearly fell out of the car when I saw you standing there in front of the bank."

Dolph pumped his hand. "Happy to meet you, Mayor Block."

Wally put a familiar arm around Jan's shoulders. She smiled up at him. "Dolph is helping. He's making a statement."

Wally still smiled, but Dolph had the odd impression that the big man had suddenly became wary. "What kind of a statement?"

"The usual thing. How Sergeant Block and Lieutenant Regan won the war."

"Good. Give it a lot of distribution, Jan. Come on into the back room, Dolph. Be with you in a few minutes, people."

Wally closed the door of the back room, closed out the noise of the workers, the ringing of the phones, the rattle of the typewriters. He opened a low cupboard, took out a bottle. There were two glasses on the table. He splashed a generous drink into each glass, handed one to Dolph. He was no longer smiling. He looked tired.

"Here's looking up your address, Lieutenant."

"Here's to the next mayor."

Wally sat down heavily in a frail chair which creaked under his weight. "What are you after, Regan?"

Dolph frowned. "Should I be after something?"

Wally grinned mirthlessly. "Aren't we all, boy? Only you better understand something. Every dime I've got is in this campaign. I've got to get in. And once I'm in, boy, I can't move very fast. Slow and easy will do it. I've got a lot of do-gooders to dump over the side before I can start producing."

Dolph perched on the table. "Maybe I'm stupider than I look."

"No, Lieutenant. There's nothing at all stupid about you. That's what worries me. Here I am, all set to move into the driver's seat, and you have to show up."

"I don't want to stop you."

"That's what I was afraid of. Understand what I said, I've got to move slow. The best I can give you is an appointment. Investigation deal. All it pays is per diem, but maybe I can wangle twenty bucks a day."

"Are you offering me a job, Wally? I don't know anything about city government."

"I suppose you think I do? All I know is how to get onto a gravy train. Shenck froze me out from one direction, so I'm going to be such a nuisance he's going to have to play ball. What are you doing in town?"

"Salesman on the road."

"A hell of a likely story, Lieutenant. You're the coolest one I've seen in a long time." Wally stood up. "Well, you're on the team. But I'm warning you. Don't ever get too greedy. There's enough for all."

He went out before Dolph could emerge from his confusion. It almost seemed as though Wally were mixing him up with some other person. And this gravy-train talk didn't sound exactly like Good Government.

By the time he walked out of the back room he saw Wally Block going through the front door out onto the sidewalk.

Jan came running to him excitedly. "Dolph! He told me! I think it's wonderful. It just never occurred to me that you'd be willing to step in and take a job. Most of our good people have businesses and professions they can't leave. When we start cleaning house we're going to have a terrible shortage of competent men to take over."

"Jan, I don't think I can take any . . ."

"Now you hush. I can see that you need convincing. And I'm going to talk you into it. You can't go back on Wally now."

"I want to talk to you, Jan."

"I've got scads of work to do here, Dolph. Why don't you go back to the hotel? I'll phone you just as soon as I get through."

"How late will you be?"

"Midnight, I guess. Maybe later."

It was only a bit after seven, and a relief to get out onto the dark sidewalk away from the clamor and congestion of the party headquarters. He walked back to the hotel, went restlessly down to the bar. The bar was in the lull between cocktail time and the evening drinkers.

When the bartender brought his bourbon, Dolph said casually, "Is a man named Shenck prominent around here?"

"Dilbert Shenck. Dilly to his pals. You could call it prominent, mister."

"What does he do?"

The bartender grinned humorlessly. "Well, not much of anything. I guess you could kind of say he runs this town. When the mayor wants to spit, he phones Dilly and asks if it's okay. If one of the neighborhood books starts to hold out bets, Dilly calls the Chief and the book goes out of business for a while. Dilly says what streets are going to be repaved and who is going to do it."

"Where does he live?"

"Hell, he's a country gentleman, Dilly is. Big place out Pike Avenue, couple of miles beyond the city limits. Fluorescent lights in the cow barns they say."

"Suppose a man wanted to go see him."

"Sometimes that's tough to do, mister. If I was you, I'd go out South Warren Street to the tracks and look for a big joint on the left a mile beyond the tracks. Some people say Dilly spends his evenings there. It's called Red-Top's."

Dolph finished his drink. The man at the parking lot told him how to get onto South Warren.

He had imagined a garish barn of a place, glittering with neon. Red-Top's turned out to be a long, low, ranch-type place on a knoll, with a long drive that led up to it. The sign on the highway was discreet—black cut-out letters against a pink ground-glass screen.

There were only a half dozen cars in the lot. He parked and went through the nearest door. It opened into a cocktail lounge. A woman with hair like

flame came lithely off a bar stool. She looked to be about thirty. She was
ripely and beautifully built, and she wore a dress that seemed unable to
decide whether it should be chaste or daring. The woman was at least an
inch over six feet tall, and the stilt heels of gold sandals added close to
another four inches. The flame hair was piled high in an ornate crest.

Dolph stared up into her face with something close to awe.

"Sort of takes your breath, doesn't it?" she said in a husky baritone.

"Imposing, in a way."

"Do you know what you get, Shorty?"

"What do I get?"

"A free drink for not asking me how the air is up here. Grab a stool,
Shorty. You have arrived a bit before our traditional festivities. Johnny, give
the man his pleasure. I'm Red-Top."

Seated side by side, her eyes were on a level below his. Most of that
height, he saw, was in her legs, particularly from knee to hip.

"And I'm Dolph Regan, stranger in town."

"You have come to the right place, Regan. Bourbon, did you say? Fill
mine too, Johnny."

Two couples came in and Red-Top gave them her booming welcome.
When she turned around, Dolph said, as casually as he could, "Do I have
any chance of catching Mr. Shenck here tonight?"

She studied him. "Internal Revenue?"

"Nothing so ominous. A friend of a friend."

"That, Shorty, is not what we call enough."

He took his copy of the statement Betty had typed out of his pocket and
unfolded it and handed it to her, under the edge of the bar.

Her lips moved as she read it. She folded it and handed it back to him.
"You call that a friend of a *friend*?"

"In a manner of speaking."

"Come on," she said.

She led the way out of the lounge, back along one side of the almost
deserted dining room to a door at the back. Beyond the door was a hallway,
an office at the end. She clicked on the office lights, pushed the door shut
as soon as he was in.

She kicked off her shoes and it brought her down so that she stood eye
to eye with him. Her manner had changed. "Window dressing for the sucker
trade," she said. "Have a seat."

She sat behind the desk, chin on her fists, and stared at him.

"This needs figuring, Regan. This isn't on the schedule. What do you
want to see Shenck about?"

"Where do you stand? What's your place in the picture?"

"I'm a friend of a friend." Her eyes were a gray so pale that they looked
like rain water on a window pane. Her mouth had a ripe squareness. Her
exuberance and friendliness of the bar was gone, utterly.

He stood up. "Don't bother about it. I can find him."

"What are you selling?"

"Am I selling something?"

She grinned. "All right, Regan. We'll call this a draw." She piled open a desk drawer, took out an automatic and pointed it at his middle. Her hand was not dainty and neither was the weapon. The combination had a deadly efficiency.

"I just dealt myself some new cards," she said, coming around the desk. "Turn around and brace your hands against the door."

As he was lifting his arms, his back to her, consciousness slid into fragments. There was no feeling of being hit. It was as though he saw, within his mind, one of those newsreel shots where a cliff is dynamited. It lifts, almost intact, and then slides into dust and rubble. . . .

Dolph awakened in a blackness so intense that there was no way to orient himself, nor even any assurance that he had not been blinded. He had a shattering headache, a pins and needles feeling in his bound hands and feet. His hands were tied in front of him and he lay on his side with his knees and forehead against a hard surface, hips and heels against another. As he straightened his legs, thrusting against a third surface, the top of his head slid up until it hit the fourth. The feeling was inescapable that he was enclosed in some sort of a box. The air was not good. He breathed rapidly, shallowly.

A coffin could be just like this.

Five feet of packed earth above him. . . .

He sucked in the stale air and screamed. The scream had no place to go. It filled the box like shards of broken glass. The sides of the box were compressing against him, smothering him. He screamed again.

The top lifted. Light slanting in shocked him into silence. It was Red-Top and she had lifted some sort of a lid. He stared up at her as she peered in at him, one hand supporting the lid. Her lips were pursed.

"Hush-a-bye baby," she said.

Wally appeared behind her, towering high and solid over the box. He stared down at Dolph with disapproval. From Dolph's angle of vision they were distorted, out of proportion, leaning as though they would momentarily fall in upon him.

"You disappoint me, Lieutenant," Wally said. The box caught the rumble of his voice, resonated it oddly.

"Wally, please, get me out of here," he begged. "Please!"

Wally put a heavy arm around Red-Top's waist, swayed her back and forth with rough affection. "It was just bad luck, Lieutenant. You made contact with my gal here. We would have both been real upset if you'd gotten to Dilly, wouldn't we, honey?"

"It would have been a shame," she said.

"Wally, I don't understand all this."

"Then why were you trying to see Dilly?"

"Because of what Jan told me. She said a reform group was trying to get you elected. Then you talked about a gravy train. I wanted to see what sort of a person he was."

"And then go disillusion the Holland wench? Don't try to kid me, Lieutenant!"

"Don't leave me in her! What do you want of me?"

Red-Top answered for him. "Why, Wally just wants his old pal to be his house guest. He's sent a man after your baggage and by now you should be all checked out. You're in Wally's place right now, Regan. I got you out the back way. You're a heavy little rascal."

She released the lid and it slammed shut with a sound that deafened Dolph, that left him once more in the frightful darkness.

Chapter 2

THE MOST WANTED MAN IN TOWN

E ACH TIME HE WOULD try to think, try to plan, the waves of panic would come washing over him, weakening him, leaving him gasping and shuddering. During one coherent interval, he managed to cock his head so that he could lay his left ear against the side of the box. He could hear muffled voices and could identify them as belonging to Red-Top, Wally and a third person, a man. He could not make out the words, and from time to time he heard them laugh. It was a small comfort to know that they were there, that he had not been left alone.

And then, as he listened, he heard the voices become more faint, heard the distant slam of a door and then silence. The next spasm of fear was so intense that he knew he must either find an escape or go mad.

The very dimensions of the box defeated him. It was so narrow that he could not bring his knees high enough to be able to exert the strength of his back. He could not sit up, even by bracing himself with his bound hands, because his head struck the inside of the lid too soon.

The only thing left to do was to get over onto his face. This involved getting his knees much straighter than they were. He pushed his head as far up into one corner as he could, and, with an effort that took skin from the angle of his jaw, managed to get his knees under him, his bound hands under his chest.

In that position he was able to get into a kneeling position, his shoulders against the lid. He cautiously pushed upward. The lid did not move. Then, with an effort that rolled his lips back from his teeth and dizzied him, he exerted all his strength against the lid. It came free, suddenly, with the sound of tearing wood. The force slammed it up and he struggled to his feet.

Turning, he saw that he was in a small living room. A small-boned swarthy man sat and stared at him with intense surprise. As he came quickly out of the chair, Dolph lost his balance and toppled over the side of the box onto the rug, unable to break the fall. He landed on his right shoulder and his head thudded against the carpet. Animal shrewdness advised him to pretend to be unconscious.

He lay with his eyes shut, heard the footsteps, heard the soft curse. Hands reached under his armpits and he was tugged up into a sitting position. The man cursed again and began to heave Dolph, a few inches at a time, back toward the box. Dolph, chin on chest, head lolling, waited. Now he was near enough. The small man had to lift him up and in.

The arms slid further through his armpits, and through slitted eyes Dolph saw the lean fingers almost touching. The man grunted and locked his fingers together. As he started to lift, Dolph clamped down with his arms with all his strength, and in the same moment flung his head back as hard as he could. Through the pain of the blow he sensed the sickening impact. With the arms still clamped, he struck again and again. Resistance was over with the second blow. Dolph rolled free. The man lay still, his face a wreck.

The immediate problem was his wrists. They were tied with heavy wrapping cord. At any moment the small man might regain consciousness. Dolph saw that the box was actually a sort of couch with a quilted top. He used it to worm his way to his feet. With care he could hop along.

The kitchen, he saw, was down a short hallway. Twice he almost fell. He found the knife drawer, took a knife out, put the handle inside the drawer and pushed it shut with his hip. He sawed the cord delicately against the exposed blade. As soon as his hands were free, he took the knife clumsily in numbed fingers and cut the ankle cord.

The small man had rolled over onto his back. He was holding one hand over his nose and mouth, moaning weakly. Dolph forced himself to strike the man again. He bound his wrists and ankles and tumbled him into the box, dropped the lid. Then, remembering the airlessness, he propped the lid up with a small table lighter.

He found his sample case and suitcase in the bedroom. He gasped at their weight as he picked them up. He opened the suitcase. In with his fresh clothes he found five common red bricks.

The implication was frighteningly clear. He flipped the bricks out, strapped up the bag again, took two bricks out of the much smaller, heavier sample case. The kitchen clock said ten minutes past one. He pulled Venetian blinds out from the side of the window. A silent street lay one story below.

Wally Block might be returning soon. And Wally had become incomprehensible. It was as though there were two Wally Blocks. One was Sergeant Block, shrewd, dependable, unexcitable. And this new one. Mayor-elect. Man with crazy suspicions, impossible motivations. Yet the man did not seem . . . mad. He seemed merely to possess information which he believed that Dolph shared.

Only one person could make sense of this. Jan Holland. By now she would have given him up, gone to her home. He realized he had no address for her.

Suddenly he realized the ridiculousness of burdening himself with the suitcase and sample case. He dropped them, let himself out into a narrow hall near the head of a straight flight of stairs. One dim bulb burned in the upper hall, one in the lower hallway. He looked down, saw nothing but a front door, the upper half of it glass. He went down quickly, as silently as he could. He looked through the grayish mesh curtain that covered the glass. The porch was dark.

As he touched the doorknob, a car pulled up in front. He moved to the side, still watching. Wally Block got out of the car. The car seemed packed. There were loud voices, laughter. He thought he recognized one laugh as being Jan's. The car drove away and Wally stood there for a time. A street lamp made his shadow grotesquely long.

Wally lifted his arm, made a beckoning motion. A figure came quickly out of the shadows on the far side of the street, trotted toward Wally. Wally turned and walked heavily toward the porch.

Dolph realized that he should have been hunting for a place to hide rather than standing there watching. He ran down the hall, beyond the stairs. A closet was set underneath the stairs. It opened with a rasp of hinges. He went in and pulled the door shut, stood there in a reek of rubber, a smell of rust and dust.

The front door opened and closed. Feet were heavy on the stairs. Wally said softly, "The car's in the back. I'll help you."

"Tracks bother me," another male voice said.

"If you're worried, use planks from that pile by the barn. Line it up with the biggest willow on the other bank. Deeper than hell, there . . ."

The rest of the words were lost. Dolph stood in the darkness and the closet walls were enfolding him, pushing in on him. He put the back of his fist between his teeth and bit hard, holding his breath against the scream that surged within him.

And then he could wait no longer. He slammed the closet door back against the wall as he plunged for the front door. At the first attempt his wet hand slid off the knob. He wrested the door open, plunged down the porch steps. He ran down the dark sidewalk, shoe soles slapping so hard that his feet stung, his mouth open, sucking air, his eyes bulging and blinded with the strain.

Once he heard a shout. He ran on until he could run no more, and with the last bit of his strength he vaulted a low hedge by a dark house, fell on the damp grass, rolled into the deeper shadows of the shrubbery close to the house.

Nearby a dog barked. Car tires made a silky noise on the asphalt. Wind rustled the leaves that were turning dry with autumn. A couple went by. Dolph saw them under the street light. Arm in arm. Girl's face, flower-like, upturned to his. Laughter warm and low in her throat.

After a long time he got up. His bones felt leaden. He shuffled across the grass, pushed his way through a narrow gap in the hedge. He had no idea how far he had run, or in what direction. He went to the nearest corner and looked in all directions. Far down the street to his left he saw a cluster of lights, neon so far away that he could not make out the sign.

After three blocks the neon was readable. *Grill.*

A neighborhood spot. Smeared window. Light shone through the window onto a pole outside, a pole on which a placard was tied—heavy smiling face—Block for Mayor.

He knew they would stare at him, but he went in. The bartender gave him five nickels. It was a wall phone. Numbers were scrawled on the plaster wall around the phone.

"Information."

"Have you got a number for the headquarters of the Good Government League?"

"Do you know the address, sir?"

"No. Look, it's Wally Block's campaign headquarters."

"Just a moment, sir." From behind him the clink of glass on glass, low conversation, chatter of the pinball. "That number is 33134, sir."

"Thanks."

33 1 3 4. There. Duzzzz duzzzz duzzzz duzzzz. "Yeah?"

"Is Miss Holland still there?"

"Don't see her."

"Can you give me her number?"

"It's in the book, isn't it?"

"There are seven Hollands in the book."

"Try under John J., friend."

"Thanks."

Holland. John J. 26765. 18 Walker Circle.

26 7 6 5. There. Duzzz duzzz duzz. "Hello?"

"Jan?"

"This is Jan speaking."

"Jan, this is Dolph. I . . ."

"I guess we better skip it until tomorrow, Dolph. I'm dead."

He was conscious of the listeners behind him. "Jan, I must see you. It's very important."

"Very isn't enough. It better be crucial. Earth shaking."

"It is."

"You sound . . . almost frightened. Want me to take a run down to the hotel?"

"I'm not there. I better come to your house. I have the address out of the book."

"Do you know how to get here?"

"I'll get a cab."

It was a big stone house, impressive but not cold. The window lights looked warm, comfortable. He paid the cab and went up the walk. She opened the door before he could press the bell. She wore a long dark blue robe, the belt knotted at her waist.

"I wanted to catch you before you started those darn chimes going and woke up the house," she said in a half whisper. "Come on in."

There was one floor lamp on in the big long living room. Embers glowed on the hearth. She turned her back to the embers, her hands in the pockets of the robe.

"You look sort of rumpled, Dolph. And you've scraped your face. Been sampling our night life?"

He sat down on the couch that faced the fire. He spoke slowly, distinctly. He started with the episode in the back room at headquarters. He gave her no time for questions. When he started she was standing, facing him. When he finished she was sitting beside him, her eyes wide.

"It can't be!" she said softly.

"But it is. He said it. He told me that he couldn't get in with Shenck any other way."

"He's a thoroughly honest man, Dolph. Don't you think we've checked him a thousand ways?"

He held out his hands. The red grooves in his wrists had faded, but they were still visible. She touched the mark on his left wrist with her fingertips. "This . . . is more than I can . . . absorb in one sitting." She smiled wryly.

"They planned to kill me. Put me in my car and run it off into the water somewhere near a barn with a board pile and a willow tree on the opposite bank. He was talking to a man with a high voice."

She stood up suddenly and walked two steps to stand on the hearth, her back to him. "I—I believe you, Dolph. And I'm darned if I know why. I've got to think. If all this is true, we've got to stop him. Better a devil you know than a devil you don't."

"He acts like I knew something about him, Jan."

"And you don't?"

"Only what happened tonight. Now I *do* know too much."

"When did you see him the last time? I mean when you were both in the army?"

"The war was over and we were waiting to be sent home as a unit. They gave us odd jobs to do. Running convoys of stuff back to Paris. I guess I had too much to drink in Paris. Got a knock on the head. Bad concussion. Woke up in a general hospital near Paris three weeks later. The unit had gone home. So, let me see. The last time I saw Wally was during that truck ride."

She turned and studied him for a moment. "Maybe something happened the night you were hurt. And Wally thinks you remember."

"I don't remember anything. That was years ago, you know. If I was going to remember, I would have before this."

"I suppose so," she said softly.

The door chimes began to sound, and in the middle of the melody somebody clattered the brass door knocker.

"Darn!" Jan Holland said softly.

Dolph moved instinctively to the far corner of the room. She stared at him curiously. He licked his lips. "I better not be here, Jan."

"Go through that door then and wait. The hall leads back to the kitchen." She went to the front door. He listened.

"Miss Holland?"

"Yes."

"Police, Miss Holland."

"I can see that."

"Sorry to bother you. There's been trouble. Mr. Block got hold of us. A friend of his, stranger in town, went off his rocker and killed a guy in Block's apartment. Then he ran. Fella named Regan. Dolph Regan."

Dolph held his breath.

Jan said, "Why come to me?"

"Mr. Block said you were with him earlier today. Mr. Block said he might come here. Have you seen him?"

"No, I haven't."

"Well, we got his car where he left it behind Mr. Block's apartment, and we got his luggage. Thanks. If he shows up, Miss Holland, don't let him in. Try to stall him and phone us."

A heavy voice said, sleepily, "Who is that, Jan?"

"Nothing important, Dad. Go back to bed."

"Thanks, Miss Holland. We're getting in touch with Regan's firm in the morning. We're watching the bus station and the railroad. Unless he hitches a ride, I don't think he'll get out of town."

"Thank you for warning me."

"That's okay."

Dolph heard the door shut softly, heard her footsteps coming across the rug toward him.

She looked at him. She held the back of her hand to her forehead. "You get tired enough and everything gets unreal, Dolph."

"I've got to leave. They'll find the cab driver. He'll say he brought me here."

"I keep wondering why I said I hadn't seen you."

"I could start talking about a big frame-up. I could try to tell you that Wally got so sore at the guy I tricked he hit him too hard."

"Come back and sit down by the fire. No one can see in."

"I'll sit down by the fire, Jan. There's something I have to tell you."

She sat beside him. He put his head back and closed his eyes. "You said when you get tired, Jan, things seem unreal. How unreal can they get when you can't trust the evidences of your own senses? I'm trying to say this. I'm trying to say that maybe it all didn't happen. Maybe Wally didn't say what I thought he said."

She was biting her lip. "Dolph!"

"They'll check back, all right. They'll find out that a doctor pressured the company into hiring me. It's a kind of occupational therapy. For the last couple of years I've been in and out of hospitals. It started one day in the firm. I was trying to sell a big builder and his partners on a design for a low-cost home. And then their eyes went as big as saucers and the walls started folding in on me and I screamed and ran out of there."

She touched his arm. "Don't, Dolph. Not that way. Not so bitter."

"It comes like fright. It squashes me. It turns me into a crazy animal trying to get out a trap."

"Have you ever imagined things that didn't happen?"

"This can be the first time, Jan."

"You've done a good job of imagining. You've imagined a lump behind your ear and welts on your wrists and a scrape on your face, Dolph."

"Don't get sucked in. Don't go maternal. Tell me to get out, Jan. That's your best play."

"Never tell a woman to be logical," she said.

He looked down at his fists. "What can we do? What can I do?"

"I've got friends, Dolph. All traces of what happened can't be removed. We can find enough to back up your story. Maybe you ought to turn yourself in and let me put someone to work on it. Let me get Dad in on it, too. He's publisher of the Brasher *Courant,* and the paper owns BRCX. We're not helpless."

"Tomorrow—I mean today—is the day before election, isn't it?"

A stocky, gray-haired man in a terrycloth robe came into the room. His hair was mussed. "Jan, who is this?"

They stood up. "Dad, this is Dolph Regan."

The man's eyes widened. "What's going on here? I just caught a late news flash on the bedside radio. This man is a murderer, Jan!"

"Listen to what he has to say, Dad."

"I'm not a judge. I'm not a booking sergeant. They can listen to what he has to say."

He began to move warily toward the phone.

"Dad," she begged, "Dolph can tell you that Wally is going to turn crooked the minute he's in office."

Mr. Holland glared. "Nonsense! When I put the weight of the paper and the station behind a man, you can be assured that he's sound."

"Are you afraid to listen to him, Dad? Are you afraid of what you might hear?"

Holland stopped his cautious drifting toward the phone. "Of course not. Speak up, Regan. What's your story?"

A boy of about eighteen had appeared in the doorway, unnoticed. Dolph guessed that he was Jan's brother. Dolph swallowed hard.

"It was like this. I had forgotten that this was Wally's home town. He was my platoon sergeant and . . ."

He swallowed again. All three of them were watching him. He felt the familiar roaring sound in his ears. Vision went off at a tangent. Holland's face swelled to the size of a bushel basket, seemed to press closer to him. The three of them stood at an odd angle, and the floor tilted up to where they stood. Eyes pulsing—expanding, then shrinking. The walls of the room were shifting, moving in.

He began to back away from them, shoulders hunched, arms hugging his belly. This was terror. Blindness. Holland had gone gray. Jan stood with her fingers at her throat. He could not break through to her, tell her what had happened.

Then the door handle was under his fingers and he did not remember how he had gotten out into the hallway. Running, running. Street lights marching by in orderly precision. Curb-stumble. Ankle-pain, slowly receding. Whip-slap of shoe leather and cool night air streaming against his sweating face.

Run for your life. Run from terror.

And the car was moving along, keeping pace with him. He began to run faster, looking wildly for a place to hide.

"Dolph!" she called. "Dolph, stop!"

Pain was a huge fist that tightened slowly on his left side, from waist to armpit.

"Dolph!"

He stopped suddenly, weak, sweating, panting, undone.

Jan was at the wheel of a pale convertible, the top down. He stood numbly and stared at the car, his chest heaving.

"Get in, Dolph." She leaned over and released the door. He got in humbly and pulled the door shut. She started up. "We're going back, Dolph, and we're going to get to the bottom of this."

There was strength in her, a strength he wanted to lean on. She still wore the robe. She held her chin high, looking over the long hood of the car. Her hair whipped in the night wind.

His breathing began to slow down. Suddenly she jammed on the brakes so hard that he had to brace himself against the dash. She shifted into reverse, backed into a driveway. He looked down the street and saw the sedan, red light on top, parked in front of her house. She roared the car off in the opposite direction.

"Take me to the station, Jan."

"Don't be a fool! I saw what happened to you. Do you want a padded cell for the next thirty years?"

He had to speak loudly above the whine of the wind. "Maybe that's what I need, Jan."

"Shut up, please."

She wrenched the car around many corners, then straightened it out on a highway where, for the first time, there was a certain amount of traffic. They passed all-night drive-ins.

"Where are we going?"

"To a place I know," she said. A light caught them and she pressed the button that put the top up, shut out the night wind.

"They can make trouble for you, Jan."

"Don't be such a miserable rabbit," she said.

It cut sharply and deeply. He clamped his jaw shut. Okay, baby. Take your own risks.

He guessed that they were twenty miles from town before she turned north off the highway. The dash clock said three. The night air had grown perceptibly colder.

After ten miles on the secondary road, she turned off into a lane between the trees. The car lurched over ruts. She pulled off into the brush and turned off the motor and lights.

"Now watch the path and try to follow me, Dolph."

It was not a long walk, but it was down a steep hill where roots laced the path. Ahead of him he heard her step up onto a wooden porch.

They were out of the trees and there was some starlight. Enough to see her as a moving shadow. He saw her stretch high, run her fingers along a porch beam, heard her sigh of satisfaction.

He could hear the lap of water, the creak of a dock. The lock grated and the door opened onto a greater darkness.

"Wait here," she said. She went in. He heard a sound he could not identify, a sort of pumping sound, and then saw the match flame. The flame grew into a blinding whiteness and he knew that she had pumped pressure into a gasoline lantern.

The blue-white light made harsh shadows, a cruel illumination on the wide boards of the floor, board and batten walls, huge stone fireplace.

"There's the woodbox and you can find some papers around. Make yourself useful and I'll be back in a few minutes," she said.

He laid a fire of newspaper, kindling, large birch logs. He opened the draft and lit the paper. The fire caught at once and began to roar as flames fingered up between the logs.

She came back into the room. She had changed to faded jeans, a plaid wool shirt. "Mumm. Nice fire."

"Will they look here?"

"No chance. There are only two cabins on the lake. The other is on the far side, empty now. I'm a moody guy sometimes, Dolph. I bought this myself, with money an aunt left me. Nobody knows where it is. It's my cave, sort of. I crawl into it and growl at the world."

With her hands in the pockets of the jeans, she moved over, kicked a log into better position. With her back to him, she said, "I'm your friend."

"I know that, Jan. But—"

"Even so, I'm going to lock the door and put the key in my pocket. You're not going to be able to run. And you're going to keep remembering that I'm your friend."

"What are you going to do?"

She turned out the lantern, carefully locked the door. The room was alive with flame light. "Lie down on the couch there, Dolph."

"Amateur psychoanalysis?" he said acidly.

"See how you fight against it? Go on, stretch out. Try to relax."

He shrugged. She came over and sat beside him. He moved over a bit to give her room. She bent and kissed his lips lightly. As he reached for her, she pulled back.

"That was just to let you know I'm on your side, Dolph."

"This sort of thing has been done before."

"Not by me. Not by Jan. Not by a girl you want."

"What makes you think I want you?"

"See how you try to squirm out of it—by trying to make me mad? You can't make me angry, Dolph. Shut your eyes. Think of a small enclosed place, a place you can't get out of."

"Life is a place you can't get out of."

"Skip the corny sophisms. Do as I tell you."

He closed his eyes. A small place. An enclosed place. Cold.

He felt the contraction of his muscles, the tautening of his throat.

"Say what you think of. Say the words."

"Cold," he said in a voice that rasped. "Cold, dampness. Naked. Dark. Wet stone. Cold and hurt. My head hurts."

He sat up, gasping for air. She pushed him back gently. "Close your eyes again, Dolph. Think. Remember."

"I . . . I can't."

"Think, Dolph."

His mind drifted back through blackness. "Truck," he said in a whisper. "Running, and there was a truck. I didn't know what they said. They put me in the truck with . . . all the others. Packed like cattle. Swaying. Sweat and stink. Packed so tight I couldn't breathe. All of them watching me."

"Better, Dolph. Oh, much better. You were running from the dark place and they put you in a truck. Were you still naked?"

He frowned, his eyes still shut. "No. I got clothes from someplace. Let me think. Clothes. Wait! There was a stone window, a narrow window, level with a dark alley. I wiggled through it and I hurt my chest. I knew that I had to have clothes. And I waited. There was a man. He tried to run. I knocked him down and I took his clothes because I knew I had to get away."

"Do you know how you were dressed when they took you into the hospital?"

"They told me that. My uniform was gone. I wore ragged clothes. A QM truck company officer brought me in and said he'd found me with a bunch of DPs."

"Could he have taken you off the truck, do you think? Maybe you called to him from the truck. They'd picked you up not knowing you were American, thinking you were another Pole or whatever nationality they were taking out of Paris in the trucks."

"Just vague—very vague—I have the memory of calling, of all of them in the truck, pressed close to me, watching me, laughing when I called."

"We've got that much. You escaped from a dark place through a stone window. You were naked. You stole clothes and were put in a truck with DPs. Now we have to go the other way. Back toward the beginning of it."

"No," he said.

"Dolph, we *must!*"

"I can't remember."

"Start with the trucks. Start with entering Paris."

"There was a checkpoint. We had tank trucks. Thirty of them. Thousands of gallons of gasoline, hauling it back west when it had been so much trouble to get it east, for the tanks."

"Gas was valuable, wasn't it?"

"On the black market a dollar a gallon. But don't you see, Jan? When I woke up in the hospital, the only thing I could remember was driving away from the checkpoint, sitting beside the driver in the lead truck. I had the convoy trip ticket in my hand. It had just been stamped. And after that . . . blackness."

"Why did you assume that you'd gone on a drunk?"

"That was what I planned to do. I thought I had, and had gotten into a brawl."

"Let's rest for a time and try it again, Dolph." Without self-consciousness she swung her feet up, stretched out beside him. He slid his arm under her shoulders, ran his lips along the smooth clear line of her cheek. "No, Dolph, please," she said sleepily. "Just keep trying to remember. Every minute. Keep trying."

Chapter 3

DEATH FOR TWO

H E SLEPT. There was a door. He knew, as he dreamed, that it was a door. A door for giants. The latch was a dozen feet over his head. There was a piece of timber. With it he was trying to trip the latch. It was too heavy. It kept falling. And then she was beside him, smiling, helping. Another try. Up, up. The latch clicked loudly and the door swung open. Wally Block stood there, filling the doorway, smiling down. Dolph took Jan's hand and tried to run from Wally. But the big foot lifted, blotting out the stars, ready to stamp down, smash them . . .

Dolph awoke with a gasp. The room was chill. The hearth was gray ashes. The windows were gray oblongs. His right arm was asleep. She had turned toward him, her cheek on his arm, her knees pulled up so that they dug into his thigh. Her face was calm and lovely.

With care he moved an inch at a time, pressed his lips against hers. They moved under his with a wordless exclamation and she came awake.

She pushed at his chest and sat up. She combed her hair back hard with her fingers, then buried her face in her hands.

"Compromised, hey?" she said, her voice muffled.

"Both of us so bushed. We couldn't help it."

She turned and smiled at him, slid off the couch and stood up. "How did your subconscious do while you were asleep? Did we jog it enough?"

"I dreamed that together we got a door open. Wally Block was on the other side of it. And then, as I woke up, I remembered it, Jan. In the moment of awakening, I knew what happened. I know now."

All the lethargy, the warm languidness of awakening, left her. "Tell me!" she said tensely.

"Wally was in the second truck. They pulled by me and cut me off by the curb. Wally came back to talk. It was dusk. He climbed in so that there were three of us in the cab, me in the middle. The convoy was halted. He said he'd done some missionary work and he had a buyer for the whole convoy. I told him not to be a damn fool and told my driver to get going. He laughed at me. Wally stuck a .45 in my ribs and told me to be good. He gave the route. We took the lead again. Then it was night and we were still rumbling through those narrow streets.

"We drove down an alley and through an arch into a courtyard with warehouses all around it. Men met us. The other trucks didn't know where they were going. Some of the men were AWOLS that had gone into the Paris underground, into the black market. They had weapons. Three of the drivers tried to get away. The archway was blocked. They were shot down. Just like that.

"Wally was some sort of a ringleader. He told me not to be a damn fool. He said if I cooperated I could have a thousand dollars, and information on a sure-fire way of getting it to this country. I tried to make a break for it. He ran along behind me, yelling to the others not to shoot. I turned just in time to see him swinging the flat of the .45 toward my head. When I came to I was underground, in a narrow place. There was a tiny barred door at the end. It was like a coffin with a door at the end, all made of wet stone. I'd been stripped. Wally came and told me he was sorry, but they had a use for my uniform and identification for a few hours.

"He went away. They'd even taken my dog tags. I pried one stone loose from the wall, a stone the size of a brick. I pounded on the hinges until I broke first one and then the other. I got out. I found the high narrow window and got out of it into the alley. I jumped on a man who came running down the alley. I think he had maybe escaped from the truck load. I think the others in the DP truck stared at me that way because they knew, and the French guards didn't, that I wasn't the man who had escaped, even though I wore his clothes."

She took his hand in both of hers. "Look, my darling," she said. "All this fear you've had. This blind irrational fear. See what it was due to? The trauma of that experience. And now you understand it. It won't come back anymore."

"Say the darling part again."

Even in the pale gray light he saw her flush. "Don't be a fool, Dolph. Now you see how it fits. Wally had no way of knowing you'd forgotten. He thought you were here to blackmail him. He told you that all he could do was to give you a small job. Then you went to see Shenck, the man he mentioned. That woman, Red-Top, turned out to be on Wally's side. He probably told her about you. Wally thought you were going to sell Shenck the story of that gas convoy. It would be invaluable the day before election. The answer would be to have you disappear completely. Then you couldn't sell information or blackmail Wally."

"He must have been afraid all these years that one day I'd show up."

"We've got to plan, Dolph."

"How do you plan your way out of a killing?"

"Do you think you killed that man?"

"How can I know? I didn't think so. I hurt him, I know."

"Block would be angry with him for letting you get away. Dolph, I saw him lose his temper once. It frightened me."

"Who can you trust, Jan, really trust, in the Brasher police?"

"The Chief is named Tom Rider. He's a dear old fuddy-duddy. Absolutely harmless and absolutely honest. He's one of Dad's friends. Shenck controls the police through the Commissioner, not through Tom. But you know how things are. All the ones who want to stay on the job are mending their fences, hoping that Wally won't have them thrown out if he wins."

Dolph stretched mightily and scrubbed the stubble on his jaw with his knuckles. She watched him.

"You look better, Dolph. Your eyes look better, as if you weren't seeing ghosts any longer in the back of your mind."

"That's easy to say. How do I know I still won't go to pieces when the circumstances are lined up against me?"

She went over and hooked one elbow on the mantel, scuffing her heel against the hearth. "We can't go into town in the daylight, Dolph. They'll pick you up at once. I could go alone. I could try to see Shenck."

"What would you say to him?"

"That if he wants to help us, we can ruin Wally's chances."

"How?"

"Bollinger is the mayor. He's running against Wally. If Bollinger could use all this about Wally in his last speech . . ."

"Wouldn't it sound just like another political smear?"

"You should give the speech," she said, smiling.

"Not me."

She stiffened. "Now wait a minute. Maybe that isn't such a silly idea. Wally has radio time today for a canned speech. I could get us into the station. I could keep them from taking it off the air. You could just tell the story of that gas convoy, Dolph."

He found the two remaining cigarettes in a pack, lit them both, handed one to her. He thought hard. "And that might clear me of the other thing, by showing Wally's motive for framing me."

"It's worth a try, Dolph. I was just kidding when I first mentioned it."

"Where do we go from here?"

"Roger Parry runs the station. If I told him to jump out a window, I think he would. If we can just get to him . . ."

On the outskirts of town Dolph waited in the car while Jan made a phone call from a small grocery store. When she came out she was pale and upset. Dolph was behind the wheel. She got in quickly.

"Dolph, I didn't know they were going to get so upset. Dad has called out everything but the Marines. Roger wanted to be stubborn, and let Dad know that I was okay. I guess you are supposed to have murdered me or something. We're going to have one awful job trying to get into Roger's office without anyone finding out."

"We're . . . a bit conspicuous, lady."

"Let's give it a try."

As he started up, he saw out of the corner of his eye the car that had come up beside him, the black sedan with fishpoles fore and aft, decal on the side, two uniformed men in the seat. He stared straight at them and saw, aimed at his face, the round dark eye at the end of the muzzle.

He had gone a hundred feet beyond the store. He turned in too abruptly and the left front wheel bounded over the curb. The cruiser nosed in, blocking them.

One cop came up to his window, wary, revolver ready, and the other went around to Jan's side and opened the door.

"You all right, Miss Holland?"

"Of course I'm all right!" she said indignantly.

It was a neighborhood of overgrown lots, stained billboards. Early morning traffic was heading for the city. Dolph noticed that the man by his window stood so that the gun was shielded from passing cars.

"Regan, don't try to make any trouble."

"He isn't going to make any trouble," Jan said hotly. "He's innocent, and I'm going on the air to tell how and why Wally Block framed him."

"You're upset, Miss Holland."

"I demand to be taken to my home, officer."

One cop said to the other. "Sixth precinct, Al?"

"No. Can't trust Taylor."

"What's going on?" Jan asked.

They ignored her. They seemed obscurely troubled. The one by Dolph's window said, "How about the farm?"

"That's better. Keep them quiet while I make a phone call."

The man strode away from Jan's window. The other one looked glum.

"What's this about a farm?" Dolph asked.

"We got the word, Regan. A certain party doesn't want you picked up officially until tomorrow. Anybody taking you in might get to be unpopular. Having the girl with you makes things kind of complicated. Just take it easy for a while."

Traffic snarled by and pallid sunlight began to come through the morning mist. The other cop came back. "The farm it is. Both of them. The car stays right here."

During a few moments when there was no traffic, Jan and Dolph were herded into the cruiser. The man driving took a U turn, a series of back streets, then headed south into the country.

The farm was nondescript. The cruiser went down the drive, swung to a stop between house and barn. A heavy sedan was parked near the barn and Wally Block stood leaning against it, smiling faintly.

Dolph looked beyond the barn, saw the curve of a small river, a group of willows on the far bank. A young man came out of the house. He had a soft, handsome face and a look of great evil.

Wally walked over. "Welcome to the Block homestead, folks. And thanks, boys."

"There could be a lot of trouble from this," one of the cops said.

Wally stared at him. "Don't you worry about that. There could be a lot more trouble if you'd taken him in. You know that."

"Sure, sure," the cop said hastily. "Only you never saw us."

"And neither did they," Wally said. "Come on, folks. Get out."

They got out. The cruiser swung hard and raced down the drive as though the men were eager to wash their hands of the whole thing.

"Lieutenant, you've been giving me a lot of trouble."

"That's nothing compared to the trouble you're going to have," Jan said grimly.

Wally smiled, almost sadly. "Jan, honey, you just don't understand. I can't have people rocking the apple cart when I'm this close. I haven't gotten to too many of the cops. It was just luck that a couple of my boys picked you up. Otherwise you two might have been making statements."

"What makes you think I won't make statements when you let me go?" Jan demanded.

"I can think of a lot of ways of stopping you, honey. Want to hear a few? I could have that kid brother of yours worked over. Or I could arrange some nice glossy prints of you that you wouldn't want shown around. Or I could promise to have somebody frame that noble old man of yours. Want some more?"

Dolph took a step forward and said, "Block, if you hurt her in any way. . . ."

Wally threw his head back and laughed. "So it's like that! That makes it nice. That makes it easier all around, Lieutenant. You talk and she has a bad time. She talks and you have a bad time. Perfect, Lieutenant!"

"I think you're insane," Jan said in a low voice.

"Crazy like foxes, honey. Come on in and make yourself at home. Don't be wise because my friend Bobby has orders about you. Right, Bobby?"

The young man said, in a thin voice, "Oh, how right! I know just what to do."

"He was going to roll my car into that river with me in it?" Dolph asked.

"It would have been dreadfully interesting," Bobby said with a smirk.

"You disappointed the boy," Wally said.

It was the typical kitchen of an unimproved farm. A pump was set into the wooden drainboard beside the sink.

As they went through the kitchen, Red-Top came out of one of the bedrooms. The red hair was tousled and her face was puffy. She wore aqua pajamas, with a gold belt. She stared at them and through them.

"Don't mind Claire," Wally said. "She isn't civil until noon."

"Up with the chickens yet," Claire grumbled.

"Where will they be happy?" Bobby asked.

"Tie her and give him the run of the house. That ought to make it simple."

Bobby clapped his hands. "Of course!"

Claire was bending over the sink, cupping up cold water. Wally went up behind her and slapped her smartly.

"Watch it!" she snapped.

"Get your clothes on. We're leaving for town. I'll drop you."

"Nuts. I'm going to get some more sleep. I'll come in later, with Bruce, when and if he gets here."

"Suit yourself," Wally said. He went out. Dolph heard the car motor start, caught a glimpse of the sedan with Wally at the wheel as it went by the windows.

Dolph tried to move close to Bobby without being conspicuous about it. Bobby smiled and pulled his hand out of his pocket. He touched the button and the six-inch blade of the switch knife flicked out, locking in position.

"Naughty, naughty," Bobby said gently.

Jan looked shrunken, withdrawn. She was listless as Dolph, following Bobby's orders, tied her wrists to the arms of a heavy chair with lengths of clothesline. Bobby checked the knots, pulled them a shade tighter. He took a nearby chair, a pile of magazines in his lap.

He said, "Now if you don't answer when I call you, Mr. Regan, or if you try anything coy, I'll make Miss Holland very unhappy."

Claire stood in the doorway. "Dirty little animal, isn't he?"

She padded back into a bedroom. Dolph heard her heavy sigh, the creak of springs. He wandered around, looking out windows. He could see no other dwelling. Just fields and patches of woods and a road with no traffic.

Thinking vaguely of some sort of a weapon, he wandered out into the woodshed.

"Still around, Mr. Regan?" Bobby called.

"Yes," he answered dutifully. There was nothing out there that would serve. No axe. No tools. No knives in the kitchen drawers.

The long slow hours passed. It was noon by his watch when he had the glimmerings of an idea. The pump handle was bolted to a rigid support on one end. The nut and bolt were rusty. They bruised his fingers. He used a torn towel and managed to free the nut. He turned it until it came off and only the bolt held it. The piston arm, fastened to the middle of the handle was far easier. He knew that in a matter of seconds he could free the handle, provide himself with a cast iron club over two feet long.

Claire woke up and came yawning out of the bedroom. "Bruce been here?" she asked Bobby.

"I haven't noticed," he said sweetly.

Claire gave him a long look of contempt. She went back in to dress. Dolph knew that the time in which he could make a move was growing short. He dreaded the consequence of failure. Yet logic said that if Block were truly mad, his simplest answer would be the death of both Jan and Dolph.

Dolph walked casually into the kitchen again, freed the pump handle, lifted it off without a sound. He held it close to his leg. Claire was fixing her hair behind the half-open door. He glanced through the crack and saw that her back was turned. He revised his plan at once, slid through the opening of the door; and as she turned, eyes wide, he rapped her across the skull with the handle.

He had been afraid of hitting too hard, but the red hair muffled the blow. Her eyes glazed and she swayed, making no sound, reaching out to the bed post to steady herself. He took a shallow breath and struck again, stepping forward quickly to grab her around the waist as she sagged. He levered her over onto the bed.

He went into the hallway and grasped the pump handle in both hands, near the end. He rehearsed his exact moves mentally. Then he swung the handle high over his head and in the same motion sprang into the room. As Bobby came up out of the chair, his hand flicking toward his pocket, Dolph threw the handle with all his strength. It made one half turn in the air. Bobby tried to duck away from it, but the blunt end caught him flush in the hollow of his throat.

Jan screamed once and then she was still. Dolph was glad that Bobby had managed to pull the knife free of his pocket in the instant that he died. He did not think he could have forced himself to go through the pockets.

He cut Jan free. Her eyes were weak and sick.

"That . . . woman?" she said.

"She's all right. Come on."

Her fingers hardened on his wrist as they heard the car come into the drive. When it stopped behind the house they went out the front door as quickly and quietly as they could. They did not stop running until they had reached a patch of woods on the far side of a neighboring field. Jan collapsed on the ground, gagging and coughing, and Dolph clung to a tree trunk and watched the house. After a very few minutes he saw a heavy man hurry out to the car, saw Claire running unsteadily after him. The car left as though it were being pursued.

Jan had herself under control again.

"Where do we go now?" she said.

"There's only one answer to that. We go to Shenck. This is no time to be touchy about who helps us."

It was the Good Government League's final rally and banquet, and it was held in the large ballroom of the Brasher Hotel. In the dark corridor behind the curtains, Dolph could hear the enthusiasm. Shenck's people had smuggled him into the hotel. Shenck had been incredulous for a long time, but at last he had believed.

He knew that Shenck had planned this with all the care of a fleet admiral setting up the order of battle. Shenck was not a wholesome person to do business with. But he was able to produce twenty men who would follow orders.

Dolph smiled grimly as he heard portions of Wally's final speech, the speech that was being broadcast.

"Even though this should be a time of celebration, I know we are all saddened by wondering what might have happened to one of our most loyal workers, Janet Holland. I sincerely hope that she is unharmed, that the man now the object of a statewide search will be apprehended soon."

He went on to specific campaign issues. Dolph had to admit that Block was a convincing speaker. Devilishly convincing. His aura of forthrightness and honesty was thick enough to cut with a knife. Small wonder that he had hypnotized so many voters.

They stood up and cheered and applauded when he was through. Dolph turned quickly as the man came up behind him. "Okay, Regan. It's all set. You're on."

Dolph's mouth was dry. He straightened his shoulders and pushed through the curtain. Two men followed him closely. He came out onto the stage that held the speaker's table. The master of ceremonies turned from the microphone and stared blankly at the trio. Wally gave a grunt of dismay and lunged for the mike. The nearest of Shenck's men rammed a gun into Wally's middle and forced him back to his chair.

The ballroom was in uproar. Chairs overturned and people started to scurry for the exits.

"Please keep your seats," Dolph said into the mike, trying to keep his voice calm. "Please keep your seats. The doors are guarded. The men have orders to let no one out. Return to your seats, you people by the doors."

The people from the radio station were being guarded, ordered to keep the connection open. With any break at all, Jan could keep the station from taking the program off the air.

Slowly order returned to the room. Block sat still, his face pasty, sullen, his eyes hooded.

A faint roaring began in Dolph's ears. His vision began to go off. The ballroom began that familiar shrinking.

Not now, he begged silently. Not with so much depending on this! He thought of Jan, of what she had said. He shut his eyes and fought against it, fought with the sweat rolling down his cheeks. And slowly, steadily, the room returned to normal.

Dolph straightened his shoulders. "My name is Dolph Regan. In order to get a chance to speak to you and to the radio audience, I have had to use force. I regret that. You are fair people. I know that. All I want is a chance to tell my story, calmly, truthfully. And then you shall judge my case. And judge Wallace Block in the light of your new knowledge."

The trembling left his voice. His knees steadied. "I first met Sergeant Wallace Block when I was assigned as a replacement infantry officer in eastern France. . . ."

AS he went on he could feel the focus of attention. The room was very still. He told of the convoy, of coming to Brasher and seeing Wally Block in the parade, of talking to him at headquarters, of going to Red-Top's. He explained the mental block which kept him from remembering the Paris episode.

At the end he said, "And now I am prepared to give myself up to the police, confident that on the basis of a thorough and unbiased investigation, I will be cleared."

In the awed silence he stepped back.

Wally Block stood up and brushed by the gun and went to the mike.

"My friends, you have just heard the most fantastic set of lies that you will ever hear." He paused, smiling. There was no sound in the room.

"Will you believe him? Instead of me?"

There was still no sound.

Wally Block sucked at his underlip. His face darkened. There was no mistaking the unfriendliness of that silence.

With the breath-taking animal quickness some large man have, Block spun and slammed the guard to the floor. Before the man could pick himself up, Block had already disappeared through the curtained doorway.

It was more effective than ten thousand words of confession. . . .

After four hours of courteous, searching questions, Dolph was released. Flash bulbs blinded him on the dark courthouse steps.

"Have they got Block yet?"

"Twenty minutes ago, I believe. They're bringing him here. Him and the redheaded woman."

"Any statement at all, Mr. Regan?"

"Yes," Dolph said. "I cleared myself with the help of Shenck. But unless this city gets rid of men like Shenck and Block, the next man in a spot like I was in may not be so lucky."

"Some gratitude!"

Dolph smiled. "Take it or leave it, boys. Shenck helped me for his own purposes, so he could keep his hold on the town. I'm not grateful, and he knows it."

"How about you and Jan Holland?"

He saw her then, coming up the walk toward him, her head high, her smile for him alone.

"They tell me I'm going to have to make an honest woman of her," Dolph said.

She took his arm and turned to the reporters. "And that's off the record," she said.

The bulbs popped again. They fled down the walk to her car. He shut the door and ran around, slid behind the wheel.

"Honest woman!" she said. "I like *that!*"

"Many a poor guy forms a terrific emotional attachment for his psychiatrist," he said, slowing for the light at the corner.

"Save your strength, Regan. You've got a tough evening ahead of you."

"Daddy?"

"Complete with shotgun."

He pulled over into a shadowed place and turned off the light and motor. He put his arms around her. She lifted her face.

"Just one question, darling," he said.

"I'll answer anything."

"Tell me, darling, how are you going to vote tomorrow?"

He smothered her indignation in a thoroughly successful way.

Murderer's Encore

MURRAY LEINSTER

D OREN'S DYING WAS OVER too soon. Much too soon. When the
tree branch crashed down on his shoulder, Doren jerked his fat face
around in incredulous astonishment. He took the second blow slantingly on
his head and then his face went terrified. At the third blow he went down,
squealing feebly, and saw Thad Hunt for the first time. His expression took
on a look of ultimate horror, He knew he was going to be murdered and
that there was nothing that could save him from it.

There were trees all about and the rustling of wind in the foliage overhead. Somewhere a little brook made small, tranquil, liquid sounds and
somewhere the flute-like call of a bob-white quail floated over the hills. No
other noises sounded but for impacts of the maniacal blows Thad Hunt
dealt his enemy.

The frenzied satisfaction he felt almost paid him for his seven years of
waiting for that moment. It was the realization of dreams that had haunted
him in the penitentiary and filled even his waking moments since. He battered his corpulent, twitching victim in an ecstasy of hatred, panting with
the satisfaction of his lust to destroy. He wanted to smash the fat man until
he was no longer human, until he was not even vaguely recognizable as that
Charles Doren who had sent him to the penitentiary for a crime Doren
himself had committed. As a lawyer, Doren had known of tricks Thad Hunt
could not combat—and now had a document on file in the County Prosecutor's office naming him the man responsible if he should ever be found
murdered.

He'd be found murdered now! Thad Hunt panted and struck and panted
and struck, sobbing curses and revilings at the thing he battered, until no
blow, however furious, made the battered object even twitch. It was a most
complete, most satisfying vengeance.

Reluctantly, Thad Hunt stopped. He could find no zest in further outrage against his victim. Panting from his exertions he turned and stalked away.

All was peace about him. Branches rustled. Something small and gray and furtive scurried through fallen leaves, leaped to a tree trunk, and whisked out of sight. A squirrel. A cat-bird squawked raucously in the distance. Crows cawed. Thad Hunt tramped heavily through underbrush, careless of leaving a trail. Presently he stood at the edge of an abandoned and flooded quarry, unused these twenty years and more. He sat deliberately on its edge and removed the oversized boots he wore and replaced them with others neatly placed in readiness for this transfer. He put stones in the discarded boots and re-laced them. He heaved them out to where he knew the water in the quarry was deepest. They splashed and were gone forever.

Those boots were not his own. He'd bought them in a second-hand store two hundred miles away and had them heavily wrapped by the salesman he'd bought them from; had not touched them until he put them on today with gloved hands and over a double pair of brand new socks. They'd have human scent on them, to be sure, but it wouldn't be Thad Hunt's. In the remote event that bloodhounds were brought to hunt down Doren's killer, those bloodhounds would trail the killer to the brink of the quarry . . . and halt. There'd be no trail beyond that. Even if a diver found the boots, it would be impossible to link them to Thad Hunt; and besides, nobody would suspect him!

Wearing his own boots he picked his way around the quarry's edge to the other side and followed a dim trail a quarter-mile to a tiny stream that ran down toward the valley. He waded into the stream and walked up it. Now he was utterly safe.

A good two miles from the scene of the murder he left the stream and went over a rise to the home which had been left tenantless for seven years when he went to the penitentiary. Doors sagged open, shingles were missing, and the windows were lackluster though unbroken. No small boys came by here to break the windows of empty houses. Even when he'd lived here, he'd had no more than one visitor a month, outside of those in the business he'd done for Doren, and for which Doren had let him to go prison. Now that the place was known to be empty, nobody would come by at all.

He sat down on a rotting chopping log, his eyes like glowing coals. The house and few outbuildings were desolation. The inside of the house was only dust and cobwebs. Doren owned it now . . . had owned it. He'd bought it at a tax sale while Thad Hunt was in the penitentiary, to take away his last excuse or reason for coming back to his home country. But the loss of his house hadn't kept him away. He was here now. He'd come back, and Doren was a mass of pulpy, corpulent flesh two miles away, which was exactly what Doren had feared most in all the world . . . what he'd tried to prevent by filing an accusation against Thad Hunt in advance should he ever be found murdered. And Thad, sitting on the chopping log, laughed softly to himself. It was a low-pitched, not-loud, satisfied laughter sound.

Presently he smoked, in flamboyant ease. He didn't have to run away. He'd arranged to be found here. And when he was discovered, he'd have an absolutely perfect alibi. Nobody in the world would ever suspect that he'd been the one to murder Doren. Doren's filed accusation would be absurd. His innocence would be so unquestionable that actually he'd be a hero, and public opinion would turn against the dead Doren and make him out the most villainous of scoundrels, whose murder was an act of justice no matter who'd done it or why.

Thad Hunt relaxed, reveling in his memory. He could eat now, if he chose. He looked at the food he'd brought wrapped up in butcher's paper; bread and cheese only. It was the sort of lunch a man might take with him when he had to count pennies and couldn't afford even the cheapest of public eating places while traveling. But he wouldn't eat now. His revenge had satisfied his every craving. He sat and smoked leisurely, filled with the triumph of this beautifully, perfectly contrived act of retribution.

Not the least of its perfection was that he had been able to destroy Doren in maniacal, insensate fury. It was no cunning destruction he'd had to content himself with. He'd killed Doren by brute strength and Doren knew who was doing it. He'd had leisure to exhaust himself in the fulfillment of every atom of his hate. It had been just as he had pictured it a million times.

Time passed as he sat and remembered. He was waiting now to be found. It wasn't likely that anybody would come today, of course. He'd turned one of Doren's own tricks against him. A letter to the County Prosecutor, in the little town down the valley, had said that he'd heard from Doren, asking that he meet Doren up at this place, and he was afraid. If he didn't report to the County Prosecutor within two days, he should be looked for. Doren most probably would have murdered him. Doren believed he had evidence of a crime that Doren had done and had offered to make amends for past injuries if Thad Hunt would surrender it. The letter was very bitter indeed, coming from an ex-convict and accusing a prominent citizen of intent to murder him. No attention would be paid to it normally, but when Doren was missed. . . .

The long afternoon wore on as Thad Hunt lived and relived, with infinite relish, the murder of his enemy. There was sunshine upon the hills and in the valleys between them. There were birdcalls and chirping insects and the drowsy, somnolent humming of bees. All of nature was very quiet and very peaceful. Here Thad Hunt sat, with a queer twisted grin on his face, and remembered.

Night fell. Fire-flies appeared and their lamps made little streaks of greenish light against the darkness. He sat grinning beneath the stars. Seven years of hate, and now this vast contentment. He did not even care to worry about his own safety.

That letter was in the town, saying he was to meet Doren here and was afraid that he would be murdered. The letter would have been delivered to the County Prosecutor today. He'd take no action at once, of course. He'd want to ask Doren about it, Doren being a prominent citizen. But Doren wouldn't be going back to answer questions. The County Prosecutor might wait through tomorrow, or maybe not. Sooner or later, though, with Doren missing, he'd send someone up to this house to see what had happened. And they'd find Thad Hunt, and he'd tell a tale of threats and near-murder which would be infinitely convincing. He'd be practically a hero thereafter, and the finding of Doren's battered body would make no difference whatever, because nobody could possibly suspect Thad Hunt of killing him.

When he grew drowsy as hours passed, he almost begrudged the need of sleep because it meant he would not be reveling in his monstrous pleasure. But he did doze, and in his dreams he killed Doren all over again in such an ecstasy of satisfaction that it woke him once. When he dozed off again, his mind absurdly framed a dream of doom, of arrest for the murder he'd planned so long.

When day broke, he woke with contentment. Undoubtedly someone would come up here to find him today. The County Prosecutor would have gotten his letter yesterday, expressing fear that he'd be murdered by Doren. There was another letter on file in the County Prosecutor's office too, from Doren, accusing Thad Hunt in advance if he should be found dead. And two such letters from two men each fearing the other would surely produce action when Doren was missing overnight.

This morning brought no doubts and no regrets—except that Doren had not taken longer to die under his rain of blows. Thad Hunt had hardly stirred from his seat all night, absorbed in his obsessed reenactments of the killing. Now he looked out over the hills, fresh and clean in the dawn light, and laughed softly to himself. This was his home country. Five years in the penitentiary had kept him away from it, and during the two years since his release he hadn't come back because he knew the local attitude toward ex-convicts. From now on though, as soon as he was found, that attitude would be changed for him. Doren would be blamed for everything. Thad Hunt would be almost a hero, and certainly he'd be a respected citizen immediately, ultimately because he'd murdered Doren! But they'd never dream of that!

He got up and moved about. If he'd been quite sure that he'd be found today he'd have left his sandwiches intact as a pathetic indication of his presence. But he wasn't absolutely certain, and he was a little bit hungry. He ate, carefully putting the fresh wrapping paper where it would catch the eye of anyone who came. And then he was thirsty; and as it was too early for any searchers, he went out to the spring a half mile or more away. There was a well by the house—a deep well—but he did not try to get water from it. He had another use for the well.

He came back and expansively surveyed the hills and sky and all the earth. Everything was perfect. Four days before, he'd called Doren by long-distance telephone. In a disguised voice, he'd identified himself as a sportsman looking for a hunting camp in this neighborhood. He said he'd heard of this place and would buy it if the price were right. He'd made an appointment to meet Doren here.

He hadn't kept the appointment. From hiding, he'd watched Doren climb up to the house that once had been Thad Hunt's home. He'd waited downhill, hugging his anticipation to himself, while Doren waited for the mythical sportsman, until Doren gave him up; until Doren came down . . . to his death.

His plan was perfection! He'd done enough, but not one atom too much. He'd written one letter which he'd duly signed with his own name. He'd made one long-distance phone call which could never be traced to him. And he'd killed Doren going away from this house—not at it, or going to it— and he'd be found here with the most perfect alibi any man ever had. There was nothing to go wrong! He hadn't even gone into the house. Since the murder, he'd stayed almost motionless leaving no sign of a long wait here. There wasn't anything to go wrong!

The morning passed. By nine o'clock, the County Prosecutor would be thinking about Thad Hunt's letter and asking for Doren, whom he hadn't been able to locate the day before. By ten, he'd know Doren hadn't come home all night. By eleven, he'd have sent someone up to see if anything had happened.

It was a beautiful morning and Thad Hunt loafed; zestfully grinning to himself and enjoying every second of it. It was warm, almost, but not quite hot, and the smell of green things on the hillside and in the thicket was good. The sound of bob-whites calling was soothing and homelike. An occasional butterfly, a homing bee or two, now and then a discordantly cawing crow; these things spoke of vast tranquility. Now that he had sated his craving for vengeance, Thad Hunt looked forward to years and years of happy remembering, while his neighbors were extra cordial to him because of the monstrous crime they would believe that Doren had perpetrated against him.

It was almost noon when he heard a car on the dirt road far away. He went to the yard in front of the house to watch. He was careful not to show himself. He watched from behind a thicket of tall weeds.

He saw four men. They were headed in his direction. They couldn't be headed anywhere else. They must have been sent by the County Prosecutor to hunt over this place for signs that Thad Hunt had been murdered here. They had two dogs with them.

He watched them until they were less than half a mile away, downhill. He didn't recognize them, but an enormous satisfaction made him grin wildly and rather unpleasantly. He turned to go to the spot where he was to be found.

For the first tim in seven years he faced the front door of the house that had been his home. There was a folded sheet of paper stuck to it with a pin. A scrawled, penciled name was written across the folded outer surface. It was fresh. It hadn't been there long. For an instant, he was shocked. Then he realized Doren had expected to meet a mythical sportsman here. Thad Hunt had murdered him as he descended after a vain wait. He'd. . . .

Yes. Thad plucked it away from the door, grinning. The writing on the outside was simply the name of that non-existent, would-be purchaser of this house and land. Doren, after fruitless waiting, had left a note for the man he'd failed to meet.

Chuckling, Thad Hunt went across the weed-grown yard, carrying a length of rope. He heaved up a rotten board from the cover of the deep, dark well. He threw it to one side. It would be very obviously a new happening. And since they'd be looking for a murdered man. . . .

He passed the rope around a four-inch tree some two yards from the table. With the doubled rope in his hands, he went to the opening in the well cover. He let himself down carefully.

It was thirty feet to the bottom. There was a foot and a half of water there and under it, all manner of foulness and mud. He stood in the mud and pulled on one strand of the rope. The other end went up toward the rectangular patch of blue sky directly overhead. It vanished, and only one strand remained. He continued to pull. Suddenly, the rope tumbled down upon him. There was no possible way for him to climb out.

He trampled the rope underfoot, thrusting it into the mud beneath the water. It made a firmer foundation for him to stand on. He stood looking up at the long narrow, rectangular patch of sky. The men the County Prosecutor had sent to hunt over the place for a murder victim, of course, would find the broken well-top. They'd look in the well, in any case, as a place for the disposal of a body. But, besides, he'd shout hoarsely as if he'd been calling despairingly for hours. Presently, astonished faces would stare down at him, cutting off part of the sky. He'd cry out. They'd have trouble getting him up. And by the time he was on top of the ground they'd have accepted as gospel his hysterical story that Doren had left him there. Doren had demanded that he surrender evidence of one of Doren's crimes. When he protested that he couldn't, Doren had driven him down into the well at pistol point and said he'd come back to see if Thad Hunt changed his mind when he got hungry.

Everything fitted together perfectly, too. The County Prosecutor had sent to look for him because of the letter which was the perfect preparation for this tale. The tale was a perfect alibi for when Doren's body was found. Nobody would imagine that a man who had been fearful of murder would commit the insensately violent battering of Doren. Nobody could imagine that a man who'd murder Doren would put himself in the most hopelessly inescapable of traps. Nobody could doubt, from now on, Thad Hunt's story that he had gone to prison for Doren's crimes. It was utterly, absolutely perfect, and he had the memory of having killed Doren to re-live and gloat over all the rest of his life.

The four men and the dogs would be arriving here soon. Thad Hunt sent a wailing call for help up the resonant shaft of the well. They wouldn't hear it yet, but he wanted them to hear faint cries as they neared the house. He'd better begin now.

The sound of his voice was ghostly. It rang and echoed hollowly against the smooth, concrete walls of the well. Thad Hunt chuckled. He stirred, and there was a rustling of paper—the note Doren had left for the mythical man he'd thought to meet here. It had to be gotten rid of, but trampling it into the mud would be enough. It would be amusing, though, to read Doren's trustful message to a figment of Thad Hunt's imagination.

He unfolded the sheet and read it. It was addressed to the man Doren had thought talked to him by long-distance. It said that Doren had been there, and waited, and nobody had turned up. And it said that if the would-be purchaser came to his office in town they could discuss the sale of the property. Doren added that he was the County Prosecutor and his office was just opposite the court house so it would be easy to find.

Thad Hunt started to trample the note underfoot. Then he checked. His breath stopped. Doren was the County Prosecutor. . . . Then the letter addressed to the County Prosecutor would have been delivered to his office after he left . . . to be murdered! Nobody's been sent to look for Thad Hunt at his home place! His letter hadn't been opened! It wouldn't be opened until Doren was missed and his disappearance was accepted as final or his body found! Even after that it wouldn't be opened until somebody else was elected or appointed as his successor and leisurely got around to cleaning up the accumulated mail. The four men and two dogs weren't coming to this house. The men might be training the dogs for hunting, or trying them out with a view to purchase! They might. . . .

Thad Hunt couldn't get out. He knew that his only chance of living was to make those men hear him. He screamed. He shrieked. He raised a hellish clamor at the bottom of the hole into which he had lowered himself. He screamed so shrilly and so long that he could not believe that he could go unheard.

But nobody came. When it grew dark, his voice was a croak, and he knew that nobody would come. By that time, too, his hands were raw and bleeding from desperate attempts to climb the smooth, concrete wall. When night fell and the thin, rectangular bit of sky above him grew dark and cold, incurious stars looked down into the well upon him and he wept in utter despair.

He could think about the vast satisfaction he'd had in killing Doren, to be sure, but it was no comfort. He even knew that sometime, maybe one month, maybe two, or even three months hence, his letter would bring somebody here to look for him. But that was no comfort either. From this instant, until starvation ended it, he would be dying . . . slowly. In murdering Doren and arranging so cleverly to escape all suspicion, he'd been remarkably successful. No one would ever dream that he'd killed Doren. But he'd planned a single murder and it had turned out to be a double one. . . .

There was one difference between the two murders, though. Thad Hunt's own dying wasn't over so soon. In fact, it wasn't completely over until far into the third week.